Grateful acknowledgment is made to Penguin Random House UK for permission to reprint excerpts from *The Travels by Marco Polo,* by Nigel Cliff. Copyright © 2015 by Nigel Cliff.

Cover design by Renee Ciufo

Contents

Foreword

Marco Polo is a name well known, but his accomplishments are not. A man of controversy, some believe he never traveled to the Far East. However, I chose to believe what he said on his death bed: "Never will I retract my book, I didn't tell you half of what I saw!"

The indented and italicized sections are partial excerpts from his book. Some of the language used may be considered offensive or controversial by today's standards. I kept his words to remain true to the original writing. However, they do not reflect my personal beliefs about different cultures, religions, or people around the world.

Introduction

Marco Polo's book, *The Description of the World,* later known as *The Travels of Marco Polo (Il Milione)*, and a Venetian legend inspired me to write this historical adventure romance novel.

Marco Polo was born in 1254, the son of Niccolò Polo, a Venetian merchant. When he was five, his father, Niccolò, and uncle, Maffeo, left Venice and traveled to Constantinople. From there, they continued their journey on the Silk Road, hoping for substantial monetary gains. With great determination and luck, they traveled to Cathay,[1] also known as the End of the World, where they met Kubilai Khan—the man who controlled one of the largest empires in history.

Niccolò and Maffeo became Kubilai Khan's emissaries. Their first mission was to return to Venice and bring back Christian scholars from the pope to explain Christianity to him. Marco Polo was 15 by then, and Niccolò's wife had died. Several years later, his father and uncle, with Marco in tow, left for Cathay, having fulfilled most of Kubilai Khan's requests. That was 1271, the beginning of Marco Polo's great adventure, which lasted twenty-four years and took him thousands of miles over lands and seas only a few had ever seen.

In 1295, after seventeen years as an emissary for Kubilai Khan, Marco performed his last duty escorting Princess Kokochin, Kubilai Khan's daughter; Princess Li of Manzi (Song Dynasty); and 100 attendees to Arghun Khan, the fourth ruler of the Mongol Empire's Ilkhanate. Completing this mission in three incredible years, Marco, with his forbidden love, his father, and his uncle, continued to Venice, arriving in Mongolian rags and barely able to speak their native language. It took a banquet and the unveiling of many jewels sewn in their coats to prove their story.

Unfortunately, a war raged between Genoa and Venice, battling over trade and control of the Mediterranean Sea. Marco became a Venetian ship commander, and in the 1298 Battle of Curzola, the Genoese captured him. While imprisoned in Genoa, Marco Polo and Rustichello of Pisa, a medieval romance writer, wrote the book *A Description of the World*—a remarkable travelogue that covers Asia, which even Christopher Columbus used.

My book is fictional; however, it is based on the authentic accounts of his travels. Throughout the chapters, the indented and italicized sections are partial excerpts from his book. The three and four dots in these sections indicate the omitted writings of Marco. I read two versions of his book—one by Ronald Latham and the other by Nigel Cliff. The excerpts quoted in this novel were taken from Nigel Cliff's version, used with permission from his publisher. Marco Polo's book did not include personal history except for small hints in the prologue. Drawing on these subtle hints, I wrote an imaginary tale that incorporated history as one of its main characters, alongside notable nonfiction and fictional figures. I wove together a compelling and complex story using the tales Marco told Rustichello about his twenty-four years of travel and the Venetian legend that tells of his first love, Princess Li of the Song Dynasty. Her ghost is said to haunt the Milion Courtyard to this day, reminding Venice that she existed and should not be forgotten.

My chapters are divided between the main characters: Marco Polo, the main thread bringing alive the remarkable times of thirteenth-century Asia; Li, the Princess of Song, who breathes life into Venice and Kubilai Khan's palace; Kim Chin-hae, a royal Goryeo[2] general and Marco's business partner and friend, who tells the history of his conquered country—a vassal of Kubilai Khan; and Lis, Kim Chin-hae's Miao shaman wife who possessed the ability to enter one's dreams. My novel follows their daring adventures, war, discoveries, forbidden love, and friendships. The characters are a perfect example of the human compass—the spiritual meaning of a compass—a reminder that you are in control and free to choose the course of your life as you wish.

---

1. China

2. Korea

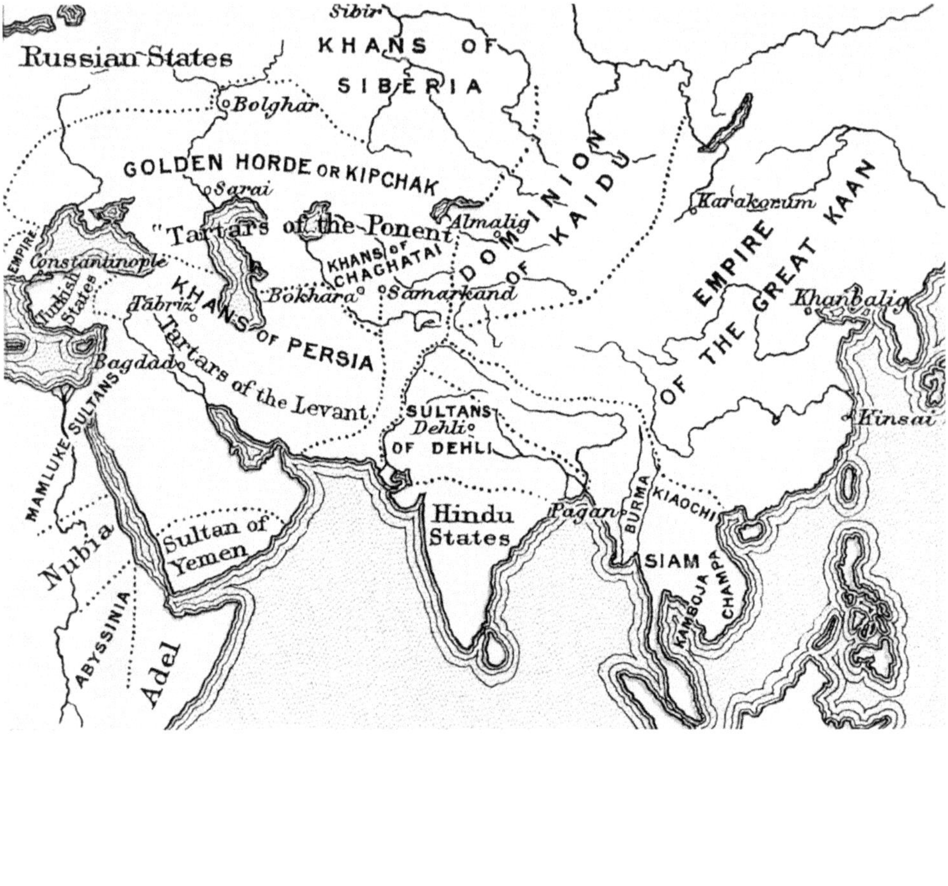

Sibir
KHANS OF SIBERIA
Russian States
Bolghar
GOLDEN HORDE OR KIPCHAK
Sarai
"Tartars of the Ponent"
Almalig
DOMINION OF KAIDU
Karakorum
EMPIRE OF THE GREAT KAAN
Khanbalig
Kinsai
EMPIRE
Constantinople
Turkish States
KHANS OF CHAGHATAI
Bokhara
Samarkand
Tabriz
KHANS OF PERSIA
Tartars of the Levant
Bagdad
SULTANS
MAMLUKE
SULTANS OF DEHLI
Dehli
Hindu States
Pagan
BURMA
KIAOCHI
SIAM
KAMBOJA
CHAMPA
Sultan of Yemen
Nubia
ABYSSINIA
Adel

The Marco Polo voyages

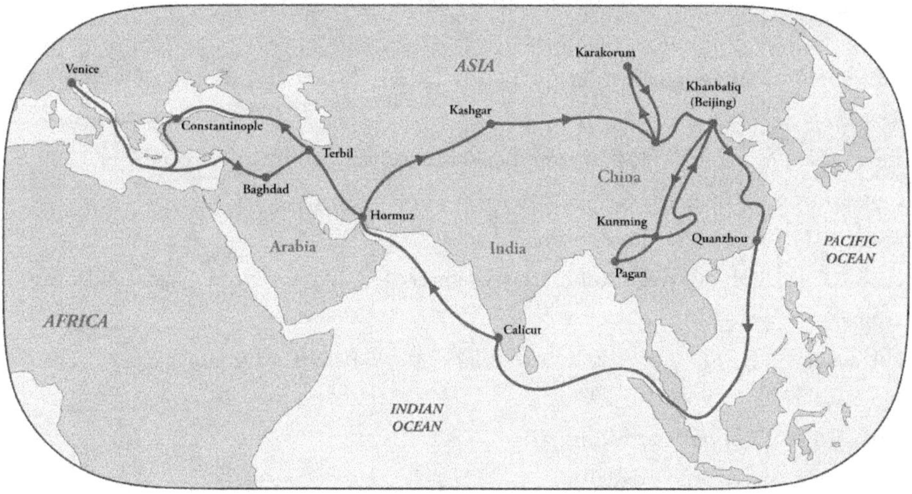

Index of Characters

NF signifies non-fictional character in history; however, some content contains nonfactual information.
F signifies fictional character.

Abaqa Khan - (NF) Second ruler of the Llkhanate, Mongolian Empire (Persia)(Reign 1265-1282)
Agnese - (NF) Marco's secret daughter; her existence was confirmed through her 1319 will, recognized by scholars in the early 2020s.
Abushka - (NF) one of the three barons
Aiyurug - (NF), also called Khutulun, the daughter of Qaidu, lover of Ghazan, and a woman warrior
Arghun Khan - (NF) Abaqa's son, fourth ruler of the llkhanate, Mongolian Empire (Persia) - Reign 1284-1291
Ashraf - (F) Marco's guide to Hormuz
Bellela (NF), Marco Polo's daughter
Bulughan Khatun - (NF) Wife of Arghun
Chinghiz - (NF) Kubilai Khan's son and the crown prince
Chungseon of Goryeo - (NF) The Crown Prince Wang Won of Goryeo, Ijir Bukhqa (Part of the Society of Three Li and Kokochin)
Dai Xiuying - (F) Marco Polo's Guide and friend
Donata - Marco Polo's wife
Ehuang-Ehu - (F) The Pearl's dealer's daughter
Eun-Ae - (F) Kim Chin Hae's mother's choice of wife
Emperor Zhao Xian - (NF) Emperor Gong of Song (Reign 1274-1276)
Empress Chabi - (NF) Kubilai Khan's favorite wife

Empress Nambi - (NF) Empress Chabi's cousin and Kubilai's wife after Chabi's death
Empress Quan - (NF) Spouse of Emperor Duzong, mother of Emperor Gong of Song
Elena - (F) Cook in Marco's palazzo and Yu's love interest.
Fantina - (NF) Marco's Daughter
Gaykhatu - (NF) Fifth Il-Khan Mongolian Empire (Persia) (reign 1291-1295)
General Atahai - (NF) Supreme Vice-Admiral (Mongolian)
General Arakhan - (NF) Supreme Admiral (Mongolian)
General Bayad One Hundred Eyes - (NF) Chinese general
General Chang Hsi - Chinese general
General Fan Wenhu - (NF) Chinese general
General Hong Dagu - (NF) Mongolian general
General Kim Bang-byeong - (NF) Goryeo general
Ghazan - (NF) Seventh ruler of the Mongol Empire, llkhanate (Persia), Kokochin's future husband, Reign 1295-1304
Grand Dowager Empress Xie Daoqings- (NF) Regent of Emperor Gong of Song Dynasty China
Guo Yu - (F) Friend, Servant, and slave of Marco Polo, the same person as Peter
Hulegu - (NF) Grandson of Genghis Khan, Founder of the Llkhanate of Persia (Reign 1256-1265)
Isabella - (F) Maffeo's daughter
Qaidu - (NF) Leader of the Chaghatai Mongolian Empire, Aiyurug's father
King Manggala - (NF) Kubilai Khan's son
Kim Ae-cha - (F) Kim Chin Hae's mother
Kim Chin-hae - (F) Marco's best friend, Lis's Husband, and Goryeo's royal
Kim Chui-hee - (F) Kim Chin Hae's father
King Chungnyeol - (NF) of Goryeo (first cousin of Kim (F), married Kubilai Khan's daughter, Queen Jangmok (Reign 1274-1298)
King Wonjong - (NF) of Goryeo -father of King Chungnyeol
Kokochin - (NF) Kubilai Khan's daughter, Li's friend, Ghazan's wife
Kono Michiari - (NF) Japanese captain, Campaign Koan
Kubilai Khan - (NF) The Great Khan of the Mongolian Empire and the Yuan Dynasty
Li - (F) Princess of Manzi or Song, Marco's forbidden love
Lis - (F) Shaman and wife of Kim Chin Hae
Luca - (F) servant of Li
Matteo - (F) current-day Venetian tour guide

Messer Alessio - (F) apothecary
Messer Maffeo Polo - (NF) Marco's uncle
Messer Marco Polo - (NF)
Messer Niccolò Polo - (NF) Marco's father
Mo Ching - (NF) fellow soldier of Kim Chin Hae
Moreta - (NF) Marco Polo's daughter, who kept his legacy alive by recording his maps
Nawrus – (NF) Ghazan's atabeg who committed treason
Pak Byeong-ho - (F) friend and fellow soldier of Kim Chin Hae
Padishah Khan - (NF) wife of Gaykhata
Peter (NF) - also known as Guo Yu, slave of Marco Polo
Physician Wu – (NF) Kubilai Khan's physician
Qoja - (NF) one of the three barons
Rustichello of Pisa - (NF) prison cellmate of Marco Polo and writer
Shikhen Tokimune - (NF) Japanese stateman, warrior (Ghenko campaign)
Son Jun-ho - (F) servant of Kim Chin Hae
Ulatai - (NF) one of the three barons
Wei - (F) Shaman Lis's mother
Yisun Timür - (NF) Kubilai Khan's grandson

PROLOGUE

Modern Day: The Venetian Legend

Matteo, an enthusiastic gray-haired tour guide, slowly began the bel canto, his imperfect rendition of his best-loved opera, Turandot's Nessun Dorma. His favorite stage stood in two little squares, the Milion Courtyard near the Church of San Giovanni Crisostomo and the Teatro Malibran Opera House near the Rialto Bridge.

Over the years, Matteo discovered his serenade would easily lure his wandering flock back to reality. Venice can magically absorb them in her past with her car-free cobblestone streets and courtyards, the gondola rowing by, and women hanging clothes on their flower-filled balconies of homes extremely worn and scarred. With one's imagination, you hear the homes call, "Come and let me tell you my untold secrets."

When Matteo was young, he would sing at his parish, but as he grew older, he took over his father's gondola, and his favorite theater became the canals of Venice. With a beautiful voice and handsome face, his reputation grew as he sang, flirted, and told fascinating stories to the passengers. Long lines of visitors waited just for him. But as his father before him, old age won, and now his son rowed the gondola. Retirement didn't suit him, so he continued with a more relaxing job—a walking tour specializing in mysterious legends and the colorful history of his beloved Venice for the curious tourists who stayed longer than a day.

When he completed his first verse, his audience surrounded him. Turandot's Nessun Dorma was a fitting opera about a strong female warrior who lived on the steppe, during the time Marco Polo lived in Cathay—China. He smiled, proud of himself. It was time to tell his treasured yet sorrowful legend. In a smooth, distinct Italian accent, he began.

"It was the midnight hour, and a soft mist lingered. I was a young man returning home through this courtyard. The fractured stucco walls, with ornate, protruding lamps that glowed gold, reflected long streaks of glittering light on the canal below. The silence of the night was suddenly interrupted by alluring, strange music—not Italian, but Chinese. It called to me. Stunned, I stopped and listened. I swear it came from that building."

He stopped and pointed at a top window facing the canal. "There." He pointed to Teatro Malibran, which shares the foundation of Marco Polo's home, destroyed by fire centuries ago.

His voice changed and became theatrically dramatic.

"I froze; a ghostly girl figure, floating above me, weaved in and out of the misty air as her white, flowing dress intertwined with the sad, crying music that filled the empty Milion courtyard."

His audience gasped, and he continued.

"I was still frozen, and her transparent body swooped in. For only a minute, her beautiful face with half-moon eyes glared into mine, then disappeared.

"From that day, I truly believed the legend I had heard my entire life... When Marco Polo returned from China, he brought home jewels, gold, and a wealth of knowledge, but his most prized jewel was his Chinese Princess. They say Marco left her to fight a war and disappeared for a year. In her sorrow, she would sit at that window and play her Chinese instrument, calling him home. Some say she jumped from that window, but no one knows for sure."

His audience all shook their heads. Matteo began singing, and soon, the crowd forgot his sad story. Again, he smiled to himself as goosebumps covered his body.

Chapter One

Marco

Marco's Presumed Lies

Venice, January 1324

An elderly Marco lay on his deathbed staring at the colorful fresco ceiling. His room faced west—displaying beautiful sunsets, the Grand Canal, and, in the distance, the Rialto Bridge. He never shared this room with his present wife—only with his long-ago lover, his soul mate. The room had remained locked and only be entered by Peter or himself when drunk and his mood was forlorn. Unique items adorned this room, keeping his memories and his sadness alive. It was not until he was dying that he moved back in.

In a dream state, he could hear his oldest daughter, Fantina. "Father, please retract your book. Tell us now before you die; you lied. It will be so much better for us."

His wife, Donata, walked over and sat on his bed. She placed her hand on his. Marco opened his eyes, looked up at her, and then around the room at his most precious assets: his wife, his daughters—Fantina, Bellela, and Moreta—and Peter, his trusted Mangi[1] friend who had served him for the last forty-two years and endured his constant drunkenness and boasting.

With a weak and crackling but gruff voice, Marco said, "No, no, no, I didn't lie; I have not told one half of what I have really seen and nothing of how I lived. "See that vase?" He pointed to a small white vase with a pale blue hue beside his bed. I have never told you who gave this to me or why. There is so much more I haven't told you. All these things in this room have stories; they are my memories."

Everyone except Peter, who knew the story, looked around. *What did he mean?* It was the memories they couldn't see.

"Donata, I am so sorry. I never loved you as I should have. My memories hardened my heart." Tears ran down his face. "I failed everyone, even myself. Please, please forgive me," he pleaded.

Donata patted his hand. "You're mistaken, Marco; you loved us by staying, never returning to Cathay."

In his weak voice, he continued. "I love you. I'm sorry I didn't tell you that enough."

"We love you, too, Marco," she said as she reached over and kissed him on the forehead.

Marco closed his eyes, remembering when he married Donata. Love for another had filled his heart. His uncle had pressured him to marry. Their business was suffering, and Donata's father was a wealthy merchant. "*Besides, Donata loves you,*" Marco remembered his uncle saying. *"We will all benefit from this marriage; we will receive the money we need to continue, and they will gain our knowledge of the Far East and our connections."*

Marco laughed inside and thought, *The rich are the same, no matter what part of the world you're from. They all sacrifice their children for wealth and power.* But deep inside, he knew he was the same. He had sacrificed the love of his life. He did not intend to, but it just turned out that way.

Voices interrupted his thoughts. He opened his eyes, and Fantina spoke again: "Father, please take back your words."

Donata stood up and gently put her arms around her. "Stop, daughter! Your father is telling the truth. Please, let's leave and let your father rest."

Marco spoke up. "Guo Yu, stay, please."

Only Marco called Peter, Guo Yu. It was his real name. Everyone else knew him as Peter.

Guo Yu came close with a tear-soaked face. He loved Marco, and Marco loved him.

Marco whispered, "When night falls, and everyone sleeps, you must do something for me. Open the wardrobe's bottom drawer. Look for a small bronze hook and lift the bottom of the drawer. There, you will find a gold box. Please place that with her. Please, Guo Yu! I don't want anyone else to touch it."

Guo Yu cried harder and nodded.

Later that night, Guo Yu went to the wardrobe and followed Marco's instructions. When he opened the drawer, he found some primitive maps and set them aside. He searched and found the hook and pulled. The drawer's wood bottom lifted. Inside was the gold box, just as Marco had said. He gently opened it. His body shook with emotion. There was a familiar scarf that was now old and tattered like the two men in the room. Picking it up, Guo Yu ran his fingers over Marco's frayed, embroidered initials and realized it held something. He unfolded the scarf. Inside were three beautiful items: a jade and gold binyeo[2] with two carved butterflies, a small knife with a pearl handle set with delicate diamonds, and an ivory comb featuring pearls and gold beads.

Guo Yu held them in his hands and cried as memories flooded his mind. Continuing, he removed a layer of gold silk, revealing a garment. Guo Yu's eyes were wide. He unfolded a delicate white V-neck silk top with long, flowing sleeves. Next, he found a long, fluid, multilayered white-and-gold silk skirt, topped with a gold silk band. The band was stitched with genuine pearls and would sit just above a woman's breast, tied securely in the back. Underneath, there was a gold silk scarf. It was circular and draped over the wearer's shoulders, falling down the back. The image of Li wearing this dress made him smile. He couldn't believe Marco still had these. Guo Yu was not prepared for what he saw next. His red and swollen eyes suddenly filled with more tears. He bent down and picked up a gold tiara with small pearls. In a soft voice, he spoke to himself. "I gave her this when she was thirteen." The following article brought more tears. It was a white baby's dress. He lifted it and cuddled it close. Now, he understood what Marco had asked him to do. They belonged with *her*.

Late that night, Moreta, Marco's youngest daughter, stood, hesitating at Marco's massive, carved door. Her hands rested on the grand, engraved bronze handles. Moreta recalled that these doors had been chained together her whole life. She quietly opened it. Peter was so immersed in his duty that he didn't hear the door open. Moreta silently watched as he pulled back the large, hanging Persian tapestry, revealing a door. Reaching into his long sleeves, he took out a gold key that glistened in the candlelit room. He opened the concealed door, gathered up the gold box, and disappeared. Moreta's curiosity overtook her. Secretly, she followed him down the dark stone staircase—lit only by the glow of Peter's candle—that led them to another locked door. Peter paused, unlocked it, and disappeared into the hidden room. Moreta paused momentarily as goosebumps and a chill ran through her body, then hastily opened the door.

Peter quickly turned and dropped the box, scattering the contents on the floor. Moreta squatted, apologizing for having scared him as she picked up the items. She stopped talking and held up the beautiful white-and-gold dress, then the tiara. Standing up, Moreta looked around the dimly lit room, realizing it was not an ordinary room but a memorial to someone. Behind Peter, she saw a table that held a large rectangular box.

"Is that a coffin?"

Guo Yu said nothing.

Moreta asked again, this time addressing him by his name, Guo Yu. "That's what Father calls you?"

He continued facing the coffin and lifted the lid. Moreta watched as Guo Yu placed the items inside.

Moreta slowly walked toward him and peered inside. Stunned, she lost her breath and fell backward. Guo Yu caught her.

"Who is that?" Moreta asked in a quivering voice.

Guo Yu silently stared at her.

Moreta regained her composure and walked closer to the coffin. She peered down. It was a woman, even though her petite body was now petrified. Her long hair was pulled back with a few thick strands brought forward over her chest, covering a small portion of a faded Cathay imperial coat. As Moreta stood staring, Guo Yu took the tiara from her hand and placed it on her head, saying, "I gave her this when she turned thirteen." Then, he gently placed the other items he had found in the scarf on her chest, starting with the binyeo.

Moreta stuttered. "Was she your wife?"

Guo Yu looked at Moreta. "No, she was your father's."

"The baby dress?"

"Your half-sister," Guo Yu answered. "She died eleven years ago."

"What? Why was she kept from us? Why weren't we told we had a sister?"

"Your father decided not to; we honored it."

"Did Mother know?"

"Yes, they thought it was best. You should try to ask your father."

Back in her father's room, Moreta sat beside her father, sobbing. "Why didn't you tell us we had another sister?" Marco remained silent.

Marco could hear someone sobbing as his mind drifted. He was unaware he was whispering out loud. "The moment the Genoese commander boarded my defeated ship—this one moment—changed the rest of my life. I had promised her I would return soon. I failed her."

Marco remembered his desperation as the prison door closed.

I stood at the cell bars yelling, "Do you know who I am? I am Marco Polo, who traveled the Silk Road and became friends with the great Kubilai Khan. I lived in Cathay for 17 years and know its secrets. It is imperative that I speak to your commander." I kept repeating myself until I collapsed on the floor, and my thoughts drifted to my love, Li.

1. South China

2. Hair stick

Chapter Two

Li

Princess Li and Marco, Butterfly Lovers

Venice 1298

On the third floor of the magnificent palazzo, an exotic beauty sat at a large western window, one of the few that didn't house stained glass. Patiently, she played her erhu—her string instrument—and waited for her love to return. This was her favorite room; it overlooked this strange city, surrounded by water, with small rivers running through it. As the sun set, intense light rushed in, illuminating the beautiful contents of her room: Marco's Morin Khuur, Turkish carpets, Cathay porcelain, Syrian metalwork, Persian silk tapestries, vases, religious paintings, and statuary. The sun slowly disappeared behind the tall, thin structures topped with rounded arches. The structures were painted in rich hues of dark red, muted yellows, and bright blue, casting dark shadows on the courtyard and canal below, leaving only a narrow escape of light that lit the way for the hurrying Venetians returning home.

As she played, she reminisced and compared her homes. The differences were profound: the landscape, the symbol of wealth, the houses, the food, the dress, and most of all, their rulers—the merchants were Venice's patrician rulers here. The other difference was the people's fear of someone who looked, dressed, and acted differently. Her country was diverse. Hundreds of merchants from around the world arrived via the Silk Road. They accepted everyone there.

But here it was different. She stood out. When Marco wasn't here, she stayed mainly within the palazzo, where she felt safe.

"Our Venetian palazzo is an architectural marvel," Marco would tell her. "It reflects my family's economic success."

Li always laughed at his statement; she would remind him she had lived in a grand palace in Cathay.

The palazzo lay on the canal where the water ran underneath it. They had water gates that allowed merchant boats to enter the ground floor, where trade goods were stored. The upper floors were the lavish living quarters. Marco had chosen his room mainly because a secret door on the ground floor led to a hidden staircase that continued to this room. Between them was a small room hidden among the foundations, where he housed his most treasured possessions. He always used this door when he returned to her.

Li's music was sweet and alluring, revealing her softer side. She played it, hoping it would call Marco home. However, this sweetness was a facade; she was strong and endured a lifetime of fear.

As the sun set and darkness fell, a young servant girl entered the room with a lit candle and began lighting the lamps and candles. Li had seen her several times and assumed she was about her age. She yearned for a female friend. In Cathay and on the long journey to Venice, she had Kokochin, whom she met at thirteen. Now, only Guo Yu existed in her life; Kokochin had been left with her new husband. Marco's cousin, Isabella, who lived in the same palazzo, despised and ignored her as much as possible and only talked to her when Marco was around. Now Marco has disappeared, fighting in a war.

The young servant girl barely looked up as she bustled around the room. Only once did she hesitate, to look at Li's musical instrument, the erhu, which leaned against the back of the chair. It was the most unusual instrument she had ever seen. Gently, she ran her hand along the long, slender neck made from beautiful red wood. At the top, an exquisitely carved white jade dragon and two large wooden pegs sat. The neck was attached to a small hexagonal box made of red wood, and its ends were covered in strange snakeskin. Two silk strings ran from the wooden pegs to the box. Next to it was a horsehair bow longer than the instrument itself. Once, she heard Li play. The sound was haunting and alluring, and Li seemed to make it cry. After her quick observations, she finished lighting the candles. She opened the door but suddenly turned and stared at Li.

Li's traditional dress, stitched with gold thread, glowed against the backdrop of the dim sunlight and the flickering candles. The girl in her native tongue whispered, "Sei Bello," and ran out the door. Li understood and smiled. She felt relieved; that was the first person who didn't look at her as a barbarian. Li hoped she would return.

Guo Yu entered the room with her dinner. He had been her servant and friend since she was five. Now that Marco was gone, he became her protector. Guo Yu knew she chose wild game over seafood and made it his job to search out merchants specializing in meat from the mountains beyond Venice. At her home, seafood was a delicacy and served only on special occasions, but here, it's an everyday occurrence. Luckily, one cook named Elena had ulterior motives and willingly prepared it for her. Li felt this person enjoyed Guo Yu's company and wasn't necessarily preparing the meat just to serve her.

Li preferred eating in her room. Guo Yu and she could talk freely in their native tongue, without feeling restricted. She wanted to know all about the war, where Marco was, and if he heard any news on the wharf regarding Cathay. The other reason is that she found Marco's cousin's conversations in the dining hall frivolous. In Cathay, she was a healer and could enter many royal women's and men's gers[1] or chambers and eavesdrop on their secrets and fascinating conversations.

The evening grew late. Guo Yu knew she wasn't like the other princesses; she preferred not to be pampered. Others demanded assistance with the bedtime ritual, but not Li; she only preserved this for Marco.

Guo Yu stood and said goodnight.

Li grew forlorn. She undressed slowly, pretending Marco was there. She sat at her ornate dressing table and, with closed eyes, removed the pins that held her long thick hair. Li imagined Marco standing behind her, sweeping her hair from her neck and kissing her gently while caressing her shoulders. Tears swelled and rolled down her cheeks as she opened her eyes and looked at the single face in the mirror. She stood, walked to the chair next to the window, and slowly picked up her erhu. Darkness had wholly consumed the streets below. She watched through weeping eyes for any glimmer of light he was returning to her. Li played her erhu as her heart and music cried. Overwhelmed with loneliness, she went to bed, longing for sweet dreams.

As she slept, her dream seemed so real: She could feel Marco's hands on her thigh, softly moving up to the arch of her back, then the weight of his body on hers, and his face touching hers. Her body trembled, waking her from her sweet slumber.

Marco gently kissed her and whispered. "I missed you."

Li slowly opened her eyes and smiled. It wasn't a dream; Marco was indeed there. Li forcefully flipped him in a quick combat maneuver. A move that her friend Kokochin had taught her. She was on top, holding his hands to the bed, her hair in his face. Marco smiled, his eyes full of surrender; Li had captured him.

Feeling scorn for her display of weakness the night before, her sweet face transformed to hardness, and she slowly spoke quietly and powerfully.

"My name is Li; I am your Song Princess. My father was the Emperor of the Song Dynasty. You are mine. I traveled half this world with you. Our love doesn't come without guilt.

Everything we were taught and understood, we denied and forgot. We didn't care. We just wanted each other. Don't die and leave me alone in your world."

Marco understood.

Her anger eroded when she saw his dirty, bruised face. She quickly released his hands and slid from his body. Li gently removed his dirt-stained clothing. He lay still, watched her, and only rose when necessary. Her hands softly followed the contours of his muscular body, examining every inch, finding only deep scratches, dirt, and bruises. Again, her eyes welled with tears, but this time with joy. She kissed him.

There was a quick knock at the door, a signal that his bath was drawn. Guo Yu had heard the water gates open.

Marco and Li rose holding hands, and entered the next room. The fireplace was roaring, and a large steaming tub awaited them.

Guo Yu knew the routine; he would prepare, and Li would continue. He greeted Marco and bowed, saying, "We are happy you returned." He turned and left.

Marco entered the tub with his bruised body, holding out his hand. Li walked over, undressed, and entered. Li felt an electric bolt flow through her as he pulled her to his body.

He whispered in her ear. "I missed you." He opened his mouth to continue. Li's love engulfed her. Her heart coveted his lips, body, and soul. There was no more speaking. Li knew he couldn't stay long; he had his duty to attend to.

After a night of love, Marco and Li rose early just as the sun peeked over the horizon, Li's favorite time. Silence surrounded them, and only they existed in their world. She knew it was the only time he entirely belonged to her. In the afternoon, he would go to his uncle, Maffeo, to discuss the war. Marco's father had died the year after their return from Cathay.

When the sun fell, he returned to her, only to leave when the sun's light fully brightened the room––a time she began to hate.

Li had to be strong. This was Marco. Her whole life, he had disappeared for months at a time—his longest, a year—but he always returned. But this was different. She tried to understand why Marco had to fight. *Why couldn't he let the others do the fighting? We had fought so hard to be together; why would he take the chance of dying, leaving me in his world?*

Marco stood at the door with his captivating smile—a smile she could never resist. "I promise I will return soon."

She ran to him, throwing her arms around him, refusing to let him go. He whispered in her ear, "I promise I will return, my love." She slowly released him, and as he walked through the door, he paused, turned, and confidently said, "I promise."

1. Mongolian home, yurt

Chapter Three

Marco

Marco's Desperate Plea

Genoa Prison 1298

Marco lay on the prison floor, mumbling continuously, "Do you know who I am?" until he blacked out.

The guard awakened him from his nightmare of Li's whispering, *You promised*, with a kick to his side and yelling for him to rise. He opened his eyes and looked up. The guard standing over him grabbed him by his collar and quickly pulled him up, saying, "The general wants to see you."

When he entered the room, he saw several uniformed men. A general spoke. "I heard you were very noisy last night, shouting that you are Marco Polo. The man who lived for years in Cathay. Is that true?"

Out of habit, Marco bowed and replied in a strange accent, "Yes!" The men looked at each other. Marco wasted no time, knowing time could make a difference between life and death. This could be his only chance. He spoke up quickly. "Let's make a deal. I will tell you everything about Cathay, the Silk Road, and trade routes over land and sea. I'll advise you on everything you need: how many days it will take you, whether natives are friendly, their religion, what each town trades, and their leaders." Marco could see greed in their eyes.

He continued. "I can direct you to the most wondrous places in the world, making you rich. Provide me with a scribe; it will be faster." Their greed glowed. *I have caught them. Now it's time to reel them in,* Marco thought.

"In return, you release me as soon as I finish. Someone is waiting for me."

The men looked at each other and nodded at the guard. He grabbed Marco and led him out of the room. Marco rebelled and spoke in Tartarian. He stopped talking and looked at the men. "That is the language of the Great Khan; I am known throughout his empire. I can make you rich."

The guard pushed him forward and out the door. Marco prayed that he ignited their imagination and greed.

The men waited until he left. One spoke up. "Do you believe him?"

Another one answered, "I have heard of him. Everyone thought he, his father, and his uncle were dead. They vanished for twenty-four years. Then, one day, they arrived in Venice wearing strange clothing and barely able to speak Venetian. I heard they had jewels sewn into their clothing and told stories of how many treasures they had left behind."

The next day, the general moved Marco from a cell that held numerous prisoners to a cell made for two. The large metal door slammed, resonating through Marco's body, and the lock sliding closed intensified it. For the first time, his self-worth faltered. Marco disgustedly walked around his dim, new home as his fingers ran along the large stone-block walls decorated with wild scribbles from past, angry prisoners. Two makeshift beds sat on each side of the room, and a foul-smelling bucket sat in one corner. Light streamed in from a barred window, exposing a man sitting in a wooden blocky chair at a matching table engraved with illegible words. He was staring out the window. A stack of clean papers and a quill pen occupied a section of the table.

He turned and spoke to Marco. "Finally, a cell with an ocean view. It's marvelous. By the way, I'm Rustichello da Pisa. They said you need a scribe. I wrote romantic books about famous warriors before I was imprisoned here. Ever heard of *Roman de Roi Artus, The Legend of King Arthur*?"

Marco looked strangely at him. "Never heard of it."

Rustichello continued. "I guess you wouldn't have. They tell me you disappeared to a land called Cathay more than twenty-four years ago. So, what do you need?"

Marco excitedly answered. "An outline of my journey to quicken my release. You will do; anyone who can write can do it. My journey could be considered a romance, I guess—a love affair with a strange and exotic land, and just like a woman, she enticed me to discover every inch of her, exposing her mysterious and vulnerable secrets."

Marco looked out the window. "Where are we anyway?"

Rustichello looked at Marco. "This place is called Palazzo San Giorgio. In 1260, it was built for Guglielmo Boccanegra, the uncle of the first Doge of Genoa. Just like the Doge's Palace in Venice, he built prison cells on the bottom floor. This palazzo and his ideas were intended to separate and elevate the temporal power of the Republic's government from the religious power of the clergy. He failed and was deposed in 1262, then exiled to France. Since then, it's been a prison."

Marco shook his head. "What a fool. Let's start."

Rustichello hurriedly grabbed his paper and pen.

"In 1271..." As Marco retraced his footsteps, Rustichello listened. After an hour of Marco's passionate rattling, Rustichello interrupted him and looked up from his notes. "Marco Polo," he said excitedly, "I know they hired me to take down information, but I think we can both make money if I write your story. You know, write an actual book."

With a severe face, Marco looked at Rustichello. "I need to be released as quickly as possible. This needs to be direct and to the point."

Rustichello spoke up. "We can do both. Your tale needs to be told. You could call it...*Il Millione...the Description of the World, the Travels of Marco Polo.*"

Marco hesitated momentarily and said, "I like it." He could never turn down the thought of money. It was one of his faults he had inherited from his father and uncle.

"Let's start again."

Marco stared at Rustichello. "Again?" he hesitated. This will take too long."

"Tell me names and details, and I will do the rest," Rustichello said as he held his pen ready.

Marco started.

> *"My father, Messer Niccolò, and uncle, Messer Maffeo, left in 1260, the year Kubilai Khan was elected the Great Khan. They were traveling merchants. They had established trading posts before I was born in Constantinople. . . My father left my mother with a promise of his quick return. After arriving in Constantinople, business was brisk. Their quickness faded away. They resided in the Venetian quarters for several years until rumors began to spread that the political situation was becoming increasingly dangerous. They moved their business farther east. This was the beginning of their remarkable story, and how their fate changed my fate and life. They traveled by ship to Sudak and bought a house, but ventured further. Their decision paved the way to the ends of the earth. They met Berke Khan, lord of part of Tartary, living in Bolghar and Sarai.*[1] *This man, delighted, received them with great honor. My father traded him*

the jewels they had brought with them, and in exchange, this man gave them goods worth double and told them where to sell them. They became partners. My father and uncle could never turn down knowledge with the possibility of gaining a fortune, so they stayed a year meeting influential people. While they were there, a war broke out between Hulegu, Kubilai Khan's brother, and this Khan. The loss of life on both sides was terrible, but Hulegu was the victor. Again, my father and uncle could not return to Constantinople for fear of being abducted. They questioned their future again. So, after much discussion of the unknown that lay before them, their imagination of obtaining great wealth won, and they pressed forward. So, they went even further east with their goods and greed for adventure and money. They made their way to Ukek, a city on the western limit of the Western Khan's land. 1262, they crossed the Tigris and journeyed through a desert for seventeen days, arriving in the finest city in Persia, Bukhara. The ruler's name was Baraq, who in 1266 became the Khan of the Chagatai Khanate in Central Asia and fought its de facto ruler, Qaidu, Kubilai Khan's nephew and rival. A truce was called, and they divided the lands into two parts. Qaidu became ruler of the Chagatai Khanate of Middle Asia, and Baraq became Khan of the Ilkhanate of Persia, who Abaqa then defeated."

Rustichello interrupted Marco. "Stop."

Marco looked up at Rustichello, who looked confused and overwhelmed. "Who are these people?"

"Listen and write; I will explain later as we go. We have lots to cover." Marco continued.

"My father and my uncle, Maffeo, ended up staying three years as the route to return was marred by a war that raged between Hulegu and Baraq, and in the future, a war between Kubilai Khan and his younger brother, Ariq Boke, made both trips impassable. While they were there, an envoy sent by Hulegu, the lord of the Levant, stopped on their way to see the Great Khan of the Tartars, Kubilai, who lived in the east-north-eastern direction at the end of the earth (1266). Hulegu was Kubilai Khan's other brother. He had sided with Kubilai in the civil war. This envoy was so amazed when they saw my father and uncle, as no Latins had been seen in this part of the world. They surprised my father and uncle with the request to trust the leader of the envoy and travel with them.

'Sirs,' the leader said, 'you will find it incredibly conducive to your profit and honor. The great lord of the Tartars has never seen any Latins and is eager to meet one, so if you accompany me until we reach him, I assure you he will be happy to see you and treat you with great honor and liberality. And with me, you will travel safely and without hindrance.' When my father and uncle heard this, they couldn't believe what they heard. Their first decision, to continue east six years ago instead of returning to their families, led them to this place. That decision had determined their destiny, so they agreed to follow them."

Marco finally stopped and looked at Rustichello. "Remember the name Abaqa, his son Arghun, and grandson Ghazan; they will play a large part in my return to Venice years later." Marco, remembering his father's story about the envoy, continued. "A young lad, maybe around eight, rode with the envoy. He was a miniature soldier, wholly dressed in uniform; his demeanor was confident and proud. Two men rode next to him. My father noticed during the day that the young boy continually stared at them. Then, one night, the curious lad escaped his escorts, found them, and sat down around their campfire.

"'My name is Arghun. What's yours?'

"My father and uncle stood and bowed. 'I'm Messer Niccolò, and this man is my brother, Messer Maffeo.'

"The young lad stood, bowed, and sat. 'I have never seen a Latin before. You are Christian; my mother was a Christian. Tell me about your homeland.'"

Marco continued. "My father knew Arghun was important but not just how important he truly was. It wasn't long before a man with a frantic face ran over to their camp. 'Your Highness, Sartaq Noyan will be looking for you; it is almost time for your lessons. You promised!'

"Shocked, my father and uncle quickly stood. The young man remained seated and spoke as he pointed. 'This is Jochigan Noyan, my atabeg. I suppose you're curious about who I am. My atabeg spoiled my secret. Abaqa, the khan of these lands, is my father. My name is Prince Arghun. I must go now.' He stood and asked his atabeg, 'Can I return another day? It could be part of my lessons.' His atabeg looked at them and nodded yes. The prince smiled.

"My father and uncle saw the young prince on and off that year as it took them a year to arrive at Kubilai Khan's court in Karakorum.

"As the envoy said, the Great Khan was delighted to see them. He held lavish festivities in their honor; they were sure it was not just for them but for the young Khan Khuu Prince, his great-grandnephew. The last day they saw the young prince, he told them, 'We will meet again.'

"Kubilai Khan's joy astonished my father and uncle at their arrival and his curiosity about the other parts of the world, such as our kings, how they maintained authority, their justice, and how they went to battles. Kubilai Khan then asked them about the customs of the Latins and their religion. My father told him of the Lord Pope and all the practices of the Roman Church. They answered his questions with a firm grasp of the Tartar language, speaking honestly and wisely; the khan was delighted. So pleased, he sent emissaries to the pope and wanted my father and uncle to undertake this mission with one of his barons, Kogatal. My father and uncle agreed and left with letters written in Turkish asking the pope to send as many as a hundred men. Kubilai Khan wanted learned men in the Christian religion who were versed in the seven arts (grammar, rhetoric, dialectic and arithmetic, geometry, astronomy, and music). And he wanted oil from the lamp of Christ's sepulcher in Jerusalem."

Rustichello stopped Marco. "Maybe we should add that Kubilai Khan wanted these Christians to demonstrate plainly to idolaters that their religion was utterly false. All household idols they worship are the devil, and Christianity is superior to their faith. Maybe the readers will accept this book more freely."

Marco looked up with a serious face. "That could be true, but Kubilai Khan accepted all religions and treated them all fairly. I want the world to know. Let's continue."

Rustichello nodded and held his pen ready.

"They left with the baron, the letters, and a remarkable gold tablet inscribed with instructions that the three men, wherever they went, were to be provided accommodations, horses, and men to escort them from place to place. In 1269, three years later, they arrived—minus the baron who had fallen ill—in Acre, the kingdom of Jerusalem. Unfortunately, they found the Pope had died, and it seemed it would be a while before a new Pope was elected, so they returned home to Venice to see their families. From Acre, they went to Negroponte[2] and boarded a ship to Venice."

Marco fell silent. Rustichello looked up from his papers and spoke. "And...?"

Marco continued after much thought. "I was only five when my father left, ten when my mother died, and fifteen when he returned—discovering his wife, my mother, had died. Not once had he written her a letter, yet my mother never lost faith or her love for him. She taught me to be prepared for his return. 'Show him you have studied hard, and you know precious goods, their cost, the trade routes, and the important merchants in town. Listen, learn languages, and study.'

"On the day of his arrival, I wasn't sure how I felt. Did I want to meet him? The only memories I have of him are those my mother shared with me. He had shown no loyalty to either of us. Only out of respect for my mother, I tolerated him that day. My father seemed genuinely saddened by my mother's death and concerned about my future. However, I could tell he wasn't sure what to do with me: take or leave me? Kubilai Khan and the Far East awaited him. Yet, my uncle made it clear I would be a hindrance if I came along. Besides, I hadn't decided if I wanted to go. There wasn't much love between us, and I knew he only felt responsible because I was his only son. I felt the same way, as he was my only father.

"That year, my father and uncle purchased an impressive, large palazzo near the Grand Canal with their newfound riches. After we moved in, every evening, we sat around a large table and they reminisced about the treasures: gold, jewels, spices, and the silk they had seen, the money to be had, and the amazing man they met at the end of the world—a man who controlled the largest empire in the world. My father would say. 'Just think of the numerous trading posts we could control, where others aren't allowed, if we deliver his wishes.' Excitement flowed around the room. My heart pumped faster, and my blood boiled with the contagious excitement. Suddenly, I desired to experience it myself and meet this mysterious man. How could I not? I had the same greedy, adventurous blood running through my veins. Except I had my mother's instinct: love, learn, and make yourself needed.

"Finally, one night, he sat me down. 'If you want to go with me, you must learn as many languages and dialects as possible and the ability to script each. Your job will be to remember and recite our journeys to the Great Khan in a fascinating way.' I agreed in Turkish, impressing my father; I earned my place. My mother's steadfast determination had taught me well.

"By the year's end, my father and uncle couldn't wait any longer for the election of a new pope. Our journey began."

---

1. The capital of the Golden Horde, north of the Russian city of Astrakhan

2. Chalcis

Chapter Four

Marco

1271 Middle East

Genoa Prison 1298

> *"So, in 1271, we left and headed for Acre. We met up with the legate of the Roman Church for the entire kingdom of Egypt, Theobald of Piacenza. My father and uncle told him the story of Kubilai Khan and his request. He understood their dilemma and wrote letters to the Great Khan, testifying that my father and uncle had tried to fulfill their mission, explaining that a new pope had not been elected. However, they obtained the requested oil. With the letters in hand, we started our return trip. We had traveled a short distance when we received news that a new Pope had been elected, the same man who had written the letters, Theobald of Piacenza. He asked us to return as he would fulfill the Khan's wishes: two friars would accompany us with the same authority as himself to ordain priests and bishops along their way.*□

> *"After meeting the new pope, we finally set off on our journey. Unfortunately, when we arrived in Bunduqdari, the Egyptian Sultan had invaded Armenia and devastated the country. The friars feared for their lives. They no longer wanted to continue; they gave us the privileges and letters and went off with the Grand Master of the Templars."*

Marco recounted the journey by day. However, at night, his mind returned to his love and the friends he had made, and it was then he decided to exclude them. They were his secret. He held them close to his heart and didn't want to share them with anyone. Only Kubilai Khan would be brought alive; he wanted the world to know what one man had accomplished.

The next day, Marco continued.

"There are two Armenias, the greater and the lesser. The lesser is where Ayas is located, a coastal city where trade is bustling with merchants from Venice, Genoa, and all over the world buying spices, clothes, and all other valuable things from the interior that were sold here. Additionally, if you plan to head into the interior, your journey begins here. Their ruler is a king who rules with wisdom and justice and is subject to the Tartars.

"Then there is Turkey; there are three races of people. First is Turkmen. They worship Muhammad. They are nomads searching for good pastures as their land consists of mountains and plains. They are known for horses and mules, which fetch high prices. The other races are Armenians and Greeks, who live among the Turkmans. Their most important cities are Konya, Kayseri, and Seivas."

Marco pauses for a moment. "You know, the finest and the most beautiful carpets in the world are woven in Turkey." Rustichello nodded and kept writing. Marco stood and walked around the small cell. His mind was racing. *How can I tell my story fast? There is so much to tell. So many men have never seen what I have seen. So many won't believe my fantastic tale.*

Rustichello interrupted Marco's thoughts. "Marco, continue if you want to finish fast."

Marco looked at him seriously. "There is so much to tell!"

"Just talk. I will choose what to write."

Marco sat on the floor facing Rustichello and rambled on.

"The next province is the vast Greater Armenia. I will begin with a city called Erzincan. It is the seat of an archbishop. They are known for the best buckram in the world... There are beautiful baths fed by the best springs.... There's a village between Trebizond and Tabriz[1] called Bayburt...a great silver mine. The Tartars of the Levant spend their summers here because of excellent pasturelands for their animals. In winter....snow falls in immeasurable amounts and brings freezing weather; no animal can survive.... In the middle of Greater

Armenia....a mountain very high, shaped like a cube, which they say the Noah's Ark rested.... To the southeast, Greater Armenia borders the kingdom of Mosul. Its people are Christians.... To the north is Georgia; a spring gushes oil at such a rate that a hundred ships can load at once. It is not good to eat but burns well and is used as a salve for man and animals. Men come from far off to fetch this oil... In Georgia....King David Malik, subject to the Tartars.... Alexander the Great constructed a tower and fortress known as the Iron Gate here... There are numerous towns and villages. They have a great deal of silk and weave gorgeous clothes of silk and gold....best goshawks in the world... All things are abundant, and the people live by trade and industry.... The province's landscape is mountainous with narrow, secure passes. The Tartars have never entirely been able to enforce their authority.... In its vast mountains, the entire forests are box trees...."

Rustichello stopped Marco. His hand ached. He needed to collect his thoughts; his mind was full. "Let's continue tomorrow. I'll write later tonight after I rest."

Marco also felt drained. He lay on the makeshift bed and drifted in and out of dreams and thoughts of his first meeting with Abaqa in 1272 on his way to Kubilai Khan. So many years had passed, and he was only sixteen then... Everything was so new and exciting.

Tabriz was the home of Abaqa Khan, lord of the Tartars of the Levant, and Kubilai Khan's nephew. His palace, Takht-e Soleyman, blended the surrounding culture and Mongol tradition. It had beautiful, pleasant gardens and a lake, surrounded by mountains that sloped to lowland plains, rich with grasslands. Here, my father gave Abaqa the letter from the Lord Pope, which granted us his aid and favor so we could visit the lands beyond the sea. Abaqa's gracious greeting surprised us. More surprising was that one of his wives was Christian from the Byzantine imperial family. When she entered the room, Lord Abaqa introduced his wife, Marie Palaiologos. "She is now called Despina Khatun, our spiritual leader." But that wasn't the only surprise; Abaqa mentioned that he knew my uncle and father through letters from his son, Arghun.

"My son wrote he enjoyed visiting you. You expanded his imagination and vision of the future."

Marco remembered the conversation so clearly.

“I am honored, my Lord,” my father said as he bowed.

Abaqa turned and looked at me and asked my father, “Who is this young man?”

“This is Marco, my son,” my father answered.

Abaqa continued talking to me. “You must be almost the age of Arghun?”

“I might be three or four years older,”

“Do you have a son, Marco?” Despina Khatun asked.

I tried not to be shocked. “No.”

The king said proudly, “Arghun has a son; our line continues! His name is Ghazan.”

“You must be proud,” my father answered.

“Yet, you are lucky, Messer Niccolò, to have your son by your side,” the king responded.□“I will grant whatever you need for a safe journey through our lands.”

I saw my father smile. “We are grateful. We would like to go to the great port of Hormuz, hoping to board a ship to Cathay.”

Abaqa replied, “I will issue you a letter, and when you reach the city of Kerman,[2] *look up, Ashraf, an honest man. Most likely, you will find him at the most significant caravanserai.*[3] *This letter will instruct him to be your escort. You will need protection when you reach the province of Rudbar; you could encounter the Qaraunas.” The king paused. “I will check where my son, Arghun, is.”*

This scene led Marco’s mind to another and another: to Ghazan, then Kokochin. Marco smiled. Ghazan and Kokochin grew up a great distance apart, but they were culturally raised in the same way: the Tartar way.

After seventeen years of service, Marco’s last mission for the Great Khan was bringing the young Princess Kokochin to this palace. He fondly remembered Kokochin, Kubilai Khan’s daughter, standing beside her new husband, weeping as Marco, Li, his father, and uncle left her. Marco continued thinking.

I had been in Cathay for four years when I met this bold little girl, Kokochin. It was February 1279 in Khanbaliq,[4] *the winter capital. At dawn, a glimmer of light peeked over the eastern wall. The Khan’s men opened the outer south gates that led to the grand palace.*

The White Feast, a New Year’s tradition, began this day. The people of the empire gathered by the hundreds to observe the beautiful white horses racing through the city streets. Many of the horses were given as gifts to the Great Khan. Then, a procession of 5,000 elephants entered the city, each draped in white silk embroidered with birds and beasts. Embellished gold and silver boxes on their backs sparkled, carrying incredible white apparel for the court. Crowds roared with excitement. Following the elephants were numerous camels draped in white silk, packing food and drinks for the honored guests, who were also lavishly dressed in white and gold, bearing great gifts of gold, silver, pearls, precious stones, and refined white cloth for Kubilai Khan. And as they offered these magnificent gifts, they said, "May this year bring luck to you and success in all you undertake."

It was also a tradition that each guest made white and gold gifts and offered them to all the other guests, whether friends or foes, hoping that the gifts would bless them with prosperity and happiness throughout the year.

I stood beside Kokochin's brother, Chinghiz, the crown prince, dressed in white and gold, observing the grand parade. Kokochin had escaped from her mother and ran to me. I must have looked strange to her. My hair was long and curly, and I had a thick, curly beard. Kokochin tugged at my clothing. Bending down, I looked into her soft eyes. She slowly reached up and touched the hair on my face. I laughed, as everyone else did. She had stolen one of her mother's presents from her basket and handed me a white jeweled box filled with ancient seashells intended for another. Her mother was too embarrassed to retrieve the present. Later, I returned it minus one seashell that I had kept. Our friendship started that day.

Marco stopped recalling. His heart ached. The room was so quiet he could hear Rustichello's pen scratching the paper as he swiftly wrote. Marco closed his eyes and tried to sleep. Morning would soon be here.

The next day began as the last, with stories.

> *"There is a monastery called St. Leonards where the miraculous occurrence I will describe takes place. There is a great lake that collects the water from mountain streams near the church, but not a fish can be found throughout the year, with the sole exception that on the first day of Lent, they begin to arrive and keep coming every day of Lent until Holy Saturday or Easter Eve... His province looks out over two seas: the Black Sea lies to the North and the other Sea of Ghelor Ghalen to the east....it's not a natural sea....2800 miles in circumference....surrounded by mountains and the rivers, Euphrates, the Tigris, and the Gihon that flow into it. There are many islands. Refugees fled to them because of the invasion by the Tartars. Genoese merchants launched ships to purchase Ghalen silk. Near this province is Tbilisi, a substantially fine city; the inhabitants are Christians, Armenians, Georgians, Saracens,[5] and Jews.... Silks and other fabrics are woven, subject to the Great Khan of the Tartars...*

"I have told you about Armenia's neighbors to the East... Next, we will talk about the lands to the south and east. Mosul...large kingdom.... There, the race is Arabs, who worship Muhammad. Another race observes the law of Christ but not the rule of the Roman Church, for they are misguided in many parts. They are Nestorians and Jacobites...which are all the Christians I met. The cloth of silk and gold known as mosulin is made here.... There are renowned merchants, known as Mosulin, who export precious spices in vast quantities.... And in the mountains, a race called Kurds, Christians, and Saracens.... They are bold and wicked people, very fond of robbing merchants...□

"The next province is Mus and Mardin....where cotton grows in abundance.... They manufacture many wares on a grand scale....and many merchants and artisans are subject to the king of Tartars.

"Now, let's leave these kingdoms to speak of the great city of Baghdad. Baghdad is a vast city where the caliph[6] of all Saracens has his seat, just as the head of all the world's Christians has his seat in Rome. A great river flows through the middle of the city, which flows directly to the Indian Ocean.... Merchants are constantly going and coming....taking 18 days....between Baghdad and Kish...a great city. Basra stands on the river....finest dates in the world are grown. Many kinds of gold and silk fabrics are woven in Baghdad, including nasich and nakh, which feature elaborate works with figures of animals and birds... Pearls exported from India to Christendom are pierced in Baghdad... They study the law of Muhammad, necromancy, physics, astronomy, geomancy, and physiognomy.... Moreover, the caliph of Baghdad possessed the most fabulous hoard of treasure in gold, silver, and precious stones of any man."

Marco stopped reciting and looked at Rustichello. "Do you want to hear a story about when the great Tartar lord, Hulegu,[7] marched onto Baghdad in 1255? Do you remember Abaqa, whom I met in Tabriz with his Christian wife? Hulegu was his father. Hulegu was one of four brothers, the grandsons of the Great Genghis Khan, who were Tartar lords who ruled his empire. The eldest one, Mengu, was then the Great Khan. Later, Kubilai.

"By 1255, the brothers had already subjugated Cathay and other adjoining countries with overwhelming force, but far from being content with these conquests, their ambitions were so great they had made up their minds to fulfill their grandfather Genghis Khan's dream to conquer the whole world. And in the end, they divided it into four parts. Kubilai was to go east, conquering Cathay to establish the Yuan Dynasty, and Hulegu was to go to the southwest. The Empire of the Golden Horde was to the North, and Qaidu, the Empire of Chagatai, ruled Middle Asia.□

"The southwest fell to Hulegu; he set out before the others and embarked on a bold campaign of conquest in those regions until he came to Baghdad. Being outnumbered and lacking strength, a consequence of Baghdad's immense population, Hulegu used a cunning tactic. Hulegu commanded at least 100,000 cavalry but wanted the caliph, the Muslim ruler, and the people inside the gates to think they were few. So, before they approached the city, half stayed in the forest, and the other half galloped to the gates. The caliph, thinking Hulegu had very few men, vowed to defeat them by relying on anything but the banner of Muhammad, and he charged out of the city at the head of soldiers. As soon as Hulegu saw this, he retreated and made the caliph come out to the forest where his other men lay in ambush. He surrounded them, crushed them, and they captured the caliph. When the city fell and Hulegu entered, he found a great tower belonging to the caliph, filled with treasures of gold, silver, and other prizes. It disgusted Hulegu that the caliph had become a great miser by not sharing his wealth with his soldiers, who defended him and the city. Hulegu asked him why, but he could not answer him. Hulegu continued. 'Caliph, since I can see how dearly you love treasures, I will give you your own to eat.' They then locked the caliph in this tower without food or drink with the instructions: 'Eat your treasure since you are so fond of it. You will eat nothing else again.' They left him in the tower for four days, where he died."

Rustichello hesitated momentarily. "I guess he learned a deadly lesson that day. A less greedy man would have given away his treasures to defend his land and people, rather than die despoiled with all his people." Marco nodded. "Greed." Suddenly, he thought of his life and his father's, also driven by greed. *I now sit in a prison cell, something like a tower. Will I die the same way?*

He closed his eyes and continued reciting. "Next, I'll tell you about Tabriz." Marco stuck to the facts, eliminating any personal story he had recalled the night before:

"Tabriz is a large, noble city in a province called Iraq. The people live by trade and craft.... Fabrics of gold and silverware were woven here.... Merchants from many places, including Latin, travel here to buy goods from foreign lands.... Precious stones are found in great abundance.... Orchards surround the city....excellent fruit.... Traveling merchants make great profits in this city. The Saracens of Tabriz are wicked and treacherous.... Their prophet Muhammad permitted them to do as much harm to those who did not share their faith. If they are killed, or in any way by Christians, they become martyrs.... They are converting the Tartars and many other nations to their laws because it gave them great license to sin..."

He continued with Persia. "It is a twelve-day journey from Tabris."

"It's a vast province comprising of eight kingdoms.... Fine horses are bred in many of these kingdoms, and they sent many for sale to India from the cities of Kish and Hormuz. They sold for at least 200 livres tournois each. Also, they sell the most beautiful asses in the world. They sell for more than the horses because they eat little, carry heavy burdens, drink little, and cross over deserts that horses can't endure.... They also use camels.... These kingdoms are brutal and bloodthirsty people; they are forever slaughtering each other. If not for the Authorities and the Tartar, lord of the Levant, merchants would be in great harm... He decreed that people who live along the most perilous routes must supply at the merchants' request capable guides to protect them in return for payment.... In these cities, there is much cotton....plenty of wheat, barley...pantic grass, grains, wine, and all kinds of fruit....□

"Leaving these kingdoms, we come to Yazd, a splendid city....busy trading centre.... Silk fabric yasdi is manufactured in large quantities and exported. They worship Muhammad.... The traveler who leaves this land journeys seven days without caravanserais except in three places...Zein ud-din, Kerman-shuhan, Shamash. There are beautiful groves of dates, wild

game....partridges, and quails....beautiful wild asses. And at the end of the seven-day journey lies a kingdom of Kerman on the edge of the Lut desert....Tartars' rules.... Stones called turquoise are produced in the mountains and are found in great abundance.... Dug out of rocks....plentiful seams of steel.... Skilled artisans make a full range of gear for soldiers....bridles, saddles, and spurs....swords, quivers, and every sort of armor. The gentlewomen and their daughters are superb needleworkers, embroidering animals and birds...figures on silk of every hue....for nobles and great men....quilts, cushions, pillows.... The best and swiftest falcons in the world are bred here....smaller than peregrine falcons, with red feathers on their breast and under the tail.... No bird can out-fly them with their incredible speed."

Marco paused. "I didn't tell you about King Abaqa. We met him in Tabriz. He gave us a letter naming an escort we should find upon reaching Kerman. After asking numerous merchants, we found Ashraf—his name meant "the honorable one"—in a large caravanserai outside the town. The caravanserai was a large rectangular building built around a massive courtyard where large, colorful groups of merchants and their camels, oxen, and asses could rest without fear of being robbed. It was also where merchants like ourselves connected with other merchants, making deals and trades for their services when moving your merchandise to further outposts was impossible.

"Ashraf was a broad-shouldered and stout-looking man, taller than Tartar. His name was Persian, so we assumed he was of mixed heritage. He carried a large, simple sword, and a considerable scar ran down his left cheek. A friendly and confident man, but his aura seemed severe and stern. My father greeted Ashraf with the letter. He looked at our group and roared with laughter. 'How could I refuse?'

"We joined his caravan the next day and continued our journey.

"Leaving Kerman....the caravan traveled for seven days, continuing across cities and towns.... Riding was good....plenty of game....but when you travel across the plain for seven days, suddenly you come to the division of the lands....a significant drop which takes two days' ride through orchards heavy with fruit to reach the bottom....where now only nomads live grazing their flocks.... Winters are so bitterly cold they can barely endure even by piling upon layers of clothes and furs...."

Marco finally stopped talking, feeling tired and disillusioned with the process. He questioned himself, *Will this work? Will I be released as soon as I'm finished?*

Rustichello looked up. His face and hands were black with ink. The writing desk overflowed with mounds of papers, and the floor beneath him was white like snow. His black index finger pointed at Marco. "Why did you stop?"

The exhausted Marco, walking around the cell, sat on his bed and stared at Rustichello.

"There is so much, and this is just the beginning. Maybe I made a mistake. This is impossible. I don't have my notes or Li's, and my head hurts. She's waiting, and I promised her."

"She will continue to wait if you don't continue," Rustichello said unsentimentally.

Rustichello greedily thought to himself, *Even if he finishes, I doubt they will release him, but I will have an outstanding book!*

"OK, Marco. Rest. We will continue tomorrow." Rustichello felt a tinge of guilt and thought, *I do feel sorry for him.*

Marco lay down on his side, facing the wall, and closed his eyes. He envisioned Li. She was so beautiful. What is she doing now? The thought caused him pain. His despair grew, turning to silent sobs. Marco's self-pity continued until he thought of Kim Chin-hae, his friend. *Kim never gave up and returned to his love, Lis.* Drawing from Kim's strength, he thought, *I must do this!*

Marco recalled his day of storytelling. There were so many stories he had not told—things that didn't pertain to anything the generals would want, but stories that could make an exciting book. Like the town of fire worshippers in Kala Asthparastan and the experiment, the wise men performed for the king of Kerman to prove that evil comes from the soil.

Tomorrow, he promised himself, *I will continue!* As he lay, his mind returned to Li.

---

1. Greater Armenia

2. South-East Iran

3. An inn with a central courtyard for travelers in the desert of Asia.

4. Beijing

5. Muslins

6. A chief Muslin ruler

7. The empire of the Ilkhanate

Chapter Five

Li

1298 Li, Luca, and Kokochin

Venice 1298

All alone, Li sat at her dressing table, gazing at her reflection instead of sitting at her window. A feeling she had never felt before came over her—a fear that she might never see Marco again. Shivering as darkness crept around her, she knew a servant would soon come. Li hoped it would be the same young servant. She liked her and wished they could become friends, wanting to share her story with someone.

A knock interrupted her brooding. The door opened. Li looked up and smiled. It was her. The girl shyly smiled back and quickly walked around the room, lighting the candles. Li wasted no time, thinking she had nothing to lose. In her Cathayan accent, she asked, "Are you happy being a servant to a wealthy family? Would you change your situation if you could? Would you risk everything to have a different life?"

Before Luca answered Li, she hesitated and studied Li. Luca had been told she had the talent to read people's faces. She had heard from the other servants that this person never spoke to anyone. *Why is she asking me such a personal question? Is it a trap?* After a few minutes, while Li stared at Luca, waiting for the answer, Luca could see that this face was lonely and sad. With boldness and curiosity, Luca lowered her guard and asked, "Who are you, really?"

Li didn't hesitate and, with honesty, answered, "I am not much different from you. I, too, am a servant, but of a different kind. My family was rich and powerful, and my father had been an emperor of a vast dynasty called Song, but a more powerful man named Kubilai Khan conquered us. At five, I was his captive and belonged to him." Tears swelled, and a memory she held deep in her heart came rushing back.

Li continued in a soft voice. "I would begin a new life in the palace of Kubilai Khan. Fortunately, Kubilai Khan's favorite wife, Empress Chabi, was kind, took pity on me, and adopted me. I lived in her chambers. Her kindness allowed Guo Yu—Peter to you—to remain my servant. During that time, I became a Tartar and a ghost to survive, as the other women in court despised me. At nine, Empress Chabi died. Again, I felt alone and had no one except for Guo Yu.

"When Empress Chabi died, I was as scared as the day my mother killed herself—the day the Song dynasty surrendered. I remembered the words of a kind stranger who rescued me. This same man escorted us to Shang-du where Kubilai Khan's summer palace stands. In the Hall of Great Peace, Kubilai Khan stripped my grandmother and stepmother of their titles and awarded them a home in Khanbaliq. My half-brother, Emperor Zhao, was no longer an Emperor but received the title Duke of Ying. He was then married to a princess of Kubilai descent, Lady Borjigin. At the time, I was too young to understand any of this.

Li stopped talking, opened a small drawer, pulled out a silk scarf, and ran her fingers over the initials embroidered on one corner. "Look, I still have his scarf. His words, even though I could not understand them, were comforting. His voice and face were gentle and full of sorrow. I felt he understood. I still see the vivid image of this man squatting in front of me with his hands on my shoulder, speaking as Guo Yu translated the man's words. His words still ring true: 'I was a little older than you when my mother died. Like you, I was alone in this world and had to depend on others. My mother loved me with all her heart, and her words were my saving grace. She stressed this daily and even on her deathbed: *"You must listen carefully to the world around you, pay attention, learn what is important to others, become valuable, and seek information, never become their victim. This way, you will survive this cruel world."* I listened to my mother, and I hope you will listen to me now. Have courage and strength, and you will survive. Perhaps your life will surprise you as mine did. After he spoke those words, I didn't see this man again for numerous years.

Li went silent, thinking about Marco's words. *I am alone. Again, I should listen to his words.* Li didn't want to talk about herself anymore, so she started talking randomly about Kokochin.

Luca interrupted and asked. "Who's Kokochin?"

"She was a loyal friend. I met her when I was thirteen," Li answered, then mumbled. "I wish you could be my friend; I need one."

Luca questioned Li. "What did you say? I couldn't understand the last thing you said."

Li didn't answer her as she looked out the dark window and continued. "The stars are bright and celestial as Kokochin, but she, too, was a servant—a servant to traditions of her ancestors, her father, her mother, and to an empire. But she embraced her destiny. On the other hand, I chose a different path. I am a servant of my desires, my love, and my decisions. They belong to me and no one else."

It surprised Luca to find Li to be a very human and ordinary girl—not a pagan who was going to hell, as the other maids warned her. Luca never thought of Li as a servant like herself. The whispers she heard from the other servants when she entered the chambers of Isabella—Marco's cousin—made Li out to be an evil, manipulative monster. The household distrusted Li. *How could Marco bring this barbaric woman to our home? How can he love a pagan?*

Isabella and Maffeo's other daughter, too, had been left by their father, but unlike Marco, who joined them in their travels, they continued to be raised by their aunt and uncle. Their lives were surprisingly happy and normal. They married well. Isabella's husband had died several years before, and she had moved back with her father, who lived in Niccolò's home—now Marco's.

As Luca listened, she dreamed of changing her destiny, but she had never thought it was possible. Now, she wanted to hear more.

Li continued. "From the time Kokochin could understand, Kokochin's mother would tell her the story of her people. Kokochin knew from an early age that marrying for love was not an option; one could only hope it would come with the marriage. Her father had many wives, consorts, concubines, and children." Luca had to stop her there. "Her father had many wives. Is that allowed in your culture?"

Li thought for a moment before answering. "Yes, her mother was one of many. Kokochin was a Tartar; her mother was from the Bayaud tribe, also known as the Forest people. She was a beautiful and skilled survivor. Her tribe came from the beautiful valleys of the Jida River, a contrast from the steppe, the home of her father, the Emperor of the Yuan Dynasty. Her tribe, since the time of Genghis Khan—Kokochin's great-grandfather—had married women from the river. The purpose of the daughters of the Great Khan, especially from this tribe, was to marry to form alliances willingly. It was their duty to give birth and raise great men worthy of becoming the next Great Khan or daughters who would become wives of kings.

"Kokochin was born the year Marco arrived in our world. I'm pretty sure it was the year 1275. Her mother never had a son, but she was proud, ambitious, and strong like her ancestors. She was well-taught by her mother, who knew her purpose: to groom her daughter to become a great man's wife. Her mother started her plan the day Kubilai came to her quarters to name his new daughter. A Han monk who accompanied him took one look and said she was celestial with her bluish skin, and her name should be Kokochin. From that day, her mother groomed her to become Kubilai Khan's favorite daughter. Han scholars taught her as her father preferred. Also, she could never forget she was Tartar. Kubilai Khan loved hunting and horses, and his daughter would, too. Her mother saw to that."

Just then, there was a gentle knock on Li's door.

It was Guo Yu. "I have your dinner."

Luca looked at Li with disappointment. "Can we continue tomorrow?"

Li smiled happily; she had made a friend. "Of course, tomorrow."

Luca walked over to the door and opened it. As Guo Yu walked in, she walked out.

Guo Yu could feel that Li's sad mood had lifted. He didn't want to take this away, but it was his job to protect her. "Li, please remember the chamber life in the palace. Trusting can be a perilous game. This place can be the same as the inner chamber." Li just nodded as they sat and ate their meal.

Chapter Six

Marco

The Enchantment

Genoa prison 1298

Marco had finally fallen into a deep slumber and woke up with a clear, refreshed mind, ready for a new day. He looked over at Rustichello, asleep at his desk. His head rested upon the mounds of papers. Marco rose, walked over to him, and shook his shoulder. Rustichello lifted his head. One side of his face was imprinted with writing.

Marco smiled. "I'm ready. I will tell the story of when I almost died. It was around the year 1272 as we traveled to meet Kubilai..."

Rustichello shoved the paper aside, found a clean sheet, and said, "Let's start."

> *"When we left Kerman, and at the end of the two-day descent, you find yourself on a vast plain....a city called Kamadin....neither big nor fine, but had been repeatedly ravaged by the Tartars' invasion...scorching hot on the plain. The province is called Rudbar....they produce grains, and their fruit grows on the slopes of the mountains...dates, pomegranates, lemons, apples, and many others that cannot grow in colder climates... This plain is home to different birds: a francolin with mottled black and white plumage with red feet and beaks....and an ox so enormous and entirely white as snow.... The hair is short and smooth....horns short and thick....and between the shoulders a round hump two hands high... They're the most beautiful sight in the world....they lie down when you load them like camels....surprisingly strong....and sheep as big as*

asses....tails thick and plump and weigh a good thirty pounds....make excellent eating.

"As you crossed over the plains, there were no longer caravanserais. The honorable Ashraf rode beside us as we passed towns and villages surrounded by thick and tall earthen ramparts. We questioned him about the ramparts. Ashraf answered. 'It's because of the Quraunas who infest these parts. These ramparts are the only protection against them. This is the main reason the king instructed you to find me. I am known for my luck, fighting, and honor. You will arrive safely at your destination, Hormuz.' He then rode off.

"That night, we sat around the slightly more prominent campfire, surrounded by tall and thick earthen walls with our weapons nearby. Trying not to show fear, I questioned my father about the Quraunas. My father, who could hear the fear in my voice, tried to comfort me but knew little about them. That's when an old toothless man who sat beside his camel stood and joined our camp. He sat down without being asked and started talking. 'Quraunas are mixed breeds, sons of Indian mothers and Tartar fathers.'

"He wove a frightening story. 'They have the power of black magic, turning daylight into darkness that takes seven days to cross. They know the lay of the land inside and out, so they ride side by side when they summon the darkness. No one in their path can escape them. They butcher the old men and sell young men and women as slaves in other countries. They lay waste to everything around them.' Everyone sat silently, and finally, I spoke up. 'I want to hear more. Tell us.'

"'They come from Dilivar.[1] They ride 30 to 40 days to get here because of merchants like you. While you wait for ships to arrive from India, your mules and camels graze in the plains, fattening their poor, overtired bodies. This is Quraunas' favorite time of the year.'

"I looked at my father, who looked at the old man and declared, 'I think we heard enough. Isn't it time to retire?' Everyone agreed.

"The old man smiled a toothless smile, stood, and returned to his camel. My uncle spoke, looking at my father. 'Do you believe they hold the knowledge of enchantment?'

"'No.' my father sternly said as he put more dung on the fire. 'Let's go to sleep; we have a long day tomorrow.'

"The next morning, Ashraf joined us. 'Did you sleep well?' He had a sly smile on his face. 'Did the old man tell you about the Quraunas' ability to turn day to night?' He could tell from my face that he did. His smile turned into roaring laughter. After he exhausted himself, he turned to us. 'Imagine a storm of 10,000 racing horses pounding the dry earth, thick swirling dust clouds rising, reaching for the sky, and concealing your world around you. So, after the thundering horses pass, their lingering power remains in the air for days, making it impossible to see.' He turned to me. 'It's a dust storm; the Quarunas used it to their advantage. The old man was correct when he said they knew the land inside and out. You understand, now?' Ashraf said in a half-laugh. My father nodded and, in a concerned voice, said, 'I hope we don't experience the thundering horses.'"

Rustichello stopped Marco. "I like the word enchantment better; it sounds more exciting and mysterious."

Marco didn't care how Rustichello wrote it; he kept talking.

"Unfortunately, the next day, as if the old man knew, the cloud appeared on the horizon. We covered our faces with scarves and our bodies with blankets, huddled beside our animals by the earthen wall, and prayed. After the heavy dust passed, we still couldn't see 100 paces in front of us because the air was opaque, as the older man said. Within the day, wild men were upon us, unmercifully killing. Unable to see, we only heard women and children screaming, sword blades ringing as they struck another sword, men grunting, and tortured animal sounds. We continued to pray that Ashraf was the lucky, skilled swordsman he claimed to be. We had our swords drawn, and our horses and camels surrounded us. We squinted, trying to see. The ringing and grunting came closer and closer. In a swift moment, the body of a dark man with a long scarf covering most of his face fell under the horse's feet. Blood oozed from beneath the scarf; someone had slit his throat. Another man in a military uniform, whom we hadn't seen before, started yelling for us to follow him. We grabbed the reins of our animals and quickly followed.

"Minutes later, several other uniformed men and Ashraf on horses surrounded us. We stayed as close to them as we could and ran. We didn't stop until we reached the village of Kamasal."

Marco stopped talking here. The candles had grown short; they had been at it all day and most of the night. Marco lay down. Rustichello watched, shook his head, blew out the candles, and retired. It had been a long day.

In the room's quietness, Marco's mind wouldn't be still, even though he was weary and needed rest. His thoughts returned to the young man, Prince Arghun, who led them to safety.

Prince Arghun was several years younger than I, but his fighting skills were remarkable. When we arrived in Kamasal village, the air was more transparent. I looked at the men responsible for our rescue. I only recognized Ashraf and three of his father's men. Others were unknown soldiers. One walked over to my father and spoke, "Messer Niccolò, Messer Matteo. Nice to see you again."

I recalled my father staring at the confident young soldier; his pondering face instantly turned to a look of surprise. "Your Highness!" he said as he fell to his knees, and everybody else followed.

The young man laughed. "You didn't do that eight years ago. Please stand."

As my father stood, he apologized. "I'm sorry I didn't recognize you; you are no longer the young boy I remembered. How did you know we were here?"

"My father sent word of your return, knowing I would want to see you. Luckily, I was buying horses and equipment for our mounted soldiers in Kerman. I must have just missed you when you went through."

"We are grateful you found us; you saved our lives."

Ashraf interrupted. "I told you I was lucky."

My father started looking around. "I'm afraid we had your luck, but it seems so many didn't. Are we the only ones left?"

Ashraf sadly answered, "Everyone else except the seven of us are dead or kidnapped."

"Let's leave this sadness behind and find someplace to stay, eat, and talk," Prince Arghun said.

As everyone sat around, my father introduced me to Prince Arghun. I had impressed the prince with my skill in the Persian language. And the prince, I found pleasant and quite admirable; he was so young yet held such responsibility.

"I can escort you to the plain of Hormuz," the prince told us. "You will pass through a dreadful road plagued by robbers. The more of us, the better. As I said earlier, I was in Kerman, buying supplies for my army. Kerman's artisans make the best bridles, saddles and spurs, swords, bows, quivers, and every sort of armor, as they have abundant iron and steel in their mountains. They will finish my order in a month, and then I must return to my father's encampment. So Messer Niccolò, while I escort you, tell me about your world and what has changed since I last saw you."

That night, drinking and eating were accompanied by pleasant conversations, while Ashraf tried to find more men. He completed his mission, and we continued our journey the next day. During the following days, Prince Arghun and I grew a friendship.

The young prince left us after we passed the dreaded road, notoriously known for robbers, and safely reached the plain.

I kept wondering if I would see him again. Six years later, I did, and much later, I would meet his son, Ghazan.

Marco finally drifted to sleep.

The following day, Marco woke Rustichello. Words flowed without mention of the prince.

> *"After we left the village of Kamasal, the plain stretched South for five days; then, there was another slope where the road dropped steadily for 20 miles. It is a horrible road full of robbers. If you are fortunate, you will reach the bottom, find the spectacular Plain of Hormuz, and travel through beautiful rivers, date palms, francolins, and parrots. After two days, you reach the ocean and the coastal city of Hormuz, where merchants wait for the ships from India that bring all sorts of spices, precious stones, pearls, silk, elephant tusks, and many other magical things. It is a great trading center but also a city filled with wailing.... Any day of the week, the eerie sound of wailing is heard throughout the city as a woman mourning her husband's death wails once a day for four years.... The king is Ruknuddin Ahmad... They drink date wine, but it is only consumed by natives unless you are prepared for purges.... People are black.....worship Muhammad.... They sow wheat and barley in November and harvest in March. Nothing else is grown after that except date palms....as the climate is horrid... scorching heat....and in summer they travel to their summer garden homes where there are plenty of rivers and lakes....or they would die from the fierce heat... They build trellis platforms over the water, one end attached to the shore and the other to pilings. A canopy of leaves decorates the roof to ward off the sun. But sometimes that is not enough. A horrid wind can blow from the direction of the sandy desert, bringing a wind so scorching hot it will kill you unless you submerge your body into the lake, neck high, as soon as you feel it is coming."*

Marco paused as he remembered something. The last time he had been in this city was when he returned from Cathay. It hadn't been that long ago. The first time, he was a naïve young man, filled with adventurous dreams. So much had happened between his first visit and the second. He returned a wiser, seasoned, and changed man who had experienced a world never seen by many—a world so different and magnificent. Huge bustling cities with grand roads and bridges. Scholars with their printed books, manuals, and recorded medicinal procedures. He feared no one would understand or believe him when he retold his stories in Venice; he found his fears were correct. But most of all, he feared he would long to return to Cathay and leave his Venice forever.

Rustichello called out to Marco. "Hey, are you going to continue?"

His thoughts interrupted, Marco quickly returned to Rustichello.

"My father and uncle had hoped to go by ship to Cathay, bypassing the struggles of the Chagatai Empire and Kubilai Khan and crossing over "The Top of the World" to reach Kubilai Khan."

Rustichello questioned Marco, "Top of the World?"

Marco answered:

"A merciless mountain range of great altitude and severe cold. No houses or inns are found; all travelers must carry their food for forty days.

"My father and uncle had been gone so long from Cathay; if we could go by ship, we could cut our traveling time. But the ships were terrible. The ships were not fastened with iron nails but wood pegs and sewn together with thread made with coconut husk that had been soaked until they became like horsehair. The husk does not rot in saltwater and lasts incredibly well. They are not caulked with pitch but with fish oil. The ships have one mast, one sail, one rudder, and no deck. After the cargo had been loaded, they covered it with skin. The skins are strong enough to hold the horses going to India as they go on top. But this makes sailing these ships very precarious and deadly. After a few days of observing and rumors of the ruthless storms of the Indian Ocean, it was unanimous that we would return to Kerman and continue overland. We traveled to Kerman on another route, and when we arrived in the city, we headed north for seven days to Kuhbanan. Then, for the next 38 days, we traveled through arid deserts where water is short, and you must carry it. Then, you pass through the northern border of Persia, Tun-Qaen, where the Dry Tree sits, where Alexander and Darius battled. They are a handsome race, and the women are extremely beautiful. From there is Mulehet, where I heard the story of the Man of the Mountain, the former home of the Grand Master of the Assassins. Here, you ride through beautiful plains, valleys, and hills covered with lush grass, and all things are abundant. Next is Sheberghan....rich in many things...., the best melons in the world...dried and sweeter than honey.

"Then you arrive at Balkh, the imaginary boundary, the end of the lands of Tartars of the Levant, our friends, Abaqa and Arghan, and the beginning of

the Chagatai Khanate empire, the land of Qaidu and his amazing daughter, Aiyurug. Our letters no longer protected us here."

Marco stopped, looked at Rustichello, and said,

"I spent a year in this empire. I was ill, and when we reached a province called Badakhshan, I could not continue. The Chagatai Khanate ruled this empire, yet some kings were vessels of the Khan. Where we stayed, the hereditary King Zulkarnain, the royal line of the descendants of King Alexander the Great, and the daughter of King Darius ruled the land. The country was high in the mountains on a broad plateau where grass and trees grew thick, and great springs of the purest water stocked with trout and many other kinds of fish flowed over the rocks to the valleys below. And beyond this plateau are tall mountains filled with many precious things. The Balas rubies came from the mountain called Sighinan. Another mountain, the most prized lapis lazuli in the world, is mined along with silver, copper, and lead.

"My illness disappointed my father and uncle. However, once they discovered the rubies and lapis, their resentment turned to opportunity. They had a year to make trusted connections with other merchants who lived there or passed through and who would deliver these precious stones to them in Shang-du. Initially, obtaining the Balas rubies appeared to be a challenge. Only the king could possess them; anyone else would be beheaded. This was a concern to my father until they discovered anything was possible.

"While in this empire, I heard many stories from the villagers; the surrounding mountaintops possessed healing powers. The air was so pure, and the streams flowed with healing sulfurous waters that a man could cure his ailing body from fevers and other things in a short time. That year, I traveled to these places, and within the year, I banished my sickness and restored my health.

"During that year, I also spent hours learning about Qaidu and his daughter, Aiyurug, which in Tartar meant 'Shining Moon', and sometimes she was called Khatulan. It meant ALL

WHITE. I was curious about this name. Was it because her skin was as pale as the moonlight, as well as her hair?" Marco continued his tale.

> *"Qaidu was a Tartar and lived in the interior between the Khan of the Levant to the west and Kubilai Khan to the east. The Empire of the Golden Horde was to the North, and the Indians to the South. His kingdom's capital was Samarkand. War hardened his warriors and allied with large numbers of the Tartars. Qaidu opposed Kubilai Khan's central rule and never made peace with him. Qaidu felt Kubilai had lost his Tartarian ways and didn't trust him. They fought many battles while guarding their borders. This argument started when Kubilai refused to pay him his share of the conquests when they defeated parts of the provinces of Cathay and Manzi. Kubilai would have, but Qaidu rejected Kubilai's request to appear in his court or bow to him like the others. He caused much havoc along the Silk Road."*

Marco paused and smiled. "And this havoc would save my Li much later."

Rushichello interrupted, "How?"

"Oh, that story comes much later. I'll tell you another time."

Rustichello gave Marco a dirty look and commented. "Why did you mention it then?"

Marco smiled and continued. "That same year, I saw Aiyurug for the first time while I rested by a stream bordering a thick forest, as large boulders camouflaged me. Soldiers arrived and dismounted to water their horses. Instantly, I recognized Qaidu from the stories I had heard. I had assumed he had come to the plateau to visit King Zulkarnain. Qaidu was a man of average height who held himself erect. His face was almost naturally clean of hair. I had heard his habits were stern, and he never drank the most loved Airag, the fermented mare's milk. Alongside him was a young girl. Her figure was powerful and large. Her hair was light, as was her skin. I had never seen a girl like this, riding next to a leader as if she were one of his warriors. I had heard rumors that this was his daughter, Khatulan. Now that I had seen her, I preferred Aiyurug. She was like the Moonlight. I was in awe. This land was becoming more of a mystery." Marco stopped. He had decided he had talked enough. Besides, talking about Qaidu brought back memories he didn't wish to share."

Rustichello had become accustomed to Marco stopping in the middle of a story. *Marco has become so predictable,* he thought to himself. He set down his writing quill. "I guess you're ready to stop."

Marco didn't answer. He returned to his bed and closed his eyes, envisioning the next scene. When he started talking, he surprised himself and Rustichello.

"After the horses had rested and filled their bellies with fresh water and grass, Qaidu, Aiyurug, and the remaining soldiers mounted their horses and rode slowly toward the palace. I wanted to follow; I wanted one more glimpse of this unusual girl. Not to be seen, I rode along the stream hidden by the forest until the distance between us was far enough that I wouldn't be noticed. When they entered the palace of King Zulkarnain, I waited, hoping they wouldn't stay long. Suddenly, the girl rode out of the king's palace alone. Blinded by curiosity, I hopelessly followed. Aiyurug rode her white stallion fast and disappeared into the forest. I stopped and thought, *What am I doing?* and turned my horse around, riding toward the village. Suddenly, pounding hooves were behind me. Before I could turn around, someone knocked me off my horse. Quickly, I stood and saw Aiyurug and her powerful stallion racing toward me. I froze, her gray-blue piercing eyes locked into mine while she passed. She brought her horse to a lurching halt, turned around, and made a dash toward me, and like a hawk pouncing on a bird, I was seized and thrown across the saddle in front of her.

"My heart raced. And I wondered, *Is she taking me to her father? Had they known all along I was following them? What a fool I had been.* Abruptly, she brought her horse to a hard halt, turned her horse around, and raced to the forest. We hadn't gone far in the forest when she threw me to the ground, landing on my stomach with a thud. Lifting my head, I saw her muscular body walking toward me. In moments, her foot was in the middle of my back, and her hand held a large amount of my hair, yanking my head up. In a more feminine voice than I expected, she asked, 'Who are you? Why were you following us? Are you a spy for Kubilai?' Trying to be confident, I answered, 'I am a merchant. My father, uncle, and I have been here for a while because I was ill. I heard stories about you and your father, and was curious. I have never seen a woman warrior. Your appearance is rare, and you are beautiful.' I could feel her hand slowly releasing my hair and her foot releasing me. 'You are a scrawny one,' she sarcastically said, walking away. As I scrambled to my feet, I stupidly decided to show her I was stronger than she thought. I tackled her, and she fell to the ground with me on top, but not for long. She flipped me over and dug her knees into the soft part of my upper arms, with her hands holding my wrist and her face a foot from mine. She proudly boasted, 'I can't believe you haven't heard I am the best wrestler in my country, or you wouldn't have tried that stupid trick.' I was defeated mentally and physically. A slight smile appeared on her face. I wondered if she was amused or if I was about to be beaten to death. She leaned in closer; her water-colored eyes sparkled as her lips met mine. I thought, *Is this the kiss of death?* I kissed her back, thinking, *If it is, I should at least die kissing a beautiful girl.* Her body softened, and her knees slid from my arms. She stretched out over my body. My pleasant feeling abruptly ended. A horrible thought crossed my mind. *Is her father somewhere close?* In fright, I pushed her to the side and scrambled to my feet. She started laughing and held out her hand. Rashly, I grabbed her calloused hand and pulled. Instead of rising, she strongly yanked me to her. Aiyurug's infectious laughter spread, and I soon joined her. She was as curious about me as I was about her. We spent the rest of the afternoon talking, and she laughed as I tried to speak her language..

"She told me the story of her birth as her father, Qaidu, told her and why she had spent her whole life learning the Tartars' arts of riding, combat, wrestling, and war:□

"The day I was born, my father entered my mother's ger to meet his newborn daughter. The midwives were whispering and looked frightened. My father, concerned, walked over to my mother, who held me close, and slowly pulled back the blanket, exposing my tiny body. His eyes widened, and he stepped back. His stern voice ordered for a shaman. The housemaid whispered, 'We have called her already.' My father hated the thought that his child could be cursed. I didn't look like the others. My skin was white, and so was my hair. My father paced the floor until the shaman arrived. As she entered the room, the midwives and housemaid scattered. The shaman walked over, grabbed me from my mother's arms, and removed the blanket. Looking at my father, she boldly instructed him to follow her. She rewrapped me, and they hurried to her ger. With frightened eyes, my father watched me and the shaman. I wailed as she laid me on a pile of animal furs.

"Confidently, the shaman walked over to a primitive table covered in strange herbs, stones, and relics of withered creatures, and drank from a bowl of liquid. Her eyes rolled back into her head. She slowly started chanting. My father told me his heart pounded with fear as she walked toward me. Removing the blanket, she exposed my white body, and I instantly ceased crying and opened my eyes. My father stepped back in shock. My fair eyes were piercing, and I stared back at the shaman. The shaman stopped chanting, and her head dropped. The entranced shaman broke the silence with an eerie voice that rang out, 'Keep this child by your side. She will be a great warrior and your protector. Teach her well, and only trust her. Her bravery will lead you to many victories.' The shaman raised her head after she regained her senses and opened her eyes. She picked me up and handed me to my father, saying, 'Her name is Khatulun,' which means 'white one.' My father stood wordlessly and thought, 'How could this be? I have fourteen sons; how could a daughter be the chosen one?' However, he didn't question the shaman. From that day forward, I entered my father's ger with a nursemaid. And to this day, with disgruntled brothers, I have remained by his side."

"We both suddenly realized the day was almost gone. Aiyurug spoke up. 'We lost your horse. What are you going to do?'

"'I thought you would give me a ride back.'

"She laughed. 'You trust my father not to kill you. We have been gone for hours! On the other hand, my father did give me the privilege of marrying as I pleased.'"

Marco recalled the moment. "I went pale."

"Aiyurug enthusiastically continued. 'However, that man must be able to subdue me through sheer strength. And we know you aren't that man. So, we can be friends. My father and I will be staying for a few more days. He has business with King Zulkarnain, my father's vassal, but prefers to stay in his ger, so we won't always be with the king. I will find you if we have the chance to see each other again. Now, I must report to him that you are not a spy.'

"I stopped her. 'I must tell you; before I fell ill, my father, uncle, and I were on the way to see Kubilai. My father is on a mission for him.' Her face hardened, and she spoke sternly. 'I thought you said you were a merchant?' Not waiting for my answer, she mounted her horse and rode off. From then on, I only saw her from a distance in the great plain practicing. She was an amazing warrior."

Marco stopped talking momentarily to gather his thoughts, then continued. "I would see her again six years later in 1280. Kubilai Khan had summoned me to the palace. At that time, I lived in Yangzhou, a city south of Khanbaliq, and my friend Kim Chin-hae lived in Ningbo, preparing for the invasion of Cipangu.[2] Kim Chin-hae had also been summoned. We were thrilled; we would be traveling together to Khanbaliq."

Rustichello interrupted Marco. "Who is Kim Chin-hae?"

Marco sharply answered, "Later, I will tell you who Kim Chin-hae is." Marco quickly continued his story.

"Kubilai heard from a trusted baron that the Khan of the Llkhanate, Abaqa's son, Arghun, was participating in a wrestling match with Qaidu's daughter, Aiyurug. Kubilai Khan was sending me to the Great Plains of Qaidu to observe this contest. The outcome could result in a marriage. The thought intoxicated Abaqa with this perfect union—his son and the daughter of his enemy. Maybe there could be peace, and Kubilai thought the same thing. Arghun had spent years defending the borders between the two kingdoms. This marriage could solve the problems of the wars that caused constant travel interruptions on the Silk Road."

Rustichello interrupted Marco again, questioning. "This is the same Arghun that saved your life?"

Marco nodded yes and continued. "Arghun had grown into a gallant, accomplished warrior, and defeat was inconceivable. He had heard of her strength but was arrogant. Many times, he had proven he possessed great power and prowess. Defeat could never happen, especially by a woman. Kubliai wanted me to encourage Arghun not to disclose his identity. It turns out that Abaqa, his father, had the same idea. So, the plan was deceit; Abaqa would send his son disguised as a son of the Kingdom of Pem, a distant kingdom, just in case of defeat. His son's shame would only be shared between his most trusted servants. When Arghun arrived, an exquisite entourage and 1,000 horses accompanied him instead of the required 100.

"The thought of having his daughter marry a prince delighted Qaidu. There was a rumor that he secretly urged his daughter to fall victim and allow the prince to win. Horrified by her father's statement, her answer was, 'Never in this world would that ever happen.'

"When I arrived, finding Prince Arghun's camp wasn't hard. I looked for the most impressive ger. At the entrance, I presented my gold tablet to his guard and declared, 'I am here to see your lord.' The guard entered the tent and returned quickly. Kubilai and Abaga were allies. When I walked in, Arghun was busy preparing for the match. He turned around, and I bowed. When I looked up, he smiled. 'Messer Marco, what a pleasant surprise. I wouldn't have recognized you except for your wide eyes. You have advanced well, and you no longer resemble a Latin but one of us.'

"Arghun was now 22 and a commander of his army. Aiyurug was 21 and wore around her neck a gold, engraved disc plate—*a paiza*—usually worn by men, showing her power and independence. *A couple made in heaven*, I thought.

"'I have come to wish you luck, Prince Arghun. Six years ago, I met the fury of your opponent.' I said, laughing to myself. 'Also, the Great Khan demands victory.' I bowed.

"Arghun smiled and responded quickly in a playfully sarcastic tone. 'Do I look like someone who needs luck?' Arghun didn't wait for my answer. He was more fascinated by my success. 'You carry the gold tablet in the name of Kubilai. How?'

"'Thanks to you and many more, we finally made it to Shang-du. I impressed Kubilai with my storytelling, and he appointed me as his emissary. I travel throughout his kingdom as his eyes and ears, just like today. I will report the outcome.' Arghun, for an instant, looked worried. 'I hear she has never met defeat.' But quickly, his confidence recovered. 'She is a woman, how can I lose? I can't believe her other suitors lost. They must have been spoiled nobles and inexperienced wrestlers.'

"A guard entered the room, interrupting our conversation. 'They are ready for you, my lord.'

"I smiled, bowed, and excused myself. Arghun spoke up. 'Come back later. Let's celebrate my victory.'

"A great crowd had gathered in the royal tent pavilion. Aiyurug entered first, and the crowd went wild. She wore a deerskin just enough to cover her womanly parts, exposing her tall, beautiful, muscular body. My heart fluttered. Six years ago, she was a young girl. Now, she was a magnificent specimen of a woman giantess.

"Next, the vigorous Arghun entered, wearing deerskin covering only his manhood. His body was slender but rippled with muscles hardened by war. His handsome face portrayed confidence and an unbeatable presence.

"The crowd roared again as they stood face to face. Their beauty matched. They spoke to each other, smiled, and backed away about ten paces. In a swift moment, Aiyurug attacked. Her brute force caused Arghun to lose his footing and tumble to the ground. I laughed as I remembered the day that had happened to me. Surprised by her power, Arghun's face turned red, and you could see his anger rise. He stood, and a threatening, robust laugh echoed in the arena. He raced toward her, and the battle began. As they tossed each other to the ground repeatedly, the crowd cheered. Someone beside me said, 'This is the most prolonged battle yet.' Her father was exuberant. *Finally, she would be wed.* His exuberance didn't last long. The crowd went silent. Arghun was on the ground with Aiyurug's powerful hands wrapped around his chin and neck. She swiftly came to a powerful squat, causing his back and neck to strain to an unbearable arch. The battle was over. Her disappointed father rose and went to his tent.

"I could see Arghun's face riddled with shame. The crowd shared his grief. He was now grateful that only a few knew his real identity. His entourage left immediately. I never saw him again, but I heard of his brilliant victories, and his most significant one was against his uncle, Lord Ahmad, who had robbed Arghun of his lordship when his father died.

"Aiyurug, Aiyurug," Marco repeated her name, then continued. "The desire to see her overcame me. My truth had scared her at our last meeting. I hoped she had forgiven me. I roamed the royal grounds for a few days, hoping to see her as the festivities continued. Aiyurug was a hero, except to her father and brothers. I never found her, so I packed my bags and began my return trip. Not traveling far, I heard a familiar sound of horse hooves coming from behind, and without time to turn around, she knocked me off my horse. Jumping up, I saw Aiyurug riding her white stallion straight toward me. Before I knew it, I was in her clutch and thrown over her saddle. This time, I was smiling. She rode until we were hidden among trees that grew by a wild stream. She threw me off her horse, slid off her horse, walked over to me, and offered her hand. I accepted it, knowing it was my turn. With all my might, I pulled her. She was laughing and didn't resist. She landed on top of me. As before, she kissed me. It was not the kiss of a young girl but of a woman. And again, I kissed her back. Our connection proved to be a powerful force of desire, not love. We were two people, foreign in this world, and found comfort in each other's arms. She will always have my admiration and kindred love. I would never know a woman like her. Years later, that admiration turned to gratitude."

Marco turned red and spoke to Rustichello. "You can eliminate that part of the story." Rustichello let out a gruff moan.

Another tedious day passed. Marco was tired, and his head hurt. He needed to rest, and he needed Li. Marco went silent. Rustichello looked up from his papers and called out his name. Marco didn't answer, so he shook his head and blew out the candle.

Marco imagined Li in her usual position, curled up into his body, stroking his hair with her fingers. He thought of the first time he saw her—it was such a long time ago. *Tomorrow, I will tell Rustichello the story,* he thought as he fell asleep collecting his thoughts.

---

1. Dilivar, Lahore, a land in east Pakistan

2. Koan (Japanese invasion of 1281)

Chapter Seven

Marco

1276 Saving Princess LI

Genoa prison 1298

Marco woke up early and was excited. He shook Rustichello and told him to get up. He had a story to tell. Rustichello rubbed his eyes. "Couldn't you wait until after breakfast?"

"No. They might not even bring us breakfast."

Rustichello stumbled out of bed, walked to the corner of the room, and relieved himself. He shuffled to his desk, arranged his writing paper in its rightful place, and picked up a pen. "Ok, I'm ready, start." Marco looked at Rustichello. "Just listen; no need to write."

"In 1276, I had lived in Cathay for over a year. Over that year, I had gained the confidence of Kubilai Khan. Like my mother, who carefully listened when I recounted my day at the docks, Kubilai did the same when I returned from my missions. Maybe this was our connection.

"I was unaware I had also gained Empress Chabi's—Kubilai's favorite wife—trust. I had just returned from a mission observing the advancement of Kubilai Khan's armies toward the Song Dynasty's capital, Lin'an.[1] The empress sent an urgent note instructing me to meet her at the Green Mound, a place of much beauty found on the grounds of the Winter Palace in Khanbaliq.

"The next day, I followed her directions to the north side of the palace, and as always, I was in awe at the palace's beautiful grounds. I walked through stretches of stately trees and green pastures filled with a great variety of game. A bridge appeared, and as I crossed over, I looked below. Swans and an array of waterfowl swam peacefully in the crystal-clear water, distorting the images of the colorful fish below them. *Their unity is so different from the outside world*, I thought.

"In a bowshot distance, I saw Kubilai's creation, a mound 100 paces high and a mile in circumference. As I continued my journey, it became apparent why the name Green Mound was chosen. Every tree was an evergreen, never shedding a leaf, and under these massive trees, the entire ground was covered with crushed stones of intense green lapis lazuli. As you climb to the top through this unique forest, a green palace appears, a beautiful vision that can only exist in a wonderful dream.

"There, I found Empress Chabi. She seemed happy I had found her. The conversation was short and sincere. Her religion, Tibetan Buddhism, was strong, and her compassion was evident. She summoned me because she was concerned about the royal family of the Song Dynasty, who would be surrendering soon in Lin'an. She was afraid that even though she surrendered, they could be injured. The soldiers had been at war for a long time. Their emotions were high, and cruelty could arise. She requested, 'Please escort them back to the palace. We will be in Shang-du by that time.' I could see her concern; however, I was hesitant to agree. I never knew where Kubilai would send me. She could see this. She quickly responded, 'I'll talk to him.' She reached for my hand and held it gently. I understood. We parted.

"A few days later, Kubilai summoned me. Empress Chabi was sitting beside him. She smiled. Immediately, I knew he agreed with her plan. I was to leave at once. The surrender was imminent. Empress Chabi knew I spoke several languages, but my knowledge of Cathay and Manzi was limited. She feared the Song empresses would mistrust me if they couldn't understand me. The day I left, she arranged for a much-trusted Manzi interpreter from her court, Guo Yu, a eunuch, to accompany me. He was around my age."

Rustichello interrupted, "The same Guo Yu you have been talking about?"

Marco nodded yes and continued.

"We left Khanbaliq traveling south carrying Kubilai Khan's gold tablet. The gold tablet made it easy for us to travel and receive necessary provisions. We rode hard for days, stopping only at the Khan's outpost for food and fresh mounts. That's when Guo Yu, an emotionless Mangi, told me his story of the Song Dynasty's defeat. 'The tartars forged this war long before you arrived in Cathay. It began under Ögedei Khan, Kubilai's father, in 1235. The incredible manpower, ships, and weapons assembled on both sides were astounding, but so was the death toll. However, the sheer determination of Kubilai Khan's warriors proved to be more powerful than the military prowess of an ancient civilization, and they overtook most of our country.'

"At that last meeting, Kubilai Khan could hardly contain his excitement. With this defeat, he would become the first man to seize all of Cathay, become the Khan of the largest empire in the world, and become the Emperor of the Yuan Dynasty.

"I, too, was excited. Kubilai favored world trade, and his victory provided an opportunity for the merchants. We would have access to all of Asia." Marco smiled and continued. "This mission would change my life.

"By February, we could see the peaks of Phoenix Mountain in the distance, sometimes called Fenghuangshan. The Song's palace lay east of these mountains in Lin'an alongside beautiful West Lake, but our destination was just west of it. That's where General Bayan, also known as One Hundred Eyes, the general in charge of the invasion and surrender, would be.

"On the last night of our journey, we faced the western horizon. It was ablaze, not because of the setting sun but with thousands of campfires. That night, as we sat next to the campfire, Guo Yu told me the legend of the mountains in his no-nonsense voice. 'The mountains you see are the earthly remains of a great mythical golden phoenix and a fierce jade dragon. Their fiery love gave birth to a magnificent pearl. From a distance, an evil queen goddess desired it. She sent her henchman and stole the pearl after a ferocious battle. Heartbroken, they attempted to save the pearl from the evil queen. After a horrible mishap, the phoenix and dragon caused the pearl to fall from heaven and turn into the lake below, West Lake. Devastated, the phoenix and dragon lay beside their beloved pearl, forever becoming the mountains.'

"I listened contentedly. I loved these legends. It made this country so mystical and exciting. I wanted more. That night, I lay under the stars and drifted into deep thought. *Would I ever find my pearl and be by her side forever?*

"The next afternoon, we rode into camp, meeting a sentinel who escorted us through thousands of Tartars and Han soldiers who had surrendered to Kubilai Khan. They both looked tired and worn. In the past years, they had fought many bloody battles where many of their fellow soldiers had been mercilessly killed. They now hoped the Grand Dowager Xie Daoqing would surrender, which seemed possible.

"I reached General Bayan, One Hundred Eyes, who sat on his silver chair as I presented him with a sealed letter. His face stiffened, and with an emotionless glare, he nodded and opened the letter. The letter allowed my entrance into the Song's palace after the surrender and instructed General Bayan that I would be in command of transporting the emperor and empresses to the Shang-du. The commander-in-charge typically had complete control, like Kubilai himself. He curiously looked up at me. I had always been an oddity to Kubilai Khan's officers, even to his son—Crown Prince Chinghiz—who was standing next to the general. Their feelings were obvious. *Who is this young foreigner who has gained Kubilai's respect and confidence?* I, too, have often wondered. The general nodded, and I let out a sigh of relief.

"Days before, General Bayan sent word to the Grand Empress Dowager Xie Daoqing and Empress Quan demanding the surrender of the four-year-old Emperor Zhan Xi'an and the imperial seal. The general, the other officers, and the soldiers had been waiting. We arrived just in time. The Grand Dowager Empress Xie Daoqing's emissary rode out to meet the general the next day.

"The day the Empress Xie Daoqing received word, she asked the name of the enemy commander. When she was told it was General Bayan, One Hundred Eyes, she instantly recalled her astrologer's prediction that a man with a hundred eyes would be the ruin of her kingdom. Hearing his name, she lowered her head in despair and knew she had to surrender.

"General Bayan, speaking Manzi, barked the demands of surrender to the emissary: 'All twelve gates are to be opened. All your soldiers shall march out of the city through the Juegan Gate, placing your weapons in a pile and yielding to the great Khan's army. Our soldiers will then enter Lin'an, secure the city, and escort Grand Dowager Empress Xie Daoqing and Emperor Zhan Xi'an in their royal carriage to Jingling Palace, where they will meet me. Together, we will ride down Imperial Street, showing her defeat to her subjects. Then the empress, the young emperor, her court, and the Royal Seal will travel to Kubilai Khan and surrender personally.' General Bayan continued, 'The empress has until tomorrow at noon to agree to my terms. At that time, your towering bell towers with their great bells shall toll throughout the city, singing a sad song of defeat: Lin'an has surrendered to the Great Khan. The Song dynasty has crumbled. If your bells fail to toll, a battle will commence.'

"The negotiation was one-sided—our side. The emissary bowed and turned. He walked toward his horse with a slight grin on his face. He saw me looking. His smile ceased. He mounted his horse and rode back to the palace. It turns out that General Bayan was unaware that the Empress's two older sons and some generals had escaped to the sea, continuing the dynasty further south.

"General Bayan looked confident as soon as the emissary rode off, knowing she wouldn't refuse. He knew the internal fighting of the barons had also left them vulnerable. They had crumbled within. I imagined what General Bayan was thinking—*Finally, I would take control of the Yangtze River, taking over Song's massive ships and weaponry. I have finally won.* With increased optimism, his voice echoed to his other generals. 'Order your soldiers to surround the city and wait for the bells. But be prepared. The battle will begin if we have not heard them ring by noon.'

"The general knew the city would be difficult to penetrate without this surrender. I'm sure he hoped and prayed to hear the bells. The location was a natural defense. To the west was a vast lake, the Pearl, and to the west of the lake were mountains, the Phoenix, and the Dragon that wrapped around to the north. To the south, the city was protected by a river that flowed eastward and a giant mound that helped protect the city from flooding, as well as the vast ocean.

"Lin'an, a magnificent city, had a population of one million. The location also limited their expansion, so the city's many wooden buildings were built four to five stories high. However, over the past years, massive fires swept through the cities, burning the structures and killing many people. For this reason, the government built the bell towers to warn the residents. This time, the bells would toll, not for fires but in mourning for the death of a nation.

"That night, I wandered around a solemn camp. Usually, there would be loud conversations, laughter, eating, and wrestling, but that wasn't the case that night. General Bayan posted most soldiers near the city, and the remaining Tartar and Han soldiers were silent. They seemed to be mentally preparing themselves for the future. I imagined that the Tartar soldiers wondered if the Han soldiers would turn on them, and the Han wondered if the Tartars would kill them after the surrender.

"I often wondered how these Han soldiers felt. They conquered the Song Dynasty while fighting their own kind. Over time, I eventually recognized that Kubilai understood men. He could buy some with their lives, money, or women, yet he never trusted the Han or Song, even though he admired their culture and knowledge. They would never hold prominent positions. They would be appointed the lowest. Only Tartars and foreigners like me held those. This had to infuriate their citizens. As years passed, one of my jobs was to travel throughout Cathay and report to the great Khan, who was unloyal.

"I am sure many Tartars thought the same about me. *How can he be trusted? He is a foreigner. He shares no blood, and can he be easily bought?* But what they didn't know, I truly admired and loved Kubilai. He had shown me loyalty I had never known—what love between a father and son should be. As I said earlier, my father deserted my mother and me for 15 years while traveling for adventure, money, and his desires. Within this time, my beloved mother died, and I was left to be raised by my aunt and uncle. Even when he returned, he was distant, and only by my sheer persistence would he decide I could go along on his next adventure. But Kubilai Khan was a different man. He was ambitious, loved power and money, and could be brutal, but he was a fair man. Kubilai was progressive, accepting of all religions, and loved knowledge and bravery. He was fiercely loyal to the ones he loved and always expected loyalty and bravery from you. If you proved yourself, his world was yours.

"Nevertheless, neither one of us was fools. We both knew we would benefit from each other. And for me, it was financial. As a merchant, Asia's connections and wealth were at my fingertips and mine for the taking.

"The night before the hopeful surrender, I slept short and woke as the sun invaded the darkness. The sun's aura created a glowing gold light in the sky, and the mountain's silhouette radiated hues of deep purple. I watched as the sun slowly threw its light upon the bell towers and the western mountains. I felt at peace for a moment. It ended quickly as my eyes returned to my immediate surroundings. The fierce soldiers stood erect, their faces stern and fearless, ready for battle. In the distance, the horsehair violin's strange, intimidating sound, mixed with a loud, baritone guttural throat singing—a Tartar battle chant—reverberated. As the sun rose higher, the singing intensified, intimidating their enemies. My anxiety grew. Finally, the sun was directly above us; the faces of the soldiers never changed. Tension filled the air; I could hardly breathe. When I thought I would faint, the bells rang out. The soldier's tense body slumped, and their voices rang out with excitement and relief. That was the first sign of emotion I had seen all morning.

"Guo Yu and I mounted our horses and rode to the Northern gate to watch. General Bayan stayed behind, waiting for the Song soldiers to exit and his soldiers to secure the city. The twelve gates slowly opened, and the Song soldiers marched out, dropping their weapons in a pile and herded like cattle to the enclosed corrals. As the last Song soldiers exited, thousands of Khan soldiers and their commanders marched into the city.

"Lin'an was a very rich and beautiful city. It was a vast trading city that traded in salt, tea, spices, and jewels. The revenue from this one city would make Kubilai and his empire extremely wealthy financially and culturally. The soldiers were instructed not to ransack the city, only to secure and search out any hostile citizens and kill anyone who threatened this surrender.

Kubilai Khan wanted this city to remain intact so that trade would continue uninterrupted.

"There was very little resistance. A rider dashed from the gate and rode toward the camp. He carried the news that the city was secure, and Empress Xie Daoqing was in the royal carriage. General Bayan and Crown Prince Chinghiz mounted their snorting and nervous stallions and rode to the city. Entering through the northern gate, Chinghiz and the general stopped at Jingling Palace and waited for her arrival.

"We rode in next. An eerie quietness and emptiness consumed the city. We only saw our soldiers as they lined Brick Street to the Guan Bridge. As we waited, my greedy side appeared. I asked Guo Yu to tell me about Lin'an's great wealth.

“In a soft voice, Guo Yu began, ‘This section is narrower than the main center street. To the left,’ he pointed, ‘stands the famous Examination Hall, where thousands of scholars from all over the country come to participate in the national examinations. Next is the county school, then a weaponry compound. Between wine shops, warehouses, bookstores, and Buddhist and Taoist temples are homes.’

“It seemed like hours before we saw the Emperor’s carriage with open curtains. Inside was the Emperor, a small child, seated beside the Grand Empress Xie Daoqing and Empress Quan, all three of them solemn and expressionless. The general and the crown prince rode up to the carriage on their magnificent stallions and nodded. There was no need for words. The carriage turned around. The proud General Bayan started his victory march to Lin’an’s grand palace.

“For a moment, my heart felt heavy with sadness. Defeat of any kind is never easy to accept, but to lose your country must be almost unbearable.

“As we rode down the street to Guan Bridge, it seemed we had entered a ghost town and the ghosts were peering down at us with their secret weapon—hate. The feeling was chilling, and I couldn’t help glancing over my shoulder and from side to side, just in case the enemy attacked. When we crossed over the bridge, the street turned left. We entered the main road, the Imperial. It was 40 paces wide; six wagons could travel simultaneously. An ingenious 2-pace gravel path ran down the middle for rain runoff, keeping the road flood-free. The stories told had not been exaggerated. The city was beautiful.

“Our soldiers still lined both sides of the street, and that intense, eerie feeling remained. I leaned toward Guo Yu and whispered. ‘Tell me more. I need something to erase the eyes.’ As Guo Yu whispered, the city came to life. ‘This area is the washi.’ My ears perked up: Entertainment and brothels. As we traveled over another bridge, he quietly continued. ‘This area is called the Center of Five Flowers; day and night, enormous marketplaces are bustling with customers. Hundreds of trading premises dealing in gold, silver, tea, pearls, jewels, and salt are present, and in between were pawnshops operated by wealthy households. Gambling establishments, various food sellers, and more homes, some five stories high, that are packed together, ’

“It was amazing; everything I had heard was true. As we approached the grand palace, we passed through the Chaotian Gate, ‘The Gate before Heaven,’ Guo Yu whispered. ‘The Royal family members and the very rich live here. There are government buildings and the grand ancestral temple. Hundreds of street vendors sell luxury items in the early morning, and multitudes of markets sell pearls, jewels, treasures, rarities, fresh flowers, fruits, seafood, wild foods, marvelous implements, and utensils.’

"In my mind, I saw this city alive. It reminded me of home, the Venice of Asia, with its canals and bridges. We then approached another gate, known as Hening Gate. 'The Gate of Peace,' which is actually the back entrance to the imperial palace,' Guo Yu explained. Momentarily, I thought the name had lost its meaning. He continued. 'The Lizheng Gate is the front.' Gui Yu's knowledge was astonishing. Later, I learned that he was originally from here.

"The three enormous doors of the Gate of Peace were normally closed and secured by the Song Emperor's guards, but today, they were open, and the Khan's guards stood guard. When we entered the courtyard, I saw the most splendid palace I had ever seen. All twenty large, broad-fronted pavilions sat slightly on a plateau with the Phoenix and Dragon overlooking them. Painted columns embellished with gold and the finest azures supported their roofs. Guo Yu continued. 'The palace is private, enclosed by tall, battlemented walls. Wildlife, beautiful gardens with fountains, fruit trees, and lakes with abundant fish primarily filled the grounds.'

"As the royal carriage halted, General Bayan and Kubilai's son Chinghiz dismounted. We waited until Emperor Zhan Xi'an, the Grand Dowager Empress Xie Daoqing, and Empress Quan stepped out of the carriage. General Bayan escorted them up the expansive, sprawling steps that led to the center pavilion. We followed behind. When we reached the top, my eyes were no longer on the Emperor but the palace itself. It was outstanding with its gilded columns, embellished gold ceilings, and walls painted with beautiful paintings that depicted stories of former kings and glorious images of beasts, birds, knights, and ladies in brilliant colors. We made our way to the largest and grandest pavilion, where the elevated throne was situated. I heard that every year, in reverence for their Emperor, an elegant banquet was given in this hall. The emperor hosted a sumptuous feast for 10,000 people of great importance, which lasted ten to twelve days. Chief lords, leading magnates, and the wealthiest craftsmen would attend dressed in silk and gold and adorned with many precious stones.

"Guo Yu and I observed the young, demure Emperor walk to his huge throne. He was obviously frightened, but his demeanor reflected authority. His mother had taught him well. His grandmothers and mother stood next to him as the general spoke. The empresses turned and stared in our direction. We locked our eyes, and Grand Dowager Empress Xie Daoqing nodded. We came forward and bowed, and Guo Yu asked her in her dialect if we could enter. She pointed to splendidly carved doors behind her, the entrance to the secret inner chambers. We bowed and entered. The first chambers belonged to the Grand Empress and the Empress. Our job was to find the remaining court ladies and escort them with the empresses. An eerie silence signaled dread and sadness as we moved through the halls and courtyards. Most of her court seemed to have left."

Marco paused momentarily, drew in a deep breath, then continued. "We walked through the beautiful rooms, but the sights were the opposite. We found pale, limp bodies of beautiful women dressed in stunning, colorful silk lying on the blood-filled floors. Overwhelmed, we continued to walk from chamber to chamber. Our eyes filled with tears; the rumors were true. Some would choose to escape, but others preferred death. These women feared the stories were true; captives, especially beautiful ones, would be gifted to the commanders or soldiers who excelled in this campaign.

"Guo Yu and I separated to speed up our search for any living women. As I moved down the hallway, I heard a slight noise. I quietly slid open a door; a delicate, crumpled body lay on the floor, surrounded by her pooling blood. As I walked toward the body in the corner of my eye, I saw movement behind the bed's silk curtain. Quietly, I moved toward the bed with my sword drawn. I whipped open the curtain. A young, beautiful child with half-moon eyes, wide with fear, stared back at me. Her left hand clutched a small ornate knife that pointed toward me. Her small lips were pursed, and her face exhibited anger. Our eyes met, mine filled with sorrow, hers with hatred. I knew one aggressive move; she would lunge toward me. I stood motionless, even though I could overtake her tiny body. My heart ached; my eyes welled with tears. I, too, was an orphan, but I didn't become one so violently. Memories of my dying mother overwhelmed me. I didn't notice she had lowered her hand, dropping her small knife on the bed. Her face had softened, and her eyes, too, filled with tears. She slowly moved toward me and wiped my tears with her small hands. She was comforting me. At that moment, we made an unusual bond."

Marco paused. Rustichello said, restless, "What happened next?"

"Guo Yu's voice awakened me from my trance, just like yours, with 'Hurry, Messer Marco, I hear soldiers.' Quickly, I picked up the knife and placed it in my pocket while removing a scarf. Hurriedly, with the scarf, I covered her eyes and swept her up. Holding her close to my chest, I walked through her mother's blood. I met Guo Yu as he was opening the sliding door. He stared at my small prisoner. We nodded and left the chambers. Guo Yu had several court women with him. We continued to the main room.

"General Bayan was still talking to the empress. He stopped and looked at me carrying the child. He walked over to me and whispered. 'Special gers for the empresses, emperor, and her remaining court have been assembled.' He motioned one of his men over. In an unexpectedly soft voice, he ordered him to assist us and take the captive court ladies back to their temporary home. He turned to me and spoke. 'The royal family will follow shortly.' I was hesitant. I was the responsible one. Guo Yu touched my arm, and I nodded. I followed General Bayan's man to the royal palanquins, which took us to luxurious gers in the middle of General Bayan's camp. Soldiers were already standing guard. The beautiful, scared women followed us inside and huddled to one side.

My small prisoner rode silently, never lifting her head from my chest or releasing her tightly clasped arms around me. Her short labored breathing and pounding heart echoed through my body. "I gently tried to pry her arms from my chest when we arrived. She held steadfast. Guo Yu spoke. She lifted her head and released me. I gently sat her on a cushion and removed the scarf. She grabbed the scarf from my hands, tucked it into her sleeve, and looked up at me. Her eyes told me, 'Thank you.' As I walked away, the warmth of her body and heart left a lasting impression on me. Guo Yu continued talking to her as I left the ger. From that day forward, Guo Yu would serve her.

"Guo Yu came to me after she fell asleep and told me her name, Princess Li. Her name meant pretty. Her facial features were delicate and soft, yet she had a great force about her.

"The following days, we prepared for our return trip as Guo Yu selected the guards and soldiers he felt were trustworthy. For the next two months, we escorted Princess Li's family, including her grandmother, the Grand Dowager Empress Xie, her 4-year-old half-brother, Emperor Zhao Xian, his mother, Empress Quan, and the remaining relatives, as well as concubines, to Kubilai Khan's royal court. First, we traveled on the Grand Canal, then on horseback to Shang-du, the summer palace.

"Guo Yu stayed close to the young princess, and I stood guard. I only caught glances of her occasionally. However, at times, I felt I was being watched. During our trip, I wondered what her life would be like. For some reason, she tugged at my heart, and I felt responsible for her like a older brother.

"One night, as the ship drifted silently on the man-made river and the reflected ship's lights met the reflections of the lit shore and gently melted together, Guo Yu and I sat and talked. I asked him what was going to happen to her. Guo Yu replied, ' If the Gods show pity, her life will resemble the beautiful lights we peer upon, a blending reflection. Kubilai Khan always tries to rule as his grandfather, Genghis Khan, did. The tradition is to treat their surrendered captors well. He wants their loyalty, and hopefully, their people will follow. The Grand Dowager Empress Xie surrendered so he would be kind. But to the sons who escaped, he would not.' Guo Yu continued, 'I hope Empress Chabi will see Princess Li as unique and want this delicate, beautiful child to be her daughter. This is usually their tradition. She is young enough to be molded into a Tartar. She is the daughter of an Emperor; her blood is royal, and she has worth. With love, she would be less likely to become a leader of an uprising.' I nodded and thought, *The word worth rubs me wrong, but it is reality.*

"The closer we came to our destination, an urgency overcame me; I had to speak to Princess Li. Guo Yu brought her to me. At first, she was shy and hid behind Guo Yu. Suddenly, she bolted, ran, and wrapped her arms around my legs. Stunned, I looked around, hoping no one was looking. I unwrapped her arms and fell to my knees. I held her at an arm's distance. She smiled, and my heart melted. I quietly spoke while Guo Yu interpreted and spoke in Manzi 'I was a little older than you when my mom died. I was alone in this world, like you, and had to depend on others. My saving grace was my mother's words, who loved me with all her heart. She stressed every day, and even on her deathbed, that I must listen carefully to my world around me, pay attention, learn what is important to others, be useful, seek information, and never become their victim. This way, I would survive this cruel world. I listened, and I hope you do, too. Have courage and strength. You will survive, and maybe your life will surprise you like mine.' I wasn't sure she understood my words. She seemed to. Her eyes never left mine. When I finished, she smiled, pushed my hands from her shoulders, wrapped her arms around my neck, and hugged me tightly. I knew then that she had become part of my life. From afar, I would watch her and somehow protect her. When we arrived at Shang-du, Kubilai Khan had arranged a full banquet in their honor in the Hall of Peace. I had never experienced such a thing: A conqueror presenting his conquered, a feast fit for an Emperor. Then, stripping them of their titles, he gave them a home and land in Khanbaliq tax-free out of respect. This was a strange land indeed. Guo Yu had been right. Empress Chabi adopted her, and Li was to live in her chambers. I was even more relieved when Guo Yu was selected as her servant. I knew then it would be possible to watch over her."

Marco stopped talking and silently thought, *So much has changed since then. For the first time, I have failed her.* He tried to reassure himself that it was only temporary, then shook himself back to reality. "Let's continue my journey."

Rustichello hesitated and mumbled, "What a fascinating life he has had. Will people believe him?" He rustled around the papers and picked up his pen. "Ok, I'm ready."

---

1. The ancient name for Hangzhou

Chapter Eight

Marco

The Introduction—Kim Chin-hae

Genoa prison 1298

Marco started. "As I said earlier, I stayed a year in Badakhshan, recovering, and where I met Aiyurug..."

> *"While there, I learned that if you travel south for ten days, you will arrive in a province called Pashai. They are idolaters who worship idols. They are dark-skinned and well-versed in sorcery. The men wear earrings and brooches inlaid with gold, silver, pearls, and precious stones. They are a spiteful lot.... The climate is scorching....and if you travel more days southeast, you will arrive in Kashmir.*

"This is where the evil men who raided our caravan live, the ones they say cast spells that change the weather and summon up deep darkness." Marco laughed. "The ones who fool.

> *"From this place, you can reach the Indian Ocean. While you travel to the ocean, I hear the people are dark and slender, and the women are beautiful.... They eat milk and rice.... Temperate weather, plenty of cities and towns....woods and deserts....have independence....holy people.... If we go further, you will cross into India.... I won't go into that because my story about India will be told in detail later.*□

"After a year, I was finally well enough to continue our journey."

Rustichello interrupted Marco. "Yesterday, you mentioned a friend named Kim Chin-hae."

With a sincere voice, Marco looked up at Rustichello and said, "Kim Chin-hae was my friend and business partner. I saved his life, and he saved mine."

Rustichello responded with curiosity. "That's a different name; where was he from?"

"Goryeo, a conquered country, a vassal of Kubilai Khan. It lay east across the large bay from Khanbaliq. Let's continue with our real mission," Marco said sadly.

Rustichello was now very curious, wanted to know more, and urged Marco to tell the story about Kim Chin-hae.

Marco disregarded him and continued.

> *"Finally, we left Badakhshan. We traveled 12 days toward east-northeast up a river valley that belongs to the brother of the lord of Badakhshan....many towns.... tough-hearted people....worship Mohammad.... Finally, you reach Wakhan....you can cross in three days....their own language....great warriors....wild breast, game, and hunting of all kinds....*
>
> *"Leaving this place, we traveled for three days northeast across mountains, one so high it is called The Top of the World. When you reach these heights, there is a plain called Pamir between two mountains with a vast lake that feeds a river....best pasture in the world.... A skinny beast will grow fat in ten days.... Many wild beasts....flocks of sheep with horns, six hands high, minimum three or four....shepherds make vessels for bowls.... Wolves kill many, and horns and bones are scattered all around.... They use them as markers, directing travelers when the ground is covered in snow....*
>
> *"It takes twelve days to cross this plain, and as you climb higher, there are no longer houses or inns, and you need to carry your food.... Birds cannot fly here....great altitude and cold...fire burns less brightly with a different hue...., and food does not cook well.*

"After you have traveled twelve days, you ride east-north-east for 40 more days through mountains, hills, and valleys, crossing many rivers and deserts. Again, there are no houses, inns, or food. This country is called Bolor.... Residents live at a very high elevation....idolaters....live entirely by hunting and dressing in animal skins, and are very fierce.

"You will arrive in Kashgar...once owned by Qaidu but nowadays ruled by the great Khan Kubilai.... People worship Muhammad....live by trade and crafts, such as cotton weaving.... beautiful orchards....vineyards.... fertile land....produce, and staple crops. Many merchants start from here, selling their wares all over the world.... They're Nestorian Christians observing their own religion....own language."

"Oh yes, I forgot about...

"Samarkand lies further to the northwest. Qaidu's palace is here....a splendid city....inhabited by Christians and Saracens.... A great miracle occurs here. Then you travel five days to the province of Yardland... They worship Muhammad...also Christians...subject to Qaidu.... They have many things, especially cotton, and craftsmen. A strange fact is that most people have one large foot and one small, swollen leg... and have goiters in their throat brought on by their water, I heard.... Let's move on.... The next province is Khotan, which lies east-north-east, eight days away... It is the subject of the Great Khan....worship Muhammad.... The finest city is Khotan....grow cotton...flax, hemp...grain....vineyard....farms.... People live by trade and are not warlike."

For the first time, Rustichello grew tired and somewhat bored. He stopped Marco and said, "Tell me a story. I want to hear about your friend Kim Chin-hae."

Chapter Nine

Marco

A Tiger and Kim Chin-hae

Genoa prison 1298

"We met on the road sometime around 1279." Marco stated. "Kubilai Khan had sent me on a mission to Zapton.[1] The Song Dynasty had finally been defeated, so this magnificent city now belonged to the Great Khan. He wanted to make sure the defeated citizens remained loyal.

"Zapton excited me as I heard stories that this city held great wealth. It lay south and more than 1000 miles away from Khanbaliq. It had the busiest trade port in the world. Ships arrived from India carrying costly wares, precious stones, and large prized pearls. As a merchant, I had to see this with my own eyes.

"As I traveled through different towns, I noticed a mysterious man several times. He seemed familiar. This man was about my age, richly dressed, handsome, and he toted a large ornate sword. *He must be very charming, as beautiful women and wealthy men always surround him in the evenings,* I thought. He spoke several languages, including Tartarian, Kubilai's language, and another language I wasn't familiar with.

"It was apparent he also noticed me. One night, while he ate with his friends, he acknowledged me with a nod. As I nodded back, he rose and walked toward me. He spoke first in Cathay. 'I'm Kim Chin-hae from Goryeo.' Suddenly, I recognized his face. He was the man I saw in the Kubilai palace a year ago."

Rustichello interrupted. "You met him in the palace? Why?"

Marco smiled, "You'll find out in time." Marco was a storyteller; he knew when to leave a mystery.

Marco continued his story. "I stood and started my introduction. Kim Chin-hae interrupted. 'You are Messer Marco Polo, the great Khan's emissary who carries his gold tablet. Your reputation precedes you. I heard you were young, handsome, and a foreigner who had won the Khan's trust and heart with your stories. Are you that trustworthy or a great game player who desires power, hoping to fill your pockets with the Khan's great wealth?'

"His frankness surprised me, as it did my guide and guard, Dai Xiuying. He placed his hand on his sword. I touched his arm; his hand left his sword. I swiftly replied. 'Isn't power and wealth everyone's desire? It depends on where your loyalties and your integrity lie. That's what matters. Even the great Khan knows that!'

"By this time, the whole restaurant was silent! Everyone was watching. Kim Chin-hae smiled—part of his charm—bowed and returned to his seat. I watched him walk away and thought, *Who is this mysterious man?*"

"My guard, Dai Xiuying, and I rose early the following day and left for Chuzhou, a large and beautiful city. It was the last city in the kingdom of Xingzai before we entered the realm of Fuzhou. We traveled through mountains and valleys with many cities, towns, and villages. It was rich in resources that made life bearable. However, scary stories circulated that great fierce tigers could pounce on you as you passed through the forest, and the residents ate human flesh if you died from unnatural causes. As I traveled, the only thought that kept me going was that I only had fifteen more miles before reaching Zapton. It was during this time that I met the mysterious man again.

"With his ornate sword in his hand, Kim Chin-hae barely stood as blood streamed down his face, and his left arm's skin was torn, exposing a large part of a mangled muscle. His guard or servant and a tiger lay dead on the ground. Kim Chin-hae bravely stood ready for his last battle, his eyes wild as another tiger crouched and prepared to pounce. I quietly slid my arrow and bow from my quiver. Without a word, I took aim and shot. The tiger hit the ground with a thud. Kim Chin-hae looked up, saw me, smiled, and crumbled."

Rustichello's mouth flew open. "Was he dead?"

"Who, the tiger or Kim Chin-hae?" Marco replied, half laughing. "Of course, the tiger."

"Frightened that more tigers would smell the blood, I instructed Dai Xiuying to bury the dead man. As he picked up the man, he moaned. 'He's alive,' Dai Xiuying excitedly said. The injured man kept mumbling. 'How's Master Kim? How's my master?'

"Kim Chi-hae lay frightenedly still. I bent over and placed my ear to his chest. His heart raced. I nodded to Dai Xiuying, who softly told the other injured man that his master was alive. Swiftly, I retrieved a vial filled with Yan Hu Suo for pain and bandages from my medical bag. Forcing Kim's lips open. I poured in the liquid. Then applied salt water to his injuries and wrapped his injured arm. Then, I cared for the other man while Dai Xiuying threw the dead tigers over the guard's horse.

"Why the tigers?" Rustichello asked.

"No way could we leave the tigers behind. Kubilai Khan would be charged with this story and would love the hides of these massive tigers."

Marco continued. "We gently placed the guard on Dai Xiuying's horse, and Kim on mine. We rode fast until we came to a cliff that looked down into the valley, hoping to see evidence of a village or town. Fortunately for Kim Chin-hae, who was profusely bleeding, I saw smoke billowing above the trees. Letting out a sigh of relief, we quickly descended and rode in the direction of the smoke. We left the forest and the main road, and rode through a river to fields submerged in shallow water planted in rice. In the background, the rice continued up the mountain slopes, ingeniously terraced. As we entered the village, the villagers weren't Song. Their clothing was heavily stitched, beaded, and full of color. Dai Xiuying said, 'Miao.'[2] I arrogantly flashed my gold tablet to the first person I saw. The villager was either unaware of its importance or didn't care. Dai Xiuying spoke up, knowing I couldn't speak their language, 'Kwa tshuaj, a herbalist, Kws khawv Kook, a magical healer,' as he pointed to the men. The villager stared at Kim Chin-hae. His reaction shocked me. *Does he know him?* The excited villagers started shouting. Several men ran to help, leading us through a long string of rustic bamboo houses with tall, thatched roofs. Pigs and strange-looking chickens roamed freely. The other villagers, with sad faces, stopped what they were doing and watched us pass. *They must know them. But how? He is a man of importance. How can he possibly be known in this primitive village? It is so off the beaten path.* The villager finally stopped at a gate decorated with animal skulls. Next to the entrance were tall wooden stakes topped with faded, colorful strips of cloth that swayed in the soft breeze. The gate led to a frightening hut. Dai Xiuying stopped and refused to go any further. Frowning, he said, 'Triv ua Neeb, a shaman. They talk to spirits and souls. You go in. I'll find someone to help with the dead tigers.'

"I found his actions funny. He was so brave against a sword," a smiling Marco said.

He then continued his story. "The villagers stepped up and helped Kim Chin-hae and his man. *He is going to owe me, this mystery man,* I thought. My heartbeat increased as I stepped onto the porch. Benches sat against the wall, large ceramic pots filled with water at each end, and small pots filled with herbs sat around the edges. All kinds of skulls sat around, colorful ribbons tied to each exposed rafter, and bags of dried herbs swung in the slight breeze. I didn't have time to be fearful, even though I had heard horrid stories of shamans, and in the past, the Song Dynasty had made them unlawful.

"Suddenly, the door swung open. An old, bent-over woman with deep wrinkles and piercing eyes stood before me. My heart pounded harder as she motioned me to come in. Inside, filtered sunlight streamed through the cracks of the walls. The rafters held drying fruits, corn, meat, and herbs. An open fire pit sat in the middle of the room. The smell of smoke, mingled with medicinal herbs, had a soothing effect. A large altar with more skulls stood at one end of the room. The old woman instructed me to place Kim Chin-hae on the straw bed. 'I've been waiting for you,' she said in a crackling voice. Confused and frightened, I put him on the bed. The villagers carried the other man and placed him on another bed. She immediately covered her face with a red mask and started chanting as she circled Kim Chin-hae. Watching intently, I didn't hear another person enter the room until she walked behind me and whispered in my ear. 'She is calming his souls. His heart must beat slowly so the bleeding will stop. Last night in my dreams, I saw him fiercely fighting the tigers and you saving him. I called you with the billowing smoke. I will always be indebted to you.'

"Looking down at the fire pit, an unnoticed enormous ash pile overflowed the surrounding area. She continued, 'When he awakens, he will only see me. It is our destiny.' The hair behind my neck stood up as she spoke; goosebumps covered my entire body, and I shivered. I could no longer refrain; I bravely turned. Standing behind me was a beautiful, petite, young woman. I was slightly relieved, but her mysterious aura that surrounded her made me shiver.

"The chanting stopped; I looked back. Kim Chin-hae's face had changed. He wasn't so pale and no longer bleeding profusely; he looked peaceful. *How could this be?* The old woman turned to the other man and did the same. The young woman passed me carrying a basket of herbs, jars, and wrappings. She sat down next to Kim Chin-hae and calmly removed the bloody clothes and my bandages. Without hesitation, she took out a bottle of unknown liquid and poured it on his wounds.

"I saw a strange amulet around his neck. The young woman, smiling, picked it up and held it for a moment. She lovingly kissed him on the forehead. Then she applied a paste made from dark green herbs to his head and, with delicate, loving fingers, rearranged his mangled shoulder and arm muscles, replacing the skin in its rightful place, and applied more paste. Carefully, she wrapped his wounds.

"The old woman carrying a tray that held a steaming tea bowl slipped by and began chanting again, then stopped and handed the girl the tea. The girl slipped her arm behind Kim Chin-hae's head, lifted it, parted his now pink lips with the bowl, and poured. She did this several times. Suddenly, his eyes opened. He looked only at her! His lips curved into a smile, and she smiled back. With his undamaged arm, he reached up and touched her face and affectionately whispered her name, 'LIS, my Lis, so strong and powerful.'

"Their smiles alleviated my skepticism about leaving him there," Marco told Rustichello.

"Lis turned toward me and smiled as she laid Kim Chin-hae down. Walking over to me, she laid her hand on my shoulder. I felt love radiating from her hand, warming my heart. 'Thank you for saving his life. We will meet again as we are forever connected as we were in the past.'

"Ignoring what she said, I bravely introduced myself. 'I'm Messer Marco Polo.'

"Lis answered, 'I know.'

"'You know,' I said, stunned.

"Not waiting for a response, I walked out of the dimly lit room, seemingly in a trance. The bright sunlight brought me back to my senses as I walked away. Looking back at the house, I wondered what had just happened. Shaking my head, I continued down the dirt road, looking for Dai Xiuying. I found him sitting on a porch having a drink with some villagers. They invited me to sit, and I politely accepted. A woman served me a steaming bowl filled with broth, a whole black-skinned boiled chicken with pieces of ginseng, and a floating reddish seed that resembled a date."

Rustichello interrupted Marco. "A black-skinned chicken and ginseng?"

Marco answered, "You remember, I mentioned strange-looking chickens earlier. Their feathers resemble the fur of a cat. It is called a Silky. Their black meat is delicious. Ginseng is a prized medicinal root found in the mountains, and the reddish seed was a Zao.[3]"

Rustichello shook his head in disbelief.

Marco continued his story. "We finished our meal. The villagers told us they would find us and bring the tiger skins another day. I didn't argue or ask questions. I wasn't even sure I wanted the skins. We bowed and thanked our host as we mounted our horses and left. Zapton was only miles down the main road.

---

1. Quanzhou, known as Zapton during the 11th and 14th centuries by merchant.
2. Ethnic hill tribes of Southern China mountains
3. Jujube fruit

Chapter Ten

Kim

Lis and Kim Chin-hae

Meanwhile, back in the Shaman's Bamboo Cottage...

Lis sat beside Kim Chin-hae, gently touching his face as he slept. He slowly opened his eyes and affectionately looked at her. Sorrowfully, he said. "I'm so sorry I took so long." She sweetly answered, "When I married you, I knew your country owned you, not me. I accepted your life when I said my vows." He smiled as tears slowly rolled down his cheek. "I missed you so much."

Lis put her small hand over his lips. "Shhhhhhhh... Sleep. We will talk tomorrow." Lis said while rising and walking over to a table that held a pot. She carefully poured some liquid and walked toward him. Kim Chin-hae's eyes opened wide. Her face was beautiful, but something had changed. She walked with a slight waddle, and her figure had grown. *Is he dreaming, or is she with a child?* Before he could open his mouth to speak, she held the bowl to his mouth. "Drink; we will talk tomorrow when your mind is clearer." She sat beside him, kissed his full lips, and held his hand as he drifted into a deep slumber.

When he opened his eyes the next morning, his vision was blurry, and his head was spinning. *Where am I? The last thing I remember is the attacking tigers.* He jerked upright with alarm. His eyes focused. His fear subsided, and his body softened as the sights and smells around him became familiar. As Lis moved about the room, his memory rushed back. She stopped, looked over at him, and smiled. His heart overflowed with love. Lis placed her hand over her swollen tummy. Kim Chi-hae's mind swirled. He never thought of this. Immediately, sorrow devastated him. *I might never be able to see my child grow up; I had made a deal with his majesty to fight in the Wa*[1] *invasion.*

Lis walked over and placed his hand over her swollen belly. "Don't worry; I will protect you! Can you feel life? You will watch your daughters grow." It startled Kim Chin-hae. *She is a witch!* He grabbed her and pulled her down to the bed, wrapping his unharmed arm around her. "Do you know how much I love you?" Before Lis could answer, he quickly said, "Daughters? How do you know?" Immediately, he felt stupid. Lis looked into his eyes; she could see her reflection and, in an authoritative voice, said, "Our clan only has daughters. A son has not been born in so many years that we lost count."

Kim Chin-hae smiled. "That doesn't matter to me. I love the thought of being surrounded by little girls like you!"

She laughed and stood. "I'll make you something to eat." Kim Chin-hae reached and grabbed her wrist. "Stay; I only need you next to me to heal." Lis lay and snuggled into his body as close as she could. Kim Chin-hae held her tightly as they both fell into a peaceful sleep. Late that evening, Kim Chin-hae awoke with Lis still in his arms. He softly kissed her. The kiss caused her to wake up, even though it was not intentional. Lovingly, she kissed him back, then unfurled and rose. "You are hungry; I hear your stomach grumbling. Let's eat and talk."

They spent the next few days discussing the man who had saved him and their future. Lis did most of the talking. "We will go to Zapton to meet Messer Marco. He holds a piece of our lives, and we hold a part of his. I can feel it. You should be healed enough to travel in a week."

Kim Chin-hae didn't argue or ask for an explanation. Lis continued, "The babies will be born next month's full moon. I know you must return to your post; your life calls you. Nevertheless, I wish you to stay until then." Again, he didn't argue. When he left his post, he informed the general that he was embarking on a mission for his king and Kubilai Khan. He would return to Ningbo in late August after meeting his cousin, the king, in Khanbaliq[2] with his report.

Lis continued. "It will take us a week to arrive in Zapton as we will travel slower than usual. We must find Messer Marco Polo and present him with gifts for saving your life." Without skipping a beat, she continued. "We will buy a house there. Your future lies in Zapton."

By this time, Kim Chin-hae was seriously staring at Lis. He couldn't believe what he was hearing. He interrupted Lis. "You didn't tell me you were so bossy when we married. You act like a general or my cousin issuing orders."

Lis started laughing, and Kim Chin-hae followed. Her swollen tummy jiggled up and down, and he stopped laughing, becoming concerned. "How are you going to travel in your condition? We will barely be able to return before you give birth."

"It will be fine, trust me," Lis replied. Kim Chin-hae nodded his head and tried to believe.

Then he asked, "Why a house in Zapton? We have one in the village. We agreed that you would never leave the village, and I assumed our children wouldn't either."

Her answer was simple, "Our future is in Zapton. I saw it in a dream. After the invasion, you will live there, and eventually, so will I."

She could see Kim Chin-hae's face turn white. He interrupted Lis. "How did you know about the invasion? I never talked about that! You are a witch?"

Lis shot back, "I'm not a witch but a shaman. I see things in dreams, and most likely, so will our children!"

She laughed. "Actually, Son Jun-ho, your servant, told me."

But hidden behind the laughter, she was lying. She had seen the battle, and she was scared. Now, she wanted to go to Zapton and ensure Messer Marco became his partner. They would need him for their future.

---

1. What the Goryeo called Japan

2. Also called Dadu

Chapter Eleven

Marco

To Zapton and Partnership

Genoa prison 1298

"After I left Kim Chin-hae, our remaining seven miles to Zapton were uneventful, except, I couldn't shake the sensation of the woman's hand touching my shoulder. I found it strangely comforting. I wondered if I would ever see him or her again."

Rustichello interrupted Marco," Did you?"

"Wait, I'll get to that," replied Marco. He was a skilled storyteller and wanted Rustichello to yearn for more. He continued his story of Zapton.

"When I saw the massive, fast-flowing Luyang River and the famous Luyang Bridge, my mind returned to the main reason I traveled here. Zapton is the most prosperous city in Cathay and the home of an incredible port. I only had to cross this remarkable, three-mile stone bridge to experience it myself. My father, my uncle, and I had dreams: We could become one of the wealthy merchants with numerous ships that docked here. Even though the Great Khan took half of your revenue in duties, your profits were still so large that you could have your ships come back every hour with another cargo.

"Making my way to the harbor, I sat on the docks feeling like a child again; listening to my mother's voice echo: 'Watch and learn.' I had only two weeks to wander the wharf and entertainment districts to spy for Kubilai and fulfill a personal quest of determining which captain or merchant might want a partner if the stakes were high enough."

Rustichello interrupted Marco. "Entertainment district?"

Marco smiled at Rustichello. "Drinking loosened the tongue." Marco continued. "I drifted in and out of cheap and expensive inns and tea houses close to the port, eavesdropping and striking up casual conversation while dropping large amounts of money. The ones who ignored me had something to hide or didn't want partners. However, I was most interested in those who engaged in polite conversation and met the small fleet quota. Trustworthy merchants and stern captains—who were fair and had a good rapport with their crews, which ensured the crew's loyalty—were what I was looking for. The two weeks passed quickly, and I met several good partner prospects. I also had several names the Khan would be interested in."

Rustichello stopped Marco with a question."Several names the Khan would be interested in?"

"Remember, Rustichello, my mission for Kubilai was to spy on the Song citizens and discover the disloyal ones. He never trusted them."

Rustichello nodded.

Marco hesitated momentarily and spoke out of context. "I swear I could feel Lis's touch during those weeks, making me stop and think of Kim Chin-hae and her, but with my busy schedule, the feeling would soon be lost."

Marco shook his head and continued, "While in the city, I secretly stayed in a small obscure inn beside the harbor. The morning before I was to leave, there was a knock at the door. To my surprise, it was a maid delivering a note. I didn't think anyone knew where I was staying. Suspiciously, I scrutinized the note before opening it. The quality of the paper and the seal seemed to belong to royalty. Extremely curious, I tore open the letter. It was a dinner invitation. I was to meet an escort downstairs at six pm. The letter wasn't signed.

"By six, my curiosity was so enormous that I raced downstairs. An elegantly dressed servant met me, directing me to follow. We went down the street to one of the neighborhood's most prestigious teahouses. As I entered, Kim Chin-hae was seated at the head of the table, finely dressed and remarkably healed, with his injured servant behind him. Beautiful women, wealthy businessmen, and generals surrounded him. He stood when he saw me. His servant motioned everyone else to do the same. I knew this mysterious man's name but not the man. Suddenly, my body warmed; I felt her touch. Shivers went down my spine. Kim Chin-hae motioned me to sit in the empty chair to his right. Then announced, 'This is the man who saved my life and Son Jun-hos. The crowd clapped. The sliding door to the private room was then closed. The man behind Kim Chin-hae bowed low to me, and Kim spoke up. 'This is Son Jun-ho, my servant, my most loyal friend.'

"In a soft voice, he responded. 'Thank you, sir. I will always be indebted.'

"Kim Chin-hae sat, and everyone followed. A feast with entertainment, food, and drinks began and continued for hours. The conversations were casual, and laughter filled the room. After the last course, Kim Chin-hae stood and clapped his hands. The sliding doors opened, and two servants carried in a large, gold, ornate box and placed it between Kim Chin-hae and me. Chin-hae walked to the beautiful box and lifted the lid. Three small objects, wrapped in beautiful silk, sat on the notorious tiger's fur. He picked up one of the items, handed it to me, and said, 'It was made from the earth where my blood was spilled, where you saved me.'

"I carefully unwrapped it, exposing a delicate five-inch porcelain jar with a glistening azure tint. It had four rolls of intricate relief patterns: the top and bottom were petal-like motifs, and the middle two were floral scrolls. It had a short neck with four small loop-shaped lugs. The second gift was an exquisite, dark green jade bracelet carved with a fierce dragon featuring a solid gold clasp. The third was a gold binyeo with a delicately carved lavender jade peony and two intricately carved butterflies on one end.

"'Please accept these gifts with Son Jun-ho's and my gratitude; we will be forever indebted to you,' Kim Chin-hae said.

"I was speechless; we stood facing each other, and I bowed a deep bow. Kim Chin-hae did the same. Son Jun-ho motioned everyone to stand with their cups in hand. The servants filled their glasses. With an outstretched hand, Kim Chin-hae clicked my glass. 'May this be the beginning of a great friendship.' Everyone cheered. Then he excused all the guests except me.

"Kim Chin-hae sat back down and motioned me to do the same as he spoke. 'I guess it's time for a proper introduction.' He rattled off a lengthy one. 'I am Kim Chin-hae. My name means the depth of the ocean. My father is Kim Chui-hee, the younger brother of Queen Jeongsun, the grandmother of Crown Prince Wang Won of Goryeo, who lives in Kubilai's palace. His father is King Chungnyeol of Goryeo, my first cousin.'

"My mouth dropped, and I quickly stood up and bowed. Kim Chin-hae laughed and gestured for me to sit. 'When I said I was grateful and wanted us to be friends, I meant it, and so does Lis.'

"Just then, a back door to the room slid open. It was the girl from the village. She wasn't dressed in ethnic clothing; she wore a beautiful silk dress typically worn by women in Cathay. However, her hair was delicately pulled back into a bun typically worn by women in Goryeo with a beautiful jade binyeo that resembled the one given to me. An outstanding jade norigae[1] and her hands rested on a bulging belly as she entered the room. I tried not to stare. Kim Chin-hae stood, and I followed. 'This is Lis, my wife.' He motioned for her to stand next to him.

"I could feel her touch. The unexpected sensation brought chills again, but her presence and aura also brought warmth at the same time. Seeing her, I remembered his injuries. I apologetically looked at Kim Chin-hae. 'I forgot to ask about your health. You seemed to have recovered completely.'

"Kim Chin-hae unbuttoned his robe and lowered it past his shoulder, exposing his injury. Amazingly, there was hardly a scar.

"'Your wife must have powers,' I told him.

"Kim Chin-hae stared at me and said, 'More than we will ever know or want to know!'

"Again, goosebumps crawled down my arms!

"We sat, and Kim Chin-hae suddenly changed the subject. 'I am a general in the Goryeo Royal Navy with no interest in continuing my service in the royal military, a future in politics, or marrying the girl of my parents' choice. After I complete my mission, the Wa Campaign, my future lies with Lis, our family, and you. My informants tell me that you were spying for the Khan and yourself, seeking a partner to expand your trade routes by sea. I'm interested!'

"Kim Chin-hae's handsome smile was captivating, and he almost caught me. But I stopped myself. It was the second time I had been surprised by his frankness and impressed by his honesty and openness. *Or is it honesty?* I thought. I learned early that some men possess the heart of a snake. Kim Chin-hae could be working for my enemies, trying to prove I had ulterior motives and wasn't loyal to the Khan. However, my enemies didn't know that the Khan and I had an agreement. As long as the Khan came first and my desires second, there wasn't a problem. I needed to know this man and where his heart lay. *Is this man willing to sell information for financial gain or personal benefit?* But at that moment, I felt the mysterious, warm touch of Lis on my shoulder and answered, 'That's possible!'

"I surprised myself and instantly thought, *Am I possessed?*

"Kim Chin-hae spoke with his rich, baritone voice, bringing me back to reality. He stood and lifted a wine-filled cup toward me, motioning for me to do the same. 'Here's to our new partnership and friendship.' As our glasses chimed, Kim Chin-hae and my eyes locked; it was as if we could see deep inside each other's souls. We mirrored each other—a life on fire that never wants to be extinguished. Stories, dreams, goals, and laughter filled the remaining night.

"By morning, we both realized it would be a while before our dream was realized. But it was a start. We were happy, understanding that our previous obligations had to be completed, and the right timing was necessary to succeed. Our integrity lined up. It was what made us trust each other more. I never had a brother, and I hoped I had found one.

"Kim Chin-hae spoke words that rang true. 'Permanence, perseverance, and persistence despite obstacles, discouragements, and impossibilities—if we accomplish these three things, we can only succeed.'

“When I returned to my room, I fell upon the bed. My body was exhausted, though not my mind. It kept returning to Lis. I was mesmerized by her and her touch and wanted to know her story. Kim Chin-hae’s words kept circulating in my mind. ‘She likes you; she says you have a soft heart and you love deeply. I could be jealous, but she says you have met your soulmate, and it's not her. Lis instructed me to buy the jade binyeo. It belongs to her, your soulmate. There will come a time you will recognize her and give it to her.’ Kim Chin-hae rose, walked over to the box, lifted one of the silk pieces, and unrolled it. He carefully held the binyeo and said, ‘The butterfly is sipping nectar from the peony. Do you know what that means?’

“I nodded no. Kim Chin-hae’s voice became low and seductive. ‘Just a butterfly means long life, beauty, and elegance, but the two together on the peony means lovers tasting joys of passion.’

“My face turned red. Kim Chin-hae didn’t notice; he was looking at Lis.”

Marco looked up at Rustichello and started laughing. “Then he asked me if I knew my soulmate, Lis was referring to. “‘No.’ I disappointedly told him.’

“Kim Chin-hae smiled, saying, ‘You do; you haven’t recognized her. It will be a while. Anyway, that's what Lis says.’”

“Our evening ended here, and Kim Chin-hae’s servant walked me back to my inn.”

---

1. Traditional Korean ornaments, typically used as a good luck charm or fashion accessory with the hanbok

Chapter Twelve

Kim

Lis and Twins

Lis and Kim Chin-hae strolled from the teahouse, stood before an exquisitely carved wooden gate, and pushed it open. A servant rushed to meet them as they entered their beautiful compound, protected by a tall stone wall in front and open sea on the other three sides. It was located on a small peninsula. A U-shaped wooden house with intricate sliding doors, large wooden columns, and a tile roof sat in an impeccably landscaped courtyard. The back and side sliding doors opened to view Zapton's famous wharf with its ships unloading their valuable merchandise and the rising sun. Inside was elegantly decorated with imports from around the world. It was the first time Kim Chin-hae had taken advantage of his royal blood. Lis staffed the house with servants and guards she could trust. They would spend the night and start their return journey to the village the following morning.

Kim Chin-hae awoke to an empty bed. He rolled over where Lis had slept. He inhaled her remaining scent. His heart pounded as he rose to find her.

Lis stood on the sandy shore, watching the pastel sunrise as gentle waves rolled in. Kim Chin-hae quietly approached from behind and gently placed his arms around her swollen belly. He could feel life and thought, *Our babies are restless to meet us.*

Lis turned and faced him. She snuggled into his body as close as possible and gently kissed him. "This will be one of our last remaining quiet mornings. We should enjoy this immensely." They held each other until Son Jun-ho interrupted them. Smiling at each other, they held hands and walked to their home, which would remain empty except for the servants until they returned. Neither one of them knew when.

Lis's timing was hauntingly correct; her contractions began as soon as they arrived back in their village. The village was in a constant state of celebration. Son Jun-ho and his friends drank, and

Kim Chin-hae paced on the bank of the warm water pond, flickering with the moon's light as it rose above the trees, Lis's favorite spot. Suddenly, a crying baby filled the night air, and then a second one joined in. As he raced to his cottage and entered, everyone stared down at Lis and the babies. Everyone was crying. *Is something wrong?* He thought as he walked closer. The midwives separated, allowing him to enter the circle. Lis was handing an unwrapped baby to her mother, Wei. Her look was disbelief as she stared at the unwrapped baby. Still bewildered, she rewrapped the baby, handed it to Kim Chin-hae, and spoke. "Blessed is this child; only girls have been born into this clan for generations. You possess a powerful seed. Meet your son!" Everyone's tears soon turned to laughter, and they started leaving, including Lis's mother. Kim Chin-hae sat on the bed next to Lis. They held their babies and cried.

Exhausted and relieved, Wei walked to the river and recalled the birth of the first. It had been a painful labor. With great restraint, Lis resisted the desire to push until it was time. She was strong. Finally, Lis's body was ready, and she pushed. The crowning of the firstborn appeared. Wei remembered the sensation she had encountered: her body tingled, and small bumps covered her skin. With the next push, a small head appeared, and the eyes were open. The baby's mouth opened, and a fierce cry filled the room as if to say, "Be prepared; I am here!" With one more powerful push, while the midwife manipulated the broad shoulders, the rest of the body slid out. Everyone gasped. Lis spoke confidently without seeing. "It's a boy, right? I told you this union was favored." Suddenly, labor started again, and the urge to push overwhelmed her body. "Another crown," the midwife announced. This time, a beautiful face appeared: calm and silent. Lis was tired, and it took several pushes before the tiny body slid from her body. The baby lay silent. Wei remembered how she felt Lis's fear and heard her inner voice speak loud and clear—*This baby is alive. I felt her soul inside me for the last months.* Without hesitation, Wei picked up the baby by the heels and gently rubbed down her back. Still no sound, she glanced at Lis. And with one swift motion, slapped her delicate behind. A roaring cry penetrated the room, announcing she was alive and had entered this world.

As Wei continued her walk to Lis's favorite place, she thought, *Two babies—a son and a daughter, two different personalities, one verbal and fiery and the other calm until provoked; only then would her fierce anger be shown. Wei smiled: A perfect combination that's needed in this cruel world.*

As Kim Chin-hae and Lis observed the new lives, Kim thought to himself, *It is a day of joy; Lis is my life, and my life has just become larger.* Kim Chin-hae cried silently inside as he stared down at the tiny faces of his son and daughter. He had made promises to her and his king. He hoped he could keep both.

Lis placed her hand on his arm. He looked up to her. Her face was severe, yet it possessed a certain calmness. Lis slowly spoke. "Rest your mind. When we married, we knew our lives were full of other obligations. Remember? We promised each other to accept these. You must return to your duty. When your war ends, you can make your decision. I'll be okay, and so will our children. Their life has been determined just like mine. We will be here when you return."

Kim Chin-hae nodded. "But I didn't know this feeling when I spoke those words." Lis squeezed Kim's arm harder until it hurt. "Stop tormenting yourself; reality is pressing. Fulfill your duty quickly, and then our dream can start."

Kim Chin-hae thought his dream had been his own. Only once did he think it could be shared. He had been wrong. This time, it was different; his dream meant nothing without her. He hugged her tighter. She was his dream.

That day, he thought about home across the sea. He was uncertain how to tell his mother about his marriage and now his children. She wanted a grandchild so badly. Lis would never be accepted; he knew this, but he recalled how Lis fought for him, and he would do the same when the time came.

Lis lay frozen; she had lied. She was scared, but she would never let him know. She had to be his strength. Besides, she was a shaman who could follow him in her dreams and always feel him, even in his last breath. Their blood had mixed; he would always be hers. "I will protect you with my life," she whispered as she drifted off to sleep.

The following day, the two new screaming lives beside them awoke Lis and Kim Chin-hae to their new reality.

Kim Chin-hae only had a couple of days before he left. He would enjoy his time now without worrying about what was to come. The most important thing now was to name their son and daughter.

The next day, they took their babies and Lis's mother to the sacred cave to meet their ancestors. As they approached the cave, the sun disappeared behind the expansive clouds, a soft mist fell, and the air stood still. A sudden burst of light filtered through the mist, and a beautiful rainbow led them to the secret opening. The air smelled stale and ancient, just as he remembered. The darkness surrounded them until, suddenly, a bright light glowed from a large stone bowl. Then he could see Lis's mother walking to the other stone bowl, waving her hands over them and magically igniting flames. The light displayed Lis's panicked look. As she turned to Kim Chin-hae and saw him successfully hide his fear about what he was seeing, Lis looked proud. They slid from their horses, and Lis's mother took both babies and walked up the stone stairs to the large stone boxes. At each sacred container, she stopped, spoke, and bowed. Each time, it seemed the cave took a breath and exhaled cool, fresh air into our stale surroundings.

Kim Chin-hae could see the excitement on Lis's face. She turned to him, smiled, and spoke. "Our children are blessed. They will fulfill our legacy."

Lis's mother then walked to the small extension of the cave where Lis had taken Kim Chin-hae's blood and placed it in a ceramic box. They followed; she removed the blanket from their son and daughter and laid them on the old wooden table. They were disturbingly calm. Wei took a small needle and vial from a bag around her neck. She pricked their son in the heel. He let out a loud whimper, and she comforted him instantly with her voice while she filled the vial with his blood.

"Your blood contains the sacred blood of a shaman, yet your father's blood carries power, as we have not had a male born into our clan in decades. Your name is Kim Yang Da- lou. You will become a powerful elder of our clan—a master. You will walk this earth with your father's and my father's names. You will show great strength. And with your sister, our clan will survive." She handed the vial to Kim Chin-hae and continued performing the same ritual on their daughter. As she withdrew the blood, she spoke, "Your name is Kim Mei-caihong, which means rainbow. You will always lead our clan joyously, even during difficult times. Just like a rainbow, you represent new beginnings. You see new opportunities through loving eyes."

Kim Chin-hae looked over at Lis. Tears were streaming down her face. For the first time, Lis's mother glanced at him with approval. Their blood was placed in the same box as his, one wrapped in a double blue ribbon and the other in red, then placed in the same cavity.

On the third day, Son Jun-ho and Kim Chin-hae left. It was a sad and hopeful day. They pretended he was a dutiful husband going to work and would return shortly. The villagers lined the roadway smiling, waving, and saying their goodbyes.

Chapter Thirteen

Marco

Letters to Li

Genoa Prison 1298

Marco looked at Rustichello. “That's how I met my friend and his shaman wife, Lis. Now, we should continue my trip to the Great Khan.”

Rustichello, in an excited voice, said, “You can’t stop there. Tell me more. Why was he in the palace the first time you saw him, and why did he have to meet the Khan later? And how did he meet Lis?”

Marco shook his head. “That can be another time when we grow tired of this report. Let’s continue; where did we leave off? I have forgotten.”

Rustichello was disappointed; the story was getting interesting. “Okay, let’s see. You were leaving Khotan and traveling to a province called Pem.”

“OK, OK, OK, Khotan. I forgot to say that this city is situated at an intersection where the Silk Road branches to a major route leading from India through Tibet to Central Asia.

> *“The province is a five-day journey and lies east-northeast. They worship Muhammad and are subject to the great Khan. There are many cities and towns, and the finest is the capital called Pem. A river....with large quantities....stones, jasper, and chalcedony are found.... Cotton grows plentifully... They live by trade and crafts....and have the strangest custom....”*

Marco laughed. “Most men in our society would hate this.”

Rustichello looked up, and Marco started describing.

> *"When a woman's husband leaves her to travel for more than twenty days, she has the right to take another husband as soon as he takes off, and the man can take a new wife as well."*

Both men laughed.

Rustichello stated, "I am not sure I could accept that arrangement. What happens when he returns?"

Marco never answered but continued laughing. He thought to himself, *It feels good to laugh.* Then, he continued with his story.

> *"The next province is Cherchen in Turkestan, which lies to the east-northeast. Before the Tartars badly terrorized this land, it was proud and fertile. They worshiped Muhammad. Rivers have plenty of jasper and chalcedony, which is traded in Cathay for a handsome profit. This entire province is a tract of sand....*
>
> *"Most water is bitter and bad, but some places have sweet and good.... They have been ravaged by their enemies so much that they often flee when men pass by; luckily, the enemies can never find them because of the sand and wind. Even friendly men they hide from. In fear, they will kill their flocks for food, and they even store their grain in caves in the sand, bringing it back home only as needed.*
>
> *"After leaving Cherchen, you journey for five days through sandy wastes where the water is terrible; then you arrive at the entry point of the Great Desert of Lop, which belongs to the Great Khan.... They worship Muhammad.... People planning to cross the desert stay here for a week to refresh themselves and stock up on a month's worth of food and water for themselves and their beast.... This desert is so long it could take a year, but the shortest point is a month. That was the path we took.... It was all mountains, sand, and valleys....nothing to eat...but in a day and night, you find drinking water not enough for a huge party but for fifty to a hundred men and beasts.... It seems that throughout the desert, after a day and night, there is water. In some places, the water is bitter, but there are 28 places where the water is good.... There are no animals or birds, as there is no*

food.

"But this desert has stories. The fact is, if you are riding at night, and you are unlucky to be left behind or become separated by falling asleep, there are stories where you hear spirits in such a way that they seem to be your companions. If you follow the voices and stray from the path, the traveler most likely will never be seen or heard from again. Some people hear spirit voices during the day, accompanied by sounds like musical instruments, such as drums, or people rushing away from them. They follow before realizing the spirits have tricked them. Then, they are lost forever. Sometimes, they see spirits charging toward them, thinking it is robbers. They turn and flee, becoming lost and dying of hunger.

"For these reasons, travelers have learned to stick together and set up a sign pointing in the direction of travel before they sleep. You also learn to put bells around the necks of all your beasts so people can find you.

*"So, after thirty days, as I said, you have crossed the desert, east-northeast, you arrive in Shazhou, province of Tangut....subject to the great Khan....idolaters and some are Christians....live off their profits from grains they harvest.... They have many abbeys and monasteries filled with idols to whom they make sacrifice and do great hono*rs....*reverence."*

Marco stopped. "I'm tired."

Rustichello knew what that meant. He laid down his pen. "Let's start with a personal story tomorrow. I won't write it. I want to hear the real story behind all these words."

As Marco stretched out his body on his bed, he quickly sat up. "I should write a letter to Li. Do you think the commander will deliver the letter?"

Rustichello grunted and held out a piece of paper. "Why not? What do you have to lose? There is always a chance."

Marco rose and took the paper. He pulled up a chair at Rustichello's table, grabbed his pen, laid the paper before him, and stared at the blank paper. He thought, *What a fool I am. She was right; we sacrificed so much to be together, and now I have ruined it.* He could feel his emotions building up inside him. It hurt so much that his body began to shake, and he could feel tears rolling down his cheeks.

Rusichello reached over and put his hand over his. "Write a simple note saying you're alive and will return soon."

Marco, with a shaking hand, started writing.

> My Dearest Li,
>
> I'm sorry, I find myself in an unfortunate situation. The Genoese have taken me prisoner. I am being treated well. It shouldn't be long before I hold you in my arms. So please don't worry.
>
> I love you,
> Marco

After the ink had dried, he folded the paper. Then Marco asked for another piece of paper. The next letter would be to his Uncle Maffeo.

> Dear Uncle Maffeo,
>
> Please take care of Li. The Genoese captured me and took me to Palazzo San Giorgio, but I made a deal with them. Hopefully, they will keep their promise, and I will return soon. If you don't hear from me again, please use your influence with the Doge to help me.
>
> Best regards,
> Your nephew, Marco

He folded Li's letter inside this letter. "Tomorrow, I will ask to see the commander, begging him to forward the letters to my uncle in Venice. Also, I will tell him about the progress of our report. Hopefully, he has started making arrangements for my release," Marco said confidently.

Rusichello tried to look positive. He had become exhausted listening to Marco's emotional plea. "I'm turning in. I look forward to tomorrow's story," he said as he stood and stretched. He went to bed sad, hoping this would work out for Marco.

Marco walked to his bed, thinking of Li. *What is she doing? I haven't seen her in a month. She must be worried.* He tried to sleep, only finding peace as he thought of Li.

Chapter Fourteen

Li

Thirteen, Now a Women

Venice 1298

After Li's ritual, playing her erhu at her window, she lay in bed. Li had begun to worry; she hadn't seen Marco for a month. She hoped her music would call him home. Marco always loved her music and often requested that she play it. It was the only thing, besides the art of herbs, that she learned at court. When Marco rescued her from her mother's chamber, Guo Yu also rescued her mother's erhu. The sympathetic Empress Chabi granted permission for her to learn.

That night, she prayed that daybreak would bring news. The palazzo was beginning to feel like a prison; she had been locked inside way too long. Inhaling a deep breath, she thought, *Tomorrow, I will dress like a man. No one pays attention to an Asian man, but a woman is a different story. Luca, Guo Yu, and I will walk the path Marco and I usually take.* Luca had become her friend. She loved to hear stories about Li's home. Guo Yu had learned to trust Luca and no longer feared she was a spy for the cousins. A week ago, Li requested that Luca become her private servant, and Marco's Uncle Maffeo agreed.

Marco's cousins hated it when anyone in the household showed the slightest interest in her. Li was a black mark on their family; they tried hard to act like she didn't exist. Her nonexistence had become much easier since Marco's departure.

Luca acted disgusted with her new role in the presence of the cousins, especially Isabella, so they did not ask her any questions.

The morning sun shone bright, and Li was excited about her decision. She waited for Guo Yu to bring her breakfast. He was less enthusiastic than she was. Guo Yu was always worried that something would happen and Marco would be livid. But he was her servant, and he discovered early that changing her mind was impossible once she had made up her mind.

When Luca arrived, she was ready for a new story. Li learned storytelling from Marco, and Luca found her stories fascinating.

Li promised to tell her the story of when she came of age and was allowed to enter Kubilai Khan's court for the first time. However, Luca wasn't disappointed when Li told her they would go out instead. She loved the strange places they visited. Luca went to the trunk and took out the Cathayan's manservant's clothing. Luca would lead as the Venetian, and the other two would follow.

Venice was the wealthiest city in this part of the world. Thousands of ships entered its harbors. The ships' arrivals had slowed as the war that Marco was fighting raged, but commerce continued. The streets and bustling shops were stocked with exquisite goods as the Silk Road brought beautiful silks, spices, and other unique treasures from Li's home and other amazing places. The city residents were diverse as sailors and merchants arrived from the Byzantine Empire and the Muslim world. As long as they knew their place, they were accepted. The city was an intricate web of waterways that weaved the city together with its grand palaces, artful bridges, shops, and beautiful architectural buildings. These waterways were alive, with gondolas transporting goods from place to place.

Li had been born in Lin'an, the city Marco Polo declared the "Venice of the East." She would think of Marco and their story every time she walked through the city. Today, their first stop would be the *Alla Testa d'Ora*, an apothecary at the foot of the Rialto Bridge. It was recognizable by the golden head above the large arched doorway of a brick building. At the entrance were pewter cauldrons containing the famous Venetian Treacle. Venetian apothecaries were known to produce the powerful cure-all teriaca. The name was a Greek word meaning wild beast because it was a cure for poisonous bites of the beast, and its main ingredient was viper's meat. It was initially from ancient Greek times, but Andromaco, Emperor Nero's physician, improved the recipe. Since then, Venetian apothecaries, with the many herbs and spices brought in by Venetian merchants, created this version, which contains as many as sixty ingredients and is considered the best in the world. Every time she approached these shops with their pewter pots, it reminded her of Lis, Kim Chin-hae's shaman wife. Lis once told her about the potent concoction, Gu, that the women from her tribe made from poisonous reptiles. It was how Lis met Kim Chin-hae, Marco's best friend.

This apothecary was Li's favorite place. Marco brought her here many times after they first arrived, of course, as a man. Li's knowledge of herbs astounded the apothecary. They became friends fast. Now, sadly, she came without Marco.

Messer Alessio, a gentle and slightly gray-haired man with a tidy beard, greeted them at the door with a warm smile. Marco had told her his name meant help. *It is a very appropriate name*, Li thought. The room was filled with pots and tools, and behind the counter were shelves covering the wall with glass jars filled with mysterious contents: Gutti, acido benzoico, Emoglobina, Agurina, and more. Learning the different names took Li a while, but she was determined.

She entered the back of the store by a small doorway leading to Messer Alessio's workroom, where he mixed his creations. He always welcomed her help as she knew different herbs than he did. Li loved to spend time here while Guo Yu and Luca waited for her. For a short time, she could forget Marco.

That day, something strange happened. For the first time, he addressed her as Lady Li. She was shocked; she had been unaware he knew she was a woman.

His smile became larger. "Messer Marco told me the last time he was here."

Li's eyes began to water. *Messer Alessio has become my Physician Wu.* She could hardly speak. "So, you don't care if I am a woman?" she whispered.

He answered, "I am a man of medicine. My only concern is to heal people, and you make it even more possible. You are always welcome."

Li walked over to him and softly squeezed his arm. "Thank you." She continued walking to the hidden chamber.

Messer Alessio, with a smile, offered Luca and Guo Yu some tea. Li had noticed Messer Alessio was overly kind to Luca. Li often thought, *He likes her*. Guo Yu and Luca sat contentedly at a small table facing a window and watched the courtyard come alive with Venetian residents. Everyone was in a rush except them. Luca was content. Her life had changed since she met Li. For the first time, her life had color, not the black-and-white life of a servant. She was excited to be alive, and Li had made this possible.

Several hours passed, and Li appeared from her favorite room. Her face had changed.

She's happy, Luca thought.

Li sat at the table and excitedly asked, "Where shall we go next?" But they knew the answer; Li always went where Marco took her.

The day went fast, and the sun was setting when they returned to the palazzo. They quietly climbed the stairs, hoping not to meet anyone. Luca followed her routine and lit the candles. Guo Yu went happily downstairs to the kitchen to request dinner. He was always delighted with this time of day. Elena was there.

Li removed her man clothes and slipped on her simple evening dress. When Guo Yu returned, they sat around a small table and ate. Luca looked at Li with a questioning face. "Are you too tired to tell more of your story?"

Li looked over at Guo Yu and then turned to the window. Her fixed eyes stared into space; she was searching for what to say. Suddenly, she started to speak. "After Marco delivered me to Kubilai Khan, it was eight years before I saw him again. I was thirteen. Li turned to Luca. "You did guess that the kind man was Marco when I was five."

Luca smiled. "I figured that."

Li continued. "I was unaware that he kept abreast of me through Guo Yu, and he was one of the reasons I ended up at the palace to live. Li smiled and continued. "You are considered a woman when you turn thirteen. My life had been so consumed with finding my purpose that I hadn't thought about what that meant. When Empress Nambi told me to start preparing for the White Festival, the New Year's celebration, I dreaded the whole affair. I would be introduced as the adopted daughter of Empress Chabi."

Luca interrupted Li, "Who is Empress Nambi?"

"She was Empress Chabi's cousin; she was now the empress after Empress Chabi died."

Luca nodded.

Li continued. "Her motive was to find a husband for me. Important barons or kings would attend, looking for wives for themselves or their sons—a perfect chance to seal an alliance with Kubilai Khan. The entire city was bustling. The White Festival was one of the most exciting festivals of the year, except for the Great Khan's birthday. All the years before, by early morning, I would be at the gate watching the elephants' procession, the horses running, and the grand barons, generals, and perhaps kings of other lands dressed in their finest. However, unfortunately, I would be the one displayed that year, so my dressing was my only concern."

Li watched Luca frown. Li frowned back at Luca and continued. "Guo Yu entered my room carrying a beautiful, wrapped gold and white present. I looked curiously at him."

He replied, "From an old friend."

"At first, I thought he meant himself. All day, he helped me prepare my unique gifts for special people. The gifts could only be in white and gold. Guo Yu had become my surrogate mother and father, and I love him." Li looked over at Guo Yu and smiled. "He had patiently taught me the Tartar language and its customs. At that time, I didn't trust Empress Nambi or her court ladies. I spent most of my time learning herb skills and playing the erhu rather than socializing and doing frivolous things. They thought I felt they were beneath me. That was far from the truth; they scared me."

Li continued. "Slowly and carefully, I unfolded the beautiful, delicate gold silk surrounding the gift. It was a beautiful dress, but on top was a small, white pearl-handled knife with embedded delicate diamonds and a gold blade that shimmered in the light. Tears swelled in my eyes as I lifted it from the wrappings. I knew who the dress and knife were from—my savior. The knife belonged to my mother; the one Marco took from me when I was five. I was frantic; I hadn't prepared a gift for him. Quickly, I went to my dressing table and pulled out 'the scarf.' This could be his gift. But I hesitated as I slowly brought it up to my face and placed it over my eyes. Gently, I put it back in the box where I found it and continued shuffling through my drawers. I had to have something, something I treasured. In the bottom drawer, an ivory comb with pearls and gold beads appeared, a gift from Empress Chabi. This would do. Carefully, I wrapped it in the necessary gold and white silk and placed it in my baskets of other presents.

Guo Yu handed me the open gift box; I ran my fingers over the dress and smiled. Slowly unfolding it, I began to dress. Its beauty entranced me. A delicate, white V-neck silk top with flowing long sleeves came first. Next, I slipped into a long, fluid, multilayered white and gold silk skirt topped with a gold band stitched with gorgeous genuine pearls. It would sit just above my breast and be securely tied in the back. Guo Yu handed me a gold silk scarf. It was circular and draped over my shoulders, falling down my back.

I stood before him. Guo Yu smiled, 'You are all grown up. Today, your life will change.'

"Guo Yu then instructed me to sit at my dressing table. He helped me pull back a large portion of my long black hair into an intricate bun with wispy sections flowing around my face. Yu handed me another present—his. Enthusiastically, I tore it open. Inside was a delicate gold and pearl tiara. I placed it strategically upon my head. Guo Yu smiled, just like now."

Luca turned and looked at Guo Yu, thinking, *His smile expresses so much love, like a proud father.*

"Then he said the frightening words. 'Come, it's time.'

"As we waited to enter the imperial court, I was penetrated with staring eyes. Some were filled with envy, some with approval, and others with daggers. I knew then who my friends were. Finally, the servant ushered us in after a much too long and complicated protocol. Guo Yu reminded me never to step on the threshold as I entered the imperial court. It is a no, no. This one protocol causes many foreigners much embarrassment. However, the interesting part is that the guards are much more lenient at the end when guests have consumed too much alcohol."

Luca giggled. Li continued. "I was seated with the other ladies and was overwhelmed by the beauty of this overflowing large room filled with rich and influential people. They glowed with their white and gold clothing and were richly adorned with jewels. The disciplined servants served outrageous amounts of food and drink. I tried hard not to let it show that this was my first time in court.

"Nonchalantly, my eyes roamed the room, looking for Marco, wondering if I would recognize him. It had been eight years. At five, I remembered his face being youthful, easy to look at, and gentle. Maybe that's why I wasn't afraid of him.

"Kubilai Khan's sons and generals were seated to Kubilai's left, laughing and drinking. Next to Crown Prince Chinghiz, a different-looking man sat. He was dressed as the others, but his hair was not straight. His dark, curly hair was partially pulled back and braided with gold beads and white pearls. The rest hung loose on his shoulder. His eyes were round. My heart skipped a beat. This was the face I remembered and had wiped the tears away. The man who carried me to safety and shared his secret with me. The man who had not forgotten me. His face was older but still possessed gentleness. His charismatic smile and laughter seemed to capture the men around him. Amazingly, he no longer looked like a foreigner; he looked more Tartar. He was proof of his words, gaining great power and position in lands different from his own. I wondered about his age.

"Suddenly, he looked my way as if he knew someone was staring at him. His eyes met mine, and he smiled. Embarrassed, I lowered my head, trying not to look back. As the evening continued, the drinks flowed, and the entertainers and music monopolized the room. Voices and laughter increased. Everyone then began to move around the room, handing out their gifts. Guo Yu motioned for me to do the same. Moving about the large room, I delivered my gifts and found him. His gift was the last one. The closer I came, my stomach swarmed with butterflies. I could hardly catch my breath and felt my face turn red. I stopped, turned around, and walked the other way when I felt a soft touch on my shoulder. I turned, meeting his eyes, and with his contagious smile, he said. 'Have you forgotten me?' Flustered, I stuttered, 'No.' Before I could say anything else, he spoke again. 'I hope you liked your dress and your other gift.' Without hesitation, I reached into the sleeve of my dress and slid out the small knife.

"'This was the best present I could ever receive. Thank you.'

"'You have grown up to be a fine young woman. Physician Wu told me you have become quite an herbalist at your age. I am happy you listened.'

"I smiled; my butterflies landed. I reached into the basket and handed Marco his gift. Without opening it, he bowed and left. I was sad; I had more to say!"

Li smiled at Luca. "That was the beginning of my obsession with Messer Marco Polo.

"When Empress Chabi died, I was of no concern to anyone; I had freedom that the other girls didn't have. Being a "Ghost" had its benefits. In fact, my interest in medicine started when

Empress Chabi fell ill. The royal court physician, Physician Wu, would come to her. I stood in the corner, watched, and followed him when he left, asking him questions about her illness and cures. He was a kind, patient man and always answered me. After her death, he asked if I wanted to learn more. This was life-changing. Maybe I was still a ghost to others, but I stopped being a ghost to myself. Guo Yu would escort me daily to the royal herbalist garden and the physician's quarters. After the White Festival, these walks turned into my reconnaissance mission, looking for Marco.

"I was unaware that Marco and Guo Yu had remained friends since our first encounter. Guo Yu found my interest in Marco amusing but warned me of the necessity of silence. It could be dangerous for both of us. At thirteen, I was naïve. *Why would anyone care?*

"Marco was seldom in the palace. I was so disappointed. Marco's face constantly crept into my thoughts as I played my erhu, studied, and slept. Guo Yu told me that Marco's job was traveling throughout the empire. He was the ears and eyes of the Great Khan. His next trip would be to Burma and Champa, and he would be gone for four or five months. Even though I knew this, I continued my childish search for Marco, hoping Guo Yu was wrong, and continued my ghost act, weaving in and out of the palace grounds, hoping for a glimpse.

"It was during this time my curiosity grew beyond Marco. I had an advantage. My apprenticeship under Physician Wu made the palace my playground and workplace. The palace was grand, with numerous rooms filled with wall paintings that displayed its history and the people who lived there. The grounds were a mystery with so many nooks and crannies, perfect for secret rendezvous. So, the simple yearning to see Marco turned me into a spy, and through this spying, I soon discovered that within the palace walls, its grounds, and the residence held many secrets. I wanted to know them."

Li stopped talking and stared out the window. The moon was shining directly in the window. She lowered her head. "I'm tired; let's talk later." Li stood and walked toward the large window that faced the illuminating moonlit canal. Her favorite chair and erhu awaited her. The crying music began. Luca and Guo Yu listened for a while and, with tears in their eyes, left quietly, closing the door behind them. Li's music filled her room, and slowly escaped to the hallway. Unfortunately, Marco's cousin, Isabella, approached them, holding her candle high. Her face distorted with disgust. She spoke loudly, hoping Li could hear her. "Do I see tears in your eyes, Luca? Have you fallen for that pagan's trick like Marco? I can understand Guo Yu; he is the same as her. That music makes me sick! If Marco doesn't return soon, I might lose control and throw that disgusting instrument in the canal."

Luca's mouth opened to speak. Guo Yu secretly touched her arm. Luca closed her mouth, bowed, and hurried away. Guo Yu stared at Isabella with defiance. He had more power than

Luca. A quick smile appeared on Guo Yu's face. "I'm sure your father and Marco would disapprove. How much is your allowance?" With a disgusted face, Isabella stared at Guo Yu and began walking down the hall. But Guo Yu could hear her mumbling as she walked away. "Someday, someday!"

Guo Yu returned to his room concerned, and hoped Marco would return soon.

Chapter Fifteen

Marco

1272 Marco, Top of the World

Genoa prison 1298

The next morning, Marco was excited. He stood at the prison cell's door and waited for their breakfast. It seemed to take forever before he began to hear the clanging of metal of the small food doors opening and a gruff voice yelling, "Breakfast." It would be his turn soon. The guard opened his door; Marco quickly grabbed their breakfast and handed it to Rustichello, placing his other hand through the small opening before the guard could close it.

"Please, I need to talk to your commander; I have something to tell him."

The guard's answer was a grunt before the door slammed on his hand. Marco walked back to their table with a disappointed face. "Damn this place! What a fool I am! Li must be going mad! Do you think I will hear from the commander?"

"You are at the mercy of the gods, Marco. You can try again tomorrow," Rustichello said in a reassuring voice. "Let's continue; the more you write, the better. Later, I hope you can tell me more about Kim Chin-hae."

Marco questioned Rustichello. "Where were we?"

Rustichello repeated the last paragraph:

> *"So, after thirty days you had crossed the desert, you arrived in Shazhou, province of Tangut....subject to the great Khan....idolaters and some are Christians....live off their profits from grains they harvest.... They have many abbeys and monasteries filled with idols to whom they make a sacrifice and do great honors....reverence."*

Marco remembered and started.

"Oh, you should know that all idolaters in the world are cremated when they die. When the corpse reaches the place of cremation, the relatives take images of men and many animals, cut them out of pieces of paper, and burn them with their bodies while their relatives with instruments make loud music. This will ensure the deceased will have as many slaves and animals. All this is done based on the rank of the deceased and the requirements of their station. Next, you travel northwest near the edge of this desert to a province that was once a Kingdom called Kamul. It lies between deserts; on one side is the Great Desert, and on the other is a little desert, a day's journey across.... People are idolaters and have their own language....live off the fruits of the earth....sell them to travelers who pass their way.

"They are satisfied with their life and enjoy just playing instruments, sing, dance, and indulge in carnal pleasures. They are a strange lot. Strangers who seek a place to stay can enter any home. The man of the house is very happy. He orders his wife to grant the stranger his every wish. The husband leaves his house, goes about his business, and stays away for two or three days or more. The owner of the house provides anything the guest desires, but, of course, the guest pays for the items. And his wife lies with the stranger as if it is her husband in a state of ecstasy. This happens all over the city and province, and they are in no way ashamed of it. The women are very beautiful and lively. Now, it did happen that the Mengu Khan, lord of Tartars, was reigning and tried to put a stop to this adultery, even putting heavy penalties. "

Marco laughed. "It didn't work," he then continued.

"For three years, they obeyed, but when they realized their lands stopped yielding their normal amounts and their households had misfortune after another, they pleaded with the king, even sending gifts, begging him to let them resume the tradition their ancestors had given them. They explained their misfortunes, and finally, the Mengu Khan, hearing this, said, 'Since you desire your own shame,

you may have it. Go and live according to your customs.' The whole population rejoiced, and still today they uphold this custom."

Rustichello stopped Marco. "I am not sure how that would work, but we will add this story; I'm sure the generals would be enticed to stop there."

Marco stated, "My father was." Marco slid right back into his story:

"From Kamul, if you travel north and then northwest, you reach Uyghuristan.... This is a large province subject to the Khan.... The chief city is Kara-Khoja....worship idols, but some Christians who follow Nestorian ideals... intermarry with Idolaters."

Marco stopped and looked at Rustichello. "They have a strange belief that their first king did not come from human birth. He sprang from a fungus called Esca that grows out of the sap of trees. I didn't question this much. The idolaters appeared knowledgeable about their laws and traditions and were very diligent students of education. I didn't want to offend them."

Rustichello looked at Marco and shook his head. He held his pen with his head down, waiting for Marco to continue. Marco understood and continued.

"The land produces grain and outstanding wine....very cold winters. The next province, Gingin Talas, lies on the edge of the desert north-northeast direction. It extends the length of a sixteen-day journey. It belongs to the Great Khan...plenty of cities....three types of people, the majority idolaters, then Turks and Nestorian Christians."

Marco hesitated momentarily and continued. "The commanders will be interested in this; on the northern border of this province is a mountain with rich veins of steel and ondanique."

Rustichello stopped Marco. "What is ondanique?"

"A steel so precious that a sword created from this steel must be treated like a jewel for its value surpasses all others. It seems its fame started in India. It is said that it is impossible to find anything to surpass the edge you obtain from this steel. Metal from the heavens, it's called."

Marco's face saddened, and he fell silent momentarily. "The Great Khan gave me one. It was my first real sword." With a quivering voice, he continued, "I have failed many people with my decisions." Marco quickly recovered and continued talking.

> *"But something else came from this mountain. It was a vein of a substance in which Salamander is produced. It is not an animal, as you might think, but something of great importance. I was told by one of my Turkish companions, named Zulfiqar, who had been employed by the Great Khan to oversee the salamander extraction, as well as the ondanique and steel. That every three years, a baron is sent by the Khan to the governor and oversees the extraction, as Salamander is the most extraordinary thing I have ever seen.*

> *"I witnessed its production and the outcome. It is dug out of the mountain and then torn and broken up, but the pieces contain twisted fibers that look like wool. Then they let it dry, pound the pieces in a huge copper mortar, and wash. The remaining wool-like fiber is then carefully spun and made into cloth. Now, the most interesting thing about this cloth is that it doesn't burn. When it's dirty or stained, you place it in a fire for a while, and it turns white as snow, ready for use."*

Rustichello put down his pen and looked at Marco with disbelief.
Marco spoke up.

> *" What I have told you is the truth. I can tell you one of these clothes is now in Rome; it was sent to the pope by the great Khan as a precious gift."*

Rustichello picked up his pen and continued writing as Marco spoke. "Can you imagine armor made from this? Warriors would never burn. Ensure you add this to the report; the commander would find this important."

Marco stopped; his stomach growled. He walked over to the door and listened for the clanging. "I'm starving. How do they expect you and me to write? Surely, food will come tonight."

Returning to Rustichello's table, Marco placed his hand on the letters. "These need to be delivered." His heart ached for Li, and his hunger disappeared.

He paced back and forth, continuing to talk.

> *"You continue for another ten days to the east-northeast. There is very little habitation and not much to talk about for the next ten days until you reach Suzhou.... The people are Christians, idolaters, and subject to the Great Khan. Rhubarb grows here, and the merchants buy and export it across the world.*
>
> *"Also, a traveler must take care, as this is a poisonous herb that grows in the mountains. They can only use animals born here. For they recognize the herb and avoid eating it, for if they do, their hooves will fall off."*

Rustichello shook his head and commented. "This is indeed a dangerous world."

Marco continued:

> *"The people live from the fruits of the land, and trade is null. The whole province is healthy and brown-skinned."*

Marco stopped talking and looked expressionlessly out the barred window. It was nightfall, and his stomach growled. "Where are the guards?" Marco stormed the door and started banging and yelling. "Hey, hey, hey, is anyone here?" The more he yelled, the louder he became. His voice echoed down the long stone hall; moments later, he heard other prisoners yelling. He smiled. "Well, that will wake up those lazy bastards."

Rustichello spoke up. "Your yelling is fruitless. Stop! If you don't, we might not see food tonight or tomorrow." Still glaring at Marco, he lowered his pen, thinking about how to take Marco's mind from his hunger and anger. "I'm tired. Let's talk about your friend, Kim Chin-hae. Why was he in the palace?"

Marco calmed down, knowing Rustichello was right. *Yes, okay.* Marco thought, *The next part of his travels would be a lengthy story. We stayed in Ganzhou*[1] *for a year. How much am I going to tell Rustichello? This was where my father and uncle decided their future for the next 17 years, even if they didn't know it at the time.*

Marco sat on his bed and stretched out his tired, hungry body. Looking up at the ceiling, he thought about Kim Chin-hae and began. "When my father, my uncle, and I first arrived in Khanbaliq in 1275, rumors were still circulating the city of Kubilai Khan's failure to defeat Cipangu.[2] But in Kubilai's court, it was a different story. The invasion was just a warning.

Kubilai hoped they would recognize his strength and agree to be his vassals without further invasions. That was the first time I heard of the country of Goryeo, a vassal of the Great Khan. Kubilai Khan's ships sailed from there to invade Cipangu. I also learned Kubilai Khan's daughter would marry the Goryeo's crown prince.

"The first time I saw Kim Chin-hae, I was waiting to see Kubilai in his chamber, around 1277 or 78. I had returned from one of my trips. Kim Chin-hae exited Kubilai's chamber with someone who looked very important and a servant carrying a child. These people turned out to be Kim Chin-hae's cousin, King Chungnyeol of Goryeo, and his son, Crown Prince Wang Won, who would live in the palace and be raised as a Tartar like Li.

"The second time, as you know, is when I saved him from the tiger. It would be two years before I saw him again. He was stationed in Ningbo, an eight-day ride from where I lived in Yangzhou. We would meet occasionally to discuss our business plans and dreams. Kim Chin-hae's life was complicated, and his family obligations in Goryeo were troublesome. He was a general in the Goryeo military, and the second Cipangu invasion was being planned. He also married someone from a different country and race, and his parents didn't even know. As I said, his life was complicated. It was one of these nights that, after many drinks, he began telling me his story."

---

1. Zhangye

2. Japan

Chapter Sixteen

Kim

Kim Chin-hae, The Beginning

Kim Chin-hae sat at the table, staring at Marco through blurred eyes. *I've drunk too much. Maybe by telling Marco my story, my drunkenness will disappear.* He started from the beginning.

"My father's family has always been powerful merchants, trading gold, silver, porcelain, and ginseng. They were also great leaders in the military and deeply entrenched in politics. I was expected to follow in their footsteps. As a young man, I attended Gukjagam, the highest educational institution in my country. My parents' dream was for me to become a scholar and enter the political circle, but I had no desire for politics, which was a big disappointment to my mother.

"My aunt, Queen Joengsun, my father's older sister, had been married to the newly elected King Won Jong of Goryeo to legitimize his rule. Her mother's side was the Choe Clan, the Ubong Choe Military regime, which fought for 30 years to prevent the Mongol from taking over but lost after the leader of the Choe was assassinated by Kim Injoon, one of their military leaders. Goryeo was now a vassal state and a compulsory ally of Kubilai Khan's Yuan Dynasty, rather than being under the Choes' military dictatorship. Both sides decided that power and wealth could be obtained and maintained by accepting their circumstances peacefully rather than through battle.

"I lacked the desire for politics, which frightened my mother. She feared I would follow my heart—the sea. Shipbuilding and navigation were my passions, even though I excelled in all subjects, including languages and politics. Our country was already advanced in cartography; however, our southern neighbor, Song, had new technology—the magnetic compass and watertight bulkheads. Goryeo was investing in this new knowledge, and I wanted to be a part of it. Our seas were perilous with strong tidal currents, so having stronger ships meant more cargo could be delivered and the richer my family would become.

"For a long time, I dreamed of owning a fleet of the most remarkable ships ever built. I had book knowledge but needed more hands-on experience; I knew this would be the only way to improve our ships. Of course, my mother disapproved. She pressured me to stay behind a desk, but that wasn't for me. When school was not in session, I secretly traveled south with Son Jun-ho, my servant since birth, to the sea disguised as a commoner. Wandering the shipyards, I met a master shipbuilder and his son. They lived such a different life. It wasn't an easy life, but it was uncomplicated and straightforward. Not only did I learn to build ships, but I also learned to have respect for the common people.

"So, in 1271, when I finished school, I entered the Royal Navy as a Sakua, an officer under General Hong Dagu, a good friend of my parents. My mother was heartbroken. I would be gone for long periods fighting the Sambyeolcho forces, the Goryeo Choe rebels, and defending our segongseon[1] and merchants' cargo ships. That included my family's, from the Waegu[2]—the Wa pirates on the southern and eastern coast, who constantly robbed our cargo ships.

"But her worst fear was the upcoming Wa invasion.[3] The night before I left, she cried openly as we sat at the table full of my favorite foods and rounds of drinks were poured. I tried hard to change her mood, making jokes that her handsome son would return with honors because of his bravery. The whole table laughed, including the servants, because I never portrayed extreme bravery; I feared water and insects.

"My mother retired early, exhausted from sadness. My father sat up and talked, reminiscing about his military battles against Mongols—something I found curious. *How could he be their ally?* However, he never discussed it, and I was too respectful to ask. But that night, he did talk about the Sambyeolcho. 'You will be fighting your grandmother's relatives.' I never thought of that. My father continued. 'You know that the Sambyeolcho are remnants of the former Military regime that revolted in 1270. They selected a descendant of the royal family as their king. They abducted government officials and their families and even commoners fleeing south to the islands of Jindo and Jeju. But what you don't know is that they had approached our family to betray your cousin, Crown Prince Wang Chong,[4] but I denied them. I was tired of fighting. Your cousin even sent troops to our house to guard us for a while. So, it will be dangerous for you if you are captured. The Sambyeolcho could use you as a hostage, demanding I join them.'

"For the first time, I realized how naïve, protected, and spoiled I was. I never realized our family had such deep, treasonous roots. Lowering my head, I promised I would be careful.

"That night, I didn't sleep. I watched the sunrise, the beginning of a new day, and my new life. Son Jun-ho helped me dress in my uniform. My father and my crying mother sat at the table. We ate and drank tea slowly. I rose, bowed low, and walked out. My father followed, and when I sat on my horse, he looked up at me with tears. 'Be Brave; remember that bravery is not lack of fear but the ability to move forward despite fear.'

"I rode south for numerous days to my commission in Masanhappo. We trained for the first couple of weeks and received a brief introduction to the ship, its weapons, and combat training. As an elite, I had been instructed in swordsmanship and archery for years, but combat fighting felt different. The day I stepped aboard the ship for duty, I felt excitement. That excitement soon became a realization: I could die. I tried to remember what my father said the morning I left.

"As time passed, I thought less of dying and gained more admiration for my fellow men. Most had come from poor families. They were abducted into the military without pay, had to supply their own weapons provided by their families, and were then expected to fight with loyalty. I was surprised most did.

"The Waegu were fierce and relentless, and so were the Sambyeolcho. I slowly gained my fellow soldiers' respect, becoming a natural leader and an exceptional fighter by staying alive. However, I failed to overcome my fear of the water."

Kim Chin-hae smiled and continued. "Eighteen months passed, and the Sambyeolcho were finally subdued. That same year, in early 1274, a rumor of a Wa invasion circulated the ship."

Marco interrupted Kim Chin-hae. "The battle Kubilai lost."

"Yes, I was twenty, not ready to die. King Won Jong summoned me to return home. I was met by my father, mother, General Hong Dagu, and my first cousin, the king's son, Crown Prince Sim, who wore a traditional Mongolian dress. I was bewildered but stayed silent.

"My mother could hardly contain her joy, and my father stood with pride as I was promoted to Busajik.[5] Following the ceremony, we had an intimate dinner with the king. That evening, we discussed the upcoming invasion of Wa.

"My cousin, the king, informed me I wouldn't be returning to my ship; I would be occupied with shipbuilding and mobilization of troops. During that year, I thought about my men. *How many had survived the year?* I was surprised at myself; I missed my camaraderie with them.

"And then it happened, I was ordered to return to my ship. The invasion would begin. That day, death monopolized my mind. My life's dream could end here. I belonged to the sea but not as my tomb."

Marco, with wide eyes, picked up his goblet and drank fast. "Tell me, what happened?"

Kim Chin-hae closed his eyes and began. "Even though the Samurai fought admirably and gallantly with their long swords and ironclad armor, they were no match for Kubilai Khan's army. We had more soldiers, and our battlefield strategies, conveyed by drums and gongs, were superior. Our weapons—gunpowder grenades fired by catapults, double-horn bows, and individual shields—were much more advanced than the Wa's. In 18 days, we owned Hakata Bay. Then, suddenly, General Hong Dagu and General Lui ordered a retreat. I was confused. *We were winning. Why would we retreat?* It couldn't be possible that this campaign was a way for Kubilai to warn the Kamakura shogunate.[6] General Hong Dagu argued that our men were exhausted, and supplies were low. However, I agreed with Commander Hogun, the vice general, who wanted to continue advancing, as victory was apparent.

"Commander Hogun lost; we retreated, and our ships turned north, returning home. Unfortunately, the day after, black rolling clouds raced toward us. Now, we were facing death by nature. We had no control. At least on the battlefield, we faced death with our strength and failures. And defeat or victory was up to us. Now, we face death with fate only. All I could do now was hope death was not my destiny.

"A giant wave swept over our seemingly miniature ship amidst the great angry sea. My salt-burned eyes saw only blurred men scrambling on their stomachs, holding on to anything tied down. Deafening winds howled, mutilating the voices of the screaming men. Only one voice could clearly be heard: Commander Hong Dagu shouting, 'General Lui is dead!' Panic and the ocean controlled the ship.

"I was disoriented and uncertain of what to do. As my ship transcended a giant wave and hugged the sea, I had a moment of clarity. A rope dangled from the mast. I tied it to my waist and threw myself on the floor, just in time before another crashing wave smashed my head against the mast. Everything went black.

"I gained consciousness with heat and brightness surrounding my body. *Is this a dream, heaven or hell?* Slowly opening my eyes and squinting, I saw the top of the mast, blue skies, and the sun. *I am alive!* Blood rolled down my face. I could hear someone calling my name, muffled by my pulsating head. The brightness was overshadowed as General Hong Dagu stood over me with a bittersweet smile. 'You are alive; it would have been devastating to inform the king and your mother of your death. Find the doctor and take care of your head.' I sat up slowly, and the general extended his hand and pulled me up. The ship and crew had survived the terrifying storm but not without injuries and damage.

"The now calm blue sea hosted remnants of mangled ships—mostly Mongols, dead bodies, and men screaming for help as they floated on battered wood. I forgot about my head, found a deserted oar, and joined in rowing as other men hung on the ship's edges, rescuing the half-frozen men. The dead Goryeo, Han, and Mongols bodies were collected and placed on a large flat segment of a destroyed ship, which was tied to our ship. The following day, the Goryeo and Han men's bodies would be set aflame while floating out to sea, releasing their souls to be reborn quickly. The Khan's men, as per Yuan custom, were left to be absorbed by nature, returning their souls to where they came from. Amid this, drums and gongs penetrated the air, calling to any remaining ships. In the distance, we could hear the lucky ones answer. By evening, the sunset displayed glorious hues of color playing backdrop to the found ships. My spirit was lifted, but the feeling was short-lived. Guilt and sadness returned as I hopelessly wandered the ship with torn, freshly blood-stained clothing, looking for my friends and fellow officers—so many had perished.

"Before darkness surrounded the ship, the ship's doctor stopped me, instructing me to sit. He gently wiped the fresh blood dripping down my face and bandaged my head. 'Rest!' he told me as his slumped, broken body walked away.

"We limped back to Masanhappo. Our losses were heavy; out of 26,000 men, we lost half our men and many ships. On arrival, I was dispatched to Kaesong,[7] the capital of Goryeo, with a report. I rode for days with a heavy heart; I had lost so many friends. When I reached the Goryeo Imperial Palace, my sadness had turned to anger. My father greeted me. His loving eyes showed worry as my facial expression and walk displayed my festering anger.

"Since the reigning King Won Jong died unexpectedly four months ago, my father had become the new advisor to the new king, Crown Prince Sim, his nephew. As king, his name changed to King Chungnyeols. I hesitated before entering the king's chamber as my father whispered, 'Greet your cousin, King Chungnyeols, respectfully; hand over the report and talk only if spoken to.' My father's words didn't surprise me as his role had changed. But his dress did. He no longer wore the Goryeo uniform but the Mongolian one. I stared at my father and entered.

"The king sat at his writing desk. I fell to my knees and bowed, and he smiled, motioning me forward. 'I'm happy to see you alive. However, I see a scar on your handsome face.' We both laughed. When the laughter stopped, the atmosphere changed. The king's face turned stern. 'You have something for me?' I presented him with the report. My eyes focused on his new royal Mongolian dress as he unfolded the pages and started to read. *Things have changed since I left*, I thought. His reading seemed to be unending. When he finally looked up, his face was blank and hard to read. I expected my cousin to be disheartened by the news and ask me questions and my opinion. His only words were. 'We will talk later. Go see your mother.'

"I clenched my fist and lips, forcing myself to be silent while facing my cousin. I bowed, turned, and walked out. Questions flooded my mind. *Did he know we were to withdraw before we left? Why didn't he mention the storm? Didn't he consider it a bad omen? We lost so much. Why didn't he ask me anything?* For five years, his father and Kubilai Khan planned this invasion. It was his failure now. He showed no remorse. My world as I knew it had ended. He had been my mentor, a respected older brother. Now, disappointment surrounded him. Early on, my mother had warned me that things could change when he became king. I wouldn't believe it. Maybe it was true. Disappointed, I left the palace with my father. He patted me on the shoulder, telling me he was proud of me as we walked home in silence.

"My mother, Kim Ae-cha, stood at our home's entrance like a statue. I saw tears streaming, but not a word was uttered. As I faced her, she stood on her tiptoes and gently touched my injured forehead. 'Your poor beautiful face, what will your admirers think?' She wrapped her arms around me as I did her.

"For a moment, we comforted each other. My mother reluctantly released me, grabbed my hand, and led me inside. The servants laid out my favorite foods on a banquet table before me. We sat as a family for the first time in months, only exchanging pleasantries and remaining silent about the cruelties of war and the politics that came with it.

"My father rose, bowed, and left us. We were lucky to have him this long. My mother sat silently for a few minutes, then rose, walked over to me, and placed her hand on my shoulder. 'I prayed every day that you would return safely. I realize some families weren't as blessed. But please see it as their destiny! Don't cause problems for your father or the king.' She walked out of the room. I sat at the table and poured myself a drink and another and another. This was the first time I was disappointed in my mother and the first time I faced the truth: our country belonged to Kubilai Khan.

"The next morning, my head wasn't pounding from my injury but from the alcohol. I'm not sure when I went to bed or how much I drank. I was in conflict. Kubilai Khan attempted diplomacy multiple times over the past five years, sending emissaries to Wa in the hopes of a peaceful surrender. When this failed, the invasion proceeded. I couldn't believe they would sacrifice so many lives just as a warning. *Our lives meant nothing to them?* I prayed that my cousin didn't know and that the general was sincere. *The reason we didn't continue was the lack of supplies. And the terrible storm was just bad luck and a bad omen to heed.*

"Suddenly, there was a knock at my door. It was my mother; she had a note from the king. He wanted to see me. My mother left the room, returning with a fresh new Busajik uniform. She was so proud. On my way out, she stopped me. 'Show respect and remember your father and I are part of this. Don't embarrass us.'

"My mind was racing as I entered the king's chamber. I kept reminding myself what my mother said.

"The king greeted me with a smile. His mood seemed more relaxed than at our last meeting. Maybe he thought my anger had cooled, but that was not the case. I bowed, and he motioned me to sit. I could not refrain any longer; my nights had been filled with men screaming and dying.

"'Why? Did you know?' I said in an angry voice."

"King Chungnyeol's face soured. 'Know what?'

"'We were winning.' I said fiercely.

"My mother's voice entered my head. *Careful.* I softened my voice. 'We withdrew even though we were winning. We conquered the two Wa islands, Tsushima and Iki. Our men fought valiantly. We outnumber them by 20 to 1. Both armies lost numerous warriors, but in the end, their people were butchered by Kubilai Khan's warriors. Then, we went to Hakata Bay as planned, creating a perfect bridgeway. Undoubtedly, if we had proceeded, we would have taken the country. Isn't that what Kubilai wanted? Were we used as a warning? To show them our strength? Ultimately, they won, not by their hands but by nature.'

"King Chungnyeols sat silently, seemingly calculating his next move. This time, he spoke more like a caring cousin: 'I understand you're young, and this was your first invasion. You lost friends and saw many atrocities. But you are a soldier by your choice; this is your life. You are to follow orders and not question. I'll answer your question only because you're my cousin. Yes, the plan was to withdraw and send emissaries to talk about surrender. Unfortunately, we lost to unforeseen circumstances.' His voice became sterner. 'Question answered? From now on, never question me! I won't be so forgiving! Go home now and spend time with your family. You will return to the Royal Navy in Masanhappo in a few days until your next orders are determined.'

"As I exited, I felt guilty; I hadn't given much thought to him. He had recently lost his father, and he had lost his first invasion. King Chungnyeols, my cousin, grew up with war, especially the first 20 years of his life. He had become hardened. The Mongols constantly invaded our country for 35 years, ending only in settled peace 15 years ago. His father ascended to the throne with the help of Kubilai Khan and even sent troops when his throne was threatened. King Chungnyeol's loyalty now sided with our conqueror, his imperial father-in-law. He had just married his daughter, Queen Jangmonk, and she was carrying his child.

"In a couple of days, I left for Masanhappo, our navy garrison, and for the next three years, I fought and defended our cargo ships out at sea. The Waegu attacks were rising because the defeated Wa islanders were starving. Wa would never forget Kubilai Khan's invasion.

"Besides improving my fighting skills, my understanding of ships grew after the invasion. In the evenings, I designed new ships and, on free days, searched out master shipbuilders. My thirst for knowledge helped me forget the past and bequeath hope for my future dreams.

"One evening in 1275, I was summoned to our general's cabin. As I walked toward his cabin, several other officers were headed in the same direction. My concern heightens as I enter the room. The already sitting officers displayed much seriousness. General Kim Bong-byong motioned us to sit. 'Today, we received news from Yuan. Kubilai Khan attempted diplomacy again with Wa and failed. He sent five emissaries demanding tribute. Unfortunately for the emissaries, they waited for four months to see the Shogunate, who beheaded them right on the beach. Another Wa invasion is in our future, though probably not until Kubilai Khan defeats the Song Dynasty, but we should prepare ourselves.'

"The room hummed with discussion. Some were in disbelief, and others were happy for an upcoming invasion. My cousin had sent many letters to the Shogunate demanding they control the pirates, but to no avail. After that night, my life continued with battles, and my secret dream of building my merchant ships dwindled. We received monthly updates on the war between the Yuan and Song Dynasty. Finally, at the beginning of 1276, Commander Bayan of the Yuan Dynasty won a significant battle, and Grand Dowager Xie Daoqing of the Song Dynasty surrendered Lin'an. It was becoming apparent the Song Dynasty was going to be defeated. It was just a matter of time before the second Wa invasion would occur.

"Over those three years, my heart had grown cold without knowing it. I no longer dwelt on the men I killed. I had become numb, concentrating on staying alive and safeguarding our ship, as well as my men, who were loyal to me because I was loyal to them. I had mixed feelings when the letter from King Chungnyeol arrived, requesting that I return. I had become accustomed to this life. For the last year, I had completely forgotten about my dream. It was not until I started gathering my possessions that I realized the stacked papers—my dreams—sat on my desk collecting dust. As I shuffled through the pages, my body stung like needles that penetrated every inch. It was like my whole body had been asleep and suddenly awoke. I no longer dreaded going home. But I felt guilty leaving my men and friends. Sadness filled my goodbye, and I wondered if I would ever see them again.

"The closer I came to home, the more I thought about my mother, Kim Ae-cha, and father, Kim Chui-hee; my heart warmed. Yet, I couldn't control my mind as it returned to my angry past, but perhaps that anger kept me alive. I matured over the past three years, gaining a deeper understanding of my father, mother, and cousin. My illusion of fairness and righteousness had its place, but if our country was to survive, it sometimes had to be set aside. I'm sure that's why the king sent me away for so long. He wanted me to learn the difficult part of life. I yearned for revenge for the first few years, but it slowly slipped away.

"My aged father greeted me when I arrived at the palace. His face looked worn, and his tired eyes welled with tears that he fought back. I respectfully bowed and asked. 'Is this meeting about the second invasion?' He didn't answer. When I entered the king's chamber, my cousin genuinely looked happy to see me. 'Again, you return safely. I heard brilliant reports on your service, outstanding battle skills, and leadership.' I bowed.

"He motioned me to sit. 'We have lots to talk about.' His voice softened as he continued. 'I have a son; he's three.' Just then, Queen Jangmonk entered the room carrying their son. I quickly rose and bowed. The king took his son, and the queen sat. 'Meet Wang Won, the crown prince of Goryeo,' my cousin said proudly.

"The young boy seemed timid and sat quietly in his father's lap. I couldn't resist; I ignored the king and made a funny face at my new relative. The crown prince smiled and giggled. I reached into my pocket and retrieved a carved ship I had completed during my return trip. Smiling, I handed the toy to Crown Prince Wang Won. That was it. I had made a friend.

"The king seemed relieved. 'I brought you home for three reasons—first, your well-deserved promotion. You have been promoted to Hogun Kim Chin-hae. Congratulations! Your father and mother should be proud. Second, you will escort my son and me to Dadu[8] to meet Kubilai Khan. Wang Won will be living there for a while.' I looked over at the queen. Her face held no emotion. She quickly spoke. 'I want him to be raised Mongol. His Mongolian name is Ijir Bukhqa. Besides, his grandfather wants to see him.' She smiled, but I thought I saw a small tear gently stream down her cheeks. I thought, *but we want him to be King of Goryeo, not a servant to Yuan.*

"Wang Won began to squirm. The queen clapped; a maid quickly entered the room, whisked him up, and exited. My eyes followed him. He turned and waved with a broad smile. The queen smiled, 'I'm happy he likes you. I know you will protect him now.'

"The king continued to talk. 'We will leave in a month on the Royal Ship. The queen will stay here as my substitute. We will have numerous attendees to care for my child. We will cross the Bay and the Bohai Sea, then disembark at Tianjin Port. From there, we will continue to Dadu by horse. It will take us about a month to arrive. You will be very interested in this trip. The last time we met, you were displeased with me. I hope this helps. Kubilai Khan and I will negotiate different terms to better our country.' He laughed, and I didn't, but he continued. 'We will have plenty of time to discuss them on our journey. And the third and last reason is the invasion of Wa. I desire to become the Minister of Jeongdong Haengseong and Goryeo, to be appointed the Eastern Field Headquarters. Your commander told me you are an accomplished ship designer. While performing your duties, you made many discoveries that will lead to improvements. Be prepared; you will be one of the appointed generals responsible for constructing our ships.'

"I sat astonished. I was unaware the commander even knew of my designs. The ship must have eyes. This whole conversation made me nervous. I felt sweat beads forming on my forehead. I hoped my cousin didn't notice. In such a short time, my life changed; I was thrust into politics—my mother's wish—and I had no choice."

"'I see sweat beads.' The king continued.

"I smiled shamefully and quickly wiped my forehead.

"'I know you have no interest in politics, but your country and I need you. Go home now, and we will talk later. I have arranged for you to spend a few weeks with your family. I hear they have news for you.' *News,* I thought, *that couldn't be good.*

"I rose, bowed, and quietly left. My father was waiting for me. His face reflected questions, but he was silent as we walked home.

"Again, my mother stood as a statue at our gate. Like my father, the three years had aged my mother as much as they had aged me. My face showed tiredness, but thank goodness, it only flaunted the old scar, though my body had countless hidden scars. So did my soul.

"My mother placed her hands on my face, looked into my eyes, and cried. She guided me to my room and had Son Jun-ho draw a bath for me. He entered the room with a contagious smile. He could always make me feel better. Unaware of how tired I was, I went to bed without dinner. I lay in my bed, surrounded by childhood memories, feeling safe for the first time in years. I slept, really slept, but the reality of the day before invaded my happiness when I awoke. The king's words echoed in my mind, and I knew I faced a new beginning. It wouldn't be swords this time, but words, which could be sharper.

"I wasn't prepared for what was going to happen next. As soon as I rolled out of bed, I accidentally bumped into a table. Son Jun-ho knocked and entered my room with fresh clothes. It appeared he had been waiting for any movement."

'Hurry, your mother is waiting for you. You slept way too long.'

"I looked at him and murmured, 'What's the hurry? The enemies aren't approaching!'

"I was mistaken. Son Jun-ho insisted that I hurry and dress. 'A luncheon has been prepared for you and some special guests. Hurry, they are waiting.'

"Entering, I scanned the room. My father and mother were entertaining a minister of the royal court and his wife. I walked forward and bowed to my father. He introduced me to Park

Jae-bong, the powerful Minister of Trade, and his wife, Park Bon-hwa. As I bowed, I heard a young woman's voice confess her sorrow over being tardy. I looked in her direction. She was delicately small, soft-spoken, and her face, well, beautiful. The minister apologized for her tardiness and introduced his daughter, Park Eun-ae, which means grace with love. We both bowed while our parents smiled.

"My mother was the first to comment. 'What a beautiful couple! We will be blessed with many beautiful grandchildren.'

"My heart leaped and sent electric shocks through my body. So, this was the news the king was talking about. I was caught off guard. Most of my home friends were married, but I avoided an arranged marriage by joining the Royal Navy. For six years, my only concern was safeguarding my men, my dream, and myself. Now, marriage sat on the table, and the bride was being served! I wondered how she was feeling. I had no intention of marrying, especially in an arranged marriage. My grandmother had been a pawn in the game of power, and this marriage was no different.

"My fate had changed in a day, first by the king and now by my parents. We all sat at the table. Park Eun-ae sweetly smiled at me. I couldn't look at her. Instead, I stared intensely at my mother; my mind was racing. She was behind this. She wanted grandchildren. But most of all, she wanted me to be home and involved in politics.

"A sweet, polite, but commanding voice lured me back to reality. It was Park Eun-ae asking me to show her around the gardens. It was spring, and my mother's cherry trees were in full bloom. They were my mother's passion, besides me. Park Eun-ae was not only beautiful but bold. I assume that's why my mother liked her. My mother, with her calculating nature, saw her as an asset to my career.

"Her father spoke up. 'Eun-ae, quiet! I haven't even talked to General Kim Chin-hae. Remember your place.'

"Park Eun-ae sneered at her father, but he didn't flinch and continued. 'Kim Chin-hae, congratulations on your promotions. Your parents must be proud. To advance so young is impressive. I heard stories of your handsome face, but to encompass bravery and skills is remarkable.'

"'Thank you, sir, but my men should receive the credit. They are very loyal, and their loyalty makes me excel,' I answered. Minister Park Jae-bong quickly responded. 'Ahhhh, not only brave but humble. I hear you will be escorting the king to Dadu.'

"'Yes, sir. We leave in four weeks. The first two weeks I will spend at home. The other weeks will be spent at the palace preparing for our departure. I will be gone for at least two and a half months.'"

'Will you be discussing the Wa invasion?' the minister continued."

"'Sir, I am not at liberty to say.' I answered."

"'Ahhhh, not only humble but tight-lipped. May I ask, what is your life ambition?' he asked.

"I hesitated, looked at my parents, and in a confident voice, I answered, 'Trade, sir, shipbuilding, having my own fleet, and sailing to faraway places.'

"He looked firmly at me and said, 'And politics?'

"'No, sir!' I strongly answered.

"'Ah, maybe my daughter can change that!'

"Quickly, Eun-ae rose, her face red, directing her words to her father. 'That's enough, father!'

"'Kim Chin-hae, I'm rescuing you, come with me!'

"I instinctively stood; I smelled danger. Eun-ae grabbed my wrist and hurried out the door.

"I was never so happy to be rescued.

"As we ran, I knew my mother had been planning this for a while; Eun-ae was too familiar with the surroundings as we fled to the garden.

"Later, I learned from Son Jun-ho that Park Eun-ae's father apologized for his strong-willed daughter after we left and that it would take a strong man to control her. My mother firmly answered. 'Well, I hope SHE is strong! There won't be a marriage unless she convinces him to forget his ridiculous dream.' Then, Park Eun-ae's mother joined the conversation. 'Eun-ae is a very determined, strong woman and seldom retreats. I know you recognize this; that's why we are here. Besides, this marriage benefits both sides. We all must do our part to make this work.' My father sat in silence. When Son Jun-ho told me this, I knew what my father was thinking: *This is Ae-cha's plan. She loves Kim Chin-hae more than her life. Every time he leaves, she spends her time at the temple praying for his safe return. Now, she has found a new champion.*

"I confess that while we stood face to face laughing among the falling cherry blossoms, she was breathtaking, and her beauty bewitched me for a moment. Thank goodness, I quickly remembered the danger; it was a setup.

"Yet, I failed to cease; I enjoyed Eun-ae too much. Never had I been in the presence of a beautiful woman who catered only to me. After that day in my mother's garden, we took long walks through the surrounding forest and the city streets, stopping at tea houses and spending hours discussing my dream. She seemed genuinely interested in shipbuilding, listening to my stories of faraway places and my ideals of acquiring great wealth through trading. *Just maybe*, I thought, *she could be part of my dream.*

"I found myself dreading the end of these two weeks. Discussing statistics and politics with my cousin would be boring for the next two weeks. The only part I was looking forward to was planning our journey to Yuan and meeting Kubilai Khan. However, I found my heart was growing fonder. I even thought, *Am I going to miss her?* Even my mother's eyes reflected that she had accomplished her goal. However, my mother didn't know that I never intended to change my dream; it would just include Park Eun-ae. Confidently, I held my ground."

***

Meanwhile, Eun-ae also held hers. As the rising sun warmed her room, she snuggled deep inside her silk blankets and thought, *I never anticipated I would find him so charming and enjoy his company so much. He was exciting and loyal to all he loved; more remarkably, he was a feast for the eyes, making my heart flutter.* Eun-ae smiled and continued thinking. *This business deal never mentioned love; it only mentioned power and wealth.* Eun-ae smiled again and thought, *But it would make the deal sweeter.* She continued to think confidently. *I can change Kim Chin-hae's dream; I have never lost. The game is going splendidly; I have already manipulated his time, and now it is time to weave my web of deception to conquer his heart. He's easy prey and innocent in love. I must become a gentle seductress these last two weeks, persuading him that living without me would be unbearable. His heart must ache with passion and desire, willing to do anything for me, even if that meant giving up his dream.*

Eun-ae's brain kept working. *My parents and I will prepare a banquet before Kim Chin-hae goes to the palace. The guest list will include many influential government officials. It will be a perfect time for introductions. Eun-ae knew these men, as her father didn't have a son. She was trained early in politics and taught the necessity of marrying a vital man. But she had her pride and insisted on arranging her marriage. Of course, there must be several eligible young men; jealousy is often a good starting point for manipulation.* Eun-ae's mind returned to the party. *I must be perfect. I'll bathe in jasmine oil imported from Persia and have my dress designed by the top dressmaker in the capital. I'll make him mine.*

***

Kim Chin-hae kept telling Marco his story: "At the end of the first two weeks, my parents and I were invited to a banquet at Minister Park Jae-bong's home on the day I entered the palace.

"That day, I spent time with the king—my cousin—discussing our trip to Dadu. He surprised me with the news that he had arranged for my men to join us. They would arrive in a week. I was elated. I needed people on my side, having been outnumbered since I arrived home.

"The king and I rode out to the royal ship. We reached a hill overlooking the Byeongnando Harbor, where the king anchored his royal ship. Its beautiful body was not the block shape like the ships I had been on, but slender with a curved bow. The king stayed on shore as I rowed out to the ship. Stepping onto the ship, I walked to the stern with my hand sliding along the smooth, curved side walls. The design was beyond words. Standing for a while, I admired the details of the ship and strode to the bow and below. Preparation had already begun, and I felt my heart race. I would not easily forget this journey."

***

The king could see the excitement in Kim Chin-hae's eyes and thought, *My uncle will have a hard time convincing him to give up his dream.* As they returned to the city, the king thought, *I will discuss politics later. I must convey to Kim Chin-hae that I am the same person I was when I was young, even though I am king now. I must regain his trust and friendship.* Feeling guilty for his manipulation, he continued thinking. *His parents and I want him to experience power and what power can bring him. But in reality, I desire Kim Chin-hae because of his loyal nature. I need him and as many trusted people as possible.*

***

"After I left my cousin, I suddenly remembered the party. I had to hurry; My mother would be furious. She was a stickler regarding proper protocol. When I arrived home, Son Jun-ho was waiting, directing me to my room, where the entire staff hustled around. Son Jun-ho drew my bath and laid out my military uniform. Disgusted, I snorted, 'What is this? I've been dressing myself for the last five years. I am not a young child. Everyone out, except Son Jun-ho. I'm not wearing my uniform, either. The party is not a military or royal event.'

"'But your mother...' Son Jun-ho said.

"'My mother, what?'"

"'She wants to show you off. Many important people are attending.'

"'I am only going because Eun-ae asked me. I'm wearing the silk robe I recently bought. It will be the last time I can wear my country's attire. After tonight, only Mongol[9] dress will be allowed.'

Standing before the mirror in my snow-white silk sokgot[10] Son Jun-ho helped me with my hair. For the past years, while in uniform, I pulled my hair in a high tail and a manggeon[11] around my head. Tonight, I told him, 'I'll wear my hair down except for the front. I will leave a small portion for side bangs, and the rest of the front will be pulled up in a sangtu and embraced by a gold cage.'

"Next, he helped me slip on a long, light blue silk jeogori[12] weaved with faint, raised flying cranes and clouds. A royal blue border encircled the small, raised collar and extended down the front edges and along the long, flowing sleeves. It crossed over my chest and tied at the side. A shimmering royal blue, silk brocade durumagi[13] with faint gold and delicate pink clusters of flowers—arranged like a painting—was added. The robe was edged with gold brocade and lined with the same light blue silk. It draped over my shoulders with wide three-quarter sleeves, exposing the flowing light blue sleeves. The robe fell just above my ankles, showing my baji*. Around my waist, I wore a wide pleated gold silk belt. Son Jun-ho, with an admiring face, stood back. 'Master Kim, you were right. You don't need a uniform to impress anyone.'"

Marco interrupted Kim Chin-hae, laughing. "I didn't know you were so fussy."

Kim Chin-hae ignored Marco and continued his story.

"My mother and father restlessly waited for me; we were late. When I exited my room, I smiled a rebellious smile. My mother looked at me in awe. I had met her approval; she was proud even though I didn't wear my uniform."

***

Ae-cha, Kim's mother, stood silently, admiring her son. *He is tall and handsome, with a chiseled face, dazzling eyes, and full lips that tilted up in a radiant smile. His jet-black hair caresses his broad shoulders and hangs to the middle of his back. How can any girl resist him?*

***

"I interrupted my mother's pride as I grabbed her hand. My father and I mounted our horses, and my mother entered the palanquin. Her maids walked along as four servants carried her to the minister's home. The minister's guards met us as we approached the house and took our horses. My mother's servant opened her palanquin and helped her rise.

"I watched my mother smile when we entered the crowded room occupied by many influential people, and I knew what she was thinking. *It is perfect; everyone stopped talking and stared. My son is now the center of attention. Maybe he is not as naïve as he seemed.*

***

Eun-ae couldn't believe how nervous she had been all day, and his lateness increased her nervousness. She had driven everyone crazy with her obsessiveness, trying to make everything perfect, including herself. She spent hours dressing. Her hanbok turned out beautifully: the dressmaker created a watery pale-green, waist-length jeogori with a raised collar that continued to cross over her chest and was tied to the side. A shimmering, multilayered chima[14] of green and pink silk gauze flowed to the ground. Her maid added a long, several-layered, pale-green, silk gauze robe. A border of pale pink fabric embroidered with delicate pink peonies and intertwining pale green vines ran down the front and along the edges of the long, flowing sleeves. Eun-ae picked up a pink silk belt with the same embroidered peonies and placed it around her tiny waist. She smiled and said, "I do look beautiful." When she exited her room, she saw her mother staring at her. Knowing her well, she knew what she was thinking: *You look so sweet and innocent with your hair pulled back, adorned with jeweled butterflies and dainty pink flowers. Your lips are moist and pink. You look like an angel, not like the seductress you are.*

Her mother smiled an approving smile.

Eun-ae was in another room entertaining friends when her maid tapped on her shoulder and whispered, "He's here!" Her heart skipped a beat. She hesitated a minute and thought. *What's the matter with me? Why am I acting like this? Am I becoming the silly girls I despise?*

Eun-ae tried to control her anger within her. She smiled and went in Kim Chin-hae's direction. On her way, she located a male childhood friend, gently grabbed his arm, smiled, and nudged him along. Her friend was caught off guard and looked at her, bewildered. His bewilderment changed when he saw a handsome young man staring at him. He whispered, "Shall I play along? You will owe me." Eun-ae smiled, nodded, and walked arm-in-arm toward Kim Chin-hae. From the corner of her eye, she saw her mother and her father walking fast to meet the guest of honor.

***

"After Eun-ae's parents greeted us, I tried not to be obvious as I skimmed the room for her. She was walking toward me with a partner. Leaving my parents' side, I met them halfway. I stopped, bowed, and smiled, thinking, *No way will I fall for this childish jealousy trick, even though she makes my heart pound with her angelic face and beauty*. Meeting them, I spoke, staring at her friend. 'Hi, I am Kim Chin-hae. Your name is?'

"'I'm Jin Bum-gi. So, you are General Kim Chin-hae. I've heard a lot about you from my father. I hope you are leaving soon; my friends and I won't have much chance with the maidens with you around.' Jin Bum-gi and I laughed; Eun-ae didn't. She was disappointed; I was being too cordial. Jin Bum-gi continued, 'Eun-ae and I have been friends since we were five.' Eun-ae dropped Jin Bum-gi's arm and walked away. I refused to watch her. Jin Bum-gi and I continued talking."

***

As Eun-ae walked away, she made a wager with herself. *He'll be mine by the end of the night*. She thought about his mother and her last words: "He would be all you need to attract powerful people."

As the party progressed, Eun-ae realized Kim Chin-hae didn't need a woman or any introductions. Just his presence commanded the room. Her guests swarmed him like bees to a beautiful flower. Eun-ae continued to mingle as long as she could endure and thought, *Not once has he even looked my way. This is definitely different from what I had planned.*

Eun-ae didn't notice Kim Chin-hae walking toward her. He tapped her on her shoulder and asked, "Would you like to join me for a walk?"

"No!" she said and started walking away.

Gently grabbing her hand, he led her outside, thinking, *The room will go wild with chatter as soon as the door closes.*

Under the stars, her eyes sparkled. She looked beautiful. "Thank you for such an entertaining night," he commented.

Eun-ae didn't waste any time. She reached up and kissed him with her sweet, moist pink lips.

Kim Chin-hae placed his hands on her shoulder and gently pushed her away. He stared into her starlit eyes. “Why did you do that?”

“Because I wanted to!”

“What else do you want, Park Eun-ae? I've talked for the last two weeks, and you've listened. It's your turn. What is your dream?”

Eun-ae found his words confusing. She wasn't expecting that question. *Most men never cared about what I wanted or what my dreams were.*

Suddenly, she seductively blurted out. “I want you.”

Kim Chin-hae became stern. “Can you live with my dream? My mother chose you, so I doubt you want the same thing.”

Eun-ae's eyes teared, and her head dropped. *Why is it so hard to lie to him? It's never been hard before. It's not a lie,* she told herself. *I want him, just not his dream.*

In a moment of weakness, Kim Chin-hae gently lifted her face, wrapped his arms around her, and passionately kissed her seductive lips.

Coming to his senses, he released her. His mind whirled. *What are you doing? You know she is your mother's plan, and this will only be if she agrees with your dream.* Frustrated with himself, he tried to make light of the kiss and quickly stuttered. “I'm sorry. Your beauty in the moonlight overwhelmed me.”

He turned and started walking back into the party, thinking he had made a grave mistake. *Before I am entangled in this trap, I should leave.*

Eun-ae was ecstatic and thought, He is mine!

***

“Trying not to be nervous, I calmly approached the host and bowed. ‘Goodnight.’

“Eun-ae seemed surprised; her face reflected hurt, and she questioned why I was leaving.

"My answer was short. ‘I have meetings all day with the king.’

“I retrieved my parents and left. Silently, my father and I rode home. When we arrived home, they questioned me why we left so quickly. I made an excuse by saying I had received a note from the king asking me to return. That wasn't true, but I didn't want to have a discussion. My mother's face said it all. She wanted to know what happened.

“The days at the palace before our departure were anxious and long; I yearned for the sea. Life was much simpler there. I tried not to think of Park Eun-ae. But when I did, I couldn't help thinking of that kiss and how I allowed myself to fall prey to my mother's and Eun-ae's manipulation. When my father showed up with Eun-ae at the palace, I had to face what I had done. It was time to speak to her alone.

"Greeting my father and Eun-ae with a bow, I wasted no time, grabbed her arm, and left the palace. We stood before the main gate, and her face radiated sweetness. Falsely confident, I started. 'Politics is not my life dream. If you can't accept this, our relationship will remain as friends only.' Eun-ae said nothing."

***

Eun-ae was paralyzed and thought, *He is so blunt. He has yet to fall into my web. It is partially my fault; I couldn't lie to him.* Her positive attitude quickly recovered. *I might have lost the battle today, but I have time, for the king and Kim Chin-hae's parents are on my side.* She smiled at Chin-hae, turned, and walked away.

***

"Surprisingly, I felt relief and remorse as I watched her walk away. Fortunately, my men had arrived and walked toward me as she walked away. They were laughing and watching her walk away. They spoke first. 'Is this the same commander we know? A woman?' I laughed and ran to them, never so happy to see familiar and friendly faces. We spent the rest of the afternoon drinking, and they joked that I looked soft and needed to toughen up.

"In the following days, my only concern was preparing my men for their new duty. They worried that they were incapable of being royal guards. Confidently, I stated that everything, except their uniform and ship, would stay the same. Eagerly, I waited to return to what I considered normal.

"Park Eun-ae faded. She disappeared like a bright setting sun that fades into the sea, leaving only a temporary, beautiful memory; I forgot the sun always rises.

"The days passed quickly, and our departure finally arrived. I went home one last time. Saying goodbye to my mother was a dreaded situation. She was a strong and opinionated woman, but her heart was soft when it came to me. Our goodbyes were always tearful.

"My heart stopped when I arrived home. Eun-ae's palanquin with four servants was resting at my gate. This awkward situation made me mad. My mother and Eun-ae were determined to change my future. However, I was just as stubborn and gallantly entered with confidence.

"Approaching my mother in the dining hall, I smiled and bowed. Eun-ae sat beside my mother. She looked stunning. My mother instructed me to sit as the servants brought food, placing it before me. My mother spoke. 'Eun-ae prepared this for you.'

"So, this is their new plan, I thought. *Eun-ae is going to play the perfect wife*. She tempted me, and I savored the thought. But I quickly came back to my senses.

"Eun-ae shyly smiled. Smiling back, I informed them. 'My men are waiting for me. I came to say goodbye to my mother. Thank you, Eun-ae, for thinking of me.'

"In a tense voice, she replied. 'You have to eat.'

"My mother gently touched her, and Eun-ae's voice softened. 'Please, I prepared it just for you.'

"Feeling guilty, I ate and commented how delicious it was, and asked. 'Did you make it yourself?'

"'Yes.' she answered. I knew she lied. She was finally herself.

"As I ate, I thought, *She is beautiful and impressive. Am I making a mistake? She would make my mother happy. But I would be lying to her and myself. I would never give up my dream.*

"Returning to reality, I rose slowly, apologizing that I must leave. I walked to my mother and bowed low. As usual, her eyes were filled with tears and worry. 'Mother, please, I will return soon.' My mother stood and sweetly touched my face. I turned to Eun-ae and bowed.

***

Eun-ae was furious as Kim Chin-hae crushed her ego. *He is so arrogant. How dare he walk away from me? He will pay for this.*

***

"I left happily, thinking, *From today on, a new life journey begins.*

"When I returned to the palace, my father met me and inquired if my mother had won. Shyly, I smiled. 'No, but I hope I won't regret my decision later.' My father grabbed my hand. 'Please, protect our king.' I nodded, and he continued, 'We'll await your return.'

"I turned; my men looked impressive in their new uniforms. The young crown prince clung to his mother. The queen's face was emotionless, and my heart ached knowing she had no choice. *My mother cried when I left, but the queen is not allowed.* My cousin walked over to his queen and took his son. The queen courageously held her emotions, knowing he would be a man the next time she saw him. The crown prince's attendants hurried to take the crying child from the king as he walked to the carriage.

"I bowed to my father, who kept a brave face. The king, the crown prince, my men, and I rode to the ship and sailed with the next high tide.

"Our crossing was calm, peaceful, and the most luxurious trip I and my men had ever experienced. What a contrast from our last three years. I couldn't help but think that my parents had planned this. They wanted me to experience power, status, and money.

"As we sailed, my king left his identity behind one afternoon, and my cousin returned. We sat on the deck, surrounded by miles of ocean, which separated us from all our responsibilities. It was during these afternoons that my relationship with the king changed.

"'Did you know Kubilai Khan saved my father and his reign?' My cousin began. 'My father, King Won Jong, was under siege by the military leader Im Yeon, who attempted to instate a new king. I owe Kubilai Khan my father's life; he sent 3000 soldiers to oust the enemy forces. That's when I learned the concept of give and take. My father knew that the Goryeo nation couldn't fight Kubilai Khan or manage the inner conflicts for control. Our country was dying, and so were our people.'

"Neither my cousin nor his father ever gained complete support from the many influential Goryeo citizens—some held hostile sentiments when Goryeo became Kubilai Khan's vassal. Sometimes, I felt the same way, but after spending time with him, my eyes were open to his views.

"Kim Chin-hae continued. My cousin explained. 'Until now, my father had always given. I was one of the first offers. My marriage to Kublilai Khan's daughter was planned years ago. When I married Princess Jeguk, I earned the title of imperial son-in-law. My father knew this would strengthen our ties with Yuan and stabilize my kingship. With this marriage, I was instantly transformed from the head of an independent Goryeo court to a member of the imperial family of great strength, giving me a voice in the inner circle of the Yuan court. But it also benefited Kubilai. It helped Kubilai Khan prevent the expansion of his cousins' power, the three kings who controlled the east of the northern border.

"'I know some of our ministers and citizens hate me. They think I am giving away my right to be king, especially when I am called a leader—not king—when I ask to be appointed Minister of the Eastern Expedition Field Headquarters. It only means I will rule over an agency controlling the Wa invasion. And then, when I changed the national dress, some hated me more. I didn't have a choice. My father taught me early that you will gain more negotiating power if you gain Kubilai Khan's trust.'

"By this trip, my cousin had earned enough respect and gained enough power; he could now negotiate with Kubilai Khan, and it was time to take. After our conversation, I realized he planned to engage in a battle of wits with Kubilia Khan. It was a dangerous game. I held high hopes that he would play well enough to negotiate issues that would benefit our country. It became apparent that both the king's father and he had sacrificed their lives and their sons for our country. I lowered my head in shame; *I fear I'm not capable of making that sacrifice.* "After that day, I had a newfound respect for my cousin. We spent hours discussing our meeting with Kubilai Khan. My cousin's list of requests was long. We both wondered what Kubilai Khan would agree to.

"I spent the other hours with my small cousin, the crown prince, roaming the incredible ship together. He had unbounded curiosity and a large heart. We made an undeniable bond at that time.

"When the day ended, I would sit at the bow and watch the sunset. I loved being at sea. Its vast, ever-moving blue water, crowned by endless blue skies, made me hope one's dreams could resemble this: endless, colorful, and magnificent. Life was so simple on the ship, and it made me happy. *Why couldn't our lives always be this way?*

"A month at sea was just what I needed to reconcile my decision. The union between Eun-ae and me was impossible. I arrived in Yuan knowing I had won and Eun-ae had lost.

"In the middle of May 1278, we arrived and disembarked on the shore of Yuan. We traveled by carriage and horses alongside the Grand Canal—which was being completed by thousands of enslaved people—to the capital city, Dadu. From there, we traveled to Shang-du, Kubilai Khan's summer palace, where our negotiations occurred before the Yuan court.

"My cousin succeeded, winning the withdrawal of Mongol troops occupying territory on our lands, the cessation of Mongol, Han, and Song soldiers being stationed on Dunjeon lands, and the end of Mongol Darughachi officials constantly monitoring us. He even managed to get a formal concession from Yuan, allowing Goryeo to stop sending household registers to Yuan.

"We stayed a while in Shang-du, and that's when I saw you, Marco, for the first time. Remember, we had exited Kubilai's chamber, and you were waiting to see him. Instantly, I knew you were the man Kubilai said I reminded him of. 'He is the same age, and you both have handsome and ambitious faces.' He told me your name, Messer Marco Polo, a Latin, from a faraway world. That's why I knew you that day at the restaurant."

Marco nodded and waited for Kim Chin-hae to continue.

"Before leaving Shang-du, I went to my young Crown Prince Wang Won's quarters. His attendees were doing their job, and he seemed happy with all the attention. His principal eunuch was dressing him to meet Kubilai Khan, his grandfather. I said my goodbye and handed him a carving of the royal ship we had arrived on. He loved ships as much as I did. He smiled and put his arms around me. As I held him, I thought, *I have always had a dream, but this little boy lives a life he would never own.*

"The king's goodbye to his son tore at my heart, but my cousin seemed numb. He had no choice and had already resigned himself to the fact that his royal obligations came first. My cousin only spoke of his son once as our ship left the shore. He looked at me and said, 'I hope he will understand someday that sacrifices are necessary for people like us; our life belongs to our people.' That was the last time he talked about his son.

"On the way home, he was enthusiastic about his successful trip. He won some of his demands—several important ones. Kubilai Khan was brilliant and an expert in manipulation. But so was my cousin.

"We also discussed the upcoming Wa invasion, which would happen after Kubilai Khan completely conquered the Southern Song dynasty. He had significantly weakened their army in 1276, and now complete defeat seemed imminent.

"My cousin prepared me for my next duty. 'You will be stationed at the port in Masanhappo, south of the capital, with your men, planning and organizing the shipbuilding with the other generals until I call for you.' My new mission was perfect. When we landed in Goryeo, I left the king and went home for only one day. This way, my mother couldn't plan other meetings with Eun-ae.

"Arriving home, I was full of conversation. My parents loved hearing that I enjoyed being with the king. It gave them hope for my future."

***

Meanwhile...Eun-ae's servant woke her up with news of Kim Chin-hae's return. Excitement filled her body as she jumped out of bed. Eun-ae whispered, "There's no note from his mother?" She didn't want her mother to hear, as they disagreed about Kim Chin-hae. Her mother told her she was wasting her time because he was a man who knew his mind and would not fall for her seductive ways like other men.

The servant's answer disappointed her, and Eun-ae returned to bed. The servant returned a few hours later. She found Eun-ae dressed but disheveled, with swollen and red eyes. The servant slowly approached and directed her to sit at the dressing table. She gently combed

Eun-ae's hair as she softly spoke, "He is leaving tomorrow morning. Kim Chin-hae's mother told the household there would be no visitors. His mother wants him to herself."

Eun-ae couldn't believe her ears. *His mother and I had an agreement. Why can't I see him?*

The rest of the day, she stayed in her room. By evening, her father grew tired of Eun-ae's sulking and wanted to enter her chamber. She could hear her mother. "Leave her be. Her heart is broken, but it's up to us to cure it. Who is the next suitable candidate?" Eun-ae heard her father gasp, grunt with disgust, and speak. "Do you think she will give up that easily?"

"Does she have a choice? She will be past her marriageable age if she waits for him," her mother answered sternly, and then continued, "She is our only daughter, our only bargaining tool! We can't waste it."

Eun-ae frowned with repugnance. By late night, her stomach growled with hunger as she lay in bed. She sat up, reached for the food her maid had left, and mannerlessly devoured it. *I will rise early and wait for him at the crossroads. My heart hurts. I must see him.*

Calling for her maid, who quickly entered, Eun-ae demanded. "Bring me some of my father's riding clothing, something you think will work for me."

The maid looked puzzled.

"Don't think—just bring them without my parents knowing."

***

Kim Chin-hae continued his story. "It was late when I retired to my room. My father and mother stood strong as we said our goodbyes. I reassured them I would return home safely."

***

That night, Ae-cha lay in bed; her mind drifted to her son. *Have I made a mistake arranging this marriage? Now, he doesn't want to stay or come home. Is having my son more critical than prestige?* She had to think!

When she rose the following day, she knocked on Kim Chin-hae's door and entered. He was gone. She sat on his bed and cried. She knew the answer.

***

"As the sun rose, Son Jun-ho, my men, and I left for Masanhappo. I didn't want to see my mother cry as she always did. But this was harder; I knew it could be years before I returned.

"Riding away, I remembered the king's words to Kubilai well: *'I think that Wa has not yet learned the virtues of an emperor. Therefore, an emperor's order should be issued to use the army, warships, and provisions for this purpose. If you, Kubilai, commission your vessels to do it, we will do our best to support the imperial army.'"*

***

Eun-ae rose before the sun and dressed in her father's clothing. Standing in front of the mirror, she admired her image. *It works. I look like a man.* She smiled, hoping he would never recognize her. Quietly, she left the house and went to the stables. Mounting her favorite horse, she rode off in search of Kim Chin-hae. Her search didn't last long. In the distance, she saw a group of riders approaching. Immediately, she recognized his tall, thin stature, which towered above the other men. She recognized his deep, full laughter. *Only he sounds like that.* Riding toward them, she thought, *I will pretend to be a visitor from the neighboring village.* Overwhelmed by the desire to speak, she wondered, *Do I dare take the chance? I will wait until I am close enough to see his eyes and only talk if he doesn't recognize me.* As he was passing, she looked at him directly. He nodded cordially, without recognition. She stopped and spoke. "Excuse me, my lord, do you know where the Parks live?"

Kim Chin-hae stopped and backed up his horse. He was now face-to-face with her. Nonchalantly, he answered with the directions. He bid goodbye and then asked, "Do you live around here? You look familiar." Eun-ae stopped breathing; her palms were sweating, and she could have sworn her heart stopped beating. "No, I am visiting from the next village," she answered in the manliest voice she could muster." He looked at her questioningly and continued on his way. Eun-ae's eyes filled with tears, and she thought, *What is wrong with me? What a fool I have become.*

***

"As we left my parents' home, *we* discussed the upcoming invasion and why we were going to Masanhappo. The Khan had instructed us to build a whole new fleet. That meant cutting all the timber on our southern coast. I met a young man asking for directions. I could have sworn

I knew the young man. I later learned that it had been Eun-ae. I didn't realize then how much she desired me.

"In March 1279, it was apparent that Kubilai Khan would defeat the last of the Song Dynasty. That same month, I received an envelope containing two letters from the king. One letter informed me which ports the invasion would originate from — Masanhappo in Goryeo and Ningbo in Yuan. It also stated that I would travel to Ningbo and meet General Fan Wenhu, the principal general, who was to lead the invasion from Yuan. My primary job was to conduct reconnaissance for my cousin, as he needed information to support his strategic plan as the director of the Eastern Headquarters. Also, his letter included a notation: No need to wear your uniform; wear your everyday clothes. You are working for me. The other letter was written by Kubilai Khan, personally introducing me to the general, omitting that I was also an officer. They both agreed that General Fan Wenhu would accept me and not be threatened if I were a relative to the king, rather than a military officer.

"Excitement electrified my body; Ningbo was world-renowned for its shipbuilding. The *Wanhu Shenzhou* super-ships, the best ships in the world, were built in the Zhaobao Mountains near Ningbo. This trip also brought relief. I needed a change of scenery. I missed sailing, and this trip would be an excellent opportunity to discover new places and meet people who could help me achieve my dream.

"I left within the week, hoping to miss the typhoon season. Space on the ship was limited, so only Son Jun-ho and two of my men from the garrison—Pak Byeong-ho and Kang Ji-yoo—came along. On the 40th day, we could see land. We arrived with only minor damage from the storms. I loved the sea, but I understood its power. The violent weather we encountered during the first Wa campaign still invaded my sleep, and with the coming of the second, it seemed the nightmares increased.

"As the land grew closer, the crew shouted and pointed to the Tian Feng Pagoda. It sat high on a hill near the town center. In a short time, we could see the world-famous wharf. *What a dream place for a shipbuilder to be,* I thought. As we disembarked, a stern Han soldier met us. We weaved through the crowded and bustling wharf as enormous ships unloaded their treasures, which made my heart beat faster. As he escorted us to our inn, I had to remind myself of the real reason I was here. We arrived at an affluent guesthouse used by Goryeo envoys, not a naval post. My men joked. 'It's nice to travel with royalty.'

"'General Fan Wenhu will be here tomorrow morning. He thought you might need rest,' the Han soldier said.

"I thought to myself, *This was my cousin's doing. He never missed the opportunity to show me what power and prestige brought. The king and my parents were naïve; it would take more than this to change where my heart lies.*

"The extra day allowed us to walk around the area, discovering the Yong Feng Stonehouse, where they house the treasured Celadon wares for trading along the Maritime Silk Road. Just entering the Stonehouse made my dream seem more real. Not knowing how long I would be here, I hoped to use every opportunity to scout every inch of this outrageous country. It was the first time I realized I didn't belong to Goryeo; I belonged to the ever-expanding world and its people, and I wanted it all.

"The following day brought me back to reality and the primary reason I had come. It began with the arrival of General Fan Wenhu—an intriguing man. He was a surrendered officer of the Northern and Southern Song Dynasties. During our voyage, I heard his story. I wasn't sure why Kubilai Khan trusted this man.

"I handed General Fan Wenhu the letter, and he read it slowly. He looked up from the letter and visually appraised me from head to toe. His face displayed slight hostility and a suspicious look. I assume he thought, *Who is he? A spy. A spoiled royal who's never seen a battle. What right does he have here?* However, he had no choice but to accept me; he had direct orders from the Khan. From that moment forward, our relationship was far from friendly."

---

1. Government tax boats
2. Japanese pirates
3. Also known as Bunei Invasion—the first Mongolian invasion of Japan
4. King Won Jong
5. Joseon Dynasty military official position
6. The leader of Japan at the time
7. Located in the southern part of North Korea
8. Goryeo word for Khanbaliq
9. Also know as Tartar

10. Undergarment

11. Headband

12. Long jacket

13. Overcoat or robe

14. Skirt

Chapter Seventeen

Marco

1278 Marco's Ganzhou Tea Secret

Genoa Prison 1298

Marco stopped telling his story of Kim Chin-hae and looked at Rustichello. "That was the end of his story that night. His head lay on the table as he spoke. 'Let's sleep. I'm tired and drank too much. Let's continue another time. Now you know how I ended up in Ningbo.'

"'But you never told me how you met Lis, and that's the most essential part.' I whined to Kim Chin-hae.

"He never said another word." Marco laughed as he envisioned the next scene and continued. "I had to carry Kim Chin-hae's tall, damn body back to the Inn, mostly dragging him."

Marco smiled and continued, "Let's start tomorrow with my journey; we have wasted enough time. Even though I enjoy talking about Kim Chin-hae. My reminiscing saddens me. I miss him."

Rustichello looked disappointed when Marco stopped. "OK, tomorrow after dinner, if they bring us some. You can continue the story of Kim Chin-hae."

Agreeing half-heartedly, Marco continued talking to Rustichello. "We need to finish this report first. So much time has passed. Everyone will be worried. If only the commander would meet me again, I could show him what we have written. Surely, after he reads my report, he will deliver the letters to my uncle."

He didn't wait for Rustichello to respond. Marco walked to his bed and lay down, stretching out his body. His stomach growled, and he began thinking.

Hopefully, they will bring us breakfast. Tomorrow, I will continue with our arrival in Ganzhou.[1] *I will treat it like all the other cities. I won't mention what we did that year. I will not talk about our business venture here. It was our secret. The generals don't need to know this information. Ganzhou meant so much more to us than other places. It was the beginning of our future business. When we arrived, my father, uncle, and I were captivated by this amazing, noble city and its beautiful, rainbow-colored mountains. Culturally, it surpassed many cities we had traveled through with its music, fine literary works left behind by famous poets, and elaborate Buddhist monasteries—one which housed the largest reclining Buddha I had ever seen.*

Ganzhou lies in the middle section of the Hexi Corridor, a 620-mile-long strip of land that unites the east with the west. It is surrounded by snow-capped mountains to the south and snow-capped mountains to the north, with a deadly desert on all sides. The terrain was flat with fertile soil, grasslands, and fruit flourished as the Hei River flowed through. It was indeed a desert oasis. Its beauty captivated me, and I soon discovered that this magnificent city was a hub for the tea trade. Tea was a very lucrative commodity, highly desired throughout the empire. My father wanted a part of this; however, obtaining a permit to trade tea was complicated, and one was considered a smuggler without it. If caught, the punishment was death.

My father's first trip resulted in deals with Kubilai: if he brought back his requests—holy oil and a priest from the pope—he would be given permits to trade. He returned with the Holy Oil, but his failure to bring the priest was a concern.

We stayed a year in Ganzhou and explored all our options, making friends and connections with other merchants and outpost owners, just like in the other five cities we chose along the Silk Road—Constantinople, Tabriz, Kerman, Badakhshan, Kashgar, and now Ganzhou. It is a large tea-trading city that collects tea from Chengdu and disperses it to other traders around the world. Or, if you traveled south from Ganzhou through the Qilian Mountains using an icy and dangerous pass called Biandukou, you would connect to the Horse Tea Road in Chamdo, which continues to Lhasa. If you continued further south, you would reach Dali and Pu'erh, where highly praised tea grows. Not only is tea found, but salt and gold are also found. Learning about the Biandukou Pass, we bypassed the middlemen and became more prosperous. Later, I learned that the kingdom where Pu'erh tea grew was called Qarajang,[2] *and its king was Kubilai Khan's grandson, Yesün Temür. The capital of Qarajang was Yachi, where powerful merchants lived. Here, the Yangtze River crossed, and merchants transported their costly merchandise to Chengdu, the hub of trade for the empire.*

My father and uncle were determined and confident that obtaining the trade permit was possible. I didn't know how determined they were until we stood before Kubilai. This was when I learned how shrewd my father and uncle were. I would become their bargaining chip.

Marco's aching stomach invaded his thoughts. His mind traveled to Li, hoping to forget his pain. Like every night, he whispered, "I love you and see you in my dreams."

---

1. Zhangye
2. Yunnan

Chapter Eighteen

Li

1285 Li, Kokochin, and Ijir Bukhqa—Crown Prince Wang Won of Goryeo

Venice 1298

Like Marco, Li lay in bed, looking out the window. The high moon reminded her of their love and the giant glowing moon they sat under on a faraway island. *Good night, Marco. Come home soon; I need you,* she thought to herself.

Her day at the apothecary had been fantastic, but the afternoon became more daunting. Marco's cousin, Isabella, met Guo Yu and Luca in the hallway on their return. Their encounter worried her, and she knew Guo Yu was, too. She hoped Guo Yu's words brought fear to Isabella; money meant everything to her.

The following day, she awoke happy. Marco monopolized her dreams, holding and kissing her. I must have entered his dreams. But worry took over her happiness. *Where are you, Marco? Are you safe?*

Luca arrived early, interrupting Li's worry, and spoke to Li. "Isabella was so angry." Li comforted Luca and spoke with confidence. "It will be fine. Marco will be back soon. I know it. When Guo Yu brings us breakfast, I'll continue with my story. Where did I stop?"

Luca responded. "Something about an advantage. The palace grounds had become a playground and workplace."

"Now I remember. I'll tell you how I met Crown Prince Wang Won.[1] In Kubilai's palace, they called him Ijir Bukhqa. He was Kim Chin-hae's second cousin.

Li settled in her favorite chair and began. "The weather was warmer than usual, and the sun shone brightly above the vast palace grounds as I excitedly started my day. I wandered the palace grounds like a ghost, fulfilling my daily missions, looking for Marco, spying on others, and gathering winter herbs. Suddenly, a guard cornered me. Never having experienced this before, I was frightened as the guard pushed me toward a small pavilion where a young boy was sitting. Apparently, he was important; guards and court ladies stood guard around him. Books, brushes, ink, and paper surrounded him. He looked a couple of years younger than me. His eunuch quietly spoke to him, and with a soft voice, the young man introduced himself as Ijir Bukhqa.

"I quickly responded, 'I'm Li.'

"He responded, 'That's not a Mongol name, but Song.'

"I hesitated momentarily and said, 'I know.' The boy looked surprised and curious at the same time.

"'Are you spying on me?' the young boy asked. Taken aback, I giggled with nervousness. And I thought, *Spying...that's what I did daily, but it wasn't intentional this time.*

"'No, of course not. I'm an apprentice to the Royal Physician Wu. It's my duty to collect herbs.'

"As I walked closer to him, a guard stopped me, but Ijir Bukhqa nodded, and I continued walking and observed his work in front of him. 'Your calligraphy and drawings are beautiful.' He frowned, 'What would you know? You are just an herbalist apprentice.'

"From that moment, I decided not to discuss my identity or to stay long. Ijir Bukhqa seemed rude, arrogant, and harsh. I said my proper goodbyes. His eyes reflected disappointment. That didn't last long. He nodded and continued his drawings.

"When I arrived at the royal infirmary, Physician Wu was seated at his desk. I couldn't wait to ask him about this person. 'Who is Ijir Bukhqa?' He looked up at me with concerned eyes and answered. 'He is Crown Prince Wan Wong from Goryeo.' Physician Wu continued, 'He is one of the great Khan's favorite grandsons. His father is the king of Goryeo, and his mother is the Khan's daughter.'

"'I'm curious. If he is from Goryeo, why is he here?' I asked. Physician Wu's answer differed from what I expected.

"'I see you lack knowledge of the political aspects of Goryeo and seemingly of the Yuan history. I think you need some lessons. The prince has lived here since he was four and will remain until he grows up, learning his obligations to the Yuan dynasty and the Mongol ways. Then, he will marry a royal descendant of the Khan, just as his father did. Again, ensuring Goryeo's loyalty.'

"After my first lesson, I realized this boy and I had much in common. He, too, came from a conquered country. Part of me felt sorry for him. However, I decided to avoid the pavilion where the crown prince sat on my next excursion. He seemed incorrigible, and I didn't want to share my time. I just wanted to enjoy the palace grounds and daydream about Marco. The next day, I stopped to sit on a tree stump. Lost in thought, I didn't hear someone approaching me until someone stood beside me, tapping my shoulder. Startled, I looked up. It was Ijir Bukhqa, the crown prince. This time, it was my time to ask. 'Are you spying on me?'

"He laughed and seemed to be in a better mood. *He must have escaped his entourage,* I thought.

"This time, he questioned, 'Who are you, and why do you live in the palace?' I wasn't accustomed to talking about myself and felt uncomfortable. I was a ghost. He persisted, and I finally answered. 'I was brought here when I was five from Lin'an.'

"Suddenly, we heard frantic people talking and footsteps coming closer. He put his finger to his mouth. 'Shhhhhhhhhh.' Whispering, he said, 'Don't talk.'

"I was right. Ijir Bukhqa was hiding from his entourage. Quietly, he rose and disappeared. I was relieved, but thought to myself. *He, too, wanted to be a ghost.* In moments, his eunuch appeared, followed by his guards. The eunuch's face looked pale and worried. With a shallow bow, he asked if I had seen the crown prince. I nodded and pointed in the opposite direction from where he had fled. They hurried off. Immediately, the prince returned, smiled, and thanked me as he left. Suddenly, I realized someone had discovered me and my ghost act, and I became concerned. It would never be the same, and part of me was happy. Ijir Bukhqa and I often met to discuss his drawings, and I shared my knowledge of herbs with him. For the first time, I had a friend.

"Then, in June, like every year, most of the palace left Khanbaliq's hot and humid weather for Shang-du, the summer palace. Our impressive caravan, displaying the Khan's moon and sun banners, left as multiple fierce warriors surrounded us. It would take us almost a month to arrive.

"The empresses, the court women, and small children rode in their ornate carriages, as young women and men rode horses, and the servants followed behind in carts filled with supplies.

"That year, I turned thirteen. For the first time, I had freedom—a new sensation I had never experienced. All the years before, as was customary, I rode in a carriage; my vision had been confined, defined, and simplified by a simple square window. Now, as I sat upon my horse, an expanded world was before me. I was mesmerized by the expansion and beauty of my newfound surroundings. Giant herds of horses roam the rolling ocean of green grass with the towering snow-covered peaks in the distance that shimmer with the setting sun. Daydreaming, I was unaware that my horse had slowed to barely a crawl, stopping and eating the fresh, tender grass tips, falling behind Guo Yu's carriage. A confident but youthful voice called out and awoke me.

"'Hello, my name is Kokochin. What's yours?'

"I turned, and a sweet-faced girl, maybe around ten, peered from a passing carriage. Her carriage suggested that her mother held a prominent position, possibly as a favorite concubine or consort of Kubilai Khan, and she was a princess.

"I smiled. 'My name is Li.' Then, I nudged my horse to pick up speed, returning to Physician Wu and Guo Yu.

"At night, we would set up camp. Our royal ger was very lavish, and warm furs surrounded us. In the evening, it wasn't quiet; laughter echoed through the campfires. I enjoyed the casual atmosphere and the camaraderie. It seemed to be a time when the entire court returned to their roots.

"Before we left the winter palace, Marco had come and gone again. Guo Yu had told me he wouldn't return for some time. His absence always made my heart heavy and left me feeling lonely. However, I wasn't as lonely as before because I had the prince, my new friend. When our trip began, I hoped to see him along the way."

***

For the first time, Ijir Bukhqa was excited to travel to the summer palace. He usually dreaded the move. But this time was different; he had a new friend, Li, and hoped to see her. His first concern was to find her in the caravan, but he soon discovered that losing his bodyguards during the day was difficult. However, the nights were different. He discovered that they were more interested in nighttime activities than they were interested in him. So he took a chance. Dressed in black, he molded his bed into a body shape and slipped out the back of the tent. Standing under the stars, he closed his eyes and wondered, *Is she in front of me or behind me?* He chose forward and began his search, running and peering from the back sides of the gers, hoping no one would notice him. Ijir Bukhqa soon realized everyone was too occupied. The men were wrestling and gambling, and the women were cooking and gossiping. Suddenly, his heart raced; he found Li sitting by the fire, looking at the stars and daydreaming: *Her favorite pastime besides looking for herbs.* He often wondered what occupied her mind. Suddenly, someone poked him in the back, and his heart sank. Someone had discovered him. He slowly turned around and released a sigh of relief. It was Kokochin. They had known each other for a while.

"Where did you come from?" he sternly asked.

Kokochin giggled. "I have been following you for a while. I was curious about where you were going so secretly. Now I know. Her name is Li," Kokochin whispered proudly.

"How do you know her?" Ijir Bukhqa asked.

"I met her en route a couple of days ago," Kokochin replied.

***

Li continued speaking to Luca. "One evening, as I sat by the fire, gazing at the stars and dreaming about Marco, I heard whispering. I quickly rose, pretended to enter my ger, and snuck around the backside. Kokochin and Ijir Bukhqa were so busy talking that they didn't notice me standing behind them. I poked them both. 'What are you two doing? Spying on me?' They turned, and their scared faces quickly turned to relieved, happy ones.

"'How do you two know each other?' I asked.

"Kokochin proudly answered, 'When I was younger, I would follow and pick on him because he was shy. Maybe he is not as shy as I thought. He has been looking for you! Do you two like each other?'

"Ijir Bukhqa turned red. 'No!' answering with an embarrassed tone.

"'Then why are you spying on her?' Kokochin asked.

"'It's a game we play in the palace,' the prince answered.

"'I want to play!' Kokochin answered excitedly."

Li looked at Luca. "I liked Kokochin from that day; she had spunk. I wished I were more like her. Kokochin differed from the Ijir Bukhqa and me. She belonged there.

"From that day forward, we would meet secretly and spy on others. It was the start of the Society of Three."

Luca clapped. "Tell me more!"

"One evening, under the vast starlit night, Kokochin told us the story of the Mongols[2]—a story her mother had recited to her as soon as she could understand."

"The Mongols were my people who lived far from the sea under azure, celestial skies, among rolling oceans of green grass, snow-peaked mountains that shimmer, the rivers, lakes, and valleys covered in alpine forest. To the south, when you experienced sandstorms, you reached the end of our lands.

"Fierce tribes with fierce warriors and their descendants roamed this land with magnificent herds of horses, hunting, fishing, and warring. We never stayed in one place; we were wanderers and moved in search of fresh grass for our herds or if we felt danger in the winds or when the days grew short and winter was upon us. This was our life. We were one with nature, and when nature talked, we listened.

"Our women differ from here; we own our gers. We would pack our two-wheel black carts with our belongings: tools, furs, and food. Then, we would carefully dismantle our homes. The wool-felt blankets that covered our gers sheltered us from rain, snow, and sun. It also protected our spirits. These blankets once belonged to our mothers-in-law and were called Mother's Felt. But after years of pounding new wool fibers into the old—immersed in our sweat, tears of joy or sadness—they became ours, the Daughter's Felt. And this tradition has been passed down from generation to generation. As a young woman, my grandmother swore that in the silence of darkness, she heard the whispers of past souls revealing their secrets.

"When the carts were packed and ready, the women drove them. Young children, old men, the ill, and the elderly would ride in the carts. The carts were drawn by woolly yaks, oxen, or even a white camel, depending on whether she was a queen or a mother of a khan. The young women and men would ride the horses. When the day's journey ended, the duty of rebuilding a new village began.

"The women, young girls, and boys of our tribe unloaded their carts, and they rebuilt the gers. The entry of each ger had to face south and was about four feet tall. We draped the felt blanket over our ger as shelter from nature. In the center was a tame, continued fire of dried animal dung—a symbol of life. The smoke rose and escaped through the only opening above.

"The ger was a place of peace; everyone who entered whispered and moved gently so as not to dismantle the low-ceiling rafter or break a much-needed item. The women sat on the east side of the door where she kept most of her tools and work took place. The Mongol men sat on the west with their bodies tightly balled, one leg under his body and the other bent at the knee, pulled up to his chest. His arms wrapped around it, and sometimes his chin would rest on the knee. We preserved the north side opposite the door for the honored. Above their heads, dried beef or yak hung on the rafters. If fresh meat was unavailable, these could be quickly made into a nourishing meal by adding warm water. Milk, food, and water were always ready if a lost hunter, a chilled herder, or a returning warrior needed food or human closeness.

"The strongest and most feared in our lands were the Turkish ethnic warriors. They captured women, killed, and ravaged the other tribes. They became the leaders of the different tribes and married their women. Allies were made this way. They traded their women like horses.

"But unbeknownst to all the tribes of the plateau, rivers, and forest, a tribe of outcasts held the great khan, my great-grandfather, Genghis Khan, who would change our lives forever. His father was Yessugel, the chief of the Khamag Mongols of the Borijin clan. They were hunters from the far northern lands of lakes and forests. After many generations, we found a new home in Mount Burkhan Khaldun, the mother source of the Onon and Kherlan rivers on the steppe. The other tribes of the steppe despised us. They considered us intruders, and we were shunned as we stole animals, women, and whatever else we needed when hunting was bad. We looked different with our round faces, high cheekbones, bowed legs, and ashen skin. Our cheeks turned so red in the bitter cold that we became known as people with faces of fire and piercing cat eyes. Most of the time, the other tribes hated us, but knowing our skills as warriors and herders, they would hire my ancestors.

"Hoelun, my great-great-grandmother, the mother of Genghis Khan, was beautiful, and her body possessed the fertility shape men desired. Her beauty captured Yessugel; he had seen her on the banks of the Onon River among the evergreen trees. She smiled at him, and he knew she was the one, but she was promised to another. That didn't matter; he stole her on her wedding day on the path to her new village. Yessugel made her chief wife. She loved him and was honored. She knew this meant her sons would become his heirs. Her first son was Temujin, named after a Tartar warrior his father Yessugel had killed. But when he was nine, another Tartar killed his father, Yessugel. Instead of comforting and protecting Yessugel's wife and five children, his family dishonored them. They confiscated his animals and banished Hoelun and his children to the steppe, where they would starve and freeze.

"My great-great-grandmother was strong, intelligent, and determined that her children would survive. It was her destiny—as she had been told in a dream—that she would become a great leader's mother. She took control, built a forest shelter, and hid in the northern Khentii. She hunted, fished, gathered roots and berries, and taught her children to do the same. She taught them the importance of unity, love, and supporting each other. 'Seeds sown with love grow strong and whole and produce abundantly like children born out of love who grow in body, spirit, and truth and lead with commitment.' Their mother loved them more than herself, dedicated herself to them, and always gave them wise advice.

"In the years following his father's death, a seed of knowledge was planted within Temüjin—Genghis Khan—a seed that grew strong. He understood that bloodlines sometimes couldn't be trusted and vowed that someday he would have a great army of brave spirits called the baatuud, and they would conquer the world. To him, it didn't matter if you were family, male or female, rich or poor, or young or old. Your heroism, loyalty, knowledge, and honor gained you a place with Genghis Khan. Over the next few years, this philosophy grew. Temüjin won battles,

lost battles, and rose to the chieftain of a small part of the Mongol tribe. He then became Genghis Khan—the Indomitable and Supreme Khan.

"My great-grandfather lived believing his strength grew from Heaven and Earth. His inspiration and destiny were called Mighty Heaven. But they were carried through by Mother Earth—the sky inspired; the earth sanctioned. And it was a terrible sin to insult either one. He spent most of his life on his father's land, the male mountain where he relied on its spiritual alms, but he had been rescued in the land of his mother, where the female waters flowed. He spent his entire life trying to balance the two perfectly.

"He never betrayed women; they were never to be traded like animals or property. Women motivated him, and he admired them. He never had more than four wives at a time. As a new leader of all the tribes, his most important task was to divide his newly conquered lands and select rulers. Instead of giving this honor to his sons or generals, he gave it to his wives. Borte, who was Genghis Khan's number one wife, was his most trusted advisor. He formed allies from the marriages of his daughters. This philosophy has mostly continued with my father."

"As Kokochin told her story, Ijir Bukhqa and I listened, and I thought, *I hate that a daughter's purpose was just to create perfect allies. There had to be more to life.* But Kokochin truly believed this was her purpose. I guess her belief made her life more bearable. I couldn't bear the thought of that happening to me. I also wondered about Ijir Bukhqa, the crown prince; his life also seemed planned.

Li sighed.

Luca spoke up. "Did she find her king? Was she happy?"

"That story will be another day."

Li continued, "When we finally arrived at the summer palace, I was sad as I loved the open space filled with crisp, sweet air and the vast, starry sky. For a time, I was free. But if I couldn't be on the steppe, the second-best place was the summer palace, Shang-du. Everyone was more relaxed as Kubilai hunted and reminisced about his days on the steppe, which brought him closer to his roots.

"In Shang-du, Kubilai Khan's vast palace was built of marble and other stones. The palace sits on sixteen miles of land in the middle of the city, enclosed by a wall. The land is home to springs, rivers, forests, lawns, and a variety of wildlife, including red deer, stags, and roebucks. You can only enter the grounds through the palace as it is a playground for the royals and his court. Once a week, Kubilai rode around this walled park on his horse with his beloved leopard by his side. On a whim, he let it go so it could catch a deer, then he would give it to his huge collection of gyrfalcons and falcons."

Li looked over at Luca; her eyes were wide, and her mouth was open. Li was delighted that her storytelling amused Luca. She continued. "Arriving at the palace, my training continued. The surrounding forest and rivers were filled with abundant, powerful roots and fungi that didn't grow in Khanbaliq. Physician Wu and I spent hours harvesting and preparing them to take back with us.

"During one of our outings, Kokochin, a short distance away, was practicing her riding. Her aura radiated her free spirit, strength, and determination as she rode like a true Mongol. Besides riding, she was learning archery on horseback. Mongol culture differed from Song culture; women could be warriors and learn to be self-reliant, thinking for themselves.

"As Physician Wu and I watched, suddenly Kokochin's horse tripped, and she flew over the horse's head. Our hearts stopped as she landed with a thud, motionless and face down. Her instructor, servants, and a young man rushed to her side. We ran and yelled, 'Don't move her.' I beat Physician Wu, slowly lifted her wrist, and checked for her pulse. She was alive. Sighing with relief, I gently rolled her over. Her eyes were closed. Suddenly, her bleeding lips turned into a smile, then a giggle, which turned into laughter. She jumped up and, walking with a limp, checked her horse. She had been lucky. Only her beautiful face, hands, and arms were scratched and bruised, and her right hip was slightly damaged.

"Her instructor yelled forcefully. 'That's not a joke! Never do that again.' The more he yelled, the more her stance became defiant, and she looked fearless.

"Then I noticed the laughing young man beside her was Ijir Bukhqa. He looked at me and said nothing, nor did Kokochin. Our friendship was a secret."

"Suddenly, Ijir Bukhqa pointed toward the palace and jokingly said, 'Boy, Messer Marco Polo is going to be mad at you. Isn't that him riding toward us?'

My heart skipped a beat just hearing his name. I looked in the direction he was pointing.

"A blurred-faced rider raced toward us and suddenly became recognizable. It was Marco. With a concerned face, he brought his horse to a quick halt and quickly dismounted. 'Are you all right?' Kokochin was laughing and didn't answer. 'Your father will punish me, not you. I'm the one who convinced him you were old enough to practice archery while riding. Go with Physician Wu and care for your scratches, especially on your face,' Marco said sternly.

"Marco headed for his horse. Before he mounted, he turned. 'Forget seeing your father. Don't show your face until the scratches have healed.' Kokochin immediately argued. Marco just shook his head, mounted, and rode off. Ijir Bukhqa raced after him.

"I was so disappointed; Marco didn't even look or acknowledge me. Deep inside, I knew why; just like the Society of Three, we had decided long ago that my relationship with Marco was a secret. But I was surprised that Kokochin and Ijir Bukhqa knew Marco; it seemed like a close relationship. *How?* I wondered.

"Physician Wu and I gathered our bags and mounted our horses, directing Kokochin to do the same. We rode to the palace stables, left our horses, and continued to the infirmary.

"I assisted him as he treated Kokochin. Her face seemed perplexed as she watched me move around the room.

"'You're good for a girl,' Kokochin smirked.

"'Thank you. You're an outstanding rider for a girl, too.' I laughed teasingly.

"My curiosity overtook me, and I thought, *During the journey to the summer palace, neither Ijir Bukhqa nor she mentioned Marco.* I had to ask!

"'I'm just curious; how do you know Messer Marco Polo?' I blurted out.

"Physician Wu's face turned serious, and he stared at me. "'Kokochin laughed. 'I have known Messer Marco since I was four. My mom said I thought he was handsome and stole one of her White Festival presents to give to him. We have been friends since. One of Messer Marco Polo's missions is to find a king for me to marry. But Messer Marco tells me I am too pigheaded to win a husband!'

"She laughed again and continued speaking. 'Ijir Bukhqa told me he knows Messer Marco Polo through his cousin. Supposedly, his cousin and Messer Marco Polo are best friends.'

"Kokochin looked inquisitively at me. 'Do you know Messer Marco? You say his name like you know him.' I nervously put away the medicine containers and answered, 'No, I just heard about him.' Kokochin wasted no more time. She looked down at her legs. 'Are you finished?' As soon as Physician Wu answered yes, she jumped off the table and started out the door. Suddenly, she unexpectedly turned to me and said, 'See you later!' Then ran out the door."

"'You know her?' Physician Wu asked.

"I confessed I did. He warned me to keep Marco a secret.

"My heart fluttered with excitement at the thought of Marco and the possibility of seeing him. He had been gone so long from the palace. Footsteps interrupted my thoughts; someone was coming into the infirmary. I couldn't believe my eyes; it was Marco."

***

Kokochin hadn't gone far before she turned around. She saw Messer Marco entering the infirmary. Her first thought was that he was checking on her. She laughed. *He must fear my father!* With no more thoughts, she continued to the stables to check on her horse.

***

"My face felt flushed. I hadn't seen Marco in months. He greeted Physician Wu with a low bow, turned to me, smiled, and asked how I was. He turned again to Physician Wu and asked about Kokochin. Marco was very pleased with his answer and continued. 'She is such a bold girl; I must work hard to find a king who can control her.' Both laughed.

"I was so disappointed. Marco didn't even notice my face was bright red or ask why. He didn't even notice I had become a woman or that my heart was about to explode with love, and I had missed him so much."

Li stopped telling her story and walked over to her window, staring at the canal. Without turning, she sadly said, "I was so naïve."

Continuing her story, she turned and stared at Luca. "Marco only stayed a few more minutes before bidding his goodbye. He bowed low, walked over to Physician Wu, and grasped his hand. 'Thank you.' Then, turning to me, he bowed and left.

"I was devastated; he was friendlier with Kokochin and Ijir Bukhqa. Didn't I mean anything to him? Like a fool, I started after him, overlooking the other assistants staring at me. Physician Wu quickly called out my name, returning me to my senses. I stopped and turned around. 'Oh, I was just going to ask if he needed his medicine bag refilled.'

"Annoyed, Physician Wu answered, 'He will return if he needs anything.'

"He looked around the room, and all the assistants had returned to work. Our response worked. I was ashamed of myself. *What was I thinking?* I returned to cleaning, and Physician Wu went to his office.

"A little later, he opened his door and came out with some bags, calling me to follow. Without emotion, he turned to the primary assistant. 'We never finished our search for herbs because of Kokochin's accident. We won't be back in the infirmary today.'

"I gathered up my belongings and mindlessly followed. We mounted our horses and headed toward the forest. Physician Wu seemed nervous. He kept looking over his shoulder and to the left and the right. As we entered the forest, he seemed relieved. We didn't stop until we reached a small decrepit hut covered by several fallen branches, moss, and vines. Mother Nature was winning; she was taking back what belonged to her. We tied our horses to the barely remaining porch with the other horses. One horse belonged to Guo Yu, but who owned the other? I wondered. We carefully entered. My heart stopped; Marco was talking to Guo Yu. They looked up and smiled. Anger filled my heart. *Why didn't he tell me he was going to see me later*? My anger didn't last long; instead, I wanted to throw my arms around him. Guo Yu sensed this; he grabbed my arm and saved me from making a fool of myself. Marco was unaware of my infatuation, and so was Physician Wu. I gained my composure and smiled at Marco. He motioned all of us to sit at the small table covered in drinks and food. Before I could sit, Physician Wu instructed me to retrieve the bag tied to his saddle, which contained more food. I reluctantly left. That's when I noticed Marco's old, ragged medicine bag that hung from his saddle.

"Returning, Marco apologized for the meeting place. 'This was the best I could do at the last minute. I didn't want people talking.'

"Now I understood his coldness. Feeling ashamed of my immaturity, I looked at Physician Wu and whispered, 'How did you know?' He pulled out a note, showed it to me, and said. 'Remember the handshake.' *Impressive,* I thought. It's just like the game Kokochin, Ijir Bukhqa, and I played. I was too young to realize this was real.

"Guo Yu, instead of sitting, walked out the door. 'He will stand guard,' Marco told Physician Wu. Marco turned to me. 'I came to see how you were. Guo Yu told me you missed me. Let's see, it's been four months since the White Festival.' Marco laughed. I couldn't believe my ears. Embarrassed, my defiant side arose, and I spoke back. 'I didn't arrange this meeting. You did. Who missed who?' Physician Wu laughed. 'Marco, you better be careful; she has a sharp tongue.' Seconds later, we all started laughing and enjoying the food and drink.

"Marco talked about his merchant business that his father, uncle, and Kim Chin-hae ran while he went on missions for Kubilai. 'Our business is flourishing with Kim Chin-hae's help. Before he made peace with his mother and Park Eun-ae, he brought spices from faraway islands. Now, he brings ginseng, celadon, and gold from Goryeo, while my father brings tea and salt from southern Cathay. However, this year, our deliveries to Persia have been delayed.'

"Marco stopped and looked at Physician Wu. 'You remember me telling you about Arghun, who fought Qaidu's daughter and lost? He had to fight his uncle, Teguder, who had stolen his throne after his father's death. Finally, he defeated him and took control of the Ilkhanate.[3] His son, Ghazan, will now protect their borders from Qaidu. The Silk Road will return to normal for now. But I always fear it won't last long. Qaidu is always causing problems. We are considering moving our trade routes to the sea.'

"All this talk was so fascinating. *Who were all these people?* Marco had seen so much. Suddenly, Marco looked at me and asked me to take Guo Yu's place. I tried to argue; I wanted to hear more. Losing, I went outside and retrieved Guo Yu.

"Sitting on the shabby porch, I looked through the thick forest canopy. The sun's filtered sunlight broke through the forest, creating beautiful sunbeams that resembled a starburst falling from the sky. The beautiful scene momentarily captured my curious mind before my strong spying tendencies took over. I silently stood, put my ear to the door, and listened instead of guarding. Marco was talking about Kubilai Khan.

"Kubilai has not been well since Empress Chabi died. He's been drinking and eating excessively. It's very concerning. Have you noticed Physician Wu?'

"Physician Wu didn't have time to answer before Marco continued. 'Kubilai seems obsessed with continuing his advancement in Champa. Last year, he captured the citadel of Mou-cheng, but now his troops are stagnant. The men suffer from heat exhaustion, illness, and a lack of supplies. We are losing men and money daily. Kubilai is no longer involved in battles, unlike in the past. That's what happened to the 1281 Cipangu invasion. Empress Chabi died that year. I could understand him then, but it has continued. Now it is four years later. I'm afraid he's losing the support of his ministers. This worries me immensely.'

"As I listened, Physician Wu seemed surprised at Marco.

"'Messer Marco, you have always trusted Kubilai.'

"'Yes, I know, but I am concerned. Can you keep an extra eye on him for me?' Marco asked. Physician Wu answered yes, but then his voice turned playful out of the blue.

"'You mean as I do for Li?'

"Everyone laughed, easing the seriousness of the conversation.

"I was confused. *What did Physician Wu mean?* That was the first time I realized Marco had been watching out for me. *Was it his idea that Physician Wu take me under his wing?* My love for him just grew more.

"Marco didn't answer and continued. 'Soon, I will travel south to Champa, maybe even Cambodia. Kubilai wants me to make a deal with the king of Champa. He thinks the king might be as tired as we are.'"

Li stopped talking to Luca and giggled at the thought of what happened next. Guo Yu smiled.

She continued, "I thought I heard something in the forest; I quickly moved, making a slight noise."

Guo Yu interrupted and took over the conversation. "'Shhhhhhhhhh,' I whispered, causing Marco to be silent. 'She has big ears and loves to spy.' Marco rose, walked to the door, and pulled it open. Li fell flat on her face. Everyone roared with laughter except Li."

Luca had to do the same. Li, embarrassed, turned red as she playfully slapped Guo Yu's hand.

Li then continued her story. "We left after Physician Wu told Marco he would monitor Kubilai. Physician Wu, displeased with me, grabbed my arm and pulled me out while I said goodbye. He lectured me as we mounted our horses. 'One day, that spying will get you in trouble! Be silent and repeat nothing you heard. Messer Marco Polo could get into trouble, and you could, too. I shouldn't have brought you along. It was a last-minute decision. You always accompany me when I collect herbs. I thought it would be suspicious if you didn't come.'

"My behavior embarrassed me, but it didn't stop me from asking more questions! 'What did you mean, "As I do for Li?" Messer Marco asked you to watch over me? And who are Ghazan and Arghun?'

"Physician Wu never uttered another word. We rode in silence, but his face said it all. He was serious when he told me, 'It's late. Go straight to your chambers and remember, for Messer Marco's sake, repeat nothing of today.'

"When he put it that way, I felt guilty! I would've died if anything happened to him because of me. As I returned to my chamber, I thought, *I can't wait till Guo Yu returns. I'll ask him the questions. He could never refuse me.* As Guo Yu prepped for my bedtime, I asked the questions.

"That night, I learned that Guo Yu and Marco had decided I should stay with Physician Wu in the royal herbal garden as much as possible and keep learning. Guo Yu also told me that he and Physician Wu were worried about Kokochin and Ijir Bukhqa, the crown prince. They feared our friendships could erupt into problems later. But they understood I needed friends; I was alone, and they could see how happy they made me. Because of this, they didn't mention this to Marco that night."

As night approached, Li awoke from her trance. She looked at Luca and said, "I have been talking so long. I'm tired and ready to call Marco home."

Mesmerized by Li's story, Luca had not noticed the sun was setting. She jumped up to light the candles, and Guo Yu moved around the room to set up for dinner, asking Li not to play her erhu tonight.

Luca moved around the room. She stopped and asked Li, "What else did Guo Yu tell you?" Li looked out the window. " Not much, except Ghazan's father was the khan of the western empire."

Li continued, "Marco didn't find out till much later that Ijir Bukhqa was my friend. That's a whole different story that includes Arghun and Ghazan. That will be another day. I also realized that night that I had another society, The Society of Four: Marco, Physician Wu, Guo Yu, and me.

While they had dinner, Li continued her story. It was short, as she longed to play.

She started. "After that night, Marco made himself scarce. It would be August 28 before I saw him again, the day the court always leaves Shang-du for Khanbaliq. This day, without fail, the Great Khan performs the *Ritual of the Milk*."

"Ritual of the Milk," Luca repeated. "What do you mean?"

Li didn't answer directly but kept talking. "Vast blue skies surrounded us. The backdrop was snow-capped mountains that reached high into the heavens, and the sea of green grass turned amazingly white as a magnificent herd of snow-white stallions and mares passed by. Their numbers were dumbfounding, at least 10,000 mares. Marco proudly rode beside Kubilai and his sons. Marco looked so grand, and I was amazed at how important he had become. Behind them were Kokochin, Ijir Bukhqa, and other royal court members watching the massive herd run by."

Luca again interrupted. "Tell me about the ritual?" Li finally answered. "It was first performed by Kubilai Khan's grandfather, Genghis Khan. It's said these horses are so revered that only those of the imperial lineage could drink the milk of these horses. Later, astrologers and monks told Kubilai that he must douse the air and the ground with their milk on this day each year so the spirits and idols could drink their share and extend their protection to all that belongs to Kubilai, the men and women, beasts, birds, grain, and everything else. So, he departs the summer palace on this date to perform this milk sacrifice with his own hands."

"How exciting," Luca said in a high-pitched voice, clapping her hands.

Li stopped talking for a moment and then continued. "I think I am ready to play my erhu."

Guo Yu looked at Li, "Please refrain from playing tonight and go to sleep."

Li didn't answer. Guo Yu and Luca rose and cleaned up.

Li went to the window but didn't pick up her erhu. Guo Yu took a deep breath silently, relieved.

As they said their goodnights, they opened the door. Isabella almost fell to the floor. Guo Yu caught her just in time. In this embarrassing moment, instead of apologizing, her only comment was to Luca. "Why are you listening to this nonsense?" Luca didn't answer. She just nodded, bowed, and walked fast down the hallway.

Isabella looked at Guo Yu and talked in a high-pitched tone. "She's not playing that disgusting instrument tonight. It makes me want to scream!"

Guo Yu looked over at Li, who was watching. Li was silent as Guo Yu directed Isabella out.

Guo Yu turned to Li and spoke in Manzi, "Please don't play tonight. Lock your door, just in case Isabella returns."

Li nodded, and as soon as Guo Yu walked out, she quietly locked the door.

Guo Yu heard the click and frowned. He knew his words meant nothing.

A few minutes later, the crying music began. Isabella stomped down the hallway, cursing.

Guo Yu continued walking to his room, thinking *Marco had better return soon.*

1. King Chungseon of Goryeo
2. The Secret History of the Mongol Queens by Jack Weatherford
3. An empire in the expansive Mongol Empire, ruling over Persia and parts of the Middle East between 1258-1335

Chapter Nineteen

Marco

1274 Marco's Slavery

Genoa Prison 1298

The clanking of metal awakened Marco. He woke up with a smile; in his dreams, he held Li all night. He jumped up and met the guards at the small window for breakfast. They handed him food, commenting that the commander wanted to see him that afternoon. Marco could hardly contain his happiness. He grabbed the food quickly, spilling part of the thin gruel upon the floor and sending the stale bread flying. He rushed to Rustichello, picked up the bread, and joyously said, "Eat fast so we can continue. I want to write as much as possible. Our journey is finally coming to an end."

Rustichello grumbled, "You spilled most of it, so it won't take long."

Marco wasn't listening. Thoughts of Li consumed his mind. He gobbled down his food. He was brought back to reality by Rustichello's voice. "We left off at Ganzhou."

Marco remembered perfectly and began reciting.

> *"It was a vast, noble city. It is the capital and administrative center. The people are idolaters and worship Muhammad, and there are Christians....three fine churches, and the idolaters have many monasteries. They had many idols, some made of wood, clay, and stone. They were all covered in gold."*

Rustichello excitedly spoke, "Gold!"

"Yes, Gold," Marco said nonchalantly.

"They lavished their idols with gold more than themselves and followed and lived more virtuous lives than others. They avoid lustfulness but do not regard it as a great sin. They believe that if a woman invites them to make love, they can lie with her without sin, but if the men make the first move, it is counted as an act of sin, and if a man has unnatural intercourse with a woman, they condemn him to death."

Rustichello cringed, and Marco continued.

"And now I will tell you if a rider travels for twelve days to the north, you arrive at Ejina, the beginning of the sandy desert. It is a province of Tangut. They are idolaters.... They have many camels and cattle. They breed lanner and saker falcons and live off the land and their flocks... They are not trading people. In this city, you must gather food for a journey that takes 40 days through this desert where there are no houses or inns. In the valleys and mountains, there are wild beasts and many wild asses.... There are pine woods and rivers full of pike and other fish. When you cross this desert, you reach Karakorum. This city is three miles in circumference and surrounded by a great wall of earth, as there are no stones. It is the first seat of Tartars."

Marco paused, looked up at Rustichello, and said, "It was here that the great Khan sent his couriers to escort us and attend to our every wish for the next forty days."

Rustichello looked up and questioned Marco. "Why?"

"The Khan had awaited my father and uncle's return for six years. Our arrival overjoyed him." Marco answered and continued.

"When you leave Ganzhou and travel east, you will go through a country alive with spirits who can be heard talking, especially at night."

Rustichello stopped Marco." What do you mean, Spirits?"

Marco didn't answer; he just kept talking.

"Then you finally arrive in Erguiul....[1] *It belongs to the Great Khan....part of Tangut... The people are Nestorians, Christians, idolaters, and worshippers of Muhammad....plenty of cities...*

"If you travel southeast from here, you come to a place with many cities....part of Tangut and subject to the great Khan.

"I mention this because there are wild oxen,[2] *as big as elephants, and beautiful. They have hair except on their backs. They are white and black, and their hair is three palms long, finer, and whiter than silk.*

"I brought some back, plus the musk I will tell you about now. Many oxen are captured and domesticated and multiplied by breeding.... beasts of burden and pull plows....twice as strong.... This country produces the finest musk....obtained from a small animal the size of a gazelle....hair like deer....feet and tail like a gazelle. Four long slender teeth, two up and two down.... When a hunter catches one, he finds a little blood sac near the navel and removes it....this sac is where the musk is full of pungent perfume.... The people live off trade and crafts and grow a great deal of grain.... Giant peasants with tails ten palms long... Other birds with beautiful and colorful plumage.... People are idolaters... They are fat...small noses...black hair.... Most have hairless bodies, including women with delicate white complexions, and are very beautiful... Great barons or magnates marry them even though their families are poor and give their mothers large amounts of money.

"I will stop here. That is enough about this region," and let's continue to our original track.

"You will find many cities when you leave Erguiul and travel eight days to the east, which is still Tangut. The capital is Alashan.... People are idolaters, but there are three churches for the Nestorian Christians....subject to the great khan.... They make the finest and most beautiful camel hair camlets, some mixed with white wool. The merchants export them across the world, especially Cathay.... Leaving this province and heading east, you will enter the Preston John domain, known as *Tenduk. Anyway, the people are subject to the great Khan.... His*

daughters or other female relatives always enter marriage with the reigning kings of the lineage of Preston John... Lapis Lazuli is found here.... They have camel hair camlets....They live off their flocks and the fruit of the soil, and some trade and industry.... The rulers are Christians, but there are plenty of idolaters and worshippers of Muhammad.... Also, you will find a class of people called Argon, which in our language means 'Half Castes.' Both natives of Tenduk...they worship Muhammad....very handsome and intelligent....great at business than most."

Marco let out a long sigh of relief. Their three-year journey was nearing its end. Shang-du was only days away.

"Just 13 more days," Marco announced.

"You travel seven days across Tenduk province....more cities and towns...Saracens, Idolaters, Nestorian Christians.... They live by trade and crafts...weave fine golden fabrics called nasich and nakh and many gold silk cloths....subject to the great Khan.... There is a city called Xuandezhou where equipment for armies is made.... In the mountains is a place called Ydifu....a prosperous silver mine. Then you travel three more days to Chagan Nur, also known as White Lake in our language. A grand palace belongs to the Great Khan here....plenty of lakes and rivers stocked with swans....plains team with cranes, pheasants, partridges, and many kinds of wildfowl. He feeds them, and they are fat. When he desires to eat them, they are brought to him wherever he is. Finally, you arrive in Shang-du when the traveler journeys north-northeast for three days."

Marco let out another sigh of relief. He had finally reached their destination—Kubilai Khan's Shang-du. Just then, he heard the prison door open. A nervous Marco stood erect. It was time to see the commander. Instead of showing his nervousness, he walked confidently over to Rustichello and grabbed the needed papers, including the letters. He thumbed over them, making sure everything was there. He smiled, and as he walked toward the door, he tried to rearrange his unlaundered clothing and ran his fingers through his tangled hair. *This must work. It must!* He mumbled to himself.

As he walked down the long, dark stone halls, he could hear moaning as disgusting smells permeated the air. *Do I smell this bad?* The walk to the commander seemed to last forever.

Marco knocked, entered the door, and saw the same men waiting for him. With confidence, he strolled to the commander and handed him the report. The commander thumbed through the papers just as he had done with the first ones, then commanded him to sit. The commander glanced around at the other men. Marco hoped this was a good sign. The commander returned to the report and continued to read page after page. Appearing fearless, Marco sat erect and confident, even though his heart pounded and his body shivered inside. Something he had learned from the past. *You never show fear, only confidence, if you want them to believe and respect you.* Never in his life had he wanted something so bad, except Li.

The commander looked up. "You have more?"

Marco swiftly answered, "Yes, much more! Did you see the letters? I beg you, sir. Please deliver them to my family. I have been gone for two months without a word. My family must be thinking the worst."

"After the next meeting, I will consider," the commander smirked. One man in the back spoke, but the commander halted him. "I will see you in another month, and Messer Marco Polo, I expect you to be finished!"

Marco stood up. A fire had ignited and erupted in his body as his anger rose. He felt intense hatred. Again, wise words from his past—words from his dear friend, Kim Chin-hae—filled his mind. *Never show that you are angry; this shows you are weak. Stand strong.* Marco bit his tongue and bowed.

"I will be back sooner than a month!" he hissed. With weak knees, he headed for the door. He turned and glared at the officers one last time before he left.

After Marco left the room and the door shut, the other men approached the commander, circling and bombarding him with a multitude of questions. Only one spoke about Marco's letter. "You should send his letters. Isn't it a gentleman's agreement, especially between generals?"

Everyone stopped talking and looked at him, horrified. The commander was not a person you questioned. The commander glared at him and answered the other men's questions.

They were all captivated by the report. They could see their futures becoming richer.

The same man didn't stop asking him. Irritated, the commander finally answered. "In due time. This way, he will write more if he has fear and hope simultaneously."

Marco fiercely walked to his cell. This time, he didn't notice the smell or the groaning. His fire inside was growing, and he was ablaze when he returned to the cell. Here, no one of importance could see his weakness. He released his anger, and Rustichello just watched. After Marco had exhausted himself, he put his thrown bed in its place and collapsed.

Rustichello sat silently, worked on his book, and waited for Marco to speak first.

Marco was in disbelief. *How could he refuse me? My report was excellent; besides, it was a gentleman's courtesy, a general's courtesy, to deliver my letters to my family.* He had not felt this much rage since his father gave him to Kubilai Khan. Strange, this was where he was in his story.

Marco suddenly started talking. Rustichello listened momentarily before pushing his book aside and quickly switching to Marco's report.

"As I said..." Marco began.

> *"When you leave this city, White Lake, and travel north-northeast for three days, you come to Shang-du. Kubilai Khan built a vast palace of marble and other stones in this city. Gilded images of birds, animals, trees, and flowers cover the halls and rooms. The Shang-du palace had an outer wall that enclosed an area of sixteen miles in three directions, featuring rivers, springs, and lawns. You can only reach the park through the palace gates. There, Kubilai kept all kinds of animals for hunting. He remains during June, July, and August to escape the heat of Khanbaliq. He calls it 'The Summer Palace.'"*

Marco stopped and looked at Rustichello. "When we arrived, the convoy directed us to Kubilai Khan in a vast hall. We entered from the south door as Kubilai's throne always sits on the north wall. He sat on a raised platform, high above the many barons present. The platform held a huge wooden chair at least three paces in length. Each arm was extravagantly carved with a leopard's head in gold, and their bodies rose to the back of the chair.

"My father and uncle fell to their knees; I followed, and we crawled the rest of the way until we could see his slightly red, handsome face. We knelt before him and showed our utmost respect. Surprisingly, he asked us to rise and received us with honor. He asked how we fared on the long trip and if our health remained good.

"'We indeed managed well, but we are even better since we find you well and flourishing,' my father answered.

"Kubilai immediately started asking questions about our trip. My father's words were dull and lacked color. They were skilled businessmen but lacked my ability to tell stories. My mother taught me to observe people and the land around me. Most of all, by God's grace, I was blessed with the ability to memorize faces, names, numbers, and places, and I had the talent to use these things to weave an exciting tale. Interrupting my father, as I could tell Kubilai was becoming distant, I took over speaking in Kubilai Khan's language. Kubilai's face changed from irritation to delight. After a while, he stopped me and directed his words to my father. 'Who is this young man?'

"I could see my father in deep thought. He didn't answer him. Instead, he quickly presented Kubilai with the privileges and letters the Pope had sent. Kubilai was greatly pleased. Then my father handed over the holy oil, and you could see the joy in Kubilai's eyes. Surprisingly, my father fell to his knees, apologizing that he could not present him with the requested priest.

"Kubilai instructed him to stand and sternly asked again. 'Who is this young man?'

"'Sire, this is my son and your liege man.'

"My heart stopped. I couldn't believe what I had just heard. *Kubilai Khan's servant, which meant slave? Did I hear that correctly?* My shrewd merchant father had seized a newfound opportunity, exchanging his son for the absent priest for the desired tea, salt, and other permits. Again, my father abandoned me.

"Kubilai Khan sat in silence as he watched me. Even though anger boiled deep inside me and sadness consumed me, I stood confidently and proudly. At that moment, I grew up and abandoned my father, and my desire to obtain his love disappeared.

"Kubilai understood my father's motive. He had been trading his daughters to obtain allies for some time. But a son was different.

"'So, Messer Niccolò, you willingly give me your son in lieu of the priest, hoping to obtain permits?' asked Kubilai.

"Before my father could reply, I answered. 'It would be an honor to serve you, my lord.'

"Kubilai smiled at me. 'You are heartily welcome. It looks like I have gained a son!'

"Everyone in the room went silent. Kubilai's smile turned to roaring laughter, and the merriment began, and all the court welcomed our arrival. We stayed at court and had a place of honor above the other barons.

"When we went to our new quarters, my father tried rationalizing his actions. I could hear some guilt in his voice, but his greed shone through.

"After a sleepless night, I couldn't imagine throwing away your son. I arose as a new man, dreaming of acquiring wealth and knowledge. I would use my father, uncle, and Kubilai like they planned to use me. However, I would do this with honor, loyalty, and respect. My father sometimes hated this over the next seventeen years, but he learned to accept it.

"Several weeks passed as we waited for the permits. While waiting, Kubilai invited us on a hunt. We would stay overnight in his temporary palace in the middle of a beautiful grove."

> *"Its beauty astounded me. This palace was constructed entirely of cane. It was all gilt inside and decorated with images of beasts and birds. It stood upon beautifully gilded and varnished pillars. The pillars are adorned with gold dragons, their tails coiled around each one. The head and outstretched arms held up the ceiling. They also made the roof of cane, three palms in girth, and ten to fifteen paces long. They are split into two, creating two tiles so heavily varnished that no amount of water could penetrate them. The unique part was that silk cords held it together, which meant it could be placed and disassembled entirely at his whim.*

"During the first evening after a very successful hunting day, Kubilai Khan announced my first mission. 'Prove your worth! You are to go to the Kingdom of Qarajang as my emissary. When you return, I will decide on the permits,' Kubilai Khan said and nodded toward a soldier.

"The soldier beside him handed him two thick envelopes and a shoulder bag. As Kubilai held them, he spoke to me. 'Deliver this one to King Manggala in Chang'anfu. Wait for an answer and bring it back to me when you return. The second package goes to King Yesün Temür in Yachi. Just as with the first one, give him the envelope and await his response. The packages contain important private letters and my paper money. Do not open them and protect them with your life.'

"I bowed as I received them, placed them in the shoulder bag, and carefully put the strap over my head. My face must have looked confused.

"'Question?' Kubilai asked.

"'Paper money?'

"Kubilai Khan nodded to his servant, who walked over to him and handed him pieces of rectangular black paper of different sizes, marked with many seals. 'This is money, legal tender. All kingdoms and lands where I rule accept these sheets in payment for anything, never refusing for fear of losing their life. The smallest one has the smallest value. Kubilai continued holding up each size, explaining its worth.

"'This size, a whole silver groat[3] in your land. This one is two groats, the next one, five groats, next ten groats, next one, gold bezant, next, three gold bezants, and so on, up to ten bezants.'

"Kubilai Khan noticed my working mind, having never seen paper money. Kubilai spoke up. 'When you return, I will have someone take you to my mint.'

"I nodded at Kubilai and asked no more questions, thinking I would ask someone else. I found out...

"They made the paper from the bark stripped from mulberry trees. Mulberry trees grew there in abundance, and the silkworms ate their leaves. The thin layer closest to the tree is then ground, pounded, and pressed with glue into sheets, similar to cotton paper, which is black in color. And then cut into rectangular shapes.

"The vital part is that several times a year, large parties of merchants arrive in Khanbaliq with pearls and precious stones such as gold, silver, silk cloths, and other precious items. Twelve experts then graded them on their worth and exchanged them for paper money. That's how Kubilai Khan accumulated all the gold, silver, precious stones, and pearls from all his lands.

"I left Kubilai proudly. My knowledge of Tartar customs, language, and writing prepared me to 'Prove my worth.'

"When we returned to the summer palace after the incredible hunt, I disappeared. My father and uncle were too busy packing to notice, excited to meet new traders and set up outposts as they always did.

"I made a decision and had to see Kubilai Khan. Receiving permission to enter,

I crawled to Kubilai Khan.

"Kubilai asked me to rise. 'What does my new son request?'

"'I request to go on my mission without my father and uncle.'

"Kubilai stared hard at me and then called over a servant and whispered in his ear. The servant then turned and left the room. Kubilai never said another word, and I awkwardly waited. When the servant returned, he broke the awkward silence, asking to enter. With permission, he entered, followed by my father and uncle. Instantly, they fell to their knees.

Kubilai instructed them to stand. Their faces reflected concern when they saw me standing beside Kubilai.

"Kubilai said one brief statement. 'Your son will go without you. This is his test! You will receive your permits upon his return if I am satisfied.'

"My father's mouth opened to speak, and my uncle laid his hand on his shoulder. He quickly closed it. I could see by his expression that he was disappointed. I smiled at him. *He deserved this.*

"After Kubilai dismissed them, Kubilai asked me, 'Are you sure this is what you want?'

"Confidently, I replied, 'Yes, my lord, my life belongs to you now. I will prove my worth. You will be happy with your decision as I am no longer a boy but a man with a mission. For three years, I prepared carefully and observed my father and uncle. Now I will do it my way.'

"Kubilai motioned to his servant, who handed him a gold bar the size of a small, slender woman's hand, stamped with letters and a dangling, looped silk cord attached on one end. Kubilai, in turn, handed it to me and softly said, 'This gold bar indicates you represent the great Khan, and you may travel freely throughout my dominion and receive any provision for yourself and the soldiers who will accompany you.' With two hands, I happily accepted this remarkable item; this marked the beginning of our unusual, loving friendship, which lasted until the day I left.

"When I returned to my room, my angered father awaited me. 'Did you make this decision on your own? Are you that sure of yourself? You're an arrogant kid. Our future now lies in your hands! Let me see those envelopes in the shoulder bag.'

"I looked emotionlessly at my father. 'You mean *my future*? I no longer belong to you! Kubilai gave these envelopes to me, and they are private. Only the owners will open them, and no one else. I gave my word.' Silently, my father left, shaking his head.

"The following day, I left with my new guide and guard, Dai Xiuying, and a few soldiers."

Rustichello put down his pen. "So, your father gave you to Kubilai Khan. What a fantastic story."

Marco smiled slightly and replied. "That was the best thing to happen to me. I was no longer under the emotional control of my father and grew into the Marco I am today."

Rustichello continued, "Did you ever forgive your father? And what was up with the letters and paper money?"

Marco answered his first question. "Yes, after many years, I forgave my father. And the answer to your second question: the envelopes were the test."

"Test?" Rustichello repeated.

"Yes! It's a long story. Let's continue tomorrow. Aren't you ready to hear more about Kim Chin-hae?"

Rustichello was thrilled; he had been waiting for this. "You told me how he came to Ningbo, but I want to hear how he met the shaman."

Marco lay on his bed talking. "Let's see. I told you how I met Lis when I saved Kim Chin-hae's life and how he came to Ningbo." Marco stopped talking, closed his eyes, and thought back. "Ok! It was the night at the inn when I was the guest of honor. With intense curiosity, I bit my lip all night until finally, it became uncontrollable. 'I'm sorry, Kim Chin-hae, but I must know how you two met: a royal with a Miao Shaman.' Kim Chin-hae hesitated; he had never told the story to anyone. He looked at Lis, who smiled. While looking at Lis, he started..."

---

1. Liangzhou

2. Yaks

3. Coin

Chapter Twenty

Kim

Down the River of Love

"As you know, I am a general in the Royal Navy of Goryeo. Seven months ago, I traveled to Fuzhou with a Han general named Hsin-tu and my servant, Son Jun-ho. We were recruiting additional troops and checking how many ships had been built or redesigned for the upcoming invasion against Wa.

"The sun was low in the sky when we reached the Min River, our destination, Fuzhou. The next day, we were to meet General Zhang.

"At the city entrance, a stout bamboo cage housed a curled-up animal in the corner. The fur resembled a caged wolf: thick, brown, and matted. Food was thrown about the cage, and a puddle of dirty water occupied the opposite corner. A horrific smell permeated the air. Something compelled me to stop. The general, Hsin-tu, continued riding. Suddenly, the creature unfurled before my eyes, and the beast transformed into a person; I saw slender arms with dainty hands reaching from under the matted, thick fur and flipping it back, exposing the most captivating face I had ever seen. Her eyes pierced through me like a spear.

"A guard that had left his post was running toward me, shouting, 'Don't look upon her. She is a shaman with bewitching powers. We have caged her as an example. Her kind is not wanted here.'

"It was too late. Our eyes melted into each other, and I couldn't turn away. Ahead, the general had stopped and commanded me to hurry. Brought back to my senses, our eyes unlocked, and I urged my horse forward.

"'That was a woman,' I whispered to the general. His response was, 'We are here for soldiers and ships. That's not our business.'

"The rest of the evening, my mind kept floating back to her. That night, lying in bed, I slowly drifted into a dream-like state. Before me, I could only see her face with sad eyes and succulent lips, speaking in a hypnotic voice, 'Please help me. Please help me.'

"I opened my eyes, shaken. *Is she calling me? Is it true? Has she bewitched me?*

Rolling over, I told myself, *Don't be ridiculous*. Sleeping was impossible; I tossed and turned for hours. Finally, I sat on the edge of my bed and quietly rose, dressed, and slipped out of the room. In a trance, I slowly walked toward the caged woman. It was a beautiful night; the moon was bright and full. The closer I came to the edge of town, the faster my stride increased, and I started looking around, making sure no one was watching. Approaching the cage, I saw the guard crouched down, leaning against the tree, sleeping. The girl stood with her hands on the bamboo bars, her face peering through a small open space, watching me walk toward her. Frightened but unable to resist, I no longer had any doubt; she had called me.

"By the time I reached her, I belonged to her, and she belonged to me. I gently placed my hands over hers. We spoke with our eyes; I found Heaven. She touched my shoulder and smiled. 'Your soul is gentle although scarred many times. I have been waiting for you. You are mine.'

"I felt warm all over. Cautiously, I looked over at the guard, who still slept. She placed her index finger to her lips, not saying a word. Her eyes looked at my sword and the ropes that held the cage together. I understood.

"Afraid the sword would cause a sound, I quietly removed a small dagger from my boot and sliced the ropes. I caught the bars one by one and held them in my arms until I created a small opening. She stepped out. Under the moonlight, she whispered, 'I will find you.' Then she disappeared into the forest.

"My heart flip-flopped. I had a powerful urge to follow, but suddenly, the feeling disappeared. I returned to my quarters and sat on the edge of the bed, thinking, *Had the guard been correct? Have I been bewitched?* Not caring, I lay down and instantly fell into a peaceful slumber.

"The following day, men shouting outside awoke me. I rose and opened the door. Guards headed toward the generals' quarters, shouting, 'She escaped! She has disappeared...'

"Smiling to myself, I followed the soldiers. That's when reality struck. It had been me. I prayed that no one had seen me, and with feigned confidence, I entered the quarters. A discussion between General Hsi-tu and Commander Zhang was underway. I silently listened.

"'Someone helped her escape by cutting the ropes,' snarled Commander Zhang.

"He looked over at General Hsin-tu suspiciously and continued talking. 'The Song Dynasty's emperor, before Kubilai Khan conquered them, passed a law that shamans were illegal unless registered with the government, especially the mountain Miao. They are dangerous. We are sure someone hired her to poison one of our captains. We don't have proof yet; she was under investigation.'

"The guard from the cage stood with his head down and suddenly fell to his knees. 'I'm sorry, my punishment should be death.

"I spoke up without thinking. I couldn't help myself. 'You treated her like an animal while under investigation. Was that right?'

"General Hsin-tu shot a look to silence. Commander Zhang stopped and looked my way. His mouth opened, and before words came out, soldiers entered. His attention flew to them. 'Did you see any tracks?' he shouted.

"'Only animals, no humans.' The soldiers answered.

"Commander Zhang sneered, half laughing. 'She's probably a shapeshifter.'

"The soldiers' faces appeared fearful, agreeing with him.

"I was thankful I had the common sense to cut a branch and wipe the tracks leading into the forest and my own as I returned to my sleeping quarters.

"The commander continued. 'Even if she's an animal, she probably won't survive. Tigers overrun our mountains.' My heart sank. I didn't think of that. Commander Zhang dismissed the soldiers and looked at General Hsin-tu. 'We have more to discuss than an escaped Miao Shaman.'

"He turned to the guard on his knees. 'I will contend with you later.' The guard rose and, with his head down, hurried out.

"Commander Zhang looked over at me. 'Who are you exactly?'

"'My name is Kim Chin-hae,' I said as I bowed. 'My primary duty is the ships. I am a representative from Goryeo. My king oversees the Eastern Expedition Field Headquarters. Kubilai Khan named him minister of the Jeongdong Haeng Seong, overseeing the upcoming invasion.'

"Commander Zhang looked at General Hsin-tu and me in disgust. His expression indicated that he couldn't accept that the Song Dynasty had lost to Kubilai Khan. Just our presence caused him pain. However, his attitude changed quickly, and he began disregarding his personal feelings. He smiled and, with a hint of sarcasm, began discussing the upcoming invasion. His words became honey-coated as we ventured to the shipyard, where numerous defeated Southern Song dynasty ships docked. He asked, 'How many men and ships do you need?' I didn't answer as excitement ran through my body. The Song ships were far superior to the Mongols. I couldn't wait to examine these remarkable ships and implement as many new ideas as possible in the new Goryeo fleet.

Commander Zhang found himself enjoying my enthusiasm and admiration for his ships. That didn't last long; he felt guilty enjoying anything about me. He suddenly snorted, 'You didn't answer me. How many ships and men do you need?' He didn't give General Hsin-tu time to respond, so he answered his own question.

"'Take what you want. Do I have a choice? You came in the name of Kubilai Khan.'

"General Hsin-tu and I understood Commander Zhang's attitude. Our presence reminded him of the loss of his country. Song[1] for the first time in history had been defeated by a foreign nation. Many soldiers refused to surrender and hid in the mountains. The general's new duties were to capture his people, and with us recruiting his soldiers, it just made his job more arduous. How will he control any new uprisings?

"But, we also had no choice. Kubilai had commanded us to complete this task, and we accomplished it. After his outburst, the commander gained control of his anger and returned somewhat cordial.

"By the end of the day, I had grown restless; too much cloying conversation, mixed with sarcasm, occurred that day. My mind had become clouded; all I could think about was the girl and the flesh-eating tigers. As we walked back to our quarters, my mind was racing. *What would be my excuse for leaving and searching for the girl?*

"Suddenly, a lie poured from my mouth. 'Sir, my servant has reminded me of the king's request to visit an old friend in Zapton. I need to leave as soon as possible.'

"General Hsin-tu looked annoyed but nodded with approval. However, in a harsh voice, he said, 'Be back as soon as possible. I shouldn't have to remind you; your king and Kubilai will be waiting for your report."

"'Yes, I understand.'

"My obsession with this mysterious girl frightened me. I even lied to the general. *Is it true she is a witch?* That didn't seem to matter. Hurriedly, I packed, wanting to leave before dark to look for her. Son Jun-ho, my servant, knew I was lying. He didn't care; his concern was only for me, and he would follow me anywhere. That was his duty.

"Commander Zhang, I worried, would become suspicious when he heard I left before General Hsin-tu. I remembered his facial expression when I remarked on the woman's treatment; I feared he would think I helped her escape.

"Son Jun-ho and I slipped into the forest where she entered. Son Jun-ho erased our horses' footprints, and we waited just out of sight to see if any men came after us. I was correct; five soldiers raced toward the main road, stopped at the empty cage, and glared into the forest. We held our breath until we heard them say, 'There are no footprints,' and continued down the road. We had to hurry before they realized they should have caught up with us and turned around.

"The sun hadn't even set, and the forest was becoming darker by the minute. I thought to myself, *Am I crazy? What are my chances of finding her?* Once she entered the woods, I had no idea which direction she took. She said she would find me, but I couldn't wait.

"We blindly traveled a short distance. Fortunately, the forest's damp, mossy ground held a footprint. Son Jun-ho pointed to it, and then he found another. She was heading west toward the river. My hope heightened. I had the advantage; She was on foot, and I was on horseback.

"In the darkness, Son Jun-ho walked with a torch until the moon rose, and with its filtered light beaming through the forest, traveling became swifter and friendlier. The forest leaves danced in the moonlight and the settled dew shimmered with its light. A small creek snaked over large and small stones, creating small pools before rushing forward. As I rode past it and looked down at the water, I swore I saw her face with soft eyes that followed me."

Lis interrupted Kim Chin-hae's story, and she continued. "For a night and a day, I traveled through the forest and headed toward the river. The forest was like a second home to me. From an early age, my mother taught me what plants were edible and how to collect water. On the other hand, I did fear wild animals. My first thought was to find the herbs that would conceal my scent.

"As I walked, I kept thinking, *I was born able to read faces and knew when they were easy prey to bewitch. Chin-hae possessed one of those faces.*"

Lis smiled at Kim Chin-hae and continued. "Many men fell prey to my spell when I needed help. Yet, this was different; I could not erase your face from my memory like the others. Time didn't help. I couldn't shake the image of the man who saved me. Initially, I just needed your help but your face kept appearing—a handsome face, no, a beautiful face. My mother warned me that this could happen someday. *Have I been bewitched?* I kept thinking."

Kim Chin-hae grabbed Lis's hand as she continued. "I became disgusted with myself. With every step I took, the urge to turn around became unbearable, even though I knew returning to the city was too dangerous. The commander was looking for me. If he caught me again, he would ensure I remained in the cage until I rotted. They accused me of using Gu, a poison, to kill a captain who had deserted his pregnant lover.

"What was I to do? I had no intention of finding you. However, on the second night, I stood on the riverbank and looked down the flowing river that would lead me safely home. My feet wouldn't take another step. I was paralyzed for the first time in my life. *Have I really been bewitched?* I found myself not caring. As I knelt on its bank, the moonlight reflected my frightening image. *How long had I been trapped in that cage?* With cupped hands, I washed my face and hands, pulled back my hair, and twisted it until I could tie it in a knot. I looked again into the river at myself; your imaginary face appeared next to mine. Looking up at the moon, I knew it was true; I had been bewitched. I entered the river and cooled my body. That night, as I drifted in and out of sleep, my dreams were only of you. You felt so close. By morning, I knew I would see you soon."

Kim Chin-hae then took over, speaking to Marco. "As the moon disappeared and the sun rose, Son Jun-ho and I stood on a ridge on the second day and looked at the river below. It would take us a day to arrive. As we rode toward the river, we frantically searched for traces of her existence. By the time the moon rose on the third night, we sat on the bank of the river. Emotion had overwhelmed me. *Now what?*

"Son Jun-ho collected firewood as I stared into the river. The moonlight brightened my distorted reflection caused by the rippling river. Suddenly, Lis's reflection appeared next to mine. In disbelief, I closed my eyes. Slowly, I reopened them and peered back into the river. Her face still stared back at me.

"Quickly, I turned. *Could it really be her standing next to me?* In disbelief, I touched her face. I watched her lips move and whisper."

Lis interrupted. "I told you I would find you."

Kim Chin-hae smiled and continued speaking, staring at her. "She no longer looked like the wild animal in the cage. Her eyes were soft, her hair was partially in a bun encircled by dainty flowers, and the other half flowed down her shoulders. The animal had transformed into a mystical forest fairy.

"For a moment, we just looked at each other, neither one of us understanding the feeling that radiated from our hearts. A warming sensation rushed through our bodies until our skin felt on fire. It seemed our heartbeat and breath had melted into one.

"Abruptly, our bond was broken when an excited Son Jun-ho shrieked as he returned with the firewood. 'YOU found her!' Embarrassed, we moved apart, and I went to assist Son.

"Son Jun-ho whispered, 'How?'

"I whispered back, 'She found me.'

"'How?' he answered back.

"I shrugged my shoulders!

"Lis walked over to us. 'I can hear you! I'm not a murderer or witch, but a shaman who sees the future in dreams and heals. As you know, I can also coerce people.'

"Listening silently, I thought, *I am a man of science, a scholar. How can I believe her?* I knew women, including my mother, who believed, but never me. Still, this woman possessed powers

I could not explain. I had illegally released an imprisoned person and lied to General Hsin-tu. Yet I didn't care. This was not me. *Had she bewitched me?*

Lis cut in and directed her conversation to Marco, "His face reflected disbelief. I walked closer to him and whispered, 'For the first time in my life, I, too, have been bewitched. I should have followed the river home yesterday instead of waiting for you. It's too late for regrets; come, I have everything ready."

Kim Chin-hae continued the story. "'*Ready?* What do you mean?' She grabbed my arm and urged me to walk along the river's bank with her. She pulled some herbs from her pocket. 'Rub this on your clothes and pass it to your servant. It conceals your scent from wild animals.' I obliged, and we proceeded forward. Son Jun-ho grabbed the horses and followed.

"As we walked, I only asked her name."

Lis took over. "I answered, 'LIS, and yours?'"

"'Kim Chin-hae.'" I answered. "We nodded to each other as we walked until we reached a well-organized camp. A fire pit with a small blaze sat in its center, ready to cook fish and gathered wild greens that lay on large leaves.

"For sitting, horizontal logs sat on one side, and three makeshift beds of branches and leaves sat on the other side. I thought, *She was expecting us. She is a witch.*"

Lis giggled and slapped his hand. "I told you I'm not a witch but a shaman." She turned to Marco. "It has been a long-time joke."

Kim Chin-hae smiled and continued. "It had been days since I ate; I was famished. Lis scurried around the fire, placing the fish she had stuffed with greens over the fire. Poking the fire, she dug wild tubules from the coals. She peeled the burnt skin and handed it to me. Sliced wild ginseng sat on the other side of the fire. 'For energy!' she noted. I couldn't help but think she was at home in these primitive surroundings. *So different from my home and the women I know.*

"Son Jun-ho rose and went to his horse, pulling out a bag of rice wine. We ate and drank quietly. I had so many questions but felt so peaceful that I didn't want to disturb this wonderful feeling. Shortly after, intense sleepiness overwhelmed me. I stood and looked down at her; she was unusually beautiful. It was hard to explain.

"'Thank you, please excuse me. I need to lie down,' I told Lis. I collapsed on one of the makeshift beds, closing my eyes for the first time in three nights and only opening them shortly as I heard Son Jun-ho and Lis stand. Son hurried to the horse for a blanket and Lis for a light branch. They met at my side. Son Jun-ho glared at Lis. 'I have cared for him his whole life. I will kill you if you hurt him!'"

Lis interrupted. "I responded, 'I will protect him with my life.' Satisfied with my answer, Son Jun-ho lay beside Chin-hae and me on the other side.

Lis continued. "As the moon set, a colorful early dawn filled the sky. I suddenly awakened and reached over, shaking Chin-hae. 'Wake up, they are coming, hurry!'"

Kim Chin-hae took over the story. "I replied in a sleepy voice, 'Who?'

"'The soldiers! Hurry, we must go.' Lis said.

"I sprang up, looking at Lis. 'How do you...?' I stopped in mid-sentence. I knew how!

Lis was already disposing of our beds as I woke Son Jun-ho, who jumped up and saddled the horses. I extinguished the fire, threw the rocks that encircled the fire pit into the river, and covered the ash. Lis gathered branches and started rubbing out our existence until I lifted her onto my horse. Son Jun-ho picked up Lis's branch and continued her job. I hurriedly got on behind Lis, holding the reins of Son's horse as we entered the river. He continued until he entered the river.

"The horses traveled slowly through the water. Time seemed to disappear into the depths of the surrounding forest. The warmth of Lis's body against me stirred emotions I had never felt. My mind wandered to Park Eun-ae. *She was beautiful and had been my mother and father's choice. If only I had felt this with her. My life would have been easier.*

"Lis rested her head on my chest and placed her hands on my hand; my heart pounded. I knew then that I didn't care. From that day forward, LIS was my life. Eun-ae vanished; she would rise again, not as a lover but as someone who would make trading in Goryeo difficult.

"That's when I looked down at her hands, and I noticed a bandage. 'What's this?' I asked."

Lis jumped in and took over. "I told him it was a minor necessity and I doubted we would see the soldiers again. 'We can probably go to shore.' Chin-hae stopped his horse, unwrapped my bandage, turned my body toward his face, and asked again. 'What happened?'

"'I slit the palm of my hand and dripped my blood around our camp. The soldiers will find our camp, but so will the tigers.'"

"I knew then she was my protector, not the other way around. We later heard that the soldiers had returned to the cage and entered the forest, where they found our tracks. It disappointed the captain that they had wasted a day. He had pushed his men hard until they reached the river. Our horse tracks had disappeared. But not the scent of Lis' blood, which had aroused the hungry tigers. In the fury of a violent battle, the soldiers disappeared."

Marco cringed.

Kim Chin-hae continued. "When we returned to shore, I dismounted. As I lifted her from the horse, I looked into Lis's eyes. I pulled her body to mine, and our lips met. It was Déjà vu; our heartbeat and breath melted into one."

Lis's face turned red as Kim Chin-hae continued the story. "Son Jun-ho was just as embarrassed as Lis is now. Then Son spoke in a low tone, 'This is going to be trouble. Your mother will never accept this.'

"Suddenly, out of nowhere, a woman with a deep voice called Lis's name. 'I was worried. Where have you been? I heard you escaped; you should have been home yesterday.' Lis stepped away from me, her eyes wide, as she looked at the woman shamefully. Her voice quivered as she responded, 'Mother!'

Mortified, I stumbled backward.

"Lis ran to her mother, wrapping her arms around her and speaking a tribal dialect. They seemed to argue, and the older women looked at me. She bowed and spoke in Song. 'Thank you for saving my daughter!' I bowed and was about to speak when she turned, grabbed Lis's arm, and dragged her down the trail.

"Reality returned. I wasn't from this country and was unaware of the local customs and protocols. I didn't care and motioned for Son Jun-ho to come, and we followed Lis. Her mother kept looking back and would walk faster each time. Lis walked forward, never turning. An hour later, we arrived at a minor road where the forest ended, and the river flooded the earth. Rice was planted in remarkable terraced rows that climbed the mountain to its highest point. We continued to a small village of bamboo huts where chickens and pigs roamed freely. The women villagers brightly dressed in heavily beaded blue dresses and men in blue shirts stopped what they were doing and stared.

"Son Jun-ho whispered, 'It's a Miao village.'

"We followed Lis and her mother until they stopped at a hut surrounded by a bamboo fence. Every few feet, the fence included a wooden stake topped with colorful cloth strips, now faded, that whirled in the soft breeze. Lis and her mother walked through two prominent posts decorated with animal skulls, leading to the hut. Son Jun-ho let out a loud moan. I turned and gave him a rude look. Lis looked back and smiled as her mother pulled her inside the hut; I got the notion she wanted me to follow. Son Jun-ho and I tied the horses to the fence and entered the grounds, each of us wondering what to do next. We could hear Lis's mother's angry voice from within. Nervously, we sat at the outside table and waited.

"Son Jun-ho spoke first as I was staring at the door. 'Do you think this is a good idea? I'm scared not only of that woman but your mother. She's not going to be happy. I am with you because of her orders. Don't you think we should go back to Ningbo? The general will be waiting for you. You have your duties to your country and your family.'

"I wasn't paying any attention; my focus was on Lis. Son Jun-ho sighed heavily. It wasn't the first time I had ignored him.

"Son Jun-ho continued, 'You know nothing about this girl. She knows nothing about you, even what country you are from and that you are royalty.'

"I turned to him and, with a straight face, answered. 'She knows my name and that I love her. And I know she loves me.'

"Son Jun-ho answered in an anguished voice. 'Now, I know you are bewitched. You're not talking sense at all.'

"'Jun-ho, just stop talking,' I commanded.

"'No! What are you going to tell your mother?'

"'I'll worry about that when the time comes!' I replied confidently."

Lis stepped in. "I'll tell you about this part. Inside, my mother and I faced each other like two fighting cocks. It was the first time I was going against my mother.

"'Who is this man who has stolen my daughter's heart?' my mother bellowed. 'He's not dressed Mongol, Song, or tribal. Where does he live? What does he do? Does he know what you are?'

"My answer was short. 'We have bewitched each other. How often does that happen? Our union will be special. All the other details are pointless.' My mother looked at me in disbelief. 'Nonsense. Have you forgotten how important you are to our people?'

"'Mother, it will be OK!' I answered, self-assured."

"'No, it won't be. He is from a different world. He looks rich. What will his parents think?' cried my mother.

"'It will be okay, trust me!' I said again confidently."

"'OK, I will see. He must leave now, and if he returns in six moons, I will consider it.'

Kim Chin-hae took over speaking. "The door opened. Lis's mother, Wei, walked out. Her face was stern, and even though her body was tiny, her presence was bigger than life. Son Jun-ho and I rose. He backed up, bowing and walking backward to the horses, saying. 'Come, Master Kim. She is going to put a curse on you, come!'

"I stood firm. Wei came one foot from my face. 'My daughter says she loves you, and you love her!'

"'Yes, that's true.'

"'If that is true, your feelings won't pass. Come back in six moons!' Wei said forcefully.

"I backed up. I wanted to say no, but I wasn't sure what to do. Was this her way of accepting me or a trick to get rid of me? I saw Lis from the corner of my eye, and her face was expressionless. Bowing low, I walked to my horse and mounted.

"That's when I heard Lis's voice. 'Wait!' She ran toward me. Her mother tried to stop her, but Lis outmaneuvered her. 'Six moons aren't that long; I'll be waiting for you!' she cried.

"'My life isn't that simple,' I said. 'My country owns me.'

"I could see the disappointment in her eyes; my heart ached. 'I will be back! It could be longer than six months, but I will be back! Watch for me in your dreams!'

"I bent and kissed her forehead. With tears streaming, Lis reached for my hand and held it as long as she could as I sped up my horse. I rode to the crossroads and stopped, looking back, with eyes clouded with tears. I could see her in the middle of the road. Son Jun-ho demanding. 'Master, let's go, don't stop!'

"Deeply sighing, my shoulders scrunched as I placed my hand over my pounding heart. It felt like someone was tearing it out.

"In desperation, I turned my horse around. My legs tightened around the horse's stomach, and I dug in my heels. My horse neighed and burst into a full gallop. I slowed as I approached Lis. I slid off with my horse still in motion. My eyes never left hers."

Lis interrupted. "He enveloped my body with his muscular arms, held me close, and romantically said, 'The sun won't rise if you are not by my side. I can't leave you like this.' He released me, grabbed my hand, and we walked back side by side in unison. Son Jun-ho followed behind, shaking his head in disbelief. And as we approached my home, my mother sadly watched. Chin-hae and I entered the gate and walked straight into the house. My mother followed with her head down."

Then Kim Chin-hae took over. "I was not prepared when I entered Lis's home. Never having been in a shaman's dwelling, I understood Son Jun-ho's and Lis's mother's objections just for a moment. Our two lives were two worlds apart. But as I gazed upon her face, my bewitchment returned; I didn't care. I would make it work somehow. I fell to my knees and bowed low to Lis's mother as she entered. This probably was not their custom for forgiveness or acceptance, but I knew no other.

"Neither Lis nor her mother could believe their eyes. Lis approached me and fell to the ground in the same position. Her mother walked to us, touching our shoulders. 'I accept you, but I fear this union will bring you to your knees many times. I hope your love is strong enough to endure, especially for my daughter's sake.'

"That evening, we sat around the fire with Lis leaning against me. I tried to erase Lis's mother's last statement about our union. *Would it bring us to our knees?* Guilt monopolized my thoughts. *Lis knows nothing about me. Am I being fair to her? I would only be at her side sometimes, maybe much later. Did she understand this? Did she know the probability of my mother accepting her was null? Or if I would survive the upcoming invasion.*

Lis spoke up. "I could feel his tension. I surprised him when I said, 'Please settle your head. I understand.'

"Chin-hae questioned me. 'Do you? You don't even know who I am.'

"'Isn't it too late to worry about that? If you think it will make you feel better, please tell me. However, I would prefer tomorrow. Tonight, I want your arms around me and be absorbed in your love.'"

Kim Chin-hae spoke. "After I heard your words, I closed the door to guilt. Do you know how hard that was? Only you could make me."

Lis smiled. "He tightened his arms around me, and we slowly fell asleep."

Kim Chin-hae butted in. "In the night's quietness, I woke up and only heard and felt Lis's rhythmical breathing. The moonlight crept through the cracks in the bamboo walls, illuminating the smoke-filled room and its dirt floor. My eyes roamed the room. In one corner was a shrine decorated with animal skulls. A weird smell of dried herbs, corn, and meats that swung from the rafters penetrated the room. Large and small jars, wooden bowls filled with fungi, dried reptiles, and stone mortar and pestles were placed around the room on tables. My guilt returned. *Would Lis survive our differences or understand what it means for our lives?* I would never release her unless she wanted to be. Even then, I didn't know if it would be possible. When I fell to my knees, I sealed my commitment to love Lis and change my life forever."

Lis touched Kim Chin-hae's hand; she had something to say. "As I lay next to him, I could feel his thoughts. I understood, as I had fears, too. I would always be by his side, but not in the way he envisioned it. Sometimes, we would be in two worlds, with only our hearts entwined, with dreams and thoughts. I had my duties, and he had his. I hoped our two worlds would someday collide, creating a singular universe. Chin-hae held me tighter; He knew I had heard him. We both took a deep breath, released it slowly, and drifted off to sleep."

Lis continued, "As the sun rose, I unwrapped his arms and slid free. I carefully dressed, wanting to look beautiful. Then, I prepared food to go, as I planned to take him to my favorite place, high in the mountains that would plateau into a field of wildflowers. From there, a trail leads to a sacred cave that only shamans know. Maybe he would then understand my importance."

Kim Chin-hae took over. "I awoke alarmed by the emptiness of my arms and house. Jumping up, I went outside. Lis looked up when I opened the door and spoke. 'It's about time. We have a long day ahead of us.'

"'Are we going somewhere?' I asked as I looked at my saddled horse. 'Where are Son Jun-ho and your mother?' Lis laughed. 'I think they are somewhere conspiring against us.' I joined her laughter."

Lis continued. "The morning was perfect; the air was crisp, the sun shone brightly, and everything around me seemed happy and content. I packed our lunch in the small, woven boxes and tied them to Chin-hae's saddle. I was ready. He lifted me onto his horse and jumped on the back, putting his arms around me as I wrapped my arms around his. We rode through the village, ignoring the loud chatter and intense stares. I directed Chin-hae to a faded trail that ran through a dried rice field, leading us toward the forested mountain. We were silent until we entered the thick, dark forest. His deep, smooth voice rang out. 'Alone at last.' I giggled, and he tightened his grip. He started talking as we climbed the mountain.

"'Say nothing until I'm finished. OK? I'm a—'

"I interrupted him. 'I know you aren't from here because when you and Son Jun-ho are together, you speak a language I don't understand.'

"Chin-hae laughed at me and said, 'I see you don't take orders well. Please listen! I am a general in the Goryeo Navy.'

"'Goryeo?' I questioned him. 'He told me he was from a small country that lay toward the rising sun, and like mine, his was a conquered country controlled by the Great Khan.'

"'My cousin is the king of that country and is married to Kubilai Khan's daughter. Soon, the Khan will invade a country named Wa. They sent me here for soldiers and ships.'

"'Stop, what? Who are you?' I asked, alarmed. Chin-hae hesitated, I guess, to think about what to say. Before he could continue, I told him. 'It seems we both have mountains to climb.' He hugged me hard and agreed. 'We will climb them. We won't give up, right?'

"'Never!' I cried.

"Ahead, as the tree tunnel ended, a massive amount of sunlight opened to a sea of wildflowers sweeping over the land like a wave. I whispered, 'We are almost there, a place I love!' Before Chin-hae could halt his horse, I slid off and hit the ground running.'

Kim Chin-hae interrupted Lis. "With her hands in the air, she swirled and danced among the wildflowers. I watched her transform—with her blue skirt and blue top embossed with colorful beads—into a flower blowing in the wind under the canopy of heaven. It was the first time in my life that I stopped thinking about myself and my dream. *From now on, she would be first.* I jumped from my horse and ran after her. We tumbled to the ground laughing and stared into the vast blue sky. I sat up on my elbow and looked upon her face. With her dainty fingers, she touched my face, first my eyes, then my cheeks, and last my lips. I leaned into her, and my lips touched hers. *This is heaven*, I thought. Suddenly, she pushed me over and rolled on top of me."

Embarrassed, Lis placed her hand over Kim Chin-hae's mouth. "Shhhhhhhhh."

Kim Chin-hae smiled at Lis and continued. "She held my arms to the ground and kissed me. I opened my eyes, whispering. 'I surrender; do as you wish!'

"Lis, in full laughter, was ambushed when I flipped her and rolled on top of her, holding her hands to the ground. I kissed her. She smiled, 'I also surrender! Do as you wish!'

"I told her, 'I wish to marry you!' Lis's face became serious. 'Now?' she said.

"Releasing her hands, I rolled on my side, propping up on my elbow. Lis did the same. As we faced each other, our personas changed. Our playfulness disappeared. Lis spoke first. 'Are you willing to go against your parents? Your parents will never accept me. Are you willing to accept that and that I will never be a normal wife because of who I am?'

"I stared at Lis and said, 'My parents and I have never agreed on my future. The first day our fate intertwined, I accepted the consequences and sealed it when I fell to my knees. Didn't you? That was the first time in my life that I wanted someone more than my dream. We can fulfill our destinies together, maybe sometimes separately. And if the Heavenly Gods see fit someday, they will allow us to blend our destinies and soar forward together. Now is the time to join hands and promise one another that we will always be on each other's side, no matter which road destiny takes us.'"

Lis smiled at Kim Chin-hae and then at Marco. "I told him, 'I will always be by your side, whether you are physically with me. I love you.' I reminded him I was a shaman with the power to see him. So, he better be by my side always! Or I would curse him!"

Kim Chin-hae halfway laughed; then, fearing Lis, he said, "I believed you then and now. I will always be by your side, I promise."

Their faces were humorless as they thought about what happened next:

Chin-hae rolled onto his back and pulled Lis onto his chest. Lis rested her head on his chest. He looked up to the heavens. Lis raised her head and slowly pulled her body until her face faced his. They kissed until everything blurred, and they disappeared into each other.

Kim Chin-Hae finally spoke. "I feared God would punish me; my heaven was her."

Lis squeezed Kim Chin-hae's hand harder and continued. "For a while, we just lay there in each other's arms until I spoke. 'We have one more place to go—*the most important.*' I stood up and held out my hand."

Kim Chin-hae recalled the following scene: *Reluctantly, I took Lis's hand and playfully pulled her back down. I wanted to feel my heaven again. She struggled with strong determination, and I laughed, letting her escape.*

Lis left out that part as she continued. "‘ I started running fast toward the mountains, leaving him behind, yelling ‘Come Kim Chin-hae."

Kim Chin-hae cut in. "I jumped up, slung myself onto my horse, and raced after her. Lis looked back, turning, as she outstretched her arm. I did the same. We double-gripped each other's arms, and I slung her onto the horse behind me. I maintained a fast speed as we approached the jagged cliffs of the mountain. I started slowing. She heeled the horse. I yelled, ‘What are you doing? Trying to kill us?'

"‘Go! Don't you trust me?' she whispered.

"I dropped the reins and closed my eyes. Fear heightened my senses. Intense darkness and cool, moist air mixed with a strange smell slapped me in the face. *What has just happened?* Lis picked up the reins and brought my horse to a stop. I opened my eyes to darkness. Lis dismounted. I heard a clicking sound, as if two stones were being struck together. In a few moments, there was light, and I could see Lis walking around, lighting piles of wood and straw in large stone bowls scattered throughout the darkness. I nervously laughed. ‘We are in a cave. I'm not dead. What is this place?' I asked with a quivering voice as I slid from my horse.

"Lis walked over to me and threw her arms around me. ‘You trusted me; this was your final test. We can get married now.' I looked at her. ‘A test! What would have happened if my heart stopped beating and I died from fright?'"

Lis interrupted. "I told him while we both seriously looked at each other, ‘I would say you failed the test.' Kim Chin-hae, somewhat disappointed, continued with a nervous giggle and asked, ‘So where are we?'

"‘This is my ancestral sacred cave, where we perform our most powerful rituals. Most importantly, it's our burial grounds. All my grandmothers who possessed shaman's powers are buried here. I will be buried here, and our children who are blessed with powers.'"

Kim Chin-hae remembered his face turning red; he hadn't thought of that.

Lis continued. "I followed his eyes as he scanned the surroundings. He stopped when he saw a large, flat, raised rock in the center of the stone room. ‘That's for animal sacrifices,' I remarked. He gulped and continued to scan the room. Along the sides of the cave were cut steps that led to a top-level, which housed human-size rock encasements with colorful fabric laid over each one. ‘Those are my ancestors.' I whispered. I grabbed his hand and climbed the stairs."

Lis hesitated and let Kim Chin-hae continue. "The cave's air was stale but alive with a life force; my body tingled as goosebumps covered my body. I could feel a rush of wind around my body. Shivering, Lis put her arms around me and tightly held me. She whispered, ‘Trust me.'

At each encasement, Lis bowed low and introduced me to each one. Out of respect, I bowed. She told me, 'We buried them with their drums. I haven't received mine yet.'

"When Lis finished introducing each one, we returned to the cave floor. I was relieved; I imagined meeting one of her angry and disappointed ancestors. Then she told me. 'We have one more place to go.' I lowered my head and thought, *Now what*? I couldn't take much more. I have experienced fear many times, but this was a different kind; my enemies, I could see.

"Lis took a torch and walked through a small opening in the cave wall. It opened into a small room with rows of carved cavities. In each niche, there were square-shaped ceramic boxes, some with ribbons and some without. An old wooden table sat in the room with mortars and pestles. Lis reached into her intricately embroidered bag that hung over her neck. She pulled out a small knife, a tiny glass vial, silk thread, and ribbons. She walked over to me and, in a sweet voice, said, 'I need a lock of your beautiful black hair, OK?' Before I could answer, she lifted my hair, exposing the soft underneath, slashed a 6-inch strand, and tied a silk thread around it. She then cut a piece of her hair and did the same with silk thread. And in her bossy voice, she ordered me to hold out my hand. 'Why?' I skeptically asked. 'Please, I need your blood,' she said firmly. I slowly held out my hand palm-up, and she quickly made a small incision and tilted my bleeding hand so the blood dripped into the small vial. She removed a soft cloth from her skirt and gently blotted the remaining blood. Holding out her hand over the same vial, she slit hers. I could have sworn the blood boiled as her blood dripped into mine. But in the dim light, I wasn't sure, except I was sure Lis was thrilled. Wiping the blood from her hand, she turned her attention to the bundles of hair and the blood vial, placing both in a ceramic box and tying it shut with a blue silk ribbon. She then returned the box to its cavity."

Lis smiled at Marco and, in a mysterious voice, said. "Now I can find him wherever he goes." Kim Chin-hae and Marco didn't understand what she meant at the time, but they would much later. Lis didn't give them time to ask questions, and she continued the story.

"I walked to the corner of the small cave room, pointed to a ceramic jar on a large rock, and told him, 'That's why I was in the cage. That's Gold Silkworm, Gu, a poison we, Miao, are known for. They said I used it to manipulate a jilted woman's lover. I did not. I was in the city buying supplies for my mother.' I looked at Chin-hae, trying to read his face. *Did he believe me?* I left the cave room before he said anything. We needed to go before dark."

Lis hesitated. Kim Chin-hae continued. "I helped her on my horse and mounted behind. I whispered, 'I believe you.' I could feel Lis's excitement. As we exited the cave and rode some distance, I looked back. *Where is the opening?* I thought. Lis read my mind and answered. 'It doesn't matter the season or time of day; a shadow is cast upon the entrance, creating the illusion of solidness. If someone stumbles across the opening, the stakes with animal skulls and strips of colorful material at the door show it belongs to a shaman. They would be a fool to enter.'"

Kim Chin-hae recalled wrapping his arms around Lis's waist. *Her stomach was rumbling. Lis and I laughed. We needed to eat. Lis opened her food baskets as we rode home, and we devoured her simple food in peaceful bliss.*

Kim Chin-hae continued. "When we returned to the village, the sun was setting. Lis slid from the horse, met her mother, and entered the house. I followed, but Son Jun-ho stopped me. 'We need to talk. Our time is running out. Don't you think we should return to duty?'

"'NO!' I answered.

"'OK, then. Shall I tell you what I have been doing today?' He said."

"'Sure,' I said as I unsaddled my horse.

"'Preparing for your wedding! You really will marry without telling your mother and father?'

"I turned to him. 'Preparing? How did Lis's mother know I would pass the test?'

"'Test? I know nothing about a test, but I have been building a bamboo house with two family friends all day.' Son Jun-ho replied.

"'House?' I was startled.

"'I assume Lis never mentioned the marriage ritual?' he stated. 'It seems you need a house. Additionally, I understand that we will likely bypass some rituals since you don't have any family members here. However, Lis's mother has appointed me to participate in some necessary rituals.'

"I stared at Son Jun-ho and laughingly spoke. 'Well, I guess you should take me to my house!' I picked up my horse's reins, motioning Son Jun-ho forward. With a disgruntled face, he said, 'Follow me.' We walked to the end of the dirt road and turned left. Son Jun-ho pointed to a newly constructed bamboo cottage on stilts overlooking the river.

"'Lis's mom told me this was Lis's favorite spot. Apparently, this house is yours. It's not completed. Tomorrow, your new friends will come back,' he said sarcastically.

"'New friends?'

"I wasn't prepared for this. We followed a well-defined trail lined with dark red wildflowers. Reaching the cottage, I walked up the primitive steps. My new home was empty except for small tables, candles, stools, and beautiful silk covers folded in the corner.

"Son Jun-ho began talking as he walked across the room and sat at the small table. 'All day, they drilled me about the wedding and what we will do.' Son Jun-ho motioned for me to join him. On the table sat a container of rice wine and two cups. He poured us a drink and started talking. 'Your mother will never forgive you or me for letting this happen.'

"'She will never know until the time is right. Lis understands this. Let's not talk about my mother.' My face turned from fearful to smiling. 'Now, tell me what I need to do.' You could tell from his face that he thought I was crazy and bewitched! He poured himself another drink and explained the next steps."

Lis interrupted Kim Chin-hae. "Back at my mother's hut, we discussed the upcoming marriage. She expressed again that marriages outside the clothing color, language, or dialect were uncommon and could be difficult. I didn't care. I wasn't an ordinary girl, and villagers knew this. I only participated in mass courting ten years ago during the holidays. All the girls from the host village would gather to sing antiphonal love songs with young men from neighboring villages. If they found love, they exchanged love tokens. I found it embarrassing. Most of the boys feared me. In my culture, I am well over the courting age, but I always knew that the right man would come into my life. It finally happened. 'Do you think the villagers would have the nerve to say anything?' I told my mother. She answered, 'I'm not worried about them, but you. If you do this and something happens to him, you will not have a clan to worship you when you die.'

"'Did you worry about that? We belong to our own clan, Mother, you know that. I will worship you, and my children will worship me.'

"With tears in her eyes, my mother said. 'I wanted you to have more!'

"'Mother, he loves and trusts me, and will always be on my side. That's what counts. He understands my duties to our village, and I understand his duty to his country. We will see each other when we can! This is what I want!' I firmly replied.

"Still with tears, my mother agreed, but said firmly, 'The moon's darkness has begun. You will wait until the new crescent moon graces us with her beauty, symbolizing new beginnings. When the moon grows, so will your happiness. The coming weeks will be yours and his time to go inward, say goodbye to old ways, thoughts, and emotional pains, and clear your mind to allow new love and dreams to enter.'

"'Yes, we will have our courtship.' I said confidently.

"My mother, with satisfied eyes, said, 'Let's prepare. I already talked to his servant about our customs.'"

Kim Chin-hae stared at Lis. He had never heard this before.

Lis smiled and continued her story. "That day, I opened an old wooden chest. Inside was my mother's ceremonial wedding dress and hairpiece. I had waited a long time for this. I delicately removed the royal blue blouse and a matching blue ankle-length skirt. Down the middle of the skirt, a ten-inch wide red apron embroidered with beautiful flowers hung to the ground. Then, on top of that apron, a four-inch, deeper red, embroidered strip also fell to the ankles. The same embroidery circled the skirt. On the other side of the wooden chest was a large, ornate silver-beaded necklace that would consume the wearer's chest and a large, weaved silver crown with delicate silver flowers protruding upward, frozen in time. Beautiful, looped silver earrings that her father had given her were carefully wrapped in silk, along with silver bangles and two double silver rings. I placed one onto my finger."

Kim Chin-hae took over the story. "Meanwhile, Son Jun-ho explained to me the marriage wouldn't take place until the crescent moon began to grow, and I needed to come up with a bride price. Wei, Lis's mother, told him silver and animals were preferred. Son Jun-ho questioned me. 'Does she know who you are?'

"'Yes! We understand each other's lives.' I told him.

"'Kim Chin-hae, I mean her mother.'

"'I'm not sure if she will tell her. It will probably make her mother worry more.'

"I stood, went over to my bag, and pulled out pieces of gold. 'Do you think this will do? What's next?'

"'You will also need a love token, which should be delivered soon.'

"Without returning to my seat, I went through my bag. I pulled out a beautifully carved piece of white jade with blue silk tassels, my mother had given me. It's perfect. 'She can wear it around her waist. Let's go.'

"But before I could reach the door, someone knocked. I swung open the door, and Lis stood smiling at me. She waltzed in the door with a basket.

Lis took over the story. "I told him, 'Our courtship starts now. I have brought my love token. The moon changes quickly, and our wedding approaches fast.'

"Son Jun-ho, smiling, stood and bowed to me. 'It's time for me to leave! I will see you tomorrow.

"His face reflected mischief. Son Jun-ho didn't explain that our courtship began with exchanging our love tokens and perhaps making love."

Kim Chin-hae wasn't listening to Lis, thinking about what had happened that night.

My heart pounded with excitement when I saw Lis at the door. She entered, put down her basket, looked around the room, and smiled. She waltzed over to me and grabbed my hand. "Come, I will take you to another favorite place." With the other hand, she grabbed a lantern and some blankets and started for the river. I saw Son Jun-ho in front of us, turning and smiling. He must have known what was going to happen.

When she reached the river, she put down the lantern, illuminating clouds of steam that rose from a pool surrounded by large, flat rocks. Lis released my hand, dropped the blankets onto the flat stones, and started walking toward the water, undressing. Stunned, I closed my eyes. Lis turned around laughing and said, "Come, I told you our courtship started." I still couldn't move. Lis walked back, looking up at me, caressing my face with her eyes. She started undressing me, and I finished what she started. We walked hand in hand into the warm water. She whispered, "A warm water spring feeds this pool." I wasn't listening; lost in thoughts of her. The water could have been freezing. It didn't matter; my body was on fire. As the water deepened, Lis could hardly touch the bottom. She turned and wrapped her slender legs around me. As our two fiery bodies collided, we extinguished our passionate fire together. Our bodies softened, and we held each other tight as we looked up at the tiny sliver of the moon.

Lis quietly spoke. "This moon favors endings. We will close the door to our past and will no longer hold on to things or people we no longer need. We will close the door to bad luck and open the door to good fortune. This is the end of our old selves. And as the days pass and the waxing crescent moon rises, we will stand together as one, a powerful force to reckon with." I carried Lis to shore. I picked up the blanket and draped it over her shoulders as I wrapped my arms around her. Looking into her eyes with a soft, seductive voice, I whispered, "My heart is you; my love is you." Lis's eyes filled with tears; she never dreamed she would be so blessed in her lifetime. We sat on the bank of the river, intertwined in each other's arms until our passion again took over our bodies. Time passed quickly, and the moon had begun to set. We picked up our clothes and the lanterns and slowly made our way back to our cottage.

Lis, touching his hand, brought Kim Chin-hae back to the present. Marco and Lis were looking at him. Lis smiled. The embarrassed Kim Chin-hae joined the conservation. "Did Lis tell you about our love tokens?"

Lis answered instead of Marco. "No." Lis turned to Marco, "Chin-hae gave me a small wooden box, and inside was the beautifully carved white jade pendant of two cranes and a waterfall carved within the mountain surrounded by clouds. He told me--" Kim Chin-hae spoke up before Lis could finish. "In my country, the cranes represent a long marriage, happiness, and eternal life, as well as mountains whose appearance and shape never change and can withstand the weight of time. The water is the symbol of life, and clouds, harmony."

Lis smiled and continued, "I gave him a double silver ring with open ends belonging to my father." Then Kim Chin-hae opened his shirt and pulled out a soul lock. "She also gave me this unusual padlock-shaped silver pendant."

Marco observed it. It was two inches wide and four inches in length, with hammered designs of flowers and geometric shapes. Large, looped silver rings that resembled snails with their heads together sat on top, one on the left and one on the right.

"When she placed the piece around my neck, she said, 'This is a talisman, a soul lock. Never take it off; it protects and locks in your souls in case of illness, accident, or spiritual distress.'

"Souls?" Marco asked.

"Yes, we believe that humans have several souls. Chin-hae has beautiful ones; I want him to always return to me whole."

Kim Chin-hae smiled and pulled her close. He continued. "I presented Lis's mother with numerous animals and gold. I finished our house with a fancy, outside cooking area while waiting for our wedding day. My effort overwhelmed Lis's mother; she liked me despite her desire to hate me. I finally won her over; she understood why her daughter loved me.

"Every night, we walked to our favorite spot—the warm water pond—and revisited our first night together. We watched the moon phases change, bringing us closer to our marriage day. Two days before our wedding day, I walked alone to the pond. Sadness surrounded me. I was in conflict; I wanted to marry her with all my heart, but I hated that our marriage meant my departure was also approaching. I would have to leave her."

Lis took over. "I could always feel his moods. I stopped what I was doing and followed Chin-hae's thoughts to the pond. I sat beside him. 'We agreed to follow our dreams and destiny. I do not want to be responsible for you not following them.'

"'But they have changed,' he told me, 'I only want you!'

"'You know you will become restless and resent me,' I answered.

"I slid my hand into his. 'We are committing to help each other discover the fullness of our being.' His grip on my hand tightened. I changed the subject. 'Have you written your love song? You know you must sing to me.'

"Chin-hae's mood became lighter, and said, 'You know I can sing!'

"I laughed. 'But I can't.' He laughed. His mood had changed. I grabbed his hand and pulled him to his feet. 'Come on and help me. I am making rice cakes. We make special ones for the wedding.'"

Marco thought to himself, *Will I ever find this kind of love?*

Kim Chin-hae continued the story. "Our wedding day finally came. In the field of wildflowers that covered the grounds of our new home, we stood in front of Wei—Lis in her mother's wedding dress and I in my Goryeo silk clothing. Lis's mother, with her red mask and drum, chanted as the entire village silently listened. Wei went silent for a few minutes, staring at us. Then, with Wei's powerful voice, the ceremony began.

"'Before me are two people from two different worlds. They wish to marry. Their journey won't be an easy one. But their relationship is genuinely and deeply karmic. They found each other when it should not have been possible. You are soulmates, but Lis and Kim

Chin-hae, please remember that a soulmate is not a person like you, but rather the other half of you, who will help you become a whole person. You must trust one another and practice genuine gratitude for each other. Show your underbelly without fear of showing your scars and sorrows. You must also embrace each other's differences. Lis and Kim Chin-hae, you must acknowledge, respect, and contribute to each other's power without feeling threatened. Love unconditionally by honoring each other. Accept each other even though you come from two different worlds. Respect each other's voices and learn to listen to each other's advice without fear of offending or being offended. Support each other's vision of your journey in the world. And most of all, love each other deeply. Then your love will thrive in the most challenging times, and your relationship will evolve.'

"As Lis listened to me repeat our vows, she smiled at me and whispered. 'I am so happy I am bewitched. My heaven is knowing only my reflection is in your eyes."

Kim Chin-hae squeezed her hand harder and continued. "Lis's mother started chanting one more time, and then said, 'I hope my daughter will be happy. Long periods of separation will scar this relationship; be strong.'"

Kim Chin-hae and Lis looked at Marco. "We have been strong. The future will be harder." He continued. "When Wei's chanting finished, Son Jun-ho handed Lis and me special cups filled with Jiaobei spirits. We crossed our wrists and drank the wine. Then, he served us special glutinous rice cakes decorated with dragons, phoenixes, and Feng dolls. Lis's mother chanted one more time. After the chant, she stared at us. Her solemn voice echoed. 'The beginning of your wholeness has begun.'

"The crowd clapped and cheered. We held each other close, and the party began—singing, dancing, eating, and drinking. But it wasn't long before I interrupted the party and said, 'I am told in your tribe that couples sing love songs to each other during courtship. Our courtship was not typical.' Everyone laughed. 'Over the past weeks, I have written a song.'

"I held Lis's hand shyly and looked at her. I began singing a simple tune and words.

'You are my heart,
When you walked into my world.
I call you my miracle.
You are my breath,
I want only to remember you,
Only feel you, treasure you.
Stay close to you.
You are my heaven in my eyes.

Heaven is in your voice.
As it sings the truth.

Your kiss is my heaven.
Even though tears fall.
In the vast world, you're the only one.
Your smile is heaven and the only smile under the sky.

All day, I dream
With deeply closed eyes
cry out your name.
I smile.
It's a day that everyone dreams of.
You are heaven in my heart and eyes.'"

Lis, with tears in her eyes, spoke. "His words penetrated my soul, his words became mine, and we sang in unison as we stared into each other's eyes."

Kim Chin-hae looked at Marco and said, "I knew then that she had powers beyond my understanding, as I had never shared my song with anyone."

"The evening was late, and the moon was setting before we walked the path to our house. It would be the first night Lis slept in my bed."

Lis's face turned red.

"Two days passed after our wedding." Kim Chin-hae continued. "Son Jun-ho scurried around the cottage, packing. The day had arrived for me to return to my old life. Lis and I stood facing the pond. Lis held her jade pendant over her heart. I pulled out my amulet. I promised I would always wear it. We were afraid to look at each other. She reached for my hand, lifted it to her lips, and slowly kissed it. I wrapped my arms around her. Our eyes never met. I walked back to our cottage and immediately mounted my horse. I looked down, and our eyes finally met. We both had decided we would be strong; There would be no tears. We were going to test our marriage vows.

"'I'll be back,' I whispered. And Lis said, 'I'll wait.'

"I spurred my horse and galloped away, never looking back."

Lis took over the story. "I stood, watched for a few minutes, and walked to our house. I tried to be strong. Remembering our vows, I had to be strong and continue my life as before I met him. But his leaving broke my heart. I lay on our bed, and his scent penetrated the blankets, and I cried. The next day, as the sun rose, I rose to my old self. There would be no more tears.

My daily life returned quickly. The neighboring villagers wandered into the village, looking for remedies for healing and spells. Sometimes, I would stop what I was doing, feeling Kim Chin hae's presence; I would smile."

Kim Chin-hae took over and looked over at Lis. "Son Jun-ho and I rode fast. I had been gone way too long. When I approached Fuzhou, where the cage stood, my heart ached. I rode faster and faster. With pounding hooves, dry earth, and billowing dust, I disappeared. When I finally slowed and emerged, thick red dust coated my face. Rivers of tears left valleys of sorrow as I left you behind."

Lis stared at Chin-hae; she remembered that day clearly and understood.

Kim Chi-hae continued. "Son Jun-ho finally convinced me to stop. He needed rest, and so did the horses. The second day, I was still unreasonable and spoke only when spoken to. Jun-ho understood that my life without Lis would be almost too much to bear. However, by the third day, I had become more reasonable. I started talking and convinced myself I would return quickly. We rode a 22-day journey in 16, trading for fresh horses in different towns. As I got closer, I panicked. *What am I going to tell the general?* The only story that finally seemed reasonable was that I fell ill in Zapton and was unable to ride. When we arrived in Ningbo, the distant and cold General Fan Wenhu's only concern was that my cousin, the king, had become restless and sent several messages for me to return with the report.' It devastated me; I never dreamed I would leave Yuan so soon. In two days, Son Jun-ho and I walked to our ship, passing under the stone gate constructed with four pillars with Song letters carved on the upper part, meaning safe sailing. While the townspeople blessed us, we boarded a ship for Goryeo. I prayed that this blessing would help; the monsoon season was expected to start in the last two weeks of sailing. I stayed too long with Lis. As the ship pulled away from shore, I clutched my chest."

Kim Chin-hae looked at Lis. "Leaving you felt like my heart was being ripped out."

Lis sweetly interrupted. "I felt the same. The moment you left this land, my heart felt it and cried."

Still looking at Lis, Kim said, "I stood on the ship's bow, watching everything and everyone become miniatures until they finally disappeared. I whispered, 'I will return.' I didn't know it would take so long. I'm sorry."

"You shouldn't be sorry. You returned, and just in time." Lis said as she squeezed Chin-hae's hand.

Kim Chin-hae continued his story. "I kept my mind busy with my report and refining my notes about the ships I had seen. Only late at night, my mind would shift to you. Even though I initially knew I would be forced to leave, I didn't realize how much it would hurt.

"The only saving grace was that the weather held, and I arrived in Masanhappo with little difficulty. As Son Jun-ho and I disembarked from the ship, the king's servant met me. I was relieved. This meant my cousin, King Chungnyeol, was in Masanhappo. During the entire trip, I feared that if I had to continue to the capital, I would no doubt face my father, mother, or Park Eun-ae. Lying was never my nature, but it wasn't time to tell them about our marriage.

"Relieved, I followed the servant. On the way to the king, I noticed my other men, whom I had left behind, waving. Their presence lifted my spirits. I nodded and continued. When I entered the king's chamber, my cousin smiled slightly, and I recognized the Mongol General Hong Dagu and Goryeo General Kim Bang-gyeong, who sat at a table to the king's right. Both men were familiar, having served under them in the first invasion.

"The king advised me that General Hong Dagu and General Kim Bang-gyeong would command the Wa Invasion from Masanhappo and that Supreme Commander General Arakhan, a Tumen[2] general, would command the entire operation from Yuan. I nodded. 'Yes, I heard that from General Fan Wenhu.'

"The king continued. 'We have been anxiously waiting for your arrival with your report.' Walking over to the king, I handed him the report. 'General Kim Chin-hae, please sit and tell us what you saw.'

"Confidently, I began, 'After observing Kubilai's ships, I found Goryeo's ships are the strongest, although small. 'Our fleet leaving from Goryeo has a much better chance of returning. Yuan's Fleet has thousands of ships, maybe around 2500, but most are river ships. The best ships were those belonging to the Song Dynasty, built in the South—the ones used for sea travel and cargo with a v-bottom—but there were not nearly enough. To build them would take way too long and be very expensive.'

"'Your solution, General Kim Chin-hae?' General Hong Dagu asked.

"'The only solution I see is redesigning and refitting the river and merchant ships. That will be the fastest and least expensive. But I am not sure if they will withstand the long journey over open ocean and bad weather. The Mongols' ships lack quality. I am worried about our men's safety.'

"Again, I was overwhelmingly disappointed when my cousin told me, 'That's not a worry now.'"

Kim Chin-hae turned from Lis and started talking to Marco. "General Kim Bang-gyeong wanted to know how many soldiers he could expect and if their condition was satisfactory. I relayed what General Fan Wenhu arrogantly told me. 'We have at least 100,000 soldiers plus sailors, including the soldiers from the defeated Song Dynasty, plus the northern soldiers.' However, General Fan Wenhu failed to mention that two-thirds of the soldiers were state farm soldiers, and all the soldiers' conditions were worn out and bitter; there had been too many wars.

"I continued. 'General Fan Wenhu is organizing the suppliers for the grain, horses, and weapons, and he informed me that Kubilai Khan's ships will carry all the supplies since their ships are more significant. My other concern is the distance between Goryeo and Yuan. How will we handle the lack of communication and the weather situation? Our timing will be of great importance while coordinating this vast campaign.'

"I sat in silence, waiting for my cousin, King Chungnyeol, to respond to these last issues, praying he would suggest I return to Yuan as his eyes and voice. That didn't happen. They all agreed that I did an impressive job. Then my cousin told me to rest and that we would talk later. I stood, disappointed; he didn't say what I wanted to hear.

"Before I exited his chamber, I turned back. My cousin was watching me. Knowing my cousin well, I'm sure he was thinking, *I desperately want to win this invasion; I put my reputation on the line when I encouraged Kubilai Khan to elect me as Minister of Jeongdong Haengseong. I could gain higher status and negotiating power if I accomplished this win. I must win for Goryeo. Were Chin-hae's assumptions correct?*

"Son Jun-ho and my men anxiously waited for me. Finally reunited, we walked back to the barracks. They talked all at once, asking questions about Ningbo and my trip through southern Yuan. My ears hurt, so I playfully told them to shut up and that I needed to rest and sleep in a steady bed. They laughed and left me as I entered my room. I collapsed, and the last thing I remembered was Son Jun-ho covering me.

"That night, Lis, you filled my dreams."

Lis smiled and thought, *I was with you.*

"I woke up refreshed; I had a newfound hope that I would be returning to you soon.

"That same morning, Pak Byeong-ho—the soldier who traveled to Dadu with me—entered my room while I dressed and told me the king had summoned me. My heart flip-flopped. Turning around, I exposed my spirit lock."

"'Why do you have a spirit lock?' he asked.

"Instinctively, I grabbed my lock with my left hand; I surprised him more. I had forgotten to take off my wedding ring.

"'Now I have two questions: spirit lock and ring?' Pak Byeong-ho stuttered.

"I changed the question around. 'How do you know about spirit locks?'

"'In Dadu, I wandered the backstreet alleys and came across an old store that seemed to call to me. They carried spiritual items, herbs, dried reptiles, and tea. It was eerie—like black magic—and shamans surrounded me.'

"Laughing, I told him, 'I understand.' Lis gave Kim Chin-hae a dirty look.

"Pak Byeong-ho continued his story. 'Inside, there were old women dressed in beaded blue dresses. They insisted I come in. As I entered, my whole body turned to chicken skin. But I couldn't leave. It seemed like someone or something had grasped onto me.' Pak Byeong-ho stopped and shivered momentarily, then continued, opening his shirt. 'Look, I have one.'

"I couldn't believe it. I laughed. 'I have a different story,' I said as I envisioned Lis dancing in the wildflowers in her blue beaded dress.'

'Someday, I will tell you when the time is right,' I said.

"He stared at me. 'But what about the ring?'

"I never answered and continued to dress. I slipped my ring in a hidden pocket next to my heart as I walked out the door. Later, I would hear his whole story."

As Lis sat and listened, her mind wandered to when Kim Chin-hae left her.

Every night, I would walk to the warm pond, enter, look at the moon, and think, 'It has been four moons since he left. As I cupped my hands and brought the warm water to my face, my bare body glistened in the moonlight. I placed my hands on my stomach; a new life had entered me. I smiled, but my heart ached. It had been so long since I felt his arms around me. Suddenly, I felt life. I caressed my body. The life within me was part of him. My heart warmed, and the ache subsided, as I felt his presence.

The next morning, the arrival of soldiers abruptly eliminated my happiness. A villager had run to alert us. My first thought was, "Why have they come? Are they looking for me? I thought the tigers killed the soldiers. But wait, these soldiers are counting the young male villagers. Why? What did this mean?" My mother wasted no time finding out. So, without fear, my mother, with her wild gray hair and eyes, stepped out the door dressed in shamanic attire and holding her drum in her hand. I desperately tried to stop her. "These soldiers have no love for shamans," I whispered. My mother stared at me. "Go to your husband's house. Someone might recognize you. That could be a problem. But for me, the Song's Emperor is no more. Their laws don't exist any longer."

As Mother entered the dirt road, she chanted and played her drum. The soldiers stopped counting and turned to her. The officer in charge was agitated. "How dare she confront us?" he thought. But the other men were unnerved. They had heard stories about evil shamans, their curses, the captain who had died of poison, and the soldiers who mysteriously disappeared. But their captain wasn't threatened. He had to show strength in front of his men; his dignity had to be upheld. He arrogantly rode his horse up to her. With her penetrating eyes, she looked directly into his horse's eyes. His horse stopped, backed up, and neighed. The officer, embarrassed, jumped off his horse and walked up to her. His soldiers watched, impressed by his courage. As he came closer and their eyes met, he felt fear; his legs wobbled, and he felt tremendous pressure on his shoulders as if someone was pushing him down. He no longer stood but fell to his knees. She walked to him and stood over him. He looked at her in disbelief, as did his men. She firmly spoke. "Leave and never come back. We need our men more than you do."

He tried to stand, but it was impossible until she released her eyes from his. She turned and walked toward her home.

He bounced to his feet, his face hosted outrage. He withdrew his sword and ran toward her.

I was hiding and watching. I tried to warn my mother, but the words wouldn't come out. My mother turned, lifted her arm, and pointed her long-crooked finger at him. The officer dropped his sword, his hand burning. He fell to the ground, yelling at his men, "Arrest her! She can't fight us all!" But his men were not sure of this. The other officer walked over to him.

"I hear Kubilai Khan favors shamans with his Mongol ways. I don't think this is the time. Maybe we can use her to our advantage, telling Kubilai Khan of her strength."

Agreeing but feeling degraded, the officer mounted his horse and rode out of our village with the other officer and his men, but not a single villager.

I followed my mother home, astonished by her power. I, however, found myself fearful. That man has become an enemy. My mother had destroyed his image.

My mother always used her power for healing. For the first time, I saw her genuine powers and now understood why significant people came to see her or why sometimes she would leave the village with them. But these thoughts left me as I felt the life within me. Something was different. I felt another soul. It differed from the one I had felt before. Unlike the daughter I knew I carried, it had a masculine force and boldness. My family only had females. Could it be that I am carrying two lives within me? One a boy? I wondered. I already questioned whether my daughter would be as powerful as my mother or more like me. Only time will tell. I smiled and thought, "How would Chin-hae handle having a child with powers? Now two, one a miracle—a son. Double threat!"

Kim Chin-hae patted Lis's hand and asked, "Lis, are you listening? I wanted you to hear this."

Chin-hae brought her back from the past. Lis nodded.

He continued, "When I returned to the palace and entered King Chungnyeol's chamber, it was just him, my cousin, not the king.

"'Sit, I'm happy to see you arrived safely. You pleased the generals and me with your report. You must return to Yuan.' My heart pounded. I tried not to show too much excitement. 'Yes, Your Majesty.'

"My cousin continued, 'We need eyes. Periodically, you can return to Goryeo with updates. If you decide to go, I will write a letter to Kubilai Khan. You must deliver it to him. Fortunately, you escorted me to Yuan, and he liked you. He gave his permission for your last trip, but this mission has greater importance. Hopefully, he will agree that you are beneficial in ensuring communications and are needed to achieve the timelines. The letter will specify my desire for you to work with General Fan Wenhu, assisting with provisions, ships, and any essential planning details. Kubilai must be the one to tell him. This way, you won't have problems with him. You are not under Fan Wenhu's command but mine and Kubilai Khan's. I will ask Kubilai Khan's permission to allow you to come and go as you please, gathering information you think will be important to me. It would be best if you continued to be in Kubilai's and Fan Wenhu's good grace.'

"But my cousin didn't know General Fan Wenhu already had growing animosity against me, and even I didn't understand why. I remained silent.

"My cousin continued, 'You understand?'

"'Yes, I am becoming your eyes and ears even more than I did on my last trip.'

"Kim Chin-hae looked into Lis's eyes. "Inside, I was ecstatic. I would be returning to you, Lis. Nothing else mattered."

Lis sweetly smiled. Kim Chin-hae continued.

"Then my cousin became serious. 'I have one more thing I would like to discuss with you. General Kim Bang-gyong and Hong Dagu suggested that you follow General Fan Wenhu to battle on his ship. They worry he will not stay on course. Your father and mother will be upset about this arrangement. But I need you. My father lost the last invasion, which became my loss. I must not lose this one. We must achieve victory. You know the dangers. You have said it yourself: the Goryeo fleet is stronger. I will give you time to think.'

"I didn't hesitate. 'I will go back to Yuan and fight beside General Fan Wenhu! After the victory, I will retire.'

"My swiftness surprised my cousin.

"'Your parents will be happy to hear about your retirement. For years, they hoped I could convince you to retire from the military and follow your father in politics.'

"Momentarily, I felt a tinge of guilt; he didn't know why I was retiring."

"I asked him not to mention anything to my parents; I didn't want to worry them. My cousin agreed, and with a sly smile, he continued. 'Now, you and men of your choice will escort me back to Koesang, the capital. You can visit your parents and any other special person you'd like to see. After that, you will return to Masanhappo to assist the generals with the shipbuilding schedule and any other details until the monsoon season ends. Then you will sail to Yuan.'

"I was barely listening; my mind couldn't stop thinking of you.

"My cousin interrupted my thoughts. 'Kim Chin-hae, Kim, are you listening to your king?' I was embarrassed. 'Ohhhh, I can return to Yuan when the monsoon season ends.'

"My cousin laughed. 'Your mind must have been on the special someone.'

"He was correct, but the special someone was wrong. Then reality struck: *How will I handle Park Eun-ae and my mother when I return home?*

"Quickly, I spoke up, 'I don't want to stay long in the capital. I should return immediately to work with the generals, studying their plans to understand their thoughts before I return to Yuan.' My cousin looked pleased; I'm sure he thought he had chosen the right person for the job.

"'We will leave for Koesang in two days. While there, I will write a letter to Kubilai Khan, and you can perform your son's filial duties,' my cousin said, smiling. 'Then you can return to Masanhappo, then Yuan.'

"Cowardly, I avoided everyone as much as possible while in Koesang. After a few days, my men, Son Jun-ho, and I returned quickly to Massanhappo. When the monsoon weather ended, I boarded a ship to Yuan and successfully delivered the letters to Kubilai Khan. I then traveled to Ningbo and handed my orders to General Fan Wenhu. Then I immediately left for you, Lis."

Kim Chin-hae looked at Marco. "I was returning to Lis when you saved me from the tigers."

---

1. What the Goryeo called china

2. A general who commands over 10,000 soldiers

Chapter Twenty-One

Marco

Marco and Rustichello

Genoa Prison 1298

Marco stopped talking and looked up at Rustichello. “I can still see Lis’s face. She was stunned; she never knew the circumstances of his return.

“After that night, I saw him in Yangzhou several months later. We met for drinks, and he told me about Lis and his babies. He was the typical proud father, bragging and such. After that time, we met numerous times, not only as business partners but as friends. I helped him with his upcoming invasion. The amount of food and supplies needed were outrageous. As the invasion became closer, his fear increased, and he returned to Lis, using the excuse that he was recruiting more men, finding suppliers, and watching over the alterations of the ships. He wasn’t lying about his fear. That night, he told me as he rode closer to her, his veil of fear and darkness lifted, and he was happy.’

Marco looked at Rustichello and said, “After meeting Kim Chin-hae and Lis, I dreamed that someday I would find what they had." Marco paused and sadly said, "I finally did but a persuasive request and a thoughtless and arrogant nod, 'yes,' led me here, where my future with Li is unknown."

Rustichello nodded as if to agree.

They sat quietly, and Rustichello was the first to speak up. “Let's sleep and continue your trip to Qaraiang tomorrow. The part where you proved your worth. Your father must have been furious.”

Marco smiled. “He deserved it.”

Marco lay in his bed, organizing his thoughts. *What would I say? How much would I tell the commander? Qaraiang was the center of Kubilai Khan's wealth, as well as ours, while we were there.* These thoughts only momentarily held his attention; he drifted to Li. He wondered if he would ever see her again. Tears rolled down his cheek. He consoled himself with the image of her. *She is so beautiful.* Then he wondered. *What is she doing?*

Chapter Twenty-Two

Li

The Medicine Bag

Venice 1298

Li sat at the window, smiling, and played her erhu, delighted that her playing infuriated Isabella. She played longer and louder than she intended. Before long, a loud banging on the door interrupted her. The doorknob rattled as Isabella screamed. Li's smile grew; she was happy she had locked the door. The banging stopped after a while. Li continued a little longer and louder. Finally, she set down the erhu, walked over to the door, and put her ear to it, listening. She could hear Isabella stomping down the hall. Smiling, she walked to her bed and fell across it, thinking of Marco. Sadness replaced her happiness. *Is he still alive?*

The following day, a gentle knock awakened her. Rising, she questioned who was there. *Could it be Isabella?* Guo Yu and Luca answered back. Relieved, Li happily opened the door. Guo Yu's face displayed worry, an image Li was accustomed to.

"I heard you last night. Must you torment her?"

"She deserves it."

Guo Yu opened his mouth to speak, but Li placed her small, delicate hand over it. "Let's have breakfast, and I will continue telling my story." Luca clapped as she rushed around the room, helping Guo Yu.

Li, eating, started her story. "We returned to the winter palace in August just in time to prepare for the Khan's birthday, the 12th of September—by far the year's largest celebration. The only other celebration compared to that was the White Festival. At the festival, I will most likely see Marco again. I could not think of anything else. The year before, his gift surprised me. This time, I wanted to surprise him and make it myself. My skills and knowledge of herbs were prolific, yet I had learned little about the skills of weaving or embroidery. After months of thinking, I finally had a plan. Luca, do you remember me telling you about his worn medicine bag at the Summer Palace?"

Luca nodded yes.

"I decided to make him a new one, showing him his words flowed through my heart and helped me daily. As I gathered, dried, and ground herbs into teas and salves, I repeatedly said, 'Be safe, come back. I love you.' I hoped every time he used them, his heart would hear my words, and he would not forget me." Li looked out the window. Tears slid down her face, and she thought, *Be safe, come back to me. I love you.*

She quickly wiped the tears and continued. "My grandmother had left me money for my marriage. But I needed it now. Guo Yu took me to the market, where I found beautiful, woven gold-thread bags with white silk ties. I instructed the merchant to stitch specific herb names on each bag along with a unique symbol: a tiger for courage, bravery, and strength; five bats for long life, riches, health, love of virtue, and natural death; a tortoise for immortality; a crane in a pine tree for power and wealth; a dragon for royalty; and the last one with two butterflies for love. On the other side of the bags, I had him stitch the herbs' use.

"I located ivory vessels for salves. Lastly, I found a beautiful, soft, white leather bag with a long strap so Marco could place it over his shoulder or hang it over his saddle. On the front, I instructed the merchant to stitch a golden-winged lion to ward off evil. But inside—always to be hidden—by his side, I was bold. I had the artist paint two golden carp swimming in a stream covered by lotus as two butterflies sipped nectar on dew-drenched peonies along the shore. When the artisan finished, he smiled. 'Your confession of love?' I smiled and shyly nodded."

Li shyly looked at Luca. "Two carp are for love. A lotus because the beautiful flower rises from the mud in exquisite beauty. It symbolizes the perfection and purity of both hearts and minds. Two butterflies sipping represents lovers tasting the joys of passion."

Li paused. "It would be many years before he saw this." Then she continued. "The bag was closed by a flap, held down by a beautiful, yellowish gold jade carved with the rabbit on the moon, which symbolized the markings of the elixir of life and herbal medicine.

"When I returned home, I prayed he would never need these as I carefully placed the herbs in their appropriate gold bags and the salves in the carved ivory vessels. Still praying, I put these items and small tincture-filled bottles, bandages, scissors, a small sharp knife, a needle and silk thread, and a leather case of acupuncture needles into his new leather medicine bag. Very proud, I wrapped it in gold silk, tied it with white silk ribbons, placed it in my gift basket, and waited for the White Festival to arrive. The day finally came, and a beautiful, wrapped box arrived again. Guo Yu smiled. My heart fluttered as I quickly opened his gift, finding a beautiful dress and a knife with an intricately carved handle, more significant than the one I had received the previous year. I feared he thought someday I would need these knives.

"Guo Yu's present was just what I needed: a beautiful pair of gold silk shoes." Li looked down at her feet. *My feet haven't grown since.* Guo Yu smiled at Li as she continued.

"I was lucky my mother never bound my feet, and the Tartar didn't practice this custom."

Luca interrupted Li. "What do you mean, bound?"

Li, looking at her feet, cringed. "It is a practice my people practiced. If the empress had not surrendered, eventually, my mother would have been forced to have my feet broken a little at a time and then tightly bound with cloth strips. It changes the shape and size of your feet. It is excruciating. They thought it was a status symbol and mark of feminine beauty."

Luca cringed along with Li. "I'm happy that didn't happen to you."

Li nodded. The horrible custom sent shivers down Li's back.

Li continued her story. "After slipping into my new dress, I admired myself in the mirror. Touching my face, I thought, *I look older, and the Gods have been kind to me. Marco has to notice I am pretty.* Guo Yu and Physician Wu were concerned. It was only a matter of time before jealousy in the royal court would erupt as the eyes of important men fell upon me. The other girls' mothers only wanted these eyes on their daughters, not someone who was no one. The inner chambers could be horror chambers if the wrong person decided you were a threat.

"Entering the royal court, I wasted no time looking for Marco. Immediately, I noticed hundreds of gazing eyes were upon me. Becoming self-conscious, I lowered my head and walked to my seat. As the evening progressed, I gained confidence, looked up, and started looking for Marco again. I found him engaged in a seemingly serious conversation with Kubilai. My imagination erupted. *What is so important?* Eventually, the guests started circulating the room with their gifts. This was my chance; I circled the large room twice, but Marco was nowhere in the crowd. My heart hurt. From that moment, time crawled, and I was devastated by the night's end. Returning to my chambers, I sat at my dressing table. Guo Yu interrupted my sadness with words I couldn't believe. 'Marco wants you to meet him at the royal herb garden tomorrow. You can take your gift.'

"That night, I was sleepless. *What does this mean? Why does he need to talk to me?* My imagination grew. *Is he leaving the palace for an extended time? Is that why Kubilai and he looked so serious earlier that evening?* Even though I only saw him a little throughout the year, I still caught glimpses of him and sometimes spoke to him. *Does this mean never now? Did Kubilai Khan dismiss him from the court? Marco looked so severe last night. Is he planning to live outside the palace? He could be injured, and I wouldn't be able to use my skills to heal him, or he could even be killed. Does he have a lover or a wife?* The thoughts devastated me.

"By morning, my despair had turned to anger. *Why do I have to be so young?* My worries and desires meant nothing; they were a young girl's fantasies. At birth, my life was already destined, and this could never be. But I didn't want to think of that.

"I pulled myself together and walked with dignity to the garden, carrying his gift. Marco greeted me with a smile and patted my head as if I were a little girl. My expression must have been obvious; he apologized. Marco was unaware of how deep my infatuation ran. I was happy about this but saddened at the same time. He thought of me as his ward, and I should have been grateful, as I needed as many people on my side as possible. But I yearned for more —something to look forward to, a dream that made my life more bearable. What he didn't know was that it was him. Holding back my tears, I smiled and handed him my gift, insisting he open it to see his expression. *He needs to know I have listened and how I have grown.* We sat on a side bench surrounded by healing plants and herbs—the only thing that made me truly happy, except Marco. He carefully opened his present. His facial expression said it all. With amazement, he opened the medicine bag, pulling out the contents one at a time. I showed him the back of each bag, explaining its use.

"'You are really beyond your age. I will always keep this by my side. Tomorrow, I am leaving on a mission and will be gone for a while.'

"'Where?'

"'To Champa.'[1]

"I thought for a moment. *I heard that name before while spying at the rundown hut in the forest.* Marco sweetly continued. 'Champa is a country many miles away. Kubilai Khan's armies are fighting with little success. My mission is to convince their king to surrender.'

"I must have looked sad; he quickly held my hand and reassured me not to worry with convincing words. 'I will return safely.' Shortly, Physician Wu approached us and motioned for me to leave. 'You have work to do.'

"Reluctantly, I stood, smiled, and ran away with tears. After Marco left the palace, I continued my ghost-like ways with Kokochin and Ijir Bukhqa. It was fun. Guo Yu warned me that someday, that fun could turn into danger. 'People could get the wrong idea; you are no longer children. You could hear or see something you shouldn't.' I promised him we were always careful. We roamed untraveled routes. With a sour face, Guo Yu said, 'So do the people with secrets.'

"One day, Guo Yu's words came true. I was on the way to meet my Society of Three on an untraveled route. Turning the corner, I heard people talking in a serious, low tone. Stopping, I listened as usual. Normally, it was simply court gossip. This time, what I heard scared me.

Pressing my shivering back against the wall, I held my breath and looked to see if anyone had seen me. Guo Yu had been right. What was I going to do?"

Luca gasped and interrupted. "What did you do?"

"I took a chance and backtracked slowly down the hall, then walked toward the gossiping people, humming loudly, hoping the people around the corner heard me. I prayed that no one else saw what I had done! Moments later, three people came around the corner, their heads down. I recognized them; two were court ladies of Crown Prince Chinghiz, Kubilai Khan's son, and the eunuch from Kubilai Khan's chambers. As we passed, they lifted their heads and slightly nodded. I smiled childishly, bowed, continued humming, and hurried down the hall. I finally reached the next hallway and fell to my knees as sweat beaded on my forehead. My heart was beating so fast I thought it would leap out of my chest. After I caught my breath, I rose and ran toward the Royal Physician's office. I forgot about Ijir Bukhqa and Kokochin.

Luca spoke up. "What secret did you hear?"

"It was about Kubilai Khan's son, Crown Prince Chinghiz—who was well respected in the empire—becoming the Khan. I couldn't hear everything, but they said some powerful court ministers wanted the aging Kubilai Khan to abdicate. The ministers had even confronted Crown Prince Chinghiz to take his father's place; now, he was terrified. If his father heard this, he would be furious, even though the crown prince had no intention to follow through. It seemed the court ladies were fishing for information from Kubilai Khan's eunuch. I also heard Marco's name mentioned. They were wishing he were in the palace. I now understand why Guo Yu warned me. The game we played could be dangerous. I was confused and frightened. *Is this true? Do they want Kubilai Khan to abdicate?*

"When I arrived at the Royal Physician's office, my face must have been white. Physician Wu instantly grabbed me by the sleeve, pulled me into his office, and shut the door. Quietly, he asked, 'What happened?' As I explained, his face appeared frightened. 'Forget what you heard and never repeat it, not even to your friends.'

"For the first time, I didn't question him. I understood. The next month, I stayed close to Guo Yu and Physician Wu, who had twice been summoned to Kubilai Khan's chamber. Since Chabi's death, he has become even more reclusive, despite marrying Empress Nambi. I heard he never was the same. As Marco said in the summer palace, his excessive drinking and eating were out of control. His health was failing, and he wasn't the only one. Crown Prince Chinghiz seemed to be in the same state as his father. Physician Wu told me that neither of them would talk to each other. It was sad to see father and son fear each other. Again, over power."

Li stopped talking and looked at Luca. "I am always talking about myself. I know nothing about you, Luca, or your family."

Luca solemnly answered. "You did once, but I did not answer you. My mother is a slave, so I am a slave. Our family was from Armenia many years ago. You asked me once if I had the chance to change my life, would I? I don't have your courage."

Li could see Luca's sadness and quickly changed the subject. "Let's go out today. Please bring my man clothes."

Guo Yu replied with a cautious voice. "Today will be a busy day; the slave ships are in! Rialto area will be bustling, and Alla Testa d'Ora will be overrun."

"Let's all be brave and face our reality," Li said as she dressed.

Guo Yu lowered his head and thought, *I wish Marco would return soon.*

Li sent Luca down first. She didn't want to run into Isabella, ruining her day. Li and Guo Yu waited at the top of the stairs for Luca to signal that everything was clear. As Luca motioned, they ran down the stairs, out the front door, and entered the streets. Guo Yu had been right. The street was teeming with people. The closer they came to the Grand Canal and the Rialto Bridge, the more ships they could see lining the canal. They were unloading hundreds of men, women, girls, and boys of all nationalities. People stood and watched like hungry wolves. The three weaved in and out of richly dressed people, stopping periodically to watch the bidding as they made their way to the apothecary.

Messer Alessio was surprised when they entered the apothecary; Li never came on the slave trade day. Immediately, he noticed Li's face reflected disgust at what she had seen. Luca's and Guo Yu's faces were blank. They had seen this many times. Li quickly recovered, but secretly, the sight had shaken her deep inside. *What would happen to me if Marco didn't return?* She stopped and put that thought high on a shelf in her mind. She forced herself to repeat what she had said earlier. *Let's be brave and face our reality.*

"Messer Alessio, I have a favor to ask. Today, let's do something different. I want Luca to learn about herbs," Li said.

Trying not to look surprised, Messer Alessio nodded yes. He opened the small back door and instructed Luca to follow. Startled, Luca hesitated a moment, then went inside. Li smiled at Luca. "Today, you can change your fate! Are you interested?"

Luca stared at Li. Saying nothing, she imitated Li. She boldly picked up the apron, placed it around her waist, and said, "I'm ready. Let my life begin."

Li smiled, picked up vessels, and called out names and purposes as Luca listened. Then Li taught her how to grind herbs. Li walked over to Messer Alessio and quietly asked him questions as Luca ground up herbs. "Where do all those people come from, and where are they going?"

Messer Alessio quietly answered, "Some are brought or captured mostly near the Black Sea; then they are sold to Egypt, Morocco, Crete, and Cyprus. Unfortunately, they sell the young boys and girls as concubines." Li understood this. She had seen this her whole life. She and Kokochin weren't sold but given for the same purpose.

Luca was a talented student. Her memory was astonishing, and she showed promise.

Before long, Guo Yu knocked on the door. "Li, we should go home. It's late." *The time passed so quickly*, Li thought. *It was fun teaching.* She dreaded returning home. When they entered the street, the crowds were gone; the ships were gone; only memories of the suppressed remained. They made their way home and up to her room without a scene. Luca lit the candles, and Guo Yu went to the kitchen for dinner. Li, tired, stood at the window and watched the sunset between the colorful buildings. She had been so naïve. Marco had protected her from the outside world since they arrived. She didn't realize Venice was so like her world. The conquered existed everywhere. Today, she saw the real Venice; they thrived in the human flesh trade, and her favorite place was in the center.

That night, Li didn't play her erhu. She lay in bed and thought about Luca, Guo Yu, and her life. They were lucky they belonged to Marco.

---

1. Vietnam

Chapter Twenty-Three

Marco

1274 Marco's Worth Proven

Genoa Prison 1298

The next day, Marco rose early and was ready to continue his report for the commander.

Rustichello was already at his desk writing. They could hear the clanging of metal. The guards served breakfast, and a tattered-dressed prisoner emptied the foul-smelling bucket.

Marco started talking. "I now belonged to Kubilai Khan, and it was time to prove my worth. I could not fail."

> *"If you travel west for ten miles outside Khanbaliq, you will come to a large river called Pulisanghin (Sanggan) that flows to the ocean. Many merchants sail this river carrying large cargo. You can cross this river by a magnificent bridge.*[1] *It is no less than 300 paces long and eight paces wide. Ten horsemen can ride across side by side. Beautiful marble lion sculptures and other sculptures adorn this bridge. After crossing, the traveler continues west for thirty miles, passing splendid inns, vineyards, and fertile fields until you reach a large and beautiful city called Zhuozhou.... Many Idolators and abbeys make their living through trade and crafts....fabrics of silk and gold....fine sendal."*

As Marco recounted his trip, which had taken him six months, he thought of his father.

He died only a year after our return to Venice. We had reconciled, and I understood him a little more now. But when I left on this trip, I despised him. For the three years we traveled to meet Kubilai, I had tried to win his approval. And in an instant, my father threw me away for money. I was determined to win Kubilai over, not for my father's sake, but for my own. Kubilai Khan was the key to my success. I had heard Kubilai dispatched many emissaries to various parts of the world, and they returned with uninteresting accounts of their trips. I was determined to ensure this did not happen. I would pay attention to every detail, including the residents' exciting customs and stories, and I wouldn't be shy. Kubilai Khan wanted to be entertained, not only informed, and I would tell Kubilai every detail, even if it included beautiful women, deceit, and loss.

> *"I traveled west through the kingdom of Taiyuanfu, a great center of trade and industry. This province produced equipment for the emperor's army, wine, and abundant silk, for they had a profusion of mulberry trees and silkworms, as well as the next city of Pingyangfu, where many wealthy merchants lived. From there, you come to a beautiful castle built many years ago by a king called the Golden King.*
>
> *"Then, when you leave this castle, you travel west for twenty miles to a river called Qara-Muren.[2] A river so large that a bridge could not be built to cross it. It flowed to the ocean, and on its banks, many cities were built filled with merchants thriving on trade. Birds were in abundance, and a huge cane grew on its banks. Two days beyond this magnificent river is another splendid city called Hezhongfu. It is a thriving city of trade and industry. I should also say that all the citizens of Hezhongfu are Idolaters. This city has a great deal of silk and spices, such as ginger, galangal, and spikenard, that never reach our world. They made silk and gold fabrics of large quality. After leaving Hezhongfu, you travel westward for eight days until you come to a great and noble city called Chang'anfu."*

Marco stopped talking, looked at Rustichello, and excitedly said, "I finally arrived at my first destination. As I rode through this city, Dai Xiuying informed me it was the capital of the kingdom and the center of trade and industry in the empire.

> *"They had a great deal of silk and gold and silk fabric of all kinds woven here, along with all sorts of military equipment manufactured. All necessities*

of life in great numbers made their way to this great city and were sold to many merchants, Idolaters, Turkish Nestorian Christians, and Saracens at little cost. They then traveled east and north, selling their merchandise at a significant profit.

"When we left the city, we continued to the palace where my first envelope was to be delivered. The palace sat on a great plain watered by rivers, lakes, pools, and springs. The grounds were enclosed by a thick, high wall that ran five miles in all directions, creating a square. At the entrance, soldiers stood guard at a huge wooden gate while others stood on a high, thick wall crowned with battlements. The soldiers stopped us. I confidently spoke. 'I am here to see your king.' With their stone-cold faces and confidence, the soldiers disregarded me and motioned for me to leave. Suddenly, the gate opened, and a man dressed in a beautiful silk robe appeared. The soldiers bowed to him and moved out of his way. I pulled out the gold bar and presented it to him. 'My name is Messer Marco Polo, and I have a letter for King Manggala from the Great Khan.' The surrounding soldiers mumbled as they backed away, bowing to me.

"The man spoke up. 'My name is Aigua. I have been waiting for you.'

"I wasn't sure what he meant, waiting for me. *Did he know I was coming? How?*

Aigua said little as he entered his carriage, except for us to follow. We traveled several miles through the park-like grounds, which were stocked with wild animals and game birds. In the distance, a large, grand palace appeared. When we arrived, Aigua directed us to dismount and for me to follow him. Other soldiers seized my soldiers and Dai Xiuying.

"'They will be given food and allowed to rest.' Aigua spoke before I could ask. 'Please, Messer Marco Polo, follow me.'

"We walked through a beautiful hall and entered an exquisite, decorated room featuring beaten gold, the finest azures, and countless colored marble. Several beautiful girl servants stood about the room. 'They are here to serve and prepare you to meet the king. The king has arranged a dinner in your honor,' Aigua replied."

Marco turned to Rustichello. "I was confused. They seemed to know I was coming, but that confusion disappeared as total pampering began. I felt like royalty for the first time, and I liked it."

Marco only told Rustichello about the dinner experience, the envelope, and the two days the beautiful girl, Ling, escorted him. "When I met the king, who sat above the rest on a decorated, carved wooden chair. I bowed low and fell to my knees. He asked me to rise as he stood and walked down from the platform.

"'I am King Manggala. Your name is Messer Marco Polo, and you have a letter from the Great Khan, correct?'

"'Yes, my Lord,' as I handed him the letter.

"He looked at it and handed it to Aigua without opening it." 'Thank you. Let's eat while you tell me of your journey.'

"The king never mentioned the letter again. Our dinner lasted for hours and was full of conversation. At the end of the evening, he asked if I was pleased with my room. Quickly, a mischievous smile appeared on my face.

"'I see you are.' He rose and began to exit the room, but suddenly turned. 'I hope I will see you again.' Before I could answer, he disappeared out the door.

"For the next two days, I walked around his city with Ling as my guide. Everywhere I went, I heard only good things about the king. He ruled his kingdom with great justice, integrity, and much love for his people."

Rustichello stopped Marco and asked. "Who is Ling?"

Marco turned red and whispered as if Li could hear him. "Ling was my first lover; she is hard to forget. On the last day at the palace, I rose, and she dressed me in my now clean traveling clothes. I said my goodbyes to my other servants, who handed me a silk bundle that contained the beautiful blue silk robe I wore at the king's dinner. 'A gift from the king.' They left the room, and only Ling remained. She walked over to me, put her arms around me, and whispered, 'Never change, even in this cruel world. Your trustworthiness and gentleness are your armor and power.' I remember my puzzlement. *What does she know about my trustworthiness?* Before I could ask, she reached up, kissed me, and led me from my room. Marco looked up at Rustichello. "I wondered what she meant the day I left. 'Never change, even in this cruel world. Your trustworthiness and gentleness are your armor and power.' I found out later." Marco laughed, and then his face went serious. "I was so young and naïve.

"I met up with Aigua, who handed me an envelope. 'This is for Kubilai Khan from the king.' He looked at me sternly, 'This is only for the Khan's eyes! Do you understand?' I nodded and bowed. He then took me to my men and Dai Xiuying. We left, traveling west for three days across a glorious plain, passing through many villages and towns. They live by trade and industry and have much silk."

Marco then continued his story. Rustichello continued writing, but curiosity was killing him. He finally spoke.

"Did you ever see Ling again?"

Marco answered. "Our paths crossed several times."

Only in the silence of darkness did Marco recall the true pampering.

On the day we arrived in my quarters, one girl walked over and shyly nudged me toward a hot steaming bath. A powerful scent of musk filled the room. She giggled as she undressed me, exposing my youthful body. I stopped her and asked her name. She softly answered, "Ling." Just the sound of her voice resolved my embarrassment. The other girls giggled as they undressed and entered the large tub. Ling removed her clothes, entered, and sat next to me. She sweetly kissed me with her succulent lips. I watched her nod to the other girls. Playfully, they scrubbed me until my skin turned red. The other girls, except Ling, rose and slowly dried so I could watch. Their bodies were dainty, and the curves of their bodies revealed their femininity and beauty. They wrapped themselves in robes and left the room. Ling turned to me, touched my face, and spoke. "I have never seen a man with so much hair on his face or body." Suddenly, Ling rose from the tub and held out her hand. I stared at her. Her skin was as smooth as silk and as white as freshly fallen snow. With a sweet voice, she said. "I want to see your whole face. Your eyes are gentle and loving. Is the rest?"

Marco smiled and continued thinking.

It was my first time being with a woman. I grabbed her hand, and she helped me out of the tub, wrapped a silk robe around me, and walked toward the dressing table. Following, I saw her long, black hair fall loosely down her elegant, slender back. I was her captive, and I didn't care. She directed me to sit as she stood in front of me. Her dewy skin glistened in the light of the many candles. Reaching for a cutting instrument, she proceeded to cut my long beard. Then, with a sharp knife, she shaved my face. Her beauty captivated me as my eyes only watched hers.

"Your face now matches your eyes, gentle and loving," she said as she reached for an ornate bottle that contained sweet oil. Softly, she applied it to my face and neck, and then, urging me to stand, she slid my robe from my shoulder. I watched it slowly fall to the floor. She continued with my shoulders, back, buttocks, and down the back of my legs. Turning me around, she exposed my manhood, and she continued down the front. She smiled and gave me the bottle. "It's your turn." Taking the oil, I restrained myself from grabbing her and carrying her to the bed. My instinct told me to be slow; she wanted sweet caresses. Twice, she had said my face was gentle and loving. I tried hard and patiently applied the oil over her entire body. Her fingers ran down my arm. She reached for my hand and guided me to the bed. Playfully, she pushed me, and as I fell onto the bed, she gently fell on me, kissing me with her succulent lips. Her body manipulated my virgin body until my instinct took over. We made love for the next hour until there was a knock on the

door. I wasn't ready to let her go. She rose and gathered the robes. I was reluctant to rise, but she promised we would have more time together. Now, it was time to meet the king.

The other girls entered my chamber. They giggled, and I could hear them comment on my newly discovered face. They combed my long, curly hair, pulled the front part back, and braided and adorned the braid with gold threads and jewels. The remaining part flowed down my back. Aigua entered the room carrying some silk garments. Ling carefully helped me dress layer by layer until the last piece—a beautiful black silk robe with small, gold floral and geometric designs. Ling then placed a gold silk belt around my waist. I stood before a mirror, smiling, and the beautiful Ling smiled.

I will never forget my first exotic bath, my first lovemaking, and the first time I resembled a Tartar. For many nights, as I felt my beard growing back, I thought about Ling's soft body next to mine.

The next day, Marco continued his story.

> *"Traveling three more days, you come to high mountains and deep valleys in the Guangyuan province. There are cities and towns across the mountains and valleys; the people are Idolaters, Christian Turks, and Saracens. Their livelihood is farming, forestry, and hunting. The woods teem with abundant wild boar, tigers, bears, fallow and roe deer, lynxes, and other animals. There are plenty of fine inns where a traveler will find comfortable lodges until you reach a province called Aq-baliq Manzi [3]that comprises one great plain. The capital is also called by the same name: "the white city on the borders of Manzi." Here, they grow ginger. They export this crop throughout Cathay, making great profit. They also live by trade and crafts and have an abundance of wheat, rice, and other grains at a meager cost. This plain takes two days to cross, and then you come to mountains and valleys, which take twenty days to travel with many cities and towns. They live from the fruit of the land. It is very beautiful here. They have many beasts and an enormous number of small creations that make musk. You will continue west for another twenty days and come to a plain and province called Chengdufu, which lies on the border of Manzi. The capital is also called by the same name. Before Kubilai Khan conquered this city, it was twenty miles in circumference, and it was a very great and noble city of powerful and wealthy kings. Several large rivers run through this city, carrying fresh water from the mountains above, providing excellent fishing. These rivers encircle the*

city and branch across it in various directions. The river's width varies, but the rivers are very deep, and countless stone bridges span them, all huge and splendid. These bridges are eight paces wide and flanked along either side by fine marble columns supported by grand wooden roofs, elegantly decorated and painted in red and topped by tiles. From one end to the other, they lined these bridges with exquisite little booths and stalls where all manner of trades and crafts are sold, which are removed every evening. The Great Khan's custom house is at the end of the bridges, where his dues are collected from the goods sold. It is amazing; the duties taken on these bridges amount to no fewer than 1000 gold bezants."

Marco stopped talking; his stomach was growling. He hadn't taken the time for breakfast. He walked over to where Rustichello sat, and his fingers fumbled over the remaining food.

"Let's take a break." Marco moved to his bed and lay down. His mind wandered, and he wondered what he would tell Rustichello next. From the beginning, he decided not to talk about Zhangye, Gansu, and its importance to his father and uncle. He continued thinking.

"From Chengdufu, I travel to Chamdo. From this city, if you traveled north, you ended in Zhangye, and south, you intercepted the Horse and Tea Road, one of Cathay's highest, most dangerous trade routes. It wound and wandered over the wildlands and the forest of the Rooftop of the World, which could only be traveled by foot and horseback. Most merchants had to hire guards as the road was treacherous because of the landscape, which hid many murderous bandits. It rivaled the Silk Road in importance, spanning the western side of Sichuan and Yunnan provinces, and southwest Tibet. It continued west through Bhutan, Sikkim, Nepal, and India. Then you reached the Middle East, the Red Sea, and the coast of Egypt. It carried precious tea from Pu'erh in exchange for horses in Tibet and many more precious, desired cargo, gold, and spices."

My father and uncle wanted a permit for this route and the dangerous pass. They would take tea and more to Gansu. There, they would sell their treasures to merchants who continued to Kashgar and further west, or those who sold in Khanbaliq and further North.

While in Chamdo, I met with my newly acquired friend and future partner, Huizhong.

Marco thought out loud. "He was so surprised to see me."

Rustichello looked up from his papers and said, “Are you speaking to me?”

“No, no, no, talking to myself.”

Marco remembered that conversation clearly.

“Where are your father and uncle? Huizhong questioned him.

“They are waiting for me in Khanbaliq. I am on a quest for Kubilai Khan. If I complete it, we will have our permits!”

An enormous smile—exposing his numerous, crooked teeth—came across his face, and without breaking his smile, he commented with a concerned voice, “Do as he says if you want to live!”

I questioned him about what he meant. Huizhong never answered. He politely discussed their business plans and expressed his enthusiasm for doing business. He would be the one who ran our outpost and arranged the caravans and the guards. His name meant loyal and wise, as he would say. We had hoped that was true, and as the years passed, he proved it: Huizhong, royal and wise. I never told Huizhong I belonged to Kubilai Khan. I was afraid Huizhong would mistrust me. My father taught me only to answer the questions asked and never to volunteer information.

We left on a pleasant note, and Huizhong told me again, “Do as he asks!” He was the second person to say that; I was beginning to fear for my life.

Marco opened his eyes. He had heard the metal clanging. He could see the sun setting through the barred window. It was dinnertime.

The days passed quickly, and he hadn’t heard a word from the commander. *Has the commander sent my letters to my family? Li must be so worried. How long has it been?* The days were running together. His cousins could be cruel, even if they received the letters. *Would they show it to Li?* Standing, he walked over to the door and waited for the small window to open. Finally, it opened, the guard shoved in the food, and the window closed before he could speak. In a raised voice, Marco yelled. “Hey, hey, hey, come back!” He could hear the continued clanging while the footsteps continued down the hall.

Marco placed the food on Rustichello’s table and pulled up a chair. He had eaten little today. Hungry, he shoved the food in his mouth impatiently and spoke with a full mouth. “Let’s continue.”

Rustichello pushed the food over, picked up his pen, and looked at Marco.

“I left off at the bridges, right?”

Rustichello nodded yes. Then repeated where Marco had left off.

"The Great Khan's custom house is at the end of the bridges, where his dues are collected from the goods sold. It is amazing; the duties taken on these bridges amount to no fewer than 1000 gold bezants.

Marco remembered and continued.

"As these rivers flowed out of the city, they joined to form a vast river named the Yangtze. This river flows for an eighty- or hundred-day journey to the ocean. There are countless cities along the way with countless ships that sail this river carrying vast merchandise up and down that a man in this world would not believe without seeing it for yourself. It is so wide that it seems like a sea, not a river."

Rustichello's mouth dropped, and he said, "Is that true?"
Marco nodded. "I will talk about this river later."

"From Chengdufu, you travel west for five days to Kangding and then more days to Chamdo. Then, after another twenty days of traveling through many towns, villages, and hamlets that have all disappeared, just ruins remain. You will have crossed into a devastated province called Tibet. It had been defeated by Mengu Khan's army somewhere around 1266. As a man crosses this country, a traveler must bring enough supplies for himself and his animals in case he doesn't find a place to replenish his supplies. After twenty days, you will find yourself in a region with many villages perched on precipitous crags. And in these parts, they have the most peculiar custom."

As Marco spoke, he remembered the deep ruts created by the horses' hooves and altars alongside the road, engraved with religious scriptures and mottos that continued to Lhasa.

Marco changed the subject suddenly and turned to face Rustichello. I would return here 12 years later, taking Li's half-brother, Emperor Gong of Song, to the retiring monastery.

Marco's face turned grave.

Rustichello questioned Marco. "Why the serious face?"

Marco turned red; it would be the first time he confessed to anyone.

"Well, when I returned from a trip, Li always wanted to hear about my adventures. She loved hearing about the world outside of hers—especially this one involving her brother. I was totally in denial. Part of me saw Li as a curious, young friend, and my other half recognized that she had grown into a beautiful woman. Even though I suspected her feelings ran deeper than a friend, I refused to accept it. I wanted to keep her my secret, someone I protected and innocently loved, enjoying how things had been so uncomplicated. This time, I failed and would fail many times later. When I told her this story, I wanted to tease and embarrass her, but after that, I was the one embarrassed."

Rustichello spoke up. "Now, you have made me curious. Tell me."

"Let's see." Marco started.

> *"In these lands, the fact is that nothing on earth would induce a man to marry a virgin, for they say that a woman is worthless unless she has been intimately acquainted with many men. They thought that a woman or a girl who had not laid with a man had offended the gods, so she was shunned and despised. So, to prevent this, the old women from the villages would approach any foreigners who pitched a tent in the area with their daughters, twenty or forty at a time, offering them to the men. They would beg them to have their way with them. The chosen girls would stay, and the others would leave disappointed. The men were free to take pleasure with them, but not allowed to take them when it was time to go. At that time, he would give the woman he had slept with a jewel or a token so she could prove she had had lovers. Custom dictates that before she can marry, she needs twenty of these tokens, which are worn around her neck, showing she is esteemed, prized as a wife, and blessed by the gods."*

Rustichello interrupted, "What happens if she becomes pregnant by one of these men?" Marco replied.

> *"Her new husband would raise the child as his own. Also, from the day he marries, he will never touch another woman, and this custom is scrupulously observed."*

Marco continued, “I intentionally included my recommendation for any man sixteen to twenty-four to visit this country when I told the story to Li. She was not amused or embarrassed.

"Her face was blank. She turned and walked away. I followed her, and then she turned and looked me directly in my eyes. ‘Why would you tell me such a story? I hope you enjoyed yourself.’

“I didn’t answer. But I was surprised, secretly enjoying her response; Li was jealous. I watched her walk away, and I cringed. “What was I thinking?”

Marco spoke with his head down. “I think that was the beginning of my betrayal.”

“Betrayal?” Rustichello questioned.

“Yes, to Kubilai Khan and Li.” Marco quickly changed the subject and continued his story.

“During those 17 years, my father and uncle often traveled this route for business and pleasure.

> *“Tibet is a vast province. The people are Idolaters and are completely depraved because of their devastation. They deem it no sin to commit robberies and other crimes. That is why guards are needed to protect the merchants.*
>
> *“They live by hunting, breeding cattle, and by the fruits of the earth. This country has an animal that produces musk, which in their language is called gudderi. I will never forget this scent that hangs over the land. They are overrun with these animals, and with every full moon, they discharge this musk from an engorged sac around their belly button. They do not use Khan’s paper money, but instead use salt as a form of currency. They dress in animal skins, canvas, and buckram. And speak their language and call themselves Tibetans. But the worst is the wild beast, so dangerous that it forces them to find a method to protect themselves, especially at night. Luckily, a giant cane grows in this country. The girth is at least three palms in circumference and a good fifteen paces long. The traveling merchants gather the green canes during the day, chopping them into usable sizes, and when night falls, they have a roaring fire, and they throw them in. They create a popping noise so loud it can be heard miles away, spreading terror to everyone who has never heard them. Even their horses need to have their eyes bandaged and their feet fettered.*
>
> *“In many places, gold dust is found in rivers, lakes, and mountains. Cinnamon*

and many other spices that have never been seen in different parts of the world grow abundantly here. Amber and coral are traded at a very high price and worn on the wives and idols, considered a precious jewel.

"I can also tell you that their enchanters and astrologers are the best in the world. They can summon tempests, lightning, and thunder, starting and stopping them at will. Their marvels are without end, but I think it's best not to speak of them in this book."

Again, Rustichello stopped and questioned Marco. "Have you ever visited one?"

"Truthfully, yes. The astrologer spoke terrifying things. Things I didn't want to hear. She told me a monk from this area would conquer and remove the great Khan's heirs from Cathay. I stopped her; it would be considered treason if she said more."

Rustichello could hear Marco whispering to himself. "I committed treason."

"What did you say?" asked Rustichello.

Marco didn't answer the question but started rambling. "Let's move on. I need to finish this." Marco circled the room, flinging his arms in the air. "How long have I been here? Time is running together! Will the commanders release me? Did they deliver my letters to my family? I am going insane! So many questions, so few answers."

Rustichello could hear the urgency in Marco's voice. He needed to make Marco focus. "Tell me more. Where did you go next? Did you deliver the next letter?"

Marco stopped circling and wringing his hands. He ran his fingers through his thick, curly hair and stood straight. "Ok! Let's begin. The next province is Jiandu,[4] whose capital is named the same. It also lies in the west."

Marco hadn't talked long before his voice became a whisper. He was talking to himself again; mentioning treason made his mind spin. *Did Kubilai find out what I had done*? Marco tried to reassure himself. *No, he couldn't have. Ghazan and Qoja owed me, and the others vowed silence for money.* Marco, swept up in guilt, thought, *Is this my punishment?* He always hated his father for his lack of loyalty and loved Kubilai for his. Now, after all, it seemed he was his father. Marco's head fell in disgrace.

Rustichello interrupted Marco's moment of disgust with a yell. "I can't hear you! What did you say?"

Marco's voice returned to normal as he picked up where he left off.

"Jiandu was formerly ruled by its king, but Kubilai had conquered and made it his own, sending his governors. The people were Idolaters and lived in many cities and towns. In this province was a great Salt Lake where pure white pearls could be found. They weren't round but knobby, as if four, five, or six were clumped together. The great Khan forbids anyone from harvesting them unless he gives his permission. This way, they keep their value. If you dare, they will put you to death if caught.

"There is also a mountain[5] *filled with beautiful turquoise stone. But Kubilai's law also covets these. As you can see, all the provinces and regions in this report belong to Kubilai Khan, except the lands that belong to the son of Arghun and his cousins. This province also follows the same customs as the other provinces regarding their womenfolk, as I described earlier.*

"The most important thing to tell you is that there is gold. They used it as their currency, weighed it in saggio, and valued it in accordance with the weight. There are no coins stamped with a die. For change, the emperor agents boil salt water for an hour until it forms a stiff paste workable enough to press into a mold the size of a two-penny loaf, creating blocks stamped with the emperor seal. They are flat on the bottom, round on the top, and weigh a pound. They placed these blocks on red-hot stones beside a fire, where they dried and solidified. Eighty of these blocks are worth one saggio of fine gold. Merchants travel the very rural areas in the mountains, exchanging these salt blocks for the abundant gold found in the mountains and rivers.

"They have plenty of gudderi, tigers, bears, and fine fish. They make wine from wheat flavored with many spices that grow wild there."

Rustichello stopped Marco and, in a very excited voice, asked, "Let's go back to the gold. Really, that much gold?"

Marco didn't hesitate. "Yes, and if you travel ten more days from the capital, you reach a river called Brius that runs into the sea. The locals call it the Gold Dust River. This river borders and divides the provinces. After you cross the river, you enter Qarajang Province, which is so large that seven kingdoms comprise the area. After months of travel, I understood why Kubilai

Khan sent me on this journey for my first quest. He wanted me to see his empire's lifeline—the gold, tea, and salt—and learn its importance.

"In this province, my second letter was to be delivered. As I crossed the river, my memories returned to my first letter delivery. *Would I experience the same pampering?* I was hoping, as the last months had been long, tiring, and filled with fear. The tales of the thieves and bandits around every corner had taken a toll on me. I carried a letter from the Khan, whose deliverance held my future and life. Anticipation ran through my body as I headed to meet Kubilai Khan's grandson, King Yisün Temür. He couldn't be much older than me. His father was King Hukechin, who died in 1271.

> *"The money that ran through here was of great importance, and the man who controlled this area had to be strong, trustworthy, and powerful. After traveling for five days, I arrived in Yachi,*[6] *a large and splendid city renowned for its many merchants and artisans. The people are a mixed bunch: some Muhammad, Idolaters, and a few Christians and Turks who followed the Nestorian creed. There was plenty of wheat and rice, which they ate, and they made wine with a mixture of spices. Besides gold and salt, they have different types of money. They use white cowries that are found in the sea. Eighty cowries are worth one saggio of silver, which equals two Venetian groats. Eight saggis of fine silver are worth one saggio of fine gold.*
>
> *"A vast lake,*[7] *a good hundred miles in circumference, lies next to this city. Enormous amounts of the finest fish of numerous varieties in the world were found. Next, I would travel for ten more days to the Kingdom of Qarajang.*[8] *As we rode closer, it was apparent that the city had been ravaged by the Kubilai Khan's army about twenty years ago. Many buildings still lay in ruins. It is surrounded by mountains, rivers, and lakes, where abundant gold can be found.*

"My anticipation had grown so large I couldn't sleep. I would finally deliver Kubilai Khan's last letter. When I reached the king's palace, I was exhausted. Again, greeted as if they expected me by a man named Delun, which meant virtuous order. He looked at me and ordered the servants to help me to my room."

Marco stopped talking and walked around the room. He looked at Rustichello and spoke. "I feel just like I felt then. I need rest. Let's finish later. Wake me up if they bring us food."

As Marco lay on his bed, his mind kept racing. *I would have been terrified if I had known the truth about those letters.*

His mind carried him to that day and the following week. He wouldn't talk about tea with Rustichello. From the beginning, he had decided that personal things would not be included and that if he told Rustichello anything personal, it would be in strict confidence; Rustichello had agreed.

Marco started talking, almost like he was sleep-talking.

Rustichello put down his pen and listened.

"They laid me on an immense bed dripping with silk. Beautiful girls surrounded me. Their giggles became quieter and quieter as I drifted off to a deep sleep. It was two days before I awoke. My bodyguard, Dai Xiuying, sat beside me when I opened my eyes. I remembered my disappointment that it wasn't Ling. But mostly, I recalled how happy they were when I awoke. They jumped up and brought in a strangely dressed man. In a strange tongue, he announced I was healed and left the room.

"I questioned my men about this man; their faces displayed concern, and they answered. 'When we arrived, you fainted. We called for a physician. They sent a magician—a devil charmer. He came with his instruments and immediately struck up a tune, danced, and leaped until he fell to the ground, foaming at the mouth and looking like a corpse. That's when other magicians entered the room, and started talking to the devil charmer. He told the other magicians that a Devil had entered your body and said you had displeased a spirit, causing your illness.' Dai Xiuying continued. 'Before he could continue, I stopped him. I asked Delun to remove the magicians, and we have been nursing you ever since.'"

Marco smiled at Rustichello. "Starting from that time, Dai Xiuying became my trusted guide for the next 17 years." Marco continued his story. "Delun entered the room when he heard I had awakened, followed by several beautiful servants directing my men to leave. Delun smiled and said, 'Welcome back, Messer Marco Polo. The king awaits you. He has prepared food for you. You must be hungry.'

In the present, Marco placed a hand on his stomach; he was hungry. Trying to forget his hunger, he continued his story.

"Delun brought me new clothing, and the servants helped me dress." Then Delun escorted me to the king. Yisün wasn't a large man, but his presence was noble. His stance and face reminded me of his grandfather, and in my imagination, I was standing before a young Kubilai Khan. Yisün was magnificently dressed in a gold and purple silk robe and wore his hair in the Tartar style, and a dangling jewel earring adorned his right ear. I bowed and fell to my knees, my forehead on the floor, the letter snug against my heart. I waited, and finally, with a commanding voice, he directed me to rise and come closer. He stood and walked down the steps. I was right; he was my age.

I reached for the letter and held it with two hands as I presented it. 'This is a letter from your grandfather. He instructed me to present this to you.'

"He looked at the letter and then at me. Smiling, he handed it to his servant without opening it, like the last letter I gave to King Manggala. The servant left the room. The king commanded the servants to bring food, and while we sat and ate, he wanted to hear about my trip and what I thought of their lands. Our conversation shifted to Kubilai Khan. The young king started slowly and cautiously asked. 'You are working for my grandfather?'"

Now lying in prison, Marco remembered that he had answered as cautiously as the king had asked the question. *We were both afraid.*

"I told him, 'Only if I pass your grandfather's test, I will work for him, and my father will receive what he wants.'

"'What work will you be doing?'

"'If I understood him correctly, I would be an emissary, traveling to different parts of his empire delivering letters and requests just like now and then, when I return, tell him a story of what I saw.'

"'What does your father receive?' the king asked.

"This was when I hesitated. *Is this a trick question? Am I saying too much? Can I trust this man?* His eyes looked into mine. I took the chance, and for the first time, I believed I could read men; his face looked wise and sincere.

"'Permits,' I replied.

"The palms of his hands pounded the table like drums. 'Well, let's go on a trip. I will introduce you to some important men and show you my land.'"

Yisün was relieved by Marco's answer. He was being honest and not secretive. Marco was passing his grandfather's test. But it wasn't his place to tell him. That would happen when he returned to Dadu if he continued to follow instructions.

Marco remembered questioning him.

"Will I pass the test?"

"I have faith in you, Messer Marco Polo."

Marco continued his story, "Our friendship began then. Yisün called his servant. 'Prepare for a trip. We will follow the Lancang River and see the tea trees.'"

As he lay in bed, Marco remembered how delighted he was. *This had been my father, uncle, and my plan since Gansu. I had to give my father some credit, but I never dreamed I would be the bargaining chip. However, my father never saw what was coming.*

Marco continued, "We left the palace the next day with a long line of the king's soldiers, his attendants, Dai Xiuying, and my men. It was definitely a change; traveling as royalty had its advantages."

Marco smiled and said, "If we were close to a city, we would set up camp before we arrived. The king dressed in disguise, wanting to enjoy the town or village without bringing too much attention.

"We traveled westward for five days through the fertile landscape with its heavy rainfall and humid, warm climate. Yisün proved to be a man involved in his kingdom and his surroundings. As the heavy rain fell, Yisün continued to ride, unafraid to feel nature. He pointed to the thick and full tea trees, stating that the climate was the perfect growing condition for cultivating the perfect tea. Our first stop was in the province of Zardandan.[9] The capital was Yongcheng. He pointed to some men. 'They come from high in the mountains. They consider themselves gentlemen but occupy themselves with nothing except warfare, hunting, and falconry. Look at their teeth.' As we passed, one man smiled. I could see they were all gold.

"Yisün continued. 'The women do all the work along with their slaves. These people do not have idols or churches but worship the head of the house, saying, 'We are begotten of this man.'

"We ate here. They served us meat, in abundance, raw or cooked, accompanied by rice, and a rice wine flavored with spices. Yisün paid with silver. The server rushed to the owner, who peered at us and bowed. I was confused, and then Yisün explained that they only have gold and love silver. The silver mines are five months away, so traders come here with large quantities of silver and exchange it for gold. They make a huge profit and a fine living from this."

Marco remembered that he had made a mental note of this. *I would tell Kubliai Khan and my father.*

Marco continued. "From we traveled south along the Lancang River to Lincang. Not only was this area known for tea, but it was also a gold route to the southeastern parts of Cathay. Yisün explained that his dream was to expand the tea from Pu'erh to here. He explained that the ground produced rich, mellow, smooth tea that many desired. It was also here where one of my exciting stories took place. My lust for gold almost left me footless or devoured if it hadn't been for the young king.

"One late afternoon, as the sun set, I stood atop the flowing Lancang River's steep bank. The sun's brilliant rays made the river's entire bottom sparkle. *Is the story true that gold nuggets as large as a baby's fist covered the river's bed?* Approximately twenty feet away, my imagination and desire for a better view grew. Foolishly, I began my descent, following a large furrow that ended at the river edge. Only a pace from the river, I heard splashing. Stopping to look around, numerous hideous creatures with wide, flat heads and large, lumpy snouts slid into the water from an islet. They had gigantic heads, outcropping teeth, and bulging eyes with hoods that rose just above the water. The bodies were ten paces long with two short legs and only three claws as feet—two small, one large like a falcon—and their bodies tapered to long, slithering tails. I was stunned as they raced toward me—some with wide-open mouths so large that they could easily swallow a man in one gulp. I couldn't move, but suddenly, I felt an arm around my waist pulling me backward to the top of the riverbank. It was Yisün laughing as arrows whistled by. As I scrambled to my feet, all I could say was. 'What are those creatures? And thank you!'

"'Jiaolongs,' the king quickly answered and continued speaking. 'But they weren't your only enemy.'

"'What?'

"'You were lucky that the furrow you followed didn't have traps. Look at the one next to it.' The king said frankly. 'These creatures sleep during the day because of the heat. They come out at day's end to drink and eat, leaving those large furrows in the sand as they crawl. The hunters look for these ruts. Look carefully, just a little farther down. Do you see something rising from the ground?' I shook my head yes. 'The hunters pound stakes in the ground with a sharp blade attached to the top. When the Jiaolong slithers at high speed to the river, it impales itself upon the blade with such great force that the stomach is gashed and ripped to the navel, and dies. That could have been your foot or somewhere else on your body.' Horrified, I deeply bowed and said, 'I owe you my life and will always be indebted to you.' He laughed. His response surprised me, 'Since I was twelve, I too, have owed someone my life. That someone is still owed. I never made that mistake again, and I learned a vital lesson: greed could end your life unexpectedly. Be cautious!'

"My next question was, 'What do the hunters use these horrid creatures for?' As we returned to our horses, he explained. 'They skin them on the spot, remove the gall, and sell it at an exorbitant price. The gall has powerful medicine for mad dog bites, difficult births, and sores. Besides, the flesh of these creatures is a delicacy and fetches a high price.'

"We then left the Lincang area and headed south for Pu'erh. Excitement overtook my body; I had waited for two years to be here. Since I visited Gansu, I have heard that ancient Pu'erh tea trees grow in this area. Yisün proudly showed me Zhen Yuan, a supposed tea tree that was thousands of years old. When we arrived in the city, hundreds of tea farmers leading horses loaded with Pu'erh tea waited for processing. Some came from the Xishuangbanna area further south, where mountains of ancient tea trees grew, along with many legends. King Yisün introduced me to Chaoxiang, who managed the tea trade office and oversaw permit checks. 'Remember and learn from this man well. His smile comes easily, but his mind is cunning.'

"It was here that I learned the process of tea and its importance. We sat around the open flame at night, not for the heat as the weather was pleasing except for the rain, but for the warmth of friendship. The king explained, 'The Song Dynasty owned this land once, but when my grandfather defeated them, they lost an important piece of their empire. Great Song families lost their tea, a large part of the salt revenue, and their ability to maintain their armies. They also lost control of the Tea Horse Road that led to Tibet, where they purchased Tibetan horses for war in exchange for tea. Our complete victory over the Song Dynasty moves closer. We are battling them south of the Yangtze River as it flows into the sea, with General Bayan leading them. Victory will be ours soon. When this happens, our empire will be the largest in the world, and world trade will belong to the Great Khan. My grandfather is planning to loosen tea restrictions. That's why you are here, right? Tea will be available for all, not just for the rich. He believes that more money will be had if merchants like you are allowed to trade, and our land's riches will travel west freely, opening new markets. His riches will increase manyfold.' For the first time, I saw Kubilai not only as an emperor but as a businessman. Yisün stopped talking and stretched his muscular body. 'I'm tired. Let's retire. Tomorrow, I will show you tea.'"

Marco, lying in his makeshift bed in prison, stopped talking; his stomach ached with hunger. "Are they ever going to bring us food?" Then, he thought, *It would be almost a year and a half before General Bayan, one hundred eyes, conquered another part of Song. That was when I found Li.*

Rustichello responded. "Continue talking; work relieves the hunger pain."

Marco frowned and continued speaking. "The next day, I learned about tea while walking around the ancient tea forest. A forest so different from what I had ever seen. Here, the forest looked like a jungle from another world, not Cathay or the mountains known as the Top of the World, where snow fell deeply in the mountains. Here, Yisün, who passionately loved tea, rambled for hours as we walked through the evergreen and lush forest.

"'The first person to discover tea was Shen Nong, who lived 5,000 years ago. You can call him an herbalist, but his name actually means 'divine farmer,' and he was considered the father of our medicine. They say he wandered the forest tasting hundreds of herbs for their medicinal value. Legends say he was conceived when his mother, Nu Teng, swallowed a celestial dragon's vapors. Nine days later, he was born with a transparent belly and internal organs. In seven more days, he was a powerful man and the leader of his tribe.' Yisün laughed and looked at me. He could tell by my facial expression that I thought maybe he was slightly crazy if he believed this. He assured me that the rest of the story seemed more feasible. 'So,' Yisün continued, 'Shen Nong saw how his people suffered from hunger and numerous illnesses, and he felt for them deeply. He was determined to find safe food and remedies, so he went hiking through the mountains, tasting hundreds of herbs. Using his see-through belly and organs, he could observe how herbs, in every part—root, stem, and leaf—worked within his body for their medicinal value. Then, he wrote his observation. Then, one day, he encountered 72 poisonous herbs. His body became so weak that he could hardly stand. Only by a miracle did he build a fire with twigs from the trees above that still held their dry leaves. These are the same ancient trees. The hot air carried the tea leaves from the burning tea twigs up, then fell, landing in his cauldron of boiling water, which he drank. Their healing powers saved him, and he named the plant Cha. The word means to examine or check, but when written in our characters, it means 'tea'. Since then, tea has been used as a medicinal plant, but now it is also used for pleasure.

"'I own his book.' Yisün said proudly. 'For generations, people remembered his works in stories. Finally, they were written down in a book called, Shennong Ben Cao Jing.[10] It is the oldest book of traditional medicine.'

"Marveled by his story, I asked if I could see it if I returned to his palace. Yisün was pleased. Our friendship grew more that day.

"Evening approached, and we returned to Pu'erh at twilight. The sun retreated, and the stars twinkled in the vast, darkening skies. We sat at an open platform table where two beautiful teapots' steam escaped and melted into the air. A young girl stood alert, hovering over the king, who would instantly pour tea at Yisün's slightest hand motion.

"Yisün spoke softly. 'This tea is made from the freshly picked young leaves of the Gusthucha.' He lifted the lid, took a whiff, and directed me to do the same. 'Smell the aroma. Eventually, you will learn the smells of different teas.' He placed the lid back on and directed the girl to pour. A yellow-green liquid emerged into the cups. The king picked up the cup and spoke before it reached his lips. 'This is best when the weather is hot.'

"I followed. Yisün lowered his cup, and the young girl poured a second cup from the other teapot. This time, a dark amber liquid appeared. Yisün looked at me. 'I prefer this one. It has been dried and fermented. The flavor is rich and earthy; some say drinking gushu Pu'erh is like listening to music. No one desires a single-note melody but wants to listen to a symphony. This is what this tea is.'

"Smiling, I thought, *This man is as complex as this tea.* I never really thought of tea this way. I drank tea that had been mixed with different herbs. It was different drinking it pure.

"Lost in thought, I didn't hear Yisün speaking to me except for the last sentence. 'Which do you prefer?' I apologized for my lack of attention and then told him I preferred the second one like him."

Suddenly, Marco's thoughts returned to his present time. A clanging of metal echoed down the halls. *Is dinner finally being served?* He jumped up and stood at the small door window, starving. He thought of Li as he stood at the door. He would give anything to be drinking tea with Li. The door opened, and they shoved the food in his face. Marco quickly responded and shouted. "I want to see the commander." But the guard never turned or answered as he continued down the hall with loud, pounding feet. Marco walked over to Rustichello, who was writing. Marco plopped down his food and pulled up a chair. As he shoved food in his mouth, he reminded Rustichello. "Remember, only write the stories I want to be told!"

Rustichello stared at Marco and cockily answered, "Of course." He dropped his quill and started shoving food into his mouth. With a full mouth, he requested Marco to continue. "I want to know more about tea. I tried it twice, once at an herbalist for medicine and once at a friend's house in Venice who always bragged about importing strange food and drinks."

Marco thought for a moment where he had left off and continued. "The night was long. Yisün talked most of the night. 'Some tribes living here pound the fresh tea leaves into a paste and mix them with ginger, pepper, salt, and boiling spring water. They call it tea porridge.'

"Yisün clicked his fingers, and two girls carried two bowls and placed them on the table.

"'This is it.' The king lifted a bowl, slurped it down, and looked at me. He motioned for me to do the same. I lifted the bowl and drank. 'It's pleasing.'

"I had already decided I wouldn't insult him in any way. I wanted him to share his knowledge with me.

"Yisün continued. 'The process of tea has been advancing. At the beginning of tea, the people of Wei knew how to make tea cakes, but the tea cakes had a strong grass smell and tasted bitter. Eventually, they found how to eliminate the grassy odor. They steamed and pounded the tea leaves into cakes. Then they bored a small hole, strung them in a thin line one by one, and dried them. Unfortunately, this didn't improve the taste. Over time, it was perfected by the Tang Dynasty, which managed tea cultivation and followed the tea process created by the famous tea saint Lu Yu. His approach is outlined in his book, *The Classic of Tea,* which led to the creation of a more pleasant-tasting tea. After the Tang, the Song Dynasty indulged in tea drinking as an art. They also used it as a tribute to their emperors and have introduced many new teas, such as the Tuan Cha.'

"Again, Yisün clicked his finger, and a girl arrived with a plate containing an irregular tea ball marked with dragon and phoenix symbols. Their process consisted of six steps: streaming fresh leaves, cooling them with cold water, squeezing out the excess leaf juice, pounding the leaves with water in a pottery mortar, shaping them into a dragon or phoenix mold, and then drying.

Marco looked at Rustichello and replied, "I was so naïve; tea was much more complicated than I ever dreamed. Yisün read my face. He smiled and said, 'I have lived here most of my life and am still learning. Eventually, if inclined, you will continue to learn about cultivation and begin to recognize the quality and types of tea by its aroma. I have one last thing to show you, and then we will eat.' Yisün enthralled me to the point that I forgot my hunger.

"Yisün again snapped his finger; the girl brought a plate piled with dried, loose tea. Yisün continued. 'You must have noticed the tea process had become quite complicated, time-consuming, and expensive, so the Song decided on this newer method instead of molding the tea. It is ground, making it easier to add the different herbs. I watched one tribe take loose green tea and place it in a hot cauldron with coals. They roasted the leaves this way, removed them, placed them in a pot, and poured hot water over them. It was excellent.'

"At that moment, Yisün went silent. He wasn't looking at me. I turned to see what he was looking at. A line of beautiful girls waltzed toward us, each carrying a bowl or tray. Our table soon became topped with a multitude of assorted foods. Yisün pointed at each dish and spoke. 'Rice noodles, yak meat, steamed pot chicken, wild mushroom noodles, grilled fish, and Baba, one of my favorites. It's a Tibetan snack, a thick, soft bread served plain or filled with minced pork or red bean paste.' A jug was placed on the table. 'You will need to try this. It is how the Tibetans serve their tea. It is called yak butter tea. They value this special tea for its medicinal properties. The Tibetans mostly eat meat, and these boiled tea leaves aid in their digestion. Traders carried compressed cakes of Pu'erh on their backs, piled high over their heads; the sunlight and rainfall naturally fermented the leaves along the long, treacherous trail.

"'Remember, learning about your customers' tastes is the most important thing. We drink milk in our tea. The Songs think we are uncivilized and unrefined.' Yisün laughed slightly. 'My grandfather dismisses their attitude and knows he will soon be their conqueror.'

"After that last sentence, Yisün fell silent. We sat under the stars, drinking and eating until the expected company joined us—a thick blanket of mist. It was time for bed. The following day, I would start my journey back. Kubilai Khan's letters were safely delivered. My journal—overflowing with incredible tales—was ready for Kubilai Khan, and King Manggala's letter needed to be delivered.

"The fearful, long journey ahead created an unwelcome sleepless night. I rose early. The air was crisp, calm, and damp. Walking to an opening in the forest that overlooked the valley and mountains beyond, I saw the thick, bluish-black clouds hanging heavy, except where the tops of the mountains met the rising sun. It was a stunning sight.

"As I stood in the glory of nature, I heard Yisün's voice. 'You are up early.'

"'Yes, I must leave today.'

"'Come, have some tea. I have something to give you,' Yisün calmly said.

"As we sat and drank the warming tea, my body relaxed. My courage returned, and I became eager to return.

"Yisün motioned for a servant, who carried a tray that held a letter like the first. Yisün's look was severe as he spoke. 'Give this to my grandfather. It is only for his eyes.'

"'I understand,' I said.

"'Do you?' Yisün gravely spoke.

"I nodded stupidly.

"Yisün continued speaking. 'From here, go east; no need for you to return to my land. I've created a map for you, and my soldiers will escort you until you reach a province called Tulaman. My men will leave you at the Wu River, and you will continue by boat.'

"I bowed low and smiled. 'I hope to meet you again.'

"Yisün smiled back, 'I am sure we will.'"

Rustichello interrupted Marco. "Did you ever see him again?"

"Yes, at the White Festival and the great Khan's birthday several times!"

Marco continued his story. "Before we left, I placed the new letter in Kubilai's leather pouch with the other letter.

"For the next few days, we traveled east toward Jiaozhi Guo (northern Viet Nam). They have their own King, language, and lots of gold. As we traveled through this province, we saw men and women painted from head to toe with intricate designs of lions, dragons, and birds of various shapes. We found out later these were not done by painting but by needles. Many died from blood loss, but they endured for the sake of gentility; the more pictures they had, the more refined and desirable they became.

"From there, we traveled north/east for fifteen days to Amu, subjects to the Great Khan, who were Idolaters. The women and men lived by their herds of buffalo, oxen, cows, and the profit of the land. The women and men wore extremely

valuable gold and silver bangles on their arms and legs. Of course, the men's were of better quality and higher in value.

"Then, we continued for eight more days north to where Yisün's soldiers would leave us. The people of Tulaman were born soldiers, subjects of the Great Khan, who had their own language and were very handsome, not fair-skinned but rather brown. They have many villages located among the towering mountains and fortresses. There are few merchants, but they are wealthy traders in gold.

"They have customs when you die. Your body is burned, and the ashes are put in small caskets, which are taken high in the mountains and hung in huge caverns where neither man nor beast can touch them.

"When we reached the Wu River, as Yisün said, his soldiers said their goodbyes, and we boarded our boat and continued to our destination. We sailed by villages and towns for twelve days until we arrived in Fuling, a vast and splendid city on another huge river."

Marco stopped talking. Rustichello looked up from his papers and questioned why he had paused.

"Thinking about what to say next. It's been a while." Marco continued.

" We spent a couple of days here, and I was relieved to be in a city. The boat had gone through the lands of Wei. We had to anchor offshore at night, or huge and dangerous lions would enter the boat and drag us off to be devoured. However, the men in this land have found a way to protect themselves. They owned dogs so brave that they would attack these beasts. So, a man with a bow and arrow and two of these stout-hearted dogs would run after these fierce lions with so much courage, attacking the lion from the front and back, giving the man time to draw his bow and kill it.

"When we arrived at the city, I yearned for my feet to touch the earth. I roamed the streets. The citizens were subjects of the Great Khan and used only his paper money. They lived by trade as large amounts of silk and goods were ferried to many regions by the city's great Yangtze River.

"As I sat in the teahouses, the chatter became one of gossip. The famous General Bayan won a glorious victory on the Yangtze and besieged Song's ships. I remembered Yisün's words: 'This victory justified his confidence.' General Bayan would soon be in Lin'an, the capital of Manzi. Everything would change regarding trade. My excitement grew, and my urge to return to Khanbaliq increased. However, so did my fear. *Would I be able to satisfy Kubilai Khan and pass his test? Would we be allowed the permits?*

"The next day, excitedly, we left, traveling for twelve more days to Chang'anfu. I would meet up with a relieved Hurzhong, our partner. He was delighted that I was alive and hoped we would meet again with the good news that our business venture had begun.

"From that point, we traveled fast, as we had already passed through these lands.

"My heart had pounded as we approached Chang'anfu. My beard had grown, and memories of the young, beautiful servant, Ling, returned. The thought tempted me to stop. My desire diminished, knowing we had seventy more days before we reached Kubilai Khan."

Marco rubbed his full beard. His thoughts returned to Li. *She is the only one who tempts me now.*

Marco continued. "There had been another type of temptation along the way. At night, as I lay under the stars with the warm glow of the fire, I would take out the letters and stare at them, wondering what they said. Luckily, my mind returned to Yisün and King Manggala's strong words. 'This letter is only for Kubilai's eyes.'

"I rode into Kkambaliq the last week of September. Spectators lined the streets as the city bustled and overflowed with ornate carriages and soldiers on horses. They carried flowing banners of every baron from all provinces and regions that Kubilai Khan owned, bearing eloquent gifts. The fanfare was an amazing sight. My guide, Dai Xiuying, explained. 'It's Kubilai Khan Birthday Festival, the most lavish feast of the year, except for the New Year, the White Festival.

"My excitement lasted only a moment as my thoughts returned to my mission and whether I had passed. When I entered the palace, everyone stared and seemed to exhale an unusual sigh of relief, except for a few who showed disgust.

"Kubilai Khan's servant raced toward me. 'Our messenger sent word of your return. Kubilai Khan is waiting for you. Your father and uncle have been summoned and will arrive soon. While we wait, go to your quarters and prepare to meet his lordship.'

"Nervousness filled my body; my heart felt like it would jump out of my chest. A servant entered my quarters and prepared my bath. I unpacked the silk robe from King Manggala and rubbed my beard, wondering if I should remove the hair like before. The servant saw me and handed me a jeweled mirror and a sharp knife. I took this as a yes. Slowly, I scraped my face, revealing my handsome face." Marco laughed and continued. "The servant helped me comb my long hair and braid the front portion in the Tartar way. Then, he helped me with the layers of fine clothing. As I stood in front of the servant, he looked very satisfied. One last time, I picked up my journal and thumbed through the pages; I had read it so many times that I had memorized every word. *Reciting my stories would be easy*, I thought. Taking a deep breath, I picked up the letters from the table, tucked them safely next to my heart, and walked nervously to Kubilai Khan's court. When I entered, Kubilai Khan sat high on the platform facing south; I fell to my knees and crawled to him. His wife, Empress Chabi, sat on his left, and lower, his son, Crown Prince Chinghiz, sat on his right. Kubilai Khan instructed me to rise, and his face broke into a smile as I stood. His eyes moved up and down as he looked at my new attire. His smile grew. As Kubilai Khan lost eye contact, I discreetly looked for my father. From the corner of my right eye, I could see my father and uncle watching. They, too, were staring at me. The reason; I no longer looked Venetian, but a Tartarian.

"Kubilai Khan, in his roaring voice, spoke. 'Come forward. I hear you have some letters from my son and grandson.' I slowly removed the letters and handed them to his servant. Another attendee carried a cage of rats and set it next to Kubilai Khan.

"Peering hard at Kubilai, I dared not question but thought, *What are the rats for?* I felt panicked, and my stomach felt sick.

"Kubilai took the letters and opened each end, pulling out another letter. Shocked, they were the letters I had delivered to his son and grandson, never opened. Kubilai handed the letters to the attendee, who opened the letters and, with a pair of silver chopsticks, pulled out a letter and paper money from each. He dropped them into the rat's cage. As they floated to the bottom of the cage, the rats scrambled over them and, one by one, fell dead. Silence filled the room, then whispering, POISON. Kubilai Khan released a burst of deep, bold laughter that surrounded me. Instantly, I looked over at my father, whose face was white as a ghost, and I glanced back at Kubilai. My legs went weak, sweat glistened on my forehead, and my hands trembled. I could hardly stand. My mind raced. I now understood why everyone was surprised to see me. But I wondered how his son and grandson knew before I arrived not to open the letters. Most of all, it became clear how brutal Kubilai Khan could be. The rest of the room was silent. Kubilai Khan's voice echoed in the room. 'You passed the first test; you are alive. Proving you are trustworthy and loyal. Now tell me your story of my lands.'

"For the next several hours, I numbly stood and weaved the most exciting stories and truths I could. Laughter, awes, and clapping echoed in the hall when I finished. Kubilai smiled and clapped his hands. His servant walked over to me and handed me several pieces of paper. Carefully, I opened them as fear radiated from my body. *Could this be my death?* My eyes couldn't believe what I saw. Staring at my father and back at Kubilai, my confidence glowed. The papers were the permits for salt, tea, and gold from the Minister of Trade, with my name only—Messer Marco Polo—stamped with the royal seal.

"Kubilai Khan stared at my father. 'You should be proud of your son, but as I recall, he belongs to me now.' Then Kubilai turned to me. 'I am proud, Messer Marco. Return to me tomorrow. I have things to discuss.' Kubilai Khan stood and left the room with Empress Chabi and his son. From that day forward, I was known as Messer Marco Polo and held a seat to the right of Kubilai Khan.

"The moment he left the room, I fell to the ground. My father and uncle laughed and congratulated me as they helped me to my feet. Then, I gave my father the permits. He, with my uncle reading over his shoulder, became silent. Uncle Maffeo grumbled in disgust and stomped out.

"'How can this be? This was not the plan!' My father yelled.

"I looked into his eyes. 'It wasn't my plan to be given to Kubilai Khan either. It looks like we have to make the most out of our circumstances.'

"My father never dreamed I would be in control. My very unhappy father and I silently returned to my quarters, where Uncle Maffeo awaited us. His face radiated hate as he had never wanted me to join them, and now I held the golden keys—gold, salt, and tea permits."

Marco stopped talking momentarily, just enough for Rustichello to speak up.

"Your father and uncle now worked for you? That must have burned their asses."

Marco answered proudly. "Yes, the permits were in my name, and it burned badly. My father and uncle now worked for me. The letters from King Manggala and Yisün were intended for me, and they contained the names of important people necessary to establish my future business.

"I learned a lot during this trip and made many friends. But as I said earlier, I realized how brutal the Great Khan could be. If I or anyone else had opened the letter, they would have died. Poison coated the money and letters. A terrifying way to test my loyalty and trustworthiness."

"How did the people receiving them know not to touch them?" Rustichello asked.

"Amazingly, Kubilai Khan had a remarkable method to dispatch his messengers. Much faster than I could travel.

> *"He has many roads throughout his provinces, named after each province it lead to. There are outposts with as many as 400 horses every twenty-five miles throughout these provinces. If a messenger wishes to travel fast, he carries a tablet with the sign of the gyrfalcons, indicating he must reach his destiny quickly. As*

he approaches the next outpost, he sounds a horn, and fresh horses are saddled and ready to go by the time he reaches it. He can travel 250 to 300 miles a day if it is necessary. When the rider can no longer ride, another one takes his place."

"Amazing!" Rustichello excitedly said. Marco stopped and looked at Rustichello. "This is where my personal story begins. Don't you think we have written enough to hand over to the commander? Anyway, I'm tired; the night is almost over. Dread surrounds me. Am I really going to be released?"

Unexpectedly, Marco asked Rustichello. "How long have you been here and why?"

Rustichello was surprised. Since the beginning, Marco had never been concerned about his life. He was in such a hurry to write this report.

"Fourteen years," he whispered.

With a crazed look, Marco yelled. "What did you say?!"

"I said fourteen years. They captured me in the Battle of Meloria in 84. The Genoese have been insisting on controlling commerce since then."

Marco thought back to his return to Venice. When they had left Cathay, they had no idea what was happening in their old world.

Rustichello continued. "If I worked for the commander and helped you write this report, they might finally release me. That was my agreement with him, anyway."

Marco's heart sank. *Have I been fooling myself? Will they really release me? Did they deliver the letters to my family and Li?* The fourteen years kept swirling in his head. *What would happen to Li?* He fell onto his bed with his back to Rustichello and closed his eyes while tears fell.

For the first time in a very long time, Rustichello felt a pang of pain. Over the years, he became numb. Standing, he straightened out his tired, hunched body and the papers on his desk, blew out the candles, and fell into his bed facing the wall, thinking back to his first year in prison. He resembled Marco's, so full of hope and urgency, but time had changed him; he grew cold as ice. Marco's pain was melting the ice. As tears filled his eyes, he thought, *I have spent my life fighting as a crusader, fighting for Pisa. My love affair was war and telling stories of warriors, never experiencing love like Marco.*

The darkness of the night concealed the two grown men, but not the sound of sorrow.

At daybreak, Marco awakened Rustichello, shouting. Rustichello rolled over and saw Marco screaming at the top of his lungs at the door. "I want to see the commander now. Someone, anyone, I order you to take me to the commander. My report is ready."

Voices from the other cells echoed through the halls, "Shut up, you asshole, shut up! The sun hasn't even risen yet."

Rustichello stood and approached Marco, putting his hands on his shoulders and turning him. "Come on, Marco. This is not the way. The commander will see you when he wants."

Marco's swollen, red eyes sadly looked at Rustichello. "I can't believe you have been here fourteen years. How can you be so calm? You, too, must want to see the commander; your release could be possible."

"The one thing I have learned here is that things will happen when the time is right. Like you coming into my life, I felt hope for the first time in a long time."

Marco shoved Rustichello's hands off his shoulder. "I can't be as patient as you. I must get out of here. He turned to the door and, with his calloused fist, started banging and yelling until his fist bled and his voice disappeared.

Rustichello sat down, picked up his pen, and started writing. The whole place had turned into a shouting battle between all the cellmates. Something would happen, but from experience, it would differ from what Marco wanted.

Suddenly, the shouting became quieter, and Rustichello heard different voices in the mix, more commanding. The other prisoners' shouting turned to screams and then silence. Suddenly, their cell door opened, and two guards grabbed Marco; one smashed his face with his fist. Blood flew around the room as the guard's fist repeatedly hit Marco. The guard released Marco, and he fell to the floor. They looked at Rustichello viciously as he lowered his head. The guards stomped out of the room, shouting, "Shut up, or the next time we return, we won't quit."

Marco lay in a puddle of his blood and whimpered incoherent words. Rustichello sat for a while and watched Marco before he spoke. "I warned you; patience is the key here. That's how I survived. You are no longer Messer Marco Polo, under the protection of the Great Khan." Rustichello walked over to Marco, squatted, gently wiped Marco's face, and repeated. "Patience, patience, patience, only then will we prevail." He then helped Marco up and sat him at the table. "Ok, let's continue, Messer Marco Polo."

Marco's swollen and split lips turned upward in a distorted smile, and he began slowly.

"Like I said, my uncle's face radiated hate, and my father's face displayed disappointment and concern. We sat at the refined, decorative wooden table with permits in front of us.

"My uncle, with a sharp, angry voice, finally spoke. 'Where does your allegiance lie, Marco, with the Khan or us?'

"I calmly answered, 'My allegiance lies with myself. I will remain true to myself and what I believe to be correct and fair. In his cruel way, Kubilai Khan showed me what he expects:

loyalty, trustworthiness, and the consequences if I falter. You were there, you saw. This doesn't mean you and Father are out of the picture. It means there are three partners instead of two, and I have become the most important one. Tomorrow, I will meet with Kubilai, who will disclose my next mission. When I return from his chamber, I will determine the handling of our business.'

"My uncle stood, his eyes undeniably coveted the permits as his hands rested upon them. He stared down at me and sternly said, 'I have heard enough. You are just a boy, and I will never accept you as a partner.'

"He stormed out of the room. My father watched him leave and then turned to me. It was the first time my father looked slightly proud of me. 'I will talk to him. After all, I am the one responsible.'

"'You must convince him, Father. Uncle Maffeo has no choice but to accept me or become a criminal in the Khan's eyes. You and Uncle will still be the merchants. I will be busy with other duties. Who cares whose name the permits are under as long as we have them?'

"My father understood, but my uncle took some convincing. He continues to have a silent resentment to this day.

"The next morning, Kubilai Khan's eunuch arrived, requesting that I follow him. Fearfully, I followed; it would be my first time alone with the Great Khan. I never dreamt this was the beginning of a genuine friendship. He would treat me as a son, and I would treat him as a father. Many enemies were made that day, but so were friends.

"You know what the title Khan means in our language.

> *"Great Lords of Lords. And he certainly had every right to this title. He was a mighty man, whether in respect of his subjects, or of territory, or of treasure. He is indeed the greatest lord the world has ever known."*

Marco sounds like a proud son, Rustichello thought. *Why did Marco leave?* Rustichello decided not to interrupt. He just listened.

> *"He descended from the direct imperial line of Genghis Khan; for only one of those lineages may be Lord of the Tartars. He began his reign in 1256 and continued until he died. He won his lordship by valor, prowess, and good sense, even though his kinsfolk and brothers tried to dethrone him. He proved he was the finest, wisest, boldest in counsel and strategist the Tartars ever had."*

Marco stopped talking, looked at Rustichello, and continued in a much sadder, muffled tone. "If any man had told me, I would someday betray him. I would have killed him on the spot."

"What did you say? Betray? Betray who?"

"Never mind!" Marco answered. "You will understand later."

Marco continued. "When I entered Kubilai's chambers, his surroundings were opulent. He was sitting by himself at a small table with numerous food bowls. Again, I fell to my knees with my face to the floor. His eunuch reached down and pulled me to a stance. He whispered in my ear. 'When the Khan invites you to his private chambers, and he is by himself, that's unnecessary.' He directed me to sit. I was so nervous; my heart was beating fast and loud. I was sure he could hear it."

"'Good morning, Messer Marco Polo. Have some breakfast. Let's discuss your future,' he said as he poured me a cup of tea. In turn, I poured him a cup. Kubilai looked at me. 'You have learned well!'

"'Your grandson was very informative as I poured milk in his tea.'

"Kubilai Khan was very straightforward. 'How's your father and uncle handling the news?'

"I decided I would be the same—direct. 'Not happy.'

"Kubilai's face reflected pride. 'I took a chance with your life, and you won. Over the years, I have encountered many treacherous and disloyal individuals across Cathay and other lands, perhaps even within my own family. I demand loyalty from those who work for me. Your eyes were young and innocent, but I wasn't sure of your father's loyalty. You had little time to grow jaded or greedy. That comes with age. Now that you are mine, I have things to tell and show you before you go on your next trip, but not before my birthday festival.'

"As I sat before Kubilai, I studied him as he had done to me. His body was well proportioned, neither small nor large, but of medium height, and muscles covered his body. Cheeks, red as a rose, glowed on his white face. His eyes were black and beautiful, and he had a shapely and well-set nose.

"As I sat before him, I thought, *Never in my wildest dreams as we traveled here did I imagine I would sit privately with the Great Khan.*

"I returned to reality when the conversation turned to General Bayan and the war raging south in Song. 'Yes, I heard the battle was ending, and the Queen Dowager could surrender soon.'

"'That's your next assignment, as soon as my birthday celebration ends, to travel to Lin'an. But not before you meet my twelve barons, who oversee and examine the captains and soldiers, especially in the expeditions and battles. You must observe the barons and the defeated for their honesty and loyalty. You are then to report the results to me without the barons knowing. Dai Xiuying will again be your guide. You will travel on the east side of my empire, heading south to Manzi. Before you leave, we will meet again with more instructions, and I have a place I'd like to show you. By the way, your quarters will remain here. I want you close. But for now, you should visit your father. I heard he found a house on the city's west side.'

"I stood and bowed. Kubilai Khan smiled. 'Prepare yourself for my birthday. I will send you new clothing.'

"I smiled and wondered if he invited my father. I left his chamber, remembering the fanfare I had seen when we arrived in the city. My excitement grew."

---

1. Lugouqiao or Marco Polo Bridge
2. Yellow River
3. Most likely Huazhong in SW Shaanxi province
4. Xicheng
5. Mount Emei (Emeishan), located in Sichuan Province, China
6. Kunming
7. Dian Chi Lake
8. Dali
9. Baoshan
10. *The Classic of Herbal Medicine*

Chapter Twenty-Four

Marco

1280 A Story Intertwining the Lives of Marco, Kim Chin-hae, and Li

Genoa Prison 1298

Marco stopped talking. His swollen eyes had turned black, and his intumescent lips had become crusted with blood. His freakish smile diminished, and he sat silently, hungry and exhausted, mentally and physically. The sun sat high in the sky. He hadn't eaten since last night.

"Remember when I rescued Li?" Marco didn't wait for Rustichello to answer. He strayed from his question. His mouth opened and, in a whisper, asked again, "Do you think we will get out of here?" The thought of fourteen years was ripping out his heart. *Li can never exist without me.*

Marco stood and bolted to the door, screaming at the guards. Rustichello quickly ran to him, putting his hand over his mouth. "Shut up, shut up. We will never eat or get out this way. He pulled him back to the table and pushed him to sit. Tell me about Kim Chin-hae. What happened to him? We haven't talked about him in a while." Rustichello hoped talking about Kim would make him forget his pain.

Marco stared into space, and like a madman, he started repeating Kim Chin-hae's name. "Kim Chin-hae, Kim Chin-hae, Kim... Maybe Li and I'll end up like Kim Chin-hae and Lis."

Rustichello urged him on. "Tell me about Kim Chin-hae. What do you mean, end up like Lis and him?"

Marco settled down slightly and whispered. "You remember, right, why he was in Cathay? Let me think, where did I stop?" Marco stared into space. His mind marched backward.

Rustichello had an excellent memory. Besides, he was more sane than Marco right now. He spoke up first. "You told me how Kim Chin-hae met Lis and married her. What happened next?"

Marco nodded; he remembered. "After that night, we met often in Yangzhou, where I worked for Kubilai Khan, observing the salt trade and the sea trade routes in Ningbo. It amazed Kim Chin-hae how quickly I had become Kubilai Khan's right-hand man.

"Kim Chin-hae and I were business partners, but our partnership went beyond that. I helped him with his upcoming invasion, gathering information and acquiring supplies.

"As the year passed, Kim Chin-hae returned twice to Masanhappo, filing his report with his king and General Kim Bang-gyong, avoiding going home at all costs. He had no idea how he would handle his personal situation. He was a coward, and he knew it. Besides, he didn't have the time or energy to face his parents or Park Eun-ae. His primary concern was the upcoming battle and how he would survive.

"Like I said in one of my past stories, in June 1280, Kim Chin-hae and I rode to the Summer Palace. He had received word from his cousin, King Chungnyeols, that he would arrive in August for a meeting with Kubilai Khan. He wanted Kim Chin-hae to meet him there. He feared that this meant the invasion was imminent.

"I, too, was summoned to the Summer Palace to meet the Khan. We left with my guide, Dai Xiuying, and Kim Chin-hae's soldier, Pak Byeong-ho, and his servant, Son Jun-ho. The days were hot, humid, and thunderous. Several times, huge thunderclouds crossed our path, and torrential rain soaked us as we traveled along the river, passing thousands of exhausted men slaving on the extension of the Grand Canal. The area we traveled through was the richest agricultural land in Cathay. As Khanbaliq grew, Kubilai Khan's citizens needed more rice and supplies, and Kubilai Khan's dream of extending the canal made that happen. Kubilai Khan always looked to the future. This extension would be the second golden waterway next to the Yangtze River. When completed, it would be over a thousand miles long, carrying the necessary supplies to Khanbaliq. Unfortunately, this canal held the hearts and souls of thousands of men who perished while laboring for their kings or conquerors for the last 700 years.

"Kim Chin-hae gasped when he heard this and said, 'What men endure for their kings!'

"I stopped my horse and looked at him. He was shaking his head; his face seemed distorted with pain. In a quiet voice so that his men could not hear, he said, 'Man always seems to be at the mercy of their king's power and greed. My memories of the last Wa invasion still cause me pain, all the screaming and dying men. Will I face the same situation this time? Will I feel the anger as I did then?'

"Kim Chin-hae didn't wait for my answer. He continued in a happier tone. 'How long do you think this extension will take?' I shook my head; I didn't know."

Marco looked at Rustichello. "By the time I left Cathay in 1292, they had almost completed it."

Marco continued with Kim Chin-hae's story. "Kim suddenly changed the subject and asked me why Kubilai Khan summoned me. I laughed. 'I'm going to a wrestling contest between the Khanate of Persia's son, Arghun, and Qaidu's daughter, Aiyurug.'

"Swiftly, Kim Chin-hae's head turned. 'What? Did I hear correctly—a woman?'

I laughed hard. 'Yes, a woman warrior, a large, beautiful woman, white as moonlight or shining moon. That's what her name means. When we originally traveled to Kubilai, we traveled through their territory. No man can beat her in wrestling; if he does, they will marry. This marriage would be a perfect solution to peace. Kubilai Khan is sending me to observe and report the results to him.'

"Kim Chin-hae noticed my smile and boldly said. 'So, it seems you know this woman personally.'

"My face turned red.

"Kim Chin-hae laughed. 'Yes, I believe my assumption is correct. Did you tumble with the women warrior and lose?'

"Dai Xiuying boldly laughed. My face turned redder. A roar of laughter surrounded us."

Marco continued. "Travel was slower than usual because of the rain. As we sheltered, we talked. Most of the time, I let Kim Chin-hae tell his story. That was my hidden talent; making you feel at ease, and information poured out. But on this trip, I also talked. Maybe Kim Chin-hae had the same talent. He was the first person I ever told how I obtained our permits.

"After I told Kim Chin-hae the story, I stared at him momentarily, hoping he understood this was a warning and he needed to be careful. Kubilai Khan could be brutal. Kim Chin-hae sat emotionless and never responded.

"The night before we arrived, I talked about the young Li and how I had rescued her four years earlier when the Song Dynasty fell. 'She lives in the palace with Kubilai Khan's Empress Chabi,' I told him.

"Kim Chin-hae noticed my persona changed and asked more questions.

"'I secretly watch over her using her servant, my friend Guo Yu. The day I found her, I made a strange bond and felt responsible.'

"Kim Chin-hae mentioned he also had a special person who lived in the palace. 'My cousin's son, the Crown Prince Wang Won, Kubilai Khan's grandson. They call him Ijir

Bukhqa in the palace. Later, his name will change when he becomes King. His name will contain the word Chung. When Goryeo became a vassal of Kubilai Khan, we were no longer allowed to use our family name, Wang. Chung means loyalty to the demands of Kubilai Khan.'

"You could see his sadness as he told me. Then I remembered the first time I saw Kim Chin-hae at the Winter Palace. A servant held a small child next to him. *So that's who that was.*

It was a strange coincidence that we both had young beings in the palace we were concerned about.

"The day we arrived, we went our separate ways. We met in the garden only once as he played with the young crown prince, in a decorative pavilion. Kim Chin-hae was still waiting for his cousin, the king, to arrive. The young prince was mature, royal, and solemn as he sat at his small, ornate desk, surrounded by ink and paper. He had a talent for drawing, and I heard it was the only thing that consoled him when his father and Kim Chin-hae left two years ago. I was in a hurry, but slowed when Kim Chin-haeand and I saw each other. He excitedly said. 'This is my cousin, Crown Prince Wang Won, I told you about.'

"I bowed and introduced myself. 'I am Messer Marco Polo.' The young prince maturely introduced himself. 'You can call me Ijir Bukhqa.'

"Kim Chin-hae didn't know, but I understood children who felt deserted. It didn't take long for us to become friends, which made Kim happy. He wanted someone close other than the young prince's eunuch and attendees, knowing they could be bought and cause harm to the young prince.

"After becoming friends with the young prince, Kim Chin-hae noticed my impatience and asked if the fair maiden was waiting for me. 'The beautiful warrior, perhaps?'

"'That's later. Now, I am on a mission for my young princess. I need to speak to the Royal Physician at the infirmary.'

"I didn't volunteer any other information, and he didn't pressure me, knowing one day I would tell.

Marco continued. "Guo Yu had been Li's servant for four years by then and came to see me when I arrived at the palace. It was a joyful reunion, but I saw worry in his eyes. Urgently, I questioned him if something was wrong with Princess Li.

"'No.'

"'So, what's with the worried look?'

"Guo Yu spoke softly; he didn't want anyone to hear. 'Empress Chabi is ill. Li is worried about what will happen if she dies.'

"I understood. Empress Chabi had always been Li's champion. And when I left her four years ago, I was relieved that she had an important person on her side. *Now, what are we going to do?* I wondered and asked Guo Yu.

"He quickly answered as if he had already been planning. 'The trip to the Summer Palace was difficult for the Empress Chabi. Li rode in her carriage with Physician Wu. Even though the Empress talked, her commanding voice was weak, her skin was pale, and she had a horrible cough. Li knew she was terribly ill. She sat quietly and curiously watched Physician Wu treat her with his strange teas and herbs. As he poured the tea, his voice would rise. 'Empress, this is Gang Shi-Tang; it contains Bei Mu, Jie-Geng, and Xing-ren for your lungs. Sometimes, Physician Wu would stare at Li, but he never said a word and continued with his herbal remedies.'

"Guo Yu continued, 'Physician Wu seems to be interested in her. Maybe that's the answer. It is fitting for girls to learn herbs.'

"Perking up, I thought, *That's it. I will talk to Physician Wu and Empress Chabi.* That's where I was heading when I met Kim Chin-hae in the garden.

"When I arrived at the infirmary, I wasn't sure what to say. The Royal Physician and I had never met. Surprisingly, upon my arrival, there was no need for introductions. Physician Wu greeted me graciously.

"'Messer Marco Polo, right? I heard you are an important man in Kubilai Khan's court. What can I do for you?'

"'I'm not sure where to start, as I have no right to ask you, but I need your help.'

"'Maybe from the beginning.' Physician Wu responded.

"As I studied his face, he looked kind and trustworthy, so I decided to take a chance. I told him of Li's rescue and how I delivered her to Empress Chabi.

"Come to find out, Physician Wu had always been curious about this young Song princess. Now he understood.

"'Again, what can I do?' Physician Wu asked.

"With a serious, almost pleading face, I answered. 'Please take Li under your wing. She needs another champion. I fear Empress Chabi's days are limited. I can't explain, but I feel responsible for this little girl. Teach her herbs and medicine; she will have a chance then.'

"Physician Wu studied me. 'I will test her. She has been present many times when I treated the Empress. If she shows talent, I will train her.'

"'Thank you, thank you! She is a bright child, Guo Yu assures me.'

"Physician Wu watched me leave. I was sure he was thinking, *What a strange connection those two have*. I hoped he would be lenient with her.

"My next mission was Empress Chabi. I stood outside her chamber and waited for permission to enter. Her servant said she would meet me at the cane palace in an hour. Nodding in agreement, I left. When I arrived, her servant led me to a flowing river among a beautiful grove of trees, where she sat. She looked pale. I bowed low and apologized for interrupting her peaceful moment. She smiled and motioned for me to sit. 'I needed some fresh air; besides, my chambers have many listening ears. Why did you ask to see me?'

"'Feeling powerless but hopeful,' I answered. 'Princess Li needs another champion. I hope you will allow Princess Li to learn medicine under Physician Wu. He agreed to instruct her if she showed talent and interest. But you need to approve. This knowledge could be helpful in her future.'

"'I see, you think I am dying like the rest.' The Empress answered emotionlessly.

"Stunned by her comment, I fell to the ground, apologizing profusely.

"'We all die,' she said as she placed her hand on my head. 'Rise and sit. The rumors are correct; my health is failing. I will fulfill your request if you fulfill mine,' she declared.

"I looked up at her with a bewildered look. I wasn't expecting a deal.

"'My request is for you to stay true to Kubilai. Stay by his side now, and when I pass. Please encourage him to marry my cousin, Consort Nambi. She will be faithful to him; her heart is pure. He will be sad, but she will soon make him forget his sorrow. Please make sure.'

"I nodded and promised with uncertainty regarding his marriage to Nambi.

"Empress Chabi continued talking. 'I find your concern regarding Li strange. What makes a man from a different world worry about a child from our world?'

"Without hesitation, I explained my childhood story and how my mother taught me to be resilient and have a purpose. She nodded with understanding. 'I will wait till Physician Wu has tested her. If the outcome is positive, I will give my permission, and my cousin, Nambi, will be told.'

"Empress Chabi started coughing hard. Instantly, her servant appeared and walked her back to the cane palace. Empress Chabi turned and smiled. 'You promise, and I will promise.'

"Guo Yu told me a few days later, Physician Wu entered Empress Chabi's chamber and asked for Li. Li shyly walked up to him, and he asked one question: 'What herbs do I give Empress Chabi?' Li, with her child's voice, answered. 'Gan-Shi-Tang with BEI Mu, Jie-Geng, and Xing-Ren.' Her future changed at that moment.

"The next day, I left for the wrestling match, feeling relieved; Li had passed the test. The following year, in March, Empress Chabi passed away.

Marco momentarily hesitated to say a quick prayer and continued talking about Kim Chin-hae. "Months later, maybe in January, I met Kim Chin-hae outside the South Gate of Ningbo on the famous Nantang Street. Kim Chin-hae and I sat at our favorite teahouse, listening to two local entertainers spin a comic tale on the regional news. We savored the taste of a remarkable tea from the Pu'-erh ancient trees as I shared the story of the female warrior. It was the first time I had seen Kim Chin-hae laugh in a long time. However, as the comics continued, we both found their news not comical. The room whirled with news of Kubilai Khan's upcoming invasion, and warships that occupied the harbor. It was hard for us to laugh or to listen, so we moved to a private room. He started his story.

"'Lis fills my nightly dreams. She is calling me. My heart aches. I haven't seen her in months.' After hesitating for a moment, he started smiling. 'Marco, just your face gives me courage. Tomorrow, I will inform General Fan Wenhu that I am going south to Fuzhou. When I return, I will make the final report, and two men will carry it to Goryeo. As I initially said, I won't return to Goryeo before the invasion.'

"With that statement, it seemed he had made a long, self-debated decision. Kim Chin-hae continued his story of what happened when he met his cousin, King Chungnyeols, in Khanbaliq."

Chapter Twenty-Five

Kim

1281 Plans of Second Invasion of Wa

"When King Chungnyeols arrived at Shang-du's Summer Palace, I met my cousin enthusiastically with the young Crown Prince Wang Won at the main gate. I became ecstatic when I realized the king had brought my men. Tears filled everyone's eyes, but proper protocol had to be maintained.

"My men and I temporarily composed ourselves and agreed to meet later in my chamber. The desire to share my family with everyone increased when I saw the king with his child. But I knew better. This was not the time. Maybe before the king left, I would find the right time.

"For my cousin, it was only after the chamber doors were closed that the tender moments commenced. The young prince jumped into his father's arms, and I greeted my cousin as a friend. After the crown prince retired, the king and I discussed the report.

"'Our meeting tomorrow will be in the main chamber with all the ministers,' I informed him.

"My cousin walked over to an ornate box and opened it. Inside, a folded piece of paper lay, and he handed it to me. 'These are the requests I plan to discuss with Kubilai Khan.'

1. The Quelpart Isle[1] soldiers will be included in the invasion.
2. Decrease the number of our soldiers and increase the size of Kubilai Khan's army.
3. I continue to head the eastern expedition.
4. All Goryeo officers to have badges.
5. All Han and Manzi who live on the seashore should be helmsmen and sailors.

"'What do you think?' My cousin asked.

"I agreed, and our discussion continued until late in the evening. Finally, my cousin, overcome with tiredness, said, 'Your men are waiting for you. Tomorrow will be a stressful day. I need sleep.'

"I left with adrenaline flowing through my body with mixed emotions: excitement to see my men, and fear of the next day.

"As I entered my chambers, my excitement overcame my fear. Soon, disappointment overcame my excitement; vases of rice wine were scattered around the room, as were the passed-out men. I picked up a cup and started drinking until the bottle was empty. Pak Byeong-ho, lying in my bed, sat up. 'They waited as long as they could. We can talk in the morning.'

"I pushed Pak Byeong-ho out of my bed, slid into it, and drifted off to sleep, imagining Lis was in my arms.

"The following day, when I opened my eyes, my men hovered over me. I jumped out of bed, cursing and laughing. We spent the morning talking over past times, eating, and wishing the future would be filled with many moments like this.

"In the afternoon, I followed my cousin, fully dressed in a royal navy uniform, to Kubilai Khan's throne hall. He sat high on his ornate chair as we entered the room. The ministers stood, bowed, and respectfully greeted my cousin. Proudly, I stood. My cousin, King Chungnyeol of Goryeo, had made it happen; Yuan ministers respected him. We sat next to the ministers. Supreme Commander Arakhan sat closest to Kubilai Khan. His appearance worried me; Arakhan looked frail. General Fan Wenhu, who was staring at me, sat next to him. I had forgotten he had never seen me dressed in uniform. He knew I was an emissary for the king and Kubilai Khan, but now he realized I was a general in the Goryeo Navy. He looked concerned.

"I held my breath as my confident cousin walked forward with his report and handed it to the Supreme Commander Arakhan. This report contained all the information I had gathered in Yuan, as well as the progress of our fleet in Goryeo. Then, my cousin handed Kubilai Khan his requests. Kubilai Khan unfolded the paper and slowly read, making grunting sounds. My heart raced as I held my breath. He handed it to the Supreme Commander Arakhan. 'Make sure they fulfill his requests.' My cousin's pride beamed. He had finally gained the respect he had dearly wanted. I released my breath.

"The supreme commander only thumbed through my report pages and handed it to Kubilai. To me, Arakhan didn't have the energy to read it. This was a concern. Kubilai Khan, instead of reading the report, started asking questions.

"In a stern, bold voice, Kubilai spoke to my cousin. 'We must be victorious. Are your ships built? How many men do you have?'

"My cousin continued with confidence. 'We have 900 ships, 15,000 sailors,10,000 soldiers, and 110,000 seoks of grain. My Generals, Hong Dagu and Kim Bang-gyong, await your orders in Goryeo.'

"Kubilai Khan turned to General Fan Wenhu. 'Are you ready?'

"The general sarcastically spoke as he stared at me. 'General Kim Chin-hae, maybe you should answer that question. It seems you have been spying for your king regarding our readiness. Do you think we are prepared?'

"Directing my answer to General Fan Wenhu, I said, 'General, my job here was to oversee the incredible logistical problems that will arise with a massive seaborne invasion coming from two directions, and to inform my king of the problems that might arise. I have no complaints regarding you or your preparedness.'

"I continued. 'I do have a concern about the weather, which is our greatest enemy. Fighting in the first invasion, I witnessed firsthand the devastating impact of a great storm on a powerful fleet and the consequences for a substandard one. The Southern Fleet is substandard except for the Song Ocean fleet. The rest are mostly river ships that have been refitted for ocean travel.

"'General Fan Wenhu!' Kubilai Khan said firmly, interrupting our conversation. 'I asked you. Are you ready?'

"General Fan Wenhu looked slightly embarrassed. 'Our 3000 ships, the grain, and supplies to support the Eastern Fleets will be ready by May next year. This will lessen General Kim Chin-hae's concern regarding storms. We will have plenty of time to defeat the Shogunate before the monsoon season begins in November.'

"That seemed to be all Kubilai Khan wanted to hear. He directed Supreme Commander Arakhan to terminate this meeting and arrange a private meeting with all generals and King Chungnyeols to discuss the invasion in detail.

"Kubilai's favorite wife, Empress Chabi, was ill, as you know, and his mind was not on the invasion but on her.

"However, that day, I wondered if General Fan Wenhu would continue his contempt for me or if my words eased his concerns.

"The next day, my cousin and I, with fallacious confidence, entered the home of Supreme Commander Arakhan, where General Fan Wenhu, General Chang-Hsi, and several other generals met us. I whispered to my cousin. 'I regret Commander Hong Dagu and General Kim Bang-gyong are absent.'

"A pretense of respectability and hope lingered in the room. An invasion of this magnitude had never been attempted. Three nations miles apart, the conqueror and two conquered, traveling with thousands of ships, soldiers, and large-ego generals joining hands to conquer a fourth nation.

"We were all seated, and the meeting began with Supreme Commander Arakhan handing my king's request to General Fan Wenhu. 'The Khan has agreed to all his requests. Make sure this happens.' The general looked sour but agreed.

"My king sat, and Supreme Commander Arakhan directed me to speak regarding my idea of the invasion. 'I agree, May is a good month. On the first lunar moon, the Goryeo navy, with 900 ships, will travel to Tsushima to take control of the strait. In July, we will meet up with the Eastern Fleet on the island of Iki, carrying supplies and food, God willing.'

"General Fan Wenhu, jealous, interrupted me. 'I am sure you are aware...' He looked at me resentfully and then redirected his conversation to King Chungnyeol. 'We have thousands of ships, including 600 from lower Pu Shou Kang. These are strong ships that will carry 100,000 troops. I am sure General Kim Chin-hae told you our men are bitter and worn, but I can assure you they are ready for battle. They are seasoned soldiers and will fight to the end. Our large cargo ships are of much better quality than yours and very capable of transporting supplies and grain to the front lines.'

"General Chang Hsi interrupted him and changed the subject to prevent any more ill feelings between us. 'We have heard from our spies that the Shogunate has been preparing for this invasion since the 1274 invasion. They have constructed forts, enormous stone walls, and other defensive structures at landing points. We should be prepared for this. But with our supreme manpower, weapons, and thousands of ships, defeat is impossible.'

"I continued, trying to dismiss Fan Wenhu's jealous words. *I guess I made an enemy instead of a friend,* I thought. I then repeated. 'Supreme Commander Arakhan, the Eastern Fleet will wait for you at Iki, and when we arrive, we will continue together to Hakata Bay and then to their leader, Shogunate, in mainland Wa, I mean Cipangu in your language. We must prepare ourselves for their defensive measures. I will let Goryeo's generals know this. The king has also decided I will fight on your ship, General Fan Wenhu.'

"General Fan Wenhu's face went stiff, and he responded quickly. 'As a Goryeo spy on our lacking ships? What is your wife going to say?'

"My cousin stared open-mouthed at me! I didn't flinch and kept on the current subject. 'I am not a spy; I am a communicator. I speak for my king and Kubilai Khan. The distance is far; a great sea separates us. I am the connector.

"Fan Wenhu wasn't listening. He continued directing his conversation to my cousin. 'Oh, you didn't know your cousin married a Hmong Miao, a shaman at that.'

"The rest of the generals watched.

"I spoke up. 'This is a personal affair, General Fan Wenhu.'

"General Fan Wen-hu wasn't finished.

"Finally, Supreme Commander Arakhan sternly said, 'General Fan Wenhu, this meeting is to discuss our invasion, not personal issues.'

"Supreme Commander Arakhan tried to change the subject. 'I agree with King Chungnyeol's decision, General Fan Wenhu. General Kim Chin-hae will fight on your ship. It's time to end this meeting. We still have time for more discussions.'

"The other generals left first, leaving my cousin, Supreme Commander Arakhan, General Fan Wenhu, and me. I turned to Fan Wenhu. 'How did you know?' My cousin and Arakhan listened.

"General Fan Wenhu answered. 'You were always leaving and going South. I became suspicious and had you followed.'

"I lowered my head and turned to my cousin. 'I wanted to tell you myself.'

"My king stood and motioned me to follow. 'It's time to return to the Kubilai Khan's palace.'

"The trip back was silent. When we arrived, I followed my cousin to his private chamber. His face showed anger. 'So, that's why you easily agreed to return to Yuan. It wasn't for your country, but for love? Your mother was right; you are a dreamer, and your life is only about you and your dream.'

"I stood with my head down. 'My punishment should be for my deceit. But I am not ashamed of my decision. A person has the right to live their own life. I am risking my life for our country, but I don't believe I should give you my whole life and soul forever. I will survive, and then my life will be mine.'

"My king sat down, stared at me momentarily, and motioned me to sit. He poured rice wine into a cup, and I poured one for him. He consumed the drink in one gulp, and then I slightly turned away from him and did the same. He set down his cup, and I refilled it, and he did the same for me. We did this three more times. The atmosphere became kinder. The king disappeared, and my cousin appeared with a smile. His voice was softer. 'Tell me about her!'

"Turning red from the drinks and feeling much more relaxed, I blurted out. 'Lis is my heaven.' I then poured him one more drink. 'So are my children.'

"This time, my cousin put down his cup and motioned me to pour him another. 'Your mother will not approve. Children? You haven't been here that long.'

"The rice wine slurred my words. 'I have twins, a girl and a boy, Kim Mei-caihong and Kim Yang-dalou.'

"My face transformed; I was no longer happy. Fear surfaced and exposed the frightening question I had hidden from Lis and myself: *Will I be able to keep my promise to Lis and live my own life?*

"Still slurring, waving my cup for more, my chest suddenly ached. 'Please, cousin, please understand. My dream only included me until the day I met her. I chose my destiny when I saw a wild animal unfurl in a bamboo cage and released her.'

"'What?' my cousin said, looking confused.

"'Someday, I will explain. Just understand that my life changed that day. Every decision made after that has been driven by love, and that will never change. For now, let's forget my life and concentrate on victory. Not my life! That includes my parents. I will deal with them later.'

"Standing up, my body swayed back and forth. My cousin rose and caught me just in time before I hit the floor. He called for Son Jun-ho. That was the last thing I remember.

"Later, my cousin told me that as he watched Son Jun-ho and Pak Byeong-ho carry me from his chamber, he remembered the day he had taken me to see the royal ship; he questioned his ability to change my heart in favor of his aunt's dream. Now, he couldn't help but wonder if my dream, decision, and reckless love would cost me my life. As a king, he should only be concerned about winning, but as a cousin, he wanted me to live."

Kim Chin-hae put his head down, wondering if his cousin was right. *Would my love cost me my life?* He shook his head as to clear it. *Why think? I made the decision long ago.*

He continued his story. "The meetings the following week always returned to a power struggle and mistrust. I attempted to raise the issue regarding the food supply. Floods during the rice planting season destroyed the rice fields on the eastern coast, as well as in the north and south of Yuan.

"'We must be prepared to talk to Kubilai Khan about gaining access to his rice and grains from his royal storage. We should know by November if necessary,' I told the assembly.

"General Fan Wenhu rejected almost everything I said, even though many other generals agreed. I tried to convince General Fan Wenhu that I was not a spy but a string that tied both sides together. He was not buying it. Trying to ignore his comments, I assured my cousin and the others, I would do my best to achieve victory. On the last day of the meetings, I shyly reported to my cousin I would not be returning to Goryeo before the invasion. I would send two of my men back with the last report.

"Son Jun-ho told me later that my cousin was so concerned that before we left the Summer Palace, he called for Pak Byeong-ho and three of my best soldiers. He told them with tears in his eyes, 'No matter what, make sure he survives. That is your king's order, and never mind what he says. Do you understand?' Pak Byeong-ho told him, 'I will protect him with my life.' And the other three repeated the same. I am blessed to have such friends."

Kim Chin-hae continued. 'We left the Summer Palace on August 28th, the day of the milk ritual. I know you know that day well. My cousin's queen wanted her son blessed. 'Please make sure our son drinks the sacred milk of the mares. He has the Great Khan's blood; only those with it may drink. He will be blessed and guarded by the Gods.' My cousin wanted to please her. She, too, had given up her life for her country.

"After the ritual, my men and I bowed and said our goodbyes to our king, returning to Ningbo. I saw the king nod and stare at Pak Byeong-ho, who smiled and nodded in return. At that time, I had no idea what their deal was.

"When King Chungnyeol arrived in Dadu, he immediately set sail for Goryeo, missing the monsoon weather. On his arrival, I am sure my father met him at the harbor, and I can envision my father's disappointment that I didn't return with him. I hoped my cousin would keep his promise and let me tell them my secret.

"When we arrived in Ningbo, I approached General Fan Wenhu and tried to convince him. 'Even though I am a general not under your command, think of me as a partner, not a spy. I will observe the progress of the ships and weapons as you recruit more men.'

"There were times I disagreed with some of his recruitments. Some were poor farmers forced to enlist, but most were defeated Song soldiers. My men heard it was Kubilai Khan's way of eliminating disgruntled, defeated soldiers. General Fan Wenhu was one of the defeated Song soldiers—a general who surrendered to Kubilai Khan early in the Song War and became very loyal to the Khan. I often wondered how Kubilai could trust him as much as he did.

"The first year I arrived in Ningbo and stood on the famous pier, the early morning mist lay heavily on the numerous cargo ships awaiting their turn to be unloaded or loaded with their precious cargo. Now, as I stood dressed in uniform, the early morning light and the heavy mist weaved between thousands of white sails, not cargo ships but war ships awaiting battle. My concern about the food shortage weighed heavily on me. I feared my fellow soldiers from Goryeo would starve. My country is mountainous and cannot supply the amount of food needed. They would depend on the food from the Southern Fleet."

***

Marco looked at Rustichello. "It was then he asked me to talk to Kubilai and said, 'General Fan Wenhu is stubborn; he insists there will be plenty of food by the time we depart for Wa. I don't believe him. The stories on the street tell the truth: the November crop failed. We will need the extra rice from Kubilai's storage.'

"Kim Chin-hae knew the khan would be aware of this as Kubilai had messengers throughout his lands that reported if any of his people suffered crop failure due to flood or pests. He exempted them from taxes and shared his grain if he had enough. Kim Chin-hae found this extremely generous and admired Kubilai Khan for it. He was confident he would do the same for his soldiers.

Marco continued. "I agreed and returned to the palace. When I arrived, everyone was on pins and needles. Empress Chabi's health had declined rapidly. The devastated Kubilai Khan became unreachable, refusing to leave Empress Chabi's side. No one, including me, was able to see him. Another rumor was also circulating in the palace. Supreme Commander Arakhan, head commander of the Cipangu invasion, had fallen severely ill. Concerned for Kim Chin-hae that night, I wrote a letter to him.

> Dear Kim Chin-hae,
>
> The illness of Kubilai Khan's beloved Empress Chabi has devastated him, making it impossible for me to talk to him. I will not give up. Another disturbing news is that the supreme commander is very ill. The necessity of a new commander has not been determined. I will send news if I hear further information.
>
> I am hoping to see you off, my dear friend. I will pray for your safe return.
>
> Your friend,
Marco

Marco stopped Kim Chin-hae's story and looked at Rustichello. "I waited days outside Kubilai Khan's chamber until I finally gave up. Several weeks passed, and after Empress Chabi died and the funeral was over, Kubilai finally agreed to see me. I desperately wanted to see him, not only for Kim Chin-hae's sake but because I also promised Empress Chabi to be by

Kubilai's side. She had kept her promise; Li was safe in Empress Nambi's chamber, and she had started her studies in herbs and medicine with Physician Wu.

When I entered Kuiblai's chamber, he sat silently. His larger-than-life self looked small and frail. Empress Chabi's death had deflated him. Saddened by this sight, I walked slowly and knelt before him. Kubilai spoke flatly without emotion. 'Rise, sit, and tell me a story. Do not be sad; be yourself. Brighten my day with your never-ending energy, and fill my soul with your boundless overflowing spirit.'

"I could hear Empress Chabi's words steering me as I forced myself to speak cheerfully. I retold the wrestling match. He loved the story, and even though the battle ended in Qaidu's favor, Kubilai didn't care.

"'My Lord, the match was incredible. The crowd cheered as Qaidu's daughter—an amazing, beautiful, sparsely dressed warrior—entered the arena. They even cheered louder as the young warrior Arghun entered.'

"Kubilai perked up. For a short time, my story made him forget his sorrow, inflating his deflated body just a bit. We talked for the rest of the afternoon—nothing serious—just talked. Time passed quickly, and soon it was late afternoon. Kubilai's servants brought in food and drink. The evening went faster, and before long, Kubilai had slumped in his chair. He had fallen into a much-needed slumber. I called his servant and left. The next day, I would return and attempt to discuss the upcoming invasion and food situation. Kim Chin-hae had been waiting way too long."

Rustichello interrupted Marco. "Did Kim Chin-hae return to his shaman wife before the invasion? Marco laughed. "You really are a romantic. Your main concern is Kim Chin-hae and Lis, not the invasion. I thought you were a man who wrote about warriors!"

Rushichello snickered. "My life has been primarily about war. But it's refreshing to hear about love instead of hate."

Marco thought to himself. *He's been locked up too long and needs a woman.* He then continued his story.

"Yes, we met again a few days before Kim Chin-hae departed for battle. This time, we met at a place that served his favorite home food and drink. He wondered if this would be his last time to enjoy them. That day, I changed his forlorn mood by asking about Lis and the last time he saw her. He began his story on a happy note, slurping his rice and chicken soup and sipping his soju one after another. But it soon turned frightening."

1. Jeju Island

Chapter Twenty-Six

Kim

1281 Dreams

"My journey south would take twenty or more days to reach Lis. Son Jun-ho, Pak Byeong-ho, and five of my men, who salivated over the Cathay cities and the money that could be made, accompanied me. Pak Byeong-ho was more interested in me. He saw the excitement in my eyes. Unaware of my secret, he curiously asked why. I never answered. The closer we came, the faster I rode. When we reached Fuzhou, our supposed destination, I stopped at the intersection—one way to the city, the other straight to Lis. The abandoned bamboo cage still stood at the crossroads. I stopped, and Pak Byeong-ho observed me staring at the cage. He asked why we stopped. 'Are we not going to Fuzhou?' I slowly answered in a soft voice. 'This is where my life and dream changed.' Without another word, I nudged my horse forward. Son Jun-ho motioned for my men to follow. 'It seems General Kim Chin-hae feels it is time for you to learn his secret.'

"My men quickly caught up with me. I rode fast until I reached where the tiger had attacked me. I stopped. Son Jun-ho and I jumped off our horses and walked around. My men watched curiously. I looked at my men. 'This is where I met Messer Marco Polo when he saved Son Jun-ho's and my life from a huge tiger.' My men's heads twisted in all directions, scared.

"The next stop was the mountain crest that looked down into the valley. Marco, you know which one. The same familiar smoke rose from Lis's small village below. I pointed and told my men, 'That's where we are headed.'

"As we approached the village, I saw the damaged fields from the relentless rains. Disappointed, we continued. Suddenly, in the distance, a small figure appeared in the middle of the road. My excitement shot an electric bolt through my body that transmitted to my horse, who reared and took off. I could hear Son Jun-ho laughing and my men questioning him.

"In full stride, I dismounted without a stumble, running toward Lis, picking her up, and swinging her in circles. We were hugging and crying when Son Jun-ho and my men arrived. At the same time, the entire village was circling us. Pak Byeong-ho asked later, 'How did they know we were coming?' No one answered him.

"Facing Lis, I apologized, 'I'm sorry it took so long.'

"Lis placed her small hand over my mouth. 'We wrote and said our vows knowingly.'

"I nodded, then asked. 'Where are they?' Lis's mother stepped forward carrying two beautiful plump babies on each hip. They had grown so much in seven months. More surprising was the way they instantly took to me. Hugging Lis and my babies tightly, I cried. We strolled to the village, with all the villagers following us. My men trailed behind, completely stunned, except Son Jun-ho and Pak Byeong-ho, who now understood my urgency.

"My men whispered when we reached Lis's mother's hut. 'That's a shaman's house.' I laughed to myself. We continued to the end of the village, where the trail ran through the field to my house. The open field was decorated with burning fire pits and low platforms for dining. Three men ran over to Son Jun-ho, hugging him, and the village women started bringing out the prepared food. Still, in disbelief, Pak Byeong-ho and the other men unmounted and approached me. Smiling at them, I introduced my family. 'This is my wife, Lis, and my son, Kim Yang Da-lou, and daughter, Kim Mei-caihong. I then pointed to my small hut. 'Welcome to my home.'

"Pak Byeong-ho smiled back. 'Now the ring and the Soul Lock make sense. This is your secret. Now I understand why you have avoided your father, mother, and the beautiful Park Eun-ae.'

"Lis's face went serious. 'Park Eun-ae!' she repeated. I shot a disapproving look at Pak.

"'It's the girl my mother chose.' I quickly changed the subject and spoke to my men. 'Please enjoy yourselves; Son Jun-ho will be around to assist you with your sleeping quarters. Lis and I have lots to talk about.'

"Lis interrupted me. 'We can't be rude. The village has been working hard preparing for your arrival. Let's enjoy the evening. We will eat, drink, and sing in honor of your return.'

"Lis could see the disappointment on my face. She stood on her tippy toes and kissed me on my lips. My face turned red, and my men laughed. Laughing, I ordered the feast to begin. Lis had won again.

"After many drinks, Pak Byeong-ho stumbled over to our table, sat next to Son Jun-ho, and blurted out. 'Tell me, how did they know we were coming? We all have made our bets.' He pointed to a table where my other men sat, each holding a money pouch. The table went quiet.

"Son Jun-ho turned serious. 'His wife is a witch; she saw General Kim Chin-hae coming home in her dream last night. She had the villagers prepare for his homecoming.' The table roared with laughter. Son Jun-ho slapped Pak Byeong-ho on the back, laughing. 'Tomorrow, we will talk.'

"Pak Byeong-ho stood up and walked back to his table. I heard him say, 'See, I told you. I would win. She is a witch.' My men became serious, then laughed and playfully slapped each other.

"The evening lasted way too long. Finally, the villagers returned to their huts. Son Jun-ho and his friends dragged my passed-out men to a small hut. Lis's mother took the twins. Now, I had Lis to myself. We walked to our favorite place next to the warm pond. The moon above us was precisely half."

Kim Chin-hae stopped talking to Marco. He thought of that moment.

Lis faced me, wrapped her arms around me, snuggled into my body, and whispered. "The moon is exactly half. This is the time for decision-making." My decision was easy: I wrapped my arms around her and seductively pulled her in closer, knowing that wasn't what Lis was talking about. Lis could now feel every inch of my hard body. She surrendered. Hours later, we returned to the cottage, exhausted by love, and slipped into bed.

Kim Chin-hae smiled shyly and continued his story. "Late that night, Lis's thrashing arms and mumbling my name awoke me. Gently, I awoke her sweat-covered body. She frantically grabbed me and tightly held me close while sobbing. 'You can't go, you can't fight the Gods.' I lifted her face from my chest and softly kissed her numerous times, trying to comfort her. 'I'm not fighting the Gods but the Wa.'

"Gloomily, she whispered. 'In my dream, a black ominous cloud shaped like a haunting face loomed over your ship, and the winds carried thousands of chanting voices. A white heron in the sky carried an arrow in its beak. Hundreds of flying arrows, ships burning, waves crashing, dead men floating. But I couldn't find you.'

"Smiling, I jokingly told her, 'That means I am still alive, right? I wasn't among the dead men. Remember, you told me yourself you could always find me. Have faith in your power, I do.'

"For a short time, she relaxed and found comfort in my arms, telling me, 'Yesterday morning, I awoke from a wonderful dream and told our babies, "Your father is coming today." Mei-caihong giggled and tried to stand. Yang Da-lou surprisingly stood and took his first step on his own. He grabbed my hand and spoke plainly: "I saw."'

"Lis continued, 'When we married, I always wondered if we had a child, would it have my shaman's ability? I now know.'

"Lying motionless, I thought, *Months ago, I realized that my children would be different.* Patting her hand, I told her it made me happy. But the ominous cloud dream frightened me. Seven years ago, a mysterious storm during our first invasion destroyed our fleet. It couldn't happen again. Trying to dismiss my fear, I found solace in Lis's arms. We drifted into a sweet slumber. But by early morning, Lis frantically awoke. Her dream returned.

"Lis jumped from the bed, and I followed, stopping at the door. She stormed out of the cottage and walked down the trail toward her mother's cottage. At the door, I noticed Son Jun-ho and my men eating and watching Lis from one of the platforms. I walked down the stairs and joined them. Pak Byeong-ho jokily said, 'That didn't last long. What did you do wrong?' Everyone laughed except Son Jun-ho and me.

"One of the laughing soldiers spoke with a full mouth. 'Pak Byeong-ho supposedly won the bet last night. Your wife is a witch?' I didn't even look up and said, 'She is, well, not a witch. Lis would be mad if she heard me using that word. She's a shaman who sees things in dreams. That's how they knew we were coming. Her mother is the one with the powers. That's where Lis is going. Lis had a dream last night.'

"Son Jun-ho and Pak Byeong-ho looked over at me worriedly. The other soldiers shivered and continued eating. I rose and walked toward Wei's cottage.

"Lis waited for me to arrive before she opened the door, and I entered. The twins were snuggled in her bed; the bed she slept in when I was gone. Her mother sat at an old wooden table. Wei didn't flinch when Lis opened the door. She was expecting us. 'Sit. Tell me your dream,' Wei whispered to Lis, not to wake the twins.

"As we sat, Lis's mother grasped her hand and said, 'I feared this would happen.' Wei looked at me, then turned to Lis and continued. 'Kim Chin-hae's souls are not at ease. I felt that when I touched him. His old fears have returned and lie heavily upon his heart as they should. Your spirit feels them and is searching for the answer for his survival.' Wei closed her eyes, still holding Lis's hand. 'I see your dream.' Wei looked at me. 'Take me to the man who wears a spirit lock, the soldier who understands you and has no fear of us.' I was confused, not knowing who she was referring to. Wei rose, and Lis and I followed her to the platforms where my men ate. She walked around the sitting men, laying her hand on each one until she came to Pak Byeong-ho. Her hand stayed on his shoulder the longest. 'Come with us,' she said in a commanding voice. He stood, looked at the other men, and followed. In silence, we walked to Wei's house."

***

Pak Byeong-ho stopped at the gate. His heart raced. He hadn't entered a shaman's house since leaving his mom's home to become a soldier.

***

"We were opening the door when we noticed Pak Byeong-ho was not with us. Sternly, we looked back at him. He took a deep breath and followed. Lis squeezed my hand and smiled. As we entered, Wei had already prepared her drums, and the red scarf sat on the table. Her appearance had changed from the night before. She was no longer a loving mother; now, her aura unnerved you, and you felt the power that encased the cottage. The twins sat in bed motionless. Pak Byeong-ho broke out in a sweat, and I fearfully held Lis's hand. Wei played her drums intermittently while mixing a strong-smelling potion, a powerful drink that helped her enter a trance. When she finished mixing, she placed her scarf around her face, exposing only her eyes. Then, she slipped the bowl under the scarf and drank, and her eyes fell on Pak Byeong-ho. Suddenly, her eyes rolled back to see inward, toward her souls, looking for answers. For a moment, her body distorted, and then it relaxed as if she had found her answer.

"Her crooked finger pointed to Pak Byeong-ho. 'I sense shaman blood running through your veins. You are transparent to me; you have known your destiny since birth, but have denied it. The day you met Kim Chin-hae, you knew you had met a man who had denied his given path, just as you had. You knew your purpose the day you saw his spirit lock and have been loyal to him since. You will be loyal to him till you die.'

"She became quiet, and she turned to me. 'Beware, powerful divine voices chant to their gods. I hear them now; they will only become louder as their defeat grows. Their gods will hear their voices. A divine tempest will be upon you, destroying a fierce fleet. All will be lost except for a few. One general is a coward, and the other, a brave hero. The coward will be the one to return to Yuan. Your honor will only be saved if you remain with the hero.'

"Wei fell to the ground. Lis stared at me. Her eyes filled with tears. She walked over to her mother and helped her up, saying. 'Mother, what else did you see? That can't be all. Tell me!'

"Wei walked away from Lis, hiding her concern. Her heart ached for her daughter. Wei turned and faced us three. In a solemn voice, she replied. 'That's all I see, but remember, destiny has many twists and is determined by many. The future is unknown.'

"Lis panicked, 'Mother, there has to be more.'

"Grabbing Lis's hand, I said, 'Come, let your mother rest,' and pulled her to the door. Looking back, I saw my babies sitting quietly in the corner. Smiling, I walked over, picked them up, and exited."

***

Pak Byeong-ho glanced at Wei and thought, *I had denied my birthright my entire life, and was always happy I had. Being responsible for others frightened me, but now I know you can never run.* He turned and followed Kim Chin-hae.

***

"Lis leaned into me, and we solemnly walked to our cottage, where Son Jun-ho and the other soldiers sat at the table. They yelled for us to sit and join them. Only Pak Byeong-ho returned to the table. Lis and I, with our family, continued down the path to the warm springs."

"Son later told me Pak Byeong-ho sat and, as he stuffed his face with the leftover food, looked like he saw death. He questioned him, and Pak Byeong-ho stopped chewing and looked at Son Jun-ho. 'I have seen death!' he mumbled, lowering his head and falling silent. The other men, who were chatting among themselves, stopped. 'What did you say?

"'Nothing,' he said, 'but you better enjoy this next week. Who knows when we will have this kind of moment again? Let's go hunting or fishing and bring dinner to our host.' Everyone agreed, and the laughter started again.

"Lis, the twins, and I sat down on the flat rocks by the warm pool, watching the sun rise higher in the sky. The morning air was still cool, and Lis shivered. I put my arm around her as the singing stream brought us temporary peace. The twins squirmed to be released, and as they left our embrace, she looked up at me with tears in her eyes. 'I know I promised I would never ask you to stay.'

"Gently, I kissed Lis's sweet lips, whispering, 'Don't then. To be free from my obligations, I must do this. I will return to you, I promise. Your dreams warned me; I will be prepared.'

"Lis laid her head on my shoulder, and I kept talking. 'Lis, you are stronger than I. Do not falter now. I need you whole. Let your love and strength empower me.

“With those words, Lis’s body melted into my body, and I could feel her strength enter me. I held her tighter to squeeze out every drop I could absorb. Finally, I exhaled; I felt renewed, not knowing what I was doing to her.

“The week went by fast. Lis held her feelings deep inside. She had the same dream every night until the night before my departure, when something changed. She saw me on a ship with a torn and bloody uniform, staring toward a strange land she didn’t recognize. Lis was trembling. ‘What does that mean? I will go and ask my mother.’

“Lis went to rise, but I wrapped my arms around her, pulling her down. ‘Don’t leave yet,’ I whispered, not to wake the twins. Slowly kissing her, Lis met my kiss with the most passion and fire she had ever had, as if she were saying, ‘I will never let him die; his body will burn for me every day until he returns.’”

***

Pak Byeong-ho returned to Wei several times. It had been a long time since he felt the comfort of a shaman. He didn’t realize how much he had missed his mother. He promised Wei that after this battle, he would return home.

***

“Our departure radiated dread throughout the village. Everyone along the road waved and yelled, ‘Come back safely!’ Lis, with the twins, stood in the middle of the road and watched as I left. I didn’t look back, and as I turned onto the main road, my heart didn’t ache. It was full of love, strength, and determination. I felt relieved and full of false hope, unaware.”

***

Lis turned and went to her mother’s, where she collapsed instantly. Every ounce of her life went to Kim Chin-hae. Wei dragged her to bed while she cried hauntingly. ‘I told you not to give so much.’

***

"By the time we reached Fuzhou, our actual destination, the hour was late. We would stay the night and inspect the remaining fleet the following day. I told my men not to mention anything about the village. Commander Zhang had always distrusted me from the first time we met.

"The following day, I found most ships had left for Ningbo, occupied with soldiers. Everything was coming together, somewhat consoling my sorrow.

"When we arrived in Ningbo, it was the beginning of the third week of March. Posters and black ribbons lined the city; the Empress Chabi had died. Dread swept over me. I had a feeling my luck was wavering."

***

Marco stopped talking, stood up, and walked around the small cell. He continued. "Kim Chin-hae paused his story and looked around. Most customers had left the food stall, and the owner stared at us. Kim Chin-hae stood and bowed to the owner, laying too much money on the table. Unbalanced, he grabbed my shoulder. Standing, I helped him balance. We bowed to the owner and slowly walked back to the inn.

"With slurred words, Kim Chin-hae continued. 'Marco, when I returned from seeing Lis, one of Kubilai Khan's postal riders was waiting for me. The rider handed me a letter and told me he had been waiting for days. "Messer Marco Polo instructed this letter only to be placed in your hands." Hurrying to my room, I ripped open the letter. As I read your letter, my heart sank.'"

> Dear Kim Chin-hae,
>
> The illness of Kubilai Khan's beloved Empress Chabi has devastated him, making it impossible for me to talk to him. I will not give up. Another disturbing news is that the supreme commander is very ill. The necessity of a new commander has not been determined. I will send news if I gather further information.
>
> I am hoping to see you off, my dear friend. I will pray for your safe return.
>
> Your friend,
> Marco

Chapter Twenty-Seven

Kim

1281 Ningbo, Kim's Nightmare

Rustichello, with a restless voice, asked, "Then what happened?"

Marco continued. "As Kim Chin-hae and I stumbled back to the inn, his mood intensified. Like an insane man without restraint, he loudly yelled out of nowhere. 'General Fan Wenhu is a bastard!' Then, like a sane man, he continued."

***

"Worried by the news in your letter, I went to see General Fan Wenhu. Perhaps he had other information before I wrote my final report, which had to be sent out the next day if my soldiers were to arrive before the Eastern Fleet departed. Pak Byeong-ho and I walked to the garrison together. The weather was hot for this time of year—another worry. The food already stored could be ruined if our delay was too long.

"General Fan Wenhu stood on the wharf and looked over the large fleet. Cautiously, I approached him. Knowing he disapproved of me, I announced myself farther back than usual.

"'General Fan Wenhu, I have returned.'

"Without turning, he sarcastically spoke. 'You finally grace us with your presence, General Kim Chin-hae. How was your shaman wife?'

"He then turned slowly and faced me with a menacing smile. My face turned red with anger, and Pak Byeong-ho calmly touched my shoulder. This was a gentle reminder that this was not the time to cause a problem.

"Facing the general, I bowed and answered, 'My wife is fine. I appreciate your concern.'

"Changing the subject, I asked him, 'Have you heard the news regarding the supreme commander?'

"'I see you have your informants.' He barked.

"'So, you know. Will someone else be chosen soon? Should we postpone the invasion? I am writing my last report to the king, and deciding what should be included. Is there anything else I should know about?'

"He looked at me, then walked away, saying, 'Ask your informants!'

"'I'm asking you.' He kept walking, and I followed.

"'If the Supreme Commander cannot join us, will we wait until another commander is chosen?' He never answered.

"Pak Byeong-hu saw General Chang-Hsi looking around the corner of the main garrison office, listening. He walked toward us when General Fan Wenhu disappeared. As we bowed to General Chang Hsi, he looked warmly at me and spoke. 'General Fan Wenhu isn't your friend nor enemy, but feels threatened by your presence. He's a prisoner of his own heart. He surrendered to Kubilai Khan and became a traitor to his country. He sees and feels hostile eyes everywhere.'

"I hesitated momentarily, thinking about what the general said.

"'My king didn't send me here to judge. I am here to ensure my soldiers will survive this invasion and that our armies move in perfect harmony even though we are hundreds of miles apart. Kubilai Khan successfully controlled this vast empire by fostering cooperation, unity of effort, competent leadership, and effective strategic communication. General Fan Wenhu has none. I do not understand why Kubilai Khan trusts him so much.'

"General Chang Hsi studied me for a moment. 'Tell your king to postpone their departure by two or three weeks. That is my opinion. I, too, have heard that Kubilai Khan has been inaccessible. Communication with him has been difficult. It will take some time to solve some issues that have arisen.'

"General Chang Hsi bowed and walked away. I watched him leave and then turned to Pak Byeong-ho.

"'What do you think?'

"'I believe him.' Pak answered.

"As we returned to the inn, Pak Byeong-ho asked me, 'Is he our hero, General Chang Hsi?'

"'Only the heavens know.'

"At the inn, I sat to write my final report. Uncertain what to write, as thoughts kept whirling around in my head. *The logistics of this long-distance invasion are turning out to be a nightmare. There is still time for the supreme commander to recover and for the needed supplies to arrive. Was General Chang Hsi correct? Are two or three weeks enough or too short? There are so many things that could go wrong.*

"I never agreed with Kubilai that state farm soldiers could replace the legendary cavalry, who were absent, controlling the Qaidu's rebellion in the middle of the empire.

"Kubilai decided that after we defeated the Wa, the state farm soldiers would stay and farm Wa's rich soils, sending the crops back to Dadu. Another worry was that we were still waiting for the thousands of tools to be made and loaded onto the ships. Additionally, following the recent defeat of the Song Dynasty, many disgruntled soldiers were being forced to fight against the samurai, who were fiercely loyal to their country. I had a terrible feeling. After hours of debates with myself, I wrote the report. *Delay departure for two weeks.*

"That night, as I tried to fall asleep, my mind returned to Lis and her mother, Wei. My lousy feelings disappeared as if they were guiding me to serenity. I fell asleep, lost in Lis's imaginary arms.

"The following day, I issued the report to my two men, who headed overland to Masanhappo, where the king awaited.

"The original departure date was creeping up. I hadn't heard if a replacement for Supreme Commander Arakhan was needed or if additional food was coming. For a short time, the arrival of some supplies uplifted my spirit. But as I previously said, the weather was scorching, and some soldiers fell ill. I hadn't received any information on whether my men had safely delivered my message to the king. Now, I could only hope the heavens favored me.

"The days passed quickly as I waited for you to gather more information. My worries caused me to become frantic. General Fan Wenhu remained distant. Thank goodness for General Chang Hsi. His relationships with his soldiers were commendable, and he tried to show confidence and strength that relieved their fears and mine. The departure date was only weeks away when word arrived that the supreme commander was too ill to join the invasion. A replacement now has to be approved by the Khan. The departure date came and went. Devastated by this, I found slight solace in my trust in General Chang Hsi. I did not know if my men arrived safely or if the king and generals listened to me. If they didn't, the Eastern Fleet would arrive at Ike Island, with the Southern Fleet nowhere in sight. Their food would be short, and decisions would need to be made. They would also conclude I had failed my mission.

"I found peace at night with thoughts of Lis. She seemed so close, but during the day, I lamented, believing the Heavens had forgotten me. That's when the Khan's messenger arrived. General Chang Hsi rushed in with the news. 'Khan has approved the replacement of Arakhan with Vice Admiral Atahai. Your friend, Marco, will arrive with the additional food, and Vice Admiral Atahai will be here in a couple of days. Now, we can leave.'

"I thought to myself, *We are weeks late.*"

***

Marco looked at Rustichello. "Pak Byeong-ho and Kim Chin-hae excitedly rode out to meet me when I delivered the supplies.

"'Marco, my friend, you have finally arrived,' Kim Chin-hae said. A counterfeit smile crossed my face; I knew I could soon lose my friend.

"Kim Chin-hae stayed at the pier for days, ensuring his soldiers unloaded every wagon filled with rice and other food items and reloaded them onto the ships. Finally, Pak Byeong-ho and I dragged him from the wharf back to the inn, where we met Son Jun-ho.

"The adrenaline-driven Kim Chin-hae needed sleep, but he needed to quench his fear more. 'Let's have drinks. It could be our last for a long time. Tomorrow afternoon, I will meet with Vice Admiral Atahai and the other generals to discuss whether we will sail in two days with high tide and the full moon guiding our way,' he nervously said.

"That evening, Kim Chin-hae, Pak Byeong-ho, Son Jun-ho, and I sat at Kim's favorite drinking place. My heart was heavy, but I could tell Son Jun-ho was dying inside. He sat with a forced smile and laugh. Everyone told stories of the past, but never once mentioned what was to come. We all denied our feelings by laughing and pretending this moment would never pass.

"I noticed a general sitting in the corner enjoying our party. It was General Chang Hsi who stood and walked to our table. No one else noticed until he stood over, glaring at us. Kim Chin-hae jumped up first, apologizing for their inappropriate behavior. Everyone else followed. Kim Chin-hae introduced me. 'Messer Marco, this is General Chang Hsi, one of the generals who will lead the Wa Campaign.' The general bowed, sat, and the party resumed at another level. After several hours, General Chang Hsi stood and handed Kim Chin-hae something. 'Give them to your men. It could save their lives.' He bowed low. Kim Chin-hae rose and bowed lower. The general turned and hurried away before Kim Chin-hae could examine the items. We watched him exit the building, and then Kim Chin-hae looked. It was four Song officer badges. It confused Kim Chin-hae, and he spoke to Pak Byeong-ho. 'Is he our hero?'

“The day the fleet departed was hectic. Son Jun-ho, Dai Xiuying, and I walked onto the bustling wharf, passing under the wooden structure that wished safe journeys for would-be travelers. We stopped under this structure, bowed our heads, prayed, and then quickly continued our search for Kim. We found him and his men standing at the gangplank, waiting. I walked toward Kim, projecting as much positive energy as possible. ‘Kim Chin-hae, I am expecting you to return quickly. You have been neglecting your business partners and business. I can’t do it alone, you know.’

“Before Kim Chin-hae could answer, I no longer restrained myself. While tears fell, I grabbed him by the shoulder and hugged him. ‘We will all be waiting for you.’ Releasing him, I motioned Dai Xiuying forward. He handed me my sword, and as I faced Kim Chin-hae, I spoke. ‘This is the best steel in the world, from the heavens, they say. I discovered it on my travels to Kubilai Khan. One night, as I visited Kubilai, I couldn’t stop talking about it. The next time I saw him, Kubilai presented this sword to me. Take it, Kim Chin-hae; protect yourself against the famous samurai.’

“Kim Chin-hae slid the sword from the decorative sheath. Its removal was silent except for a faint musical whistle, and the blade glittered in the moonlight, reflecting his handsome face. He couldn’t speak, but I could see his emotions in his eyes.

“‘I expect the sword back.’ We both faked a smile. As Dai Xiuying and I walked away, I looked back. Son Jun-ho stood slumped, staring at Kim Chin-hae, unable to speak. Kim smiled, and I heard him say, ‘I’ll be back, I promise you. Your job is to watch over Lis.’ He slapped him on the shoulder and ran up the gangplank.

“Son Jun-ho caught up to us, and we slowly walked off the wharf. We found a spot on the shore where the full moon highlighted thousands of ships departing—a magnificent display of military power. As far as the eyes could see, white sails billowed toward the dark horizon. Three large Song Ocean ships led the way: General Fan Wenhu’s, Supreme Commander Vice Admiral Atahai’s, and General Chang Hsi’s.

“The next day, I returned to Yangzhou, and Son Jun-ho traveled with a guide to Lis. He would remain with her until, hopefully, Kim Chin-hae returned.”

Rustichello looked over at Marco and asked with urgency in his voice. “So, did he return to Lis? Did he survive?”

Marco lowered his head. He could feel a thrill rise in his body. It had been a long time since he felt this way. Again, he had proven his storytelling skills.

“You must wait, Rustichello,” he said with a twinkle in his eye. “It would be a while before I heard his story.”

Chapter Twenty-Eight

Kim

1281 The Wa Campaign

Kim Chin-hae and his men boarded General Fan Wenhu's ship early that morning. As expected, General Fan Wenhu was cold and avoided them as much as possible. Still, Kim Chin-hae could feel his eyes on him.

Pak Byeong-ho approached Kim Chin-hae and whispered, "I fear General Fan Wenhu has no trust in you."

Kim Chin-hae whispered, "It is my job to prove him wrong."

It surprised Kim Chin-hae how much he had missed the sea. The salt spray on his face was invigorating, and the smell brought back good and bad memories. He roamed the ship, working with the sailors, especially the navigators. They had left 30 days late, and he prayed they could make up for lost time. As the sun rose and the full moon disappeared, he could no longer see land in any direction. It was just an open sea filled with the illusion of floating tree carcasses identified as battleships for scared and brave men. He was both.

When the Eastern Fleet of 900 ships was being built, every tree in the southern region of his home was cut down. He prayed for victory in fear; hopefully, they did not cut the trees in vain. His countrymen would suffer for years to come. He wondered if Kubilai Khan realized the sacrifices they made to fulfill his lust for power.

At the bow of the ship, he thought about Lis. His heart pounded with a mixture of fear and sadness. He looked down at the sword Marco had given him and thought, *Sword, please save me; use your heavenly powers. I must return.*

Pak Byeong-ho came up next to him, interrupting his troubled heart. "The sky is clear, and the winds are perfect for sailing. Maybe Lis's mother was wrong."

"Who are you fooling, yourself?" They both turned to the open sea, standing erect as statues.

From the helm, General Fan Wenhu observed them and thought, *They are a perfect image of the brave Goryeo warriors. Yet, I would never let them know that.*

***

Meanwhile, Lis was walking on the wildflower-lined path to her cottage when her heart started pounding. She grabbed her chest, and tears began streaming down her cheeks. She ran to the warm pond and slowly submerged, finding solace as the warm water surrounded her. It was as if Kim's warm body consumed her. He was no longer on land; the water was the only thing connecting them.

***

For Kim Chin-hae, the days passed slowly. Some days, the wind blew strong, and others, the ships floated aimlessly in the sea. The only sounds were rowers grunting loudly as their muscles strained, moving the wooden ships with only their power, and the captain's voice yelling, "Faster! Harder!"

On one of the slow days, Kim Chin-hae retold the meeting of 1279 as Pak Byeong-hu and his men listened: "When word arrived that the Song Dynasty had fallen, and this invasion was converging, my commander sat us around his table on the ship and told us how surviving soldiers of the first invasion lived on a deserted island off the coast of Wa. They secretly spied on the Wa and employed Goryeo's fishermen as couriers to deliver information to the king. The brave soldiers met their demise when they stole a fisherman's daughter, who escaped and reported them to the shogunate. All died, but not before we learned the Wa had been preparing for this second invasion, building forts and a large two-meter stone wall along the coast of the potential landing points, especially at Hakata Bay. The Wa also drove large stakes into the mouth of the river to prevent us from landing."

Pak Byeong-hu spoke up. "Is this why you insisted on bringing tall wooden poles?"

"Yes, when we arrive, we will build large platforms on the ships, rising above the walls, and meet our enemies fairly."

His men cheered him, but Kim Chin-hae didn't feel he deserved this. "Do not praise me. We owe this to the brave survivors stranded on the islands."

He lowered his head and whispered to himself, "So many men died during the first invasion. I was one of the lucky ones; I made it home. Yet, I lost respect for our king and Kubilai Khan that day."

"What?" one of his men asked.

Kim Chin-hae didn't answer.

Suddenly, General Fan Wenhu approached them and sarcastically spoke. "Having a private meeting?"

All the men rose, and Kim Chin-hae answered. "No, we are discussing the preparedness of the shogunate."

In his most controlled voice, Kim Chin-hae asked, "Would you like to join us?"

"No," he snarled, "but I have a question. What did your shaman wife tell you?"

Pak Byeong-ho placed his hand on Kim Chin-hae's shoulder. He glanced at Pak Byeong-hu and carefully answered.

"My shaman wife has a name. It is Lis. She told me she heard a thousand voices chanting, and her mother told me a divine tempest would destroy us and save the Wa!"

General Fan Wenhu laughed boldly and sneered at him. "You believe that nonsense?" Promptly, he walked away, laughing, but deep inside, he felt fear. He also heard they had built numerous shrines and temples, obtaining hundreds of monks to pray and chant when the invasion began. He would never admit to Kim Chin-hae, but *maybe his wife had powers*, he thought. Fan Wenhu assured himself, thinking it was too early in the season for a storm.

The other men stared at Kim Chin-hae and Pak Byeong-ho and asked, in a shaky voice, "Is this true?"

Kim Chin-hae spoke in a serious voice. "I want you men to stay on this ship. You will survive. Do not follow me, no matter what!"

"What do you mean?" Pak Byeong-hu said, staring at Kim Chin-hae.

"I have my destiny, and you have yours. You know that! Keep the men safe."

"What are you planning to do?" Pak Byeong-ho questioned with concern.

"I'm not sure now. I will know when the time comes!"

The conversation went silent. Pak Byeong-ho thought back to the king's request and Wei's prophecy. *Yes, I know my destiny.*

Kim Chin-hae slept very little at night, but when he did, it was only dreams of Lis. It was as if her dreams resonated within him. He heard her voice every night, "Save your honor and your life."

It was early dawn, the 15th of June; the sun peeked above the horizon when Kim Chin-hae was awakened by yelling sailors' voices. "Land, I see land." The Mongols' horns filled the air, announcing they had reached their destination to the other ships behind, and another low blast was sounded to prepare for battle. He jumped from his hard bed and met Pak Byeong-ho and General Fan Wenhu at the bow. They strained their eyes and saw land in the distance—but no Eastern Fleet.

Vice Admiral Atahai commanded the Southern Fleet to anchor off the coast of Noko and Shiga—two small islands five miles from Ike—and called for General Fan Wenhu and General Chang-Hsi. After a deep discussion, they made a decision.

General Fan Wenhu returned to his ship and called for Kim Chin-hae. "The Vice Admiral needs information. Board General Chang-Hsi's ship with your men. Your mission: locate the Eastern Fleet and discover what's happening." Wasting no time, Kim Chin-hae and his men boarded General Chang-Hsi's ship and set sail immediately. By nightfall, their search was over; they found them. The sky was bursting with flames, explosions, and men's screams. With each explosion, they could see small enemy wasens[1] attacking and samurai boarding the Eastern Fleet, even though the aerial bombs repulsed most.

As they came closer, General Chang Hsi became irate and disgusted by the Kubilai Khan's warriors' cruelty and disregard for orders. It was apparent that the Mongols' ships had conquered some islands. When the explosions lit the night, they observed numerous prows decorated with bloody corpses of men, women, children, and the elderly.

However, the Eastern Fleet was now in a difficult situation. The disappointed Kim Chin-hae thought, *They didn't wait. My men didn't arrive on time, or Commanders Hong Dagu and Kim Bang-gyong didn't listen.* General Chang-Hsi anchored his ship and ordered General Kim Chin-hae and his men to obtain information. With a smaller side boat decorated with red flags, they oared toward a Goryeo ship that temporarily resided beyond the attacking samurai. Kim Chin-hae prayed that the Goryeo's sailors would recognize the red flags and that someone from his past would be on board.

As they glided up to its side, hostile sailors met them, ready to defend their ship. Kim Chin-hae and Pak Byeong-ho screamed in their native tongue, disclosing their identities. One sailor from Masanhappo's garrison recognized them. His uniform was bloody and torn, but his thin body was unscarred.

"General Kim Chin-hae, is that you?" he said as he held up his hand, ordering the others not to fire.

"Yes," replied Kim Chin-hae. The sailor, relieved, held out his hand and helped them aboard. After moments of joy, the sailor urgently asked them if they had food. The soldier continued before they could answer his question. "The little food we had, we consumed or it spoiled. You do have some, right?"

Kim Chin-hae enthusiastically answered, "Yes, we have food on the ships waiting on Shiga Island. Take me to your commander; I need information."

The Goryeo commander, standing on the bow observing the battle scene in the distance, quickly turned as the sailor announced, "Commander, General Kim Chin-hae is here."

He turned, his face tormented. "General Kim Chin-hae, we have been waiting for you! You're late. Our fleet has been living on sparse provisions, yet the generals wouldn't wait. We defeated Tsushima, but the islanders lied about Hakata Bay being undefended. We have been attacking for weeks without success. Unfortunately, General Dagu Hong and General Kim Bang- gyeong are battling each other instead of the enemy, trying to prove who will be victorious and obtain the glory. The fierce samurai have held their ground, preventing our soldiers from going beyond their walls, and not allowing some to return to the ships. An added disaster, the smaller wasen have relentlessly attacked us from behind."

"You were to wait," Kim Chin-hae said as they faced each other, displaying frustrated looks. You never received my dispatch to wait?"

"What dispatch?" The commander shouted with concern.

Kim Chin-hae lowered his head. *My men didn't arrive on time?*

"I sent a letter explaining we were having problems with supplies, and the supreme commander was ill. You were to wait at least two more weeks before departing."

"We saw no such dispatch." The commander replied.

In an apologetic voice, Kim Chin-hae said, "Two of my men left in March, heading overland for Masanhappo. I wonder what happened."

The commander thought for a moment. "A huge snowstorm blanketed the earth with outrageous amounts of snow, making travel impossible. Most likely, the fleet had already left when they reached Southern Goryeo."

General Kim Chin-hae interrupted. "It is too late to be sorry. Our concern now is to inform the Goryeo generals of our arrival. We have supplies, as well as long poles for building scaffolding, so our archers, armed with their arrows, can stand above the protective walls on Hakata Bay. The scaffolding will level the odds, allowing the fighting men trapped on the small strip of beach between the shore and the walls to escape and return to their ships. We need to rendezvous. Maybe somewhere along the shore of the Imari Bay, where we can combine our fleets."

The Goryeo Commander moaned with slight gratitude and commanded his sailors. "We need to inform the generals! Get ready to sail."

In the night's darkness, Kim Chin-hae and his men returned to General Chang Hsi's ship and informed him of what they had found. General Chang Hsi patted Kim on the back, "Your idea to bring long poles was brilliant."

Kim Chin-hae felt a sense of relief; something was working right.

They sailed back to the Vice Admiral Atahai and General Chang Hsi, informing them of the situation. Immediately, Chang Hsi, Fan Wenhu, and numerous ships sailed toward Hakata Bay, and on the way, they built the platforms.

Kim Chin-hae, Pak Byeong-ho, and his men didn't stay on General Fan Wenhu's ship. They chose General Chang Hsi's ship, which sailed up front, disobeying his king's order and Kim's initial plan. When the time to fight came, they stood bravely on the frames and fired upon the enemy.

The two Generals—Fan Wenhu and Chang Hsi—watched General Kim Chin-hae from their ships. They had different emotions or thoughts. Fan Wenhu: resentment and hate, and General Chang Hsi: admiration.

After hours of relentless fighting, the men on land escaped to their ships and sailed to Ike Island and Imari Bay on Kyushu Island, uniting the entire Eastern Fleet. They continued to Shiga Island to meet the Southern Fleet.

Meanwhile, General Chang Hsi and General Fan Wenhu, along with their fleet, sailed to Shiga and met Vice Admiral Atahai.

Several days later, men cheering from the next ship woke them. Kim Chin-hae and General Chang Hsi rushed to the side of the ship. In the distance, they saw numerous ships illuminated by the rising sun. One sailor climbing the mast yelled excitedly, "It is the Goryeo Fleet!" Mongols' drums from the Southern Fleet reverberated, celebrating their reunion, traveling far beyond their ships, and alerting the samurai on shore.

The following day, the first day of the seventh month, bright blue skies and a glowing sun welcomed both fleets as the flagships landed on Shiga Island, where the southern and eastern generals met. The Eastern Fleet received the much-needed food and supplies. Kim's old commander, General Kim Bang-gyeong from Goryeo, happily greeted him. They hadn't seen each other in over a year. Both had been seriously concerned about whether their counterpart was still alive.

"I am still responsible for you, General Kim Chin-hae. Your mother, father, the king, and Park Eun-ae will have me beheaded if you die." They both laughed.

Kim Chin-hae paused. "Park Eun-ae?" He hadn't heard that name or thought of her in a very long time.

"Oh, yes, her father constantly reminds me of your upcoming marriage."

"Marriage! I think there has been a misunderstanding." Kim quietly said as he moved General Kim Bang-gyeong to the side for privacy.

General Fan Wenhu followed them, and General Kim Bang-gyeong greeted the general with a low bow. "Thank you for the assistance."

General Fan Wenhu bowed back and sarcastically said, "I see General Kim Chin-hae has deceived you, too." Just then, General Chang Hsi grabbed the surprised General Fan's arm and pulled him away.

"Why are you always belittling him, Fan Wenhu?" whispered Chang Hsi. "What has he ever done to you? He's a skillful warrior, and his intentions seem noble."

"I see him as a man with too many life advantages. Plus, I just don't like the man. Do I have to?" answered Fan Wenhu.

"No, but you should respect a fellow officer."

"He is only an officer because of his relatives. He's probably never fought in a battle in his life," snorted General Fan Wenhu.

"That's not what I heard," replied Chang Hsi. "I heard he had spent most of his adulthood fighting the Waegus. He is not involved in politics as his family wishes."

Fan Wenhu stared at Chang Hsi and then walked away, thinking, *Am I wrong?*

---

1. Small Japanese boats

Chapter Twenty-Nine

Kim

1281 Kim and the Fiery Battles

After their rendezvous, the Southern and Eastern Fleets sailed their ships toward Hakata Bay, where countless Wa waited on the other side of the wall, with their bows, spears, and swords drawn. Beyond the narrow strip of land that met the sea and their parapets, which held thousands of wind-blown banners, the Wa observed a vast fleet with the blood-red flags of Kubilai Khan. Fear ran through their veins.

The Great Khans' ships' decks were armed with weapons and immense men. The intimidating fleet with arrows flying from their ships forced most of the Wa to stay behind the walls, but the Mongol forces also could not breach the enemy's wall. Smaller and faster wasens of the fierce samurais cut Kubilai Khan's warriors' small detachments short. Thousands of Mongols were driven back immediately or were left headless on shore by the relentless samurais' swords.

The battle became a stalemate until one early morning. Kim Chin-hae and Pak Byeong-ho stood on the platforms and noticed samurais boarding their boats and advancing toward them. They sounded the alarm and stood ready to signal when to fire. Kim Chin-hae lowered his arm—a shower of arrows and enormous stones launched from their catapults on the decks. Many of the samurais died.

In the middle of the chaos, Kim Chin-hae and Pak Byeong-ho became horrified when they detected a group of samurais swimming, escaping the hurling arrows, and boarding the ship nearby. Fierce samurais beheaded the entire crew before anyone could help them. This small victory energized the enemy. The small and fast wasens kept coming day and night despite their horrendous and numerous deaths. If the wasens made it to one of Kubilai's ships, the crew would pull alongside and lower their mast to create a bridge that allowed easy boarding. With their incredible daisho[1] swords, the ferocious samurai would remove their enemies' heads in one swift motion and set fire to the ships before any other ship could assist.

Panic-stricken, the Yuan generals and Goryeo generals gathered to analyze the situation, making a swift decision: their ships would become the new battlefield, connected by chains and large planks along their hulls, where archers, spearmen, and swordsmen would await their enemies. At night, large lanterns lit the ships brightly. From the shore, the glowing ships became a floating city ready for battle.

On land, Kono Michiari, a samurai captain, refused to hide behind the wall. So, with his 500 soldiers, he camped along the shore. He was devastated that he arrived late for the first battle with the enemy. Now, he prayed to the gods for another chance. At night, he wrote his prayers on paper and set them on fire, watching as they rose high into the sky. The remaining ashes he swallowed. Knowing the samurai's bravery and success the day before, his desire to honor his family with his courage and skills grew. While scheming his next move on how to invade the new fortification of Kubilai Khan's ships, a white heron appeared high in the sky and landed on top of the turret where the samurais placed thousands of arrows. The heron plucked up an arrow with its beak, flew toward the enemy's ships, dropped it upon one of the most imposing ships, and mysteriously disappeared.

"It's a message from God!" yelled his men.

Kono Michiari was ecstatic and spoke. "He who, through this miracle, has revealed to us that we shall storm the enemy's flagship. Protected as we are by God, how shall we fear the devil's arrows!"[2] Quickly, he filled two wasens with men, instructing them to hide their weapons, and rowed toward the unnerving fleet.

On shore, the Wa warriors cried, "He is mad!"

Kim Chin-hae had prepared his men: "Remember the Sambyeolcho and the Waegu we spent years fighting? These samurais are more dangerously fierce, but we know how they fight. It's time we show them." However, Kim Chin-hae wasn't prepared for what he saw next: a white heron flying toward them with an arrow in its beak. He soared above General Fan Wenhu's ship, dropping the arrow upon his deck. Kim Chin-hae's heart sank with deep fear. *Wei's prophecy!* he thought. Pak Byeong-ho, too, watched in horror, knowing what was next! His shaman blood ran deep—he never doubted—next, the Divine Tempest. Kim Chin-hae turned to Pak Byeong-ho and saw him gazing up at the sky. He followed. The sky was clear, and not a single cloud graced the sky.

The sailors yelling and pointing toward the land brought Kim Chin-hae and Pak Byeong-ho back to reality. They looked in the direction the men were pointing and yelled, "How bold for two little wasens of unarmed men to approach our great fleet. Indeed, they are coming to surrender." Everyone was watching, assuming the same. Not an arrow flew.

Kim Chin-hae and Pak Byeong-ho stared at each other, remembering where the heron dropped the arrow. Without a word, they took off toward General Fan Wenhu's ship with their men trailing. Kim's long legs stretched forward, springing gracefully along the large planks that connected the ships. He resembled a large stag, bravely heading toward his opponent at full speed.

General Chang Hsi watched, growing increasingly concerned. *Why are they running?* The scene moved in slow motion.

Before Kim Chin-hae could reach General Fan Wenhu's ship, the samurais, who were only oars away, withdrew their hidden weapons and cut their wasen's mast, making it fall on Fan's ship. With lightning speed, they climbed their mast, boarded his ship, set it on fire, and fiercely dismembered their enemies with their swords even before they fired an arrow. Finally, the Mongols awoke from their nightmare and began firing, injuring Kono Michiari on his shoulder and arm. Kono's courage was commendable. His injury didn't even faze him as he killed multitudes of the enemy, heading for General Fan Wenhu, who was no match for Kono Michiari. Kono immediately captured him.

General Fan Wenhu's ship was ablaze when Kim Chin-hae and Pak Byeong-ho reached Fan's ship. The smoke swirled and concealed their vision, and they only heard the swords clashing. They made their way to the stern. With a passing breeze, the smoke cleared for a moment. Kim Chin-hae saw Fan Wenhu in Kono's hands. Kim Chin-hae raced forward with his enormous sword. Kono, a small man bleeding profusely, didn't hesitate to release General Fan Wenhu to meet his opponent. Kim Chin-hae and Kono, like two stags, charged; their swords were their antlers. Kono and Kim's swords met. The force surprised the samurai; his razor-sharp blade couldn't match the strength of Kim Chin-hae's sword, which was made from heaven's metal. Besides, Kono's loss of blood had weakened his samurai power. His men could see this. They attacked Kim Chin-hae. Pak Byeong-ho and his men raced to him. After a brief battle, the retreating samurais dragged Kono to their boat and rowed toward shore under the cover of the smoke.

Stunned, General Fan Wenhu stood and watched, his face distorted with anger as the Wa's cheering voices echoed across the sea. His blood boiled, and he was unaware of Kim Chin-hae briskly walking toward him, grabbing him by his arm, and yelling, "We need to leave! Your ship is burning!"

He quickly knocked Kim Chin-hae's grasp from his arm. His pride wouldn't allow him to humble himself in front of him. Kim Chin-hae understood. He bowed low to Fan Wenhu and, as he was rising, said, "General, we will go down with the ship if we don't leave. My men are dismantling the chains as we speak; we must leave. I will escort you to General Chang Hsi's ship. I fear the stalemate is over by the sound of motivated war cries. Their insignificant victory has brought vitality to the samurai garrison."

The arrogant General Fan Wenhu snarled at Kim, stepped up, and led the way through the smoke-filled ship while Kim Chin-hae and Pak Byeong-ho followed. They saw numerous Wa's wasens entering the sea. It was inevitable that they would assault the fleet in all directions.

General Fan Wenhu, Kim Chin-hae, Pak Byeong-ho, and their men swiftly crossed the planks from ship to ship; General Fan barked orders. "Prepare for battle, prepare for battle!" He sensed a newfound fear sweeping through his men.

When they reached General Chang Hsi's ship, Kim Chin-hae quietly excused himself and joined the other men on the planks, preparing for the oncoming enemy. General Chang Hsi squarely looked into General Fan's eyes. "You are a lucky man that General Kim Chin-hae was so intuitive."

"Intuitive, you say; he is bewitched," General Fan Wenhu answered.

"I don't understand you. General Kim Chi-hae just saved your ass."

Fan Wenhu didn't have time to retort; wasens, like ants, swarmed the ships. The samurais, with their daisho swords and flaming arrows, surrounded them with lightning speed.

With drawn swords just in case, General Chang Hsi and Fan Wenhu watched the battles from the bow. Kim Chin-hae and his men amazed Chang Hsi. He spoke his thoughts out loud. "They move like graceful dancers with their swordsmanship precise and daring, cutting the enemies down one by one. They're sword dancing; it's beautiful." General Fan Wenhu watched in silence.

By sunset, many brutal fighting machines, Mongol warriors, were fighting by Kim-Chin hae's side.

General Chang Hsi admired him more. General Fan Wenhu hated him more.

They battled throughout the night. By early morning, dead, bloody bodies were so thick there wasn't an inch of flooring left; they were the floor. The samurais retreated at sunrise. Kim Chin-hae and his men stood covered in blood and watched them go. His warriors cheered. The enemies' losses were heavy, and so were theirs. The Mongol generals nodded in agreement. Their plank plan had worked; they had survived. However, sadly, victory didn't belong to either side.

On land, the shogun's reinforcements flooded in from the empire, increasing the number by the hundreds. The monasteries and temples throughout the country became overrun with Shinto monks, and the populace prayed and chanted to their God, Hachiman, to destroy their enemy and save their country. Even the emperor and ex-emperor went solemnly to the high priest. They wrote their prayers and sent them to the shrines at Ise.

The increased chanting resonated and mingled with the winds, transporting the sound far out to sea.

Kim Chin-hae stood on the bow with Pak Byeong-ho, General Chang Hsi, and Fan Wenhu. The salt-filled wind slapped them in their exhausted faces. The men witnessed Kim Chin-hae's pale face as he fearfully looked at Pak Byeong-ho and asked him. "Do you hear it?" Kim Chin-ha's heart pounded as he remembered Wei's prophecy.

"Hear what?" General Chang Hsi asked.

"Listen to the winds. It's alive with the voices of the Wa's people praying to their gods!" shouted Kim Chin-hae. A violent tempest will come!"

Pak Byeong-ho looked into the skies, remembering Wei's words. General Chang Hsi and Fan Wenhu followed. There was not a cloud in the sky, only the brilliant sun. Chang Hsi looked confused.

General Fan Wenhu sarcastically declared as he walked away, "I told you he was bewitched." Then, he thought, *I would never dare act as if I believed.* But he trembled; he felt fear greater than when the samurais attacked him. *It can't be true.*

General Chang Hsi wanted to believe Kim Chin-hae but wondered, *Could prayer conjure a divine wind*? He immediately disregarded his thoughts.

During the day, restless Kim Chin-hae and Pak Byeong-ho watched the shore and the skies--the two enemies. They had tried and failed several times to convince General Chang Hsi to prepare.

Kim Chin-hae remembers the first invasion and Wei's prophecy. Coming face-to-face with his fears. He told his men, "If I order you, unchain the ships, make them ready to sail. We must make it out to the open seas to survive and, if necessary, tie yourselves to the strongest part of the ship."

His men weren't sure what he was talking about and asked why.

"Tie?"

"You will know if the time comes."

Meanwhile, the cowardly General Fan Wenhu had secretly departed General Chang Hsi's ship for Vice Admiral Atahai's ship. When he arrived, he ordered the sailors to take him to Vice Admiral Atahai, who spoke calmly to General Fan Wenhu.

"I'm happy you survived. I hear General Kim Chin-hae saved your life. I hope you thanked him." General Fan Wenhu was in no mood to discuss General Kim Chin-hae's bravery and changed the subject quickly.

"I have come to request if I can stay on your ship. When do you think the Wa will attack again? It's been a day."

"They must be regrouping; it shouldn't be long. Stay if you wish. Maybe you should rest."

General Fan Wenhu agreed, but that's not what he was planning. He walked away from the vice admiral, went to the men on the deck, and instructed them to unchain the ship. "By orders of the admiral," General Fan Wenhu slyly told them.

It was early evening, and Kim Chin-hae, still tormented by the chanting, covered his ears with his palms and prayed to Lis to make the chanting stop. General Chang Hsi was watching Kim Chin-hae when a brilliant streak of light suddenly crossed the southern sky with a sonorous thunder so loud that it vibrated the ship. An ominous darkness shrouded the setting sun as large, rolling, bluish-black clouds with intermittent internal flames marched toward them. It quickly spread over the Ghenkai Sea. An eerie quietness and stillness surrounded the fleet. Moments later, the serene wind grew violent. Sheets of piercing rain fell from the sky as if a slashing sword had slit the heavens. Frightened men hung onto anything fastened down, as huge, angry waves hurled their ships into deep water valleys and back to the crest in minutes. The deadly, thunderous waves crashed onto the shore against the Wa protective walls, deafening the men's screams. The ships cracked and moaned, with the masts snapping like toothpicks. There was no way Kim Chin-hae or his men could disengage their ship from the other vessels. The ships thrashed into each other like giant rams in mating season. Once, Kim Chin-hae caught a glimpse of a ship heading out to sea as his ship rose to the top of the wave. *I am sure it is General Fan Wenhu and the vice admiral,* he thought. *That coward. He believed me when I said, "We must make it out to the open seas to survive"—but didn't dare say so.*

It was his last thought as a flying barrel flew into him, causing him to lose consciousness.

Pak Byeong-ho crawled to him. Blood streamed from Kim Chin-hae's head. Pak Byeong-ho held him tight as he prayed to the gods and Lis. The ship violently dismantled under them, leaving only the shell of a ship.

They were luckier than most. By morning, their shell had drifted onto an island. Kim Chin-hae awoke with General Chang Hsi and Pak Byeong-ho hovering over him. With a pounding head and clothes torn and bloody, he stumbled to his feet. Corpses were piled high on the shore and continued out to sea; bodies floated with thousands of ship pieces. Kim Chin-hae was devastated. *If only they had listened*. Anger filled his heart.

"Where is General Fan Wenhu? Where are my men?" He shouted.

Pak Byeong-ho answered, "Some men said General Fan Wenhu was on the vice admiral's ship. They escaped to the west with other ships that survived. Most of our men made it because of you. They tied themselves down like you instructed. We aren't sure if General Kim Bang-gyeong and Dagu Hong's ships survived. They aren't on the island."

"Where are we?"

General Chang Hsi answered. "I think this is Taka Island. It's deserted except for the 30,000 or so survivors from both fleets." Chang Hsi pondered out loud, wondering if General Fan Wenhu would return.

Kim Chin-hae and Pak Byeong-ho knew he would. One more of Wei's prophecies had to happen. Wei's and Lis's words swirled in Kim Chin-hae's mind: *"Save your honor and integrity." Lis also said I would live, but Wei never said so. Are these my last days? Will I ever see Lis and my babies again? Will I see Marco, my parents, and the king?*

Pak Byeong-ho placed his hand on his shoulder. "You will live. It's my destiny to protect you."

Before Kim Chin-hae could answer, there was shouting from the beach. "The vice admiral's ship is here."

Pak Byeong-ho held back Kim Chin-hae as he whispered, "This is General Chang Hsi's duty, not yours."

General Fan Wenhu disembarked and told Chang Hsi to gather his men of choice and leave with him.

General Chang Hsi couldn't believe General Fan Wenhu. "You are a coward, General Fan Wenhu. We survived; we are strong. Let us unite our remaining forces and conquer our enemy. Then we can return to our great master with victory."

Kim Chin-hae instantly knew that General Chang Hsi was the hero, and Fan Wenhu was the coward. It was just as Wei said.

General Fan Wenhu argued with Chang Hsi. "This is no time to be a hero. I will take responsibility for this decision."

Chang Hsi refused.

General Fan Wenhu walked over to Kim Chin-hae. "Bring your men. You can return to your wife. I owe you that much for saving my life." Kim Chin-hae stared at General Fan Wenhu. It took all his strength not to hit the man.

"No, we are staying," Kim Chin-hae said with blatant hate.

"You are a fool." General Fan Wenhu snorted.

Within an hour, General Fan Wenhu had gathered officers who, with their followers, boarded the remaining ships and left.

General Chang Hsi and Kim Chin-hae watched Vice Admiral Atahai, General Fan Wenhu, and the remaining fleet disappear into the horizon toward Goryeo.

Chang Hsi turned to Kim Chin-hae. "You know you will probably die."

"But I will save my honor, General Chang Hsi," Kim Chin-hae said, walking away.

"Your wife will be crying," Chang Hsi said sadly.

"No, she knows the future, no matter what it is. She is prepared."

At the Miao's village, Lis went in and out of the warm pond all night, still feeling him. But by morning, she could no longer feel his presence in the water. He wasn't dead, as she felt his heart beating with hers. Instantly, tears welled. She realized she had been so happy to see him alive in her dreams that she never thought of him being captured. Her imagination gave way to the unimaginable torture he might endure and even die. With her heart aching unbearably, she thought, *This is the first time I've felt totally human.* She walked back to their twins, held them tightly, and cried.

---

1. Two swords the samurai carried, meaning "great and small"

2. Written by Nakaba Yamada from *Ghenko, The Mongol invasion of Japan*

Chapter Thirty

Kim

1281 Park Eun-ae, The Truth Revealed

When Park Eun-ae heard that the invasion was imminent and the fleet had departed from Masanhappo, her only thought was of Kim Chin-hae. She haunted her father, Minister Park Jae-bong, for days, begging and crying uncontrollably until her father gave in. They traveled to Masanhappo and waited.

Eun-ae was his only daughter, and he found it impossible to refuse her when her mind was made up. She had never given up on Kim Chin-hae. His mother blessed their union, even though her mother had pleaded with Eun-ae to give up and find another.

An excited servant awoke Eun-ae from her miserable sleep. "A servant from the king's quarters has arrived; she brought news about Master Kim." Eun-ae thought she was dreaming.

It was now late August. News traveled fast; a great storm had destroyed the fleet, and no one knew who or how many survived.

Eun-ae lifted her head. "What did you say?"

The excited servant, slightly scared, spoke. "There's news of Master Kim. Your father is calling you!"

Eun-ae sat up. The servant sadly stared at her. Eun-ae's face turned white, and tears filled her eyes as she collapsed. Covering her head, she feared the worst. *He can't be dead.*

Again, the servant told her. "Your father is waiting."

Eun-ae rose from the bed, slowly growing strong and confident, thinking, *He can't be dead.*

The servant helped her dress, and Eun-ae defiantly entered her father's study. Her father's face said it all. Eun-ae kept her composure and spoke. "I don't believe it!" But her confidence failed her. Tears fell.

“Eun-ae, pull yourself together!” He stood and walked over to her, putting his arm around her. He never showed sympathy or possessed softness, but this time, he felt compassion; her heart was breaking.

“Vice Admiral Atahai’s ship is offshore. A soldier delivered a letter to the king. A divine tempest destroyed thousands of ships. General Chang Hsi and Kim Chin-hae died. The Vice Admiral is returning to Yuan[1] with the news of their defeat.” The blood drained from Eun-ae’s face, and she went limp. Her father caught her and yelled for the servant. “Call the physician!”

The few surviving Goryeo ships were coming into port; they had lost two-thirds of their fleet. The news devastated the king, but mainly, his heart was breaking for his cousin, and he thought, *Chin-hae never wanted to be part of this political mess. But, like me, he had been born into it.*

Sadly, he called in Kim Chin-hae’s father, Chui-hee. “I am sorry to tell you—” Kim Chin-hae’s father stopped him before he could finish. “Please stop; I’m not prepared to hear it out loud.” He exited the room, stumbled to his chamber, and devastatedly sat at his desk. The news crushed his heart: *How would I tell my wife and Park Eun-ae?* He wrote a brief note to Park Jae-bong, Minister of Trade, and sent a servant to his quarters. Kim Chui-hee decided it would be best to tell his wife in person when he returned to the capital.

The king pondered whether he should tell Kim Chui-hee about Chin-hae’s family in Yuan? Then he thought about the woman, Park Eun-ae, who had been waiting for him. *It wasn’t fair; even in death, Chin-hae would cause more pain.* He decided to wait. *Perhaps a miracle could happen.*

On the island, General Chang Hsi continued to listen to Kim Chin-hae’s nonsense regarding his wife's preparedness and thought, *No woman is prepared.* He shook his head and began discussing their next move. He tried not to show his despair to the other soldiers, even though they had no food and limited weapons. Kim Chin-hae regarded General Chang Hsi as an outstanding leader, the hero Lis had spoken of. General Chang Hsi encouraged the men to repair the damaged ships and ready themselves to avenge the deaths of their countrymen.

Quietly, Chang Hsi reminded Kim Chin-hae of the badges he had given to his men.

“Have them put them on. It could save their lives.”

Kim Chin-hae questioned General Chang Hsi. “Why Song Officer Badges?”

“The Wa are soft toward the Song Officers. They know Kubilai forced them to fight, and they were previously their trade partners.”

Three days later, a horrified sentinel announced the advancement of the samurais. "They must be 5000 strong with at least 500 wasens."

Even though the Mongols and Goryeoin[2] outnumbered them, many of their men were injured and exhausted. On the other hand, the samurais, who had been re-energized by their luck, rushed in with swords raised. Injured General Kim Chin-hae, with Pak Byeong-ho and his men at his side, fought valiantly beside General Chang Hsi. After many hours of fierce fighting and numerous samurai deaths, General Chang Hsi lowered his sword in a moment of tiredness. Kim Chin-hae witnessed a samurai's sword rammed into his body. He fell to his knees, only being held up by his sword. A shogun motioned his warriors to halt. General Chang Hsi, whose blood-splattered face displayed surrender, stared at Kim Chin-hae. Their eyes met. Chang Hsi nodded and crumbled to the ground. Kim Chin-hae's heart pounded. He understood General Chang Hsi. Thousands of samurais surrounded them. They had massacred most of their soldiers; only 1,500, more or less, were still standing. General Kim Chin-hae lowered his sword and fell to his knees, surrendering, and the other men followed.

Impressed by their bravery, the samurai general couldn't kill them on the spot. Instead, he took General Chang Hsi's remaining men to Kyushu Island. Kim Chin-hae reminded his men about the badges.

On the long white beach of Kyushu Island, they faced Shogun Shikken Tokimune. His youth amazed Kim Chin-hae; he looked at least ten years his junior. Kim Chin-hae remembered General Chang Hsi speaking about Tokimune:

"He is a strict and impartial administrator of justice. A bold soldier, overflowing with physical courage, like you. He is also the one who beheaded Kubilai's emissaries."

"That's why we are at war now," Kim Chin-hae answered.

Kim Chin-hae smiled and remembered General Chang Hsi laughing.

Now, standing in the front row, Kim Chin-hae saw the leader of the samurais talking to Tokimune, who looked over at him, Pak Byeong-ho, and one of General Chang Hsi's headmen. Tokimune called them forward in Song.

Shikken Tokimune, speaking Song, surprised Kim Chin-hae. He shouldn't have been, as he had also heard he was a scholar.

"What was your courageous general's name?"

Kim Chin-hae answered in Goryeo instead of Song, "General Chang Hsi!"

Shikken Tokimune, without the slightest change in his voice, said, "You are as brave as my men say. But you are a fool. I gave you a chance." Kim Chin-hae knew what he meant; he should have spoken in the Song language, knowing the Shikken was soft on the Song generals and soldiers.

Shikken Tokimune continued. "The historians will enter General Chang Hsi's name in our records for his bravery. I heard several of your large ships turned tail and fled. You, with your General, chose to remain and fight. I admire your courage. Who was the cowardly general who fled?"

Kim Chin-hae, in a disgusted voice, said, "General Fan Wenhu and Vice Admiral Atahai."

"Record these names as cowards," Tokimune said to the historians. Then he returned to Kim Chin-hae.

"The cowards will tell Kubilai Khan many lies. Your reward for your overwhelming courage is life. You three," Shikken Tokimune said, pointing to Kim, Pak Byeong-ho, and General Chang Hsi's headman, "will go to Kubilai Khan and tell him the truth."

Kim Chin-hae stepped closer to Tokimune, and the sharp blade of a samurai's sword etched his neck.

"What will happen to the other men?"

"You are testing my patience, general. What is your name?"

Kim Chin-hae hesitated. Pak Byeong-ho touched his shoulder. Kim Chin-hae looked back at Pak Byeong-ho.

Shikken Tokimune smiled and said, "This is your second chance to lie, but I know you won't. Kubilai Khan must have trusted you, or you wouldn't have been placed on the Yuan fleet."

Kim Chin-hae answered in his native language, Goryeo. "My name is General Kim Chin-hae."

"General Kim Chin-hae, the other men will be enslaved," Tokimune said, lying, knowing all men not from the Song Dynasty would die.

Kim Chin-hae bowed and then spoke again. Pak Byeong-ho stared at Kim Chin-hae in disbelief. "The sword your samurai is holding is mine. It was a gift from a friend. I wish to return it to him as an important person gave it to him."

Shikken Tokimune held out his hand, and the samurai placed the sword in his hand. "My men say this sword is special," he said as he slid it from the sheath. "I want it for myself. I haven't seen this type of metal before. It is stronger and sharper than ours."

"They say it is from the heavens," Kim Chin-hae answered.

Shikken Tokimune carefully touched the blood-caked blade and stared at him as he slid the sheath back on.

"Who's the important person?"

"Kubilai Khan," answered Kim Chin-hae.

Shikken Tokimune handed Kim Chin-hae the sword. "I trust you will tell Kubilai Khan every detail. Don't forget to tell him the Heavens protected us with a divine wind. Twice you have tried, and twice you have failed."

Sharp memories of the first invasion flashed before Kim Chin-hae. He unintentionally nodded in agreement. Kim Chin-hae bowed and nodded as he backed up.

The next day, drained of his adrenaline, limping, and bleeding from the head, Kim Chin-hae boarded a wasen heading to Masanhappo with Pak Byeong-ho and Mo Ching.

Eun-ae awoke suddenly from an intense dream. She opened her eyes. Her father sat beside her, holding her hand. She spoke quietly. "Chin-hae is not dead. I saw him returning. I must go to the pier," she said as she struggled to sit. Her father helped her.

"It was just a dream, Eun-ae. General Kim Bang-gyeong and Dagu Hong's Goryeo ships survived, and they said the same thing. He made a name for himself; he died a hero and a brave warrior."

Eun-ae lay back down and curled into a ball. Her father left the room, instructing the servant to stay with her. When Eun-ae heard the door slide and close, she rose. "Bring my men's clothes. I am going to the pier."

Every day, she deceived her father; she woke up early, ate breakfast with him, and returned to her room. After he left for the day, she changed her clothes, slipped out the back window, and walked to the pier. She sat upon the cargo and listened to the sailors' conversations. Her heart ached as the wounded warriors and sailors arrived from the disastrous invasion. Her thoughts returned to Kim Chin-hae. *Where is he?* As darkness fell, she returned to eat with her father. One day, she saw King Chungnyeol standing on the pier. *He, too, must be waiting*, she thought.

Only when Kim Chui-hee, Chin-hae's father, arrived at Park Jae-bong's quarters during the day, requesting to see Eun-ae, did her father discover what she had been doing. Her servant stuttered and made excuses for her. Her stuttering didn't last long before her fathers's anger exploded. The maid fell to her knees, and the truth spilled out. It was then that he made plans for their departure. After a sympathetic apology to Kim Chui-hee, Eun-ae's father sat in her room until she returned. As she slid into the window, she heard her father's voice. "I know you have been going to the pier. You must face reality, or people will start talking. We are leaving with the king at the end of next week."

Eun-ae defiantly spoke. "I'm not going. He is not dead."

Her father walked out, shaking his head, wishing her mother were there, who was stronger than he was. He ordered soldiers to guard her window.

By the middle of the following week, Eun-ae became desperate to return to the pier. An intense feeling came over her. Kim Chin-hae was near. She had to go; she called her maid.

"Is my father home?" Her maid's answer gave her hope. "Give me your clothes!"

The maid shook her head. "I can't. Your father will kill me."

"Not unless I'm caught," whispered Eun-ae as she tried to undress the maid. The maid struggled.

"Stop. I will punish you if you don't stop struggling. I won't let you visit your sister!"

The maid stopped and started undressing.

"Now get in my bed. Stay there until I return."

Eun-ae held her head down and slid open the door. No one said anything as she walked out of her quarters and down the road. She stopped, looked back, smiled, and ran toward the pier.

When she arrived, King Chungnyeol, Kim Chin-hae's father, and General Kim Bang-gyeong stared toward the horizon.

A wasen flying a Wa and white flag had anchored offshore. General Kim Bang-gyeong, with armed soldiers, boarded a boat and rolled out to meet it.

General Kim Bang-gyeong recognized Pak Byeong-ho standing on the bow. *Where is Kim Chin-hae?* he thought.

Pak Byeong-ho left the bow momentarily and returned, holding up a large, slumping man. Excited, General Kim Bang-gyeong recognized Kim Chin-hae. Their boat slid next to the enemy's. Pak Byeong-ho, Kim Chin-hae, and the other man stumbled aboard. The only words spoken were those of a samurai speaking Song. "Remember why Skikken Tokimune spared your life."

Kim Chin-hae nodded, then passed out as he stood on the Goryeo boat. Pak Byeong-ho swept him up and held him as he greeted General Kim Bang-gyeong.

"We made it, sir! We have a lot to tell, but we'd better take General Kim Chin-hae to shore. Only hate has been his medicine. I think he needs the real thing now."

General Kim Bang-gyeong sighed with relief and happily grabbed Pak Byeong-ho's hand and said, "The king, his father, and a certain girl have been waiting for him. What did the samurai mean when he said, 'Remember why Skikken Tokimune spared your life?'"

Pak Byeong-ho didn't answer that question but asked, "What girl?"

"Of course, his fiancée, Park Eun-ae, the Minister of Trade's daughter. She has been here since July."

Pak Byeong-ho's mouth dropped, but no words came out. He thought, *This can't be good.*

"Pak Byeong-ho, Pak, hey, did you hear me? I asked what that samurai meant. You didn't answer me!" barked General Kim Bang-byeong.

After returning to reality, he answered. "You should wait for General Kim Chin-hae. He is the one Shikken Tokimune gave the order to."

Eun-ae saw the king and Kim Chui-hee running to the boat when they reached the shore. Two men were assisting a tall man. Suddenly, the injured man became recognizable. Without even thinking, she ecstatically raced toward them. At first, the king didn't recognize her in her maid's clothing, but Kim Chin-hae's father did. He moved aside, and she wrapped her arms around him. Delusional, Kim Chin-hae wrapped his arms around her and, in a weak voice, called out, "Lis." and then passed out. The king and the others looked confused. Only Pak Byeong-ho understood and shook his head as he carried him to his father's quarters.

Eun-ae sent word to her father. "Kim Chin-hae is alive. They are taking him to his father's quarters. I will be there."

Pak Byeong-ho gently laid him on the bed. Eun-ae stood against the back wall. Kim Chui-hee and Pak Byeong-ho removed his bloody upper garment, exposing his soul lock and a ring attached to it.

"What's this?" Kim Chui-hee asked Pak Byeong-ho as he tried to remove it.

Pak Byeong-ho sternly withdrew Kim Chui-hee's hands. "This must stay; it protects his souls!"

His father, surprised, looked at him and stopped.

Eun-ae moved forward and looked over Pak Byeong-ho's shoulder. *The pendant is no concern, but the ring?*

Kim Chin-hae's father noticed Eun-ae and directed her out of the room. "This is not a place for a young woman. I will call you when it's appropriate."

Eun-ae began to argue when she caught herself. *This man is the father of my fiancé.* Out of character, Eun-ae left the room without a word.

As Kim Chui-hee continued to undress his son, he cried. Every inch of his torso bore a scar from past battles; now he had new ones. The doctor entered the room and treated his wounds the best he could. The doctor told them it was a waiting game. "He has lost a lot of blood, his head injury is severe, and now he has a fever. He fought hard without considering his injuries.

Every hour, feed him this tea. Hopefully, it will help him recover. Make sure you keep his body cooled."

When the doctor left, Eun-ae couldn't control herself any longer. She became her old arrogant self and charged into the room, saying, "I have waited almost two months to see him. I won't leave again."

Pak Byeong-ho held his tongue; he could see the love in her eyes. At that moment, he felt sorry for her. *Her love would never be.* He stepped back, and she sat beside Chin-hae. She picked up a compress, dripped it in a water bowl, and lovingly laid it on his head. Kim Chui-hee and Pak Byeong-ho watched from the back of the room. His father couldn't stop thinking of the soul lock and ring. *What is this all about?*

At the Miao's village, Lis entered the warm pond. She felt him, but suddenly, nothing. Alarmed, she rushed out of the water. Lis placed her hand on her heart and let out a sigh. She felt his heartbeat, but it was weaker than ever. Panicking, she ran to her mother. "I must find him and give him strength! I am going to the cave."

Her mother asked, "Are you strong enough to handle what you see?"

"Yes, I will make him live!"

Son Jun-ho met Lis at the door. She could see his pain.

"Is Kim Chin-hae okay?" he asked.

"He's alive, but barely. I am going to the cave."

Son Jun-ho didn't understand. He followed her to her horse and asked, "Can I go with you?"

Lis hesitated. Her mother answered. "Yes."

Lis turned and gave her mother a questioning look.

"You will need his closest people to call him; the more, the better. The babies and I will also come. You take Yang Da-lou, and I will take Mei."

They rode off toward the mountain. Son Jun-ho suddenly recalled Kim Chin-hae's story about the cave where her ancestors were buried. Chills ran up the back of his neck, and his hair stood up. Goosebumps covered his body. *Why did I ask to go?*

When they left the thick forest, the sun was setting. They entered a field of blooming wildflowers that blended with the colors of the sunset. Lis recalled Chin-hae and her frolicking in the field when they first declared their love for each other. She rode faster and faster, calling his name.

Son Jun-ho and Wei sped up. Suddenly, Lis disappeared into the mountain. Son Jun-ho pulled his horse to a halt. Wei looked back. She slowed her horse, turned around, and rode to Son Jun-ho. "Trust us!" Then she turned around and rode straight into the mountain. Apprehensive, he kicked his horse and directed it toward the mountain with closed eyes. After several minutes, he cowardly half-opened his eyes, spied a cave opening, and halfheartedly entered it. By this time, Lis had lit the fires and climbed the stairs with Yang Da-lou to the huge stone coffins. Her mother followed with Mei. When they reached the top, Wei spoke in a deep voice.

A dialect Son Jun-ho had never heard echoed and vibrated against the walls. Son Jun-ho's goosebumps reappeared. The flames dimmed as an eerie wind blew throughout the cave, carrying a haunting sound of voices. After an hour, Wei and Lis, carrying Kim Chin-hae's babies, walked down the stone stairs. Lis motioned for Son Jun-ho to follow her. They entered a small chamber. Son Jun-ho looked around and saw many cavities that contained jars and boxes. Lis removed the box with a blue ribbon and placed it on the small, crude table. She spoke to Son Jun-ho. "This is his blood and hair. I will call him now."

Wei spoke. "Should I do this? My powers—" Lis interrupted her. "No, our connection is stronger. The first day we met, our bewitchment began, and our threads of fate intertwined. I must do this." Lis unwrapped the box and removed his vial of blood and hair. She placed the hair in the middle of the table, instructing her mother to put Mei and Yang Da-lou on each side of her, with Son Jun-ho and Wei on the other side of the table.

"Hold their tiny hands and create a circle when I tell you."

Son Jun-ho, again with goosebumps and his hair standing up on the back of his neck, observed the stillness and seriousness of the toddlers. They seemed to understand what was happening. Lis opened the vial and, with a small knife, slit her palm. Her blood dripped into the vial, swirling, blending, and boiling. Son Jun-ho's eyes grew large. She tightly wrapped her fingers around the vial and spoke the strange dialect he had heard earlier. Wei followed, and Mei and Yang Da-lou joined with tiny voices. Son watched her place the vial under her garment close to her heart. Then, she completed the circle by grabbing Mei's and Yang Da-lou's hands as the chanting grew louder. The room grew dark, and the eerie wind surrounded them, filled with haunting voices. Before their eyes, Chin-hae's hair that lay on the table ignited into a flame, and within the flame, they could see Chin-hae sit up and lie back in bed. The flame burned throughout the night as love flowed through the heavens to him. Li and Kim Chin-hae talked all night. By morning, Lis's power of love mysteriously healed Chin-hae. He would return to her.

They mounted their horses and rode back to the village to wait.

During the night, Kim Chin-hae awakened his father, Kim Chui-hee, Pak Byeong-ho, and

Eun-ae, sitting up in bed, obviously still sleeping. His eyes opened strangely, staring into space as he called out to someone. "Lis, I see you, I see you. I survived only because of you. Mei, Yang Da-lou, I see you. You strengthen me. Son Jun-ho, take care a little longer. I am coming home. Wei, I saw the heron. I then believed. I tried to tell them, but they wouldn't listen. General Fan Wenhu ran like a scared rabbit. General Chang Hsi was my hero; I was saved with my integrity intact because of him." Kim Chin-hae slowly lay down and kept talking. Eun-ae and his father looked at each other with concern. Kim Chui-hee spoke first. "It must be a dream."

By morning, they knew it was much more than that; Chin-hae, in a trance, conversed the entire night with a woman named Lis, his wife, his babies, Son Jun-ho, and another woman named Wei.

When the sun rose, Kim Chin-hae rose. His strength reverberated. His father and Eun-ae couldn't believe their tired eyes. But Pak Byeong-ho understood. Chin-hae asked for a clean uniform and water.

"I must meet with the king."

His father tried to ask him about Lis. His only answer was, "I will tell you later."

Eun-ae interrupted Kim Chin-hae. "We have the right to know!"

Kim Chin-hae turned to Eun-ae. He looked as if it were the first time he had seen her. His voice turned icy.

"Why are you—?" Before he could finish, Pak Byeong-ho spoke up. "She has been by your side all night."

Kim Chin-hae turned toward him. He then turned to Eun-ae. His voice turned warmer as he stared at Eun-ae's love-filled face, saying, "I am sorry, Eun-ae, but I thought you understood me the last time; our lives can never be shared. My life, body, and souls belong to Lis."

She didn't want to hear this, placing her hands over her ears and closing her eyes.

Kim Chin-hae took this opportunity and left the room, followed by Pak Byeong-ho. Kim Chin-hae's father walked over to Eun-ae and touched her shoulder. She opened her eyes and looked around the room, seeing that he had left. Her face contorted, her voice quavered, and tears streamed down her face as she spoke. "Someday, I will make him pay. Never will he be able to trade in Goryeo. It will never happen."

Kim Chui-hee walked from the room, leaving Eun-ae all alone. She fell to the ground, repeating, "I will make him pay. I will make him pay."

Kim Chin-hae and Pak Byeong-ho quickly walked to King Chungnyeol's quarters. Right behind them was his father.

The guard announced their arrival and opened the door. The king stood before them, surprised. Kim Chin-hae and Pak Byeong-ho bowed and fell to their knees. "Your majesty, we lost, losing so many men and ships. I am only here by the grace of Shikken Tokimune."

"I know, General Chang Hsi's man, Mo Ching, told me."

The king approached them and placed his hand on Kim Chin-hae's and Pak Byeong-ho's shoulders. "Rise! I know you did your best. Your quick recovery amazes me. It must be true. You are bewitched!"

Kim Chin-hae's father, startled, spoke up. "You know?"

The king, disappointed by their defeat and concerned for his uncle, responded solemnly. "The last time I was in Yuan, I found out. Kim Chin-hae needed to tell you. It wasn't my place."

Meanwhile, Eun-ae's father had been sitting to the side, not understanding.

Not wasting any time, Kim Chin-hae asked for a ship and men. "Urgently, we must return to Yuan and tell Kubilai Khan the truth before that bastard becomes a hero."

The king nodded. " Leave when you are ready, but return before you leave. I need to talk to you one more time."

Kim Chin-hae and Pak Byeong-ho bowed and left, leaving behind his father, who was speechless and stunned by everything. He stared at the king and Park Jae-bong. The king approached him and guided him next to Eun-ae's father. "Let's talk."

Kim Chui-hee hastily turned to the Minister of Trade and bowed. "I'm sorry you made this trip. Your daughter needs you. I left her in my room crying and very upset."

Quickly, Park Jae-bong stood and looked confused at the king, not understanding what had happened.

Kim Chui-hee spoke again. "My wife and I had hoped to become your in-laws. That is no longer possible. Please go to Eun-ae and apologize for my son's behavior. I am unaware of what their last conversation was, but there seems to be a misunderstanding on my son's part. Please accept my apologies for my wife's meddling, which has caused your daughter pain. Last night, I appreciated your daughter's concern and her help. Thank her for me. In the near future, I'm sure she will make a powerful wife for a more deserving man."

Eun-ae's father bowed, "I am unsure what happened, but I assume Eun-ae has lost. She is a very determined girl and has never been defeated by anyone. It will take some time for her to forget. I bid you farewell and will see you again." The minister turned and left, finding Eun-ae in Kim Chui-hee's room. Holding Kim Chin-hae's bloody clothes, Eun-ae was talking to herself. "You will love me; I will make you." Her father put his arms around her and led her to their quarters.

The next day, they left for the capital.

---

1. China
2. People from Goryeo

Chapter Thirty-One

Kim

1281 Returning from Hell

Kim Chin-hae and Pak Byeong-ho spent all day preparing to leave for Dadu. They returned late to his father, who obviously had questions. For a long time, Kim Chin-hae dreaded this day. In some ways, he felt disloyal to Lis; he should have been proud of their love, shouting and thanking the heavens. Yet, as a loyal son, his desires should have come second. He failed both.

Stressed, he nervously walked to his father's room, contemplating what he would say. Suddenly, he stopped, turned around, and walked into his cousin's quarters instead. Never on the battlefield had he lacked courage; he always knew what needed to be done. But these were his parents. Their goals had never been his. In the past, he always sidestepped them. This time, it wasn't possible.

King Chungnyeol's servant met him at the door and, without hesitation, boldly announced, "General Kim Chin-hae has finally arrived!" Kim Chin-hae looked at him, surprised, and thought, *My cousin knows me well and knows my bravery is wavering.*

Kim Chin-hae's heart stopped. He didn't expect his father and mother to be there. He fell to his knees with his forehead to the floor. After regaining some courage, he looked up. His mother weakly walked toward him. She kneeled before him, her eyes filled with love. "I prayed every day that you would return to me."

Kim Chin-hae rose with his arms outstretched to his mother and gently pulled her up, wrapping his arms around her. It had been a long time since he had seen her. After a long pause of love, she fought to be released. He dropped his arms, and she stood in front of him. Without tears, she spoke. "Who is Lis?"

The king interrupted. "Maybe we should have some tea or perhaps wine." He walked over to his aunt and guided her to a chair. Kim Chin-hae followed. He wasn't sure how to start. Then he thought out loud. "When did you arrive, Mother?"

"I arrived this morning. I have been traveling for days; I left the minute I heard a tremendous storm occurred. I remembered the first invasion. You really thought I wouldn't come; you are my only child!" Kim Chin-hae's mother answered.

With a high-pitched voice and a look of disappointment, she continued. "Who is Lis? I have the right to know! Your father told me she is your wife. How could you do this to me, marrying someone from a foreign land? What kind of family is she from? How are you going to pursue your political career?"

Kim Chin-hae cringed; this tone meant she was mad.

King Chungnyeol and Kim Chin-hae's father sat silently, knowing his answer.

Kim Chin-hae requested more wine and spoke in a forceful voice. "Mother, you say you prayed for my safe return; Lis answered your prayers. She saved me not once but twice. Lis and her family are powerful shamans. They guided me through this absurd political war. You should thank her." He heard his mother and father gasp. His courage grew just by saying her name.

"We have been married for almost two years and have twins, Kim Yang Da-lou and Kim Mei-caihong. A political career is never going to happen. Instead, I am pursuing my dream of being a merchant like your father's family. I have a partner in Yuan."

No one could stop him now. Words poured out of his mouth for an hour, and then he stopped and fell to his knees. "Please forgive me for my deception. We love each other deeply, and Lis accepts my dream, and I accept her life."

His mother rose and, without a word, left the room. His cousin, the king, walked over to him and pulled him up. "She will come around. She loves you; a mother's love will prevail and forgive you."

Kim Chin-hae thought long and hard about his cousins' words, then spoke. "Maybe?"

His father was still stunned; his son's dream was now his destiny, and he could do nothing about it. However, it was still hard to hear. Kim Chin-hae was his only son, and he dreamed that Chin-hae would follow in his footsteps. Standing, he thought, *I once had a dream, but my sense of duty rose above it—unlike my son's, whose dream meant more.* He was disappointed.

Pushing aside his personal feelings, he spoke. "Kim Chin-hae, what happened, and why did the Shikken Tokimune release you? What message are you carrying to Kubilai Khan? I heard a small portion from the king. I want to hear it from you."

Kim Chin-hae could hear the concerned tone in his voice. For the next couple of hours, he explained everything to them. The king and his father listened, horrified, and understood Chin-hae's love for his shaman.

King Chungnyeol spoke first. "You never said what your friend's name was? Is that the sword?

"Yes, this is the sword, he said as he pulled it out and showed it to the king. My friend and partner is Messer Marco Polo. He saved my life. That's how I met him. Someday, he will be famous. Messer Marco comes from a faraway land and lives as an emissary in Kubilai Khan's Palace. He holds permits for the tea and salt trade. We are hoping to trade with Goryeo." Just then, Kim Chin-hae thought, *Have I shot myself in the foot? Eun-ae will never forgive me.*

The king nodded and smiled, seeing Kim Chin Hae's reaction as he spoke those words. King Chungnyeol changed the subject. "Kim Chin-hae, you must prepare for your departure tomorrow. The high tide is at the monkey's hour tomorrow. It is an excellent time to leave; however, having a wife like Lis, you won't need luck."

Kim Chin-hae smiled, stood, and bowed low. "Someday, I will return."

The king stood. "I have one more order. Watch after my son."

"Like my own, my king. Oh yes, I forgot to tell you. He knows Messer Marco, who also promises to be on his side."

His cousin smiled. "Two is better than one."

Kim Chin-hae left the room without speaking to his father.

The king and his father sat in silence as reality sank in. The Wa won. *We had wasted thousands of lives and thousands of ships. We were defeated, no matter how much we planned or how many ships and men there were. It must be true; the heavens truly protected them*. Silently, they wondered what would happen next. *Would they be preparing for another battle?*

Kim Chin-hae didn't return to his father's quarters. Instead, he went to the barracks to sleep, meeting Pak Byeong-ho, who was surprised to see him. Before he could ask, Kim Chin-hae spoke. "I couldn't face my mother again."

"Your mother? Here?" Pak Byeong-ho replied earnestly.

"She arrived today. I told them everything, but I don't know if she will ever forgive me."

Pak Byeong-ho walked over and slapped him on the back. Kim Chin-hae moaned; he was still in pain.

"Sorry, man, I forgot. Your mother will someday." Pak Byeong-ho lay down.

Kim Chin-hae followed. His body ached, and so did his heart. As the room's darkness surrounded him, he thought, *I never intended to hurt them*. His tired body won over guilt; he fell asleep.

The following day, a familiar voice awakened him. He opened his eyes; his mother was looking down at him. "You didn't tell me where Son Jun-ho is. You know he belongs to us."

Kim Chin-hae rubbed his eyes, hoping he was dreaming, and looked again. It was his mother. He could hear all the men snickering. Embarrassed, he quickly rose, and with little regard for dressing, he grabbed his mother's arm and escorted her from the room, questioning his father's whereabouts. From the corner of his left eye, he saw a figure scrambling quickly toward them.

It was his father. "Ae-cha, I told you to wait for me. You can't treat your son this way in front of the men! Chin-hae, go get dressed!" snorted his father.

After dressing, he returned, and they walked down toward the pier. His mother walked far to the left. She wasn't talking. That meant she was really mad. They reached the pier in silence. His mother stood far to the left of him; the rising sun blinded Kim Chin-hae, and he could not read her face.

"Mother, please forgive—" and before he could finish, she spoke. "I will always love you, but I will never forgive you. You are a selfish child, no, a selfish man! You have kept a precious secret from your father and me for the last two years. I will never accept this woman, Lis. I cannot say if I will accept your children. You are making a horrible mistake by becoming a merchant. You could have had it all: money and power. Eun-ae's father is the Minister of Trade. You are a fool, the worst kind, a fool for love!"

Her harsh words crushed him. He moved in closer and shielded his eyes from the sun, wanting to see her face. Tears were rolling down her cheeks, but her stare was hard. He turned to his father and spoke with intensity. "I will always love you, but I will not forsake my wife, my children, or my dream for yours."

Kim Chin-hae turned and walked back toward the barracks. "I must prepare to leave," he shouted as he walked away. Suddenly, he stopped and turned. "I hope to see you before we leave at three. By the way, Son Jun-ho is mine. You gave him to me years ago. I released him. He is a free man protecting my family as he protected me." Turning, he continued to walk.

Chui-hee, Kim's father, walked over to Ae-cha, wrapped his arms around her, and whispered. "You raised a brave and good man, Ae-cha. You should be proud. He is no longer just a son. He is a husband, father, and courageous man in more ways than one."

She looked up at Chui-hee, and as tears fell, she nodded. "He is no longer afraid of me."

That afternoon, Kim Chin-hae stood on the pier waiting for his parents. His only thought was of his mother. *Will she come to see me off?*

Pak Byeong-ho could see his agony. He didn't want to rush him, but it was time. Walking over and nudging him, he said with an understanding voice, "We must go."

"Just a few more minutes." Kim Chin-hae pleaded.

In the final moment, before he boarded, he saw his father rushing toward him. His aged face looked older than usual. "I could not convince her." Holding his son's hand, he said, "Please come home. Those are worthless words, I know, but I promised your mother."

Chui-hee wrapped his arms around his son. "Be safe and happy. Someday, you never know; we will see you in your new home."

Kim Chin-hae stood on the stern of his ship. With torn feelings, his heart raced at the thought of returning to Lis, but tears flowed as his homeland disappeared.

Rumors buzzed around Yangzhou. Gossip filled every teahouse and restaurant. "A divine wind, Kamikaze, has destroyed Kubilai Khan's entire fleet."

Marco and Dai Xiuying could not believe what they were hearing. *Could it be true? The entire fleet and thousands of men perished.* Marco's heart sank. *Did Kim Chin-hae survive?*

"Let's leave for Dadu tomorrow. The news will devastate Kubilai Khan. We will use the express," Marco said, holding his gold tablet. We can make it in 10 days."

When Marco arrived in Tianjin, a prominent flagship with a flowing red flag belonging to Vice Admiral Atahai and several ships floated in the harbor. Marco headed to them, hoping for answers.

The gossip had spread like wildfire. Vice Admiral Atahai and General Fan Wenhu had arrived two days earlier and were on their way to Kubilai Khan. They were the only generals from the Southern Fleet who had survived.

Marco was in disbelief. "I must find General Fan Wenhu," he told Dai Xiuying.

They mounted their fresh horses and rode hard. It was late afternoon when they came upon Vice Admiral Atahai and General Wenhu's convoy outside Dadu. Marco wasn't sure how to approach Fan Wenhu. He had never met the man and only knew about him through Kim Chin-hae's words.

They rode into his camp, deciding that facing him head-on was best. General Fan Wenhu was arrogant, and Marco decided he must be the same.

With a demanding voice, Marco asked to see the general as he held out the gold tablet. There was no hesitation. The soldier bowed and instructed him to follow. When they arrived at Fan Wenhu's ger, he sat upon his silver chair. Marco bowed. "I am Messer Mar--"

General Fan Wenhu interrupted him. "I know who you are, Messer Marco Polo. You are Kubilai Khan's right-hand man. But you are also General Kim Chin-hae's friend. Your friend chose the wrong general. He has perished."

Marco's facial expression didn't change as he mockingly responded. "No, he chose the right side, the honorable one. I heard what I needed to hear; I know now he is not dead," Marco boastfully stated. He then bowed, turned, and walked away. He remembered what Kim Chin-hae had told him the day he departed for the invasion: "*Lis saw me alive on a ship heading toward a strange land. There would be a coward that would return, and a hero left behind.*"

General Fan We-hu's voice didn't match his response; there was fear. "Don't tell me you believe his witch wife."

Marco didn't turn around. He kept walking. He was confident he wasn't dead.

The next day, he left for Dadu. Marco debated with himself. *Should I say anything to Kubilai? I have no proof, only the word of a shaman*. He decided to wait.

When Marco arrived at the palace, Crown Prince Chinghiz met him. As he expected, the loss devastated Kubilai. He never recovered from his loss of Empress Chabi; now this.

Chinghiz, with concern, spoke. "General Fan Wenhu's courier arrived this morning with the news. The general will arrive soon with his report. Marco, Kubilai needs one of your stories to take his mind off this. He is already speaking of a third invasion. Honestly, we can't afford a third."

Marco entered Kubilai's chamber feeling guilty. He promised Empress Chabi he wouldn't leave him during this time, but his loyalty to Kim Chin-hae was strong. Marco thought, *I hadn't been gone that long*, making an excuse for himself.

A beautiful girl sat next to Kubilai, serving him airag. When Kubilai looked up, Marco fell to his knees and crawled toward him.

"Where have you been, Messer Marco? Did you hear the news? Rise, you fool!"

He turned to the young girl. "Leave us." She quickly rose and gracefully left the room.

"Marco, come sit. What have you heard?" Kubilai said with slightly slurred words.

Marco quickly sat and answered, forgetting what he had decided the day before. "I met General Fan Wenhu. I'm not sure if you should believe him, my Lord."

Kubilai looked confused.

Marco continued. "I'll tell you a story about General Kim Chin-hae, the Goryeo king's cousin. Kim was his eyes and helped him plan the invasion. I am his friend, and he is married to a shaman."

Kubilai perked up. He believed in shamans. Throughout the night, Marco retold Kim Chin-hae's story from the beginning. Kubilai listened contentedly.

Finally, Kubilai spoke. "Do you think he is alive?"

Confidently, Marco answered back. "Yes."

Kubilai sat quietly, contemplating, and finally spoke, "Marco, tomorrow, I will listen to General Fan Wenhu and the vice admiral. Leave; I must sleep."

Marco quietly left him to his servants. He passed the young girl as she entered, just as he exited.

Now, he thought, *all I can do is wait. I'll visit Physician Wu and check on Li.*

The next day, Vice Admiral Atahai and General Fan Wenhu waltzed into Kubilai Khan's court.

Marco was present but not seen.

General Fan Wenhu bowed and slowly walked toward Kubilai. Marco was surprised and thought, *Their rapport was more like friends.* The vice admiral stood back.

Kubilai Khan greeted General Fan Wenhu first. "I am happy to see my old friend survived."

General Fan Wenhu fell to his knees. "I deserve death; I have failed you, my lord. We lost everything. I am so sorry."

"Rise, Wenhu, and tell me your story."

Kubilai Khan listened carefully. General Fan We-hu's story was convincing, but in the back of his mind, Marco's story kept going around. *I need more proof of misgivings.* He respectfully dismissed General Fan Wenhu, the vice admiral, and the ministers.

Marco came out of hiding; he understood Kubilai had no other choice. Marco bowed and began to leave through the large door. Praying that Kim Chin-hae was alive.

"Messer Marco, stay!" Kubilai said in a discouraged voice. "Twice I have lost to a divine tempest. Could heaven be on their side? No way!" He yelled, answering his own question. "I will never resign to this failure. Call in Crown Prince Chinghiz, Messer Marco. Today, we will start planning my next campaign against Cipangu. This time, it will be larger!"

Marco stood speechless.

"Go, Messer Marco, bring my son."

Marco bowed and left.

He returned with Crown Prince Chinghiz. Again, Marco tried to escape Kubilai, but he ordered him to listen while Chinghiz politely tried to reason with his father.

"We are stretched too thin, Father. We have lost thousands of ships and men fighting this war. In Champa, our campaign is showing no prospects of winning. And most of our Tartar soldiers are fighting on the western borders against Qaidu."

Kubilai wasn't listening; his ambitions overshadowed reality.

Marco sulked around the palace for the next couple of days, worrying. Kubilai was obsessed with his next invasion and had no time for him. His only relief was talking to Guo Yu and the royal physician. Li flourished in her studies, making him proud.

One day, Marco saw Kim Chin-hae's young cousin, the crown prince, among the gardens. It made him sad, and he wondered if he had heard the news.

Marco spent the other days in his palace quarters meticulously inspecting the family business ledgers that his father or uncle delivered every six months. Not that he didn't trust them, but his name was on the permits.

Their relationship had improved when his father and uncle realized Marco worked mostly for Kubilai. His involvement was minimal, and they liked that. They spent most of their time in the trade outposts they had set up along the Silk Road and in the middle of Cathay, Zhangtzu, Chamdo, Chengdu, and Dali. Marco handled more of the eastern coast. It worked out well. Initially, the ledger's pile was small; now, it took him hours to manage. They were making money.

On the ship, Kim Chin-hae looked out to sea. With the luck of the monkey, their voyage was going smoothly. They were only a few weeks behind General Fan Wenhu and Vice Admiral Atahai.

The three surviving men met daily and discussed their strategy against the general. Each time Kim Chin-hae read the letter from Shikken Tokimune, his heart pounded.

It was early morning; the drums started--they had seen land. Soon, he would stand in front of Kubilai. He wondered what General Fan Wenhu had told the Great Khan.

While Marco sat and studied the ledgers, his mind was busy, and his worry declined. Suddenly, a violent knock on his door interrupted him.

"Messer Marco Polo, Messer Marco Polo."

Marco quickly rose and opened the door. A soldier stood there. "You must come, Dai Xiuying sent me. Your friend, General Kim Chin-hae, is entering the palace's gates with two other men.

Marco's heart excitedly pounded as he raced to the gates. It was true his friend was alive. Kim Chin-hae raced toward him. They met in an undignified manner, hugging each other. Quickly, they realized others were watching and resumed a dignified stance.

They stood face to face, smiling, and then Kim Chin-hae's face became severe. "We need to see the Great Khan. I bring news from Shikken Tokimune. I'm sure General Fan Wenhu told him great lies."

Marco studied his friend's face, never seeing him this serious. He knew Chin-hae's presence and news would severely affect General Fan Wenhu and the vice admiral.

"Kubilai is waiting for you," stated Marco.

Kim Chin-hae's expression changed to puzzlement. "What do you mean he has been waiting for me?"

"I told him you were alive. I believed Lis, and I told him the story about you and Lis. He believes in shamans."

Marco whispered. "Let's go."

Marco, General Kim Chin-hae, Dai Xiuying, Pak Byeong-ho, and Mo Ching walked side by side confidently toward the palace entrance. The doors opened, and they marched toward Kubilai Khan's throne hall.

Meanwhile, General Fan Wenhu, resting in his home, was alerted by a brisk knock at his door. It was his servant who handed him a letter. Relaxed, he lazily opened the letter. The servant watched Fan Wenhu's expression change from calm to terrified; his hands trembled until he could no longer hold the letter. The letter floated to the ground. General Fan Wenhu barked at his servant to leave. As the door closed, he crumpled to the floor.

The four men, Marco, Kim Chin-hae, Pak Byeong-ho, and Mo Ching, entered Kubilai Khan's court as he sat high upon his glorious chair with Crown Prince Chinghiz and ministers to his right. They fell to their knees with their heads to the floor.

Kubilai Khan's voice boomed, "Everyone, rise and come forward."

As Kim Chin-hae went forward, he held out a letter with both hands. Khan's eunuch walked forward, took the letter from him, and handed it to the Khan. As Kubilai read the letter, he glanced at Marco and General Kim Chin-hae, then back at the letter. He lowered the letter, his face turned violet-red as his anger rose. He yelled for a servant to summon General Fan Wenhu and Vice Admiral Atahai. Everyone stood like statues; only deep sighs could be heard as they waited for the general and vice admiral. The hour of waiting seemed like days.

The announcement, "Vice Admiral Atahai and General Fan Wenhu request to enter," broke the silence. The doors opened. Arrogantly, General Fan Wenhu stood at the entrance, dressed in his ornate uniform. Suddenly, he withered like a dying flower. They both fell to their knees.

Kubilai Khan rose, his chest inflated, and his face turned redder as if he were about to explode as he walked down the stairs. He stopped, facing General Kim Chin-hae, and looked down at Kim's sword. Swiftly, he grabbed it and withdrew it from the sheath. He walked, dragging the sword behind him, toward the defeated Fan Wenhu. Whispering echoed throughout the chambers. With fire in his eyes, Kubilai stopped and looked toward the whispering ministers. Instantly, silence consumed the room, and the ministers lowered their heads. Reaching Fan Wenhu, Kubilai Khan erected the sword high above his head. Loud gasping broke the silence. With a booming voice, Kubilai said, "How dare you lie to me?!" He wheeled the sword toward Fan Wenhu, missing him by an inch. "You left hundreds and hundreds of my men to die at the hands of my enemies to save your hide. You coward."

General Fan Wenhu groveled. "I deserve to die, I deserve to die," he said as he crawled to Kubilai Khan, grabbing his ankles.

Kubilai roared. "How dare you, a coward, touch me!"

Crown Prince Chinghiz immediately removed his hands and dragged him from the room. Meanwhile, Kubilai still roared. "Take him and Vice Admiral Atahai to the guardhouse!"

Disgusted, Kubilai returned to his seat and lowered his head. When he looked up, his anger had cooled.

"Everyone, leave except General Kim Chin-hae and his men. There will be a trial later."

The ministers rose, bowed, and quickly left. They were relieved they didn't see blood.

Marco slid out the door and met Dai Xiuying in the hall.

Kim Chin-hae, Pak Byeong-ho, and Mo Ching stood before Kubilai Khan. Their knees were weaker than they had been in battle. Kubilai spoke slowly. "Shikken Tokimune's letter has enlightened me. General Chang Hsi died a hero trying to do his duty. This letter states that he fought heroically, just as you men. That's why you are here in front of me. I will reward you with one wish for your bravery."

Kim Chin-hae spoke up bravely. Pak Byeong-ho touched Kim Chin-hae's hand to remind him to be cautious. Kim Chin-hae disregarded him. "What will happen to General Fan Wenhu and the vice admiral?"

Kubilai thoughtfully stared at Kim. "Is that your wish?"

"No, but—" Pak Byeong-ho touched his hand again, and Kim stopped talking momentarily.

"My wish? I want ships from Ningbo and maybe Fuzhou, and your permission to live in Zapton and expand sea routes for trading," said Kim Chin-hae.

"That's more than one wish. You are courageous and ambitious. No wonder you are friends with Messer Marco. What will I gain from such a wish?"

Confident, Kim Chin-hae answered. "Collecting lots of tax."

The corner of Kubilai Khan's lips turned up, and a loud belly laugh erupted.

"Granted." Then Kubilai turned to Pak Byeong-ho.

Pak Byeong-ho looked at Kim Chin-hae and answered. "My wish is the same as his."

Surprised, Kubilai Khan thought *that both are brave and smart.* "Granted. However, both of you will personally bring the tax money to me. I want to know that you did not waste your wish and that I was not a fool to grant it."

"Mo Ching?" Kubilai asked.

Mo Ching looked at all three and answered. "A restaurant, that's my wish. I never want to sail another ship or fight again except with a wife. My skills with a knife are as good as my sword. I was a good cook before they ordered me to become a warrior."

They all laughed.

Kubilai replied. "Granted! The same goes for you. Every year, you are to report to me!"

Mo Ching smiled, nodded, and bowed.

Kubilai Khan sat there a moment in silence, staring at the men.

"General Fan Wenhu will be demoted and exiled for some years. As far as Vice Admiral Atahai, I have different plans." Kubilai Khan watched Kim's disappointed face and continued. "Now leave. My eunuch will see you tomorrow with your proceeds."

Kim Chin-hae, Pak Byeong-ho, and Mo Ching bowed low, turned, and exited.

Marco impatiently waited. The minute he heard the door open, he rushed over. "Well???"

Kim Chin-hae smiled and spoke. "We have our ships!"

"Ships?" Marco responded.

"Come, let's go. We have lots to talk about."

The door opened, and a servant called out to Marco. "Kubilai Khan wants to see you!"

"Wait for me in my quarters," Marco told Kim Chin-hae.

Mo Ching bowed to Marco and said his farewell. "I will be on my way; I have a wife and restaurant to find. The next time you see me, I will own the most famous restaurant in the city."

Marco looked puzzled and looked at Kim Chin-hae. "I will explain later."

Marco entered Khan's court. It was just him now.

"I won't talk long. I have somewhere to go," Kubilai said. "Your friend wasn't happy hearing General Fan Wenhu's punishment. I'm sure he doesn't think it fits his crime. The general and I go back a long way. Like how you saved your friend, Kim Chin-hae, years ago, Fan Wenhu saved Crown Prince Chinghiz's life, and I granted him a wish."

Marco's mouth dropped. Now he understood.

"Vice-admiral?" Marco questioned. Kubilai didn't answer.

"Leave now. Chinghiz and I have somewhere to go. You should return to Yangzhou. I will see you at the White Festival."

Marco bowed and left quickly. He couldn't wait to talk to Kim Chin-hae.

Kim Chin-hae and Pak Byeong-hu wandered around Marco's quarters, admiring all his things while waiting for him. Kim Chin-hae was dying to thumb through his ledgers.

As Marco entered his room, he said, "Now we are really partners, Chin-hae. You'd better start examining the ledgers. That's your job now."

The men laughed.

"Tell me everything," Marco said, pouring drinks.

For the rest of the day and half the night, all three men talked, drank, and ate until they passed out. It was midday when a knock on the door woke them up. It was Kubilai Khan's eunuch. He was there to deliver their wishes. It was a gold tablet with the seal of Kubilai Khan.

The eunuch looked at Marco. "You can explain how it works. When you have accomplished your wish, please return the gold tablet and report to Kubilai Khan everything that has happened. Remember, trustworthiness is everything to him. Besides, he will know everything, anyway. This gold tablet belongs to Mo Ching. Where do I find him?"

Marco spoke. "The best teahouse in the city."

The eunuch bowed and turned.

Kim Chin-hae turned to Marco. "Pak Byeong-ho and I are leaving. Lis is waiting."

"I'll go as far as Yangzhou," Marco told him.

Kim Chin-hae nodded.

Marco asked, "Tomorrow morning?"

Kim Chin-hae smiled and nodded.

Kubilai Khan and Crown Prince Chinghiz made their way to the guardhouse. General Fan Wenhu and the vice admiral fearfully waited for him.

Kubilai Khan's soldiers forcefully pulled the admiral from the cell and forced him to his knees. He looked up at the Great Khan with pleading eyes. Kublai showed no mercy, and with one swift motion, his head went flying.

General Fan Wenhu watched in horror.

Kubilai's persona was surprisingly calm. "General Fan Wenhu, you will be exiled to a deserted island until I call for you. My debt has now been paid. There won't be another chance to escape death."

Chapter Thirty-Two

Kim

1281 The Awakening

The three men rode leisurely to Yangzhou. They agreed to meet again after the New Year, the beginning of dreams.

Kim Chin-hae rode faster and harder the day they left Marco in Yangzhou, counting down the days until he saw Lis.

When they reached the crest overlooking the valley where he lived, he saw smoke rise from his chimney. He slid off his horse and took out a bag. Watching the smoke billow, he removed his uniform and washed the dust and dirt from his body. From a bag, he withdrew ordinary clothing and dressed.

With his feet and hands, he scraped dry leaves, straw, and sticks together in a pile. Kneeling over the pile, he quickly struck two flint rocks together, creating a spark. He blew until he saw a flame. The flame grew more prominent as the sticks ignited. He stood and placed his uniform on the fire. “I have finally reached my crossroads. My life and dream truly begin now. Like a fire that sweeps across a forest, it leaves nothing but remnants of its past, and from its ashes, a new life springs forth.” Tears rolled down his cheeks. “From this moment, I will only remember the memories I wish to remember, and from these memories, my new life will bring forth great happiness.”

Pak Byeong-ho’s eyes welled with tears as he watched Kim Chin-hae.

They mounted their horses and rode fast until, in the distance, they could see the outline of a small body standing on the road. Kim Chin-hae and Pak Byeong-ho stopped; they knew it was Lis. Kim Chin-hae smiled at Pak, heeled his horse, and rode fast, leaving Pak Byeong-ho behind. Pak Byeong-ho watched Chin-hae jump from his horse and run to her. Lis jumped into his arms, and Kim Chin-hae swirled her around and around until they both fell entwined into each other’s bodies. Wei, his children, Son Jun-ho, and the villagers weren’t far behind.

They circled them, laughing and crying. Finally, they rose and walked hand in hand while all the others followed.

Chapter Thirty-Three

Marco

Prison and a Confession

Genoa Prison 1298

When Marco finished his story, Rustichello was guilty of tears. Marco kept talking in a melancholy voice. "That was the end of the year 1281. 1282 was a glorious year."

Suddenly, Marco seemed to awake from a dream. He looked around as if he needed to remember where he was.

"How long have I been talking?" Marco touched his lips and his face. The dried blood had disappeared entirely, and so had his anger. His stomach growled. "How long has it been since we ate?"

"After that last outburst, well, it's been a couple of days," Rustichello replied.

Marco walked to the barred window, gazed into the heavens, and continued to talk, forgetting his hunger. "The sea, Lis, and his children became Kim Chin-hae's country. It took years for his mother to forgive him."

Marco stopped momentarily. "I understood Chin-hae's actions. My last year in Cathay, I forsook Kubilai for my dream."

"What, how?" Surprised, Rustichello asked.

Marco didn't answer, and he continued with Kim Chin-hae's story. "The whole next year, Pak Byeong-ho and he built four ships. Kim Chin-hae spent his youth researching designs and learning crucial building techniques, the year he prepared for the invasion. Goryeo ships were sturdy, but the Song Dynasty and the dynasties before them were more advanced. Their ships were double-hulled and divided into separate watertight compartments, which saved them if they were rammed by whales or other ships. The other amazing thing is that they held drinking water for passengers and animals and had compartments to keep the fish they caught fresh."

Rustichello stopped Marco. "Really?" Rustichello's tone was one of disbelief.

Marco turned to him. "Really! That's not all. They were using sternpost rudders on the outside of their ship. They could navigate close to shore, in crowded harbors and narrow channels. They built three and four-masted ships, so they didn't need banks of rowers. The ships were 200 feet long and carried up to 500 men. They had private cabins for travelers."

Rustichello's eyes became wide. "You're lying now!"

"No, not only did we use magnetic compasses, but also printed star chart manuals for navigating by the stars. I learned all this from Kim Chin-hae; he is a natural. After they built their ships, our business flourished. Kubilai Khan not only opened trade to the world by land, but he also encouraged sea trade by building large shipyards, employing many skilled workers, and spending many years fine-tuning naval technology. That was one reason he liked Kim Chin-hae and used him."

Marco's speech softened as he dropped his head. "I wonder what he is doing." A smile flashed across his face, and he answered his own question. " Loving Lis and the sea as always."

Rustichello put down his pen and yawned. "I must sleep. Hunger disappears when you sleep. It makes time pass quickly. Before you know it, the morning will have come, and maybe our breakfast."

Marco agreed. Rubbing his caving stomach, he thought, *I have become so thin*. He lay on his bed and closed his eyes. His mind traveled to the year when everything changed, and before he knew it, he mumbled a few words: "Li nourished my hungry heart."

Rustichello, with a raised voice, said, "Are you speaking to me? If you are, speak up. I can't hear you."

Chapter Thirty-Four

Marco

Marcos' Melting Hungry Heart

Genoa Prison 1298

Marco spoke up. "After Empress Chabi died, Kubilai married Consort Nambi. I was away for most of the time, busy with Kubilai Khan's mission and my trade company, leaving Guo Yu and Physician Wu in charge of Li. Then, in 1286—an eventful year—happiness and sadness occurred. For years, Chin-hae's mother had refused to accept his marriage. She hoped her refusal would make him forsake his Miao wife, Lis, plus she made sure that he never traded in Goryeo by involving Eun-ae's father, the Minister of Trade. This didn't stop Kim Chin-hae. Instead, he sailed south to Java, Champa, and other islands, purchasing much-desired spices, medicinal herbs, and other goods. Finally, fearing she would never see him, she made peace, and our business expanded to Goryeo. This reunion was the happy part.

"However, sadness became a priority that year when Chinghiz, Yuan's crown prince, died. For a year, I stayed at the palace, allowing me to see Li more than ever, who was still a little girl to me. I had a lover who traded in pearls and lived next door to my father.

"It was two years later, at the New Year's White Festival, that I lost my heart, and my life changed. From that moment, my life spiraled out of control.

"Still in denial, I brought Li her usual white and gold dress for the Festival. This time, however, Guo Yu insisted on helping me, unaware that Li had secretly instructed him to do so. Li was seventeen now, and I was utterly naïve about Li's feelings. Guo Yu met me at the most distinguished luxury shop in the market. Li had already selected her dress and several magnificent gold and white pearl jewelry pieces for me to choose from.

“Guo Yu easily manipulated me, but I became concerned. ‘Isn’t this dress too revealing, too mature? Is she trying to impress someone? Has someone won her heart?’

“Guo Yu smiled. ‘Li is of marrying age.’

“I was horrified. ‘Li is just a little girl.’

“However, when Li waltzed into court on White Festival day, turning many men's heads, fright and jealousy ran through my body as these horrid men whispered to their friends. What was I going to do? Kubilai had informed me minutes before: ‘When the weather warms, your next mission is to take Li’s half-brother, Emperor Gong of Song, to the Sakya Monastery in Tibet, where he will live as a monk.’ The Grand Dowager had died, and his mother had gone into a nunnery. It was Kubilai Khan's way of discarding a threat. I would be gone for six months. With all my strength, I tried to shake my jealousy and fear; I avoided her for the rest of the evening.”

Marco’s story was interrupted when the prison door swung open. The general stood in the doorway. “I heard you wanted to talk to me; you completed your report?”

Excitedly, Marco stood and scrambled to the desk, gathering the papers and handing them to the general. “Did you deliver the letters to my family?”

The general looked at him. “I will if I am satisfied.”

Disgusted, Marco bellowed, “That report will make you rich! Are you playing with me? You said you would release me. You should release Rustichello, too!”

The general’s face turns wicked. “Don’t forget, you are not one to order anyone! Where’s the report? It's your only hope if you want your letters to be delivered or released!

Marco, desperate, walked to Rustichello’s desk and picked up his report, forcing an arrogant smile as he handed the general the papers.

The general turned and walked out the door, slamming it.

At the general’s office, the commander sat and read the report. A grin slowly emerged. *Messer Marco Polo is right; I could become rich.* Opening his desk drawer, he pulled out Marco’s letter to his family, slid the second half of the report on top of Marco’s first half, and closed the drawer.

The general sat for a while, staring at Marco’s letters. In a moment of righteousness, he called in an officer and handed the letters. “Deliver this to a courtier with access to the Venetian government.”

Besides, he thought, *I heard through the grapevine that the war could end within the year. He will be released then, anyway.* But he still hated giving Marco the satisfaction that his quick thinking had earned him a release. Yet, his hate turned to laughter, and he spoke out loud. "I won anyway. I am going to be rich."

Back at the cell, Marco wildly hit the desk and ran to the door, hearing a laughing commander walk down the hall. With a closed fist, an out-of-control Marco hit the wall repeatedly until Rustichello stopped him.

"This is what I want to do to his face," snorted Marco.

Rustichello wrapped Marco's hand with a piece of a torn shirt. "Come on, Marco, finish your story. It was just getting interesting."

Marco lay down on his bed, facing the wall. He slowly continued his story.

"I feared my feelings. I even told Li a disgusting story when I returned from escorting her brother to Tibet; you know, the one I told you about when she got mad at me."

Rustichello thought for a minute. "Yes, I remember the one where the fathers give their daughters to the men travelers."

"I was trying to push her away. I also tried to spend the rest of the year outside the palace at my father's, enjoying the company of the pearl trader's daughter, and only went to the palace when Kubilai Khan called me or on his birthday. Again, Li appeared with men at her side. And again, I left. It was not until the following White Festival that I utterly failed. Li entered as a queen. She wasn't wearing the age-appropriate dress I bought. When it became time to give gifts, men surrounded Li. One never left her side. When I looked closer, that man was the Crown Prince Wang Won of Goryeo, Kim Chin-hae's cousin, who followed her like a puppy. As I looked around the room, I wasn't the only person watching. Trying to dismiss my feelings and concerns, I left early to prepare for my next mission, which would take me to Java. We were to meet their king and convince him to be part of the Kubliai Khan's empire. Then, I would continue sailing the coast of Myanmar to India.

"It was the day before I left. I entered the palace to gather my belongings and bid Kubilai Khan farewell one last time. As I walked through the palace halls, court ladies and eunuchs stood together, whispering. That always indicated something scandalous had happened. A friend passed by, and I asked what the commotion was. His response: 'It's silly court gossip, something about Physician Wu's herbalist apprentice and the Crown Prince Wang Won.'

"My heart stopped for a moment. I shook it off and regarded it as court gossip. But a memory appeared, the crown prince following Li and peering eyes following them...

"When I entered my quarters, Kim Chin-hae's letter sat on my desk, confirming our meeting place for our journey. But it included a statement: 'My cousin, the crown prince, seems bewitched by Li.' At that time, I wasn't sure if Kim Chin-hae understood the consequences. Or was it his way of warning me?

"That night, I lay in bed staring at the ceiling. I wasn't sure what I felt, but my stomach felt sick like I had eaten something vile. I rose, went to my desk, and wrote her a letter."

> Princess Li,
>
> Just before tomorrow's dawn, when most people are in their chambers, please have Guo Yu escort you to the Green Mound Palace. Try to avoid being seen. I need to talk to you.
>
> Marco

Marco returned to the present, stood, stared out the prison window, and spoke in a quiet, serious voice. "But no one knew past coincidental deeds, intertwined with a dying queen's wish a thousand miles away, would sow the seeds: propagating our fateful destiny."

Rustichello hesitated a moment, staring at Marco. "What queen?"

"Buluqhan Khatun, the wife of Arghun, who is the grandnephew of Kubilai Khan and ruler of the Tartar empire's Ilkhanate. You remember he was the young crown prince my father had met on his first journey to Cathay and the one who fought the beautiful female warrior, Aiyurug, and disgracefully lost."

Rustichello laughed. "I remember!"

"Buluqhan died in the year 1286. Her last wish was for Arghun to marry a princess from her tribe, Bayaut. In her will, she insisted that no lady should sit on her throne or be his wife who was not of her lineage. Arghun was so preoccupied with civil wars that it was not until 1288 that he sent three lords, Ulatai, Abushka, and Qoja, to Kubilai Khan to retrieve one. They arrived in '89 after I had left for my mission."

Chapter Thirty-Five

Li

Li's Seduction

Venice 1298

The next morning, Luca arrived early after their day at Alessio's shop. She was more confident and felt comfortable around Li. *Today would be the day,* Luca thought. As she helped Li dress, she would ask more intimate questions. "You never told me how you finally convinced Messer Marco to fall in love with you."

Li smiled; her heart fluttered. "It is a long, complicated story. He saved me, not once, but twice." Guo Yu turned and stared at Li.

"When I was seventeen, I decided to seduce him," Li bluntly said.

Luca's face turned red.

Guo Yu lowered his head, embarrassed, and thought, *She could sometimes be shameless.*

Li started slowly. "First, I sent Guo Yu on a secret mission to help Marco buy my dress for the White Festival. A dress I chose. I wanted him to notice I was a woman."

Luca giggled. "Did it work?"

Li laughed. "Too much; he wouldn't talk to me all night. I was heartbroken and didn't understand what had happened. He even left before I could give him my present, and I didn't see him again until he returned from Tibet six months later."

"Then what?" Luca urgently said.

"Well, when he returned, he surprised me by requesting to see me. We met privately at Physician Wu's office, and he told me about my brother and their trip. Then he told me a disgusting story about this area and how it is a young man's dream to travel there. The parents give their young daughters to the men travelers to sleep with. It is their custom. The more men they sleep with, the more desirable they are."

Luca gasped; she had never heard of such a thing. "That's really not true?"

"Yes, it is. I was so jealous that I stomped out of the room while Marco roared with laughter. *How dare he*, I thought. I didn't realize he was trying to push me away."

"It was then that I decided. I must have a plan. Unfortunately, Ijir Burkhqa was part of it, even though he didn't know. The following two times I saw Marco, at Khan's birthday and then at the White Festival in February, I made sure I was stunning, and the crown prince stayed by my side. I was naïve and simply stupid; my only concern was making Marco jealous. The consequences proved to be life-changing."

Li stood at the window, looking out over the canal. "It was after the White Festival. Guo Yu handed me a note. Perplexed, I looked at Guo Yu, whose face was blank.

"'Someone from the Khan's chamber brought it.' He said.

"Afraid, I opened it slowly, thinking, *Has someone seen me spying? Did someone know how I felt about Marco? Was this a threatening letter?* Instead of reading the content, I went straight to the end. My heart fluttered, and I could feel my face burn. The letter was from Marco. My heart pounded harder as I skimmed the letter."

Li then recited the note to Luca.

"*Princess Li*—" Li stopped and looked up. "He was the only one who called me that."

Then Li continued reciting the letter.

"Princess Li,

Just before tomorrow's dawn, when most people are in their chambers, please have Guo Yu escort you to the Green Mound Palace. Try to avoid being seen. I need to talk to you.

Marco

"I remember looking up at Guo Yu. I probably looked pale.

"'What's wrong?' he asked.

"I handed him the note. Guo Yu looked worried. My heart wanted this to be a joyous occasion. All night, I tossed and turned, fantasizing about all situations. *Could this finally be a confession of love? That had to be the reason. Not that he's leaving the palace or getting married.*

“The following day, I rose early and carefully dressed; I had to look beautiful. Guo Yu arrived, and we secretly slipped out. It was cold and dark, but the palace's snow-covered grounds reflected light from the setting moon. Nervously, I walked to the place where Marco and my journey began when Empress Chabi sent Marco to Lin’an.

“We crossed over a bridge and started our incline through the evergreen forest. Everything was white except for massive brown trunks and the green needles that glittered like stars. A dim light gleamed in the distance. We walked faster and finally arrived at the Green Palace’s enormous doors. The doors squeaked, stiff with coldness, as we opened them. Following the light, we found Marco waiting for us. He greeted us with a bow, and I, with a smile, beaming with happiness. But he wasn’t smiling. The room was cold, and so was Marco.

“He motioned for Guo Yu to leave. As I stood before him, he gruffly spoke, ‘I have heard rumors. Do you like Crown Prince Wang Won of Goryeo?’ Marco grabbed my arm. ‘Do you know how dangerous that is?’

“His actions weren’t like Marco’s. *What is wrong with him?* I thought. I must have looked scared. He released my arm and backed away.

“‘Tomorrow, I leave for a long journey sailing to Java and India, checking trade routes for the Khan. You must promise you won't see the prince. His life is destined, and his destiny does not include you. His Tartarian wife has been chosen. Her mother and his chosen bride are brutal for power and will destroy whoever gets in their way. You mustn’t become an issue. You don’t have anyone on your side except Physician Wu, Guo Yu, and me. And I won’t be here to protect you. I won’t see you as a concubine, either. Now, promise me! Don’t see the crown prince again. Promise me!’

“With tears in my eyes, I promised. The cause of my tears was mixed; Marco was yelling at me and leaving me for a long mission. As I left the Green Mound and walked away, I was confused. His ravings could have belonged to a jealous lover, a worried father, or a brother. Which was it?

“As I walked through the snow-covered grounds, chills covered my body. What had just happened? I only knew I was sad; he was leaving, and I wasn’t sure if I could keep my promise.”

Chapter Thirty-Six

Marco

Coming to Terms

Genoa prison 1298

Marco continued his story to Rustichello. "Of course, I knew nothing about the queen or the three Lords. My fear and my anger stemmed from Crown Prince Wang Won. I met Li at the Green Mound the morning I was to leave. That morning, as the setting moon illuminated her silhouette through the window, I saw the real her for the first time. She was no longer a child but a beautiful woman, inside and out. I never saw it coming; Instantly, my heart stopped, reversed, and my life restarted.

"I intended to warn her. My heart was telling me differently. The thought of her with the crown prince caused me pain. I didn't understand. Was I jealous or just scared for her life?

"Throughout the night, my mind kept drifting to Li. The image of her face in the moonlight stirred a feeling I didn't know I had. Feeling ashamed, I tried to stop thinking about her this way. My only concern should be her safety. She was eighteen, and I was much older; I couldn't betray her trust.

"The following day, mentally and emotionally exhausted, I forced myself to focus on this critical exploration trip. It could change everything for the empire, my father and uncle, and Kim Chin-hae. The sea trade routes were the future, as land trade routes had been in constant turmoil. Additionally, Kubilai Khan has chosen me to be part of the convoy to help persuade Java to join his empire. Another worry: my father, uncle, and I wondered if this could be my last trip. Kubilai Khan's health and state of being had changed considerably since the death of Empress Chabi and his son. We wondered if our time in Cathay was ending.

"I left my quarters to discuss any last-minute details with Kubilai Khan. Still, after all these years, Kubilai demanded respect, especially during formal official meetings. As I entered the main hall, I bowed, fell to my knees, and explained that if God's will and fair weather followed me, the ships and I would return safely and on time. I boasted that, on my return, I would have lots of colorful and exciting stories to tell him. Khan's body jiggled as he laughed, and a broad smile appeared. He was pleased, motioning me forward. I slowly rose from my knees. He grabbed my hand, seriously looked at me, and whispered. 'You do that. I will command God.'

"You could hear a low chatter around the room. Few understood our relationship, and those who did, disapproved of it. I lost much of my support base in the last couple of years. As Kubilai Khan released my hand, my last words were, 'Please stay healthy.'

"My mind never left Li. From the beginning, my father had warned me not to get involved with her. I never understood his concern. She was just a little girl for whom I felt sorry. Our lives had crossed paths when I was still as vulnerable to loss as she was. I felt her pain. It was too late now; I hadn't listened. Unconsciously, I hurried to the royal Physician's office. I needed to speak to Physician Wu. He had been her protector for years and needed to know about the crown prince.

"When I finished explaining, I was surprised by his answer. 'Messer Marco, they have been friends for five years, Kokochin included. They have a secret bond and have vowed silence. So, I'm surprised Ijir Bukhqa, the crown prince, said anything to his cousin.'

"As he finished that sentence, his face reflected concern. 'Maybe it wasn't the crown prince who told Kim Chin-hae.'

"Before he could say more, I interrupted, 'What do you mean by a secret bond?'

"Physician Wu explained. 'It started as a simple child's hide-and-seek game. Kokochin and the crown prince hid from their guards and escorts and met Li. Then, they would playfully seek the mysteries and secrets of the palace. They were the Society of Three.'

"Physician Wu stopped talking as if our thoughts intermingled. *Have they been discovered? Have they heard someone's secret, or was it their togetherness?*

"Now, Physician Wu understood my fear. *Have the young prince's feelings grown beyond friendship? Has he become bold and declared his love to someone? Or has someone assumed it because they were no longer children?*

"'Messer Marco, I will talk to Guo Yu, and we will warn them of the need to disband their society. We will keep our eyes and ears open. If anything comes of this, we will reach out to you.'

"He was trying to make me feel better. *Reach me*, I thought about it. *They could send messages to different ports and leave a letter with the harbormaster.* I was being optimistic, but I had to try anything. I told him I would return with a list of harbors where we would be docking. Then I asked him if he could replenish my medical bag. 'Usually, Li does it. But I don't want to see her now, or it could be the other way around. Our last conversation wasn't pleasant.'

"Physician Wu nodded and left. As I waited, I became lost in the past as I gazed out the window. I remembered a young, determined Li who stood among the abundant herbs with Physician Wu, desperately wanting to learn. *She had listened. I am proud of her. Have I ever told her that?*

"Suddenly, Physician Wu's voice brought me back to reality when he returned from replenishing the medicine bag and questioned where I had gotten it. I suddenly became aware that outside in the garden, a beautiful Li was staring back through the window.

"I answered him without breaking our gaze. 'Li, it was her gift for the White Festival about five years ago. Why?'

"'Oh, I was just admiring the bag's construction and beauty...and wondered where you purchased it. Make sure you take good care of it. It's special.' His last words were to take care of myself and return quickly, as I would be missed.

"'Thank you for everything, and I will return with the list.' I responded as I hurried out the door, putting the medicine bag over my shoulder. 'I must apologize to Li.'"

***

Physician Wu stood at the window, watching them. He understood more than Messer Marco did. While he refilled the bag, he discovered an intricate painting hidden deep inside—a painting that confessed love.

***

"Li was walking away when I caught up and gently grabbed her wrist. She stopped. 'I'm sorry about the other morning. I am concerned for your safety; you are no longer a little girl.'

"'So, you have finally noticed.'

"Li looked embarrassed by her comment. So was I.

"'Never mind, Ijir Bukhqa, the crown prince is just a friend,' Li sharply answered.

"'But someone thinks it's more. So, as I said, please be careful.'

"Li looked down; I was still holding her wrist. 'Who should be more careful?'

"'What?'

"I glanced down and looked up. Our eyes met. My heart pounded as blood rushed to my face, turning it red. Her face did the same. Quickly, I released her wrist.

"Stuttering, Li said a tearful goodbye. Before I could say anything, she reached into her oversized, flowing sleeves and removed an object. She held out a small red silk bag, her hands stretching toward me. A slight breeze exposed her slender, delicate, white arms and hands. My heart melted.

"She quickly regained her poise. 'This is for you. It will protect you.'

"Reaching into the other sleeve, she removed another silk bag. 'This is wishing you success. I know this trip is essential to you. Always keep them with you, like your medicine bag.'

"She didn't wait for me to open them. She turned and swiftly walked away. As Li walked, I wondered what she was thinking. It was much later that I found out: '*I will miss you so much. All my life, my love for you had been one-sided. Has that finally changed?*'

"I stood there, holding the two silk bags, wanting to run after her, hold her, and never let go. Suddenly, guilt devoured me. *What was I thinking?* I stood steadfast and opened the first bag. Inside was a circular, red, disc-shaped amulet with symbols of Dorje, three golden lions, or three divine guardians. They represented celestial animals, including the Fu Dog, Chi Lin, and Pi Yao, which were sent to earth from heaven to safeguard the trinity—heaven, earth, and humans. Inside the second was a green jade pendant carved with a delicate heron alongside a lotus. I held it in my hand and looked up. She had disappeared. I placed both into my medicine bag and understood; she hoped they had the power to protect me."

***

Meanwhile, Physician Wu stood at his office window, watching. Unluckily, an observant, unfaithful guard outside his door also watched Messer Marco and Li. He looked around to see if anyone else was watching. It was his lucky day. He saw Kokochin and Ijir Bukhqa, who were supposedly hiding. Their faces said it all.

Early in the morning, Kokochin and the crown prince had waited on Li. They were surprised she hadn't shown up for their secret rendezvous, as she had never missed a day. A little worried, they decided Li would be their mission for the day. So, in their typical ghost-like fashion, they secretly went to the most promising location, the royal physician's office. Their assumption was correct. Li was standing in the garden, staring at Physician Wu's window.

Suddenly, she turned and walked away. Kokochin and the Ijir Bukhqa moved closer, hiding as much as possible. They wanted to surprise her. The office door suddenly opened; it was Messer Marco Polo. Startled, Kokochin and Ijir Bukhqa stopped and looked at each other. They could hardly believe their eyes. Messer Marco was practically running after her. *Did he know her?* Then, he grabbed her wrist, forcing her to turn around, and they stood face to face, having words.

Kokochin and Ijir Bukhqa looked at each other. *Are they having a lovers' quarrel?* They didn't even know Marco and Li knew each other. *Does Li have a secret life we know nothing about?*

They no longer watched Marco and Li. Kokochin could see the prince's tragic disappointment in his eyes. But the crown prince didn't see hers. Without a word, they went their separate ways.

The guard standing outside Physician Wu's office thought, *Finally! I have something to report, especially the young prince, who looks extremely upset. It was even more interesting when I observed Princess Kokochin's sad face, watching the prince's reaction. I can add this information, along with Messer Marco telling Physician Wu that he would return with a list.* The guard smiled. He felt lucky. He could smell the money.

***

Marco looked at Rustichello and continued. "After leaving Physician Wu, my heart was heavy. I should have been in a hurry; my father would be waiting. Yet, I walked to the south gate in a fog, not seeing anything around me. Time went in slow motion. My mind was concentrating on the list. *What harbors would I list? Would that even be possible?* I reached the south gate, and Dai Xiuying awoke me from my trance when he called out, 'Messer Marco Polo, your horse and pack horse are ready.'

"As we left the palace and entered the city, I looked around and spoke as if I was talking to someone visiting the city for the first time: 'It is a massive, exquisite walled city with a circumference of 24 miles. Architects perfectly constructed the streets like a chessboard with calculated rules, streets so broad and straight that you can see the end of each main street at one of the twelve gates that exit or enter the city. The streets are bustling with multitudes of refined people shopping, whether at the elegant markets, simple booths, or shop houses. They were occupied by well-mannered shopkeepers, who returned to their fine mansions with their courtyards, gardens, or inns. The Khan demands order, with soldiers parading the streets. And at night, curfew bells ring at midnight, instructing you to return home. If you have an emergency after curfew, you must carry a lantern, but if they find you in the dark, you are punished accordingly. But beyond the walls, gates lead to wards. Each extends three or four miles, touching the neighboring ward on each side. The wards are where foreign merchants and common people, honest or dishonest, preferred to live, including my father. Life is real. Dangers are blatant, and you know who your enemies are. Not like the city or palace where silent, secret enemies live.'

Marco continued. "It would take me a while before I reached my father, who lived about a mile from the city, in a notable home between markets and hostels where merchants worldwide came to trade and live. The merchants hustled their customers as their clanging wagons, the hooves of the horses, and the bleating camels echoed down the crowded streets, bringing in new merchandise. It is buzzing with life. I knew many people there, and some I would call friends. My lover, Ehuang-chu, whose name means beautiful pearl, lived here. I had enjoyed her company for the last couple of years. She was outspoken and intelligent, and her Tartar father and Han mother were pearl merchants. Her feelings for me went far beyond mine, but I was selfish. I trusted her and wanted her company.

"When I arrived, my father, angry about my tardiness, met me at the door. He and my uncle would accompany me as far as Zapton and stay with Lis at Kim Chin-hae's house. My father's angry face disappeared when he looked at my face, asking if something had happened.

"'No, are you ready to go?' I answered.

"'Ready? We have been waiting for an hour. The attendees and pack horses are restless and ready to leave.'

"'I have one more thing to do.'

"I quickly sat down at my father's desk and grabbed a piece of paper, ready to write the list of port names where the Khan's postal service would easily reach Kim Chin-hae and me. I was grasping, but a miracle could happen, I prayed. But as I sat, my hand only wrote one place: Kim Chin-hae's home in Zapton. The note read,

Dear Physician Wu,

If trouble arises regarding Li, please send this letter as quickly as possible to

Kim Chin-hae, my business partner, whose residence is in Zapton, next to the ship harbor.'

Thank you,
Messer Marco Polo

"I then wrote a second letter and addressed it to Lis.

My friend Lis,

Please find me. I am calling in your indebtedness.

With gratitude,
Marco

"I folded the two letters together, placed them in an envelope addressed to Physician Wu, and sealed it with my seal. For the first time, I trusted something intangible—powers of a shaman.

"Standing up, I turned to my father. 'I need to stop at Ehuang-chu's. I'll say goodbye and ask a favor.' My father looked puzzled and nodded.

"Ehuang-chu's excitement quickly turned solemn when she saw the pack horses, which meant I was leaving and would be gone for a long time. Casually, she walked outside to greet me.

"'I have come to say goodbye and ask you a favor.'

"In my heart, I knew she was hoping I would ask her to wait for me. But with her lethal confidence, she replied, 'It will cost you a ruby from India like the ones you always talked about.'

"I laughed. Ehuang-chu knew how to make me smile.

"'Could you please take this note to the Royal Physician Wu? It is crucial.'

"'How am I going to enter the palace?' She asked.

"'You're beautiful and intelligent. I have no doubt you'll figure it out. I'm sure of it! My confidence in you is great. Please do it today!'

"I mounted my horse, slightly fearful. I was entrusting Li's life with her. Nudging my horse forward, I never looked back. I was always a little sad whenever I left this magnificent city. But it was different this time; I had a bad feeling."

***

Ehuang-chu stood in the road and watched Marco leave. *I wish I had run and wrapped my arms around him instead of calmly walking to him. But then I noticed his normal, happy, dancing eyes looking sad. I am glad I resisted.*

When Marco was out of sight, she ran upstairs to her quarters and thumbed through her clothing, looking for something that made her look rich and important. Opening her drawer, she took out a handful of pearls. *These will come in handy.* Her mind raced as she descended the stairs. *What is so important?* In a moment of weakness, she broke the seal, pulled the letters from the envelope, and read the contents. None of it made sense. *Who are Lis and Li?* As jealousy filled her heart, it tempted her to discard the letters. But she envisioned Marco's worried face. Now, she felt guilty. Carefully, she folded the letters, slid them into the envelope, and resealed them with her father's seal. *They will never notice.* She concealed them in her oversized sleeve and walked out the door.

A palanquin waited for her. She would look more noble. Besides, the nosy neighbors would become curious if they saw her dressed so grandly. At the palace gates, she stepped out of the palanquin. The guard stepped in front of her. She smiled. "I have come to see Royal Physician Wu." Before he could answer, she slightly held out her hand and obscurely opened it. He smiled; she slipped two pearls to him. She politely asked which direction. He pointed to the left as he stepped to the side and motioned her forward. Swiftly walking, she hoped it wasn't far. This place made her nervous. Finally, she saw the herb garden. Again, she faced a guard.

"I have come to see Physician Wu; I have something for him." She opened her hand.

The bribe didn't work. The guard stood firm and answered. "He's not here. I'll deliver whatever you have."

Sweetly smiling, she answered, "No, I'll wait."

Ehuang-chu waited for what seemed to be forever. Finally, she concluded she had to trust the guard. She reasoned with herself that by staying longer, people might become suspicious. She made him take the pearls as she handed him the letter.

The guard bowed and entered the office. But instead of placing the letter on the table, he shoved it in his shirt. Smiling, he thought, *This has been my lucky day*. Walking to the corner of the office, he opened the letter. It was from Messer Marco Polo. *But what does it mean? It mentions Li. Maybe my master would understand. It is worth the chance.*

As Ehuang-chu walked away, she felt terrible. Marco had trusted her. She comforted herself by thinking, *He was Physician Wu's guard.*

When Physician Wu returned, passing the guard, he asked if Messer Marco had returned. The guard nodded no. Surprised, he wondered if Marco changed his mind.

A little later, one of his assistants entered his office, mentioning that a woman had been waiting for him, but left. Upset, he dropped his paperwork and briskly went to the guard. He was horrified to find that it was a different guard. His mind raced as he returned to the office. *Maybe Messer Marco was right. There is a reason to be concerned. Who was that woman? Was it Marco's friend? Can we ever find her? And where is the original guard?*

That evening, the guard met Buyan Kelmysh Khatun's maid. He handed her the note and retold the happenings of the day. She gave him a gold piece. The guard smiled to himself. *I did well today.* As he walked away, the maid told him, "Don't return to Physician Wu's office. Your post changed today."

Chapter Thirty-Seven

Marco

Zapton, Fearful Departure

Genoa Prison 1298

"My silence deafened my father and uncle as we rode out of the city. Father asked me again what had happened, and when I didn't answer, he stopped questioning. Our conversations over the next thirty days were brief and primarily focused on business. My overflowing sadness remained hidden, knowing my father wouldn't understand as he had never loved or committed himself to anyone, including his wife, my mother, or me. My father spent most of his life devoted to money, and when his bodily needs arose, he would spend time with paid women who pretended to love him. He understood *that.*

"When we passed through Lin'an, the city where I rescued Li, my heart ached, and my depression increased. My father saw it in my face. He now understood—*Lin'an is where he first found Li. His mood is about Li.*

"Kim Chin-hae, Lis, and I hadn't seen each other in a long while, only exchanging letters regarding business. The closer I came to Zapton, the more my spirit soared. By the time we passed Fuzhou, I was riding fast. My memory replayed the first time I met Kim Chin-hae. Finally, I smiled for the first time. My mood instantly changed when we arrived in Zapton and rode to his remarkable home—*Chin-hae understood love.* Chin-hae ran out to meet me. The twins followed, and then Lis."

Marco turned to Rustichello. "My mind left Li for the first time as we prepared for India. Lis constantly joked that I was taking her husband away. Her joking could not conceal her concern and sadness; we would be away for a long time. We sat at a large table the night before our departure, having our last meal with our families. In the distance, lights reflected the silhouettes of our ships. Lis turned to me and laid her hand on my shoulder. As usual, goosebumps traveled up my neck, and my body warmed. 'We should talk before you leave.'

"The goosebumps grew all over my body. I nodded yes. Later that night, I sat on the shoreline, watching our ships, waiting for Lis to find me. Kim Chin-hae and I yearned for this trip for years, and it was finally happening. But why did I feel so anxious? My thoughts returned to Li. I knew why.

"I heard a familiar voice: 'I found you.' Lis sat down next to me and put her hand on my shoulder.

"'Your heart is heavy, Messer Marco Polo. Are you sad about leaving your soul mate, whom I told you about years ago? She does exist. Have you ever really looked at your medical bag closely?' I hesitated and thought, *This is the second person who mentioned the bag.*

"Lis changed the subject. 'You better take good care of my husband. He better return in one piece, or I will use my powers to make you suffer.'

"'I promise!' I quickly answered, laughing, but deep down inside, she meant it.

"'You know, it will be your husband taking care of me.' We both laughed. Chin-hae was a lot better fighter than I was.

"Lis stood up, and as she walked away, I heard her say, 'I will find you!'

"'What?'

"'You heard me!' She continued to walk away.

"Suddenly, my anxiousness disappeared; I believed her."

Chapter Thirty-Eight

Marco

1289 Discovery, Li's confession

Genoa Prison 1298

"The following day, Dai Xiuying, Pak Byeong-ho, and I boarded our ship and watched Lis and Kim Chin-hae face each other with Yang Da-lou on one side and Mei-caihong on the other. With his long arms, he gathered them together and held them tight for one last hug. Their circle of love radiated. He released them, ran up the gangplank, and started barking orders to make ready to sail." Marco turned to Rustichello. "For years, I longed for this kind of love."

After a short pause, Marco continued, "My father and uncle were standing close to Lis. She leaned in to my father, saying something. My father suddenly sprinted toward the ship. He ran up the gangplank toward me, gripped my hand tightly, looked at me, and told me to return safely. Sadly, I thought, *His concern was the permits. And what would happen if I disappeared?* It was sad; we'd never shown affection toward each other.

"Afterwards, I walked to the bow and looked out to sea. My hand shielded my eyes from the rising sun. A drifting cloud covered the sun, and my hand fell to my side and onto my medical bag that draped over my shoulder. Looking down, I remembered the two conversations. Quickly, I walked to my quarters and frantically pulled out the contents, thinking, *What's with this bag? It was a gift from Li five years ago. The contents were just medicine.* Then, I remembered Physician Wu talking about the construction. I hastily turned it inside out. For the first time, I saw an ink drawing worn and scuffed. Two golden carp swimming in a stream covered by the lotus. Two butterflies sipping nectar on dew-drenched peonies along the shore. It was the same design as the hair pick Lis and Kim had given me years ago. My heart flopped; it was a confession of love.

"I have been such a fool," I said as I fell to the floor, just like now. I left Li in danger, all for money. I raced to the stern and watched the land disappear, yearning to see her again. The only thing that kept me from going mad was Lis's voice whispering in my ear, 'I will find you.'"

This time, Rustichello tried to console Marco using reason. "You were doing as your country told you. It was your duty."

Marco continued sitting on the floor, mumbling. "Kim Chin-hae told me the same thing, trying to console me. It didn't work then, and it won't work now."

Rustichello moaned. Marco was getting to him. Finally, he said, "Come on, continue your story. What happened next?"

Marco stood and walked around the room, crazed. Breathing in the stale air, and when he exhaled, he spoke in a soft voice. "As a child, I loved the smell of the sea as I wandered the docks. The salty air, mixed with decaying sea creatures, human sweat, and the voices of working men and their captain's commands, resonated with adventure, wealth, and knowledge from unknown lands, causing my heart to race. When I boarded the ship that day, it would be my first time at sea. That familiar smell followed me on board. As the land disappeared and the vast sea surrounded us, I fell deeper in love with the sea. I could only smell salt, sweet, and fresh air—free from man's greed. Its openness brought a newfound freedom and peace. Kim Chin-hae had always told me about this feeling. It was only then I understood."

Marco took a deep breath and coughed, bringing him back to reality. "Not like this disgusting place."

He changed the subject and returned to Li. "After I had opened the bag and discovered the painting, I thought back to the last time I saw her. She has always been honest with her feelings. I was the one so naïve. Putting the contents back slowly, I looked at each pouch. She had meticulously selected them all for my safety, success, and happiness.

"When I returned to the bow, Kim Chin-hae stood erect and confident, looking out to the open sea.

"'You were staring at your medical bag and disappeared. Did you look inside?'

"'Did Lis tell you?'

"Kim Chin-hae nodded and continued. 'I always found the answer when I went to sea. Keeping busy is the key. Starting today, Pak Byeong-ho and I will be your sailing instructors. Someday, you will command a ship.'"

Rustichello interrupted. "So, Kim Chin-hae taught you?"

"Yes, regretting it now. I might not be in prison now if Chin-hae had never taught me."

Rustichello just nodded.

Marco continued his story. "For the first 1500 miles, I was a low-ranking swab learning about the ship with little time to think about Li. I worked hard, and at night, Kim Chin-hae told me stories of his travels to islands that lay to the east. 'There are at least 7000 islands, most are uninhabited. But the ones that are, you must be cautious, as some islanders are cannibals. They will eat you.'"

Rustichello swallowed hard. Marco continued. "The islands were filled with fragrant wood like aloeswood, white and black peppers, and gold were abundant, making them huge profits. Kim Chin-hae and Pak were gone for a year each time, which made Lis unhappy. Eventually, Kim Chin-hae told her 'Others will go, and I will stay home and collect the rewards.'"

Marco continued. "When we arrived in Champa, I was relieved. Now, I was the person in charge. I visited Champa's king, selecting twenty of the largest and most beautiful elephants in the land for his tribute. The Champa king had 326 children; 150 were old enough to bear arms: his army. When I told Kim Chin-hae the story, he laughed. 'I have a hard enough time controlling my two children and one wife.' I snickered. 'You control Lis?'

"After we left Champa, we traveled another two months, passing several more islands. It was then that I learned navigation. Kim Chin-hae was right. As time passed, my mind was too busy to dwell on Li. It was a welcome relief.

> *"We sailed further south for 500 miles, coming to an island called Bintan, a very savage place. Its forest is entirely of trees that are heavily scented. From there, we traveled 60 miles through a strait. Here, I learned the advantages of the Cathay invention of movable rudders. At many points, the water was only four paces deep. We voyaged southeast for another thirty miles to another island kingdom called Malayu. It was a bustling trade center.*

"By this time, four months had passed; Li's existence was dimmer. My mind hadn't erased Li, but, as usual, my selfishness won. Only in the dead of night would her face appear to me. It was then that guilt and worry got to me. I still hadn't come to terms with her. She was just a child; on the other hand, the face that appeared on those black nights didn't belong to a child. Li made my heart race like the sea did. Forcefully, I would turn my thoughts to the business. We would soon arrive in Lesser Java,[1] where I would meet up and join an envoy on the way to Greater Java on a mission demanding King Kertangara's submission to the great Khan. Kim Chin-hae would wait for me here until I returned. Then, we would continue our voyage.

"Fortunately for me, we stayed too long in Champa, and the envoy continued without me. I learned later that the king's response was to cut off their ears and return them to Kubilai Khan."

Rustichello rubbed his ear. "Ouch!"

Marco smiled and continued, "Wait till you hear the other stories.

"We didn't stay long in Lesser Java; the timing was perfect to sail. Not like the second time I was there when we waited for five months."

"Five months," Rustichello repeated.

Marco momentarily hesitated. "That story is later."

"After leaving Lessor Java, we were entering unfamiliar territory neither Kim nor I had ever seen.

> *"For four months, we sailed west on a great sea, passing islands where some didn't wear clothes. They loved beautiful silk clothing of every color purchased from merchants. They would hang them from poles outside their homes as a token of their wealth. We also passed a savage island with savage people who looked like great mastiffs. They were cruel people and ate men. Their island lies in a turbulent area, and ships never anchor there. As we were told, it sweeps them into a gulf, and you can never return. Passing these islands, we sailed for the next 1000 miles."*

Marco stopped talking and turned to Rustichello. "I had become a truly impressive sailor by then, Kim Chin-hae told me."

> *"After 1000 miles, we arrived in Ceylon, where I heard marvelous stories. In all the world, precious and noble rubies are produced on this island, along with sapphires, topazes, amethysts, and garnets. We heard that the King possesses the most beautiful, flawless ruby, the length of a palm and as thick as a man's arm. It is dazzling and red as fire. Its existence had traveled as far as Khanbaliq. The Great Khan even sent an envoy insisting he had to have it. He would pay him the value of a city. The King refused, 'This is an heirloom from my ancestors. I will never part from it for any amount of money.' The men of Ceylon were not fighters, so if they needed soldiers, they hired them, especially the Saracens.*

"It was here I purchased the requested ruby for Ehuang-chu. You remember, my lover, that I asked her to deliver the letters to Physician Wu?"

Rustichello thought back. "Yes, of course."

Marco continued about his trip. "Before we left Ceylon, they told us about diamonds found in a kingdom ruled by a queen if we sailed northward along the east coast of India for 1,000 miles. We made a note about this.

> *"After we left Ceylon, we traveled west for about 60 miles and arrived in Maarbar. We were unhappy; we arrived late, and the prime time to gather pearls of great size was April through the middle of May.*

"We recorded this information for our future trips and decided to sail to the kingdom with diamonds. It was here that I started feeling uneasy and thinking about Li."

---

1. Sumatra

Chapter Thirty-Nine

Li

1289 The Offering

Venice 1298

Li walked around her room; her voice softened as she spoke. "When I returned to my chambers from the Green Mound that day, I only thought of Marco. *Why was he so angry this morning?* I forgot about meeting Kokochin and Ijir Bukhqa. Besides, I promised Marco I wouldn't see the crown prince again. Suddenly, I remembered the amulets I purchased for his protection. Urgency swept over me, and I had to find Marco, but where? My only hope of seeing him was to find him at the infirmary. Perhaps to see Physician Wu one last time. I didn't wait for Guo Yu. I ran. When I reached the royal garden, Marco stood in Physician Wu's office window. I smiled and waved; we locked eyes. My courage failed. I turned and briskly walked away. That's when someone grabbed my wrist. When I turned, it was Marco apologizing for his past behavior. My lack of courage turned to defiance. 'You told me to be careful, but shouldn't you be more careful?' I said as I looked down at his hand, which was holding my wrist. His face turned red. My defiance then led to sadness. I felt the tears roll down my face as I faced him. I could hardly speak as I gave him the amulets. I turned and ran. I wouldn't have resisted turning around that day if I had known the future. I would have run into his arms and asked him not to go. Not that that would have done any good, but he would have known how I felt."

In an excited voice, Luca asked, "Then what happened?"

"The next few months, I tried to fulfill my promise to Marco and avoid Kokochin and Ijir Bukhqa as much as possible. The crown prince wasn't easy; he was adamant and confessed his love. I had foolishly used him.

"Then, in June, gossip buzzed like bees throughout the palace. Three lords arrived from faraway lands searching for a princess for their king. Physician Wu and I were preparing herbs when an ecstatic Kokochin entered the office.

"She grabbed my hand and dragged me out of the office to one of our secret spots.

"'It's come!'

"'What's come?' I naively asked.

"'To become a queen. Throughout my life, my mother has been grooming me for this. I am a little disappointed it isn't Ijir Bukhqa. I liked him. Even though he liked you.'

"I tried to interrupt, but she kept talking.

"'Three lords have arrived from Khorasan.[1] Their Khan, Arghun, seeks a princess of the Bulagan lineage. That's me! My mother is from this tribe, and I was selected. I am only sad that Messer Marco isn't here. So I could say goodbye.'

"For the next hour, she talked about how happy she was and how exciting it would be. Her only concern was the distance. 'It will take almost a year to arrive.'

"It was hard to understand, even though I was happy for her. She willingly accepted this marriage without love. Her mother had groomed her well. Her loyalty to the empire was remarkable. This thought sent chills down my spine.

"When I returned to Physician Wu with the news, he seemed worried. He called for his assistant, asking her about a girl. *What girl?* I thought. The assistant nodded no. His anxious face got worse. I didn't understand until I returned to Empress Nambi's chambers. Guo Yu met me with tears. *What is wrong?* My heart broke as he shared the news with me.

"The next day, I entered the throne room with Empress Nambi. The three lords, Ulaatai, Abishqa, Qoja, and the shocked Kokochin, watched me enter. She searched the room, and her eyes widened. She was looking at Princess Budashiri's mother, Buyan Kelmysh Khatun, who wore a smile on her face. Then I understood. Marco was right. I was a threat. Ijir Bukhqa, the crown prince, refused to marry the princess chosen for him. He wanted me, even though I was not part of the tradition; only descendants of the Khan could marry a Goryeo crown prince. The princess's mother had a plan; sending me away would solve the problem, and the three Lords were the perfect answer. She convinced Kubilai Khan to send me along with 100 other girls as a tribute. The only advantage I had over the other girls was my royal blood, a princess of the Song Dynasty. I was destined to be his royal concubine if accepted.

"As I stood before Kubilai Khan, his voice melted away. I only heard certain words: the lords accepted me, leaving next month, concubine, King Arghun, Empire, and Kokochin—words that penetrated my soul. Mostly, I heard myself repeating, 'I will never see Marco again!'

"Empress Nambi brought me back to reality, whispering, 'Bow and act grateful.' Bowing, I closed my eyes and felt tears roll down my cheeks, and when I opened my tear-soaked eyes, tears fell in slow motion. The floor became a river of sadness. I rose using every ounce of strength I had and silently returned to my chambers. Guo Yu met me at the door. I fell into his arms, and he carried me to my bed, whispering, 'I will talk to Physician Wu. Surely, he can convince them that you are needed here. You are a talented herbalist whom he trained.' His voice was so positive that I believed him and fell asleep with hope. The following day, Guo Yu left for Physician Wu's office.

"While he was gone, I kept telling myself, *Yesterday was just a dream*. When Guo Yu entered the chamber, his face told it all: it was not a dream. He repeated what Physician Wu had told him: he had gone to Kubilai Khan, who had refused his request.

"Heartbroken, I fell to the floor. As Guo Yu helped me up, he told me some good news: he would accompany me. However, he didn't tell me Marco had gone to Physician Wu before he left—that was when I saw Marco in the garden. He planned to return with a list of harbors where he could be reached if something happened—but he never returned. Later, Physician Wu's assistant told him a woman had waited for him while he was out. They suspected she had the letter and left it with the guard. The guard disappeared, and so did the letter. They were trying to find the girl, which seemed almost impossible.

"The next month was a blur. Guo Yu rushed and prepared everything. I only saw Kokochin, never the prince—our Society of Three was broken. Kokochin's excitement oozed from every pore. Not once did she ever assume I was devastated. *Why would she?* At her age, she thought everyone felt like her. She told me that they locked Ijir Bukhqa in his chamber. And with her childlike voice, she said, 'YOU know it's your fault.' I couldn't say anything back. She was right. I used him to make Marco jealous.

"When the day arrived for our departure, the palace gates opened, and Kokochin's procession exited; the three Lords on horseback led the way. Kokochin, dressed in imperial attire, sat high on a magnificent white stallion so everyone would know she was a bride on her way to her new home and king. I was next in line, riding a sleek black stallion, followed by one hundred attendants upon their horses. And trailing behind were treasure-filled and supply wagons escorted by soldiers. The city came to a halt and watched in awe. It was a grand procession as red flowing flags whipped in the wind, and our ornate clothing and saddles shimmered in the sun. My heart sank, and my tears flowed. I looked back one last time and saw the prince beside Physician Wu looking down from the wall. His face looked like mine. I thought again, *it was all my fault.*

"As we traveled through the city, so did gossip. When we reached the city's main gates, hundreds of spectators had gathered to watch."

***

Ehuang-chu, at home, heard the gossip. It was exhilarating: A bride on her way to meet her husband, a king. Ehuang-chu fought the crowds to be upfront as she never missed a fanfare of this kind. She loved the clothing and the jewels, but mostly to read the bride's face. All her life, she had excelled in this talent. *Was it a happy bride or a miserable one?* As she fought her way, chatter filled her ears. 'It's a princess named Kokochin on her way to an empire far west.' Ehuang-chu arrived just in time to see Kokochin. *She is beautiful*, she thought. Her *face glows with happiness. But the girl on the black stallion looks like death. What's her story?* The parade ended when the last person exited the city, but not the chatter.

Ehuang-chu returned to her store. It was busy; the procession had brought out many potential clients. Behind the counter, she heard two noble ladies talking. "Did you see the girl on the black stallion? I hear she is a princess from the Song Dynasty. She has lived in the palace since she was five years old. I have to say, she looked like she was going to a funeral instead of a wedding." They both laughed and continued looking at the pearls. Ehuang-chu thought for a moment. *Why does that sound familiar?* The business became brisk, and the thought passed.

Meanwhile, Physician Wu was still in disbelief. Li was like his daughter. For the last month, he had tried everything to intervene. However, the crown prince's betrothed and her mother blocked every effort. He saw Li's tear-soaked face every night when he lay in bed. Seeing her in pain was almost too much for him to bear. If only he could reach Messer Marco Polo, who had promised to return with a letter but never did. The very same day, a mysterious lady and a guard disappeared as well. Physician Wu's only hope was to locate the mystery lady or the missing guard. Desperately, his guard continued searching for any leads.

Almost a month passed, and Ehuang-chu could not shake the feeling that the Princess of Song and Marco were connected. The story sounded so familiar. One night, Marco's face flashed before her as she lay in darkness, and she remembered Marco telling her the story.

Now, she felt guilty more than ever. The letter she was delivering to the royal physician mentioned a girl. *I'm going back. I need to make sure the guard gave him the letters.*

Rushing, she didn't plan her entry into the palace. When she arrived at the gate, the guard dismissed her. "Please, I must see the royal physician. I have something to ask him." Again, the guard pushed her aside.

"Please, it is about Messer Marco Polo."

Suddenly, another guard stepped in. Grabbing her arm, he pulled her until he reached the royal guard house. Her heart pounded. *Am I going to be arrested?* He pushed her onto a bench and ordered her to stay. It seemed like a lifetime had passed until he returned with another guard who appeared slightly kinder. Bending down, he whispered. "Are you a friend of Messer Marco Polo?" Ehuang-chu nodded shyly. *Yes!*

The guard slipped his hand under her arm and pulled her up. "Let's go!" As they left, he handed the other guard something. The guard smiled and bowed.

He never said another word until they reached the royal physician's office. "Wait here."

A few minutes passed when the guard returned. "Physician Wu is waiting for you."

Ehuang-chu entered his office, bowing. She was so ashamed. It was apparent they were looking for her. *Had I misread the guard? Was he a foe?*

Physician Wu was beside himself. "Girl, we have been looking for you. Why did you leave that day?" He hesitated for a moment. "You are the one who waited for me the day Messer Marco Polo left. Right?"

Ehuang-chu stuttered. "I waited a long time; everyone started staring at me. I was afraid I was drawing too much attention. I left the letters with the guard. You didn't receive them, did you?" She fell to the ground on her knees. "I'm sorry, I failed Messer Marco!"

Physician Wu walked over to Ehuang-chu and pulled her to her feet. With a kinder voice, he started asking her questions. "How do you know Messer Marco? How long? Why did he send you?"

He believed Ehuang-chu's sincere answers. He finally asked, "Do you know what the letters said?"

Looking ashamed, she replied. "Yes, I opened them."

"Letters?" he questioned.

"Yes, one to you and the other to someone named Lis."

"Do you remember what they said?" he asked cautiously.

Ehuang-chu looked at him and answered in a soft voice. "Of course, they were very short and strange. I also wrote it down," she said shamefully.

Ehuang-chu kept talking. "Last month, when I saw the sad princess on her beautiful, sleek black stallion and heard her story, I kept thinking I had heard this story, but it wasn't until last night that I realized it was from Messer Marco. That's when I decided to find you and ensure you received the letters."

Patiently, Physician Wu listened, and then he asked again. "What did Messer Marco write?"

Ehuang-chu proudly recited the letters. "'Dear Physician Wu, If trouble arises regarding Li, please send this letter as fast as possible to Kim Chin-hae, my business partner, whose residence is in Zapton, next to the ship harbor.'

"The second letter was addressed to someone named Lis. 'Lis, please find me. I am calling in your indebtedness. Marco.'

"That's all they said," she said as she pulled out her copied letters and handed them to the physician.

Physician Wu stared at the words for a while. It didn't contain any helpful information. *What should I do? Who is Lis?* He knew Kim Chin-hae was the Crown Prince Wang Won's cousin. He walked over to his desk and sat down with his head in his hands, overwhelmed. Suddenly, he lowered his hands, sat straight, and wrote a letter to Lis, leaving his logic behind.

> Dear Lis,
>
> Months ago, three barons took Kokochin and Li. Kokochin will become the queen of King Arghun, and Li will be a royal concubine. They travel in a large caravan on the Imperial Highway until they reach the Silk Road. Then, they will continue west. Please find Messer Marco.
>
> Thank you,
> Royal Physician Wu

He slid the letter into an envelope and wrote on the front, Kim Chin-hae, Zapton City residence, next to the ship harbor.

He exited his office and handed the letter to his guard. "Take the letter to this residence. Present it only to a person named Lis. I will expect you back in several months."

Physician Wu returned to Ehuang-chu. "Thank you for coming back. I'll have my assistant take you to the gate."

Ehuang-chu was too curious to leave. "Do you think this will help the sad princess?"

"I hope so, I hope so," he repeated as he directed her out.

As Ehuang-chu strolled home, she thought, *My life might not be rich or powerful, but I am happy and grateful that it is mine and not an object to be given away at someone's whim.*

She walked into the store, stepped behind the counter, hugged her mom and dad, and started helping the customers. Her parents gave her a strange look. She smiled and spoke. "I am happy, that's all." They smiled as they continued working.

---

1. The territory of Iran, Azerbaijan, Turkey, Iraq, Armenia, Georgia, Afghanistan, Turkmenistan, Pakistan

Chapter Forty

Li

1289 The Bad Dream

Venice 1298

Li continued her story. "The day I stood before Kubilai Khan and the three barons, everything became a bad dream; nothing seemed real. My body numbly went through the needed motions. I suddenly woke up after we stopped and changed our attire from imperial clothing to riding clothes. Outside the ger, I looked down the Imperial Road, and my old fears erupted—a feeling of loss and the unknown future. My body trembled. Guo Yu walked nonchalantly toward me and gently held me up. His eyes were stern, insisting I must be strong. Mounting my stallion, I found my place, and for the next twenty-five miles, I cried inside and out until I couldn't cry anymore, draining my soul into emptiness. I needed Marco.

"Kokochin was giddy and foolishly rattled continuously about how being Queen would be marvelous. *How childish,* I thought. *I was on this road once when I was five, when Marco delivered me to Kubilai Khan. She should realize how scary her life could become.*"

Li stopped talking and walked over to her favorite window, picking up her erhu. She whispered to herself, "I need him now."

Luca didn't want Li to play. She feared Isabella. "Li, don't stop, tell me more."

Guo Yu nodded in approval to Luca.

"Please tell me more!" Luca pleaded.

Li didn't move or look at Luca but continued speaking. "Honestly, everything for a month or so was blank. We rode through towns and cities, but I didn't see them. Kokochin still sported her positive attitude, as traveling was far from harsh. It was not until we reached Zhengye that my soul was replenished. It was one of the most beautiful places I had ever seen.

The mountain's sand layers were like rainbows; they seemed on fire when the rising sun rose and threw its light upon these grand mountains."

"Rainbows on fire?" Luca repeated.

"It was the most inspiring place I had ever seen. My sadness diminished slightly, and my happiness rekindled somewhat when I learned from Guo Yu that Marco had lived in the area for a year and that his father had a trading post there. The Biandukou Pass started here and led to another of his trading posts. I found a new purpose, however fruitless it might have been—I wrote letters to Marco and had Guo Yu deliver them to the trading post with instructions: 'Please present these letters to any traveling merchants who might be able to meet Messer Marco Polo.' As I wrote the letters, I gained a newfound strength and hope. Marco's old words resonated: find a purpose.

"Our next destination, Shazhou, was the beginning of the Gobi Desert. Our lives would become more difficult. It was a long stretch, taking thirty days or more to cross without inns to stay at or places to eat. The soldiers gathered and stored more food. As we traveled through the desert, Kokochin's demeanor changed. The talk of spirits and ghosts scared her.

"After we passed through the desert, the soldiers lowered Kubilai Khan's moon and sun flags and hid them in the wagons. We were entering Qaidu's territory. The Lords instructed us to change into ordinary clothes as we would join the merchant's caravans, camping when they camped or staying in a caravanserai when they did.

"Kokochin returned to earth, spending more time with me like the old times. She was bolder and personal, now asking me questions about Marco. I was caught off guard.

"Ijir Bukhqa and I saw Messer Marco and you at the royal herb garden. We were surprised you knew him. Every time we mentioned him, you were silent. That day, you looked like lovers quarreling, which shattered the crown prince. And frankly, so was I when I saw how upset Ijir Bukhqa was. I dreamed that someday I would marry him. That's when I realized he loved you.'

"Kokochin stopped talking and looked at me, waiting for answers. I wasn't sure what to say. For years, Marco had been my secret. After a moment of thinking, *can I trust her*? I thought, *Why not? I have nothing to lose but my life, which means nothing now.*

"During those days, I told her my story. Kokochin listened contentedly. She giggled childishly and responded. 'That's why we started our Society of Three, to search out Messer Marco? How romantic! Does he know how you feel, and does he feel the same?'"

Li stopped talking and looked at Luca. "The only answer I could give her was no.

"'That's so sad,' she responded.

"'It doesn't matter now. My life is over,' I told her.

"She cried and said, 'I wish he had known; he would have loved you, I'm certain.'

"'It was just a childish dream. You know our lives aren't ours.'

"That night, as Kokochin and I lay on our silk mats, I concluded my reality was unfair. I wanted to die. Marco was gone and wasn't here to save me this time. My tears soaked my pillow. My spirit was dissolved, and I melted into myself. But Marco's words resonated, pulling me from the dark hole: *Find a purpose, and you can survive this cruel world.*

"When I rose the following day, I decided to resume my role as a ghost and secretly use my skills to help others. And for my sanity, I would continue searching for Marco like before.

"The next night, as Kokochin slept, a reluctant Guo Yu and another female servant who hid her identity with a draped shawl entered our ger. She slid the shawl from her head. It was a girl I had treated and saved not so long ago. I smiled and handed her several pieces of silver, which she refused. We exchanged clothes. The servant slipped under my blanket. I picked up my medicine bag, draped the shawl over my head, and headed for the door. Suddenly, Kokochin sat up. 'You should cover your face. You are a ghost, right?' I froze.

"She repeated. 'Cover your face. You know you are playing with fire.'

"I walked over to my packed items and found my favorite treasure box, pulling out Marco's rust silk scarf. My fingers ran down the edge until I felt the embroidered letters MP. My finger outlined the letters. Kokochin watched and asked. 'What are those figures?'

"'They're Marco's initials in his native language.'

"I wrapped the scarf around my neck several times and then around my face, except my eyes. I looked at Kokochin. 'Will this do?'

"Kokochin nodded and, in a concerned voice, asked, 'Why help these people? Why do you care so much? You are a captive; you lost your mother, home, and country. My people ridiculed you. Don't you feel hate toward us?'

"'When I was five, a stranger, a foreigner with round, gentle eyes, saved me. It was when my country had surrendered, and all around me was death. A man entered our chamber as my mother lay on the floor with her beautiful silk dress covered in blood. I watched my mother, with tears streaming down her face, stab herself to death, and I was to do the same. This man slowly walked over to me, sat down, and spoke softly with his arm outstretched. With his calloused hand, he reached for the knife I held, pointed at my small body, and then at him. I couldn't understand his language, but his eyes spoke gentleness, and his calm face convinced me to hand over my knife. He removed a scarf—this scarf—from his pocket, placed it over my eyes, picked me up, held my head down on his chest, and carried me to the empress. It was Marco. He taught me kindness and that you must have a purpose to survive. That's why I must do this.'

"Kokochin lay back down and covered her head, fearing for my life.

"With my head down, the shawl draped over my head, and my heart pounding, I exited the ger with Guo Yu. The guards didn't even question me. After a brisk walk, I lowered the shawl, and Guo Yu ensured my face was covered as I walked among the caravan. I thought *Marco used this scarf to shield the horrors that life could bring. Now, I will face them with my eyes wide open*. I touched the scarf. For the first time, I realized this scarf was the only thing I had of his. The smell of musk—the scent of him—that had lingered for years was almost gone. In the past, when I needed him, I would take it out of my treasure box and soak in his scent. It always warmed my heart, and I needed that now.

"That night, the sky was lit up by a long line of campfires. Many languages, laughter, the smell of burning dung, unfamiliar foods, and familiar animal waste filled the air. We weaved in and out of the campfires, searching for injured or ill people and Marco. It was not long before I found my first patient and then another. My services were free, and as we traveled the Silk Road, people started searching for me. KE AI DE REN, a kind angel, became my name.

"Soon, I discovered that the Silk Road was astonishing. For thirteen years, the palace, a closed society, confined my life. The Silk Road opened my mind to new ideas and thoughts. I discovered that many merchants carried medicinal herbs; some I was familiar with, and others I wasn't. It made it easy to constantly replenish my bag.

"Guo Yu and Kokochin worried. I was becoming too well-known. What would happen if the three lords found out? No matter what they said, I wasn't stopping. Helping others made my life bearable.

"As we traveled closer to our destination, a raging war between Ghazan and Nawrus became apparent."

Chapter Forty-One

Kim

The Dream 1291

The guard rode hard, and when he arrived in Zapton, he found it easy to find Kim Chin-hae's residence. He was rich, noble, and married to a powerful shaman.

When he arrived at the house, Lis met him at the entrance. "You have something for me."

The guard, shocked, asked her name.

"Lis."

Slightly frightened, he handed her the letter, mounted his horse, and rode off. Lis walked into her home.

Niccolò and Maffeo sat busily at the table. They looked up at Lis, who appeared concerned. "Is something wrong?"

"Last night, I dreamed that a courtier from Khanbaliq would arrive with a letter written by Marco months ago. It arrived just now."

Marco's father sat silently as Lis opened the letter.

"Marco is requesting that I find him if something happens to Li. Something has happened."

His father stood up, asking where the courtier was.

Lis answered. "He left."

He ran out the door and yelled for the courtier to stop. For the first time, Lis saw concern in Marco's father. He returned, unable to stop the courtier.

Lis comforted him. "I have all I need. Before Marco left, we made a deal. I will leave for my village as soon as possible."

Marco's father questioned Lis. "What else did the letter say?"

"Three Lords have taken her to a king named Arghun, along with someone named Kokochin."

Marco's father moaned. "Marco feared this. I warned him not to become attached to that girl. But he wouldn't listen. Since she was five, he's been her secret caretaker.

Lis, straight-faced, responded as she walked out of the room while ordering her servant to prepare. "She is more than that."

Niccolò and Matteo sat silently, wondering if their time in Cathay was ending. *What would Marco do? Would he go against his great Khan for love?*

As Lis and Jun-ho traveled to her village, her thoughts were only of Marco. She was indebted to him and had waited years to pay off her debt; the time had finally come. At night, Lis tried to enter his dreams but felt resistance. *Marco must not be accepting his fate, she* thought each morning. *He is fighting his feelings.*

Son Jun-ho and Lis arrived in her village days later and wasted no time. Wei, her mother, had aged, but her powers hadn't wavered. She met Lis, ready to travel to the cave, before Lis said anything. Lis recalled the day she gave Marco the binyeo, the hair stick, for his soulmate, Li. That was almost ten years ago. Marco finally realized his true feelings.

They entered the musty cave and lit the pile of wood. Son Jun-ho's heart fluttered like the first time he had entered this mysterious and scary cave.

Lis and her mother climbed the stairs to the stone encasements and performed their ritual. Again, Son Jun-ho could hear the chatter, and the cave seemed to breathe. After their hello, they entered the small room with the cavities. Removing Kim Chin-hae's box and recovering his blood vial as she had done in the past, she slit her hand and let her blood drip into his. Removing his remaining burnt hair and placing it in the center of the aged table, she dripped her blood into the vial, which instantly began to swirl, blend, and boil. Son Jun-ho's eyes grew large. After sealing the vial, she tightly wrapped her fingers around it while speaking the strange dialect he had heard earlier. Son Jun-ho watched as she placed the vial under her garment, close to her heart. Then, she grabbed their hands to form a circle and chanted loudly. The room grew dark, and the eerie wind surrounded them, filled with haunting voices. Before their eyes, Kim Chin-hae 's hair glowed like a flame, and within the flame, they could see Kim Chin-hae sitting up and then lying back in bed. The flame burned throughout the night as her love flowed through the heavens to him. Lis told him what had happened. She recited the letters. Kim Chin-hae's face showed sadness. He nodded and answered. "I will tell Marco."

Chapter Forty-Two

Marco

Marco's Nightmare

Genoa prison 1298

"As I said, after we left Ceylon, we traveled west for about 60 miles and arrived in Maarbar. We were unhappy; the merchants told us that the prime time to gather pearls of great size was from April to the middle of May. We would use this information for our future trips. It was here that we decided to sail northward along the eastern coast for 1,000 miles; we would reach the Kingdom of Motupalli, known for its diamonds.

"This kingdom was ruled by a wise and just queen who ruled with great integrity. Her subjects dearly loved her. But we weren't going there to see her. It was for the diamonds. The kingdom had many mountains, and when it rained, the water rushed down the valleys and caverns, unearthing these precious stones. Men would search the ravines for the plentiful diamonds when the sun returned. Kim Chi-hae and I could hardly wait. But during the last fifteen days, Li lay heavily on my mind. Again, she was becoming my obsession, and I found it hard to concentrate on my business at hand.

"The morning we arrived in Motupalli Bay, Kim Chin-hae exited his chambers with a panicked face. He motioned Dai Xiuying and me to his quarters. As I entered, I saw Kim studying a primitive map on his desk. My stomach instantly felt sick. Kim Chin-hae looked up from his map and said one word. 'Lis.'

Marco, circling his cell, stopped and looked at Rustichello, "The last eight months I spent in denial. It didn't take a second for that denial to vanish.

"Instantly, a feeling of doom surrounded me; I whispered, 'You had a dream? Lis came to you in your dream, didn't she? Tell me!'"

"Kim Chin-hae slowly started. 'About two months ago, three lords arrived in Khanbaliq looking for a queen for Arghun of the Ilkhanate. Kubilai Khan selected Kokochin as his Queen, and Li to become his concubine. They left traveling west on the Silk Road.'

"My fist rammed the table. 'That will never happen. I promised.'"

Chapter Forty-Three

Marco

Marco's Mad Race

Genoa Prison 1298

Marco stopped telling Rustichello his story, and his voice became powerful. "I didn't fail her then, and I won't now!"

Rustichello's curiosity was overflowing. "What happened next? You knew King Arghun, didn't you? Did that help?"

Marco didn't answer Rustichello right away. He recalled his uncontrollable anger at himself for his past months of denial.

Rustichello's questioning voice brought him back to reality. Marco continued his story. "I was so distraught I couldn't think straight. Thank goodness for Kim Chin-hae's quick thinking; he saved the day. He immediately began calculating how far Li would have traveled and how long it would take me to reach her. 'If you and Dai Xiuying leave now, travel to Warangal and then to India's main road, Dakshinapatha, you could intercept her in Balkh in four or five months.'

"I stopped Kim Chin-hae and seriously asked. 'You don't think I've lost my mind?'

"'You're asking me, the person who gave up becoming a powerful right-hand man to the king and living a very comfortable life. And most of all, I disgracefully disobeyed my parents, all in the name of love. So, you are asking me if I think you lost your mind?"

"The room went silent; moments later, Marco and Dai Xiuying slightly laughed and nodded.

"Kim Chin-hae continued. 'Pak Byeong-ho and I will return home. Lis misses me. I will see you again in Zapton?'

"'If the heavens are on our side.'

Marco walked around the cell, fiddling with his beard. He stopped, looked at Rustichello, and continued.

"Dai Xiuying and I needed to travel fast. This route would be foreign, and my golden tablet meant nothing here. My anxiety grew, but lasted only briefly as my fear for Li overshadowed it. Kim Chin-hae's last word of advice: change out of Mongolian attire. 'Dress like India's merchants, or you will stand out too much. Marco rubbed his beard, happy he hadn't shaved in a while.

"As we disembarked in Motupalli, I heard stories of the Banyan merchants. Their honesty distinguished them, and their clothing and food choices would identify them. One thing I learned from my travels is that your travel companions are critical. It wasn't long until we joined one of their caravans traveling to Lars close to Delhi, and then we were to travel through Lahore. This city scared me. I still had nightmares about the Qaraunas warriors."

Marco turned to Rustichello. "You remember, they were the ones that almost killed me when I was a young man, and the young Arghun saved us. I heard later in '79, Arghun's father, Abaqa, defeated them."

Marco forgot his empty stomach and continued, "My heart pounded harder with each mile traveled as I came closer to Li. After we passed through Kashmir and Pashai, I only had seventeen more days if everything went well until I reached Badakhshan, a territory I was familiar with. You remember this is where we stayed a year while I recovered from an illness, and I met Aiyurug."

Rustichello nodded.

"I would finally share the same road with Li. Our plan or hope was to travel with merchant caravans and listen for any rumors regarding Kubilai Khan's caravan. If we had questions, Dai Xiuying would ask for fear of me being recognized. We didn't want Kubilai Khan to know I wasn't in India. The first night we arrived in Badakhshan, we roamed the caravans. At night, tongues became loose with wine, and it wasn't long before we heard rumors of a mysterious person who traveled with a western-bound caravan that healed people. Her name was Ke Ai De Ren, which meant kind angel. In my heart, I knew it was her. But that wasn't the only rumor. A war raged beyond Balkh, and all caravans were forced to stop.

"The following day, we left, traveling west. In three weeks, we would reach our destination, Balkh. The war stories continued, giving me hope, but anticipation killed me. Li and the caravan were probably there. Only one day from Balkh, the stopped caravans lined the road. Camping was the only option, as the inns and caravansaries in and around the city were full of merchants and travelers waiting for the Silk Road to reopen. We weaved in and out of the long train of camps and finally reached the city's outskirts. There, an enormous camp with elegant gers resided close to a significant caravanserai. Seeing Kubilai's soldiers made my heart race, and my desire to rip open every ger to search for Li became unbearable. Dai Xiuying saw my urgency and stopped me. He grabbed the reins of my horse and spoke sternly. 'We need to wait until dark. They say she appears every evening. I will find us a room.'

"'How? Didn't you notice all the people?' I asked.

"Dai Xiuying smiled as he held out his hand. 'With lots of money, of course.'"

Rustichello laughed. "I guess that's universal."

"As I handed him a large bag of coins, he politely instructed me to go somewhere and clear my head. 'If we are going to pull this off, you need to be centered. I will meet you here before sunset.'

"'There is a beautiful river beyond the city that separates the empires. Water flowing brings me peace. I need that now. That's where I'll be.'

"Dai Xiuying agreed and again reminded me. 'Meet me at sunset.'

"Riding slowly through the noble city, I recalled that sixteen years ago, parts of the city still lay in ruins, but with the rise of open trade along the Silk Road, recent growth erased the scars. The city flourished. But, this war and the continued conflict between Qaidu and Kubilai Khan could bring a new future: the sea routes. *Wasn't that the reason I had to leave Li?*

"The river running on the edge of town was the border between Arghun Khan and Qaidu's empire. I rode on its banks until I found a peaceful oasis, hidden by boulders, where I could sit, watch, and hear the water flowing, hoping to melt my anxiety.

"As I relaxed, an impressive hooded warrior suddenly appeared not too far from me. He stood on the bank, looking to the other side. Another hooded warrior on the other side rode out of the trees and entered the river, riding directly toward the other warrior. Captivated by this mystery, I couldn't turn away. The warriors met and moved swiftly into the trees. I quietly moved to spy. My heart stopped when they removed their hoods. It was Aiyurug, Qaidu's daughter, and a man who also looked familiar. They kissed passionately, talked until sunset, and then her lover rode back across the river.

***

Ghazan and Aiyurug stood on the Balkh side of the river, hidden by a few trees that lined its bank. Ghazan was handsome, young, and stood proud in his general's uniform. Aiyurug was towering, and her gold medallion that hung around her neck glittered in the escaped sunlight.

Aiyurug didn't care that years ago she had wrestled his father with the prospect of marriage. Her feelings for Ghazan were love.

Aiyurug was livid. "You shouldn't be here; my sentries could capture or kill you if you are discovered. My hands would be tied."

Ghazan touched her muscular arm. "I couldn't leave without telling you goodbye. Victory belongs to Nawruz for now. I must escape to Mazandaran."

"You should have just left. It's more important that you live. You know our lives will never join. We played with fire for the last few years and risked being found out."

Ghazan laughed. "You could marry me. It would solve all the problems between our fathers."

Aiyurug didn't laugh. "I can't give up my empire and be by your side."

Ghazan grabbed her arm and pulled her in close. His lips met hers; she kissed him back. Aiyurug never felt this way about a man. Even though he couldn't beat her in wrestling, she didn't care. Their lives were so similar. He had been a warrior and viceroy in Khorasan since he was eleven, when his father, King Arghun, became the Khan of the Ilkhanate. She, too, had become a warrior at an early age. Her father was Qaidu.

Ghazan guarded the Ilkhanate's boundaries against her father, Qaidu, as she guarded the exact borders against Ghazan's armies. They watched each other from afar for years. His men made sly remarks about her womanhood, but to Ghazan, she was beautiful, and her strength thrilled him. To her, he was the most handsome man she had ever seen. Their curiosity grew until, one day, they met secretly. That was two years ago, and they had been secretly meeting ever since. However, Nawruz, his atabeg for eleven years, recently committed treason against Ghazan. Nawruz wanted the Khorsan Territory. Ghazan had to run for his life, unable to defeat him. But she knew he would return to battle one day.

Unaware of being watched, they talked and said their goodbyes as the sun fell behind the forest. Aiyurug watched him cross the river with tears in her eyes. All of a sudden, as he neared the shore, arrows flew; soldiers were ambushing Ghazan. Aiyurug didn't hesitate; she jumped onto her horse and sped across the river. When she reached the other side, Ghazan stood alone, battling his attackers. Aiyurug never brought her horse to a halt, and at full speed, she jumped with her enormous sword drawn, attacking with all her might. From the corner of her eye, she saw Ghazan being stabbed and slashed.

Aiyurug became a wild beast that protects her young; her powerful body struck down man after man until no one else stood. Covered in blood, she ran to his side. He was still alive but unconscious and bleeding profusely. *What am I going to do now?* Frantically, she tore part of her uniform and held it tight to his wound. Her heart ached. Suddenly, she heard splashing.

Frightened, she threw her body over his and looked toward the river. A man was crossing the river. She stood with her sword drawn, her face distorted with anger and terror, and walked toward the man crossing the river. Mid-river, with her sword ready to strike, she heard her name. "Aiyurug, it's me, Messer Marco." She lowered her sword and cried. "Help him."

***

Marco looked at Rustichello. "Suddenly, out of nowhere, several warriors appeared, attacking Aiyurug's lover. I did something I shouldn't have; I mounted my horse and started crossing the river."

"Facing Aiyurug was frightening. Thank goodness she recognized me. Ghazan was partially unconscious as I set him on my horse and mounted behind him. Aiyurug followed, leading Ghazan's horse as we crossed the river, terrified someone would see us. We were fortunate that the sun was setting fast. I had questions, but decided this wasn't the time. He was bleeding and needed a physician. 'We should take him to Balkh,' I said.

"Aiyurug kept shaking her head, no. 'He is our enemy and can't be caught.'

"'Well, he will die if we don't. My guide is waiting for me in the city. I know someone there who can help.'

Aiyurug's face relaxed. Ghazan moaned, and Aiyurug jumped off her horse and ran to his side. She looked at him lovingly, and he asked, "Who's the man I ride with?"

Aiyurug touched Ghazan's leg. 'It's Messer Marco Polo, your father's and my friend. He knows someone who can treat you in Balkh.'

"Frailly, he said, 'Balkh! No! We both could be in serious trouble.'

"Those were his last words as he lost consciousness. Darkness surrounded us. We rode cautiously, terrified. In the distance, a light appeared; someone was coming. Hiding behind some old ruins, we held our breath as the rider passed. I let out a deep breath and whispered Dai Xiuying's name.

"He stopped and turned around. 'Messer Marco, is that you? Where have you been? I was worried.' As he rode behind the ruins, his mouth dropped. 'Who are these people?'

"I didn't answer. Instead, I asked, 'Did you find us a room?'

"'Yes, in a caravanserai right outside town where the Khan's gers are. The room is the best I could do on such short notice. We were lucky the merchant needed money.'

"Emotion shook my body. She was so nearby. I shut off my feelings and changed the subject. 'We need to travel fast. Ghazan's injuries are serious, and he needs Li.'

“In the night’s darkness, we stayed hidden until we almost arrived at the caravanserai. I dismounted, helped Ghazan pull his hood over his head, and placed him on his horse. ‘It will be less suspicious.’

“Entering the caravanserai, Ghazan was barely holding on. Aiyurug helped him get down from his horse, and they followed Dai Xiuying into the room, where Ghazan collapsed on the straw bed.

“Kneeling next to his bed, I informed Ghazan that Dai Xiuying had gone after a healer named Ke Ai De Ren. ‘An angel, they say, that doesn’t ask questions.’

“Ghazan slowly nodded. Aiyurug moved a stool next to Ghazan, holding his hand as he lost consciousness.

“Abruptly, there was a soft knock. Aiyurug, alarmed, covered Ghazan’s face, and I opened the door slightly. Dai Xiuying spoke, and I nodded to Aiyurug as I moved to the corner. Guo Yu entered the room, and then Li.”

Marco turned to Rustichello. “Li’s courage always surprised me. She was like Kim Chin-hae. They were so sure of their feelings and their duty. I always held things close to my heart, never letting my true feelings show. It was how I survived and continued to live in my darkest moments. I wished to be more like them.”

Chapter Forty-Four

Li

A Dream Fulfilled

Venice 1298

Li stood at her window and continued telling Luca her story. “After seven months, we reached Balkh. The caravans had come to a standstill. A war raged between two Tartar Lords beyond this grand city. Balkh was the imaginary boundary between Arghun, Lord of the llkhanate, and Qaidu, de facto khan of the Chagatai Khanate. It was an unusual war; those two weren’t fighting, but Ghazan’s atabeg, one of Arghun's generals, went rogue and was fighting Ghazan.”

Luca interrupted Li. “Isn’t Arghun the king Kokochin was to marry?”

Li nodded, turned, and looked out her window. Slowly, she began again in a soft voice.

“The night was black; the moon hadn’t risen.” Li’s heart began to race as she started her story. Tears fell out of happiness. “I will never forget that night.”

“We left our ger and started our normal routine when a young boy who stood against a dark wall walked toward us. ‘I’ve been waiting for you.’ He gently grabbed my arm and pulled me into the darkness. In a youthful voice, he said, ‘Please follow me.’”

Li stopped her story and turned to Guo Yu. “You never understood why I did not show fear that night. That’s because I felt my life was over, and I welcomed death more than becoming someone’s concubine.

“So, I didn’t hesitate; I followed the young boy who took us to the caravanserai near our camp. The young boy paid the guard, who then opened the gate, and we followed him to a room. Dai Xiuying knocked, and the door slightly opened. Dai Xiuying quietly spoke, and someone cautiously opened the door, and Guo Yu entered. A few minutes passed before a grave Guo Yu reopened the door and called me in. A young, handsome man lay in a worn bed, badly wounded, and a towering woman, whose body was more defined as a man, stood at his side. She wore a blood-soaked hooded cloak that concealed most of her face. I feared she was injured and moved in closer to remove her coat. She sternly refused, but her eyes widened as she looked at my scarf and the letters. *Why?*

"But when she moved, the cloak swung to the side, and I saw that she wore a large, heavy gold medallion with engravings around her neck. It was apparent she held a high rank and was a warrior. A glance revealed she possessed a beautiful face belonging to a woman in love and deathly afraid her lover would die.

"Guo Yu told me a story once about the daughter of Qaidu, who was his right arm and general. *Could this be her? We are in her territory, but why are they here alone? Why have they summoned me and not their physician?* I opened my mouth to ask when Guo Yu slightly touched my arm. I understood—don't ask questions.

"I laid out my medicine bag. The towering female warrior's facial expression had softened. She hovered closely over my shoulder and watched me remove his uniform. I glanced up at her and then down at him; his uniform revealed he was a general, but not on the same side. He had been slashed and stabbed with a sword. Taking out my acupuncture needles, I inserted them into prime locations to prevent pain. His pain-distorted face relaxed. I washed the wound with water and salt, then started sewing it up with silk thread and a needle. The woman warrior suddenly placed her large hand on my shoulder. Her grip hurt. I stopped and looked up at her. Suddenly, someone in the room cleared their throat. A shadow of a man standing against the wall appeared in the corner of my eye. The warrior released her grip. I continued, and afterward, I applied moistened Gan Cao and started wrapping his wound. She took over. It was obvious she cared for him. As I removed my needles, the young man opened his eyes. He stared at me and pulled down my scarf with his weak hand. Quickly, I pulled it back up.

"Faintly, he said, 'He told me you were an angel, but he didn't tell me you were beautiful.'

"My face turned red. 'Who told you?' I asked.

"The woman warrior reached for my scarf, held up the corner where Marco's initials were stitched, and said, 'This man.'

"Instantly, butterflies monopolized my stomach, and my heart pounded. Nervous, I dropped my acupuncture needles as I heard footsteps. Guo Yu held up his lantern toward the corner and gasped. Slowly, I turned around. The man in the corner moved forward, removing his hood. The light exposed long curly hair and a face full of whiskers, concealing his face except for the wide eyes—the wide eyes of Marco. I walked toward him as he walked toward me. We both stopped a foot from each other, with our eyes locked. My face grew hot. Making sure he was real, I touched his face. His hand covered mine and, with his free hand, pulled me into his body, never losing eye contact. His heart pounded as I lay my head on his chest and wrapped my arms tightly around him. All my life, I have had this dream.

"He whispered, 'I will never leave you again.'"

Li stopped talking, looked out her window, and said in a quiet, sad voice, "He lied." Li picked up the erhu.

Luca looked over at Guo Yu and then at Li and quickly said, "Don't stop now; tell me more. Who were the warriors? Tell me more."

Li cleared her throat and continued. "We held each other until the woman warrior spoke. 'I was unaware passion was involved. Messer Marco, I understand now why you hid. Ghazan could have died if she hadn't been able to pull herself together.' She laughed boldly.

"Embarrassed, I tried to regain my composure, returned to Ghazan and my bag, and pulled out some dried herbs. 'Make tea with these. It will help him heal faster. Here are some more bandages and Gan Cao. I will come back tomorrow.'

"'No need. I won't be here tomorrow,' Ghazan said softly. The woman warrior who sat next to him looked down at him. He reached up and wiped her tears.

"Marco walked over, pulled my scarf up, and sweetly spoke. 'You should return.' Then, he turned to the woman warrior. 'Dai Xiuying, my guard, is outside. He will stay until I return. We will talk then.'

"Marco opened the door, whispered to Dai Xiuying, covered his head with his hood, and motioned me to come. Silently, we walked until we found a deserted alley. Facing each other, Marco touched the scarf. 'I can't believe you still have this.'

"I slid the scarf down. 'I can't believe it took you this long to realize your feelings! My whole life has been you!'

"Marco, without thinking anymore, placed his hands on each side of my cheeks and softly kissed me. Guo Yu, embarrassed, turned away, just like he is now."

Li laughed and continued. "My dream finally came true. I wrapped my arms around him, and we held each other until Guo Yu cleared his throat loudly and spoke softly. 'Li, we must return.'

"I nodded, looked at Marco, and asked, 'What will we do now?'

"Marco stared at me with a blank face. 'For the last months, finding you was my only concern. I didn't even think past that! Now that we have accomplished that, I will devise a plan. I have a feeling this war will benefit us. Don't tell anyone about me, not even Kokochin.'

"I changed the subject and asked him, 'How did you find me? How did you know they had sent me away?'

"'Lis, Kim Chin-hae's wife.'

"'Kim?'

"'The Crown Prince Wang Won's cousin and my friend. I know you have heard his name. He is married to a shaman named Lis, who can connect to Kim Chin-hae's souls through dreams. Later, when we have time, I will tell you the entire story. You should go.'

"Marco turned to Guo Yu. 'Meet me here tomorrow morning in this same alley.'

"I had never heard such a thing, but didn't question it. The only thing that mattered was that Marco found me."

Luca clapped with excitement and squealed. "I love your stories. How romantic. Tell me more."

Li sat quietly for a moment. Tears filled her eyes, and she looked at Guo Yu. "I'm scared. Marco has been gone for so long. What if something has happened to him?"

She picked up her erhu, placing her hands correctly, and the music wailed.

Luca tried to speak to Li, who never looked up.

Luca and Guo Yu stood up. "Lock your door when we leave."

Li nodded as they walked out.

Chapter Forty-Five

Marco

Marco's Rescue

Genoa Prison 1298

Marco went silent when he heard the doors clanging. His stomach was hollow, and he felt weak. The small window opened, and Marco grabbed the food.

He heard the guards say, "We must have taught him a lesson; He has been quiet these days!" Marco could feel his temper rising.

Rustichello stood and walked over to Marco. "Give it to me before you drop it. I'm hungry."

Marco handed Rustichello his food, but dropped his on the floor, made a tight fist, and rammed the door. The sound echoed through the halls. He picked his food up from the dirty, vile floor and shoved it into his mouth.

Rustichello watched him, shaking his head. With a full mouth, he calmly said. "Marco, finish the story. What happened next?"

Marco sat on the floor among the spilled food and continued.

"When I returned to my room, the young general was sitting up. Aiyurug held the tea bowl up to his mouth, gently giving him small sips. She looked out of place. Just hours ago, she had butchered numerous men.

"'This is Ghazan, Arghun's son,' she said as she looked up at me.

"'No wonder you looked familiar; you look like your father.'

"After Ghazan swallowed the tea, in a frail voice, Ghazan said, 'Thank you for helping me. I owe you my life.'

"'One day, you can pay me back.'

"Ghazan nodded.

"'I think this woman should take most of the credit. Without her fierce temper, you might have died.'

"Ghazan laughed, holding his wound, and replied. 'I heard you met her temper years ago.'

"Aiyurug and I looked up at each other. I must have turned red. Ghazan and Aiyurug continued laughing.

"Ghazan turned serious quickly, turning to Aiyurug. 'Before the sun rises, I must leave. My men will be frantic. I must travel to Mazandaran and wait for my father's troops. Then, hell will be released.'

"Then he turned to me. 'The road won't be open for a while.'

"I nodded. That's when the idea popped into my head: *I will have Guo Yu talk to the lords, telling them they must return to Khanbaliq.*

"Ghazan caught me off guard as I was in deep thought. 'How do you know that girl? Who is she?'

"Aiyurug and Ghazan stared at me. I stared back. 'She is my secret like she is your secret,' I said as I looked at Aiyurug.

"Ghazan nodded. 'I understand—enough questions. I have one request. Help me return to the river. Aiyurug shouldn't come. I have put her in enough danger. Her brothers would love this.'

"Aiyurug argued. Ghazan looked at her. 'You know I'm right. You are too recognizable. We were lucky this time, but might not be next time.'

"I left and let them argue. As I closed the door, I said, 'I'll be back after some sleep.'

"Dai Xiuying and I found a quiet corner in the caravanserai, unrolled our blankets, lay under the stars, and talked. 'Li asked me what we were going to do now. Telling her I didn't know frightened me; I am normally a man with a plan and consider all consequences. But I did everything in the past months out of pure emotion without thinking of the consequences.'

"'Isn't that what love is?' Dai Xiuying said and continued. 'Like those two in the room, they knew the dangers, but it didn't matter. I call it Love Blindness; you no longer see nor hear the world around you. You see only the person who fires your heart. Love leaves you vulnerable. You are a prisoner of your passion. It can be a dangerous game.'

"I agreed and asked. 'How many times have you been in love?'

"'Never,' he laughed. 'That's why I am still alive.'

"We both laughed hard.

"I became serious. 'I had an idea while I was talking to Ghazan. The war is just beginning, and the road will be closed for some time. I think this is our chance. Guo Yu should ask for an audience with the lords. Perhaps he can persuade them to turn around. If he can't, I'll find someone else, maybe Aiyurug.'

"Dai Xiuying liked the first part, not the second. 'Let's sleep on it,' he told me.

"It wasn't long before Dai Xiuying's breathing became rhythmic. I lay and looked up at the stars. He was right. It was love blindness, and I was scared.

"I returned to our room before the sun rose. Ghazan was waiting as Aiyurug slept. We slipped out the door. Within the hour, we had reached the river, and the moon was setting. There was just enough light to see the other side. The dead bodies of Nawruz's soldiers lay sprawled on the shore. That was a good sign. Watching for a while, we didn't see any movement. Quietly, Ghazan turned his horse, facing the city. He placed his hand over his heart and bowed his head. After a few minutes, he whipped his horse around and charged the river. Five men on horseback met him on the other side moments later, and they raced off. As Dai Xiuying and I headed for the city, we saw a towering shadow in the forest. We knew it was Aiyurug."

Marco looked up at Rustichello from the floor. "It would be three years before I would see Ghazan again."

***

Meanwhile, Aiyurug rose after Ghazan and Marco rushed out the door. She left and rode far behind them. Hidden among the trees, she held back her tears as she watched Ghazan turn, placing his hand on his heart and bowing. When he crossed the river, her warrior-self reappeared when she saw his men. He was safe for now. She waited for Messer Marco and Dai Xiuying to leave before she rode to the riverbank. Momentarily, she stared beyond the river, turned her horse north, and heeled him hard. In a full gallop, she rode toward Samarkand while her mind kept going over what had happened. *So much deceit,* she thought. *Ghazan must have been devastated by Nawrus, who had been his atabeg for many years and now committed treason.* Her feelings were in turmoil. Ghazan and his father were her enemies, but they were honorable. Nawruz was detestable and had no honor. Aiyurug continued thinking about what Ghazan had told her. His father depended on many men to maintain his empire. When Nawruz heard Arghun's army, led by Nurin Aqa and Prince Baydu, was approaching Khorasan, where Nawruz was the de facto ruler, he knew his ruling time was over. Instead of bowing to Hulagu, he rebelled, proclaiming Hulachu, son of Hulagu, as a new Ilkhanate, banishing his ward, Prince Ghazan, to Mazandaran. *So many poisonous snakes had appeared for power and money,*

Aiyurug thought as she prayed that Ghazan would survive. And then she thought of her father. *He ruled utterly; his country survived because his control left no room for deceit.*

Sometime later, Aiyurug heard that after Ghazan reorganized his army, he fought Nawruz again but lost in Radkan. However, when Prince Baydu and General Nurin Aqa arrived with his father's army in autumn, the overwhelmed Nawruz fled, scorching the earth and destroying everything in his way that the opposing military could use. Prince Baydu marched west victorious, even though he had lost half of his men.

Nawruz fled across the Oxus to Qaidu's Empire, defeated by Prince Baydu. Aiyurug became secretly angry; she didn't trust the man. She hadn't seen Ghazan since Nawruz's men had attacked him at the river. Her spies informed her that Ghazan was still alive, and his armies had defeated this man. But she also heard Ghazan's father had died, creating chaos in his empire. Now, Nawruz has requested an audience with Qaidu.

Aiyurug and Qaidu sat and listened to Nawruz's persuasive argument. If they sent men now, they could overtake Khorasan. Nawruz left Qaidu's ger and waited for his decision. Aiyurug, her father's strategic genius, sat quietly, mulling over their next move. She hated Nawruz, but her loyalty to her father and empire ran deep. Her father noticed her silence and questioned her.

She started slowly. "Nawrus is a poisonous snake, who knows no loyalty. Putting your trust in this man could be deadly. He bit his last lord, who trusted him with his son." Qaidu stared at his daughter and asked her how she had come to know so much.

Aiyurug didn't answer and painfully set aside her heart. "Let's join hands with caution. Give Nawruz 30,000 soldiers. Sorban, Ebugen, and I will fight by his side. I will watch the snake and chop off his head if he falters." Her father nodded and didn't ask any more questions.

In the following weeks, they prepared for battle as Aiyurug prepared her heart. She questioned her loyalty. *Can I fight him on the battlefield?*

When the day arrived, Nawrus, Sorban, Ebugen, and Aiyurug marched, crossing the Oxus. Ghazan, General Nurin Aqa, Prince Baydu, and their army awaited them. The battle raged. In the distance, Aiyurug saw Ghazan once, fiercely fighting. Outnumbered, his army fell back. Nawruz laid siege and seized different parts of the province, reaching Mashhad, where Ghazan's capital stood.

After the battle, Aiyurug, bloody and tired, weaved her stallion between the dead warriors that scattered the battlefield, secretly searching for Ghazan's body. Unable to find him, she looked toward Mashhad. Aiyurug felt Ghazan's eyes upon her. The heavy weight of her heart lifted. This time, she laid her hand on her heart and lowered her head. Moments later, she rode to her camp.

Qaidu awarded Nawruz, governor of Badakhshan, for his gallant victories.

However, as Aiyurug predicted, in the next year, Nawruz abandoned Qaidu by allying himself with Uruk Temür. Her father complimented her heavily. Her brothers hated her more.

The fierce invasion slowed, and General Nurin Aqa, Ghazan, and Prince Baydu's army held the borders. Aiyurug secretly followed Ghazan as he defended his borders. She heard through her spies that he could not take his rightful place on the throne due to these invasions. His uncle, Gaykhatu, was now the Khan, thanks to the help of Prince Baydu.

Her thoughts centered on him more than any man. *Why him?* Every month, on the same day, she would ride to Balkh and sit by the river where they had last met. Staring across the river for hours, she could imagine him riding across. But that never happened. Dismayed, she would mount her horse before daybreak and ride home.

Ghazan hated Gaykhatu, who falsely sat on the throne. Ghazan was the rightful Khan, but he had no recourse, as his loyalty to his kingdom was to protect its borders, which ultimately prevailed over his pride. Not only did he hate Gaykhatu, but he also hated that he could not see Aiyurug. Their bittersweet love was disheartening. His thoughts of her entered his dreams nightly. Until one day, the heavens blessed him. A warrior who rode the borders came to him.

"When we ride on our scheduled day, which is now, to the riverbanks near Balkh, I see the same warrior on the other side of the river. Should we worry? He seems to be waiting for someone. A spy, perhaps?"

Ghazan hesitated momentarily, then strolled to his horse, not saying a word, and mounted. He could no longer refuse his aching heart. Riding fast, he reached Balkh right before nightfall.

Even though hidden in the trees, the setting sun exposed Aiyurug's glistening white skin and hair to Ghazan. Ghazan's heart pounded.

Aiyurug rode out of the forest to the riverbank, looked across the river, slowly turned north, and urged her horse forward.

With urgency, Ghazan swiftly entered the river. Splashing water awoke Aiyurug's survival instinct. She quickly withdrew her sword, turned, and prepared for battle. The descending sun made it impossible to see the face of the rider, but Aiyurug could hear Ghazan's familiar voice.

"Aiyurug!" he shouted.

Her sword fell to her side. Ghazan rode next to her. Their eyes said it all as they crossed the river. They dismounted, and with his outstretched arms, Ghazan caught her as she crumpled into his arms. She had missed him and had waited for this moment.

Unfortunately, there was another feeling: *disgrace. I'm acting like a woman, not a warrior. My brothers would experience great pleasure if they saw me.*

Deep down, she was more of a warrior than a woman, and this feeling would pass. Meanwhile, she wanted to savor the moment, as it might not happen again.

They walked hand in hand into the trees. Ghazan built a small fire, and she laid out a blanket. They sat beside each other, mulling over how their lives had led them to this point. Softly, he looked into her eyes and gently stroked her face. She did the same. Their lips met, and they no longer thought, letting their feelings consume them. Hours later, they returned to reality and talked.

Ghazan angrily spoke of his disappointment, and she listened. "My father's death, Gaykhatu's rise to khan, and the betrayal of Nawruz were almost more than I could handle. Someday, I will get my revenge."

As he stared at Aiyurug, his voice and facial expression softened, and he whispered, "Life sometimes hands you an unexpected gift . . . like you."

His look and voice became earnest. "Marry me! After I bring down Nawruz, our love could bring peace among our people."

"And after Gaykhatu," Aiyurug pointed out.

Then she snickered. "Marry you? I'm afraid that will never happen."

By sunrise, they had gone their separate ways with the agreement that they would meet every full moon.

Their love remained secret for the next couple of years, and with every departure, he asked, "Marry me?"

Chapter Forty-Six

Marco

Marco's Plan

Genoa Prison 1298

Marco continued his story. "The following morning, I met Guo Yu and told him about my plan. He was skeptical; convincing the three lords could be difficult, but he would try. Then he questioned. 'Then what?'

"Again, my plan stopped there. First things first, we need to return to Khanbaliq. Guo Yu informed me that he and Li went out every night. 'We will meet you here an hour after the sun sets.'

"Overwhelmed, I thought, *I have so much to say to her. Our relationship has changed so fast.*

"After Guo Yu departed, I found Dai Xiuying eating in the caravanserai. As he gorged his face, he excitedly pointed to a message board. A large piece of paper glued to the board read:

The war between the lords has closed the road. Merchants should return to where they come from or find alternative routes.

"My mind raced. *It's happening. Now what?*

"That evening, I met Li. My scarf wrapped around her face, exposing only her beautiful eyes, which glowed with love. She clutched my hands. Embarrassed, I brought them to my lips and kissed both. Her confidence in her love was undeniable. Mine wasn't; I feared failure, rejection, and the inability for true intimacy between hearts. *Would I let her down?* I had only loved my mother, whose love was unconditional. Kubilai Khan's love was born out of respect, and Kim Chin-hae and I shared a kindred spirit. Never had I given myself completely; I was afraid."

Marco stared at Rustichello with tears. "My fear of failure turned out to be true."

Rustichello pushed Marco to continue.

"Guo Yu was happy he did not have to face the three lords, as they had received the same notice and would start their return the next day.

"That night and for the following months, I became a ghost with her, following her as she searched for the sick. Not only did she have confidence in our love, but she was also a remarkable healer. I understood why her new name, Ke Ai De Ren, followed her. Her kindness radiated.

"It was a strange time. Li always loved me from afar. My connection was different. She was someone I protected and watched over. Her kind of love, I didn't understand.

"For the first time, we were together for many days. Surprisingly, we weren't strangers. Instead, there was a closeness and comfort I never experienced. I wanted more; she became my obsession. I no longer saw her as a little girl; she had become a woman I never wanted to leave, someone to covet and draw strength from.

"When Lis told me I had a soulmate, I laughed. Kim Chin-hae was right; his wife was a witch. I wasn't laughing anymore.

"Our love blindness grew deeper instead of fading. Dai Xiuying and Guo Yu grew more fearful. We were playing with fire in the same way as Ghazan and Aiyurug.

"My mind worked feverishly on my next move. I wondered if Kim Chin-hae made it home and where my father and uncle were. *What did they say when he told them what I had done?* I prayed every night for Kim Chin-hae's safety and that my father would be in Khanbaliq when I returned. However, Li could always extinguish my anguish.

"By the time we reached the desert, we were only two months from Khanbaliq. I decided that the only way to save Li was to leave Cathay and Kubilai Khan. My father, uncle, and I had known for some time that Kubilai was aging and that his grandson, the new crown prince, would become Khan, bringing about drastic changes. Several times, my father and uncle discussed their fears with me. I refused to listen; I didn't want to leave Kubilai. Things were different now. There was only one answer: betraying Kubilai Khan. My heart was heavy, yet my love for Li stood above all.

"It took us a month to cross the Gobi Desert. After we crossed the desert, Dai Xiuying and I decided to leave the caravan and continue to Khanbaliq. We would pretend we had just returned from India and knew nothing except for rumors of a war between the Ghazan and Nawruz.

“Li was heartbroken by my departure. The night before we left, she refused to leave my side. ‘The sick can wait. I am selfish and want you more,’ she told me. ‘My life is not complete without you. Your breath has become mine; without you, I cannot breathe.’ She grabbed my hand and led me to my ger. It would be the first time I was ever alone with her. Dai Xiuying and Guo Yu shook their heads and walked away just far enough.”

Marco stopped talking to Rustichello. Marco crawled to his straw bed. Disappointed, Rustchello picked up his pen and continued writing his story.

Marco faced the wall, and the image of Li appeared; it was the first night she had given herself to him.

Li unwrapped my scarf and dropped it to the floor; seductively, she removed her clothing, revealing a delicate, graceful body. Walking over, she placed my hands on her body. I felt her warmth, and her body shivered beneath my touch. She started removing my clothes. My body and mind forgot any restraint. I helped her. Gently holding her, I kissed her as we melted into each other. Our bodies urged each other for more until we reached the explosion of love.

As we lay with our bodies intertwined, she whispered. "I have loved you from the moment you saved me, feeling your pain as my own. My love grew over the years, and I wanted only you."

She raised her head, looked into my eyes, and asked. "When did you know?" Remembering, I felt my body grow warm. "It was when I saw the Crown Prince Wang Won following you like a lovesick puppy. Jealousy set me on fire. Then, the day Chin-hae announced Lis came to him in his dream, warning us that the lords had taken you, I no longer fought my feelings; Nothing could have stopped me. When you entered my room to heal Ghazan wearing my scarf, that was the pivotal moment. There was no turning back; I lost my heart to you forever."

She caressed my body softly. This time, I shivered, and she used her body as a blanket. Face-to-face, we lost ourselves in love. The night was bliss as she dissolved my guilt and molded our love into one.

It was strange, but with just the thought of Li, Marco felt a sense of comfort. He drifted off to sleep.

Chapter Forty-Seven

Li

Li, Luca, Isabella, and the Letter

Venice 1298

When Luca arrived early the following day, Isabella stood in the entry hall reading a letter. When she saw Luca, Isabella quickly folded the letter and placed it in her book. Isabella sneered at Luca and walked upstairs. Instantly, Luca thought her face appeared deceitful. *What is she up to?*

Shaking her head, Luca ascended the stairs to Li's room, gently knocked, and tried to enter. The locked door made Luca happy; Li listened to Guo Yu. After several hard knocks, Li finally answered the door, still dressed in the clothes from the day before. Guo Yu had heard the knocks and was coming down the hall.

They looked at Li. Her eyes were red and swollen.

Guo Yu spoke. "Let's go to the Golden Head. I think you need an outing."

Li shook her head. "No, I want to continue my story." She sat at her dressing table and looked into the mirror, trying to dismantle her muddled braid. Guo Yu sympathetically went to Li and finished combing her hair. Luca walked to her trunk and pulled out fresh clothes.

Li opened the drawer and pulled out the binyeo that Marco had given her. Li whispered in a melancholy voice. "I wore this when we married. Kim Chin-hae and Lis gave this to Marco years before he knew he loved me. It's gold with purple jade. Isn't it beautiful?" She held it out for Luca to see. "See the carved peony and the delicate butterflies. It means a lover tasting the joys of passion." At fourteen, I had the same symbol drawn in the medicine bag I made for Marco. Do you recall the story I shared with you? Again, long before Marco was aware of my love for him."

Guo Yu combed her hair, sweeping the front part into a loose bun and allowing the remaining hair to fall to her shoulders gracefully. When he finished, Li handed him the binyeo, which he gently placed in the bun.

Li looked in the mirror, smiled, and continued. "Marco was so naïve."

Guo Yu handed Li a wet cloth, and she gently blotted her face and red, swollen eyes. Slowly, she picked up her makeup pad, applied the powder, and moistened her lips with color. Finished, she stood, walked over to her fresh clothes, and continued talking. "When he found me in Balkh, it was the happiest moment in my life. He accepted his love for me."

Li went behind the dressing screen and removed her clothing as she talked. Guo Yu quickly left the room for breakfast; he was becoming uncomfortable. Li laughed. Luca sat and listened as she returned to her story.

"After the night I treated Ghazan, we saw each other every night. He followed Guo Yu and me as we roamed the caravan, healing. This time, I was not just healing strangers. We were healing each other. It was the first time we had spent so much time together. I thought we would feel awkward. Instead, we felt like one." As she finished that statement, she handed the last piece of clothing to Luca and thought, *It won't be long till my clothes won't fit,* as she rubbed her swollen belly. Luca handed her a fresh undergarment and her robe. Li walked from the screen and continued her story. "The night before Marco left to return to Khanbaliq, I decided to seduce him."

Luca gasped, and her face blushed. Li continued. "We only had a month before we arrived in Khanbaliq. That's when Marco told me he was leaving the caravan and returning to Khanbaliq. I was heartbroken. Deep down, I knew he had to, but I couldn't bear the thought. The desire to have him completely at least once grew intense. Instead of roaming the caravan, I led him to his room and undressed before him." Luca giggled, embarrassed.

Li continued. "That night, we declared our love and knew then he would do anything for me. It was the beginning of his betrayal of Kubilai Khan."

Li continued dressing and talking. "I returned to my ger later than usual. Kokochin was waiting for me, worried the lords had caught me. With tears in my eyes, I told her she didn't need to worry any longer; I wouldn't be going out any longer. Falling into bed, I wanted to tell Kokochin. But that would be dangerous. Remaining silent, I relived the night. For the first time, I felt fear. *Would Marco be able to accomplish his plan?* The next morning, as we mounted our horses, I looked around, and my heart sank. Marco was gone."

Guo Yu returned with breakfast, concerned. Isabella acted strangely, as if she had a secret, and a bad feeling lingered over Guo Yu.

After breakfast, Li looked around the room and spoke less forlornly. “You were right, Guo Yu. We should go to the Golden Head. This room is making me sad. I need fresh air and some color in my life. Luca, please bring me my man's clothes.”

When they walked down the stairs, Isabella smiled at Li. Li, Luca, and Guo Yu stared at her, and Li asked in a sarcastic and sweet voice, “What makes you so cordial today, Isabella?”

Isabella answered back in a sarcastic voice. “I have been blessed with power today.”

“I hope you use it wisely.”

“I plan to,” Isabella said boldly.

Guo Yu smirked, and Luca grew concerned. *Did it have something to do with the letter Isabella received today?* Luca decided to tell Guo Yu about the letter later, as they walked out the door.

As Li felt the warm sun and spring air upon her face, her spirit lifted. She resumed talking to Luca. “I love my small herbal garden behind the apothecary. There isn't much soil in Venice, so I grow the herbs in containers. Marco and I brought back medicinal tuber roots and seeds for tea, hoping they would grow. Some grew like Di Huang, a Cathay rhubarb used when the body is too heated and the blood is hot, or for liver disease. Also, Bai He[1] for sore throats and wheezing, Bai Lui Pi[2] for pain, and Tian Men Dong.[3] I also presented Messer Alessio the Trinity of Heaven by mixing Di Huang,[4] Tian men Dong[5] with Ren Shen[6] that we brought back from Cathay.”

The thought of her garden eased the pain of the present. As she approached the Golden Head, she smiled and forgot about Isabella.

While Li tended her garden, Luca talked to Guo Yu. “When I arrived this morning, Isabella was reading a letter. She hid it when she saw me. Do you think it was about Messer Marco?”

With a serious look, Guo Yu answered. “Maybe I should talk to Messer Maffeo.”

---

1. Willow bark
2. Tuber asparagi cochinensis
3. Lily bulbs
4. Earth
5. Heaven

6. Ginseng—humanity

Chapter Forty-Eight

Marco

1290 Marco's Betrayal

Genoa Prison 1298

Marco woke up refreshed but hungry. Rustichello was still sleeping. He walked to the wall beside the barred window, where he and Rustichello marked the days. From this window, they watched the gray skies of winter march by and the blue skies of spring arrive, Li's favorite time. She must be excited about tending her garden. He smiled at the thought. Then his face went blank, and out loud, he said, "Will they ever release me?"

Waking up, Rustichello rolled over and looked up at Marco. "You will be, and she will be waiting."

Marco whispered. "For the past years, I felt so large. Now, I feel so small. A feeling I haven't felt before. Is this my karma?"

"Karma?" Rustichello questioned.

"My fate, caused by my actions," Marco whispered back.

Rustichello jumped up and changed the subject. "Let's finish your story. Last night, I covered your food from the hungry, pesky rats. So eat. I want to hear more."

Marco uncovered his food, grabbed a hard piece of bread, and continued. "As we rode away that day, I felt lonely. Something was missing. The further I rode, the lonelier I became. I missed Li.

"When I arrived in Khanbaliq, I went straight to my father's, hoping he was there. Usually, I would have rushed to see Kubilai. Being gone for over a year and a half, my head would have been swirling with stories to tell. The need to see my father surprised me. Desperation does funny things. For the first time, I was turning to my family for help.

"As I passed Ehuang-chu's store, I felt gratitude.

"Reaching my father's home, I saw his horses. Opening the door, something happened that had never happened before. My father ran over to me, put his arms around me, and asked if Lis had found me.

"'We left before Kim Chin-hae made it home. Lis insisted we leave and wait for you. Did she find you?'

I nodded yes.

"Amazed, he hugged me harder and pulled me inside. 'Tell me what happened.'

"'No, you tell me what happened.'

"My father sat and told us that when he returned home, a desperate Ehuang-chu had rushed to greet him, inquiring if Physician Wu had found Lis and given her my letter. He was surprised she was involved and questioned her. She told him the story. He sent a relieved Ehuang-chu home, saying I had received the letter. But that was all he knew.

Then he asked me again. 'You found Li, right? Now what?'

"'Are you ready to go back to Venice?'

"His face looked relieved. 'I've been waiting for this. Your uncle and I are ready. How?'

"'I have a plan! Li is coming with us!' I blurted out.

"My father became silent and looked at Dai Xiuying, who nodded.

"'I found her in Balkh. They had to stop and turn around because of the war between Arghun, Ghazan, and Nawruz. Kokochin, Li, and their whole caravan are one month out.

Marco continued with his plan. 'Father and Uncle Maffeo, it will be your job to circulate rumors of your son's successful sailing voyage over strange seas to India. The three Lords are anxious to fulfill their duty. They must hear these rumors and make a request to Kubilai Khan that we escort them to Persia by sea.

"'Prepare your spies. We need as many people as possible to spread this rumor.' I told my father.

"My father found it hard to believe that Kubilai would let us go."

"'I smell desperation, Marco. If he goes for it, then what? The lords are not just going to give you Li!'

"'I will make it happen,' I told him. 'Everything has worked out so far, Father. It will work.'

"My father became stone-cold. 'So, you will betray Kubliai for that girl?'

"It wasn't the first time I had heard that word, betrayal. It was true; the answer was yes. I didn't say it out loud. It made it too real.

"Not answering, I left to see Kubilai. Anxiety made my heart race as I entered his chamber, falling to my knees. I feared he would hear treason in my voice. But his face shone with happiness, and he instructed me to rise and join him. His fatherly gestures wounded me. Yet, the thought of Li healed me. I was doomed. I recounted my trip with many interesting stories, such as the fact that the pole star was no longer visible in Lesser Java, the flesh-eating humans, the abundance of fragrant woods on the reclusive islands, the huge rubies of Ceylon, the pearls and diamonds of India, and the trading habits of the honorable Banyan traders.

"I never flinched as words spilled out of my mouth. I informed Kubilai that the Banyan merchants had informed me of the road closure in Balkh due to a war between Ghazan and Nawruz, and that a large caravan belonging to a khan had turned back.

"Kubilai became irate, cursing the warlord Nawruz for screwing up trade and his loss of revenue. He grabbed my hand. 'I am so happy you returned safely and had a successful voyage. It will be our future.' My heart sank, feeling a tinge of guilt—yet not enough to change my course.

"For the next several days, I stayed at the palace and visited Physician Wu. As I entered the infirmary, he stared nervously and pulled me to his office. I answered his question before he spoke. 'I found her.' He lowered his head and looked up with tears. 'I was so scared; I had failed you and Li. Then your friend, Ehuang-chu, unexpectedly came back.'

"I told him I heard the story from my father and then bowed low. Thanking him for what he had done for us.

"He asked where Li was.

"I explained what happened and that she would return soon. Physician Wu looked concerned and said, 'A guard stole your letters. I am assuming they went to the person who influenced Li's departure. They won't be happy when Li returns. And who knows, they could use the letters against you.'

"I knew then that I needed to stay far away from Li until we left. Physician Wu asked me what would happen next. I decided not to tell him. He was a loyal friend and had already risked his life and position at the palace.

"The next day, I returned to my father. On my way, I visited Ehuang-chu. Her face lit up, but quickly changed to disappointment; I loved someone else. The disappointment quickly melted when I held my hand out, and a gorgeous, large ruby lay in my palm. Her eyes beamed. She softly laid her hand over the ruby. 'I am sorry. I almost failed you, but you found Li?'

"'What? How do you know her name?'"

"'I read your letter. Thank goodness,' Ehuang-chu said, giggling, 'or you wouldn't have found her.'

"I wrapped my arms around her, and she explained again what had happened.

"When I returned to my father's, they had already set my plan into motion, and Dai Xiuying and I headed back to Li fast. Anticipation grew with each mile as I came closer. If the plan worked, Dai Xiuying would continue to Zapton, telling Kim Chin-hae to prepare his ships to sail. Not only would we be taking Kokochin to King Arghun, but we would also be trading along the way. Our ships would be filled with merchandise from Cathay to sell, and then, his ships would return, carrying merchandise from India and Persia. It was the perfect plan."

Rustichello stopped Marco. "Did Kim Chin-hae return to Cathay with the new merchandise?"

"I can only assume. The ships all left, but I never heard from Kim Chin-hae again. And now I am here." Marco's face distorted with sorrow, and he slammed his fist on the table.

Rustichello urged Marco on. "What happened next?"

Marco's face relaxed as he envisioned Li. "We finally came across her caravan, but I was uncertain how to meet her.

They weren't staying in the gers, but inns. Suddenly, I realized this would work in our favor. Silence wasn't necessary any longer. I found an inn close to the caravan and boasted day and night that I, Marco Polo, had returned safely from a fantastic voyage exploring the unknown seas. I hoped Guo Yu would find me, and the lords would hear my story.

"Several days passed when someone knocked on my door. Hoping it was Guo Yu, I opened it. Stunned, it was the Crown Prince Wang Won, escorted by his guard. Without grace, he pushed me to the side and entered my room. He wasn't the young, infatuated prince I remembered, but a man with a mission. Not a word was spoken. Instead, he punched me, knocking me to the floor. Then, with an outstretched hand, he offered me help up, saying, 'If you weren't my favorite cousin's friend, I would kill you.'

"'Have you seen Li?' I questioned.

"'Not yet. That's why I am here. When Li left, I couldn't even say goodbye to her. They locked me up, releasing me only after she left. Ever since then, I have had people following her. You owe me; I haven't exposed Li and your secret. Messer Marco Polo, you are a bold man. I realized you loved her when I saw you and Li in the royal garden. It surprised me that you are willing to risk your life for love. I didn't expect that from you. No one knows that the caravan turned around. I've been waiting here to see her. Last night, I heard you boasting about your remarkable adventure to India. That's why I am here.

Marco turned to Rustichello. "Then the most remarkable words came out of his mouth. 'You must save her. I can't bear the thought of some strange man touching her. But I can handle it if it's you because I know she loves you. It's hard to swallow, but I will accept it.'

"His next words brought tears to my eyes. 'I am powerless, but you aren't. Help her!' His pleading words hurt.

"Sympathetically, I told him he could help by not talking to her again. If the culprits felt threatened again, worse things could happen.

"'This will be my last time seeing her until I have worked my plan out,' I told him.

"His face perked up. 'You have a plan?'

"'Yes.'

"'Tell me!' he said excitedly.

"'NO, you must trust me. The less you know, the better.'

"He pleaded. 'I must know!'

"Suddenly, there was a knock on the door. We both shivered. The crown prince and his guard moved to a dark corner. As I slowly opened the door, it pushed open. I could hear the crown prince gasp as Li threw her arms around me, kissing my face many times. Guo Yu quickly shut the door.

"We heard a booming voice: 'Stop!'

"Li stepped back, frightened, and looked toward the crown prince as he walked toward us. Li gasped.

"'I never had a chance. You fooled Kokochin and me. Messer Marco Polo was your secret. That's why we ghostly roamed the palace looking for him. And during the festivals, you flirted with me, knowing Messer Marco was in the palace. It makes sense now.'

"Li's head dropped, and in an embarrassed voice, she said, 'I'm sorry.' Her voice changed fast, becoming stronger. 'What are you doing here, anyway?'

"The crown prince hesitated momentarily. 'I heard the caravan was returning, and I had to see you before you entered the palace. I surely will be locked up again. Then I heard Messer Marco Polo was in town; I came to ask for his help. I can't envision you with another man, but I can accept it if it is with someone you love.' The crown prince stared at me. 'Your plan will work, right?'

"He sounded like the young boy I knew. I looked at Li and confidently answered. 'Yes!'

"I remember both of their faces vividly. They held such hope. I felt scared; my plan could fail. We sat and discussed what would need to happen. After an hour or so, there were two knocks on the door. The crown prince stood and bowed. 'I must leave now.' Li stood and walked over to him, gently kissed him on his cheek. 'I will never forget you.'

"The crown prince's face turned red. Li continued. 'You and Kokochin were my only friends. You made my life bearable. Kokochin has always accepted her destiny. We are different. We are selfish. I am sorry I have caused you pain. I pray you find happiness.'

"The crown prince responded. 'Happiness can have two sides: selfish or selfless. Back then, I fell into the trap of wanting more. This time, I will be happy if I see you leave with Messer Marco. At least you two will have a chance. For Kokochin and me, our lives have always been destined.' Again, the crown prince begged for forgiveness. 'I am sorry, Li, I wanted you and caused this to happen to you.'

"Li turned to the crown prince and then to me, sweetly saying, 'You don't need forgiveness, Ijir Bukhqa. It made Marco realize his feelings for me. It was worth it. I should thank you!'

"The crown prince smiled, but still with tears. Li bowed low before the crown prince. He turned and left.

"When the door shut, we rushed and held each other, absorbing the requited love. I spoke first. 'This will be the last time we talk until we are on the road to Zapton. Even then, only as acquaintances. Maybe we will be together when we arrive at Kim Chin-hae's house. However, until then, our primary concern is convincing the lords that they need me. I have started the plan and assume it's working because the crown prince was here. That means, hopefully, the lords will hear too.'"

***

Ulatai, Abushka, and Qoja's journeys had been long and hard. They had been on the road for almost two years and still had not fulfilled their duty: delivering a new queen to King Arghun. They didn't know eight months ago that they would face Kubilai Khan with their failure.

As they sat in the teahouse discussing what they should do, they heard gossip about a man named Messer Marco Polo, who had just returned safely from India, voyaging over strange seas. The crowd grew quiet as they sat drinking their tea. Everyone was staring at the two men that walked in. "That's him, Messer Marco Polo, Kubilai Khan's favorite man."

The three lords looked up. He was a foreigner but dressed and possessed a Tartar air. Ulatai, the oldest one, spoke first. "He looks familiar, a lot older, but I know that person. Yes. Yes, I remember now. I met him with his Latin father and uncle years ago as they passed through Tabriz. They knew Hulegu and Arghun. He was just a young boy then."

The other two lords responded. "It seems he has become quite important now."

Ulatai stood up and greeted Marco with a bow. Everyone in the room watched.

Chapter Forty-Nine

LI

1291 The Prince's Plea

Venice 1298

The afternoon at the apothecary, Golden Head, passed quickly. Guo Yu interrupted Li as she was gardening. "The sun will set soon. We should return." Guo Yu had another motive. He wanted to talk to Messer Maffeo.

Li was happy; working with her herbs raised her spirits. Returning home brought her back to reality.

Luca noticed Li's facial expression changed as they approached the palazzo. She spoke up. "Can you continue your story? I would love to hear more!"

Li's mood swung. "Of course, I'll continue when Guo Yu brings us dinner."

Guo Yu was pleased with the dinner decision as it would allow him to talk to Messer Maffeo.

When they entered the palazzo, Li and Luca went straight upstairs, delighted that Isabella was nowhere in sight. Guo Yu went to the kitchen and heard the servants whispering. They suspiciously stopped when Guo Yu entered. A bad feeling came over Guo Yu.

"Is Messer Maffeo home?" he asked.

"He's in the dining room with his family," Elena answered.

Guo Yu walked to the dining room, knocked, and entered the room. He bowed low. Messer Maffeo cordially greeted Guo Yu.

"Messer Maffeo, after dinner, could I speak to you?" Guo Yu glanced at Isabella; she seemed nervous.

Maffeo quickly answered. "In an hour, I will be in my study."

Guo Yu nodded, bowed, and left the room. When he entered Li's room with dinner, she had changed and was already telling Luca the continuation of her story.

"When Marco left the caravan, my heart broke. I didn't know when I would see him again. Kokochin kept asking me questions and was surprised I no longer left during the evening. She didn't understand.

"A week before arriving in Khanbaliq, Guo Yu came rushing into our room. The look on his face told me Marco was close. Guo Yu nodded. It took all I had to hide my excitement.

"'Someone needs you. This evening, I will return. Be ready,' Guo Yu said and left the room.

"Waiting for Guo Yu and the servant girl almost became unbearable as the hours passed. I circled the room, trying to contain my exploding heart, which drove Kokochin mad.

"Finally, Kokochin sat up in her bed. 'Marco must be back!' My heart sank. Kokochin continued talking, and I interrupted, trying to change the subject.

"'Someone is sick, and I am needed. That's why Guo Yu came this afternoon.'

"Kokochin giggled. 'Don't lie! It's been three weeks since I smelled musk; Marco's smell. He's the one who needs you.' I sat down on my bed with my head down.

"Kokochin rose and sat down beside me. 'Don't worry, I'm not telling anyone. I like Messer Marco. He's my friend, too, remember.'

"'I couldn't tell you,' I answered apologetically. Kokochin placed her hand on my arm. 'I understand. You and Marco are tempting fate. I worry this could end badly.'

"'Yes, I know. We should refrain from discussing this from now on. I don't want you to be involved,' I answered back.

"Finally, Guo Yu opened the door. Kokochin kissed me and went to her bed, facing the wall. I changed into the servants' clothes, covered my face with Marco's scarf, and left while the servant girl lay in my bed. We hurried to an inn down the lane. My racing heart was beating so fast I could hardly catch my breath. When the door opened, I hurled myself at him and covered his face with kisses until I heard a loud 'Stop.' Shocked, I stepped away. A person walked from the corner. I went limp. Marco caught me. It was Ijir Bukhqa, the crown prince."

Luca gulped. "Why was he there?"

"He was there asking for Marco's help."

"Help?" Luca repeated.

Li looked down. "He really loved me and asked Marco to protect me. I felt so guilty; I had taken advantage of him. He didn't stay long, but at least we got to say goodbye. When I first left the palace, they locked him in his chamber.

"In the inn, Marco told us his plan. He hoped the three lords would hear of his journey and request that he be their guide, taking them by ship to Persia. Marco decided to leave Cathay for good, and for the first time, he would lie to Kubilai.

Luca let out a deep breath. "How romantic!"

Li stared at Luca. "That wasn't romantic. Marco loved Kubilai. Sometimes, I feel guilty and wonder if he made the right choice. Some days, he feels Venice isn't his home any longer."

Guo Yu, who had been listening, spoke. 'He has no regrets, Li. There was no other choice for him. It was his fate, like Kokochin's and the crown prince's destinies. It was time to leave Cathay. He found his most beloved jewel, you. If he had to leave Cathay to keep you, so be it. It was an easy choice; he chose you."

Li lowered her head and whispered to herself. "Then why did he leave me now?"

She looked up, wiped her wet cheeks, and smiled, knowing the answer. She felt sorry for herself.

Luca clapped. "Now that's romantic! Did you ever see the crown prince again?"

"No, after that night in the inn, I never saw him again. I assume he married Kubilai Khan's great-granddaughter, his betrothed. Like Kokochin, his life had been destined.

"When I left Marco that night, I didn't know when I would see him again. The day Guo Yu brought me a note, my heart nervously pounded as I opened it."

Chapter Fifty

Marco

1298 Marco's Sorrow and Epiphany

Genoa prison 1298

As Marco sat in front of Rustichello, he continued his story. "After saying my sad goodbyes to Li at the inn, Dai Xiuying and I continued our plan, boasting about our trip. We walked into a teahouse, and before me were the three lords. As we walked in, the crowd grew quiet and stared. One lord stood and bowed, introducing himself. 'I'm Ulatai from the Empire of Ilkhanate. I met you years ago with your father and uncle. Please join us.'

"I was ecstatic; this could be easier than I thought. I bowed back, and the other two lords, Abishai and Qoja, stood, bowed, and introduced themselves. We sat. The evening was filled with questions, and by the end, Ulatai had shared their story. You could hear the desperation in his voice. That's when I suggested they should travel by sea.

"Ulatai instantly answered. 'Only if you are our guide. We will pay you handsomely.'

"I didn't want to sound too excited, so I hesitated to answer. 'I'm not so sure if Kubilai will allow me to go. I just returned after a year's voyage.' They stared at me for a moment and answered thoughtfully. 'Next week, we will be in Khanbaliq. We will convince him we must leave soon, and you should be our guide.'

"'I must also convince my father and uncle to accompany me.'

Marco looked at Rustichello. "Lying was easier than I thought."

"The three lords nodded, and Ulatai answered. ' I understand your father and uncle have a great thirst for money. We will also pay them well.' I thought, *My father's reputation must have traveled far and wide.*"

"Then what happened?" Rustichello excitedly asked.

"My heart wanted to go and tell Li my plan was working. However, Dai Xiuying was logical and insisted I write a note he would deliver to Guo Yu. Then, he would ride to Zapton and prepare for our next incredible life's chapter.

"I arrived a couple of days before the caravan, excited to tell my father my plan had worked. The three lords had been easy. Now, we faced the hard part, Kubilai Khan. My father and uncle anxiously prepared. I sat, waited, and worried until the caravan arrived.

"The three lords arrived and immediately asked to see Kubilai Khan. They fell on their knees and asked for his forgiveness, as they had failed their mission. With his forgiveness, Ulaatai wasted no time.

"'On our return, we heard of Messer Marco Polo and his remarkable sea voyage. Please allow Messer Marco Polo and the other two Latins to be our guides over the strange seas. We are desperate to accomplish our mission for King Arghun.'

"They left disappointed. Kubilai wasn't in a hurry for us to go.

"That evening, I went to Kubilai. He never mentioned the lords. He desired more stories. Every night for the next several days, I did just that until one night, when I entered his chambers, Kubilai's face was red, and his voice slurred from drinking as he called out my name.

"'Messer Marco Polo.'

"I crawled to him, and he placed his hand on my head and asked, 'Do you want to leave? The three lords have requested you to escort Kokochin and her attendees by ship to Arghun.'

"My nervous stomach fluttered; this was my chance. 'Yes, my lord. I feel it's time. We have served you loyally for the last seventeen years, and if you allow me, I can serve you one more time and assist the lords.'

"He motioned me to stand. With tears in his eyes, he spoke. 'My heart is sad. I will miss you and your stories. You can leave when I return to the Summer Palace. I will notify my minister to prepare fourteen ships in Zapton with enough supplies for two years.'

"I remember my heart pounding with his words. I would finally be with Li," Marco said softly.

"Kubilai continued. 'We will celebrate the White Festival with more grandeur than any other year, and I will take you hunting one last time. Maybe I can convince you to stay. Anyway, your last memories of me will remain with you forever as the most magnificent person you have ever known.'

"Physician Wu was the one who convinced him by asking, 'What would happen to Messer Marco, or who would protect him if anything happened to you? If you love him, you should release him.' Reluctantly, he agreed.

"It was a long two and a half months. I longed to see Li so severely that I felt I was suffocating. However, no one could make a mistake, including me. Rumors circulated in the palace that Crown Prince Wang Won's guardian had locked him up again, and the same guardian watched Li around the clock. The Crown Prince's destiny was to marry Buyan Kelmysh's daughter. The crown prince had not only written to Kim Chin-hae expressing his love for Li, but he also had written to his father. Someone in his court relayed this information to Buyan Kelmysh. She knew their closeness, and the letter sealed Li's future. She became the force behind Li's departure.

"My letters, which ended up in Buyan's hands by the guard, were not understood but caused suspicion. One slip up, and this time Li could mysteriously disappear."

Marco stopped talking momentarily, and his head dropped. He looked up at Rustichello, slowly talking again. "During those two and a half months, my betrayal grew larger. Our business made lots of money. From the day I obtained the permits, I was required to exchange our business profits of gold, silver, and precious gems for Kubilai's paper money. Now, I had permission from Kubilai to change it back to the jewels, gold, and silver. Here, your ledgers and the taxes paid had to match.

"Our trunks overflowed with treasures of many years of trade. We would return with a fortune. When I went to my father's to help him prepare for our departure and saw many heavy, unlocked trunks, my betrayal became real. Lifting the lid, I saw years of hidden treasures. It was the first time I accepted my father's greed and dishonesty. I turned a blind eye, closed the lid, and helped him place them in the wagons."

Rustichello's face showed no reaction, and he urged Marco to continue.

"Kubilai ordered us to come before him the day before we left. With sadness, he said goodbye and gave us two new gold tablets, proclaiming that we could travel freely throughout his territories and receive anything we might need. He also requested that we convey messages to the pope, the kings of France and Spain, and other kings of Christendom. I left feeling shame, but not enough to stop me.

"For months, I held my breath, and finally, when our departure day arrived. I exhaled the stale air of fear and inhaled the fresh air of relief.

"We left the palace in a huge caravan. Unsurprisingly, I experienced sorrowful pains as the palace guards bowed to me. I had been an honored citizen for the past seventeen years, and Kubilai Khan's palace had been my home. I would miss this place. At that moment, I had an epiphany—I no longer considered myself a Latin but a Tartar. I would start a new life with Li in a foreign place."

Chapter Fifty-One

Li

1291 Li's Return

Venice 1298

Luca was like a kid. She was so impatient that she was bouncing in her seat. "What did the letter say? Hurry, what did the letter say?"

"It said he had talked to the lords, and the plan was working. We would soon be together."

Luca sat back in her seat and took a deep breath.

"It was months before that happened." Li continued. "We arrived in Khanbaliq at the end of December. Kubilai Khan insisted that Marco and the lords attend the White Festival in February and an incredible hunt in March. He was reluctant to release Marco and tried everything to convince him not to leave. We didn't depart for Zapton until the end of April.

Luca stopped Li. "A hunt?"

Li looked off into space.

"Can you imagine four elephants bound together with a beautiful wooden shelter sitting on their backs? The inside glittered with cloth of beaten gold, with Kubilai Khan sprawled among elegant furs, barking orders to everyone around him. They cover the outside with tiger skins. It was large enough for several people, and his twelve best gyrfalcons sat above him atop the shelter. Thousands of falconers, other barons, and soldiers who rode around him also accompanied him. It is such a spectacular sight. When Kubilai arrives in Cachar Modun, near the sea, he creates the finest residence, as if he were in the finest city. The first tent, facing south, is large enough to accommodate thousands of soldiers. Another

tent facing west is where Kubilai entertained, and superfine sable fur filled his sleeping chambers. Outside were skins of great beauty, striped with black, white, and orange, protecting him from the rains and winds. His entire house staff, physicians, astrologers, and palace officials attend. He even brings his many mistresses, housed in splendid pavilions.

"I once went with Physician Wu. Every night was a feast."

Luca laughed and clapped with excitement.

"While Marco stayed with Kubilai, I didn't take any chances. Even for the White Festival, I stayed in my chambers. Finally, the news arrived that Marco and the three Lords convinced Kubilai. Physician Wu played a crucial role, reminding Kubilai that he was aging and that, in the future, he might not be able to protect Marco. Deep down inside, Kubilai Khan knew he was right. Again, Physician Wu proved to be a worthy friend.

"I often wondered what happened to Ijir Bukhqa and Kokochin after we left them, but I hope great happiness filled their lives.

"When Kubilai and Marco returned from the hunt, Kubilai left for Shang-du, his summer palace, and our caravan left for Zapton."

Li stopped talking. Guo Yu stood and excused himself. "I must leave for a moment." He looked over at Luca. She nodded.

Li noticed the passing nods. She questioned Luca, knowing Guo Yu would never tell, but Luca was easy.

Luca avoided her and kept insisting that she continue her story.

Li finally dropped it and began her story again. *I would ask Guo Yu when he returned.*

"When I saw Marco, I thought my heart would jump out of my chest. It felt like the old days when I searched the palace, hoping for a glimpse. But when our eyes met this time, there wasn't even a smile or a nod. Marco looked away. My body trembled, and my stomach ached. My mouth opened, and just then, Kokochin rode next to me and stared concernedly. I lowered my head, knowing she was right. I would have to wait."

Meanwhile, Guo Yu walked down the stairs and knocked on Messer Maffeo's study door. The door opened, and it was Isabella. Guo Yu bowed, and as she left, they stared into each other's eyes, and she smiled slyly.

Messer Maffeo greeted Guo Yu. "You wanted to speak to me?"

"Yes, my lord. Have you heard anything from Marco? It has been so long since we have seen him."

"That's funny; Isabella was asking me the same question. I found that strange since Marco and she are usually estranged. Maybe it is true that absence makes the heart grow fonder."

Guo Yu murmured to himself. *I don't think so.* Then he continued. "I'm concerned about his whereabouts. Isn't there someone you could ask? You know important people."

Maffeo hesitated and then said in a condescending voice, "I will ask around. Hopefully, we will learn something."

Guo Yu bowed and left the room. As he walked out the door, he thought, *I'm afraid the apple doesn't fall far from the tree.* He didn't trust Messer Maffeo and wished Messer Niccolò were still with them. Maffeo had always been greedy and would love for Marco not to return. Then, he would receive his estate. His daughter had another motive: she hated Li.

Not happy, he returned to Li and Luca as Li began to tell Luca about arriving in Zapton.

Chapter Fifty-Two

Marco

1291 "The Marriage"

Genoa Prison 1298

Marco continued, reminiscing out loud. "For the next two months, as we traveled to Zapton, I hungered for Li and rode with hunger pains, unable to feast. The only thing that kept me going was my memories. Every time I passed through certain cities, memories flooded my mind. I tried to memorize everything, as most people have never seen this world. Someday, I wanted to share my knowledge, but not like this—from a prison cell.

"The first city was Yangzhou. Remember, Rustichello, I lived here for three years, spying for Kubilai and reporting back if the Manzi weren't loyal. I also ran our tea and salt business here, but most importantly, this is where Kim Chin-hae and I grew our friendship and partnership.

"But when we reached Lin'an, I became overwhelmed. It was here that my life's course altered. It was here I saved Li.

"As we traveled, Li and I imagined our lives together. The fire we had for each other had to be contained, and as time went by, the fire grew hotter, making it impossible for us to look at each other. We were afraid we would get burned, and our love would turn to ashes. Our friends helped us resist our dangerous temptation when we became weak. My father and uncle rode alongside me, ensuring I didn't make a mistake. Kokochin and Guo Yu controlled Li. Everywhere, there were spying eyes.

"The days passed slowly, and our future weighed heavily on our hearts. When we passed through Chuzhou, I thought of Kim Chin-hae once more. I met him here and will never forget that day. The arrogant, handsome man waltzed over to my table and introduced himself. We were so young and ambitious.

"When we traveled past Fuzhou, Lis entered my mind, and I felt her warm touch on my shoulder.

"Remember, Rustichello, this was where Kim Chin-hae freed her, and soon, we would pass where I saved him from the tiger."

Marco shivered and wondered what would have happened if he hadn't passed that day. *Would Lis have saved him?*

"We finally reached the ledge where I saw the smoke billowing from Lis's village that day. Again, the smoke billowed. Kim Chin-hae and Lis were calling me. They must be. I felt the warmth of her hand resting on my shoulder."

Rustichello nodded and then shook his head in disbelief.

"Were they there?" Rustichello had to ask.

"Yes, at the crossroads, waiting. I hadn't seen Kim Chin-hae since India. My excitement was uncontrollable. Everyone watched as I heeled my horse and rode at full speed toward them. I jumped from my horse, hugging and begging them to help me see Li as the rest of the caravan caught up.

"Lis laughed. 'Why do you think we are here? We have prepared a feast. It will be a perfect excuse to stop for a few days.'"

"Really?" Rustichello interrupted Marco.

"Yes, I told you she was a shaman. She saw us coming in her dreams," Marco confidently said.

Rustichello shook his head.

"Excitement flowed through my body when I heard the news. Kim Chin-hae took command and walked over to the three lords, bowing and introducing himself in Persian. 'My name is Kim Chin-hae. I am Messer Marco Polo's partner. Welcome to my wife's village. We have prepared a feast for you.'

"They looked over at me. I nodded. Kim Chin-hae continued. 'Your journey has been long, and everyone needs a respite. The caravan can camp in this open field. My guards will be on duty. This evening, the villagers will bring food, drink, and entertainment.'

"The three lords bowed, accepting Kim Chin-hae's invitation. That evening, Chin-hae kept serving the lords and their guards' drinks until they retired or passed out.

"My father surprisingly aided Kim Chin-hae. *Is my father finally on my side?*

"Late evening, Kim Chin-hae walked over to me and whispered, 'It's your turn now. Walk toward the village.'

"I looked over toward my father and uncle. Both had passed out at the table. The lords returned to their gers. Finally free, I ran down the village road."

Marco stopped talking and walked to his bed.

Rustichello shook his head as he watched Marco lie down facing the wall. The storytelling ended.

Marco's heart raced as he remembered that night.

Li was beautiful. As she walked toward me, her small torch cast a radiating light upon her face and jet-black hair. I couldn't believe it as I gathered her in my arms.

She whispered, "They prepared a hut for us."

I remembered my fear and her courage as we walked hand in hand. Finally, our fire could be extinguished.

We walked past Lis's mother's hut, continued to the end of the road, and turned toward a lone lit hut.

Li whispered, "Lis told me this is their house, but it's ours tonight."

Marco smiled to himself. He remembered Kim Chin-hae's stories. He then continued remembering.

I wasn't expecting Wei, Lis's mother, dressed in a shaman's dress, waiting for us. Confused, I looked around. Plates of tea cakes and bottles of wine covered the table.

Chin-hae and Lis opened the door, carrying packages. Lis gave Li hers, and Chin-hae gave me his. Handing his package, Chin-hae whispered, "Remember the binyeo I gave you years ago for your soul mate?"

I looked mystified.

"It's your wedding day. You need to exchange gifts. While you retrieve her gift, Lis will help Li prepare. Your horse is out front. That is where you carry it, right?"

I nodded. Chin-hae grabbed my hand and pulled me out the door. Downstairs, he insisted I open the package. Chin-hae looked proud. "It's what Miao men wear when they marry." Chin-hae directed me toward the warm pond, Lis's and his favorite place.

As we stood by the pond, my face appeared worried. The look surprised Chin-hae.

"You do want to marry Li?"

I hesitated. "I love Li but fear for her. My greed for her is too great. I am older and should be the reasonable one, protecting her. From afar, it was easy, but up close, failure is intimate. The future is so unknown."

Kim Chin-hae reflected as the pond reflected the crescent moon. "Aren't all our futures unknown? Your destinies began the day you found her and were sealed the day you rushed to her side.

"Like Lis and I, the day we crossed paths, and I rescued her, I unchained our destiny. Our lives have had many obstacles, but we have survived. Everyone should experience true love once in life, yet few people are as lucky as we are."

Chin-hae slapped me on the back. "Come to your senses. Your love is waiting for you. But you should wash first. You smell like your horse." Roaring laughter filled the air.

I entered the hut and found Li in a royal blue dress, a silver headdress, and a large silver necklace.

Chin-hae looked at Lis and smiled. Seeing the blue dress—the dress Lis wore when they married—made his heart flutter.

Li and I stood in front of Wei in our borrowed attire. The drumming and chanting began.

Marco continued to picture Chin-hae standing next to him, translating Wei's words, and Li lovingly nodding as Wei continued with our vows.

Then Li unfolded the silk material, revealing a long jade binyeo—with two butterflies on a peony carved into it—that Chin-hae and Lis had given him years ago. At the time, he was unaware that Li was his soulmate, but Lis knew.

Li stared at it momentarily. In a quiet voice, she said, "Your medicine bag."

I nodded. "That's when I knew for sure."

Li smiled and then handed me my soul lock. "It matches Kim Chin-hae's. It will protect your souls."

I placed my hand on my heart. It fluttered like the sound of a thousand birds' wings taking flight in a bamboo forest.

I can't recall every word, but there was one phrase that I have never forgotten. "Two people from different worlds wish to marry. Their journey won't be an easy one."

Wei was right. It wasn't because of our lack of love but because of other people.

Marco remembered what happened next.

I gently pulled Li in until our lips met.

Everyone in the room left. I blew out the candles and carried Li to our bed. We both cried. Our first time together was different from this one. We had said the words out loud. There was no turning back.

For the next few hours, we submerged ourselves in love, surrendering to each other's wishes as our bodies moved as one. We didn't know when the next time would come.

Marco remembered his words to her. *"I will make sure no other man has you. You have my promise."*

As Marco remembered, he moaned.

Rustichello questioned him.

Marco didn't answer. Tears slid down his face. His fists tightened. He had failed her. *Who knows what is happening now? Left alone with only Guo Yu by her side—strangers in a strange land surrounded by cruel people.* Raising his fist, he rammed into the wall. He held his bloody, aching fist, relishing his pain. He deserved it.

The next thought eased his pain, and Marco agreed with Chin-hae's words: *Everyone deserves true love once.* And Li was his.

***

Meanwhile, after the ceremony. Lis and Kim Chin-hae smiled at each other as they walked toward the pond. They looked back. The hut went black. Lis reiterated that the moon was near its waxing phase. "The moon will soon emerge with new energy. It's a time to set new goals for our lives. Reaching the pond, they faced each other. Lis and Kim Chin-hae undressed. Their eyes never left each other.

He wrapped his arms around her and whispered in her ear. "I'm going only until the first ship supplies are emptied and reloaded with new merchandise. Marco doesn't know yet. The years I was away from you and the twins became torturous. This trip will be a lot longer. Pak Byeong-ho will accompany Marco on our best ship for the rest of the trip and sail it back after they reach their destination."

Lis let out a sigh of relief. "With all my heart, I hoped I would hear these words. Today, when Mother recited their vows, our vows, I repeated them too. I never would hold you back. It had to be your decision." Standing on her tiptoes, she kissed his lips. They walked into the warm pond. The darkness surrounded them as their powerful love ignited.

Chapter Fifty-Three

Li

1291 Li's Version "The Marriage"

Venice 1298

Guo Yu wasn't gone long. Li stopped talking as he entered the room, giving him a dirty look. "We'll talk later. I was telling Luca about our journey to Zapton," Li said to Guo Yu.

"I thought my heart would jump out of my chest when I finally saw Marco. But when our eyes met this time, there wasn't even a smile or a nod. Marco looked away. I was heartbroken, but Kokochin made me understand. The following months were torturous and seemed much longer than our return to Khanbaliq. At least then, I saw Marco secretly in the evening. Now, I couldn't look at him. If our eyes met, my heart melted with the fire in his eyes. Kokochin or Guo Yu broke the spell and brought me back to reality when they rode between us.

"As we rode through Lin'an, my thoughts turned to my past. I never returned. Remember Luca, this was where I lost my mother, and Marco found me?"

Li stopped talking, walked to her favorite window, and looked down at the canal. Her voice softened. "I often wondered how my life would have been if the Great Khan hadn't defeated my country. Would I have met Marco? Or was our life always destined? That's what our teachings tell us. We make our choices before we are born. Marco followed his path; I followed mine, and we found each other. But were we destined to be together always or for only a short time?"

Guo Yu interrupted Li. "You have had more than most people, whether short or long. You found him, your soulmate.

Li turned and smiled. "But I'm greedy. I want him for a lifetime. I want him like Lis has Kim Chin-hae."

She walked back to the table and sat. Luca's face looked sad. Li patted Luca's hand.

"Lis's mother married us."

Luca's face perked up. She clapped. "Tell me how, when?"

Li looked at Guo Yu. "We were almost to Zapton when Marco raced his horse toward two people on the road. When we reached Marco, I recognized Kim Chin-hae. I had seen him in the palace a couple of times. The woman had to be Lis. Marco talked about her on our journey back from Balkh. Containing my excitement was difficult as my chances of seeing Marco grew. The three lords and Marco stood and listened to Kim Chin-hae as he pointed to an open field. Marco nodded and rode to Guo Yu. 'Tonight, and for the next three days, Kim Chin-hae and Lis have prepared a feast for us.' As the soldiers assembled our gers, my heart raced.

"It wasn't long afterward that Lis visited. Her aura was powerful, and my hand tingled when she grabbed it."

Luca's face turned pale. "Weren't you scared?"

Li hesitated. "Even though my hand tingled, and her power pierced my soul, I felt only purity. It was strange and surprisingly calming.

"Kokochin, stretched out on her silk pillows and blankets, watched with frightened eyes. I laughed. Kokochin, who never showed fear, was scared. She must have felt her aura like I did.

"'Kokochin, may Li and I join you?' Lis asked sweetly.

"Kokochin quickly sat up erect. 'Of course, how rude of me.'

"'Bring in tea,' Kokochin ordered her servant.

"Lis touched Kokochin's hand. Kokochin looked down and slowly raised her head. With a pale face, she asked, 'Who are you?'

"'I am the wife of Kim Chin-hae, the crown prince's cousin.'

"'You're the shaman that caused the excitement in the crown prince's family.'

Lis laughed heartily. 'Yes, I am that woman.'

"We sat, laughed, and drank our tea. Suddenly, Lis looked at me seriously and asked, 'Are you prepared to do the same?'

"'What?'

"'Risk everything for Messer Marco?'

"Lis's tender face suddenly turned frightening. 'We love Messer Marco, and we would do anything for him. He asked us to arrange a rendezvous between you two. I wanted to hear from you first.'

Li giggled and said, "Kokochin gasped. Just like you just did, Luca. I recall feeling a strength I had never experienced before. I answered her. "'At five, I fell in love. Since then, Marco has been my life. Without him, I wouldn't have survived. I would die for him!'

"Lis's face lit up. 'That's what I needed to hear. We have a plan.' Suddenly, Lis directed her attention to Kokochin. 'I can feel your concern. You have something to say?'

"Sweetly, Kokochin said, 'Li, you are much braver than I. I have never allowed myself to think of anything but my duty, except once when I longed to marry the crown prince. Finding my love was one-sided, I quickly returned to my old self and duty. I am satisfied with my life. Li, I am worried that Messer Marco and you could die. You have been my friend since I was ten, and I selfishly hoped you would be my companion and friend for a very long time.'

"I hugged Kokochin tightly. 'It's my destiny, Kokochin, like this is yours.'

"Kokochin hugged me back and looked up at Lis. 'What do you want me to do?'

"'Continue to be Li's friend. After the villagers serve the food, take Li and go to your ger, then wait. My husband will continue serving drinks until the three lords and the guards have passed out or retired. Then, Guo Yu will retrieve you, Li, and show you our hut. It will be yours tonight. My mother will wait for you. Chin-hae will instruct Messer Marco to walk toward the village, where you will wait for him.'

"'Why?' I questioned Lis.

"'Why? You want to marry him, right? My mother will perform the ceremony.'

"I was so shocked, I lost my breath. My face turned bright red and hot, and Kokochin choked. After I recovered, I asked, 'Does Marco know?'

"'He knows it is his destiny,' Lis answered directly.

"By this time, tears filled my eyes. It was like a dream. I feared my overflowing heart, so full of love, would expand and burst when I saw Marco, and everyone around would know.

"'Kokochin, will you help me?' I pleaded.

"Then Lis placed her hand on my shoulder, startling me. Her touch radiated a sensation I had never felt before. She told me, 'Your love runs deep. Marco is a lucky man. I will see you tonight.'"

Luca clapped louder. "Tell me more."

"The evening seemed to take forever. Kokochin sat where she blocked Marco from my view. Finally, Lis nodded to Kokochin. She tapped me on the hand. We bowed to the highly intoxicated three lords and quickly returned to the ger.

"I walked in circles, nervously wringing my hands. Kokochin, irritated, tried to hide her fear and asked me to stop and arrange my bed as I had done when I left before. I knew she wondered how this would end. Shortly, Guo Yu entered. Blood rushed to my face as my heart excitedly raced. I hadn't been with Marco in almost five months.

"Guo Yu showed me the hut and left me by a large tree on the village road. As I waited, I could hardly catch my breath. Finally, a silhouette of a person walked toward me; It was Marco.

Checking the surroundings, I ran toward him, and with his arms outstretched, he gathered me up like a greedy person gathering treasures. I melted in his arms and whispered, 'Kim Chin-hae and Lis have prepared a hut for us.' We strolled hand in hand down a trail surrounded by wildflowers that led to the lone hut."

Luca swooned.

"When we entered, Marco was surprised when he saw Wei. I realized Marco knew nothing. We hadn't noticed Kim Chin-hae and Lis were behind us. They had thought of everything: the dress and love tokens, Miao's wedding customs, soul lock for Marco, and a binyeo for me—the one I showed you, Luca."

Luca nodded. "A soul lock?"

"Yes, Lis gave Kim Chin-hae one when they married. 'We are both married to men who live dangerously. The soul lock protects their souls,' Lis said.

"The ceremony was a blur, and I can only remember the chanting and drumming. My heart couldn't believe this was happening. I spent my entire life searching for him, and now I have found him. He was by my side and belonged to me. That night, we cried together and became one.

"I returned to the ger before the new day broke. Guo Yu and Kokochin were waiting for me. She was like you now, Luca. She wanted to hear every detail.

"The next two nights became our heaven. Kim Chin-hae ensured it; he kept the three lords happy. The day we left the village, Wei invited me to her hut. Never having been to a shaman's house before, I carefully looked around and thought of Kim Chin-hae. *He, too, married a person from a different world. They have overcome.*

"Wei watched me as I slowly looked over her herb supply; most I knew. Then she handed me a bag. 'Take this with you. You might need it. It's mostly Dong Quai.'

"Dong Quai?" Luca repeated.

"'For pregnancy,' Wei told me. It would have been lethal if I were with child. Heads would have rolled."

Luca cringed.

Li continued while nonchalantly touching her growing belly. She felt life today. The last time she saw Marco, she had decided never to drink the tea ever again. So far, no one has noticed.

"The next week, we were in Zapton preparing for our departure. Marco kept his distance. It was strange. My heart ached less because I knew he was mine. We would soon be on the ship: Marco's domain, not the three lords. There, we would have more freedom."

Li stood up again and walked to her window. “I think it is time to stop.” Li picked up her erhu and sat down. Guo Yu and Luca shuddered.

Chapter Fifty-Four

Marco

Marco's Exodus

Genoa prison 1298

Marco had drifted to sleep and awoke to the rattling sound of the small door window being opened. His stomach growled. Rustichello was standing at the door, grabbing the food. Marco rose and sat at the table, waiting.

Marco, with his mouth full, started talking.

"When we arrived in Zapton, our caravan members settled in the inns near the wharf except for Kokochin, Li, the head lord, Ulaatai, and my father and uncle, whom Kim Chin-hae invited to stay at his home. That night, before they arrived, Lis served Chin-hae, Son Jun-ho, Pak Byeong-ho, Dai Xiuying, Guo Yu, and me drinks and food on the outside porch as the twins practiced with their wooden swords in the lit courtyard. We were happy, but needed time together, just us. We were a misfit group, yet our lives had been intimately intertwined for many years; our closeness ran deep. Our futures were unknown. Even though our hearts were heavy, our friendships strengthened us.

"Kim Chin-hae became serious and stopped joking and drinking. 'Before the drinks control our minds, we must discuss our journey.' The table went silent. Before anyone questioned him, he continued. 'We have fourteen ships filled with two years of supplies. I have hired trustworthy captains myself. As each ship empties its supplies, they will replenish them with merchandise from the area and then return to Zapton. I will be here to meet them.'

"I panicked. 'What? What did you say?'

"Kim Chin-hae, with moist eyes, pointed to the twins and smiled at Lis. 'In my youth, nothing interfered with my desires. Only I was important. My heart has changed. I can't leave them. Initially, I had planned to go as far as the first islands, but I changed my mind. Someone needs to take care of our business. Pak Byeong-ho and Dai Xiuying will stay with you until you reach Hormuz.'

"I was horrified. The thought of leaving Kim Chin-hae pierced my heart, but I understood the reason behind it. Our journey was going to be hard and long. How could I ask him to leave Lis for that long?

"With my head hanging low, I nodded in agreement. Lis walked around the table and poured more drinks. She stopped next to me, smiled, and placed her hand on my shoulder. Her warmth filled my body. 'We both paid our debt. It's time to go on with our lives.'

"Kim Chin-hae leaned into me and whispered. 'Let's continue the discussion tomorrow.'

"The rest of the evening, everyone drank until we passed out. I awoke with a pounding head as the rising sun poured into my window. Suddenly, a vision appeared; it was Li helping me into my room and tumbling into bed together. Our lips touched as she snuggled into my body. Fear ran through my body, and I quickly looked for Li. I was relieved; only I remained. *Or was it a dream?* I quietly rose, dressed, and began to exit the room. The minute the door slid open, a servant handed me a cup of foul-smelling tea. 'It's from Lady Li. She said it's for your pounding head. Master Kim is waiting for you in his chamber.'

"Suddenly, I remembered him telling me he wasn't coming and rushed toward his room. As I passed the outdoor deck, I stopped. Li, Kokochin, Lis, the lord, my father, and my uncle were enjoying breakfast. Standing at the door, I bowed and continued walking. Li's face looked enraptured. Lis placed her hand on Li's to remind her to be discreet.

"When I entered Chin-hae's chamber, my disappointment showed. He paid no attention and went right into the details. 'The ships will be ready to sail in fourteen days with high tide. Unfortunately, your timing is off. On our first trip, we arrived in Lesser Java, perfectly timed, and voyaged straight to India. When you arrive in Lessor Java this time, you must wait on the monsoon currents, which could be five months.'

"I reminded him it was safer there than here. He reminded me of the flesh-eating natives—an alarming situation. For the next three months, I planned how to protect us."

Rustichello cringed.

Marco continued. "Kim Chin-hae was all business and continued talking. 'However, by the time you reach there, you should have at least two empty ships. You will have plenty of time to load the empty ships with the island's overflowing treasures, the spices we never see here, and their multitude of woods, aloeswood, spikenard, brazilwood, and ebony.'

"Staring at me with a twinkle in his eyes, he told me. 'I hear there is gold in their mountains, lots of it. Five months could be fruitful.'

“I stared back. ‘If we don’t get eaten first.’

“We laughed until there were tears. Suddenly, our happy tears turned to tears of sadness. Chin-hae stared at me with watering eyes. ‘I will miss you, my friend. You made me grow and expand my world. Even though our cultures, skin color, and eye shape may differ, people are the same. We yearn for love and desire happiness. Some of us go to the extreme.’

“He grabbed my hand. ‘I’m happy I met you, and hope we meet again, Messer Marco Polo. You will remain in my heart forever.’

“ I felt the same and told him so. The room fell silent as we hid our tears. Moments later, Kim Chin-hae continued talking about business. This time, I stopped and scolded him. ‘I have been your business partner for many years. I know what to do.’

“Kim Chin-hae frowned. ‘I’m nervous, that's all.’

“The fourteen days went fast. Lis and Kim Chin-hae walked with us down the long pier to our fourteen ships and stayed until we sailed. My ship belonged to Kim Chin-hae, built to his specs, highly sophisticated, and equipped with the newest equipment. Pak Byeong-ho would be the captain, and I was his second-in-command. Like the others, it had four masts and twelve sails. But it was the only one with sails of blue displaying a qeej, a musical instrument; an object of the Miao Hmong, symbolizing their ability to communicate with the spirit world. The others flew the flags of the Khan, the moon, and the sun. Kokochin and her entire convoy would be on my ship. It had over 60 beautiful cabins and 250 sailors. Five of the fourteen carried the same number of sailors; the rest were smaller ships. All would carry supplies and cargo to sell.”

Marco slyly smiled at Rustichello. “One cabin was only for our treasure trunks, which continued to grow over the next three years.

“It took most of the day to settle in the women and the others. Li and Kokochin’s cabin sat between mine and my father's. The lords were next to my father’s.

“Sadly, we had our last meal with Kim Chin-hae and Lis on the evening before we departed. But secretly, we were all happy. So far, no one has caught us.

“With the full moon high in the sky, Kim Chin-hae, Lis, Kokochin, Li, and I stood at the gangplank. Lis, usually a strong woman, seemed weak. Chin-hae held her. Lis never uttered a word. She let her hand do that as she touched each of us on the shoulder, allowing her love to flow. Lis’s touch will remain with me forever.

Everyone went their separate way, leaving Kim Chin-hae and me alone. We stood facing each other. His servant ran over to us, handing Kim Chin-hae a sword. It was mine, the one I gave him when he sailed to war. He held it out. ‘I’m reluctantly returning this to you. It saved my life twice. I pray you won’t need this, but it will do the same for you if something arises.’

“Taking it, I thought, *I will pray too.* We stood for a moment longer before I hugged him, something Chin-hae wasn’t expecting, and then I ran up the gangplank. I turned, waving violently. ‘I hope our paths meet again, my brother.’

“Pak Byeong-ho barked orders. ‘Make way to sail!’

“The oars hit the water, and the crew worked vigorously to raise the sails. I stood and watched the life I loved disappear.

“Before we reached Venice, we heard Kubilai Khan had died. I knew then I would never return to see my friends again.”

Marco walked toward his bed and fell into it. He didn’t say another word till morning.

Chapter Fifty-Five

LI

Isabella's Rage

Venice 1298

As Li sat and placed her erhu on her lap, Luca and Guo Yu cringed, anticipating her tears and crying music that drove Isabella crazy.

Guo Yu stood to leave. Li stopped playing, stared at him, and unexpectedly spoke. "Where did you go today? I saw you and Luca nod to each other. *WHY?*" Her voice had risen an octave. "Did something happen?"

Guo Yu hesitated. "I am concerned. We haven't heard any news of Messer Marco in a while. I went to see Messer Maffeo, hoping he could ask any superiors about Messer Marco."

Li lowered her head and, in a quieter voice, said, "What did he say?"

Guo Yu lied. "Messer Maffeo agreed to my request."

Li nodded and continued to play. She knew both were lying. *Guo Yu didn't want to worry me. And Maffeo has no love for Marco. He only loves his money. He wouldn't care if he ever returned.* Her music cried harder.

Guo Yu shuddered as her music got louder as he exited. He stood outside her door, knowing it wouldn't be long before Isabella would stomp down the hall.

Luca turned down Li's bed, blew out the candles, and left the room. When she opened the door, it surprised her to see Guo Yu waiting for her. Now Luca understood. He had lied to Li. They walked across the hall.

Luca spoke quietly. "What happened?"

Guo Yu, very serious, answered. "When I entered Maffeo's study, Isabella was leaving. I had a feeling they had a secret."

"What do you think it is?" asked Luca.

He shrugged. "I'm not sure. We'll wait and see if he tells me anything."

Suddenly, they heard footsteps. Isabella was coming up the stairs, and her face resembled a bull in a rage. Guo Yu quickly moved before Li's door, preventing Isabella from entering.

"Get out of my way, you slant-eye moron."

Guo Yu's face showed no expression, and he quietly responded. "My job is to protect Li from hurtful words or bodily harm. I am just doing my job."

Isabella stopped, backed up, and faced Luca, violently slapping her. Swiftly, Guo Yu grabbed Luca's raised hand before she returned the slap.

Her reactions surprised her. Since getting to know Li, she has gained strength and courage.

Guo Yu squeezed Luca's wrist hard. She slowly lowered her hand. The fire in her eyes extinguished, and she lowered her head. "I am sorry, my lady. It was a natural response. Please forgive me."

Isabella's mouth opened to speak, but her father, Maffeo, had reached the top of the stairs and said condescendingly, "She forgives you. Isabella, don't you think it's time for you to retire? We will talk tomorrow."

Isabella's rage melted slightly, and she plodded down the hall to her room.

Maffeo nodded at Guo Yu and Luca, and he descended the stairs.

Luca fell to the floor, crying. Guo Yu gently picked her up, saying, "Go. Today's troubles will be here tomorrow. We will solve them then."

Luca frowned and left.

Guo Yu stood in front of Li's door until her music faded away. He opened the door and entered the dark room. A stream of moonlight from her window exposed Li's body, sprawled out over the bed. *She has finally quit crying*, he thought. Closing the door, he walked to his room with a splitting headache and a hurting heart. Things were getting worse. *Marco has to return soon.*

Chapter Fifty-Six

Marco

"Caught"

Genoa prison 1298

The following day, Marco didn't wait for breakfast. He sat down at the table and shuffled through Rustichello's papers. He was not really reading; he was thinking. *What would I say next?*

Rustichello heard the papers, rolled over, and looked at Marco. "What happened next?"

Marco hesitated for a few minutes, then spoke. "Li and I remained painfully careful for the next few weeks, only seeing each other late when everyone slept. But it didn't matter."

"Why?" Rustichello asked.

"One month out, during our late-night rendezvous, Dai Xiuying, standing guard at my door, was called out for some fake emergency. Suddenly, the door opened, with Li snuggled in my arms. Lord Qoja, with a sly, smiling face, walked confidently in. He quietly closed the door behind him.

"I grabbed my sword and wheeled it high above my head.

"Lord Qoja kept smiling and sat down. 'No need for violence. I am sure we can solve this peacefully.'

"I lowered my sword, and he motioned us to sit. Outside, there were running footsteps, and the door suddenly opened. It was Dai Xiuying. Fearfully, he looked around the room. I nodded, and he reluctantly turned, shutting the door behind him.

"Calmly, Lord Qoja talked in a low, soft voice. 'While in Khanbaliq, I received a letter. Fortunately for you, the servant mistakenly gave it to me. It was intended for Lord Ulaatai.

"'Fortunately?' I asked.

"'I am much more sentimental and understanding in love, especially a forbidden one. When I read the letter, I realized why you agreed to help us so quickly.'

"'Letter?'

"'You know, the letter you wrote to Physician Wu that he never received. Let's see if I remember correctly; the servant belonged to Lady Budashiri.'

"Li gasped. I turned to her, and she whispered. 'That's the mother of the crown prince's betrothed, I am sure.'

"Lord Qoja continued. 'Initially, she didn't understand the letter until she heard you had volunteered to escort us to Tabriz. The letter made sense. That's when she sent the letter to Lord Ulaatai.'

"His smile became larger. 'That's why I said, *fortunately*. Lord Ulaatai wouldn't have been as understanding and cooperative as I.' His eyes glowed with greed.

"I smiled back. 'Please accept a gift for your great understanding.'

"'You are too generous, Messer Marco Polo,' replied Lord Qoja with another enormous smile as he stood. I'm so happy we understood each other. I hate bloodshed of any kind.'

"'I will have it delivered to your room tonight,' I told him.

"Lord Qoja walked to the door and turned. 'I highly suggest you remain very careful. I am greedy, but I have integrity. My fellow lords are greedier, have no integrity, and do not understand forbidden love.'

"When the door closed behind him, Li fell upon the bed face down, crying. 'We are doomed.'

"I tried to comfort her. For some reason, I trusted him."

"Well, what happened?" Rustichello excitedly asked.

"That night, I had a trunk delivered to his room. Everything went as planned from that day until we reached Lesser Java."

"Is that where the men ate human flesh?" An excited Rustichello asked.

"Yes! Kim Chin-hae had been right. When we arrived at the northern point of Java, we had to wait five months for the ocean currents to change. I worried for months about how we would protect everyone. Unfortunately, I was unaware of what lay ahead.

"The king in Lesser Java was rich and powerful and was only nominally subject to the Khan. This, nominally at least, allowed us to disembark from our ships with about 2000 men. With these 2000 men, we built five watch towers, 4000 paces from the seashore. Behind the towers, we created a great semi-circle ditch that met the sea on both sides, hoping this would protect us from the savage tribes that would love to capture and eat us.

"Luckily, we soon discovered the islanders in this part of the island were kind and came to barter food. A mutual trust grew, and many men soon shared the islander's wine. With loosened tongues, my men soon discovered the whereabouts of the gold Kim Chin-hae talked about. Regrettably, it lay deep in another kingdom on the west side of the Minangkabau highlands. You had to travel through the realm of Dagroian. It had a king, and they spoke a different language. They were the ones who ate human flesh. Pak Byeong-ho and I forgot the gold.

"However, the stories of gold traveled like wildfire among my men. Greed caused some men, including the three lords, to disregard the Dagroian kingdom's vile custom. Later, Dai Xiuying discovered the three lords had struck a deal with some of our men. If they escorted them, they would all share the wealth. Then, they offered a large amount of silver to any islanders who would guide them through the dangerous kingdom.

"The three lords quarreled over who would stay behind. One had to stay in case misfortune fell upon them. Someone had to deliver the girls to the king. You see, I soon discovered they were fierce, fearless fighters trained in many fighting skills and thought nothing about the Dagroian. Gold consumed them, and their eyes reflected not fear but greed.

"They drew straws to see who would stay behind. Lord Qoja lost, or maybe you could say he won. Lord Ulaatai and Abishqu would go. By the time I learned of their plan, they had disappeared with 50 of my men.

"A month later, five hysterical men ran into our camp, their eyes wide, their faces deranged like men who had lost their minds. Dai Xiuying finally contained them and brought them to me with Lord Qoja, my father, and my uncle following. Lord Qoja calmly asked questions. My father and uncle stood quietly in the corner. Glancing over to my father, I saw his face reveal guilt.

"The men mumbled in sporadic sentences that made little sense. Li brought some tea that contained special herbs to calm them. Their bodies relaxed one by one, and their tortured facial expressions eased.

"'They ate them.' One man mumbled.

"Quickly, Dai Xiuying ushered a reluctant Li and Guo Yu out.

"Then another spoke louder. 'The savages ate them alive.'

"He held his hands over his ears. 'I can still hear screaming.'

"We stood stunned.

"'One by one, they ate them.' He continued to mumble.

"Lord Qoja gasped and asked about the Lord Ulaatai and Abishqu.

"'They fought bravely but succumbed to the savages. They tried to bargain. Their king dismissed them. They tied everyone alive to stakes. The king killed Lord Ulaatai and Abishqu last, making them watch as the natives with clubs beat their men until they were unconscious. They then stripped their flesh from their bodies with large knives. Even if they woke up, they just continued.'

"All the men put their hands over their ears as if they could still hear the screams.

Slowly, they removed their hands and continued.

"'Meanwhile, the women natives had placed large pots on an open fire. Dead or alive, they were stripped of their flesh one slice at a time, and the savages threw their flesh into the boiling pots. Sometimes, they would savagely eat a piece of raw flesh with salt and lemon. They seem to relish each bite. Only the king ate the lord's flesh as if he were gaining their courage.'

"Lord Qoja turned white, violently threw up, and ran out the door."

Rustichello sat up in his bed, his face white. "I think I have lost my appetite; eating is impossible."

Marco agreed. "I have tried desperately to forget this day. My guilt still haunts me. I was happy. It was a blessing for Li and me. We no longer had anyone to fear."

Rustichello nodded and asked how the five men survived.

"When I asked them, all five men lowered their heads. Finally, one man looked up. 'We escaped because we were cowards. We had already left the party and were returning when we heard screams deep in the forest. Following the screams, we came upon the village, the worst mistake we could have ever made. Forever, the screams, the slicing, the eating, and their cooked skulls placed on a stake in front of the savages' huts next to other skulls will be burnt into my memory.'

"By this time, tears ran down their faces, and quiet sobbing filled the room. Dai Xiuying placed his hand on the man's shoulder and led him out of the room. The others followed.

Rustichello spoke up. "Did you punish the men?"

"No, living with their memories was punishment enough, I felt."

"I turned to my father. 'I'm sure you were part of this by the look on your face.'

"My father didn't answer. My uncle did.

"'It's no different from what you did. You gave a treasure trunk to Lord Qoja. But for a stupid reason, love. At least our reason was for profit.'

"'You mean greed. You lost 45 of our men for that,' I scolded him.

"My uncle looked at me with an evil smile. 'But look what you gained. Peace, you no longer need to worry about LI. She is finally yours.'

“I lost it. I walked over to my uncle and grabbed him by his shirt. ‘My love was pure; now my love has a stain.’

“‘Pure? It started with a stain. The day you decided you had to have her and lied to Kubilai.’

“My father uncurled my fingers, and Maffeo stood defiantly momentarily and then walked out. I watched him leave my quarters with hatred. I hated him and myself. He was right on both accounts.

“Li flung open the door. Silently, she stood at the door and stared at me. Her face reflected love and relief. We had crossed one dangerous bridge, and one remained—King Arghun.”

Marco continued. “Lord Qoja became our friend. He never mentioned Li and our relationship again, except for a warning. ‘There could be eyes who desire favor from the king.’ We carefully heeded his words.”

Marco stood, went to the barred window, looked at the blue sky, and fell silent, thinking.

The next three months were glorious. Our love grew when I never thought it could. The island was a perfect backdrop for love. Its beauty, the balmy air, seduced us. The sun rose with its rays shining through pastel-colored clouds. Then the day turned glorious blue, and hours later, the sun fell into the sea, leaving behind a painted sky of bright orange and red. Tall, palm tree silhouettes stood proudly as the sky glowed by the rising moon. We made love with the rhythm of the crashing waves.

Marco’s face turned red.

Rustichello whispered, “Amor, Amor,” as he clapped.

Marco turned to Rustichello. “Yes, love, but I broke my promise. I can’t protect her; I have become my father and uncle. I went to war for money.”

Chapter Fifty-Seven

Li

1292 Flesh-Eating Greed

Venice 1298

The following day, Luca arrived early. When she entered the dim room, Li was still lying across the bed. Luca stood over the bed, looking at Li.

Li opened her swollen eyes. She had cried for hours, and it was hard to focus. Luca was a fuzzy image. She sat up, looked at Luca, and spoke. "For the first time, I'm scared, like when we reached Lesser Java."

"Where?" asked Luca.

"Lesser Java, an island where savages eat human flesh."

Luca gasped.

"But that wasn't the reason. Lord Qoja discovered Marco and me."

"Ohhhh!" Luca said excitedly.

"My life had turned into a nightmare. Lord Qoja walked into Marco's room when I was in his arms. I am having the same feeling now! My heart is pounding. Something is wrong, and I can feel it. What happens if Marco never returns? He promised me, he promised me!"

Luca walked over to Li, sat on the bed, and patted her back. "He never failed you in the past, did he? I know he is trying hard to return to you now."

"No, he never did." Again, Li touched her stomach.

"See," Luca said sympathetically. "He won't fail you this time."

Luca tried to change the subject. "Tell me more about Lessor Java, where savages eat human flesh?"

Li didn't go for it. "Tell me, Luca, the secret you are keeping from me. Tell me now! It is driving me crazy."

Interrupting Luca and Li, Guo Yu knocked and entered. Luca sighed with relief. *He can tell you,* she thought.

Guo Yu heard Li and contemplated what to say. He knew nothing.

The room was no longer dim; sunlight streamed through the window. Luca stood and stared at Guo Yu as he spoke to Li.

"Look at you; you're a mess. Crying like a child. What happened to the brave Song princess I knew? Messer Marco would be disappointed," he sternly said.

Li quickly answered. "Guo Yu, you are the one treating me like a child. Tell me what you know!"

He stared at Li as she stood. *She looks different. Gained weight? But how could she? She hasn't been eating.*

As Luca moved about the room nervously, Guo Yu motioned for Li to sit. "It's not much. The other morning, when Luca arrived, she saw Isabella hiding a letter in her book. Luca thought it was suspicious."

Li stared at Luca and looked back at Guo Yu.

Guo Yu continued. "Luca told me about the letter, and that's why I went to see Messer Maffeo, hoping he had heard the news about Marco. When I knocked, Isabella opened the door and left with a smirk as she passed me. That's all. That's our secret."

"That's it?" exclaimed Li. "We need to find that letter. Do you think she has hidden the letter from her father? Luca, it will be your job to find the letter!"

Luca started stuttering. "My, my job?"

"Yes, you are the only one who has access to her room and his office. We'll start with Isabella's room."

Before she continued, Li could see the fear on Luca's face. "I'm sorry, Luca, that's too much to ask. You have too much to lose. But I don't. What could she do to me? Besides, I was a spy for years; I'm good at it."

Luca and Guo Yu could hear the excitement in Li's voice. Guo Yu frowned.

Li continued. "Luca, it will be your job to tell me when Isabella leaves the palazzo!"

Guo Yu was worried. "Maybe we should wait a few days while Messer Maffeo asks around."

Li barked back. "He has already had a couple of days!" Li said confidently, no longer sad. "Luca, please help me dress. Guo Yu, bring me breakfast. I'm starving. I feel better. It was just a letter!"

But deep inside, Li felt uneasy. Yet she continued. "During breakfast, Luca, I will tell you how the Lord Qoja discovered us. Then, afterward, the man-eating savages."

Luca could see the gleam return to Li's eyes. Deep inside, Luca felt uneasy but was delighted when Li perked up.

Thinking about Li's sudden weight gain, Guo Yu wondered if Li had a secret, too.

Li, stuffing her mouth, started her story. "Marco and I, for months, tip-toed around, thinking we were careful, when one of the lords, Qoja, burst into Marco's room as I lay in Marco's arms.

Luca squealed.

"I thought we were doomed, but again, greed played a part. Marco, an expert in greed, handled it well. His father and uncle trained him well. Funny, come to think about it, it was also about a letter."

"Letter?" asked Luca.

"Yes, Lord Qoja accidentally received a letter from the mother of the crown prince's betrothed. She intended it for the number one lord. Thank goodness, Lord Qjoa's loyalty to his king was slight. He happily accepted a trunk full of treasure for tight lips. But it was the flesh-eating humans that sealed the deal.

"Sealed the deal?" Questioned Luca.

"Yes, like I said, it's all about greed. Lord Qoja kept his lips tight, but we still had to be careful of the other two lords." Li placed the last bite in her mouth. "Now, I will finish my story. Marco discovered the location of the gold as we stayed longer in Lesser Java. But you had to pass through the kingdom of the man-eaters!"

Luca nodded. She wasn't sure she wanted to hear more.

"Marco decided it was too dangerous and disregarded the gold. However, others secretly disagreed."

"Who?"

"Who do you think? Marco's father, uncle, the three lords, and the poor fifty men."

"What happened?" Luca moved closer to Li.

Li wasted no time. "Salvage natives ate everyone except five cowardly men and Lord Qoja, who had lost the draw!"

Luca screamed. "Don't tell me more!"

"So, you don't want to hear they ate them alive, raw, served with a little salt or lime," Li said with a mischievous smile.

Luca put her hands over her ears. "No more, no more!"

Slowly lowering her hands, she said, "That meant you no longer had to worry, right? That was a good thing. Right?"

"Yes, but that day, I discovered someone they called Ke Ai De Ren, meaning angel, felt only relief and greed. Greedy for Marco's love, no matter what. It seems all humans are flawed, and we shouldn't judge others."

Luca nodded. "Sometimes that's hard."

Li stared at Luca for a moment and continued her story. "For the next few years, until we reached Tabriz, Marco and I continued to be careful. Kokochin constantly reminded me. 'The two lords might be dead, but plenty of eyes exist. If they discovered your secret, they could use it against you and Messer Marco. People love power and money.'

"Kokochin was a good friend," stated Luca.

Li smiled. "She was until the day we left her with her king. I often wonder if I will ever see her again. She will always be in my heart, and I will always remember her words: 'Be happy, I am.'"

A few days later, Luca raced into Li's room with the news that Isabella had left with her friends and wouldn't be back for several hours."

Li excitedly said, "Heaven has blessed us. Guo Yu went to the market."

Luca nodded and thought to herself, *Has it? Maybe I should have remained silent, as Guo Yu told me.*

"You stand guard. I'm going into her room." Li continued.

"Shouldn't we wait for Guo Yu?" Luca said with caution in her voice.

"No, Isabella might return by then."

Li opened her door and peered down the hall. It was clear. Li's heart pounded as she exited and walked to Isabella's door, motioning the reluctant Luca to wait and watch.

Li hustled into Isabella's room, a room she had never been in. The room was slightly dim as the sun set directly overhead. Li thought, *'It's tidy and colorless, like Isabella. Cold, empty, and lacking in life, unlike my room, which is full of life and color and filled with Marco's and my treasures.'* She didn't waste any more time thinking. Hurriedly, she began her search for a book, a book that held the letter. However, that was one thing the room didn't lack. There were hundreds. Quickly and nervously, she started thumbing through the numerous books and became lost in her search.

Li didn't hear Luca whispering at the door. "Isabella is coming, hurry!"

Li's silence forced Luca to open the door and enter just in time to instruct Li to hide behind the sofa as Isabella entered the room. Luca was standing next to Isabella's bed, pretending to smooth out the wrinkles, when Isabella furiously asked, "Why are you in here?"

Luca stuttered. "Your maid asked me to make your bed."

Suddenly, the door opened, and Isabella's shocked servant entered. Instantly, Isabella asked her, "Is that true?"

The alarmed maid looked at the frightened Luca. "Is what true?" the maid asked.

"Did you ask her to make my bed?" Isabella asked.

Luca didn't wait for the answer. She dashed out the door and down the stairs. The maid and Isabella ran after her.

Li felt weak as she stood and escaped to her room. She feared for Luca. *Stupid girl, why did she do that?*

Luca opened the front door and ran. She ran until she couldn't run any longer, slipped behind a corner of a building, and peered back. No one was following her. *What am I going to do now*? *The Golden Head,* she thought. Alessio, the Apothecary, liked her not only for her skills. *He might help me*. She prayed.

Isabella and the maid stopped chasing Luca when they lost sight of her and returned to the palazzo. Isabella stomped up the stairs and straight into Li's room without knocking.

Li sat at her desk and slowly looked up. "Why do I deserve your presence?"

"You know why. I caught your maid in my room. Don't act innocent!" Isabella yelled.

Li replied calmly, "I haven't seen Luca since this morning. She said she had an extra job this morning."

"Really, she has no job now. She's considered a runaway slave. My servants are looking for her right now."

Li could hardly breathe but tried to remain calm. "I am sure she had her reasons, and she is innocent. But that's no concern of mine. She's just a maid to me."

"Nonsense, she was in there for you, looking for a bo—" Isabella abruptly stopped talking.

"What did you say? For me? Looking for what? Do you have something that belongs to me?"

Isabella didn't answer. She turned and walked out the door.

Li burst out in tears and spoke to herself out loud. "She shouldn't have done that. Isabella couldn't do anything to me except make my life a little more miserable. Why?" she kept asking herself. Still sobbing, she mumbled, unaware that Guo Yu was standing in the doorway. "I never told her I was with child."

Guo Yu's mouth dropped. "What did you say?"

Li looked at him, tears rolling down her cheeks. "Did you hear what happened? Do you know where Luca went? She was right. We should have waited for you. I'm so bad; I always think of myself. Even when Marco and I played with fire, Kokochin could have been in trouble. We were lucky then, but now Luca must pay for my sins!"

Guo Yu answered softly. "I'm asking if you are with child? Is that true?"

Li mumbled. "Yes, the last time I saw Marco, I decided I wouldn't drink the tea. Again, I was selfish. If I had a child, he would no longer leave me."

Guo Yu walked over to Li and put his arms around her. "Messer Marco will be so happy. I am so happy."

Li still sobbed. "It's been seven months since Marco left. I fear he is dead, and I fear for this child. Messer Maffeo is not our friend. What are we going to do? Sobbing harder, Li fell upon the bed. Guo Yu sat next to her, pulling her close.

Guo Yu hesitated momentarily, holding her like a father holds his child. "My heart tells me he is alive and is desperately trying to return to you. But if that is not the case, you must live for his child. Promise me you won't look for the letter. The heavens will reveal the truth at the right time."

Li nodded yes. "But you must promise me you will find Luca. She has sacrificed her life for me."

Guo Yu promised.

Luca constantly looked behind her back as she hastened to the Golden Head. She entered the Golden Head with a worried, tearful look. Alessio walked over to her and placed his hands on her shoulders. She was trembling. Alessio closed the door and locked it. Taking her hand, he gently pulled her to the back of his shop and wrapped his arms around her. Holding her close, he whispered. "What happened?'

Luca slowly told him.

Looking at her lovingly, he said, "You naïve girl, you shouldn't have protected her. Isabella couldn't touch her. You can never return now. Polo's servants are probably looking for you now."

Luca looked at him with a pitiful face.

Alessio's heart was so full of love that he had no choice. "You can stay here until Messer Marco Polo returns. He can help you then."

"What happens if he is dead? I think Li thinks he is."

"We will worry about that if the time comes. You are a talented herbalist like Li. She has taught you well. You will always have a place here with me, not only as a helper but as a wife, if you will have me."

Luca looked shocked. She never expected his response. Luca thought, *I was so naïve, like he said. Li said she felt he loved me several times, but I always brushed it off.* "How could a famous man love a simple maid?" she would tell Li. "That's because you are beautiful, smart, and loyal," Li would tell her. *But how could I, a slave, be that lucky?*

Luca gazed lovingly at Alessio, embraced him tightly, and whispered, "Yes."

It took three weeks for everything to settle down in Polo's palazzo. Li, missing Marco and now Luca, became more forlorn. Every night, she sat in her window and played her erhu. Isabella never once protested Li's playing. She ignored Li for fear that she would ask questions about the letter. Her main servant left several times to search for Luca, even going to her frantic mother. Isabella was clueless and never mentioned the Golden Head to the servant. She never took the time to know Li. From the beginning, she hated Li as she was a disgrace to the Polo family. How could Marco marry a pagan, a barbarian?

Guo Yu and Li remained home, fearing Isabella would have them followed. Their luck changed when Messer Maffeo came down with a cold and called Guo Yu into his bedchamber.

In his customary fashion, Guo Yu bowed low.

Maffeo, in a hoarse voice, asked, "Do you know of an apothecary who carries Cathay herbs? The Venetian physicians are helpless."

Guo Yu smiled to himself. He longed to go to the Golden Head for three weeks. Nonchalantly, he jumped on the opportunity. "Sir, I know an apothecary whose talents are unmatched. Shall I retrieve his special herbs?"

Maffeo nodded. "Go right away, I must feel better fast. I have an important meeting with Doge."

Guo Yu's heart skipped a beat. "Will you be asking about Messer Marco?"

Maffeo stared at him and sarcastically answered. "Of course, he is my nephew."

Guo Yu bowed low and left the room. Maintaining his composure, he strolled up the stairs to Li's room, knocked, and entered. His excitement showed throughout his body. His excitement was contagious.

"What's happened?"

"Our luck has changed. Messer Maffeo has asked for Cathay herbs. I'm going to the Golden Head." He didn't mention Messer Maffeo's meeting with the Doge.

Li ran over to him and wrapped her arms around him. Surprised, Guo Yu stepped back. Li laughed until her stomach hurt. She hadn't laughed since Luca disappeared. When she stopped laughing, she became serious. "Hurry, go. I am sure that's where Luca is. She must be there."

Guo Yu left, controlling his excitement until the door closed behind him. He raced through the crowded courtyard. The slave ships were in port. Blank-faced women, children, and men stood on the platform as their lives were auctioned away. He thought of Luca. *Would they sell or kill her if they caught her?* Weaving through the crowds, he finally arrived at the Golden Head.

Messer Alessio stood behind the counter, busy with customers. He looked up and saw Guo Yu. A slight smile appeared, and he directed him to the back with his large eyes.

With an emotionless face, Guo Yu silently disappeared into the back room. His emotion soon turned to joy. In an herbalist apprentice uniform, Luca stood at the table separating piles of herbs and bagging them.

Luca looked up, and her expression said it all. She ran around the table, and Guo Yu received a tight hug for the second time today. After a moment, he backed away, placed his hands on her shoulders, and said, "Li has been going crazy with worry. We both have. Li can't afford to be."

"Why? Is she sick? I can make up some special tea for her. Tell me about her symptoms."

Guo Yu smiled. "Look at you. You sound like an apothecary." He didn't hesitate. "Li is with child. She was so disappointed she couldn't tell you herself."

"OHHHHH," Luca swooned. Then she became serious. Tell her not to worry; it was not her fault. Anyway, it has turned out to be the best thing that has ever happened to me. Tell her she was right; Messer Alessio loves me. We will be married when Messer Marco returns."

Guo Yu clapped with excitement. But inside, he thought, *What happens if he doesn't return?*

Messer Alessio walked in, answering him as if he could hear him. "We will worry about that when the time comes. She will be with me no matter what."

"I am so happy. I know Li will be," Guo Yu continued excitedly.

Luca directed the conversation to Messer Alessio. "Li is with child; we should make tea for her."

Messer Alessio looked worried." She must be pretty far along. Marco has been gone for quite a while."

"Yes, her time is coming fast. Messer Marco must return soon." Guo Yu moaned and changed the subject. "Isabella's servant has been looking for you, but things have calmed down. Maybe Li can come soon."

Luca smiled. "I hope so. I miss her."

"We resisted coming, in fear that Isabella might become suspicious. Today, an opportunity came; Messer Maffeo has a cold and requested some Cathay herbal tea."

Messer Alessio smiled proudly at Luca. "Do your job."

Guo Yu left the Golden Head happy. He couldn't wait to tell Li.

Chapter Fifty-Eight

Marco

1292-1293 India

Genoa prison 1298

Marco sat at the table, facing Rustichello. "Over seven months, I have been in this hellhole. Every day that passes, I hurt more. Li must hate me. I hate myself. The general fooled and used me; they will never release me. What a fool I am. My only hope is if the war ends."

Rustichello nodded and tried to change the subject. "Tell me more."

Marco thought for a moment. "In September, after five months, we left Lessor Java for Ceylon, but not before we loaded two empty ships with merchandise, which headed back to Kim Chin-hae. After sailing for months, we arrived in Ceylon and made deals with King Senderman for rubies, other precious stones, and Brazilwood. I even brought back Brazilwood's seeds, but they didn't grow. We didn't stay long in Ceylon as the pearl harvest in Maabar had begun. You remember, Rustichello, we were too late the last time we arrived there, but not this time. When we arrived in Greater India, hundreds of merchants were there for the same reason: pearls. First, a license had to be obtained from King Sundara Pandya Devar."

Then Marco snickered. "Let me tell you, there was no need for tailors. The people, even the king, were naked all year long except for their private parts, for the weather was extremely hot. They even went to battle naked."

Rustichello couldn't believe it." Naked?" He questions Marco.

Marco laughed. "Yes, naked, but you won't believe me when I tell you.

"The King wore a collar beautifully decorated around his neck with hundreds of precious stones, rubies, sapphires, emeralds, and other precious stones worth a

king's ransom. Besides that, he wears a long, thin silk cord around his neck that hangs down his chest, adorned with exactly 104[1] *exquisite pearls and rubies."*

Rustichello stopped him. "Why exactly 104?"
Marco answered.

"It is his custom. He prays morning, noon, and evening using the pearls and rubies, reciting 104 prayers. The prayers simply comprise the words Pauca, Pauca, Pachuca."

Marco continued.

"He also wears three bracelets decorated with more pearls and precious jewels at three points on his arms and legs. And the most marvelous thing is that he wears the same jewels on his toes. He wears so many; his body is worth as much as a city. And it's no wonder, as all these gems are found in his kingdom.□

"He had 500 wives or concubines. I can assure you we hid our women; it was said that the moment he lays his eyes on beautiful women or girls, he wants them for himself. In fact, he stole his own brother's wife."

Rustichello interrupted Marco, "His brother's? What happened? That would cause a war here."

Marco let out a snicker. "Their mother stopped that."

"Their mother?" he questioned.

"Yes, the story goes, she held a knife to her breast and threatened. 'If you fight with each other, I will cut off these breasts that suckled you.'

"The brothers believed their mother and retreated."

Rustichello was in amazement. Indeed, Marco had heard and seen strange things.

Marco continued.

"Many faithful followers loved the king, so loved that if he died, they would follow him in death. You should know that in this kingdom, when the king dies, his body is burned, and these loyal followers would fling themselves into the flames. And not only his followers, but also his wives. Not all do, but the ones that do are highly praised."

Rustichello cringed. "That's true loyalty. I don't know if I could be that loyal." Marco continued.

"Another custom that you will find strange is when the king dies, he leaves behind great treasures. The sons who survive would never touch these treasures. They are inclined to make their own fortunes. They say, 'I have my father's whole kingdom and his subjects. Surely, I can find a way to profit.'

"King Sundara Pandya Devar did. No one could remove any large gem or pearls that weighed half a saggio or more from his kingdom. Several times a year, the king issued a proclamation instructing all who processed fine pearls and precious stones to be brought to court. He would pay them twice their value. However, this is how he amassed such a vast wealth and numerous precious stones. But even when he dies, his son will never be able to touch his treasures. That's why this kingdom has masses of treasures."

"Were you required to do this before you left?" asked Rustichello.

"Of course, we had to agree before we received our permit to harvest the pearls. But not until an expert in physiognomy read my face to see if I was of good character."

"I am sure you hated this agreement," Rustichello said as he sat writing notes.

Marco sadly nodded.

Rustichello looked up, saw Marco's sad face, and quickly changed the subject. "Tell me more."

Marco shook off his sadness.

"There are so many strange customs. They worshipped the ox and would never eat beef. They would hire a Saracen or others who did not follow their faith if they wanted beef. They bathe, women and men, head to toe, in water twice daily before eating or drinking. If you don't, you are considered a heretic. They always eat with their right hand and never with their left, as it is reserved for the unpleasant and unclean, such as cleaning themselves and wiping their nostrils. They would never drink from any containers except their own."

Rustichello stopped Marco. "They are so different from what you would think, so enlightened, so different from us in some ways..."

Marco nodded, stopped talking, looked at Rustichello, and suddenly changed the subject. "No matter where I traveled, people lived differently throughout this strange world. And in their world, it worked.

"Li would become my world. We would make it work. Li and I were more than lovers. She was my partner and friend. Li is a strong woman and someone I could genuinely trust. For the first time, we were no longer lonely. We had each other. In the evenings, Li would come to me when everyone slept. I would tell her my day. It was she who first told me to write down my travels. After many hours of writing, we would blow out the candles and disappear into the darkness in each other's arms.

"After months of harvesting pearls, we went to the king, sold the large ones, and departed. We continued up the coast to Kayal.[2]

"It was a splendid city ruled by Ashar, the eldest of the five brothers. It was an excellent port for all merchandise from the western cities, Hormuz, Kish, and Aden. The king is rich and governs with great justice, particularly with the foreign merchants. He watches over their interest with great care.

"It was here we sold more of our Cathay and Lessor Java merchandise for their country's merchandise, and again, three more of our ships sailed back to Kim Chin-hae filled with treasures.

"You should know about one of their customs. They almost constantly keep in their mouths a kind of leaf called tambur. They, and by they, I am referring to nobles, magnates, and kings. They chew this leaf with lime, camphor, and other spices

for their health and then spit out the remains when the flavor ends. They also use this to insult and taunt someone by spitting this mixture on them, which usually results in a battle of the clans."

"Ugh," whispered Rustichello as he continued writing while Marco continued.

"Then we traveled 500 miles to Kollam. They produce peppers, gathered in May, June, and July. They also have very fine indigo. I can also tell you the sun is so fierce and scorching that if you drop an egg into one of the rivers, it will boil. The merchants do a roaring trade here. They also have many strange animals. They have black lions and many parrots, some as white as snow with red feet and peaks, while others are red and blue, all beautiful. All their things are different, bigger, and better than ours. I think it's because of their extreme heat. Everything a human body needs for life is cheap and abundant, except grain other than rice.

"Then, we sailed to Kanyakumari and Ezhimala, 300 miles from Kanyakumari.

Then, we went to Gujarat, Thane, and continued to Khambhat. From there, five ships sailed to Arden with our newly acquired treasures to sell to the Christians. With their ships filled with new treasures, they would return to Kim Chin-hae. As we continued to Somnath, we heard stories about trade beyond the Arabian Sea."

"Kesh-Makran was the last province of India I traveled to before we reached the Strait of Hormuz. We traveled up the west coast of India for months. It was an experience I will never forget. Many people died. We had lost three ships to Malabar pirates, and numerous women of Kokochin's party, crew members, and servants who fell ill with a mysterious illness and died. Li became Ke Ai De Ren again, nursing as many as she could, including my father. By the time Li had healed him and we arrived, my father had come to love her as his daughter. He had softened with age. His health never recovered completely, and he died within the year of our return to Venice. The girls who lived were indebted to Li. They were forever her sworn sisters vowing never to tell our secret, which had been discovered by this time."

---

1. In the Hindu tradition, the number 108 is considered significant. However, in Marco Polo's book, the number 104 is mentioned.

2. Kayalpattinam

Chapter Fifty-Nine

Marco

1294 The Death of the King

Genoa prison 1298

“When we reached Hormuz, my mood changed. Li and I faced reality. The past years were a dream, but things could change in one or two months. Qoja, the last lord, came to me just days before our arrival with the same concern. ‘What are your plans? We need to prepare.’”

Marco looked out the barred cell window, deep in thought, and spoke slowly and softly. “It had been twenty-one years since I was in Hormuz. Memories flooded in. The first time, I was a young man, inexperienced in life, curious, and optimistic. But this time, I arrived a worldly man, knowing that life could be unfair and brutal, and my fears grew. I knew Lord Qoja was right—a decision needed to be made.

“It took a couple of weeks to sort out our merchandise in the one remaining ship. It carried the most precious cargo: Li, Kokochin, the remaining girls, and the most valuable treasures a man could obtain—jewels, gold, and items that held my memories. Only one trunk of gold remained to purchase merchandise for Pak Byeong-ho’s ship that would sail back to Cathay. I never knew if he made it or how many other ships safely returned.” Marco sadly said as he looked down at the floor.

Rustichello spoke before Marco could continue. “What did you decide?”

Marco looked up and questioned. “Decide?”

“About Li, what did you do?”

Marco hesitated and slowly began. “We would dress her like a man and tell everyone the Princess of Song died. It was a perfect plan, we thought. But again, life is unpredictable.

"As Pak Byeong-ho stood on the stern, his ship sailed away. Li, Guo Yu, Dai Xiuying, Lord Qoja, and I stood on the wharf and watched Pak Byeong-ho disappear. My heart sank. Even though I was looking forward to my new future and returning home, I watched a part of me fade as he sailed away. I looked over at Li and Guo Yu. They were waving and crying. I assumed they felt the same or worse. They didn't know what their future held."

Rustichello interrupted Marco. "What happened to Dai Xiuying?"

"My loyal guide and protector came with us. Our small caravan departed from Hormuz, and we hoped to arrive in Tabriz within a month or so. We sewed our jewels and gold coins in the linings of our clothes for their protection and placed the trunks of personal items on asses. Hormuz hadn't changed from my first visit: scorching hot. We traveled the same route as in the past. The same large plain, decorated with fields of wheat, appeared, along with the huge, pure white oxen with their round humps, used like camels. The numerous date trees and crumbling earthen walls that once stood at great height remained. We rode through flocks of turtle doves. The weather was still scorching hot as we rode through the countryside of Rudbar and arrived in the city of Kamadin. I was excited to tell Kokochin this was where her new husband, as a young general, saved our lives. Kokochin's face shone with pride. Her mother raised her well, and her dedication and loyalty to her country were evident. Never once wavering, she had the making of a royal queen.

"Li and I discussed this several times. Li was the opposite. If I hadn't rescued her, she was unsure if she could have become his concubine. She mentioned her mother, and my heart ached. Deep down, I knew what she meant. She would have taken her life."

Rustichello shook his head. "Our country is no different. We might not have concubines, but the rich and powerful use their daughters similarly."

Marco nodded. "I never gave much thought to the other girls' destinies until I traveled with them for two and a half years. Li opened my mind, and if one wanted to escape her destiny, I turned a blind eye. My loyalty to Kubilai Khan continued to disappear."

Marco continued mumbling. "As we ascended a mountain for two days, we reached the edge of Persia and a city called Kerman. It was here that we heard the news that sent shockwaves throughout our caravan. King Arghun was dead."

In shock, Rustichello yelled. "DEAD?!"

"Yes, dead. We had traveled so far and long. Kokochin was heartbroken; her king was dead. His brother, Gaykhatu, was governing the Kingdom. The remaining girls feared their futures.

"We found the same caravanserais outside the city where we had met Ashrad years before. Remember, Rustichello, our guide when Arghun saved our lives?"

He rustled through his papers. "Of course, the man with a large scar."

Marco continued. "The unexpected happened. What were we to do?"

"What did you do?" Rushicello asked.

Marco started slowly. "The pressure surrounded me like a heavy chain as I gathered everyone around a large table, and they stared at me."

Rustichello sighed.

"Finally, Lord Qoja spoke. 'Messer Marco, write a letter to Gaykhatu introducing yourself and telling him about your mission. Dai Xiuying and I will deliver it. Gaykhatu and I were friends before I left; even though I have been gone for years, he will remember me.'

"I nodded in agreement. 'Tonight, I will write the letter, and tomorrow morning, Dai Xiuying and you should leave. Your journey should take forty days. We will stay in place until you return.'

"Dai Xiuying and Lord Qoja left the room to prepare, and that's when Li, Kokochin, and all the girls who had survived asked to enter my room. Li and Kokochin sat silently as the other girls begged me with tears in their eyes. 'Please, let us return home with Dai Xiuying when he returns to Cathay. We will disappear and never reveal the truth.'

"Li placed her hand over mine and looked at me pleadingly. I nodded yes. Their faces lit up. They stood, bowed low, and left the room.

"I noticed then that one girl was not present and mentioned it to Li. 'I didn't see Jia. She must know that returning is not the best option for her.'

"Li replied, 'I fear that there is much more to Jia than she appears. My heart and Kokochin tell me she wants power, and she shouldn't be trusted.'

Rustichello interrupted Marco, "Who is Jia, and was Li correct?"

Marco hesitated, thinking what to say, and then replied, "Jia was a beautiful girl of noble birth. Her family had lost favor with Kubilai, and he sent her away as part of the family's punishment. She stood out from the other girls, always sugary sweet and eager to please, despite having every reason to be angry and sad.

Rustichell became impatient and continued. "You answered only part of my question. Was Li correct?"

Again, Marco smiled. He had captured Rustichello's curiosity. "You have to wait." Rustichello snarled.

"That evening, Li, my father, Lord Qoja, and I sat in a dim, dusty room and composed the letter."

My Lord Gaykhatu,

My name is Messer Marco Polo, son of Niccolò Polo and the nephew of Maffeo Polo. I am not sure if you remember us. In 1272, we met you on our way to the great Kubilai Khan. After spending seventeen years in his service, Kubilai Khan entrusted us to deliver Kokochin, King Arghun's requested Queen, and her attendants. Kokochin survived, but unfortunately, many attendants perished mainly due to the unforeseen circumstances of an arduous three-year journey. We are at odds over what to do with the news of the death of King Arghun. We are currently in Kerman, awaiting your decision.

Messer Marco Polo

"The following day, I handed the letter to Lord Qoja and watched him and Dai Xiuying ride away. For the next forty days, we roamed Kerman, learning its ruler was a queen named Padishah Khatun, wife of Gaykhatu. She had a gold dinar, showing her important title, Lord of the World. They praised her for her extraordinary learning, skills in calligraphy, and knowledge of the Qur'an. A scary fact: she had her brother strangled!"

Rustichello gasped. "Did you meet her?"

"Yes! A very clever woman with much power over her husband."

"Power?" Rustichello questioned.

Marco looked down at the dirty floor; his foot scraped the dirt back and forth. "Later, I learned she held Kokochin's future in her hands."

Marco quickly changed the subject. "We also heard news of Ghazan. Li and I often wondered what had happened to him and Aiyurug, and if their love still flourished like ours. It was thrilling to hear Ghazan wasn't far away in the region of the Dry Tree, commanding 60,000 troops that guarded the passes and borders from their enemies, including Aiyurug. Li and I smiled at each other.

"Meanwhile, Kokochin secretly oversaw Jia, afraid her sweetness and her readiness to please were part of a plan. Kokochin, born in the depths of the inner chambers, had seen many power-hungry women who usually came in the image of Jia. Kokochin, from the day she met Li at ten, loved Li like a sister. She was determined to protect her. Li had been a victim from the beginning, and when Empress Chabi died, she lost her champion in the inner chamber. Only Guo Yu, Messer Marco, and Physician Wu fought for her, but were powerless in the inner chamber. That's why Li was here to begin with."

***

Dai Xiuying and Lord Qoja rode fast and arrived a couple of days early. They requested an audience with Gaykhatu. They entered his chambers on their knees, bowing. Next to him was a beautiful woman. Dai Xiuying had a hard time not staring. Lord Qoja lifted his body from a bow and held out the letter.

Gaykhatu stared at Lord Qoja. "Is that you, Lord Qoja? We thought you were dead. Where are Lord Ulaatai and Abishqa?"

"They have perished like most of our caravan. Only a few of us survived," Qoja answered in a pitiful voice.

Gaykhatu ordered them to stand. "Who is the letter from?"

"Messer Marco Polo, the man entrusted to deliver Princess Kokochin, the late King Arghan's requested queen."

Gaykhatu, in deep thought, instructed a servant to retrieve the letter. He swiftly opened it, looked up from the letter, and smiled. "I remember him, his father, and uncle. He was a very young man at the time. It's amazing. In these past years, he won the respect of the Great Khan."

Then he looked at Dai Xiuying. "Who are you?"

"I am Messer Marco Polo's man, Dai Xiuying."

He nodded and said, "Messer Marco Polo's man, Dai Xiuying, take your leave. Tomorrow, you will have my answer. My servant will take you to your guest quarters."

Dai Xiuying quickly glanced at his beautiful queen, who was reading the letter. This surprised him, and he thought, *She must have power.*

"Lord Qoja, stay. I have more questions." Ordered Gaykhatu.

Dai Xiuying cringed. He looked over at Lord Qoja, who smiled. Dai Xiuying thought, *Will Lord Qoja stand loyal to Messer Marco? He paid him enough. But now he is with his people.*

Dai Xiuying bowed and followed the servant out the door and down the hallway. Another servant opened a door and directed Dai Xiuying in. He entered an elegant room filled with fabulous silk drapes and elegant rugs. He fell upon the silk bed and closed his eyes. His heart raced, and his mind swirled with questions. *Will he remain loyal?* Yet, his exhausted body soon drifted to sleep. Lord Qoja awoke him hours later, knocking loudly on the door and entering. Dai Xiuying sat up, rubbing his eyes. Not quite awake, he looked at Lord Qoja and, without hesitation, started to ask. "You were—" but before he finished his sentence, Lord Qoja put his index finger to his lips. Dai Xiuying looked around the room. Lord Qoja loudly spoke as he touched his ears and eyes. Dai Xiuying stopped talking. He understood.

"Are you going to sleep all day? Let's visit my family. I've been gone for so long. I fear it might be a week or more before we receive our answer."

"A week or more? I thought he said tomorrow."

"That was before the queen read the letter," Lord Qoja stated.

Padishah Khatun returned the letter to Gaykhatu and then lovingly touched his face.

She remained silent while Gaykhatu finished talking to Lord Qoja. Their conversation consisted mainly of Qoja's journey. It disgusted Gaykhatu with the thought of the man-eating savages, and he didn't ask many more questions. He was happy that Lord Qoja and the young girl, Kokochin, had survived.

Lord Qoja noticed that his queen, Padishah Khatun, listened attentively and watched the khan's face. As their conversation ended, Padishah leaned into him and whispered something in his ear.

Gaykhatu looked at Lord Qoja. "My decision is unclear. I will let you know when I decide, maybe in a week."

Padishah smiled.

Lord Qoja thought, *The queen is a beautiful woman in her flowing silk robe and draping veil. She controls Gaykhatu, the khan, who is naïve of her cleverness.*

Lord Qoja bowed and took his leave.

Padishah stood, reached for Gaykhatu's hand, and softly led him to their chambers.

She seductively kissed him on his lips and whispered. "My body burns for you, and I will not allow other women to touch your lips. It wouldn't be fair to this young girl who has traveled so far."

Gaykhatu wasn't listening. Padishah had captivated him since he was sixteen; she was thirteen when she and his father married. When his father died, Padishah stayed in court, trying to keep her power in Kerman. She filed a claim against a powerful minister who had supported her brother, with whom she had bitterly fought over the city of Kerman. The outcome was devastating. The powerful minister married her off to Gaykhatu and sent her to Anatolia, thus removing her from the center of power. But when Gaykhatu, who couldn't resist her, became khan, she regained her power.

Padishah pulled him in closer to her body and kissed him hard. She felt his surrender and knew Kokochin would never belong to him. Now she had to decide on her next move.

As Gaykhatu made passionate love to her, her mind wandered, but not for long. Even though he was easy to manipulate, and she used him for her selfish desires, she found him exciting and extremely handsome, and his lovemaking could easily manipulate her, too. She soon became lost in her lust.

The following day, she comfortably lay in his arms, thinking of the dilemma. Suddenly, a solution appeared. *Ghazan. Gaykhatu needs more allies. My brother's wife hates me, and I fear that her brother, Prince Baydu, could attempt to overthrow us.*

Padishah intentionally whispered out loud. "Ghazan, your nephew, resents you for taking over the empire when his father died. But maybe this could change. Ghazan, with his 60,000 troops, must be on your side."

Gaykhatu, who also lay quietly awake, heard her. "What did you say?"

Padishah slid out of his arms and sat up. "Ghazan needs to be on your side. Give the young girl to him. As Kubilai Khan's daughter, she is a powerful asset. Ghazan will appreciate this token of trust." Padishah slyly smiled.

Gaykhatu then sat up. "I do need him and his warriors. Do you think this will work?"

Padishah smiled. "I'm confident it will."

"Today, I will send a letter!" Gaykhatu said, smiling at her as he stroked her long, dark hair. "You are as smart as beautiful. But I don't need to tell you that. That's why you are the only woman in my bed." He called his servant and requested paper.

A rider, flying Gaykhatu's banner, fast approached Ghazan's camp in Tun-Qaen. Ghazan watched the rider quickly dismount and race toward him. The rider bowed low, and when he rose, he spoke. "Your uncle sends you good tidings and this letter."

Ghazan's face has turned red with anger. *How dare he*? Grabbing the letter from the man, he ripped it open. Astonished by the content, he sat and called to his servant for wine. His uncle's gift impressed him, and the news that Messer Marco Polo was only miles away delighted him. He often thought of him and the secret girl who saved him. Ghazan often wondered who she was, but it was apparent they were in love. Aiyurug and he had remained lovers for all these years, even though she refused to marry him. He understood, even though his heart ached with loneliness. She would never give up her kingdom, just like him.

Ghazan ordered his servant to saddle his horse as he dressed in his formal military uniform. He quickly mounted and rode off without a word. The men in the camp stood watching, except his guard, who promptly caught up with him. They rode until they reached Kerman. After some inquiries, they rode to the caravanserais and entered, yelling Marco's name. The merchants stared and listened in fright. *Why is a general here yelling out Messer Marco's name?* The caravanserais buzzed with excitement.

Someone knocked on Marco's door. In man's attire, Li answered the door. A concerned man pointed to the courtyard. Li heard a man yelling for Marco. She shook with fear. *Are we caught? Did Lord Qoja desert us?*

Marco and his father walked up behind her. Marco placed his powerful hands on her shoulders, gripping them firmly. In a soft, confident, and reassuring voice, he spoke. "Stay here. Everything will be fine."

Ghazan continued to stand formidably in the middle courtyard, shouting for Marco.

Marco's heart pounded as he walked toward the yelling man. As he rounded the corner, his fears diminished.

Marco's father, Niccolò, heard him release a deep breath and suddenly burst out laughing loudly. Marco ran, quickly bowed, and threw his arms around Ghazan.

Li, disobeying Marco, followed him, barely able to breathe. As she watched, her knees melted with relief. Luckily, Kokochin caught her. Puzzled, Kokochin looked at Li, who was laughing like Marco. She answered Kokochin's question without being asked. "That's Ghazan, the man I saved in Balkh. The one who loves his enemy."

Kokochin drew a deep breath, smiled at Li, and prevented her from walking toward Marco. "I am sure Jia is watching! She knows nothing about Ghazan, and that you know him. Don't give her more weaponry."

Niccolò also watched in awe. *Who is this man Marco knew so well?* He was a general who walked with arrogance and too much confidence.

Meanwhile, Jia stood behind a pillar, watching. Jia's curiosity grew. Who was this man who knew Messer Marco? Jia wasted no time and started asking around. The answer raised more interest.

Kokochin and Li quietly returned to the room and waited in an obscured corner.

Marco excitedly led Ghazan to his room. Niccolò and Guo Yu, who joined them, followed. Confidently, Niccolò quickly closed the door, nodding to Guo Yu to stand guard.

Guo Yu watched closely for prying eyes. He was disturbed when he discovered Jia peering around the corner with a smiling face. A sick feeling engulfed his body. Kokochin's intuition had been correct.

Niccolò interrupted their joyous reunion and introduced himself.

Ghazan looked at Marco and then at his father. He bowed low and rose with a brilliant smile. "I am delighted to meet the father of the man who saved my life. My name is Ghazan; I am King Arghun's son."

Stunned, Niccolò fell to his knees, asking for forgiveness. "I didn't know." He quickly added, "I assume we have paid our indebtedness?" remembering Ghazan's father saved them many years ago.

Ghazan smiled, "Well, Messer Marco did play his part, but his woman was the one who saved me. What was her name?" Ke Ai De Ren?"

Confused, Niccolò looked at Marco. Li and Kokochin stepped out of the corner of the room and bowed.

As Kokochin rose, Ghazan's eyes widened. Her astonishing beauty bewitched him. Kokochin's face burned red.

Li quickly walked toward him. He turned from Kokochin and stared at Li. His face lit up with recognition. "Ke Ai De Ren. Still in disguise, I see."

Li smiled and nodded.

Ghazan looked back at Kokochin. "I hope you are my gift. You were to be my father's queen, and now mine?"

Kokochin, surprised, looked at Marco.

Marco spoke as the rest stared at Ghazan. "So that's how you knew I was here. You were his decision?"

Ghazan nodded, still staring at Kokochin. "My mind wasn't made until now."

Kokochin's face turned redder.

Marco motioned everyone to leave. "I must speak to Ghazan alone."

Niccolò cracked open the door, and Guo Yu met Niccolò's eyes, leading his eyes to the corner of the building where Jia hid. With his hand, Niccolò motioned Guo Yu to walk in Jia's direction. As he rounded the corner, Guo Yu only saw a glimpse of her dress as she slipped around the other corner.

Kokochin and Li escaped unseen to their room.

Ghazan and Marco sat. Ghazan spoke first. "Yes, I am the solution. I'm sure my aunt had something to do with it, especially after seeing Kokochin. Padishah Khatun would never allow her in my uncle's bed. She has tremendous power over him. That girl could be a threat. However, I'm not clueless; my uncle and aunt have alternative motives for giving me this gift. They need me, my soldiers, and my loyalty. It's a great trade. The great Khan's daughter, Kokochin, will be a great asset and bring me power. However, their cleverness tells them that now is not the time because my primary concern is to protect my empire from my enemies.

Marco interrupted him. "Talking about your enemy. How is Aiyurug?"

Ghazan's face turned solemn. "We love each other, yet most people could never understand. Our lives are similar but distant as the moon is far. We will never be together. She will never be my queen, nor I, her king. When we are in each other's arms, we forget and live in the moment." Ghazan became quiet and looked down. When he looked up, his eyes were watery, and his voice sounded sad. "We know the day will come. I will leave and never return. For some reason, I feel that time is not far away. His mood quickly swung. He perked up and, with a devilish smile, spoke. "I see you still have your secret. Who is that girl, anyway?"

Marco hesitated. "She is like your Aiyurug, someone I should have never loved. We have gone beyond our destinies and tested the heavens. I hope you understand. I cannot say."

Ghazan stared at Marco and said, "Testing heaven is a desire larger than the vast star-filled skies. I hope Heaven opens its gate and shines brightly on your love, my friend."

Marco studied Ghazan, and under his breath, he whispered. "I hope you remember what you said."

Ghazan questioned him. "What?"

Marco didn't answer him back, but asked. "Now what?"

"I'll return home and write a letter agreeing to his gift."

Marco became serious again. "Please treat Kokochin with love. I have known her since she was a little girl. She's like a sister. Years ago, I promised to find her a kind and gentle king to marry. Someone she could love."

Ghazan nodded. "I promise."

Marco wanted to believe him.

"Are you returning to Khanbaliq?" Ghazan asked.

Marco's face turned solemn, and he sadly answered, "No, we are returning to our old world. Delivering Kokochin was my last mission. We have been gone for almost 24 years. We accepted this mission as an opportunity to leave Cathay. Kubliai Khan has grown old, and I fear his time on this earth is limited. Few lords have understood Kubilai and our relationship, and things could become questionable. I am sad to leave my friends and your world. Besides, my 'secret' can never be told; if I return, my secret will no longer be a secret."

Ghazan stared at Marco, and his curiosity almost couldn't be contained. He held back and smiled. "Wise men, too, can be fools regarding love. I will see you soon with my new queen."

Marco bowed low. "I know you will become a great khan."

Ghazan turned and left.

Marco was relieved that Ghazan didn't continue to question him about Li. His relief didn't last long. There was a knock on his door, and he opened it, thinking it was Li. To his surprise, it was Jia. She pushed herself in.

Without hesitation or thought, she started talking. "We have something to discuss. I want to take the place of Li, the Princess of Song. That's a better position than just a low concubine! That man, Ghazan, who just left your room, is King Arghun's son. He must be the solution you were looking for. He's handsome. Kokochin and I are lucky."

Jia's evil, power-hungry self hid behind the sugary smile. *I will expose them all. I'll be the victim, forced to take her place so they can be together. I will gain Ghazan's trust, his heart, and his power.*

Marco listened; he had no choice but to do so. His heart sank. *Kokochin had been right; Jia, greedy for power, wanted to be queen or a king's royal concubine and someday be a king's mother. She could make this happen if she gained favor by revealing Li's secret. She must be stopped.*

When Jia exited Marco's room, she boldly walked straight to the courtyard to look for Ghazan. She found him just ready to mount his fresh horse.

Niccolò saw her approaching Ghazan. His heart stopped, and he rushed after her urgently. Jia smiled, bowed, and sweetly spoke. "My Lord, I am so sorry I missed you. I am Li, Princess of Song. I traveled with Messer Marco to enter your father's court and now, yours."

Ghazan slid his foot from his stirrup and faced Jia. "I must admit, this is my lucky day. I have been given two beautiful women."

Jia sweetly smiled and was about to speak when Niccolò reached her and began apologizing for her boldness.

Ghazan smiled, bowed, mounted his horse, and sped off with his guard following.

Niccolò frowned at Jia. "What did you say to him?

"I introduced myself. Li, the princess of Song."

Niccolò's face turned bright red with anger. He grabbed her hand and dragged her to her room. "Stay here. Don't leave." Niccolò hurried to Marco's room.

Jia sat on her bed, an evil smile appeared, and a wicked laugh filled the room.

Marco, Kokochin, and Li were discussing Jia at the table when Niccolò rushed in, his face still bright red. Marco nervously listened to his father. They had no choice; that day, Jia became LI, the princess of Song.

When Ghazan returned, he wrote his letter and ordered the capture of the rare Caspian tiger cub. His men set out with the letter with a tiny cub thrown over their saddle. The letter stated,

My Dear Uncle,

My answer is as rare as Kokochin's beauty and the Caspian tiger cub I present.
I accept!

Your Nephew,
Ghazan

Gaykhatu handed the letter to Padishah Khatun, and satisfaction spread across her face as she read Ghazan's letter. Ghazan solved her problem, and Gaykhatu gained the possibility of Ghazan's support.

Gaykhatu released Dai Xiuying the next day, instructing him to return to Marco with the news. After days of travel, he found Marco and Li preparing for their journey to Ghazan. Dai Xiuying questioned. "How did you know?" But he also questioned their nervous mood. Silent, Marco stared at Dai Xiuying and spoke quietly. "The answer to your first question: Ghazan came immediately after receiving Gaykhatu's letter. The answer to your second question is that Jia is a thorn in the side and can't be trusted. She introduced herself to Ghazan as Princess Li. Our only hope is that Ghazan's friendship will prevail."

The next day, everyone bustled around their room, packing. Jia kept smiling to herself. *My life is about to change. I will become queen*. Suddenly, a knock at her door interrupted her twisted dream. When she opened the door, Kokochin stood there, surprising her as they had never been great friends. *What does she want?* Jia thought. Kokochin's face looked different. Somehow, it resembled the women of the inner chamber: brutal and cruel.

Kokochin pushed herself in, shutting the door behind her. The Tartarian blood that ran deep in her veins boiled for the first time. Her inner strength, which her father had instilled in her, took over. She learned loyalty and what it could bring from her father. But she had also learned what disloyalty brought: death. She became her father, the part men and women feared. She pushed Jia against the wall, holding a small, sharp knife to her main throbbing vein, revealing Jia's fear. Kokochin viciously laughed in a low tone. With all her might, she restrained herself, controlling the tip of the knife just enough to pierce Jia's skin so a small river of blood ran down her neck. Jia gasped.

A voice erupted from Kokochin Jia never heard. "Your game ends here. If you continue to plot, you will never be the Princess of Song. You will die."

Jia regained her composure. She, too, had learned well in the chambers never to retreat, or you would forever be a target.

Kokochin knew this and was prepared. "Jia, you will lose!"

With a stern, confident voice, Jia answered. "Why? Messer Marco, Li, and you are the deceivers. You always talk of your loyalty and your father's quest for it."

Kokochin continued to look at Jia with fierce eyes. "That's right, but who is your father? I am the daughter of the Great Khan. Who do you think Ghazan will believe?"

For a moment, Jia hesitated. Kokochin had a point. The hesitation lasted only a moment before her arrogant self returned. "Ghazan will always wonder, *Are you really Kokochin? Maybe you are the substitute. Maybe Li is the true Kokochin?*"

Kokochin thought she had a point, and it was a good one, but poor Jia didn't know the entire story. *Her desire, arrogance, and lack of knowledge deceive her.* Kokochin pressed the knife deeper, and the blood stream thickened as it ran down her neck. Kokochin wickedly whispered, "You will lose. Messer Marco and Ghazan are intertwined more than you will ever know!"

Those words burned; Jia never thought of that. For the first time, she felt pain, and she could feel the blood run down her neck. In a sudden, unexpected rush of fear, she raised her fist and punched Kokochin on her back, "Ok! Ok! Drop the knife, let's talk."

This time, Kokochin was arrogant. "I thought we were talking. I have nothing else to say. I'm waiting for your answer."

Jia wasn't someone who easily gave up, but death was the alternative, feeling the determination in Kokochin's body. A simple answer was required if she wanted to live for another day and have a chance. The words burned her lips as she spoke. "I will remain silent. I will be Li and be content."

Kokochin's body relaxed as she lowered the knife. She shoved a cloth from her sleeve into Jia's hand, raised Jia's hand to her neck, and wiped the blood from her neck. Viciously, she showed Jia the blood-soaked cloth and said, "The next time I show you a cloth, it will be the last thing you see." Kokochin turned and walked out the door, and Jia fell to the floor.

She watched Kokochin shut the door. In a low murmur, she said, "You stupid girl, you should have killed me."

Kokochin returned to her room and started packing. Her heart told her Jia was lying. Li, walking into the room, interrupted her. She smiled and told Li to pack. "I'm in a hurry. Finally, I will be queen." They both giggled like the old days.

The next day, Li dressed as a man, while Jia dressed as the Princess of Song. Marco, Kokochin, his father, and uncle, along with Dai Xiuying, left Kerman, leaving the remaining girls to wait for Dai Xiuying's return.

Li left feeling hopeful. Kokochin felt anticipation, Marco felt desperation, and Jia radiated arrogance. Kokochin peered back at Jia, and her anticipation grew.

Chapter Sixty

Marco

1294 The Trees That Held Our Future

Genoa prison 1298

Marco looked up at Rustichello and stopped talking. He gathered his thoughts to continue.

Rustichello couldn't wait. He yelled out. "What happened? What happened?"

Marco started slowly. "Our caravan arrived at Ghazan's camp quicker than we wanted. Our blessed life could end here. I felt fear many times, but this was different." Marco hesitated for a moment. "I feel the same fear now: the unknown and the lack of control.

"Ghazan excitedly waited for us, and when he heard we were only a mile out, he and a large parade of his soldiers rode out to meet us. He rode past me and straight to Kokochin. He unmounted. Kokochin wasted no time; she unmounted like a fierce and confident queen. They faced each other and gazed into each other's eyes so intensely as if they yearned to see each other's souls. Li and I watched with wonder; beyond your control, destiny seemed to happen in unusual circumstances.

"Instead of Kokochin bowing to her new King, Ghazan suddenly bowed low. He rose with a smile, saying, 'My queen has finally arrived.' Kokochin's fierceness retreated. Her face softened, and she bowed to her king. When she rose, Ghazan lovingly held out his hand. 'It's time to go home.' Kokochin left our caravan, and they rode side by side, leading their warriors.

"As she left, Kokochin glanced at Jia. The glance was so powerful, I thought Jia would fall from her horse.

"For the next few days, a wedding festival commenced. Jia again presented herself to Ghazan as the Princess Li of Song. He greeted her well, and her fictitious sweetness oozed. A week later, we prepared to leave for Tabriz. Every night that week, Li and I held each other and trembled in fear. The night before we left, my breath returned. Li and I would have achieved our great lie in a few hours.

"Unfortunately, that night, a very soft knock interrupted my confidence. Quietly, I opened the door, not to wake Li. It was Guo Yu, his face ghostly white. I lost my breath as he handed me a note from Ghazan. The letter was brief, but his writing strokes were bold and wild. Meet me at the Dry Tree.

"Jia told; I was sure of it. My head exploded with the vision of Ghazan plunging his ornate sword into my chest.

"The black night's vast sky danced with millions of brilliant stars. In the distance, I could see a speck of light on the horizon; was it the moon or a flame? The closer I came, the more I realized it was both. Ghazan's face, distorted by the torch he held, bore the truth. His anger raged. Jia told.

"The rising moon reflected light upon one side of the towering trees, making them white. The other side was black, yet you knew it was green. As I approached him, he grabbed my reins, and his eyes met mine with contempt. My breath stopped. He motioned me to dismount. Before my feet hit the ground, he spoke softly and low, full of disappointment. 'I heard an interesting story that requires death. I decided not to kill you and your secret yet, as I owe you my life. Have you ever read the *Epistola Alexandri ad Asistotelem*?'

"I nodded yes.

"'Then you know these are the two Holy Trees, the trees of the sun and the moon. One is female. She foretells your future with the rising of the moon. The other is the male who can foretell your future if the sun rises brightly. Shall we find out your future?'

"My mouth was so dry I could hardly speak. Ghazan's voice relaxed. 'So far, you will live. The moon has risen; its glow shines upon you. Before the sun rises, tell me your side. The tree of the sun will determine your and your secrets' future.'

"Staring at Ghazan, his face reflected hurt; I had broken his trust. Ghazan held his large, unsheathed sword to his side and said, 'From the beginning.'

"Slowly, I told him our story. The year I found Li, how I protected her, how I loved her, how I lost and found her, and how I betrayed Kubilai and him. He listened without saying a word as I talked for hours. By the time I finished, the eastern skies displayed long strokes of pale color that streaked across the horizon. Like the pale color and dim light, my future seemed bleak. Closing my eyes. I prepared myself to die. Suddenly, the sound of pounding hooves rushed toward us. I opened my eyes as the glaring sun's rays rose without a tear from heaven, beaming a bright light across the land and upon Li, with her long, flowing hair and beautiful face exposed. Behind her were Guo Yu and Kokochin. I looked back at Ghazan, whose face showed astonishment. The tree of the sun had spoken. Li was my future, not death.

"Ghazan walked past me, patting me on my shoulder and placing his sword in its sheath. Li dismounted and ran toward me, jumping into my arms and showering me with kisses."

***

Ghazan mounted his horse and rode toward Kokochin, who had stopped to watch. Tears flowed down her face. He stopped beside her, pulled her from her horse into his saddle, placed his arms around her, and whispered in her ear. 'I'm happy the sun shone brightly today. I was in no mood to kill any of you. Soon, it will be Jia's day.'

Kokochin shivered. Ghazan held her tighter. Kokochin thought, *I have been lucky. Would Jia?*

***

"The next day, before we departed, my father, uncle, and I stood before Ghazan, Kokochin, and Jia. We said our goodbyes with tears and smiles as the sun glowed. Jia never smiled, knowing today could be her last. The next day, the sun didn't shine. Jia's future seemed ominous. But we never knew what happened to her."

***

Kokochin stood over Jia's lifeless body, her knife dripping blood. Ghazan walked over, took her knife, guided Kokochin to her horse, they mounted, and rode toward his camp.

Chapter Sixty-One

Marco

1295 The Strangers

Genoa prison 1298

Marco looked out the cell window. The day was gloomy. *Has my bright future with Li come to an end? Have I ruined it with a decision more like my father?* At that moment, he faced his true self mournfully. It was not his father's decision but his own. *Why have I blamed my father my whole life for my misfortunes? I was a grown man and made those decisions myself. I was just like my father. Selfish.* Marco walked over to his bed and, with his foot, shoved the dirty blanket against the wall. He fell to his knees, closed his eyes, and prayed. *Please, Lord God, let me return home and protect her. I will repent, I promise you.* He repeated it with hopeful repentance until he fell over with exhaustion.

The following day, Marco awoke to the sound of clanging iron bars and men yelling. He wondered if he would ever forget this sound. He walked over to Rustichello. The sun was bright, and a stream of light hit Marco's face. "It looks like the sun is shining on me. Maybe my future will be bright." They sat down at the table, and he continued his story.

"We finally reached Tabriz. Gaykhatu and his queen, Padishah, were very interested in our future business plans and savored the possibility of filling their vaults. As I said, Padishah was a clever woman, not only in business. She often made sly remarks, smiling. 'The man who accompanies you is as beautiful as a woman.'

"After nine months, my father and uncle's instinct sensed a changing tide; the tension between Gaykhatu and Prince Baydu had grown. Fortunately, my father and uncle had a talent for reading the immediate circumstances. I think that is why we survived all those years. We quickly departed for Venice.

"Before we left, Gaykhatu issued us four gold tablets of authority: two bore the sign of the gyrfalcon, one of the lion, and one plain. Along with the tablets, Gaykhatu wrote a letter instructing all to honor and serve us throughout the land like we were the khan himself.

"My father wasn't wrong. Gaykhatu died four months later from poison, and Padishah died on her way to Ghazan. Prince Baydu, his generals, and Ghazan fought a great battle. Ghazan won, becoming the khan with Kokochin as his Queen. We also heard other stories: He won only with the help of his past enemy, Nawruz, when Ghazan forsook his Tartar ways and became Muslim in exchange for a mighty Muslim army."

Weeks passed as Marco continued his story. "As we traveled toward Venice and neared our departure from the Ilkhan Empire, our travels became more dangerous. The tablets had no meaning. Marco stopped talking for a moment to collect his thoughts. "That was a sad time. Dai Xiuying, my trusted guide and friend, died defending us and saving our few trunks from bandits." Marco hesitated as he said a small prayer. He then continued. "Li and I often wondered what happened to the girls who wished to return to their homes with Dai Xiuying." Then he continued his story.

"When we reached Trebizond, we sailed to Constantinople. It was here the news of the war between Genoa and Venice had ignited. Luckily, when we arrived, their fighting slowed, and we left Constantinople for Negropont and finally arrived in Venice. By the time we reached Venice, as I mentioned, we arrived in rags with a few trunks, looking like foreigners, Tartars with limited Venetian language skills. Our families hardly recognized us and had many doubts that our stories were real. It was not until we held a banquet and revealed our jewels and gold coins sewn into our old, torn jackets that our families finally believed."

Marco stood and looked at Rustichello and softly said, "The End."

Rustichello clapped. "What an amazing story."

Marco looked sorrowful and said, "I wish the rest of the story were amazing."

Chapter Sixty-Two

Marco

1298 The Real End

Genoa prison 1298

Marco watched Rustichello write nonstop for the next few days as he rethought the words, '*The End.*' It didn't end there, but he wished it had. Everyone was happy, especially LI.

Marco walked over to his bed and lay down. The sounds of Rustichello's hand gliding over the papers and the scratching sound of the feather's point had become familiar but would soon end. He was sad. Telling one's life in a year is relatively short. *Is there more to come, or is this the end?*

It was a stormy morning when the prisoners erupted in a frenzy. Marco stood at the cell door window, trying to hear. His heart flip-flopped. He turned and yelled to Rustichello. "They signed an agreement. The fighting is over!" His voice cracked, and tears flowed. "Will they release me? They must let me go home. I won't end up like you, fourteen more years?"

Rustichello stared at Marco with tired eyes. "You are the great explorer and merchant who opened the famous Silk Road. Your country, Venice, owes you, Messer Marco Polo."

"Right, right!" Marco kept saying, trying to believe.

A torturous week passed before Marco heard keys clanging, the lock turning, and the door opening. It was the commander. "Messer Marco Polo, you must have friends in high places! I received a letter for your immediate release."

The commander rushed out before Marco could recover from the shock. The slamming door brought Marco back to reality. "Wait, wait, you bastard!" Marco screamed. "When are you going to release me?"

As the commander walked away, he shouted. "Tomorrow!"

Tomorrow was a week later. Marco and Rustichello da Pisa were released. As they traveled to Venice, their conversation never ceased. Marco talked of Li and Rustichello about his new book.

Chapter Sixty-Three

Marco

Marco's Final Hours and Fantina Learns the Secret

Venice, Marco's Palazzo 1324

For a moment, Marco, on the verge of death, regained consciousness. He could hear sobbing. Opening his blurred eyes, he recognized Moreta sitting next to him. Her head tilted down, and tears flowed down her face. With his failing strength, he raised his frail arm and gently wiped her tears with a soft, wrinkled hand. Moreta opened her eyes and looked down at her father. Her sobbing quieted. Their eyes met. Marco weakly spoke. "I want you to know I love your mother, you, and your sisters with all my heart. Your mother saved my life. My heart indeed belonged to another once, yet your mother overlooked this love, my drunkenness, boasting, sins, and failures. Maybe God never accepted my repentance, but she did and never failed to love me."

Moreta gasped, and tears flowed again.

Marco tried to reach her tears, but was too weak.

With a soft, loving voice, Moreta encouraged her father to rest. "You can tell me more later."

Marco struggled to speak, changing the subject. "My will is simple. I am leaving all I have to your mother, you, and your sisters. Your cousins will hate you, as I refuse to leave them a penny.

"Guo Yu, Guo Yu, are you here? Yu!!" Marco continued in a less formal tone, struggling to speak.

"Yes, Messer Marco. Yes, I promised you years ago I would never leave your side," Guo Yu answered, walking to the other side of the bed and touching Marco's hand.

Marco turned in his direction and looked at him with sad, clouded eyes. "You can finally leave."

Guo Yu's emotions could no longer be contained. He bursts into loud sobbing. Marco gripped his hand and squeezed.

With much effort, Marco turned to Moreta and said, "Guo Yu is to be freed as directed in my will. Even though he has always been free to go as he pleased, it was only out of necessity that we labeled him as my slave in the beginning."

Marco's eyes slowly closed, and his grip on Guo Yu's hand relaxed. Guo Yu stopped sobbing and frantically looked down at Marco. When he heard Marco's frail voice whisper, "Guo Yu," he felt relief. "Yes, Messer Marco."

Marco whispered, "Isn't it time you just call me Marco?"

Guo Yu nodded.

"Guo Yu, your last duty is to complete Li's story. Tell Moreta about her cousin, Isabella, Luca, Li's faithful servant and best friend, and Messer Alessio." Still struggling, Marco turned to Moreta and continued whispering so low that Moreta put her ear to Marco's lips. "I will never retract my book. There was so much more to my life that I never told. But everything I wrote was true. Things I didn't understand or know will be disclosed in the future. Have faith and protect my legacy." Marco's words faded. Frightened, Moreta rose and looked at Guo Yu with concern.

Guo Yu placed his fingers in front of Marco's nose. "He still breathes."

Moreta let out a deep breath and sat again. She grabbed Marco's hand. "Father, I'm listening. Tell me about Li, Isabella, Luca, and Messer Alessio.

Guo Yu looked at Moreta. "I'll tell you."

Marco listened with an aching heart. Guo Yu has told this story many times. Whenever Marco returned to this locked room, drunk and longing for Li, he insisted that Guo Yu tell him the story. Marco wanted punishment for his greediness and selfishness. He remembered Donata rescuing him from his self-pity. At last, this would be the last time he heard it.

Guo Yu slowly started while staring out the window. Closing his eyes, Guo Yu envisioned Li sitting and playing her beloved erhu. When he opened them, only her chair and the erhu remained; her image had faded.

"Your father and I found Li when she was five. Your father was around twenty. Kubilai Khan had finally defeated her country, and they sent Marco to escort the empress, the young emperor, and any remaining court members back to his palace. Her mother, like most of the court ladies, had killed herself. He found Li, a frightened little girl surrounded by blood, ready to kill or be killed. She brought your father to tears, but it was Li who comforted him. From that day, they shared a bond that no one could break. Li loved him from that day forward. It took your father longer.

"I became her caretaker, her servant, that day. Your father secretly protected her for seventeen years until Buyan Kelmysh Khatun felt her daughter's betrothed was falling in love with Li. That's when fate took a turn. Three lords from Persia came looking for a princess to marry King Arghun, Kubilai Khan's nephew. Kokochin, Li's friend, was selected, and Li was to become his concubine. Of course, Buyan Kelmysh Khatun was the cause. Your father was in India but, by a miracle, heard of her tragedy. He traveled miles to save her, betraying Kubilai Khan. He had no choice but to leave Cathay. After many trials and tribulations, they made it to Venice three years later."

Amazed, Moreta spoke out loud. "What an incredible story. I want to hear more."

Guo Yu continued. "Li and Marco soon discovered the Polo's palazzo did not differ from the inner chamber. Marco's cousins hated her; a slant-eyed barbarian disgraced their home, and they feared their community would reject them. Your father continued to protect her as he did in Cathay. A year later, after we returned, your grandfather died. Things changed. The war between Genoa and Venice raged, and your father had no choice but to enter the war in 1297. The Genoa War threatened their trade business to a state of nonexistence. Your father became the commander of a ship and promised a horrified Li that he would return quickly. He kept his promise until late '97 when he disappeared. Li remained as strong as she could. Thankfully, that year, a new servant named Luca entered her life and helped her survive. Without her, Li's life would have been unbearable. Li spent hours telling Luca her story, longing for your father. At the day's end when the night consumed the city, she would sit in that chair. Guo Yu pointed toward the window and chair that faced the canal. Moreta's eyes left her father's for a moment, and she followed Guo Yu's finger as he continued. "Li would sit in her chair and play her erhu, brokenhearted. Her music cried as she called your father home.

Marco squeezed Guo Yu's hand harder and, in a louder whisper, said, "Tell her, tell her, tell me. I need the pain one more time."

Guo Yu sat for a moment and thought, *I have told this story many times over the past few years.*

He looked over at the chair. Again, he envisioned Li sitting there playing her erhu. She stopped playing and looked over at Guo Yu. He could hear her voice, and it was as if her soul had infiltrated his soul.

Li spoke through Guo Yu. *"I sat at my window, my erhu in my lap, straining my eyes to see the Rialto Bridge. The moon was so full and bright. My heart hurt as I looked down at the glistening canal. If only I could see a boat carrying him to me. Lovingly rubbing my stomach, I thought, 'It has been so long since I have seen you. I have something important to tell you.' Then, I returned to hurtful thoughts: 'You promised you would return to me. You have always kept your promises.' But that night, I felt something different. Tears rolled down my cheeks as I positioned my erhu to play. I promised Guo Yu I wouldn't play tonight; Isabella had become almost insane with my music. I couldn't help myself. I kept thinking, 'Maybe you are lost and can't find me.' My heart cried, and my tears flowed as my music cried. I was calling you home."*

Chapter Sixty-Four

Li

The Erhu

Venice 1299

Isabella went to the kitchen and was relieved that Li wasn't playing her horrid instrument. *Talking to Peter must have worked*. As she ascended the stairs, a sudden rush of guilt hit her. *I have never given Li the letter. Am I a horrible person to hate her so much?* But the feeling subsided as fast as it arrived. The disgusting music escaped Li's room. Without thinking, she pushed on the door, and surprisingly, it opened. Li was sitting at the window. Isabella's guilt left, and her rage took over. *That instrument has to go.*

Li was lost in sorrow when the door suddenly opened. At that moment, she remembered she had not locked it. Standing, she looked toward the door. Isabella's eyes pierced her, and Li could feel the hate.

Isabella, screaming, moved seemingly in slow motion toward her. "Marco is dead. We received the letter from the Dogie months ago. Stop playing that disgusting, screaming instrument. Marco is not coming home."

Li stood statue-like; her body wouldn't move, only her lips. "What did you say?"

"Marco is dead!" Isabella screamed.

Guo Yu had been lying in bed, praying Li wouldn't play. Isabella cornered him in the hallway this morning. Her hatred for Li had grown, and she seemed almost insane. He remembered her crazed words. "*Tell that Manzi barbaric princess I will throw it out the window if I hear it one more time.*"

When the music filled his room, he jumped out of bed and headed for Li's room. As he entered, he saw Li and Isabella's silhouettes fighting in the moonlight. In that second, the erhu flew out the window. Li's arm and then her body stretched far out, reaching, and she tumbled out the window. Isabella, sobbing, bent over the window, looking down.

Guo Yu could hardly catch his breath as he turned and ran down the stairs to the bottom floor, where the canal ran under the palazzo. Sweat dripping down his face, he stepped into the boat and picked up the oars. He thought, *I must find her,* while manically rowing out into the canal, repeatedly calling her name. In disbelief, he looked up toward the window. Isabella was gone. He then continued searching. Suddenly, a flowing white dress glowing in the moonlight caught his attention. Rowing violently toward it, through his tear-soaked eyes, he saw her face down. With as much strength as he could muster, he pulled her body into the boat. In her hand, she held the erhu. *Is she dead?* Guo Yu thought as he cried, putting his two fingers close to her nose and placing his ear on her chest. He thought he could feel breathing and hear a heartbeat. Picking up the oars, all he could think about was the Golden Head. Messer Alessio could surely save her and the baby.

Guo Yu rowed so hard his arms were on the verge of giving way. In the distance, the moon's glow directed him to the Rialto Bridge. Cautiously, he looked around, hoping no one saw him. He was grateful it was late; only drunks were sleeping under the bridge. Carefully, he rowed to the edge, gently cradled her, and stepped onto the stone stairs. Li moaned. A welcome sound; she was alive.

Discreetly as possible, Guo Yu carried Li to the Golden Head and knocked on the door numerous times, becoming more fearful with each knock. It seemed like a lifetime before Messer Alessio opened the door. Seeing Guo Yu's face at this late hour alarmed him, and then he saw the cradled, small body dripping water in his arms. He pulled Guo Yu in the door and directed him to the back.

Luca entered the room at the same time and wailed with horror. "Dear God, is she dead?"

Guo Yu didn't answer her question, but screamed instead. "Please help her and the child. She fell into the canal from her window."

Luca, in a state of shock, said, "Or was she pushed?"

As Guo Yu laid Li on a bed, a frail voice echoed in the quiet brick room. "Marco is dead, Marco is dead."

Guo Yu couldn't believe her words. "What did you say?"

Li never said another word, devastating Guo Yu.

Luca whimpered as Alessio helped her remove Li's wet, white, flowing dress, surrounded her with warm blankets, and placed warming pans beneath them. Alessio listened to Li's pulse as she had taught him, then put his ear to her chest. Her lungs rattled. He then placed his hand on her extended stomach, leaving it there for many minutes until his face drew a smile. "The baby is alive. I feel movement."

Luca hugged Li. "The baby is alive. You must live for your baby. You must live."

With gentle urges, Luca spooned teaspoons of warm herbal tea into her mouth.

Guo Yu stayed until the morning light seeped into the room. He could hear Li breathing. His anger erupted; he could no longer contain himself. Leaving without saying goodbye, he raced back to Isabella. The closer he came, the more his speed slowed, and he thought more clearly. His anger subsided, and reason prevailed. *There was no way Isabella reported this incident to the authorities, but there was a possibility. I could endanger Luca and Messer Alessio if I stormed into the palazzo.* Guo Yu stopped unconsciously and looked around. *Did anyone see me? I need to be more discreet.* In the distance, he could see Isabella standing before the door. Her face was pale, but her stance, as always, was obstinate. *Is she waiting for the authorities or me?* Slowly, he turned and walked back to Li, deciding they must disappear and wait for Marco. Guo Yu couldn't make himself believe Marco was dead.

From that day forward, Guo Yu made it his mission to find Marco, dead or alive. He tried to see the Doge, Pietro Gradenenigo, sitting for days in the hall, waiting. As hope faded, he decided on his only option, the Basilica di San Marco. Marco had a history with them, donating many precious gifts. He may be received there. Guo Yu prepared a letter and was ecstatic when the clergyman took it from him. "I'm begging you, please give it to Doge Pietro Gradenenigo."

Isabella stood on the front stoop, stunned, remembering the night before. The blood drained from her face. She felt faint; the vision from the night before terrified her: Li falling as her white, flowing dress glowed in the moonlight, swirling around in the air, followed by a large, glistening splash, then her white dress swirling as she floated. *It was beautiful*. Anger swelled. *How could I think it was beautiful?* Her lips tilted slightly upward into an evil smile. Isabella remembered thinking that Li was finally gone as she closed the shutters. In bliss, she had walked from Li's room into her room and lay on her bed, relishing the silence—no more horrible music. She drifted off to a deep sleep.

The following day brought the reality that abruptly interrupted her blissfulness. *Where is Peter? Did he see what happened? I have yet to see him. What is he going to do and say? The servants will ask questions, and even my father might. He liked Guo Yu.*

Isabella looked at her clasped hands turning red, and her knuckles turning white as she stood on the stoop. She whispered to herself, "Think, think, Isabella. You're smart." She looked up and out to the street. For an instant, she thought she saw Peter watching her. Her heart pounded. But suddenly, the vision disappeared. Her smile returned, and in her delusional mind, she thought, *He will not face me. They are gone. I will tell everyone Peter came to me late last night and told me they would leave early for the seashore—Li needed space, white sand, and the soft breezes to clear her head. They would return when she felt rested.* Fantasizing that her explanation would do, she entered the house in good spirits.

After a week, the servants began gossiping with each other. It was strange. One servant entered Li's room for housekeeping and found all her belongings scattered. She seemed to have left in a hurry. Out of curiosity, the same maid went into Guo Yu's room. His was the same; he did not even make his bed. That was unlike him. However, they dared not question Isabella. It was the day her father entered the palazzo shouting the news, "The war is ending!" Isabella faltered; her face turned white, and she fainted.

Meanwhile, the news circulated through the streets and drifted in and out of the Golden Head. "The war is ending. The Doge was meeting with the Genoese, and an agreement was in place."

Guo Yu hopefully sat next to Li, who had never fully recovered. Li lay quietly, dreaming of Marco. Her breathing had improved, except for the same rattle. The dirty canal water had filled her lungs. Messer Alessio and Luca tried every herb but failed.

Gripping her hand, Guo Yu softly spoke. "The war is ending. You must get better; Messer Marco will come home."

Li opened her eyes and struggled to sit. Guo Yu helped her. In a sad voice, while her hands rubbed her bulging belly, she said, "Do you really think he is alive? I have tried to believe."

Guo Yu hesitated and, with great confidence, answered. "Yes! He promised you, and he has never failed you."

A small smile appeared and then quickly faded. "Why did Isabella lie to me?"

Guo Yu didn't hesitate. "To hurt you. Isabella wanted to see you suffer. Isn't that like her?"

"Unfortunately, yes, and she accomplished her goal." Li changed the subject. "How will Marco find me?"

Guo Yu spoke with confidence. "Are you talking about the same Messer Marco? The man who found you thousands of miles away. How can you ask that?"

For the first time in a long time, Li giggled.

Suddenly, with her face distorted with pain, Li cried out. "It can't be. It's not time. Marco is not here."

Guo Yu helped her lie down and called for Luca, who rushed into the room. Li reached for Luca, who grabbed her hand. With a restrained voice, Li asked, "Please, Luca, stop the pain! I can't have this baby, not now."

Luca, sorrowful, looked over at Guo Yu. "OK, I'll be right back."

Guo Yu followed Luca, and they met Alessio, their concern evident in their voices. They all agreed she must have the baby now, or they both might die. "She grows weaker by the day."

Luca could no longer hold back the tears. Her knees buckled, and she fell to the ground, sobbing. Messer Alessio walked over to Luca and offered his hand. Tenderly, he told Luca, "Stand. You must be strong, my wife. Prepare tea for pain, and let nature and the heavens direct the course."

Guo Yu returned to the room. He pulled up a chair, held Li's hand, and gently patted her head with the other hand.

Luca brought in the tea, observing Guo Yu's love. Restraining her tears, she thought, *I must be strong*. He urged Li to drink the tea. Alessio entered the room. "Li, you must be strong; it is time."

Li grasped Guo Yu's hand harder and said tearfully, "Stay with me."

The day and night were long, and finally, the morning brought the penetrating wails of a newborn baby. Luca cradled the baby and handed it to Guo Yu, who tenderly wrapped the tiny, healthy baby in a blanket and laid it on Li's chest. "It's a girl, a beautiful girl like her mother."

Li's arms tightened around her newborn daughter and whispered, "Your father will be here soon. I saw him in my dream and told him to hurry. Only I can introduce you to him. Your name is Agnese, the pure one, like your mother and father's love." Without warning, her eyes closed, and her hugging arms released Agnese. Guo Yu panicked and retrieved Agnese.

Alessio rushed to her side, lifted her wrist, and felt her pulse, assuring Guo Yu, "Her body is weak, but her will to live has grown; her pulse is strong."

Luca left the room and brought back a woman named Maria, a wet nurse. She would feed Agnese until Li became stronger.

Chapter Sixty-Five

Marco

The Painful Arrival

Venice 1299

When Marco and Rustichello arrived in Venice, they parted, agreeing to meet up in a couple of weeks. As Marco approached home, he looked up at Li's window before his gondola glided beneath his palazzo. For weeks, he had imagined her sitting there, playing her erhu. *She would be ecstatic at the sight of me and run to meet me.* His spirit withered. *The window is empty.* As the gondola disappeared beneath the palazzo and reached the gates, Marco yelled for Guo Yu. A servant, Marco didn't know, answered his call. "Who goes there?"

"It's me, Messer Marco Polo, open the gates."

The shocked servant lost his breath and quickly opened the gates. Marco dashed up the stairs. As he passed, the servants couldn't believe their eyes. Marco thought, *They looked like they had seen a ghost*. Marco entered his room. It was stale and dark, and the presence of loneliness seeped into his soul. Li's things remained scattered as she had left them that day. He quickly rushed to Guo Yu's room. It was the same. When he shut his room, his uncle ascended the stairs. His face radiated a mix of emotions; his lips smiled with happiness, while his eyes conveyed sadness.

Surprisingly, his uncle wrapped his arms around him and whispered. "Come to my study; we need to talk." Marco became concerned, as his uncle had never shown him any sympathy.

Maffeo slowly started. "Li and Guo Yu left three or so months ago. He told Isabella that Li was losing her mind, so he took her to the sea to recover. They have never returned."

Marco listened, but he did not believe what he heard. Before Maffeo could say more, he said, "I don't believe it!" Marco shouted. "Where is Isabella?"

Maffeo, trying to comfort him, replied. "We will find them."

Marco backed away, saying, "Is this the first time you have tried?"

Maffeo became quiet and then spoke, "I trusted Guo Yu. Don't you?"

Momentarily, Marco hesitated. "Of course, I trust him. You know that. But things don't seem right. Where is Isabella?"

"She's in her room. Isabella has been ill for a while."

"What kind of illness? Guilt or her lack of ability to hide her happiness!" Marco snarled. "You know she never liked Li!"

"Marco! Don't blame my daughter for Li's weakness and your failure," Maffeo barked back.

Marco, raging, picked up a chair and threw it across the room. Servants who had been listening came rushing in. Maffeo's servant grabbed Marco. Marco's anger was stronger than the servant's will, so he threw the servant to the floor.

Suddenly, Isabella rushed into the room, yelling. "He's telling you the truth; they disappeared in the early morning darkness."

A stunned Marco turned. Isabella stood arrogantly, screaming. "He is telling you the truth!"

Marco gazed at her; he could see through her. *She is lying. She must be.* Marco stomped out of the house, out of his mind with grief. Through tear-filled eyes, he saw a familiar face standing in the courtyard. It was their cook, Elena.

Knowing Marco saw her, she lowered her head, placed the hood over her head, and started walking. Marco followed. She disappeared around a corner. When Marco turned the corner, she was waiting for him. Elena whispered. "You are right. Something is wrong. Li was fine the day she disappeared. Besides, Guo Yu would never leave without telling me. Another thing is that Isabella caught Li's maid in her room a couple of months before they disappeared. She, too, disappeared. I heard she was looking for a letter."

Marco could see her tears. He stood terrified. Unconsciously, his thoughts tumbled from his mouth. "What could have happened? Was it my letter she was looking for?"

Elena continued. "All of us have been walking on eggshells. Isabella is the one who's been acting like a madwoman."

Marco sighed.

"Peter told me they spent mornings at the Golden Head. Maybe they know something. I went there several times, hoping to see him. That didn't happen."

Marco could hardly contain himself. An old habit returned; he bowed low, quickly raised, and ran. The crowds were out, and it seemed forever to reach the Golden Head. He could hardly catch his breath when he reached the Golden Head and opened the door. Alessio gaped. His heart skipped a beat. He rushed to Marco, wrapped his arms around him, and whispered. "My heart sings, hallelujah, you are alive." He released Marco, quickly locked the door, and ushered him back past his herb storeroom and down a small hall. He opened the door and entered with Marco following.

Guo Yu couldn't believe his eyes. Trying to hold in his emotions, he stood and walked toward Marco. His face told the story. Marco looked beyond him and saw Li lying on the bed. She looked tiny. Her face was pale and withdrawn, yet beautiful. He felt as if an arrow had pierced his heart.

Guo Yu and Alessio exited the room and walked to the front. Luca was knocking on the door, confused. *Why is the door locked?* Alessio opened the door, grabbed Luca, and hugged her. "Messer Marco has returned."

Marco swiftly walked over to Li, sat in the chair, and whispered in her ear. "Li, my love, I'm here. I'm sorry it took me so long." He sweetly laid his hand on her cheek and softly kissed her forehead.

Li opened her eyes. "Marco, your hands have become soft, free of calluses. Did you find another princess to pamper you? Leaving me to survive your family." Li weakly giggled.

Marco's eyes welled and overflowed. His head fell to his chest in shame, mumbling, "I failed you; I'm sorry."

Li struggled and raised her hand, wiping his tears. "You haven't failed me; you are late, but you are here now. But someone else arrived earlier than planned. I told her to wait, but she didn't listen."

"She?" Marco said, confused.

Li held her hand up and pointed to the back of the room. Marco hadn't noticed a woman sitting in a chair across the room. "Our daughter. I have been waiting for you, Marco. Only I could introduce you to our daughter."

The woman stood and walked toward Marco, who stumbled to his feet. Li smiled as the wet nurse placed the swaddled infant in his arms. "Marco, this is your daughter, Agnese."

"Agnese, this is your father, Marco." Li's voice became weaker as she spoke. "Her name means pure; she is pure as our love. I wanted you to know this. You always questioned our love. That always made me sad. You were my destiny. I only lived because of you."

Marco carefully sat, holding his daughter tight with one arm, and reached for Li's hand with the other. He squeezed it tightly. "Li, you have always been my pure light, and I have followed it willingly. I will love her as I have loved you."

Li looked at Marco seriously. "You must never leave her or me again, no matter what. You understand, Marco?"

Marco sadly nodded. "I understand." Marco was momentarily silent, then, in a questioning voice, asked. "Didn't you receive my letter? I made a deal with my captor, the Genoese commander. I traced my footsteps to Cathay for him in exchange for my release. He agreed to deliver a letter to you."

"The letter, that bitch. That bitch, that bitch," she kept repeating as she struggled to sit. Her voice had more strength than she had in months.

Her anger surprised Marco. With his free arm, he helped her sit, trying to calm her. "Who are you referring to?" Suddenly, he remembered Isabella's frantic, arrogant voice, screaming that her father was telling the truth and what the cook had said.

Li started violently coughing. Frightened, Marco called out to Guo Yu and Maria, who took Agnese. Marco tightly held Li in his arms. He could feel Li relax, and her cough subsided.

In a frail voice, she whispered in his ear. "Isabella. Luca saw Isabella placing a letter in her book. She smiled strangely and acted suspiciously when she saw Luca watching her." Li's voice faded.

Guo Yu, Alessio, and Luca stood in the room, listening. Marco hugged her harder and then gently laid her down. Alessio walked over and felt her pulse. "Her pulse is weak but stronger than ever, Messer Marco. Let her rest for a while."

Marco kissed Li on the cheek, stood, took Agnese from Maria, and lovingly kissed her tiny cheek. Immediately, his persona changed as his thoughts returned to Isabella and his uncle. His tender face suddenly turned red as his blood boiled. He left Li's room with Agnese, followed by Guo Yu and Luca. When he knew Li could not hear, he roared. "What the hell happened?!" Marco could hardly contain himself. Agnese felt his anger and started crying. Hearing her, Marco crumbled and melted into a humbled being.

Luca took Agnese from his arms. Marco watched her cuddle and lovingly comfort her. "Who are you?" Marco asked.

Lovingly, Luca touched Marco's hand. "I am Li's maid and friend, Luca. Messer Marco, I have heard so much about you; I feel I know you. Messer Alessio and I live together."

Suddenly, Marco realized she was the missing servant. "You, you know the truth. Please tell me everything," he said sternly.

Guo Yu spoke first, "Marco, please be calm. You are going to upset Agnese again."

Marco looked down. Agnese's face softened his, and he smiled. "She looks more like Li, don't you think, Guo Yu?"

He answered, "I hope so."

Marco slightly laughed, his thoughts returning to Isabella. He could feel his anger beginning to erupt.

Luca called for Maria. As she handed Agnese to her, she directed Marco to follow her to the front and to sit. "Let's begin. Li missed you so much that she would sit in her window and play her erhu. She hoped it would call you home. Isabella desperately hated Li and her music."

Marco again lowered his head and listened to Luca.

"Things escalated when I told Li I saw Isabella opening a letter and acting suspicious when she saw me, quickly placing it in a book and going to her room. Li was determined to find it."

Marco stopped Luca. "It must have been the letter I wrote telling her the Genoese had captured me and I was alive."

At the same time, Guo Yu and Luca said, "Isabella knew all this time. She is heartless."

Luca looked at Guo Yu and said, "You were right; she wanted Li to suffer."

Marco's blood boiled hotter. "Continue."

Luca proceeded with her story. "Li insisted on searching Isabella's room herself.

Just then, Guo Yu interrupted Luca. "Luca prevented Isabella from finding Li and took the blame. That's why she is here. She had to run and is now considered a runaway slave. The only good thing from this is that Luca and Messer Alessio found love."

Luca's face became flushed.

Guo Yu continued and ended with the story of the night Li fell.

Marco's eyes widened. His fist slammed into the arm of the chair, and his face distorted with anger. Guo Yu became frightened and quickly spoke up, grabbing his hand. "Messer Marco, this is not the time for revenge. Li needs you now more than ever." His voice became solemn. Her days are few, and her life dangles by a thread; you are her thread. Stay by her side like you promised. Don't break your promise again. Her heart will break. She will take revenge by refusing to see you in the next world."

Marco slithered down into the chair. Everything he heard broke his spirit and filled him with more guilt, as he had been many times while in prison.

Guo Yu continued talking. "Messer Marco, there will be plenty of time for revenge, and I will help you."

Marco stood and straightened his body. Looking down at Guo Yu, he confidently said, "I promise, and I will keep my promise this time." He then walked to her room, carefully took Agnese, sat beside Li, and whispered, "I missed you so much and will never leave you again."

With closed eyes, Li squeezed his hand and whispered. "And I will always love you."

Marco slid into the bed next to Li, with Agnese in between. He had dreamed of this moment for so long.

The following day, Agnese's tiny cry awakened Marco. Li was missing. Startled, he jumped from the bed and saw Li dressing. Her face was pale, her body thin, and her movements were slow. But her essence glowed intensely.

Li heard Marco stirring. "I never thought you were going to wake up. Get ready. It's time for our revenge."

After Marco left, Isabella locked herself in her room. Her maid and she frantically searched book after book. Her father pounded on the door several times, unaware of what she was doing. He could hear a disturbed voice mumbling and the sound of objects being thrown. After several hours, he had a servant forcibly open her door. He found her sitting on the floor among hundreds of books, sobbing and, between each sob, whimpering. "Where is it? Where?"

Isabella looked up at her father with a troubled face and cried. "Who dared to enter my room? Who?"

Her father, confused, looked at the maid. "What's going on? Help her up."

Isabella refused and kept exclaiming, "It must be here."

Maffeo stormed to Isabella, forcibly made her stand, and walked her to her bed. He sternly ordered one maid to help and the other to call the physician.

Isabella fought, but the two finally managed to put her to bed. She surrendered, yet she mumbled, "Where? Who?"

Maffeo, worried his daughter had gone mad, turned to the maid and asked, "What is she raving about?"

The servant lowered her head in fear.

"Speak! Speak!" Maffeo yelled.

The servant looked over at Isabella in bed.

Maffeo couldn't believe the servant was more afraid of Isabella than him. Under his breath, he mumbled. "Has she gone mad, or is she that cruel...or both?" He instructed the maid to stay by her side and went downstairs to wait for the physician. Suddenly, he thought of Guo Yu. *Where did he go? He would know what to do.* His thoughts continued. *What did happen to Li? Did my daughter have something to do with her disappearance? She has been acting strangely since that day. Come to think of it, Li's maid also ran away.*

Maffeo felt a tinge of regret and remorse. He knew Isabella hated Li and that dreadful instrument. *Could Marco be right? Have I intentionally turned a blind eye and overlooked the situation? Has my long-time envy consumed me? Since Marco obtained the permits from Kubilai,*

I have carried a torch that burned a hole in my heart, hoping someday, Marco would experience loss and disappointment. Did I secretly really want Marco to suffer?

Maffeo was grateful that the physician's knock on his study door interrupted his disturbing thoughts. After a brief discussion, the physician left Maffeo and instructed the maid to prepare the tea he had brought. The servant had filled him in on the way over. The physician ascended the stairs with the tea and entered her room. Observing her and the room as Isabella mumbled, he decided she had indeed had a moment of insanity. He forced the tea down her throat, and her mumbling ceased. The physician instructed her maid to give her more tea when she awoke. "She needs rest to recover," he said as he left her room.

Maffeo was waiting outside her door. As they descended the stairs, the physician told him the same thing: "I will return tomorrow. Try to keep her quiet. Do you know what she was looking for?"

Maffeo stopped at the base of the stairs and called for her maid. While both watched, she trudged down the stairs, her face long and expressionless.

The physician spoke. "You want her to improve, right? Tell me what was so important."

Her eyes turned toward her father, then to the physician. "All I know is she was looking for a letter in a book. She couldn't find it."

"A letter?" Maffeo said. "How could a letter be that important?" Just saying the words, Maffeo's heart stopped. He dismissed the maid and hurried the physician out. "I will call for you tomorrow if I need you." He entered his study in shock. "It can't be." He mumbled. "She couldn't be that cruel?" Maffeo sat at his desk, staring out the large window. His lips moved slowly. "Did she know Marco was alive? Did she hide a letter meant for Li?"

At the Golden Head, Marco resisted Li's request, lying back in bed and staring at her. Li walked over and sat on the bed. She placed her small hand on Marco's cheek. He raised his hand and lovingly covered her hand. Their tearful eyes met, and Marco spoke first. "You should rest. You haven't recovered fully."

"I have rested for months waiting for you. Seeing you alive has brought me enormous strength. Just thinking of confronting Isabella fills me with an energy force. I cannot be controlled." Short of breath, Li coughed into a floral handkerchief and hid the blood. She continued. "I must do this, or my soul will never rest. The time has come. She intentionally made me suffer the unbearable, making me believe that you were dead."

Marco interrupted. "But I caused you the most pain; I left you. Don't you want revenge?"

Li took Marco's hand into hers and held it to her heart. "I knew the first night I went to you as a woman, you were loyal to your ideals and devoted to the ones you loved. That included

Kubilai and, this time, your Venice. I was never naïve; I waited for you most of my life, even though I would never come first. But Isabella intentionally meant to hurt us."

Marco could not hold back his tears. There was an urgency in his voice. "Please forgive me. I promised you; I did everything I could to return."

Li reached down and kissed him. "And you did. Now, please do this for me. Let's make her suffer. She must live the rest of her life knowing that we and others, even if only a few, know what kind of person she is: despicable. Then I will be satisfied."

"I won't be satisfied so easily until I take what she loves most: money and the respect and envy that come with it," Marco said as he sat up. He wrapped his arms around Li and whispered. "Let's get our revenge."

Marco and Li rose and dressed. Li dressed in one of Luca's dresses and tried not to show how difficult it was. Marco secretly watched; his heart ached, knowing he didn't have the right to stop her, even though this was the hardest thing he had ever done. He would forever feel unbearable guilt.

They silently slipped out of the apothecary, leaving Agnese fast asleep beside Maria. It was early morning, and the sun was peeking through the buildings, illuminating their many colors, but not enough light to cause a glint on the Grand Canal. Only a fine fog floated on its surface, undisturbed in the absence of passing gondolas and boats.

A gondola floated next to the bridge, waiting for the day's first customers, Li and Marco. As the gondola glided over the surface, the fog instantly engulfed them. For a short time, Marco and Li disappeared into a mystical land, free from the clamor of a city and the thought of revenge. They found comfort and peace in each other's arms until the sight of Marco's palazzo drew them back into reality.

"I missed you so much," Li said as she softly kissed him. Marco's return kiss intensified. For a year, he feared he would never kiss her again.

When the gondola rolled underneath his palazzo, Marco ordered the gates to open. The same servant appeared. Only the kitchen stirred. Elena looked up, stopped cooking, walked over, and hugged Li, surprising her.

"I'm assuming if you are alive, Peter is also?" she whispered. "Am I right?"

Li nodded yes.

A big smile spread across Elena's face. "The house has been in an uproar since you left yesterday, Messer Marco. Lady Isabella went completely mad, and Messer Maffeo called a physician. She tore up her room looking for a letter."

Marco and Li looked at each other and then asked. "Did she find it?"

"No, the physician administered some sleeping tea; she was insane. Messer Maffeo is still sleeping. I will send his servant to wake him. You can wait in his study. Later, I will find you."

"Later?" Marco questioned.

"Yes, when the time is right," She mysteriously said.

Marco nodded and walked toward the study. Shortly, Marco's uncle rushed in, still in his sleeping clothes, obviously distraught.

"LI, where have you been? We've been so worried!" he bellowed.

"Why don't you ask your daughter?" Li sarcastically answered.

"I did! She said Guo Yu took you to the seashore for rest."

"Yes, I left for the sea, but not how you would want to," Li answered. Immediately, her body convulsed with multiple coughs, which Li controlled with extreme effort. Marco put his arms around Li and shivered when he felt excessive heat from her body.

Li gently removed his arms. "Call Isabella and ask her," she said boldly. Abruptly, Guo Yu opened the door and slipped in quietly, standing beside Marco.

Maffeo asked Guo Yu, "What does she mean by that?"

He didn't answer but looked at Li, who continued.

"Ask your daughter how I left and about the letter she has been frantically looking for."

"The letter? What letter and why is it so important?" He calmly asked.

Marco could hardly contain himself. Li held him back by placing her hand on his shoulder. His voice quivered. "Tell your servant to retrieve Isabella now."

Unexpectedly, Isabella opened the door, her appearance disheveled and her eyes glazed. Her mouth opened to speak, but her face went white when she saw Li. She regained her composure quickly, displaying arrogance. "I see you returned from the sea."

Li's temper flared, but she subdued herself. She lived many years in the chambers and knew the tongue could be sharper than a knife. "Yes, Guo Yu saved me." Then Li looked at Marco's uncle. "Messer Maffeo, your daughter lied to me. She told me Marco was dead, even though she received a letter stating otherwise. Plus, she threw my erhu into the canal. I fell trying to catch it. Did she tell you that? She watched me fall, closed the shutters, and forgot me. Yes, I was on my way to the sea if Guo Yu hadn't saved me."

Isabella stood firm. "I did not do such a thing. And there was no letter."

Again, the study door opened, and Elena walked in. She looked at Peter, smiled, and then walked over to Marco, handing him a letter. "I told you I would see you later."

Isabella lost herself and screamed before she realized what she was saying. "You, you, you witch, you took it."

Marco stood in disbelief as he took the open envelope from Elena. He removed the letter, read it, and handed it to his uncle.

Maffeo's eyes watered as he looked at Li. "I'm sorry; I never dreamed my daughter was so cruel. But again, I never taught her love or tolerance." He lowered his head.

Isabella fell to the ground and cried out. "It's your fault, Father! How could you allow Marco to marry her and bring her to our house? Our friends have ostracized us. Our lives have never been the same since you returned."

"Only the false friends, Isabella. You are old enough not to be consumed by such hate. I lived twenty-four years in her world and was accepted by most. They do not differ from us." Then, he thought, *I am lying and guilty of another hate.*

Isabella sat on the floor sobbing.

Li walked over and took the letter from Maffeo. She read out loud only two sentences: "The Genoese have taken me prisoner. I am being treated well." As she finished the sentence, she swayed, and Marco rushed to her side, holding her close and whispering sweetly in her ear, "You did well. Let's go. You did what you came for."

Li stood defiant. "No, they forced me to leave. This time, only death will make me go. This is our home, and I have you as my strength." She walked past Isabella, staring down at her with contempt but also feeling pity. Marco and Li opened the heavy study door and went up the stairs, the servants watching.

Guo Yu looked at Elena, Peter to her. His feelings exploded; his feelings weren't one-sided. *How dense I've been, only admiring her from afar.* Her thick, beautiful black hair piled high on her head with wispy small strands that fell across her round eyes and succulent lips made his heart pound—especially when her small hands, covered with flour, flipped the strands away, and her whole body swayed as she prepared food. She wasn't talkative; she was a listener and observer. No one told her what to do; she just knew. She proved that today. He admired her for this. He never thought, in a hundred years, that this meticulous, pretty woman could love a man like him.

Over the past years, they had become friends, and sometimes, he would slowly lower his guard, only to quickly raise it again. Elena often smiled at him and prepared their special meals and sweets. He thought Marco had instructed her to do so. Then he remembered Messer Alessio telling him about the cook from the Polos' who came once a week looking but never buying. Unfortunately, he was too scared to trust her; she could be a spy for Isabella. His hope grew when Marco told him about a cook who met him in the courtyard with information, but this incident was proof and the best confession he could have imagined.

Elena waltzed over to Peter, who was in deep thought, and tapped him on the shoulder as she left the room. "Now you understand?"

He smiled and followed her back to the kitchen. Sitting down, he watched her lovingly prepare breakfast just for him. *I missed her and her cooking.* Slowly, he ate, savoring the food and, most of all, her.

Later that evening, she explained how she had the letter. "It was the day Marco arrived home. After he left the palazzo, I waited for him in the courtyard. When I returned, Isabella was still in the study. Everyone else was gossiping in the kitchen. I secretly went to Isabella's room. Next to her bed, a book lay open, and an envelope addressed to Li sat in plain sight. I took the book and the letter and ran."

Marco and Li entered their room; their essence remained, even though it was stale. Li had stood firm, but now she withered. Marco swept her up and hugged her closely. "Is this where you want to be?" Li looked around. The morning light was streaming into her favorite window, illuminating her other favorite things.

"Aren't your memories of that day too hard? Are you ready to come back here?"

Li motioned Marco to the chair, where he sat still caressing her. She comfortably sank into his arms and softly spoke. "I wanted to return here one last time and absorb our remaining love and memories that lie within this room and take them with us."

Marco held her tighter, feeling her shortness of breath and the rattle in her chest. They sat silently, wrapped up in their thoughts. Marco hated himself for failing to protect her. Li felt happiness. She cuddled deeper. Her thoughts became dark. *I will always haunt Isabella and this room.* Marco could feel her body grow tense. He hugged her tighter. Their thoughts turned to each other, and they felt the love between them.

A knock on the door, and Guo Yu's voice broke the silence. "May I come in?"

They both answered simultaneously. "Yes."

He entered, and Li spoke first. "We are going back to Agnese. I received what I came for. We have a lot to discuss with Luca and Messer Alessio."

Marco stood with Li still in his arms. Guo Yu, with sad eyes, opened the door for Marco.

Li insisted he put her down. "I am walking out of this house one last time, out the front door dressed as a Song princess."

Guo Yu dug through her trunks. "This one?"

Li nodded and disappeared behind the screen. Shortly after, she appeared exquisitely dressed, and Marco's heart never failed to flutter at the sight of her. They held hands as they proudly descended the stairs and exited. Isabella and her father watched from the study window.

Weakly, Li walked with her arm looped through Marco's curled arm on one side and Guo Yu on the other. As they strolled through the Milion courtyard toward the Rialto Bridge, her memories returned to the day Marco found her and how Guo Yu had been there, too. For the past years, these men had been by her side. Few could have been so lucky. She smiled first at Marco and then at Guo Yu. Both men fought back tears. They held her tighter as they slowly walked through the bustling crowds to the Golden Head.

Li and Marco walked to the back. Guo Yu stayed behind, as Alessio and Luca's questioning faces pulled at him. He needed to tell them what had happened.

Li walked across the room to Maria, gently took Agnese from her arms, held her tight, kissed her cheek, and strolled to her bed. She slipped into the bed, holding Agnese with one arm and the other outstretched, motioning for Marco to join them. They encircled Agnese. Li stared at Marco with a severe face. "Marco, please free Luca. That way, she can marry Messer Alessio."

"Of course," Marco quickly said.

Li hesitated momentarily before continuing. She knew the following request would be more challenging for Marco. After giving birth to Agnese, not knowing if Marco would return, she asked Messer Alessio and Luca to take Agnese as their child. Li, a healer, knew her life was hanging by a thin thread. "Marco, I have lived my destiny. You have not."

Marco put his finger over her mouth; she gently moved it. "Let me finish. I believe that our past lives are forgotten when we are born, and we begin our new lives with a fresh start. However, some of us take our regrets and lessons to our new lives without knowing it. That's why I believe people accomplish great or terrible things in their lives. Marco, you have achieved great things. Tell the world what you have seen and done."

Marco couldn't believe what he heard. He hadn't had time to tell her his story, what had happened, and about Rustichello.

Li continued talking. "I know this will be hard for you, but please do what I ask."

Marco could see the seriousness on her face.

"Marco, I want Agnese to remain with Luca and Messer Alessio. Luca will be a loving mother, something I never had. Your home will be too much like the inner chamber. You will always be her father, secretly by her side, like you were to me. Agnese will be blessed to have so many people love her."

Li could see the hurt in his eyes. "None of this is your fault; it was my destiny. Your destiny is to tell the world. I was just a small part. Just remember, when it's your time, Marco, do not take your regrets with you. That way, we will find and love each other freely in the next life. I will wait for you no matter how long it takes, but now you must take care of Agnese and do as I ask."

Marco couldn't refuse her even though he thought he would die. He nodded yes.

Li smiled, her eyes welled, and tears rolled down her cheek. Marco wiped her tears gently, kissing where the tears ran down her face.

Marco stayed by her side the rest of the day, telling her about his past year. She, in turn, told Marco about her year and that fatal night. They shed many tears, some from happiness and others from sadness.

By the following day, Li's body lay still; her soul had left her, yet her sweet smile remained. He tenderly kissed her. Devastated, he rose, carefully gathered up Agnese, and left Li, unable to cry anymore. Guo Yu, Luca, and Alessio were waiting for him.

Marco's youthful body stooped and appeared old. A forced smile appeared as he walked to Luca and placed Agnese in her arms. "This is what she wanted. I agreed," Marco said sadly. "She told me you had agreed. Of course, I will free you so you can marry. You and Messer Alessio will never have to worry about money."

Luca wailed and wrapped her arms around Agnese. Alessio wrapped his arms around both.

Marco continued, "Guo Yu, please come with me. I need to go to the palazzo and prepare, and then I will return."

"Prepare? "Guo Yu asked.

Marco didn't answer. He exited the apothecary, and Guo Yu followed. They came to a metal shop, where Marco stopped.

Marco pulled out gold pieces. "Make keys using these gold pieces for two locks," he told the locksmith. "I also need chains. I will return later." Then, he went to a carpenter shop and ordered wood planks and tools. "My servant will come for them later."

When they arrived at his house, his eyes were swollen and red. He spoke to no one as he went upstairs to their room. Rustling through her trunks, he found her Imperial dress and coat. He carefully placed it into a bag. Guo Yu started to straighten the room. Marco stopped him. "Leave it be; her room will never be touched. It will be my remembrance, my torture." Guo Yu turned and saw Marco remove her favorite blanket. He held it up to his face and inhaled her scent. He then handed Guo Yu her small Asian dressing table, which contained her favorite things. Marco looked at her favorite chair, lowered his head, and kept walking.

Marco pulled back the heavy tapestry on the wall and opened a secret door. They entered and descended narrow stairs to another door. He unlocked the door and entered a small room. Marco lit a candle as he entered, which illuminated his most treasured items—not only gold, silver, or jewels but personal items he had obtained from Cathay, his sword, his first Tartarian clothes, the small vase, and the dragon bracelet Kim had given him—things he didn't want to share with anyone. Marco surprised Guo Yu when he removed his spirit lock and placed it beside the dragon bracelet. "Cathay is no more; only memories are left," Marco told him. "Now, Li, my prized jewel, will remain with her favorite things and mine. Only you and I will know." They placed her small dressing table and imperial dress on a large table.

Marco returned to their room, sat in Li's favorite chair, and stared mournfully down at the canal. Marco whispered, "Only her erhu will sit here as a reminder of my failure."

Guo Yu continued down the steps to the bottom floor, where the canal flowed under the palazzo. He boarded a boat and rolled down the canal. Marco watched him row past.

When Guo Yu returned, it was midday. Marco again descended to the secret room. Guo Yu and Marco feverishly built her coffin. The pounding sounds echoed throughout the palazzo, creating a ghostly sound. Isabella covered her ears.

When they had finished, they returned to his room, picked up her favorite blanket, and walked out the door. Marco turned, faced the door, lowered his head, and laid his hands flat upon it, saying a long, sorrowful goodbye. Afterwards, Marco took a chain and ran it through the door handles. He clasped the lock, and the clink echoed loudly in Marco's ears, stinging his entire body, and he wept.

Isabella stood at her door, watching. Marco turned to see her and said contemptuously, "I'll be back. You will forever see my face and remember what you have done."

Isabella ran into her room, slammed the door, and fell into bed, sobbing.

Marco descended the stairs and proceeded to the canal. He took the same boat Guo Yu had used and returned to the Golden Head. He waited till early morning, her favorite time, wrapped her up in her favorite blanket as if she were just asleep, grabbed her erhu, and, while everyone slept, he carried her to the entrance of the Golden Head. His life flashed before him when he opened the door and entered the early morning mist and fog. This step was the hardest of all and the most demanding thing he had ever done. His feet could hardly move. He forced himself, remembering her words: "*In the next life, we will find each other and freely love each other. I will meet you again, I promise.*"

Tears ran down his face as he rowed through the mystical lands, pretending Li was talking and sharing her favorite time—the city's silence before it awoke.

Marco arrived and ascended the back stairs that led to the secret room. Guo Yu had lit the candles and waited outside the door of the secret room. Only Marco entered and carefully laid her down, dressing her in an Imperial dress. Her face was still beautiful, even in death. He fell over her body and cried until he thought he would die. Guo Yu entered the room and pulled

Marco from her body. He encouraged Marco to place Li in her coffin. Guo Yu peered down at Li. She looked so royal. Guo Yu wondered how her life would have been if Kubilai Khan had not conquered her home. Then he remembered her words, *"This was my destiny. It was fate that Marco rescued me."* Together, they placed the coffin lid on.

Guo Yu led Marco out of the hidden room and locked the door behind them. They then descended the rest of the stairs to the canal. When they reached the bottom of the stairs and exited the door, they turned and faced it. Marco couldn't move.

Guo Yu went to the boat, removed the plaster from it, moved Marco, and began plastering the door shut. Marco picked up the tool and helped. With the last swipe, they completely sealed and hid the entrance. Yu forced him into the boat and took him back to Agnese.

Marco stayed for days. The thought of returning to his home sent chills down his body. For months, he drank and wandered throughout the city until Guo Yu and Rustichello saved him.

Chapter Sixty-Six

Marco

Marco's Last Words

Venice 1324

Marco, with his dying eyes, looked at Moreta, gained some unknown strength, and softly spoke. "Sometimes I failed your mother; I drank and boasted, and she always brought me back. I am unsure if I fulfilled my destiny, and I never again achieved great wealth, but I think we lived comfortably. Moreta, I will never retract my book. I promised Li I would tell the world my story. She told me I would be famous because I had done great things in this lifetime. It was my destiny." Marco chuckled softly. "She also told me I should never have regrets. That's been hard."

Marco drifted off for a moment, then suddenly spoke. "Please, Moreta, believe me and tell the world. Then, I will die with no regrets."

Moreta gripped his hand. "I promise you, Father."

Marco suddenly had a strange look on his face. With his frail hands, he reached up and touched his shoulder. He thought to himself, *I feel warmth, the warmth of Lis's loving hands. She sees me. I see her. Kim Chin-hae and Lis are next to Li, smiling*. Marco's body relaxed, and his fear of death diminished.

"Father, please tell me of Agnese," Moreta asked.

Slowly, Marco spoke. "The only thing I did right in this world was never leave again, and I protected your mother and my daughters, including Agnese. Your mother helped. Agnese was hidden for protection, not because I was ashamed. That's what her mother wanted. Sadly, Agnese died many years ago, leaving two sons. No one in this family knows them." Marco's voice faded.

Guo Yu stood, walked over to Li's favorite chair, picked up her erhu, and opened the secret door one last time. He descended the stairs and entered the secret room. He opened Li's coffin and gently placed the erhu in Li's arms. "It is finally where it belongs. May your spirit play forever, not only to call Marco home but also to remind Venice you existed and are not to be forgotten." Guo Yu closed the coffin, exited the room, took a chain, looped it through the door handles, and locked it. He slowly climbed the stairs to Marco's room. When he exited, he walked to the bucket of plaster and the trowel and began sealing the door. With each stroke of plaster, the door started to vanish, and his tears flowed harder. When he finished, he walked over to Marco, kissed his hand, and placed the golden keys around his neck.

With his last breath, Marco spoke. "Guo Yu, I hear Li's erhu. Do you hear it? She's calling me home."

Moreta listened with tears, but her heart sang with the hope that her father indeed found Li.

Guo Yu smiled and walked out of the room for the last time.

Epilogue

The Legend Continues

Matteo, the tour guide, thought of his experience every time he passed through Milion Courtyard.

Several years passed, and the owners of Malibran Theater began foundation renovations. Matteo noticed an enormous group of people gathered. He pushed through the whispering crowd. His heart stopped as the whisper echoed around him; they found human remains buried in a tomb containing objects of Chinese origin, an Asian woman who wore a tiara and a Chinese imperial coat from the 13th century.

Matteo pushed his way out of the crowd. He didn't need to see or hear anything else. He smiled and thought, *I always knew the legend was true; I had seen Messer Marco Polo's Princess.*

Never the End. There's so much more to discover...

Bibliography

Latham, Ronald. *Marco Polo: The Travels.* London, Penguin Group, 1958

Cliff, Nigel. *Marco Polo: The Travels*. UK, Penguin Classics, 2016

Weatherford, Jack. *The Secret History of the Mongol Queens*. New York, Penguin Random House, 2010

Kahn, Paul. *The Secret History of the Mongols: The Origin of Ghengis Khan*. Boston, Cheng & Tsui Company, 1998

Yamada, Nakaba. *Ghenko: The Mongol Invasion of Japan*. The Ronin's Collection of Old Books, 1916

Shou-zhong, Yang. *The Divine Farmer's Materia Medica.* Portland, Blue Poppy Press, Inc, 1998

www.ingramcontent.com/pod-product-compliance
Lightning Source LLC
Jackson TN
JSHW080916040326
98784JS00008B/49
* 9 7 9 8 2 1 8 4 9 5 1 6 9 *